SEPTEMBER

"A Dance of Life!"

—*Philadelphia Inquirer*

"Enrapturing . . . wonderful!"

—*Booklist*

"Reading *September* is like unwrapping a splendidly packaged gift!"

—*L.A. Life*

VOICES IN SUMMER

"Intriguing characters . . . lovely settings . . . romantic fiction with substance . . . Pilcher displays a perfect touch!"

—*Booklist*

"Pilcher evokes the sense of contentment that flows from affection."

—*Publishers Weekly*

THE CAROUSEL

"A romantic tale imbued with several comforting lessons on loving, friendship, and family ties."

—*Booklist*

"Delightful . . . . It exudes comfort as it entertains."

—*Publishers Weekly*

"Enormous charm and warmth!"

—*Kirkus Reviews*

ROSAMUNDE PILCHER

Three Complete Novels

ROSAMUNDE PILCHER

Three Complete Novels

SEPTEMBER

VOICES IN SUMMER

THE CAROUSEL

WINGS BOOKS
New York

This 1996 edition is published by Wings Books, a division of Random House Value Publishing, Inc., 201 East 50th Street, New York, New York 10022, by arrangement with St. Martin's Press, Inc.

Wings Books and colophon are trademarks of Random House Value Publishing, Inc.

Random House
New York •Toronto •London • Sydney •Auckland
http://www.randomhouse.com/

Printed and bound in the United States of America

Library of Congress Cataloging-in-Publication Data
Pilcher, Rosamunde.
    [Novels. Selections]
    Three complete novels/Rosamunde Pilcher.
        p. cm.
    Contents: September—Voices in summer—The carousel.
    ISBN 0-517-12190-5
    1. Title.
PR6066.I38A6 1995
823'.914—dc20   94–36508
                                                                                      CIP

12 11 10 9 8 7

Contents

SEPTEMBER

May

1

IN EARLY MAY, THE SUMMER CAME, at last, to Scotland. Winter had clung, with steely fingers, for far too long, refusing to relinquish its cruel grip. All through April, bitter winds had blown from the north-west, tearing the first blossom from the wild geynes, and burning brown the yellow trumpets of the early daffodils. Snow frosted the hilltops and lay deep in corries, and the farmers, despairing of fresh grazing, tractored the last of their feed out to the barren fields where lowing stock huddled in the shelter of the drystone walls.

Even the wild geese, usually gone by the end of March, were late in returning to their Arctic habitats. The last of the skeins had disappeared around the middle of April, honking away north into the unknown skies, flying so high that the arrowhead formations looked no more substantial than cobwebs drifting in the wind.

And then, overnight, the fickle Highland climate relented. The wind veered around to the south, bringing with it the balmy breezes and the soft weather that the rest of the country had been enjoying for weeks, along with the scent of damp earth and growing things. The countryside turned a sweet and verdant green, the wild white cherry trees recovered from their battering, took heart, and spread their branches in a mist of snowflake petals. All at once, cottage gardens burgeoned into colour— yellow winter-flowering jasmine, purple crocus, and the deep blue of grape hyacinths. Birds sang, and the sun, for the first time since last autumn, brought a real warmth with it.

* * *

Every morning of her life, rain or shine, Violet Aird walked to the village to collect, from Mrs. Ishak's supermarket, two pints of milk, *The Times,* and any other small groceries and supplies needed for the sustenance of one elderly lady living on her own. Only sometimes, in the depths of winter, when the snow piled in deep drifts, and the ice became treacherous, did she eschew this exercise, on the principle that discretion was the better part of valour.

It was not an easy walk. Half a mile down the steep road, between fields which had once been the parkland of Croy, Archie Balmerino's estate, and then the stiff half-mile climb home again. She had a car, and could perfectly well have made the journey in that, but it was one of her convictions that, as old age crept up on you, once you started to use the car for short journeys, then you were in dire danger of losing the use of your legs.

For all the long months of winter, she had had to bundle up in layers of clothing for this expedition. Thick boots, sweaters, water-proof jacket, scarf, gloves, a woollen hat pulled well down over her ears. This morning, she wore a tweed skirt and a cardigan and her head was bare. The sun lifted her spirits and made her feel energetic and young again, and being uncluttered by extraneous garments reminded her of childhood satisfaction when black woollen stockings were abandoned and one felt the pleasant, draughty sensation of cool air on bare legs.

The village shop, this morning, was busy, and she had to wait for a little to be served. She did not mind, because it meant that there was time to chat with other customers, all of whom were familiar faces; marvel at the weather; ask after somebody's mother; watch a small boy choose, with painful deliberation, a packet of Dolly Mixtures, which he proceeded to pay for with his own money. He was not hurried. Mrs. Ishak stood with gentle patience while he made up his mind. When he had finally done this, she put the Dolly Mixtures into a little paper bag and took the money from him.

"You must not eat them all at once, or you will lose all your teeth," she warned him. "Good morning, Mrs. Aird."

"Good morning, Mrs. Ishak. And what a lovely day it is!"

"I could not believe it when I saw the sun shining." Usually Mrs. Ishak, exiled to these northern climes from the relentless sunshine of Malawi, was bundled in cardigans and kept a paraffin heater behind the counter, over which she huddled whenever there was a moment of quiet. This morning, however, she looked much happier. "I hope it will not become cold again."

"I don't think so. Summer is here. Oh, thank you, my milk and my paper. And Edie wants some furniture polish and a roll of paper towel. And I think I'd better take half a dozen eggs."

"If your basket is too heavy, I can send Mr. Ishak up to your house in his motor car."

"No, I can manage, thank you very much."

"It is a lot of walking you are doing."

Violet smiled. "But just think how good it is for me."

Laden, she set off once more for home, for Pennyburn. Down the pavement, past the rows of low cottages, with windows blinking reflected sunlight, and doors standing open to the fresh warm air; then through the gates of Croy and up the hill again. This was a private road, the back driveway of the big house, and Pennyburn stood half-way up it, to one side and surrounded by steep fields. It was approached by a neat lane bordered in clipped beech hedges, and it was always something of a relief to reach the turning and to know that one did not have to climb any farther.

Violet changed her basket, which was becoming heavy, from one hand to the other, and made plans as to how she would spend the rest of her day. This was one of Edie's mornings for helping Violet, which meant that Violet could abandon her house and instead get busy in the garden. Lately, it had been too cold for even Violet to garden, and things had become neglected. The lawn was looking tired and mossy after the long winter. Perhaps she should run her spiker over it and give it a bit of air. After that, a huge pit of carefully nurtured compost needed to be barrowed and spread over her new rose-bed. The prospect filled her with satisfying joy. She could not wait to get down to work.

Her step quickened. But then, almost at once, she saw the unfamiliar car parked outside her front door, and knew that the garden, for the moment, would have to wait. A visitor. Such irritation. Who had come to call? Who was Violet going to have to sit with and talk to, instead of being allowed to get on with her digging?

The car was a neat little Renault and betrayed no clue as to its owner. Violet went into the house through the kitchen door, and there found Edie at the tap and filling the kettle.

She dumped the basket on the table. "Who is it?" she mouthed, making pointing gestures with her forefinger.

Edie, too, kept her voice down. "Mrs. Steynton. From Corriehill."

"How long has she been here?"

"Only a moment. I told her to wait. She's in the sitting-room. She wants a wee word." Edie resumed her normal voice. "I'm just making you both a cup of coffee. I'll bring it in when it's ready."

With no excuse or possible escape route, Violet went to find her visitor. Verena Steynton stood at the window of the sun-filled sitting-room, gazing out at Violet's garden. As Violet came through the door, she turned.

"Oh, Violet, I am sorry. I feel embarrassed. I told Edie I'd come back another time, but she swore you'd be home from the village in a moment or two."

She was a tall and slender woman around forty, and invariably immaculately and elegantly turned out. Which instantly set her apart from the other local ladies, who were, for the most part, busy country women, with neither the time nor the inclination to bother too much about their personal appearance. Verena and her husband Angus were newcomers to the neighbourhood, having lived at Corriehill for a mere ten years. Before that, Angus had worked as a stockbroker in London, but having made his pile, and tiring of the rat race, he had bought Corriehill, ten miles distant from Strathcroy, moved north with his wife and his daughter Katy, and cast about, locally, for some other, and hopefully less demanding, occupation. He had ended up taking over a run-down timber business in Relkirk, and over the years had built this up into a lucrative and thriving concern.

As for Verena, she, too, was something of a career woman, being heavily involved with an organization called Scottish Country Tours. During the summer months, this company shuttled busloads of American visitors hither and yon, and arranged for them to stay, as paying guests, in a selection of well-vetted private houses. Isobel Balmerino had been roped into this exercise, and hard labour it was, too. Violet could not think of a more exhausting way of making a bit of money.

However, from the social point of view, the Steynton family had proved themselves a true asset to the community, being both friendly and unassuming, generous with their hospitality, and always willing to give time and effort to the running of fêtes, gymkhanas, and various fund-raising events.

Even so, Violet could not begin to imagine why Verena was here.

"I'm glad you stayed. I would have been sorry to miss you. Edie's just making us a cup of coffee."

"I should have telephoned, but I was on my way to Relkirk and suddenly thought, much better to drop in and take my chance. On the spur of the moment. You don't mind?"

"Not in the least," Violet fibbed robustly. "Come and sit down. I'm afraid the fire's not been lighted yet, but . . ."

"Oh, heavens, who needs a fire on a day like this? Isn't it blissful to see the sun?"

She settled herself on the sofa and crossed her long and elegant legs. Violet, less gracefully, lowered herself into her own wide-lapped chair.

She decided to come straight to the point. "Edie said you wanted a word with me."

"I just suddenly thought . . . you'd be the very person to help."

Violet's heart sank, envisaging some bazaar, garden-opening, or charity concert, for which she was about to be asked to knit tea-cosies, declare open, or sell tickets.

"Help?" she said faintly.

"No. Not so much help, as give advice. You see, I'm thinking of throwing a dance."

"A *dance?*"

"Yes. For Katy. She's going to be twenty-one."

"But how can *I* advise you? I haven't done such a thing for longer than I can remember. Surely, you'd be better to ask somebody a little more up-to-date. Peggy Ferguson-Crombie, or Isobel, for instance?"

"It's just that I thought . . . you're so experienced. You've lived here longer than anybody I know. I wanted to get your reactions to the idea."

Violet was nonplussed. Casting about for something to say, she welcomed the appearance of Edie with the coffee tray. Edie set this down on the fireside stool. "Are you wanting biscuits?" she asked.

"No, Edie, I think that will do very nicely. Thank you so much."

Edie departed. In a moment, the vacuum cleaner could be heard roaring away upstairs.

Violet poured the coffee. "What sort of an affair did you have in mind?"

"Oh, you know. Reels and country dances."

Violet thought that she did know. "You mean tapes on the stereo, and eightsomes in the hall?"

"No. Not like that. A really *big* dance. We'd do it in style. With a marquee on the lawn . . ."

"I hope Angus is feeling rich."

Verena ignored this interruption. ". . . and a proper band for the music. We'll use the hall, of course, but for sitting out. And the drawing-room. And I'm sure Katy will want a disco for all her London friends, it seems to be the thing to do. Perhaps the dining-room. We could turn it into a cave, or a grotto. . . ."

Caves and grottoes, thought Violet. Verena had clearly been doing her homework. But then, she was an excellent organizer. Violet said mildly, "You *have* been laying plans."

"And Katy can ask all her friends from the south . . . we'll have to find beds for them, of course. . . ."

"Have you spoken to Katy about your idea?"

"No, I told you. You're the first person to know."

"Perhaps she won't want a dance."

"But of course she will. She's always loved parties."

Violet, knowing Katy, decided that this was probably true. "And when is it to be?"

"I thought September. That's the obvious time. Lots of people up for the shooting, and everybody still on holiday. The sixteenth might be a good date, because by then most of the younger children will have gone back to boarding-school."

"This is only May. September's a long way off."

"I know, but it's never too early to fix a date and start making arrangements. I'll have to book the marquee, and the caterer, and get invitations printed. . . ." She came up with another pleasurable idea. "And, Violet, wouldn't fairy lights be pretty, all the way up the drive to the house?"

It all sounded dreadfully ambitious. "It's going to be a lot of work for you."

"Not really. The Tourist Invasion will be over by then, because the paying guests stop coming at the end of August. I shall be able to concentrate my mind. Do admit, Violet, it is a good idea. And just think of all the people I'll be able to cross off my social-conscience list. We can get everybody off in one fell swoop. Including," she added, "the Barwells."

"I don't think I know the Barwells."

"No, you wouldn't. They're business colleagues of Angus's. We've been to dinner with them twice. Two evenings of jaw-aching boredom. And never asked them back, simply because we couldn't think of anybody who could be asked to endure an evening in such excruciatingly dull company. And there are lots of others," she remembered comfortably. "When I remind Angus about *them,* he's not going to raise any difficulties about signing a few cheques."

Violet felt a little sorry for Angus. "Who else will you ask?"

"Oh, everybody. The Millburns and the Ferguson-Crombies and the Buchanan-Wrights and old Lady Westerdale, and the Brandons. And the Staffords. All their children have grown up now, so they can be invited, too. And the Middletons should be up from Hampshire, and the Luards from Gloucestershire. We'll make a list. I'll pin a sheet of paper to the kitchen notice-board, and every time I think of a new name, I'll write it down. And you, of course, Violet. And Edmund, and Virginia, and Alexa. And the Balmerinos. Isobel will give a dinner party for me, I'm sure. . . ."

Suddenly, it all began to sound rather fun. Violet's concentration drifted back to the past, to forgotten occasions now remembered. One memory led to another. She said without thinking, "You should send Pandora an invitation," and then could not imagine why she had come up with the impulsive suggestion.

"Pandora?"

"Archie Balmerino's sister. One thinks of parties, and one automatically thinks of Pandora. But of course you never knew her."

"But I know *about* her. For some reason, her name always seems to come up at dinner-party conversations. You think she would come? Surely she hasn't been home for over twenty years?"

"That's true. Just a silly thought. But why not give it a try? What a shot in the arm it would be for poor Archie. And if anything would bring that errant creature back to Croy, it would be the lure of a full-blown dance."

"So you're on my side, Violet? You think I should go ahead and do it?"

"Yes, I do. If you have the energy and the wherewithal, I think it's a wonderful and generous idea. It will give us all something splendid to look forward to."

"Don't say anything until I've bearded Angus."

"Not a word."

Verena smiled with satisfaction. And then another happy thought occurred to her. "I shall have a good excuse," she said, "to go and find myself a new dress."

But Violet had no such problem. "I," she told Verena, "shall wear my black velvet."

2

Thursday the Twelfth

THE NIGHT WAS SHORT and he did not sleep. Soon it would be dawn. He had imagined that, for once, he might sleep, since he was tired, exhausted. Drained by three days of an unseasonably hot New York; days filled to the brim with breakfast meetings, business lunches, long afternoons of argument and discussion; too much Coca-Cola and black coffee, too many receptions and late nights, and a miserable dearth of exercise and fresh air.

Finally, successfully, it had been achieved, though not easily. Harvey Klein was a tough nut, and some persuasion was necessary to convince him that this was the very best, and indeed the only way to hook the English market. The creative campaign that Noel had brought with him to New York, complete with a time-schedule, layouts, and photographs, had been approved and agreed upon. With the contract under his belt, Noel could return to London. Pack his bag, make a last-minute telephone call, stuff his brief-case with documents and calculator, take another telephone call (Harvey Klein to say safe journey), get himself downstairs, check out, flag down a yellow cab, and head for Kennedy.

In the evening light Manhattan, as always, looked miraculous—towers of light thrusting upwards into the suffused glow of the sky, and the freeways moving rivers of headlights. Here was a city that offered, in its brash and open-handed way, every conceivable form of delight.

Before, on previous visits, he had taken full advantage of all the fun, but there had been no opportunity, this time, to accept any of them, and he knew a pang of regret at leaving unfulfilled, as though he were being hustled away from a stupendous party long before he had even started to enjoy it.

At Kennedy the cab dropped him at the BA terminal. He duly queued, checked in, rid himself of his suitcase, queued again for Security, and at last made his way to the departure lounge. He bought a bottle of Scotch in the Duty-Free, a *Newsweek* and *Advertising Age* from the newsstand. Finding a chair he sat, slumped with tiredness, waiting for his flight to be called.

By courtesy of Wenborn & Weinburg, he was traveling Club Class, so at least there was space for his long legs, and he had asked for a seat by the window. He took off his jacket, settled himself, longed for a drink. It occurred to him that it would be fortuitous if no one came to sit beside him, but this faint hope died almost at once as a well-upholstered individual in a navy-blue chalk-stripe suit claimed the seat, stowed various bags and bundles in the overhead bin, and at last collapsed, in an overflowing fashion, alongside.

The man took up a great deal of space. The interior of the aircraft was cool, but this man was hot. He pulled out a silk handkerchief and dabbed his brow, heaved and humped, searched for his seat-belt, and managed to jab Noel, quite painfully, with his elbow.

"Sorry about that. Seems we're a full load this evening."

Noel did not wish to talk. He smiled and nodded, and pointedly opened his *Newsweek*.

They took off. Cocktails were served, and then dinner. He was not hungry, but ate it, because it passed the time and there was nothing else to do. The huge 747 droned on, out over the Atlantic. Dinner was cleared and the movie came on. Noel had already seen it in London, so he asked the flight attendant to bring him a whisky and soda and drank it slowly, cradling it in his hand, making it last. Cabin lights were extinguished and passengers reached for pillows and blankets. The fat man folded his hands over his stomach and snored momentously. Noel closed his eyes, but this made them feel as though they were filled with grit, so he opened them again. His mind raced. It had been working full throttle for three days and refused to slow down. The possibility of oblivion faded.

He wondered why he was not feeling triumphant, because he had won the precious account and was returning home with the whole thing safely sewn up. A suitable metaphor for Saddlebags. Saddlebags. It was one of those words which, the more times you said it, the more ridiculous it sounded. But it wasn't ridiculous. It was immensely important not only to Noel Keeling, but to Wenborn & Weinburg as well.

Saddlebags. A company with its roots in Colorado, where the business had started up some years ago, manufacturing high-class leather goods for the ranching fraternity. Saddles, bridles, straps, reins, and riding boots, all branded with the prestigious trademark of a hoof-print enclosing the letter *S*.

From this modest beginning, the company's reputation and sales had grown nation-wide, outstripping all rivals. They moved into the manufacture of other commodities. Luggage, handbags, fashion accessories, shoes and boots. All constructed from the finest of hide, hand-stitched and hand-finished. The Saddlebag logo became a status symbol, vying with Gucci or Ferragamo, and with a price-tag to match. Their reputation spread, so that visitors to the United States, wishing to return home with a truly impressive piece of loot, chose a Saddlebag satchel, or a hand-tooled, gold-buckled belt.

And then came the rumour that they were moving into the British market, retailing through one or two carefully chosen London stores. Charles Weinburg, Noel's chairman, got wind of this by means of a chance remark dropped at a London dinner party. The next morning Noel, as Senior Vice-President and Creative Director, was called for his briefing.

"I want this account, Noel. At the moment only a handful of people in this country have ever heard of Saddlebags, and they're going to need a top-gear campaign. We've got the headstart and if we land it we can handle it, so I put through a call to New York late last night, and spoke to Saddlebag's President, Harvey Klein. He's agreeable to a meeting but he wants a total presentation . . . layouts, media coverage, slogans, the lot. Top-level stuff, full-page colour spreads. You've got two weeks. Get busy with the Art Department and try to work something out. And for God's sake find a photographer who can make a male model look like a man, not like a shop-window dummy. If necessary, get hold of a genuine polo-player. If he'll do the job, I don't care what we have to pay him. . . ."

It was nine years since Noel Keeling had gone to work for Wenborn & Weinburg. Nine years is a long time in the advertising business for a man to stay with the same firm, and from time to time he found himself astonished by his own uninterrupted progress. Others, his own contemporaries, who had started with him, had moved on—to other companies, or even, like some colleagues, to start their own agencies. But Noel had stayed.

The reasons for the constancy were basically rooted in his personal life. Indeed, after a year or two with the firm, he had considered quite seriously the possibility of leaving. He was restless, unsatisfied, and not even particularly interested in the job. He dreamt of greener fields: setting up on his own, abandoning advertising altogether and moving into property or commodities. With plans for making a million, he knew that it was simply lack of the necessary capital that was holding him back. But he had no capital, and the frustration of lost opportunities and missed chances drove him nearly to distraction.

And then, four years ago, things had dramatically changed. He was thirty, a bachelor, and still resolutely working his way through a string of girl-friends, with no inkling that this irresponsible state of affairs would not last for ever. But his mother quite suddenly died, and for the first time in his life Noel had found himself a man of some means.

Her death had been so totally unexpected that for a little while he was shocked into a state where he found it almost impossible to come to terms with the cold fact that she had gone for ever. He had always been fond of her, in a detached and unsentimental manner, but basically he'd thought of her as his constant source of food, drink, clean clothes, warm beds, and, when he asked for it, moral support. As well, he had respected both her independence of spirit and the fact that she had never inter-fered, in any way, with Noel's own adult and private life. At the same time, much of her dotty behaviour had maddened him. Worst was her habit of surrounding herself with the most down-at-heel and needy of hangers-on. Everybody was her friend. She called them all her friends. Noel called them a lot of bloody spongers. She disregarded his cynical attitude, and bereaved spinsters, lonely widows, penniless artists, and unemployed actors were drawn to her side as moths seek a candle flame. Her generosity to all and sundry he had considered both mindless and selfish, for there never seemed to be any money to spare for the things in life that Noel believed to be of primary importance.

When she died, her will reflected this thoughtless bounty. A hefty bequest was left to a young man . . . nothing to do with the family . . . whom she had taken under her sheltering wing, and whom, for some reason, she wished to help.

For Noel, it was a bitter blow. His feelings—and pocket—deeply hurt, he was consumed by a resentment that was totally impotent. It was no use raging, because she was gone. He could not have it out with her, accuse her of disloyalty and demand to know what the bloody hell she thought she was doing. His mother had moved beyond his reach. He imagined her, safe from his wrath, across some chasm or uncrossable river, surrounded by sunshine, fields, trees, whatever constituted her own personal conception of Heaven. She was probably, in her mild way, laughing at her son, her dark eyes bright with mischievous amusement, unperturbed as always by his demands and reproaches.

With only his two sisters to make miserable, he turned his back on his family and concentrated instead on the only stable element left in his life —his job. Somewhat to his surprise, and to the astonishment of his superiors, he discovered, just in time, that he was not only interested in advertising but extremely good at it. By the time his mother's estate was cleared, and his share of the loot was safely deposited in the bank, youthful fantasies of enormous gambles and fast profits had faded forever. As well, Noel realized that making money with some other person's hypothetical fortune was actually very different from parting with your own. He felt protective about his bank balance, as though it were a child, and was not about to risk its safety. Instead, in modest fashion, he bought himself a new car and began, tentatively, to put out feelers for some place new to live. . . .

Life moved on. But youth was over, and it was a different life. Gradually Noel came to terms with this and, at the same time, discovered that he was incapable of sustaining his final grievance against his mother. Nourishing useless resentment was far too exhausting. And at the end of the day he had to admit that he hadn't come out of it all too badly. As well, he missed her. During the last years he had seen little of her, closeted as she was in the depths of Gloucestershire, but still she was always *there*—at the end of a telephone, or at the end of a long drive when you felt you couldn't stand the hot summer streets of London a moment longer. It didn't matter if you went alone or took half a dozen friends for the weekend. There was always space, a relaxed welcome, delicious food, everything or nothing to do. Fires flickering, fragrant flowers, hot baths; warm comfortable beds, fine wines, and easy conversation.

All gone. The house and garden sold to strangers. The warm smell of her kitchen and the good feeling that somebody else was in charge and you didn't have to make a single decision. And gone was the only person in the world with whom you never had to put on an act or pretend. Life without her, maddening and capricious as she had been, was like living a life with a ragged hole in the middle of it, and had taken, he recalled wryly, some getting used to.

He sighed. It all seemed a long time ago. Another world. He had finished his whisky and sat staring out into the darkness. He remembered being four years old and having measles, and how the nights of illness had seemed long as a lifetime, each minute lasting an hour, and the dawn an eternity away.

Now, thirty years later, he watched the dawn. The sky lightened and the sun slid up from beneath the false horizon of cloud, and everything turned pink and the light was dazzling to the eye. He watched the dawn and was grateful, because it had chased away the night, and now it was the next day and he did not have to try to sleep. Around him, people stirred. The cabin crew came around with orange juice and scalding face towels. He wiped his face and felt the stubble on his chin. Others collected themselves, found wash-bags, went to the lavatory for a shave. Noel stayed where he was. He could shave when he reached home.

* * *

Which, three hours later, he did. Weary, dirty, and dishevelled, he clambered out of the taxi and paid the driver off. The morning air was cool, blessedly cool after New York, and it was raining lightly, a dampening drizzle. In Pembroke Square the trees were greening, the pavements wet. He smelt the freshness and, as the taxi drove away, stood for a moment and thought of spending this day on his own, recovering. Having a nap, taking a long walk. But this was not to be. There was work to be done. The office and his chairman waited. Noel picked up his bag and his brief-case, went down the area steps and opened his own front door.

It was called a garden flat because at the back of it French windows opened out onto a tiny patio, his share of the larger garden of the tall house. In the evening the sun fell upon it, but at this early hour it lay in shadow, and the upstairs cat was comfortably ensconced in one of his canvas chairs, having apparently spent the night there.

It was not a large flat but the rooms were spacious. A living-room and a bedroom, a small kitchen and a bathroom. Overnight guests had to sleep on the sofa, a tricky piece of equipment which, if resolutely approached, folded down into a second double bed. Mrs. Muspratt, who did for him, had been in while he was away and so all was neat and clean, but airless and stuffy.

He opened the French windows and chased the cat away. In his bedroom, he unzipped his suitcase and took out his wash-bag. He undressed and dropped his soiled and crumpled clothes onto the floor. In the bathroom he cleaned his teeth, took a scalding shower, shaved. By now he needed, more than anything, black coffee. In his towel robe and barefooted, he padded into the kitchen, filled the kettle and switched it on, spooned coffee into his French coffee-pot. The smell of this was heartening and delicious. While the coffee filtered, he collected his mail, sat at the kitchen table and leafed through the envelopes. Nothing looked too urgent. There was, however, a garish picture postcard of Gibraltar. He turned it over. It had been posted in London and was from the wife of Hugh Pennington, an old school friend of Noel's, who lived in Ovington Street.

Noel, I've been trying to ring you, but no reply. Unless we
hear to the contrary, we'll expect you for dinner the
thirteenth. Seven-thirty for eight. No black tie. Love,
Delia.

He sighed. This evening. Unless we hear to the contrary. Oh well, by then he'd probably have got his second wind. And it would be more amusing than watching television. He dropped the postcard onto the table, heaved himself to his feet, and went to pour his coffee.

* * *

Shut in the office, in conference for most of the day, Noel lost track and sight of what was happening out of doors. Finally emerging and driving home through rush-hour traffic that did not rush but moved at the pace of an arthritic snail, he saw that the rain of the morning had been blown away by the breeze and it was a perfect May evening. By now he had reached that state beyond exhaustion when all is light and clear and strangely disembodied, and the prospect of sleep seemed as far away as death. Instead, another shower, a change of clothes, and a drink. And then he would not take his car but walk to Ovington Street. The fresh air and exercise would whet his appetite for the excellent meal that he hoped was waiting for him. He could scarcely remember when he had last sat at a table and eaten something that was not a sandwich.

The walk was a good idea. He went by leafy back roads, residential terraces, and gardens where magnolias opened and wistaria clung to the faces of expensive London houses. Coming out into the Brompton Road, he crossed over by the Michelin Building and turned down into Walton Street. Here his steps slowed as he paused to look in at the delectable shop windows, the interior decorators and the art gallery that sold sporting prints, hunting scenes, and oil paintings of faithful Labradors bounding through the snow with pheasants in their mouths. There was a Thorburn that he craved. He stood longer than he intended, simply looking at it. Perhaps tomorrow he would ring the gallery and discover its price. After a little, he walked on.

By the time he reached Ovington Street, it was twenty-five to eight. The pavements were lined with the cars of the residents, and some older children were riding their bicycles up and down the middle of the road. The Penningtons' house was half-way down the terrace. As he approached it, a girl came down the pavement towards him. She had with her, on a lead, a small white Highland terrier and was apparently on her way to the post-box, for she carried a letter in her hand. He looked at her. She wore jeans and a grey sweat-shirt and had hair the colour of the very best sort of marmalade, and she was neither tall nor particularly slender. In fact, not Noel's type at all. And yet, as she passed him, he gave her a second glance because there was something vaguely familiar about her, and it was difficult to think where they might once have met. Some party, perhaps. The hair was distinctive. . . .

The walk had tired him and he found himself sorely in need of a drink. With better things to think about, he put the girl out of his mind, went up the steps, and gave the bell a token push. He turned the handle to open the door, with a greeting ready and waiting. Hi. Delia, it's me. I've arrived.

But nothing happened. The door remained firmly closed, which was odd and out of character. Knowing that he was on his way, Delia should surely have left it on the latch. He rang the bell again. And waited.

More silence. He told himself that they had to be there, but already knew with hideous certainty that nobody was going to answer the bell and the Penningtons, damn their bloody eyes, were not at home.

"Hello."

He turned from the inhospitable door. Below, on the pavement, stood the dumpy girl and her dog, back from posting the letter.

"Hi."

"Did you want the Penningtons?"

"They're meant to be giving me dinner."

"They've gone out. I saw them going off in their car."

Noel digested, in gloomy silence, this unwelcome confirmation of what he already knew. Disappointed and let down, he felt very much ill-disposed towards the girl, as one usually does when told something perfectly horrible by another person. It occurred to him that it couldn't have been much fun being a medieval messenger. There was every chance you'd end up without a head, or else employed as a human cannon-ball for some monstrous catapult.

He waited for her to go away. She didn't. He thought, shit. And then, resigned, put his hands in his pockets and descended the steps to join her.

She bit her lip. "What a shame. It's miserable when something like this happens."

"I can't think what's gone wrong."

"What's worse," she told him, in the tones of one determined to look on the bright side, "is when you arrive on the wrong night, and they're not expecting you. I did that once, and it was dreadfully embarrassing. I'd got the dates mixed up."

This did not help. "I suppose you think I've got the dates mixed up."

"It's easily done."

"Not this time. I only got the postcard this morning. The thirteenth."

She said, "But this is the twelfth."

"No, it isn't." He was quite firm. "It's the thirteenth."

"I'm terribly sorry, but it's the twelfth. Thursday, the twelfth of May." She sounded deeply apologetic, as though the mix-up were all her fault. "Tomorrow's the thirteenth."

Slowly, his punch-drunk brain worked this out. Tuesday, Wednesday . . . damn her eyes, she was right. The days had run into each other, and somewhere he had lost track of them. He felt shamefully foolish, and because of this he instantly began to come up with excuses for his own stupidity.

"I've been working. Flying. I've been in New York. Got back this morning. Jet lag does ghastly things to your brain."

She made a sympathetic face. Her dog smelled at his trousers and he moved aside, not wishing to be peed upon. Her hair in the evening sunlight was astonishing. She had grey eyes flecked with green and milk-maid skin, bloomy as a peach.

Somewhere. But where?

He frowned. "Have we met before?"

She smiled. "Well, yes, actually. About six months ago. At the Hathaways' cocktail party, in Lincoln Street. But there were about a million people there, so there's no reason why you should remember."

No, he wouldn't remember. Because she was not the sort of girl that he would register, would want to stay with, or even talk to. Besides, he had gone to that party with Vanessa, and spent most of his time trying to keep track of her, and stop her from finding some other man to have dinner with.

He said, "How extraordinary. I am sorry. And how clever of you to remember me."

"Actually, there was another time." His heart sank, fearing to be faced with yet another social gaffe. "You're with Wenborn and Wein-burg, aren't you? I cooked a directors' lunch for them about six weeks ago. But you wouldn't even have noticed, because I was wearing a white overall, and handing round plates. Nobody ever looks at cooks and wait-resses. It's a funny feeling, as though you are invisible."

He realized that this was true. By now feeling more friendly towards her, he asked her name.

"Alexa Aird."

"I'm Noel Keeling."

"I know. I remembered from the Hathaways' party, and then for the lunch, I had to do a placement, and write names on cards."

Noel cast his mind back to that particular day and recalled in satisfy-ing detail the meal she had produced. Smoked salmon, a perfectly grilled fillet steak, watercress salad, and a lemon sorbet. The very thought of these delights caused his mouth to water. Which reminded him that he was ravenously hungry.

"Who do you work for?"

"Myself. I'm free-lance." She said this quite proudly. Noel hoped that she was not about to embark upon the history of her career. He did not feel strong enough to stand and listen. He needed food, but, more importantly, he needed a drink. He must make some excuse, take his leave, and be rid of her. He opened his mouth to do this, but she spoke first.

"I suppose you wouldn't like to come and have a drink with me?"

The invitation was so unexpected that he did not immediately reply. He looked at her and met her anxious gaze, and realized that she was, in fact, extremely shy, and to come out with such a suggestion had caused her some courageous effort. As well, he found himself uncertain as to whether she was inviting him to the nearest pub or to some grotty attic pad filled with cohabiting colleagues, one of whom would doubtless just have finished washing her hair.

No point in committing himself. He was cautious. "Where?"

"I live two doors down from the Penningtons. And you look as though you could do with a drink."

He stopped being cautious. "I do."

"There's nothing worse than arriving in the wrong place at the wrong time, and knowing that it's all your own fault."

Which could have been more tactfully put. But she was kind. "You're very kind." He made up his mind. "I'd like that very much."

3

*T*HE HOUSE WAS IDENTICAL to the Penningtons', except that the front door was not black, but dark blue, and a bay tree stood in a tub beside it. She went ahead of him, opened it with her key, and he followed her indoors. She shut the door behind them and then stooped to unfasten the little dog's lead. The dog instantly went to drink copiously from a round dish that stood, handily, near the foot of the stairs. The dish had DOG written on it.

She said, "He always does that when he comes in. He seems to think that he's been for a long, long walk."

"What's his name?"

"Larry."

The dog lapped noisily, filling the silence, because, for once in his life, Noel Keeling found himself at a loss for words. He had been caught on the hop. He was not certain what he had expected, but certainly not this —an instant impression of warm opulence, loaded with evidence of wealth and good taste. This was a grand London residence, but on a miniature scale. He saw the narrow hallway, the steep staircase, the polished bannister rail. Honey-coloured carpeting, thick to the wall; an antique console table upon which stood a pink-flowering azalea; an ornately framed oval mirror. As well, and this is what really threw him, the smell. Poignantly familiar. Wax polish, apples, a suggestion of fresh coffee. Pot-pourri, perhaps, and summery flowers. The smell of nostalgia, of youth. The smell of the homes that his mother had created for her children.

Who was responsible for this assault of memory? And who was Alexa Aird? It was an occasion to fall back on small talk, but Noel couldn't think of a mortal thing to say. Perhaps that was best. He stood waiting for what was going to happen next, fully expecting to be led upstairs to some rented bedsitter or tiny attic apartment. But she laid the dog's lead on the table and said in hostessly fashion, "Do come in," and led him into the room that lay beyond the open door.

The house was a twin of the Penningtons' but about a thousand times more impressive. Narrow and long, this room stretched from the front of the house to the back. The street end was the drawing-room—too grand to be called a sitting-room—and the other end was set up for dining. Here, French windows led out onto a wrought-iron balcony, bright with geraniums in terracotta pots.

All was gold and pink. Curtains, padded thick as eiderdowns, hung in swags and folds. Sofas and chairs were loose-covered in the best sort of country chintz, and scattered haphazardly with needlepoint cushions. Recessed alcoves were filled with blue-and-white porcelain, and a bulging *bombé* bureau stood open, stacked with the letters and paperwork of an industrious owner.

It was all very elegant and grown-up, and did not match up in the very least with this quite ordinary and not particularly attractive girl in her jeans and sweat-shirt.

Noel cleared his throat.

"What a charming room."

"Yes, it is pretty, isn't it? You must be exhausted." Now that she was safe, in her own territory, she did not seem so diffident. "Jet lag's a killer. When my father flies in from New York he comes by Concorde because he hates those night flights."

"I'll be all right."

"What would you like to drink?"

"Have you any whisky?"

"Of course. Grouse or Haig's?"

He could scarcely believe his luck. "Grouse!"

"Ice?"

"If you have some."

"I'll go down to the kitchen and get it. If you'd like to help yourself . . . there are glasses . . . everything's there. I won't be a moment. . . ."

She left him. He heard her talking to the little dog, and then light footsteps as she ran down the stairs to the basement. All quiet. Presumably the dog had gone with her. A drink. He moved to the other end of the room, where stood an enviable sideboard, satisfactorily loaded with bottles and decanters.

Here hung charming oil-paintings, still lifes and country scenes. His eyes, roaming, assessing, took in the silver pheasant in the centre of the oval table, the beautiful Georgian coasters. He went to the window and looked down into the garden—a small paved courtyard, with roses climbing the brick wall and a raised bed of wallflowers. There was a white wrought-iron table with four matching chairs, conjuring up visions of alfresco meals, summer supper parties, cool wine.

A drink. On the sideboard were six heavy tumblers, neatly lined up. He reached for the bottle of Grouse, poured himself a slug, added soda, and then returned to the other room. Alone, and still curious as a cat, he prowled. He lifted the fine net curtain and glanced down into the street, then moved to shelves of books, glancing at the titles, endeavouring to find some clue as to the personality of the owner of this delectable house. Novels, biographies, a book on gardens, another on growing roses.

He paused to mull things over. Putting two and two together, he came to the obvious conclusion. Ovington Street belonged to Alexa's parents. Father in some sort of business, sufficiently prestigious to fly Concorde as a matter of course and, moreover, to take his wife with him. He decided that they were, at this moment, in New York. In all probability, once the hard work was over and the conferences finished with, they would fly down to Barbados or the Virgin Islands for a restorative week in the sun. It all clicked logically into place.

As for Alexa, she was house-sitting for them, keeping bandits at bay. This explained why she was on her own, and able to be generous with her father's whisky. When they returned, sun-tanned and bearing gifts, she would go back to her own abode. A shared flat or terraced cottage in Wandsworth or Clapham.

With all this tidily settled in his mind Noel felt better, and strong enough to continue his investigative circuit. The blue-and-white porcelain was Dresden. By one of the armchairs a basket stood on the floor, brimming with bright wools and a half-worked tapestry. On top of the bureau were a number of photographs. People getting married, holding babies, having a picnic with thermos flasks and dogs. Nobody recognizable. One photograph caught his attention, and he picked it up the better to inspect it. A large Edwardian mansion of some bulk, smothered in Virginia creeper. A conservatory bulged from one side, and there were sash windows and a row of dormer windows in the roof. Steps led up to an open front door, and on top of these sat two stately springer spaniels, obediently posed. In the background were winter trees, a church tower, and a rising hill.

The family's country house.

She was coming back. He heard her light footsteps ascending the stair, carefully replaced the photograph, and turned to meet her. She came through the door, carrying a tray loaded with an ice-bucket, a wineglass, an opened bottle of white wine, and a dish of cashew nuts.

"Oh, good, you've got a drink." She set the tray down on the table behind the sofa, edging some magazines aside to make space for it. The little terrier, apparently devoted, dogged her heels. "I'm afraid I could only find a few nuts. . . ."

"At the moment"—he raised his glass—"this is really all I need."

"Poor man." She fished for a handful of cubes and dropped them into his drink.

He said, "I've been standing here coming to terms with the fact that I've made a complete fool of myself."

"Oh, don't be stupid." She poured the wine. "It could happen to anybody. And just think, now you've got a lovely party to look forward to tomorrow evening. And you'll have had a good night's rest, and be the life and soul. Why don't you sit down? This chair's the best, it's large and comfortable. . . ."

It was. And bliss, at last, to be off his aching feet, buffered by soft cushions, and with a drink in his hand. Alexa settled herself in the other chair, opposite him, and with her back to the window. The dog instantly jumped into her lap, made a nest, and went to sleep.

"How long were you in New York?"

"Three days."

"Do you like going?"

"Usually. It's getting back that's so exhausting."

"What were you doing there?"

He told her. He explained about Saddlebags and Harvey Klein. She was impressed. "I've got a Saddlebag belt. My father brought it back for me last year. It's beautiful. Very thick and soft and handsome."

"Well, soon you'll be able to buy one in London. If you don't mind paying an arm and a leg."

"Who plans an advertising campaign?"

"I do. That's my job. I'm Creative Director."

"It sounds frightfully important. You must be very good at it. Do you enjoy it?"

Noel thought about this. "If I didn't enjoy it, I wouldn't be good at it."

"That's absolutely true. I can't think of anything worse than having to do a job one hates."

"Do you like cooking?"

"Yes, I love it. Just as well, because it's just about the only thing I can do. I was dreadfully thick at school. I only got three O levels. My father made noises about me going to do a secretarial training, or a design course, but in the end he agreed it would be a total waste of time and money, and let me be a cook."

"Did you do a training?"

"Oh, yes. I can produce all sorts of exotic dishes."

"Have you always worked on your own?"

"No, I started with an agency. Then, we worked in pairs. But it's more fun on my own. I've built up quite a good little business. Not just directors' lunches, but private dinner parties, and wedding receptions, or just filling people's deep-freezes. I've got a little minivan. I cart everything about in that."

"You do the cooking here?"

"Most of it. Private dinner parties are a bit more complicated, because you have to work in other people's kitchens. And other people's kitchens are always a total enigma. I always take my own sharp knives."

"Sounds bloodthirsty."

She laughed. "For chopping vegetables, not for murdering the hostess. Your glass is empty. Would you like another drink?"

Noel realized that it was, and said that he would, but before he could shift himself, Alexa was on her feet, spilling the little dog gently onto the floor. She took his glass from his hand and disappeared behind him. Comforting clinking sounds reached his ears. A splash of soda. It was all very peaceful. The evening breeze, stirring through the open window, moved the filmy net curtains. Outside, a car started up and drove away, but the children who played on their bicycles had apparently been called indoors and told to go to bed. The abortive dinner party had ceased to be of any importance, and Noel felt a little like a man who, trudging across a barren desert, had inadvertently stumbled upon a lush, palm-fringed oasis.

The cold glass was slipped back into his hand. He said, "I always thought that this was one of the nicest streets in London."

Alexa returned to her chair, curling up with her feet tucked beneath her.

"Where do you live?"

"Pembroke Gardens."

"Oh, but that's lovely, too. Do you live alone?"

He found himself taken off guard, but as well amused by her directness. She was probably remembering the Hathaways' party, and his dogged pursuit of the sensational Vanessa. He smiled. "Most of the time."

His oblique reply went over the top of her head. "Have you got a flat there?"

"Yes. A basement, so it doesn't get much sun. However, I don't spend much time there, so it doesn't really matter. And I usually manage to avoid London weekends."

"Do you go home?"

"No. But I have convenient friends."

"What about brothers and sisters?"

"Two sisters. One lives in London and one in Gloucestershire."

"I expect you go and stay with her."

"Not if I can help it." Enough. He had answered enough questions. It was time to turn the tables. "And you? Do you go home for weekends?"

"No. I'm very often working. People tend to throw dinner parties on Saturday evenings, or Sunday lunches. Besides, it's hardly worth going to Scotland just for a weekend."

Scotland.

"You mean . . . you live in Scotland?"

"No. I live here. But my family home is in Relkirkshire."

I live here.

"But I thought your father—" He stopped, because what he had thought had been pure conjecture. Was it possible that he had been barking up entirely the wrong tree? ". . . I'm sorry, but I got the impression . . ."

"He works in Edinburgh. With Sanford Cubben. He's the head of their Scottish Office."

Sanford Cubben, the vast International Trust Company. Noel made a few mental adjustments. "I see. How stupid of me. I imagined him in London."

"Oh, you mean the New York bit. That's nothing. He flies all over the world. Tokyo, Hong Kong. He's not in this country very much."

"So you don't see much of him?"

"Sometimes when he's passing through London. He doesn't stay here, because he goes to the Company flat, but he usually rings, and if there's time, he takes me out for dinner at the Connaught or Claridges. It's a great treat. I pick up all sorts of cooking ideas."

"I suppose that's as good a reason as any to go to Claridges. But . . ." *He doesn't stay here.* ". . . who owns this house?"

Alexa smiled with total innocence. "I do," she told him.

"Oh . . ." It was impossible to keep the disbelief from his voice. The dog was back in her lap. She stroked his head, played with the furry pricked ears.

"How long have you lived here?"

"About five years. It was my grandmother's house. My mother's mother. We were always very close. I used to spend some part of all my school holidays with her. By the time I came to London to do my cooking course, she was a widow and on her own. So I came to stay with her. And then, last year, she died, and she left the house to me."

"She must have been very fond of you."

"I was terribly fond of her. It all caused a bit of family ill-feeling. My living with her, I mean. My father didn't think it was a good idea at all. He was quite fond of her, but he thought I should be more independent. Make friends of my own age, move into a flat with some other girl. But I didn't really want to. I'm dreadfully lazy about things like that, and Granny Cheriton . . ." Abruptly she stopped. Across the space that divided them their eyes met. Noel said nothing, and after a pause she continued, speaking casually, as though it were of no importance. ". . . she was getting old. It wouldn't have been kind to leave her."

Another silence. Then Noel said, "Cheriton?"

Alexa sighed. "Yes." She sounded as though she were admitting to some heinous crime.

"An unusual name."

"Yes."

"Also well-known."

"Yes."

"Sir Rodney Cheriton?"

"He was my grandfather. I didn't mean to tell you. The name just slipped out."

So that was it. The puzzle solved. That explained the money, the opulence, the precious possessions. Sir Rodney Cheriton, now deceased, founder of a financial empire that stretched world-wide, who, during the sixties and the seventies, had been associated with so many take-over bids and conglomerates that his name was scarcely ever out of the *Financial Times*. This house had been the home of Lady Cheriton, and the sweet-faced, unsophisticated little cook who sat, curled in her chair like a schoolgirl, was her granddaughter.

He was flabbergasted. "Well, who'd have thought it?"

"I don't usually tell people, because I'm not all that proud of it."

"You should be proud. He was a great man."

"It isn't that I didn't like him. He was always very sweet to me. It's just that I don't really approve of huge take-overs and companies getting bigger and bigger. I'd like them to get smaller and smaller. I like corner shops and butchers where the nice man knows your name. I don't like the thought of people getting swallowed up, or lost, or made redundant."

"We can scarcely move backwards."

"I know. That's what my father keeps telling me. But it breaks my heart when a little row of houses gets demolished, and all that goes up in their place is another horrible office block with black windows, like a hen battery. That's what I love about Scotland. Strathcroy, the village we live in, never seems to change. Except that Mrs. McTaggart, who ran the newsagent's, decided that her legs couldn't take the standing any longer and retired, and her shop was bought by Pakistanis. They're called Ishak, and they're terribly nice, and the women wear lovely bright silky clothes. Have you ever been to Scotland?"

"I've been to Sutherland, to fish on the Oykel."

"Would you like to see a picture of our house?"

He did not let on that he had already taken a good look. "I'd love to."

Once more, Alexa set the dog on the floor and got to her feet. The dog, bored by all this activity, sat on the hearthrug and looked fed up. She fetched the photograph and handed it to Noel.

After an appropriate pause he said, "It looks very comfortable."

"It's lovely. Those are my father's dogs."

"What's your father's name?"

"Edmund. Edmund Aird." She went to replace the photograph. Turning, she caught sight of the gold carriage clock which stood in the middle of the mantelpiece. She said, "It's nearly half past eight."

"Good heavens." He checked the time with his watch. "So it is. I must go."

"You don't have to. I mean, I could cook you something, give you supper."

The suggestion was so splendid and so tempting that Noel felt bound to make some small noises of refusal. "You're too kind, but . . ."

"I'm sure you haven't got any food at Pembroke Gardens. Not if you've just come home from New York. And it's no trouble. I'd like it." He could tell from her expression that she was yearning for him to stay. As well, he was painfully hungry. "I've got some lamb chops."

That did it. "I can't think of anything I'd like more."

Alexa's face lit up. She was as transparent as clear spring water. "Oh, good. I'd have felt really inhospitable letting you go without something inside you. Do you want to stay here, or do you want to come down to the kitchen and watch me?"

If he stayed in this chair, he would fall asleep. As well, he wanted to see more of the house. He heaved himself out of the chair. "I'll come and watch you."

Alexa's kitchen was predictable, not modern at all, but quite homely and haphazard, as though it had not been planned, but simply come together over the years. It had a stone-tiled floor with a rush mat or two, and pine cupboards. A deep clay sink faced out over the window and the little area with its steps leading up into the street. The sink was backed with blue-and-white Dutch tiles and the same tiles lined the walls between the cupboards. The tools of her trade were very evident: a thick chopping board, a line of copper saucepans, a marble slab for rolling pastry. There were racks of herbs and bunches of onions and fresh parsley in a mug.

She reached for a blue-and-white butcher's apron and tied it around her waist. Over the thick sweat-shirt this made her look more shapeless than ever and accentuated her rounded, blue-jeaned bottom.

Noel asked if there was anything he could do to help.

"No, not really." She was already busy, turning on the grill, opening drawers. "Unless you'd like to open a bottle of wine. Would you like some?"

"Where would I find a bottle of wine?"

"There's a rack through there. . . ." She indicated with her head, her hands being occupied. "On the floor. I haven't got a cellar, and that's the coolest spot there is."

Noel went to look. At the back of the kitchen an archway led into what had probably once been a small scullery. This too was stone-floored, and here stood a number of shining white electrical appliances. A dishwasher, a clothes washer, a tall refrigerator, and a huge chest deep-freeze. At the far end, a half-glassed door led directly out into the little garden. By the door, in country fashion, stood a pair of rubber boots and a wooden tub of gardening tools. An ancient raincoat and a battered felt hat hung from a hook.

He found the wine-rack beyond the deep-freeze. Crouching, he inspected a few bottles. She had an excellent selection. He chose a Beaujolais, went back to the kitchen.

"How about this?"

She glanced at it. "Perfect. That was a good year. There's a corkscrew in that drawer. If you open it now, that'll give it time to breathe."

He found the corkscrew and drew the cork. It came, sweetly and cleanly, and he set the open bottle on the table. With nothing more to be done, he drew back a chair and settled himself at the table to enjoy the last of his whisky.

She had taken the chops from the refrigerator, assembled the makings of a salad, found a stick of French bread. Now she was arranging the chops on the grill-pan, reaching for a jar of rosemary. All this was accomplished deftly and with the greatest economy of effort, and it occurred to Noel that, working, she had become quite assured and confident, probably because she was engaged in doing the one thing she knew that she was really good at.

He said, "You look very professional."

"I am."

"Do you garden as well?"

"Why do you ask that?"

"All the clobber by the back door."

"I see. Yes, I do garden, but it's so tiny that it's not *really* gardening. At Balnaid, the garden's enormous, and there's always something needing to be done."

"Balnaid?"

"That's the name of our house in Scotland."

"My mother was a manic gardener." Having said this, Noel could not think why he had mentioned the fact. He did not usually talk about his mother unless somebody asked him a direct question. "Perpetually digging, or barrowing great loads of manure."

"Doesn't she garden any longer?"

"She's dead. She died four years ago."

"Oh, I am sorry. Where did she do her gardening?"

"In Gloucestershire. She bought a house with a couple of acres of wilderness. By the time she died, she'd transformed it into something very special. You know . . . the sort of garden people walk around in after lunch parties."

Alexa smiled. "She sounds rather like my other grandmother, Vi. She lives in Strathcroy. Her name's Violet Aird, but we all call her Vi." The chops were grilling, the bread put to warm, the plates to heat. "My mother's dead, too. She was killed in a car accident when I was six."

"It's my turn to be sorry."

"I remember her, of course, but not really very well. I remember her mostly coming to say good night before she went out for a dinner party. Lovely airy dresses, and furs, and smelling of scent."

"Six is very young to lose your mother."

"It wasn't as bad as it might have been. I had a darling Nanny called Edie Findhorn. And after Mummy died we went back to Scotland and lived with Vi at Balnaid. So I was luckier than most."

"Did your father marry again?"

"Yes. Ten years ago. She's called Virginia. She's not much older than I am."

"A wicked stepmother?"

"No. She's sweet. A bit like a sister. She's terribly pretty. And I've got a half-brother called Henry. He's nearly eight."

Now she was making the salad. With a sharp knife she chopped and shredded. Tomatoes and celery, tiny fresh mushrooms. Her hands were brown and capable, the nails short and unvarnished. There was something very satisfactory about them. He tried to recall the last time he had sat thus, slightly woozy with hunger and drink, and peacefully watched while a woman prepared a meal for him. He couldn't.

The trouble was that he had never gone for domesticated females. His girl-friends were usually models, or young aspiring actresses with immense ambition and little brain. All they had in common was their general appearance, for he liked them very young and very thin with tiny breasts and long, attenuated legs. Which was great for his own personal amusement and satisfaction, but not much use when it came to being good about the house. Besides, they were nearly all . . . however skinny . . . on some sort of diet, and while able to down enormous and expensive restaurant meals, were disinterested in producing even the simplest of snacks in the privacy of either their own flats, or Noel's.

"Oh, darling, it's such a bore. Besides, I'm not hungry. Have an apple."

From time to time there had come into Noel's life a girl so besotted that she wished only to spend the rest of her days with him. Then much effort—perhaps too much—had been made. Intimate dinners by gas-fired logs, and invitations to the country and doggy weekends. But

Noel, wary of commitment, had backed away, and the girls in question, after a painful period of abortive telephone calls and tearful accusations, had found other men and married them. So he had reached thirty-four and was still a bachelor. Brooding over his empty whisky glass, Noel could not decide whether this left him feeling triumphant or defeated.

"There." The salad was ready. Now she began to mix a dressing with beautiful green olive oil and pale wine vinegar. Various herbs and seasonings were added, and the smell of these made his mouth water. With this done, she started to lay the table. A red-and-white-checked cloth, wine-glasses, wooden mills for pepper and salt, a pottery butter dish. She took forks and knives from a drawer and handed them to Noel and he set the two places. It seemed an appropriate moment to pour the wine, so he did, and handed Alexa her glass.

She took it from him. In her apron and bulky sweat-shirt, and with her cheeks glowing from the heat of the grill, she said, "Here's to Saddlebags."

He found himself, for some reason, much touched. "And here's to you, Alexa. And thank you."

It was a simple but splendid meal, living up to all Noel's greedy expectations. The chops were tender, the salad crisp; warm bread to mop up juices and dressings, and all washed down by fine wine. After a bit, his stomach stopped groaning, and he felt infinitely better.

"I can't remember food ever tasting so good."

"It's not anything very special."

"But perfect." He took more salad. "Any time you need a recommendation, let me know."

"Don't you ever cook for yourself?"

"No. I can fry bacon and eggs, but if pushed I buy gourmet dishes from Marks and Spencer and heat them up. Every now and then, if I'm desperate, I go and spend an evening with Olivia, my London sister, but she's as useless in the kitchen as I am, and we usually finish up eating something exotic, like quails' eggs or caviar. A treat, but not very filling."

"Is she married?"

"No. She's a career lady."

"What does she do?"

"She's Editor-in-Chief of *Venus*."

"Goodness." She smiled. "What illustrious relations we both seem to have."

Having devoured everything on the table, Noel found himself still peckish, and so Alexa produced cheese and a bunch of pale-green seedless grapes. With these, they finished the last of the wine. Alexa suggested coffee.

By now it was growing dark. Outside, in the dusky blue street, the lights had come on. Their glow penetrated the basement kitchen, but mostly all was shadowy. Noel was, all at once, overcome by a mammoth yawn. When he had dealt with this, he apologized. "I'm sorry. I really must get home."

"Have some coffee first. It'll keep you awake until you reach your bed. I tell you what—why don't you go upstairs and relax, and I'll bring your coffee up to you. And then I'll phone for a taxi."

Which sounded an eminently sensible idea.

"Right."

But even saying the word took much conscious effort. He was aware of arranging his tongue and his lips in the correct position to make the appropriate sound, and knew that he was either drunk or on the point of flaking out from lack of sleep. Coffee was an excellent idea. He put his hands on the table and levered himself to his feet. Going up the basement stairs, headed for the drawing-room, was even more of a trial. Half-way up he stumbled but somehow managed to keep his balance and not to fall flat on his face.

Upstairs, the empty room waited, quiet in the bloomy twilight. The only illumination came from the street lights, and these were reflected from the brass fender and the facets of the crystal chandelier that hung from the middle of the ceiling. It seemed a pity to dispel the peaceful dusk by turning on switches, so he didn't. The dog was asleep on the chair that Noel had previously occupied, so he sank down in a corner of the sofa. The dog, disturbed, awoke and raised his head, and stared at Noel. Noel stared back. The dog turned into two dogs. He was drunk. He had not slept for ever. He would not sleep now. He was not sleeping.

He was dozing. Sleeping and waking at the same time. He was in the 747, droning back over the Atlantic, with his fat neighbour snoring alongside. His chairman was telling him to go to Edinburgh, to sell Saddlebags to a man called Edmund Aird. There were voices, calling and shouting; the children playing in the street on their bicycles. No, they were not in the street, they were outside, in some garden. He was in a cramped and steeply ceilinged room, peering from the peep-hole of a window. Honeysuckle fronds tapped on the glass. His old room, in his mother's house in Gloucestershire. Outside on the lawn, a game was in progress. Children and adults played cricket. Or was it rounders? Or baseball? They looked up and saw his face through the glass. "Come down," they told him. "Come down and play." He was pleased that they wanted him. It was good to be home. He went out of the room and downstairs; stepped out into the garden, but the cricket game was over, and they had all disappeared. He did not mind. He lay on the grass and stared at the bright sky, and everything was all right. None of the bad things had happened after all, and nothing had changed. He was alone, but soon somebody would come. He could wait.

Another sound. A clock ticking. He opened his eyes. The street lamps no longer shone, and the darkness had gone. It was not his mother's garden, not his mother's house, but some strange room. He had no idea where he was. He lay flat on his back on a sofa, with a rug over him. The fringe of the rug tickled his chin, and he pushed it away. Staring upwards, he saw the glittering droplets of the chandelier, and then remembered. Moving his head, he saw the armchair, with its back to the window; a girl sat there, her bright hair an aureole against the morning light beyond the uncurtained window. He stirred. She stayed silent. He said her name. "Alexa?"

"Yes." She was awake.

"What time is it?"

"Just after seven."

"Seven in the morning?"

"Yes."

"I've been here all night." He stretched, easing his long legs. "I fell asleep."

"You were asleep by the time I came up with the coffee. I thought about waking you, but then I decided against it."

He blinked, clearing the sleep from his eyes. He saw that she was no longer wearing her jeans and sweat-shirt, but a white towelling robe, wrapped closely about her. She had bundled herself up in a blanket, but her legs and feet, protruding, were bare.

"Have you been there all night?"

"Yes."

"You should have gone to bed."

"I didn't like to leave you. I didn't want you to wake up and feel you had to go, and not be able to find a taxi in the middle of the night. I made up my spare bed, but then I thought, what's the point? So I just left you to sleep."

He caught the tail end of his dream before it faded into oblivion. He had lain in his mother's garden in Gloucestershire, and known that someone was coming. Not his mother. Penelope was dead. Somebody else. Then the dream was gone for good, leaving him with Alexa.

He felt, surprisingly, enormously well, energetic and refreshed. Decisive. "I must go home."

"Shall I call you a taxi?"

"No. I'll walk. It'll do me good."

"It's a lovely morning. Do you want something to eat before you go?"

"No, I'm fine." He pushed aside the rug and sat up, smoothing back his hair and running his hand over his stubbly chin. "I must go." He got to his feet.

Alexa made no effort to persuade him to stay, but simply came with him into the hall, opened her front door onto a pearly, pristine May morning. The distant rumble of traffic was already audible, though a bird was singing from some tree, and the air was fresh. He imagined that he could smell lilac.

"Goodbye, Noel."

He turned to her. "I'll ring you."

"You don't need to."

"Don't I?"

"You don't owe me anything."

"You're very sweet." He stooped and kissed her peachy cheek. "Thank you."

"I've liked it."

He left her. Went down the steps and set off, at a brisk clip, down the pavement. At the end of the street he turned and looked back. She was gone, and the blue front door stood closed. But it seemed to Noel that the house with the bay tree had a special look about it.

He smiled to himself and went on his way.

June

1

ISOBEL BALMERINO, AT THE WHEEL of her minibus, drove the ten miles to Corriehill. It was nearly four o'clock in the afternoon and the beginning of June, but although the trees were heavy with leaf and the fields green with growing crops, there had, so far, been no summer at all. It was not exactly cold, but it was dank and drizzling, and all the way from Croy her windscreen wipers had been working. Clouds hung low over the hills and all was drowned in greyness. She felt sorry for the foreign visitors, come so far to see the glories of Scotland, only to find them shrouded in murk and almost invisible.

Not that this troubled her. She had made the complicated journey, cross-country and by back roads, so many times before that she sometimes thought that if she were to dispatch the minibus on its own it would manage very nicely, getting itself to Corriehill and back with no human assistance, reliable as a faithful horse.

Now she had come to the familiar junction and was nearly there. She changed down and swung the minibus into a single-track lane hedged with hawthorn. This lane led up and onto the hill, and as she climbed, the mist grew thicker; prudently she switched on the headlights. To her right appeared the tall stone wall, the march boundary of the Corriehill estate. Another quarter of a mile, and she had reached the great entrance gates, the two lodges. She turned between these and bumped her way up the rutted drive lined with historic beeches and deep verges of rough grass which, in spring, were gold with daffodils. The daffodils had long since died back, and their withered heads and dying leaves were all that remained of their former glory. Some time, some day, Verena's handyman would cut the verges with his garden tractor, and that would be the end of the daffodils. Until next spring.

It occurred to her, sadly, and not for the first time, that as you grew older you became busier, and time went faster and faster, the months pushing each other rudely out of the way, and the years slipping off the calendar and into the past. Once, there had been time. Time to stand, or sit, and just *look* at daffodils. Or to abandon housekeeping, on the spur of the moment, walk out of the back door and up the hill, into the lark-song emptiness of a summer morning. Or to take off for a self-indulgent day in Relkirk, shopping for frivolities, meeting a girl-friend for lunch, the wine bar warm with humanity and conversation, smelling of coffee and the sort of food that one never cooked for oneself.

All treats that for a number of reasons didn't seem to happen any longer.

The driveway levelled off. Beneath the wheels of the minibus, gravel scrunched. The house loomed up at her through the mist. There were no other cars, which meant that probably all the other hostesses had been, collected their guests, and gone. So Verena would be waiting for her. Isobel hoped that she would not have become impatient.

She drew up, switched off her engine, and got out into the soft, drizzly air. The main door stood open, giving onto a large paved porch, with an inner glass door beyond. This porch was stacked with an enormous amount of expensive luggage. Isobel quailed, because it seemed to be even more lavish than usual. Suitcases (hugely big), garment bags, small grips, golf bags, boxes and parcels and carriers, emblazoned with the familiar names of large stores. (They'd obviously been shopping.) All of these were tagged with distinctive yellow labels: SCOTTISH COUNTRY TOURS.

Diverted, she paused to read the names on the labels. Mr. Joe Hardwicke. Mr. Arnold Franco. Mrs. Myra Hardwicke. Mrs. Susan Franco. The suitcases were heavily monogrammed, and the golf bags had prestigious club labels hanging from their handles.

She sighed. Here we go again. She opened the inner door.

"Verena!"

The hallway at Corriehill was immense, with a carved oak stairway rising to the upper floors, and much panelling. The floor was scattered with rugs, some quite ordinary and others probably priceless, and in the middle of the floor stood a table bearing a varied collection of objects: a potted geranium, a dog's lead, a brass tray for letters, and a massive leather-bound visitors' book.

"Verena?"

A door, distantly, shut. Footsteps came up the passage from the direction of the kitchen. Verena Steynton presently appeared, looking, as always, tall, slender, unfussed, and perfectly turned out. She was one of those women who, maddeningly, always appear co-ordinated, as though she spent much time each day selecting and matching her various garments. This skirt, this shirt; that cashmere cardigan, these shoes. Even the damp and muggy weather, which ruined the hair-dos of most right-minded women, didn't stand a chance with Verena's coiffure, which never wilted under the most adverse of circumstances, and always appeared as neat and glamorous as if she had just come out from under the dryer. Isobel had no illusions about her own appearance. Stocky and sturdy as a highland pony, her complexion rosy and shining, her hands roughened by work, she had long stopped bothering about the way she looked. But, seeing Verena, she all at once wished that she had taken the time to change out of her corduroy trousers and the quilted sludge-coloured waistcoat that was her oldest friend.

"Isobel."

"I hope I'm not late."

"No. You're the last but you're not late. Your guests are ready and waiting for you in the drawing-room. Mr. and Mrs. Hardwicke, and Mr. and Mrs. Franco. From the look of them slightly more robust than our usual run of clients." Isobel knew some relief. Perhaps the men would be able to hump their own golf bags. "Where's Archie? Are you on your own?"

"He had to go to a church meeting at Balnaid."

"Will you manage?"

"Of course."

"Well, look, before you whisk them away, there's been a slight change of plan. I'll explain. We'd better go into the library."

Obediently, Isobel followed her, prepared to take orders. The library at Corriehill was a pleasant room, smaller than most of the other apartments, and smelled comfortably masculine—of pipe smoke and wood-smoke, of old books and old dogs. The old-dog smell emanated from an elderly Labrador snoozing on its cushion by the ashy remains of a fire. It raised its head, saw the two ladies, blinked in a superior fashion and went back to sleep.

"The thing is . . ." Verena started, and at once the telephone on the desk began to ring. She said, "Damn. Sorry, I won't be a moment," and went to answer it. "Hello, Verena Steynton . . . Yes." Her voice changed. "Mr. Abberley. Thank you for calling back." She pulled the chair from the desk and sat down, reaching for her ball-point pen and a pad of paper. She looked as though she was settling in for a long session and Isobel's heart sank, because she wanted to get home.

"Yes. Oh, splendid. Now, we shall need your largest marquee, and I think the pale-yellow-and-white lining. And a dance floor." Isobel pricked up her ears, stopped feeling impatient and eavesdropped shamelessly. "The date? We thought the sixteenth of September. That's a Friday. Yes, I think you'd better come and see me, and we'll talk it over. Next week would be fine. Wednesday morning. Right. I'll see you then.

Goodbye, Mr. Abberley." She rang off and leaned back in her chair, wearing the satisfied expression of one with a job well done. "Well, that's the first thing settled."

"What on earth are you planning now?"

"Well, Angus and I have been talking about it for ages, and we've finally decided to take the plunge. Katy's twenty-one this year, and we're going to have a dance for her."

"Heavens above, you must be feeling rich."

"No, not particularly, but it is something of an event, and we owe about a million people hospitality, so we'll get them all off in one smashing do."

"But September's ages away, and it's only the beginning of June."

"I know, but one can't start too early. You know what September's like." Isobel did know. The Scottish season, with a mass exodus from the south to the north for the grouse shooting. Every large house filled with house parties, dances, cricket matches, Highland games, and every sort of social activity, all finally culminating in an exhausting week of hunt balls.

"We have to have a marquee because there's really not space for dancing indoors, but Katy insists we must fix up some corner as a night-club so that all her yuppie friends from London can have their little smooch. Then I'll have to find a really good country dance band, and a competent caterer. But at least I've got the tent. You'll all get invitations, of course." She gave Isobel a stern look. "I hope Lucilla will be here."

It was hard not to feel a little envious of Verena, sitting there planning a dance for her daughter, knowing that that daughter would be helpful and co-operative and enjoy every moment of her party. Her own Lucilla and Katy Steynton had been at school together, and friends in the lack-lustre fashion of children thrown together by their parents. For Lucilla was two years younger than Katy, and had a very different personality, and as soon as school was behind them, their ways had parted.

Katy, any mother's dream, had dutifully conformed. A year in Switzerland, and then a secretarial course in London. Graduated, she'd found herself a worthwhile job . . . something to do with funding for charity . . . and shared a small house in Wandsworth with three eminently suitable friends. Before long, she would doubtless become engaged to an excellent young man called either Nigel, Jeremy, or Christopher, her blameless face would appear on the front page of *Country Life,* and the wedding would be predictably traditional with a white dress, a great number of small bridesmaids, and "Praise My Soul the King of Heaven."

Isobel did not want Lucilla to be like Katy, but sometimes, as at this moment, she could not help wishing that her darling, dreamy daughter had turned out to be just a little more ordinary. But even as a child, Lucilla had shown signs of individuality and gentle rebellion. Her political tendencies were strongly Left Wing, and at the drop of a hat she would involve herself, with much passion, in any cause that caught her attention. She was against nuclear power, fox-hunting, the culling of baby seals, the cutting of student grants, and the planting of tracts of horrible conifers in order to provide pop stars with tax-deductible incomes. At the same time, she voiced much concern over the plight of the homeless, the down-and-outs, the drug addicts, and the poor unfortunates who found themselves dying of AIDS.

From an early age, she had always been intensely creative and artistic, and after six months in Paris working as an au pair, she was accepted at the College of Art in Edinburgh. Here, she made friends with the most extraordinary people, whom, from time to time, she brought to Croy to stay. They were a funny-looking lot, but no funnier than Lucilla, who dressed from the Oxfam shop and thought nothing of wearing a lace evening dress with a man's tweed jacket and a pair of Edwardian lace-up boots.

With Art School behind her, she had failed entirely to find any sort of a way in which to earn her keep. No person seemed inclined to buy her incomprehensible paintings, and no gallery wished to exhibit them. Living in an attic in India Street, she had kept herself by going out to clean other people's houses. This had proved strangely lucrative, and as soon as she had saved up enough to pay her fare across the Channel, she had taken off for France with a backpack and her painting gear. Last heard of she was in Paris, staying with some couple she had met on the road. It was all very worrying.

Would she come home? Isobel could write, of course, to the Poste Restante address her daughter had given her. *Darling Lucilla, be here in September because you have been asked to Katy Steynton's dance.* But it was unlikely that Lucilla would pay much attention. She had never enjoyed formal parties, and could think of nothing to say to the well-connected young men she had met at them. *Mummy, they're quite gruesomely square. And they've all got hair like tweed.*

She was impossible. She was also sweet, kind, funny, and overflowing with love. Isobel missed her quite dreadfully.

She sighed and said, "I don't know. I don't suppose so."

"Oh dear." Verena was sympathetic, which didn't make it any better. "Well, never mind, I'll send her an invitation. Katy would so love to see her again."

Privately, Isobel doubted this. She said, "Is your dance a secret, or can I talk about it?"

"No, of course it's not a secret. The more people who know, the better. Perhaps they'll offer to have dinner parties."

"I'll have a dinner party."

"You are a saint." They might have sat there making plans for ever had not Verena, all at once, remembered the business in hand. "Heavens above, I've forgotten those poor Americans. They'll be wondering what's happened to us. Now, look . . . the thing is"—she rummaged on her desk and produced some sheets of typed instructions—"that the two men have spent most of their time playing golf, and they want to play tomorrow, so they're going to give the trip to Glamis a miss. Instead, I've fixed for a car to come and fetch them from Croy at nine o'clock tomorrow morning and take them to Gleneagles. And the same car will bring them back sometime during the afternoon when they've finished their game. But the ladies want to go to Glamis, so if you could have them back here at about ten o'clock, they can join the others in the coach."

Isobel nodded, hoping that she would forget none of this. Verena was so efficient and, to all intents and purposes, Isobel's boss. Scottish Country Tours was run from a central office in Edinburgh, but Verena was the local co-ordinating agent. It was Verena who telephoned Isobel each week to let her know how many guests she could expect (six was the limit, as she had no room for more) and as well fill her in with any small idiosyncrasies or personality problems of her guests.

The tours started in May and continued until the end of August. Each one lasted a week and followed a regular pattern. The group, arriving from Kennedy, began their stay in Edinburgh, where they spent two days sightseeing in the Borders and in the City itself. On Tuesday their coach brought them to Relkirk, where they dutifully plodded around the Auld Kirk, the local Castle, and a National Trust garden. They were then transported to Corriehill, to be welcomed and sorted out by Verena. From Corriehill they were collected by the various hostesses. Wednesday was the day for Glamis Castle and a scenic drive to Pitlochry, and on Thursday they set off yet again in the coach to view the Highlands and to visit Deeside and Inverness. On Friday they returned to Edinburgh, and on Saturday they flew home, back to Kennedy and all points west.

Isobel was certain that by then they must all be in a state of total exhaustion.

It was Verena who, five years ago, had roped Isobel into the business. She explained what was involved and gave Isobel the firm's hand-out to read. It was effusive.

> Stay as a private guest in a private house. Experience for yourself the hospitality and historic grandeur of some of Scotland's loveliest homes, and meet, as friends, the ancient families who live in them. . . .

Such hyperbole took a bit of living up to.
"We're not an ancient family," she'd pointed out to Verena.
"Ancient enough."
"And Croy's not exactly historic."

"Bits of it are. And you've got lots of bedrooms. That's what really counts. And think of all that lovely lolly. . . ."

It was this that had finally decided Isobel. Verena's proposition came at a time when the Balmerino fortunes, in every sense of the word, were at a low ebb. Archie's father, the second Lord Balmerino, and the most charming and impractical of men, had died leaving the estate in some disarray. His unexpected demise took him, and most other people, quite by surprise, and because of this, stupendous death duties creamed off most of the inherited family wealth. With the two children, Lucilla and Hamish, in the throes of their education, the large and inconvenient house to keep going, and the lands to be maintained in some sort of order, the young Balmerinos found themselves faced with certain problems. Archie, at that time, was still a regular soldier. But he had joined the Queen's Loyal Highlanders at the age of nineteen simply because he could think of nothing else he particularly wanted to do, and although he had thoroughly enjoyed his years with the Regiment, he was not blessed with a driving ambition to succeed and knew that he would never make Major-General.

Keeping Croy, living there, come hell or high water, became their first priority. Optimistically, they laid plans. Archie would retire from the Army, and while he was young enough to do so, find himself some sort of a job. But before this could happen he was committed to a last tour of duty with his Regiment, and went with them to Northern Ireland.

The Regiment returned home four months later, but it was eight months before Archie came back to Croy, and it took Isobel about eight days to realize that any sort of a job was, for the time being, out of the question. In some desperation, through long and sleepless nights, she reviewed their plight.

But they had friends, in particular Edmund Aird. Realizing the gravity of the situation, Edmund moved in and took control. It was Edmund who found a tenant for the home farm, and Edmund who assumed responsibility for the grouse moor. Together with Gordon Gillock, the game-keeper, he saw to the burning of the heather and the maintenance of the butts, and then let the entire concern out to a syndicate of businessmen from the south, retaining a gun for himself and a half-gun for Archie.

For Isobel, to be shed of at least some of her anxieties was an enormous relief, but income remained a vexing problem. There was still some inherited capital, but this was tied up in stocks and bonds, and was all that Archie had to leave to his children. Isobel had a little money of her own, but this, even added to Archie's Army pension and his sixty-per-cent disability pension, did not amount to very much. The day-to-day expenses of simply running the house and keeping the family fed and clothed remained a constant source of worry, so that Verena's suggestion, initially daunting, was in fact the answer to a prayer.

"Oh, come on, Isobel. You can do it standing on your head."

And Isobel realized that she could. After all, she was well used to managing the big house, and accustomed to having people to stay. When Archie's father was alive there were always house parties to be arranged for the shooting, and the dances in September. During the school holidays, Croy filled up with the children's friends, and Christmas and Easter never passed without entire families coming to share the festivities.

Compared to all this, Verena's proposition did not sound at all arduous. It would only take up two days a week throughout the four months of summer. Surely that could not be too demanding. And . . . cheering thought . . . it would be stimulation for Archie, people coming and going. Helping to entertain them would give him an interest and bolster his morale, sadly in need of a boost.

What she hadn't realized, and what she had painfully learned, was that entertaining paying guests was a very different kettle of fish to having one's own friends about the place. You couldn't argue with them, any more than you could sit about in a companionable silence. Nor could you allow them to slope into the kitchen to peel a pot of potatoes or concoct a salad. The real rub was that they were paying. This put hospitality on a totally different level because it meant that everything had to be perfect. The tour was not cheap and, as Verena forthrightly insisted, the clients must be given value for their dollars.

There were certain guide-lines, printed out on a special instruction sheet for hostesses. Every bedroom must have its own bathroom, preferably adjoining. Beds must have electric blankets, and the rooms must be centrally heated. Also, if possible, there should be supplementary heating . . . preferably a real fire but, failing this, then an electric or gas fire. Fresh flowers must be arranged in the bedrooms.

(Reading this, Isobel had known some annoyance. Who did they think they were? She had never in her life put a guest in a room without seeing that there were fresh flowers on the dressing-table.)

Then there were more rules about breakfast and dinner. Breakfast must be robust and hearty. Orange juice, coffee, and tea, all available. In the evenings, a cocktail must be offered, and wine at dinner-time. This meal had to be formally served, with candles, crystal, and silver on the table, and consist of at least three courses, to be followed by coffee and conversation. Other diversions, however unlikely, could be offered. A little music . . . perhaps bagpipe-playing . . . ?

The overseas visitors awaited them in Verena's drawing-room. Verena flung open the door. "I am sorry we've been so long. Just one or two ends that needed to be tied up," she told them in her best committee-meeting voice, which brooked no question nor argument. "Here we are, and here is your hostess, come to take you to Croy."

The drawing-room at Corriehill was large and light, palely decorated and little used. Today, however, because of the inclement weather, a small fire flickered in the grate, and around this, disposed on armchairs and sofas, sat the four Americans. To while away the time, they had switched on the television and were watching, in a bemused fashion, cricket. Disturbed, they rose to their feet, turning smiling faces, and one of the men stooped and politely turned the television off.

"Now, introductions. Mr. and Mrs. Hardwicke, and Mr. and Mrs. Franco, this is your hostess for the next two days. Lady Balmerino."

Shaking hands, Isobel understood what Verena had meant when she described this week's guests as being slightly more robust than usual. Scottish Country Tours seemed, for some reason, to attract clients of an extremely advanced age, and sometimes they were not only geriatric but in a dicey state of health—short of breath and uncertain about the legs. These two couples, however, were scarcely beyond middle age. Grey-haired, certainly, but apparently bursting with energy, and all of them enviably tanned. The Francos were small of stature, and Mr. Franco very bald, and the Hardwickes were tall and muscled and slim, and looked as though they spent their lives out of doors and taking a great deal of exercise.

"I'm afraid I'm a little late," Isobel found herself saying, although she knew perfectly well that she was not. "But we can go whenever you're ready."

They were ready right now. The ladies collected their handbags and their beautiful new Burberry raincoats, and the little party all trooped through the hall and out into the porch. Isobel went to open the back doors of the minibus, and by the time she had done this, the men were humping and heaving the big suitcases across the gravel, and helped her to load them. (This, too, was novel. She and Verena usually had to do the job by themselves.) When all were safely aboard, she shut the doors and fastened them. The Hardwickes and the Francos were saying good-bye to Verena. "But," Verena said, "I'll see you ladies tomorrow. And I hope the golf's a great success. You'll love Gleneagles."

Doors were opened and they all climbed in. Isobel took her place behind the wheel, fastened her seat-belt, turned on the ignition, and they were away.

"I do apologize for the weather. We've had no summer at all yet."

"Oh, it hasn't bothered us in the least. We're just sorry you had to come out on such a day to come and collect us. Hope it wasn't too much trouble."

"No, not at all. That's my job."

"Have we far to go to your home, Lady Balmerino?"

"About ten miles. And I wish you'd call me Isobel."

"Why, thank you, we will. And I am Susan and my husband is Arnold, and the Hardwickes are Joe and Myra."

"Ten miles," said one of the men. "That's quite a distance."

"Yes. Actually my husband usually comes with me on these trips. But he had to go to a meeting. He'll be home for tea, though, so you'll meet him then."

"Is Lord Balmerino in business?"

"No. No, it's not a business meeting. It's a church meeting. Our village church. We have to raise some money. It's rather a shoe-string affair. But my husband's grandfather built it, so he feels a sort of family responsibility."

It was raining again. The windscreen wipers swung to and fro. Perhaps conversation would divert their attention from the misery of it all.

"Is this your first visit to Scotland?"

The two ladies, chipping in on each other like a close-harmony duo, told her. The men had been there before, to play golf, but this was the first time their wives had accompanied them. And they just loved every inch of the place, and had gone crazy in the shops in Edinburrow. It had rained, of course, but that hadn't bothered them. They had their new Burberries to wear, and both decided that the rain made Edinburrow look just so historic and romantic that they had been able to picture Mary and Bothwell riding together up the Royal Mile.

When they had finished, Isobel asked them what part of the States they came from.

"New York State. Rye."

"Are you by the sea there?"

"Oh, sure. Our kids sail every weekend."

Isobel could imagine it. Could imagine those kids, tanned and wind-blown, bursting with vitamins and fresh orange juice and health, scudding over starch-blue seas beneath the curving wing of a snow-white mainsail. And sunshine. Blue skies and sunshine. Day after day of it, so that you could plan tennis matches and picnics and evening barbecues and know that it wasn't going to rain.

That was how summers, in memory, used to be. The endless, aimless summers of childhood. What had happened to those long, light days, sweet with the scent of roses, when one had to come indoors only to eat, and sometimes not even then? Swimming in the river, lazing in the garden, playing tennis, having tea in the shade of some tree because it was too hot anywhere else. She remembered picnics on moors that simmered in the sunlight, the heather too dry to light a camp-fire, and the larks flying high. What had happened to her world? What cosmic disaster had transformed those bright days into week after week of dark and soggy gloom?

It wasn't just the weather, it was just that the weather made everything so much worse. Like Archie getting his leg shot off, and having to be nice to people you didn't know because they were paying you money to sleep in your spare bedrooms. And being tired all the time, and never buying new clothes, and worrying about Hamish's school fees, and missing Lucilla.

She heard herself saying, with some force, "It's the one horrible thing about living in Scotland."

For a moment, perhaps surprised by her outburst, nobody commented on this announcement. Then one of the ladies spoke. "I beg your pardon?"

"I'm sorry. I meant the rain. We get so tired of the rain. I meant these horrible summers."

2

THE PRESBYTERIAN CHURCH IN STRATHCROY, the established Church of Scotland, stood, impressive, ancient, and venerable, on the south bank of the river Croy. It was reached from the main road that ran through the village by a curved stone bridge, and its setting was pastoral. Glebe lands sloped to the water's edge, a grassy pasture where, each September, the Strathcroy Games were held. The churchyard, shaded by a mammoth beech, was filled with time-worn, leaning gravestones, and a grassy path led between these to the gates of the Manse. This as well was solid and imposing, built to contain the large families of bygone ministers and boasting an enviable garden burgeoning with gnarled but productive fruit trees and old-fashioned roses, for these flourished behind the protection of a high stone wall. All of this, so charmingly disposed, exuded an ambience of timelessness, domestic security, and God-fearing piety.

In contrast, the little Episcopal church, like a poor relation, crouched directly across the bridge, totally overshadowed, both literally and metaphorically, by its rival. The main road ran close by, and between the church and the road was a strip of grass which the rector, the Reverend Julian Gloxby, himself cut each week. A small lane led up a slope to the back of the church and to the rectory that stood behind it. Both were modest in size and whitewashed. The church had a little tower with a single bell, and a wooden porchway enclosed its main door. Inside, it was equally unassuming. No handsome pews, no flagged floors, no historic relics. A worn drugget led to the altar, and a breathless harmonium did duty as an organ. There was always a faint smell of damp.

Both church and rectory had been erected at the turn of the century by the first Lord Balmerino and handed over to the Diocese with a small endowment for maintenance. The income this produced had long since trickled to nothing, the congregation was tiny, and the Vestry, endeavouring to make ends meet, found themselves perpetually strapped for cash.

When the electric wiring was discovered to be not only faulty but downright dangerous, it was very nearly the last straw. But Archie Balmerino rallied his meagre troops, chaired committees, visited the Bishop and wangled a grant. Even so, some fund-raising was going to be necessary. Various suggestions were put forward, discussed, and eventually turned down. In the end, it was decided to fall back on that old dependable, a church sale. This would take place in July, and in the Village Hall. There would be a Jumble stall, a Plant and Vegetable stall, a White Elephant and Handwork stall, and, of course, teas.

A committee was duly appointed and met, on that grey and damp June afternoon, around the dining-room table at Balnaid, home of Virginia and Edmund Aird. By half past four the meeting was over, with business satisfactorily concluded and modest plans laid. These included the printing of eye-catching posters, the borrowing of a number of trestle-tables, and the organizing of a raffle.

The rector and Mrs. Gloxby, and Toddy Buchanan, who ran the Strathcroy Arms, had already taken their leave and driven away in their cars. Dermot Honeycombe, busy with his antique shop, had been unable to attend. In his absence, he had been given the job of running the White Elephant stall.

Now only three people remained. Virginia and Violet, her mother-in-law, sat at one end of the long mahogany table and Archie Balmerino at the other. As soon as the others had gone, Virginia had disappeared into the kitchen to make tea, and brought it to them on a tray, without ceremony. Three mugs, a brown teapot, a jug of milk, and a bowl of sugar. It was both refreshing and welcome, and it was pleasant to relax after the concentrated discussions of the afternoon and to be able to chat without restriction, enjoying the easy closeness of family and old friends.

They were still mulling over the church sale.

"I just hope Dermot won't mind being told he has to run the White Elephant stall. Perhaps I should ring him and give him the opportunity to say he doesn't want to do it." Archie was always cautious about other people's feelings, terrified of it being thought that he was throwing his weight about.

Violet pooh-poohed the very idea. "Of course he won't. Dear man, he never minds pitching in. He'd probably be far more hurt if we gave the job to somebody else. After all, he knows the value of everything. . . ."

She was a tall lady in her late seventies and very large, dressed in a much-worn coat and skirt and shod in sensible brogues. Her hair was grey and wispy, skewered to the back of her head in a small bun, and her face, with its long top lip and wide-set eyes, resembled that of a kindly sheep. And yet she was neither plain nor dowdy. Wonderfully upright, she had presence, and those eyes were both merry and intelligent, dispelling any suggestion of haughtiness. Now they twinkled with amusement. "Even pottery doggies with bones in their mouths, and table lamps made out of old whisky bottles plastered in shells."

Virginia laughed. "He'll probably pick up some wonderful bargain for twenty-five pence and sell it for some incredible price in his shop next day."

She leaned back in her chair and stretched, like a lazy girl. In her early thirties, Virginia Aird was as blonde and as slender as the day she had married Edmund. Today, making no concession to the formality of the occasion, she wore her usual uniform of jeans, a navy-blue Guernsey sweater, and polished leather loafers. She was pretty in a pert and catlike way, but this prettiness was elevated to beauty by her eyes, which were enormous and of a glittering sapphire blueness. Her skin was fine, innocent of make-up, and the colour of a delectable brown egg. A fine tracing of lines fanned out from the corners of those eyes, and these alone betrayed her age.

Now she flexed her long fingers and circled her wrists, as though performing some prescribed exercise.

"And Isobel will be the tea-lady." She stopped stretching. "Why didn't Isobel come today, Archie?"

"I told you . . . or perhaps you were out of the room. She had to go to Corriehill to pick up this week's batch of visitors."

"Yes, of course, how stupid of me. Sorry . . ."

"That reminds me." Violet held out her mug. "Pour me a little more tea, would you, dear? I can drink it till it comes out of my ears. . . . I met Verena Steynton in Relkirk yesterday, and she told me that I didn't have to keep it a secret any longer. She and Angus are going to throw a party for Katy in September."

Virginia frowned. "What do you mean, keep it a secret?"

"Well, she confided in me a few weeks ago, but she said I wasn't to say anything until she'd spoken to Angus about it. It seems that he has finally been persuaded."

"Goodness, how enterprising! A little hop, or a full-blown affair?"

"Oh, full-blown. Marquees and fairy lights and copperplate invitations and everybody dressed to the nines."

"What *fun*." Virginia was filled with enthusiasm, as Violet had known she would be. "It's lovely when people throw private parties, because then you don't have to pay for your ticket. Instead I'll have a good excuse to go and buy myself a new dress. We'll all have to rally round and have people to stay. I'll have to be certain that Edmund's not planning to go to Tokyo that week."

"Where is he now?" asked Edmund's mother.

"Oh, in Edinburgh. He'll be back about six."

"And Henry? What's happened to Henry? Shouldn't he be back from school?"

"No. He's stopped off to have his tea with Edie."

"That'll cheer her up."

Virginia frowned, puzzled, as well she might be. The boot was usually on the other foot, and Edie the person who did the cheering. "What's happened?"

Violet looked at Archie. "Do you remember that cousin of Edie's, Lottie Carstairs? She was housemaid at Strathcroy the year you married Isobel?"

"Do I *remember* her?" His expression was one of horror. "Dreadful female. Nutty as a fruit-cake. She broke most of the Rockingham tea-set, and she was always creeping around the place, just where you least expected to find her. I never knew what induced my mother to employ her."

"I think it was a case of any port in a storm. It was a busy summer and she was desperate for help. Anyway, Lottie only lasted about four months, and then she went back home to Tullochard to live with her aged parents. She never married . . ."

"That's no surprise . . ."

". . . and now, of course, they're dead, and she's been on her own. Becoming, apparently, odder by the day. Finally, she went over the top and was wheeled off to the nearest mental hospital. Edie's her next of kin. She's been visiting the poor creature every week. And now the doctors say that she's well enough to be discharged, but of course she can't live alone again. At least, not just yet."

"Don't tell me Edie's going to have her?"

"She says she has to. There's nobody else. And you know how kind Edie is . . . she's always had a great sense of family responsibility. Blood is thicker than water and all that nonsense."

"And a great deal nastier," Archie commented drily. "Lottie Carstairs. I can't think of anything worse. When is all this going to happen?"

Violet shrugged. "I don't know. Next month maybe. Or August."

Virginia was horrified. "She's surely not going to *live* with Edie?"

"Let's hope not. Let's hope it's just a temporary measure."

"And where on earth will Edie put her? She's only got two rooms in that little cottage of hers."

"I didn't ask."

"When did she tell you this?"

"This morning. When she was Hoovering my dining-room carpet. I thought she was looking a bit down in the mouth, so I asked her what was the matter. I heard all about it over a cup of coffee."

"Oh, poor Edie. I can't bear it for her. . . ."

Archie said, "Edie is a saint."

"She certainly is." Violet finished her tea, glanced at her watch, and began to gather her belongings. Her large handbag, her papers, her spectacles. "That was very nice, dear. Most refreshing. And now I must take myself home."

"Me too," said Archie. "Back to Croy to drink more tea with the Americans."

"You'll be awash. Who have you got this week?"

"No idea. Just hope they're not too elderly. Last week I thought one old boy was going to die of angina right there, in the middle of the soup. Mercifully, however, he survived."

"It's such a responsibility."

"Not really. The worst are the ones who've signed a pledge and take no drink. Bible Belt Baptists. Orange juice makes for sticky conversation. Have you got your car, Vi, or do you want a lift home?"

"I walked down, but I'd like a lift back up the hill."

"I'll take you then."

He too gathered together his papers and heaved himself to his feet. For an instant he paused and then, when certain of his balance, made his way towards them down the length of the thickly carpeted room. He limped only slightly, which was a miracle because his right leg, from a stump of thigh downwards, was made of aluminum.

He had come to the meeting today straight from his garden and apologized for his attire, but nobody took much notice because this was the way he looked most of the time. Shapeless corduroy trousers, a checked shirt with a patched collar, and a threadbare tweed jacket that he called his gardening coat, though in truth no self-respecting gardener would be seen dead in it.

Virginia pushed back her chair and stood up and Violet did the same, but much more slowly, matching her movements to Archie's painful gait. She was in no way impatient to be gone, but even if she were would never show it, for her feelings towards him were sympathetic and fiercely protective. She had, after all, known him all his life. Remembered him as a boy, as a wild young man, as a soldier. Always laughing, and an enthusiasm—almost a lust for life—that was as catching as the measles. She remembered him endlessly active. Playing tennis; dancing at the Regimental Ball, swinging his partners nearly off their feet; leading a line of guns up the hill behind Croy, his long legs covering the heather with an easy stride that left all the others behind.

Then, he had been Archie Blair. Now, he was Lord Balmerino. The

Lord and the Laird. Fine titles for a man thin as a stick, with a tin leg to boot. The black hair was now flecked with white, the skin of his face netted with lines, his dark eyes deep-set and shadowed by the jutting brows.

He reached her side and smiled. "Ready, Vi?"

"All set."

"In that case, we'll go. . . ." And then, in mid-step, he stopped again. "Oh, God, I've just remembered. Virginia, did Edmund give you an envelope to give me? I called him last night. It's rather urgent. Some document from the Forestry Commission?"

Violet was instantly suspicious. "You're not going to start planting conifers, are you?"

"No, it's about some access road they're wanting to build at the edge of the moor."

Virginia shook her head. "He didn't say anything about it. Perhaps he forgot. Let's go and look on his desk in the library. It's probably there. . . ."

"Right. I'd like to take it with me if I can."

They moved at a leisurely pace out of the dining-room and into the hall. This was even larger, panelled in pine with a massive staircase, heavily balustraded, rising in three short flights to the upstairs landing. Various items of undistinguished furniture stood about. A carved oak chest, a gate-leg table, and a chaise longue that had seen better days. This was quite often occupied by dogs, but at the moment was empty.

"I shall not come and look for Forestry Commission documents," Violet announced. "I shall sit here until you have found them." And she settled herself majestically on the dogs' bed to wait.

They left her. "We shan't be a moment." She watched them go down the wide passage that led to the library and on to the drawing-room, and on again through glassed doors to the soaring conservatory.

Alone, Violet savoured her momentary solitude, with the old house around her. She knew it so well, had known it all her life. Its every mood was comfortably familiar. Every creak of the stair, every evocative smell. The hall was draughty, but the draughts did not bother her. No longer Violet's home, but Virginia's. And yet it felt much the same as it ever had, as though, over the years, it had assumed a strength of character all its own. Perhaps because so much had happened here. Because it had been the haven and the touchstone of a single family.

Not that Balnaid was a very old house. In fact, it was younger than Violet by a few years, and built by her father, then Sir Hector Akenside, and a man of considerable means. She always thought that Balnaid was a little like Sir Hector. Large, kindly, and lavish, and yet totally unassuming. At a time when men of newly acquired wealth were constructing for themselves huge monuments to their pride of startling hideousness, castellated and turreted, Sir Hector had concentrated his able mind on less glamorous but infinitely more important features.

Central heating, efficient plumbing, plenty of bathrooms, and kitchens filled with sunlight, so that servants (and there were plenty of them) would work in pleasant surroundings. And from the day it was finally completed, Balnaid never looked out of place. Built from local stone on the south side of the Croy, with its back to the village and the river, the face of the house smiled out over a view both domestic and magnificent.

The garden was large, rich with shrubs and mature trees. Sir Hector's passion, he had planned and landscaped it himself, so that formal lawns flowed into drifts of unmown grass, daffodils, and bluebells. Azaleas, coral and yellow, grew in fragrant masses, and mown paths twisted away invitingly out of sight between tall stands of pink- and scarlet-blossomed rhododendrons.

Beyond the garden, and separated from it by a steep ha-ha wall, was an acre or so of parkland, grazing for the hill ponies; and, beyond again, the stone-dyked fields of the neighbouring sheep farmer. Then, in the distance, the hills. They swelled to meet the sky, dramatic as a stage-drop. Constant, and yet continually changing, as the seasons and the light changed: snow-clad, purple with heather, green with spring bracken, swept by gales . . . whatever. They were always beautiful.

Had always been beautiful.

Violet knew all this because Balnaid had been her childhood home, and so her world. She had grown up within these walls, played solitary games in that magic garden, guddled for trout in the river, ridden her stubby Shetland pony through the village and up onto the lonely hills of Croy. At the age of twenty-two, she had been married from Balnaid.

She remembered driving the little distance to the Episcopalian church in the back of her father's stately Rolls-Royce, with Sir Hector, top-hatted, beside her. The Rolls had been decked out for the occasion with white silk ribbons. These somehow lessened its dignity, and it looked almost as incongruous as Violet felt, with her ample frame laced into a cream satin dress of quite hideous uncomfortableness and a mist of inherited Limerick lace veiling her homely features. She remembered returning to Balnaid in the same opulent vehicle, but on that journey even the agonizing tightness of her stays had ceased to matter, because she was, at long last, the triumphant wife of Geordie Aird.

She had lived at Balnaid, on and off, ever since, and had not finally moved out until ten years ago, when Edmund married Virginia. He brought Virginia back to Balnaid to live, and Violet knew then that the time had come for her to bow out and allow the old place to welcome its new young mistress. She made the property over to Edmund and bought a gardener's derelict cottage from Archie Balmerino. This house was called Pennyburn, and there, within the estate walls of Croy, she made a new home for herself. The restoration and refurbishment of the little house had kept her happy for a year, and she was still not finished with the garden.

I am, she told herself, a fortunate woman.

Sitting there, on the dog-smelling chaise longue, Violet looked about her. Saw the worn Turkey rug, the old bits of furniture that she had known all her life. It was pleasant when things did not change too much. When she said goodbye to Balnaid, Violet had never imagined that so little would change. Edmund's new wife, she decided, would be the new broom, come to sweep away all the dusty old traditions, and she was indeed quite interested to see what Virginia—as young and vital as a breath of fresh air—would achieve. But, apart from completely revamping the big bedroom, freshening up the drawing-room with a lick of paint, and turning an old pantry into a utility room that fairly hummed with deep-freezes, washing machines, drying machines, and attendant luxuries, Virginia did nothing. Violet accepted this, but found it puzzling. There was, after all, no lack of money, and to her it seemed strange that Virginia should be content to live with the worn rugs and the faded velvet curtains and the old Edwardian wallpapers.

Perhaps it had something to do with the arrival of Henry. Because after Henry was born, Virginia abandoned all other interests and immersed herself in her baby son. This was very nice, but came as something of a shock to Violet. She had no idea that her daughter-in-law would prove so deeply maternal. With Edmund away so much, and mother and child left on their own, Violet had secret reservations about this overwhelming devotion, and it was a constant source of astonishment to her that despite his upbringing, Henry had grown into such a delightful little boy. A bit too dependent on his mother, perhaps, but still, not spoiled, and a charming child. Perhaps . . .

"Sorry, Vi, to keep you waiting."

Surprise made her start. She turned and saw Archie and Virginia coming towards her, Archie holding up the long buff envelope as though it were a hard-won banner. ". . . took a bit of searching for. Come along now, and I'll drive you home."

3

JENRY AIRD, EIGHT YEARS OLD, banged with some importance at Edie Findhorn's front door, using her brass knocker shaped like a pixie. The house was one of a line of single-storey cottages that lined the main street of Strathcroy, but Edie's was nicer than anybody else's because it had a mossy thatched roof and forget-me-nots grew in the little strip of earth between the pavement and the wall. Standing there, he heard her footsteps; she unsnibbed the door and threw it open.

"Well, here you are, turned up like a bad penny."

She was always laughing. He loved her, and when people asked him who his best friends were, Edie came on top of the list. She was not only jolly, but fat, white-haired, and rosy-cheeked, and appetizing as a fresh and floury scone.

"Did you have a good day?"

She always asked this, despite the fact that she saw him every lunch-time, because she was the school dinner-lady and served out the midday meal. It was handy having Edie doing this because it meant that she stinted on helpings of things he hated, like curried mince and stodgy custard, and was lavish with the mashed potatoes and chocolate shape.

"Yes, it was all right." He went into her sitting-room, dumped his anorak and his school-bag on the couch. "We had drawing. We had to draw something."

"What did you have to draw?"

"We had to draw a *song*." He began to undo the buckles of his satchel. He had a problem and thought that probably Edie could help to solve it for him. "We sang 'Speed Bonnie Boat Like a Bird on the Wing over the Sea to Skye,' and we had to draw a picture of it. And everybody else drew rowing boats and islands, and I drew *this*." He produced it, slightly crumpled from contact with his gym shoes and his pencil box. "And Mr. McLintock *laughed*, and I don't know why."

"He laughed?" She took it from him, went to find her spectacles, and put them on. "And did he not tell you why he laughed?"

"No. The bell rang and it was the end of class."

Edie sat on the couch and he sat beside her. Together they gazed in silence at his work. He thought it was one of his best pictures. A beautiful speedboat slicing through blue waters, with white water pouring up at its bow and a snowy wake at the stern. There were sea-gulls in the sky and, on the front of the boat, a baby wrapped in a shawl. The baby had been difficult to draw, because babies have such funny faces. No noses or chins. Also, this baby looked a bit precarious and as though at any moment it might slip off the boat and into the sea. But still, it was there.

Edie did not say anything. Henry explained to her. "It's a speedboat. And that's the lad that's been born."

"Yes, I can see that."

"But why did Mr. McLintock laugh? It's not funny."

"No, it's not funny. It's a lovely picture. It's just that . . . well . . . speed doesn't mean a speedboat in the song. It means that the boat's going very fast over the water, but it's not a speedboat. And the lad that was born to be king was Bonnie Prince Charlie, and he was grown up by then."

All was now explained. "Oh," said Henry, "I see."

She gave him back the drawing. "But it's still a good picture, and I think it was very rude of Mr. McLintock to laugh. Put it in your bag and take it home for your mother to see, and Edie will go and start getting your tea."

While he did this, she heaved herself to her feet, put her spectacles back on the mantelpiece, and went out of the room through a door at the back that led to her kitchen and bathroom. These were modern additions, for when Edie was a little girl, the cottage had consisted solely of two rooms. A but and ben it was called. The living room, which was the kitchen as well, and the bedroom. No running water, and a wooden lavatory at the end of the garden. What was more astonishing was that Edie had been one of five children, and so seven people had once lived in these rooms. Her parents had slept in a box-bed in the kitchen, with a shelf over their heads for the baby, and the rest of the children had been crowded into the other room. For water, Mrs. Findhorn had made the long walk each day to the village pump, and baths were a weekly affair, taken in a tin tub in front of the kitchen fire.

"But however did five of you get into the bedroom, Edie?" Henry would ask, fascinated by the logistics of sheer space. Even with just Edie's bed and her wardrobe, it still seemed dreadfully small.

"Oh, mind, we weren't all in there at the same time. By the time the youngest was born, my eldest brother was out working on the land, and living in a bothy with the other farm-hands. And then, when the girls were old enough, they went into service in some big house or other. It was a sore wrench when we had to leave, tears all over the place, but there was no space for us all here, and too many mouths to feed, and my mother needed the extra money."

She told him other things, too. How, on winter evenings, they would bank up the fire with potato peelings and sit around it, listening to their father reading aloud the stories of Rudyard Kipling, or *Pilgrim's Progress*. The little girls would work at their knitting, making socks for the menfolk. And when it came to turning the heels, the sock was given to an older sister or their mother because that bit of the knitting was too complicated for them to do.

It all sounded very poor, but somehow quite cosy too. Looking about him, Henry found it hard to imagine Edie's cottage the way it had been in olden days. For now it was as bright and cheerful as it could be, the box-bed gone and lovely swirly carpets on the floor. The old kitchen fire had gone too, and a beautiful green tile fireplace stood in its place, and there were flowery curtains and a television set and lots of nice china ornaments.

With his drawing safely stowed, he buckled up his satchel once more. Speed Bonnie Boat. He had got it wrong. He often got things wrong. There was another song they had learned at school. "Ho Ro My Nut Brown Maiden." Henry, singing lustily with the rest of the class, could just imagine the maiden. A little Pakistani, like Kedejah Ishak, with her dark skin and her shining pigtail, rowing like mad across a windy loch.

His mother had had to explain that one to him.

As well, ordinary words could be confusing. People said things to him, and he heard them, but heard them just the way they sounded. And the word, or the image conjured up by the word, stuck in his mind. Grown-ups went on holiday to "My Yorker" or "Portjiggal." Or "Grease." Grease sounded a horrid place. Edie once told him about a lady who was very cut up because her daughter had married some fly-by-night who was not good enough for her. The poor lady, all cut up, had haunted his nightmares for weeks.

But the worst was the misunderstanding that had happened with his grandmother, and which might have come between them for ever and caused a lasting rift, had not Henry's mother finally found out what was bothering him and put it right.

He had gone to Pennyburn one day after school to have tea with his grandmother, Vi. A gale was blowing and the wind howled around the little house. Sitting by the fire, Vi had suddenly made an exclamation of annoyance, got to her feet and fetched from somewhere a folding screen, which she set up in front of the glass door that led out into the garden. Henry asked her why she was doing this, and when she told him he was so horrified that he scarcely spoke for the rest of the afternoon. When his mother came to fetch him, he had never been so glad to see her and could not wait to scramble into his anorak and be out of the house, almost forgetting to thank Vi for his tea.

It was horrible. He felt that he never wanted to go back to Pennyburn, and yet knew that he ought to, if only to protect Vi. Every time his mother suggested another visit, he made some excuse or said he would rather go to Edie's. Finally, one night while he was having his bath, she came and sat on the lavatory and talked to him . . . she brought the conversation gently around to the touchy subject and at last asked him straight if there was any reason why he no longer wanted to go to Vi's.

"You always used to love it so. Did something happen?"

It was a relief at last to talk about it.

"It's frightening."

"Darling, what's frightening?"

"It comes in, out of the garden, and it comes into the sitting-room. Vi put a screen up but it could easily knock the screen over. It might hurt her. I don't think she should live there any more."

"For heaven's sake! What comes in?"

He could see it. With great tall spotted legs, and a long thin spotted neck, and great big yellow teeth with its lips curled back, ready to pounce, or bite.

"A horrible *giraffe*."

His mother was confounded. "Henry, have you gone out of your mind? Giraffes live in Africa, or zoos. There aren't any giraffes in Strathcroy."

"There are!" He shouted at her stupidity. "She said so. She said there was a horrible giraffe that came out of the garden, and through the door and into her sitting-room. She *told* me so."

There was a long silence. He stared at his mother and she stared back at him with her bright blue eyes, but she never smiled.

At last she said, "She wasn't telling you that there was a giraffe, Henry. She was telling you that there was a draught. You know, a horrid, shivery draught."

A draught. Not a giraffe but a draught. All that fuss about a stupid draught. He had made a fool of himself, but was so relieved that his grandmother was safe from monsters that it didn't matter.

"Don't tell anybody," he pleaded.

"I'll have to explain to Vi. But she won't say a word."

"All right. You can tell Vi. But not anybody else."

And his mother had promised, and he had jumped out of the bath, all dripping wet, and been gathered up into a great fluffy towel and his mother's arms, and she had hugged him and told him that she was going to eat him alive and she loved him so, and they had sung "Camptown Races," and there was macaroni and cheese for supper.

Edie had cooked sausages for his tea and made potato scones, and opened a can of baked beans. While he ploughed his way through this, sitting at her kitchen table, Edie sat opposite him, drinking a cup of tea. Her own meal she would eat later.

Munching, he realized that she was quieter than usual. Normally on such occasions they never stopped talking, and he was the willing recipient of all the gossip in the glen. Who had died and how much they had left; who had abandoned his father on the farm and hightailed it off to Relkirk to work in a garage; who had started a baby and was no better than she should be. But today no such snippets of information came his way. Instead Edie sat with her dimpled elbows on the table and gazed out of the window at her long, thin back garden.

He said, "Penny for your thoughts, Edie," which was what she always said to him when he had something on his mind.

She sighed deeply. "Oh, Henry, I don't know, and that's for certain."

Which told him nothing. However, when pressed, she explained her predicament. She had a cousin who had lived in Tullochard. She was called Lottie Carstairs and had never been bright. Never married. Gone into domestic service, but had proved useless even at that. She had lived with her mother and father until the old folks had died, and then turned very strange and had had to go to hospital. Edie said it was a nervous breakdown. But she was recovering. One day she would come out of hospital, and she was coming to stay with Edie because there was no other place for the poor soul to go.

Henry thought this a rotten idea. He liked having Edie to himself. "But you haven't got a spare room."

"She'll have to have my bedroom."

He was indignant. "But where will *you* sleep?"

"On the Put-U-Up in the sitting-room."

She was far too fat for the Put-U-Up. "Why can't Dotty sleep there?"

"Because she will be the guest, and her name's Lottie."

"Will she stay for long?"

"We'll have to see."

Henry thought about this. "Will you go on being dinner-lady, and helping Mummy, and helping Vi at Pennyburn?"

"For heaven's sake, Henry, Lottie's not bedridden."

"Will I like her?" This was important.

Edie found herself at a loss for words. "Oh, Henry, I don't know. She's a sad creature. Nineteen shillings in the pound, my father always called her. Screamed like a wet hen if a man showed his face around the door, and *clumsy!* Years ago, she worked for a wee while for old Lady Balmerino at Croy, but smashed so much china that they had to give her the sack. She never worked again after that."

Henry was horrified. "You mustn't let her do the washing-up or she'll break all your pretty things."

"It's not just my china she'll be breaking . . ." Edie prophesied gloomily, but before Henry could follow up this interesting line of conversation she took a hold of herself, put a more cheerful expression on her face, and pointedly changed the subject. "Do you want another potato scone, or are you ready for your Choc Bar?"

4

$\mathcal{E}$MERGING WITH ARCHIE AND VIRGINIA from the front door of Balnaid, and descending the steps to the gravel sweep, Violet saw that the rain had stopped. It was still damp but now much warmer, and lifting her head she felt the breeze on her cheek, blowing freshly from the west. Low clouds were slowly being rolled aside, revealing here and there a patch of blue sky and a piercing, biblical, ray of sunshine. It would turn into a beautiful summer evening—too late to be of much use to anybody.

Archie's old Land Rover stood waiting for them. They said goodbye to Virginia, Violet with a peck on her daughter-in-law's cheek.

"Love to Edmund."

"I'll tell him."

They clambered up into the Land Rover, both with some effort, Violet because she was elderly, and Archie because of his tin leg. Doors were slammed shut, Archie started up the engine, and they were off. Down the curving driveway to the gate, out onto the narrow lane that led past the Presbyterian church, and so across the bridge. At the main road, Archie paused, but there was no traffic, and he swung out and into the street which ran through Strathcroy from end to end.

The little Episcopal church squatted humbly. Mr. Gloxby was out in front of it, cutting the grass.

"He works so hard," Archie observed. "I do hope we can raise a decent bit of cash with a church sale. It was good of you to come today, Vi. I'm sure you'd much rather have been gardening."

"It was such disheartening weather, I had no desire to get at my weeds," Vi said. "So one might as well spend the day doing something worthy." She thought about this. "Rather like when one is worried sick about a child or a grandchild, but you can't do anything, so you go and scrub the scullery floor. At the end of the day you're still worried sick, but at least you've got a clean scullery."

"You're not worried about your family, are you, Vi? What could you possibly have to worry about?"

"All women worry about their families," Violet told him flatly.

The Land Rover trundled down the road, past the petrol station, which had once been the blacksmith's forge, and the Ishaks' supermarket. Beyond this stood the open gates that led to the back drive of Croy. Archie changed down and drove through these, and at once they were climbing steeply. Once, and not so long ago, the surrounding lands had all been park, smooth green pastures grazed by pedigree cattle, but now these had been ploughed for crops, barley, and turnips. Only a few broad-leaved trees still stood, witness to the splendour of former years.

"Why do you worry?"

Violet hesitated. She knew that she could talk to Archie. She had known him all his life, watched him grow up. Indeed, she was as close to him as if he had been her own son, for although he was five years younger than Edmund, the two boys had been brought up together, spent all their time together, and become the closest of friends.

If Edmund was not at Croy, then Archie was at Balnaid; and if they were at neither house, then they were walking the hills with guns and dogs, potting at hares and rabbits, helping Gordon Gillock burn the heather and repair the butts. Or else they were out in the boat on the loch, or casting for trout in the brown pools of the Croy, or playing tennis, or skating on frozen flood-water. Inseparable, everybody had said. Like brothers.

But they were not brothers, and they had parted. Edmund was bright. Twice as bright as either of his not unintelligent parents. Archie, on the other hand, was totally unacademic.

Edmund, sailing through University, emerged from Cambridge with an Honours Degree in Economics, and was instantly employed by a prestigious merchant bank in the City.

Archie, unable to think of any other career that he might successfully follow, decided to have a try for the Army. He duly appeared before a Regular Commission Board and somehow managed to bluff his way through the interview, for the four senior officers apparently decided that a modest scholastic record was outweighed by Archie's outgoing and friendly personality and his enormous enthusiasm for life.

He went through Sandhurst, joined the Regiment, and was posted to Germany. Edmund stayed in London. He became, to no person's surprise, enormously successful, and within five years had been head-hunted by Sanford Cubben. In the fullness of time he married, but even this romantic event added glitter to his image. Violet recalled pacing up the long aisle of St. Margaret's, Westminster, arm in arm with Sir Rodney Cheriton, and finding time to hope in her heart that Edmund was marrying Caroline because he truly loved her, and not because he had been seduced by the aura of riches that surrounded her.

And now the wheel had gone full circle, and both men were back in Strathcroy. Archie at Croy, and Edmund at Balnaid. Grown men in their middle years, still friends, but no longer intimate. Too much had happened to both of them, and not all of it good. Too many years had slipped by, like water under a bridge. They were different people: one a very wealthy man of business, the other strapped for cash and perpetually struggling to make ends meet. But it was not because of this that a certain formality, a politeness lay between them.

They were no longer close as brothers.

She sighed gustily. Archie smiled. "Oh, come on, Vi, it can't be as bad as that."

"Of course not." He had troubles enough of his own. She would make light of hers. "But I do worry about Alexa, because she seems so alone. I know she's doing a job she enjoys, and that she has that charming little house in which to live, and Lady Cheriton left her enough to give her security for the rest of her life. But I am afraid that her social life is a disaster. I think she truly believes that she's plain and dull and unattractive to men. She has no confidence in herself. When she went to London, I so hoped that she would make a life for herself, make friends of her own age. But she just stayed at Ovington Street with her grandmother, like a sort of companion. If only she could meet some dear kind man who would marry her. She should have a husband to take care of, and children. Alexa was born to have children."

Archie listened sympathetically to all this. He was as fond of Alexa as any of them. He said, "Losing her mother when she was so little . . . perhaps that was a more traumatic experience than any of us realized. Perhaps it made her feel different from other girls. Incomplete in some way."

Violet thought about this. "Yes. Perhaps. Except that Caroline was never a very demonstrative nor loving mother. She never spent much time with Alexa. It was Edie who provided all Alexa's security and affection. And Edie was always there."

"But you liked Caroline."

"Oh yes, I liked her. There was nothing to dislike. We had a good relationship, and I think she was a good wife to Edmund. But she was a strangely reserved girl. Sometimes I went south, to stay for a few days with them all in London. Caroline would invite me, very charmingly, knowing that I would enjoy being with Alexa and Edie. And of course I did, but I never felt totally at home. I hate cities, anyway. Streets and houses and traffic make me feel beleaguered. Claustrophobic. But, quite apart from that, Caroline was never a relaxed hostess. I always felt a bit in the way, and she was an impossible girl to chat with. Left alone with her I had to struggle, sometimes, to make conversation, and you know perfectly well that, if pressed, I can talk the hind legs off a donkey. But pauses would fall, and they were silences that were not companionable.

And I would try to fill those silences in, stitching furiously at my tapestry." She looked across at Archie. "Does that sound ridiculous, or do you understand what I'm trying to say?"

"Yes, I do understand. I hardly knew Caroline, but the few times I met her I always felt my hands and my feet were too big."

But even this mild attempt at levity did not raise a smile with Violet, preoccupied as she was with Alexa's problems. She fell silent, brooding about her granddaughter.

By now they had climbed half-way up the hill that led to Croy and were approaching the turning for Pennyburn. There were no gates, simply an opening that broke the fence to the left of the road. The Land Rover turned into this, and Archie drove the hundred yards or so along a neatly Tarmacked lane bordered on either side by mown grass verges and a trimly clipped beech hedge. At the end of this the lane opened up into a sizable yard, with the small white house on one side and a double garage on the other. The doors of this were open, revealing Violet's car, and, as well, her wheelbarrow and lawn-mower and a plethora of garden tools. Between the garage and the beech hedge was her drying-green. She had done a wash this morning, and a line of laundry stirred in the rising breeze. Wooden tubs, planted with hydrangeas the colour of pink blotting paper, flanked the entrance to the house, and a hedge of lavender grew close to its walls.

Archie drew up and switched off the engine, but Violet made no move to alight. Having started this discussion, she had no wish to end it before it was finished.

"So I don't really believe that losing her mother in that tragic way is the root cause of Alexa's lack of confidence. Nor the fact that Edmund married again and presented her with a stepmother. Nobody could have been sweeter or more understanding than Virginia, and the arrival of Henry brought nothing but joy. Not a hint of sibling rivalry." The mention of Henry's name reminded Violet of yet another tiresome worry. "And now I'm fretting about Henry. Because I'm afraid that Edmund is going to insist on sending him to Templehall as a boarder. And I think he's not ready for that yet. And if he does go, I'm anxious for Virginia, because her life *is* Henry, and if he is torn away from her against her will, I'm afraid that she and Edmund might drift apart. He is away so much. Sometimes in Edinburgh for the entire week, sometimes on the other side of the world. It's not good for a marriage."

"But when Virginia married Edmund, she knew how it would be. Don't get too worked up about it, Vi. Templehall's a good school, and Colin Henderson's a sympathetic headmaster. I've got great faith in the place. Hamish has loved it there, enjoyed every moment."

"Yes, but your Hamish is very different from Henry. At eight years old, Hamish was quite capable of taking care of himself."

"Yes." Archie, not without pride, had to admit this. "He's a tough little bugger."

Violet was visited by another dreadful thought. "Archie, they don't hit the little boys, do they? They don't beat them?"

"Heavens, no. The worst punishment is to be sent to sit on the wooden chair in the hall. For some reason this puts the fear of God into the most recalcitrant infant."

"Well, I suppose that's something to be thankful for. So barbaric to beat little children. And so stupid. Getting hit by someone you dislike can only fill you with hatred and fear. Being sent to sit on a hard chair by a man you respect and even like is infinitely more sensible."

"Hamish spent most of his first year sitting on it."

"Wicked boy. Oh dear, it doesn't bear thinking about. And Edie doesn't bear thinking about either. Now I've got Edie to worry over, saddling herself with that dreadful lunatic cousin. We've all depended on Edie for so long, we forgot that she's no longer young. I just hope it's not all going to be too much for her."

"Well, it hasn't happened yet. Maybe it'll never happen."

"We can scarcely wish poor Lottie Carstairs dead, which seems the only alternative."

She looked at Archie and saw, somewhat to her surprise, that he was near to laughter. "You know something, Vi? You're depressing me."

"Oh, I am sorry." She struck him a friendly blow on the knee. "What a miserable old gasbag I am. Take no notice. Tell me, what news of Lucilla?"

"Last heard of, roosting in some Paris garret."

"They always say that children are a joy. But at times they can be the most appalling headaches. Now, I must let you get home and not keep you chattering. Isobel will be waiting for you."

"You wouldn't like to come back to Croy and have more tea?" He sounded wistful. "Help amuse the Americans?"

Violet's heart sank at the prospect. "Archie, I don't think I feel quite up to doing that. Am I being selfish?"

"Not a bit. Just a thought. Sometimes I find all this barking and wagging tails daunting. But it's nothing compared with what poor Isobel has to do."

"It must be the most dreadfully hard work. All that fetching and carrying and cooking and table-laying and bed-making. And then having to make conversation. I know it's only for two nights each week, but couldn't you chuck your hands in and think of some other way to make money?"

"Can you?"

"Not immediately. But I wish things could be different for you both. I know one can't put the clock back, but sometimes I think how nice it would be if nothing had changed at Croy. If your precious parents could still be alive, and all of you young again. Coming and going, and cars buzzing up and down the drive, and voices. And laughter."

She turned to Archie, but his face was averted. He gazed out over her washing-green, as though Violet's tea-towels and pillowcases and her sturdy brassieres and silk knickers were the most absorbing sight in the world.

She thought, *And you and Edmund the closest of friends,* but she did not say this.

"And Pandora there. That naughty, darling child. I always felt that when she left she took so much of the laughter with her."

Archie stayed silent. And then he said "Yes," and nothing more.

A small constraint lay between them. To fill it, Violet busied herself, gathering up her belongings. "I mustn't keep you any longer." She opened the door and clambered down from the bulky old vehicle.

"Thank you for the ride, Archie."

"A pleasure, Vi."

"Love to Isobel."

"Of course. See you soon."

She waited while he turned the Land Rover, and watched him drive away, along the lane, and on up the hill. She felt guilty, because she should have gone with him, and drunk tea with Isobel, and made polite chat to the unknown Americans. But too late now, because he was gone. She searched in her handbag for her key and let herself into her house.

Alone, Archie continued on his way. The road grew steeper. Now there were trees ahead, Scots pine and tall beeches. Beyond and above these, the face of the hillside thrust skywards, cliffs of rock and scree, sprouting tufts of whin and bracken and determined saplings of silver birch. He reached the trees; and the road, having climbed as high as it could, swept around to the left and levelled out. Ahead, the beech avenue led the way to the house. A burn tumbled down from the hilltops in a series of pools and waterfalls and flowed on down the hill under an arched stone bridge. This stream was Pennyburn, and lower down the slope it made its way through the garden of Violet Aird's house.

Beneath the beeches all was shaded, the light diffused, limpid and greenish. The leafy branches arched thickly overhead, and it felt a little like driving down the centre aisle of some enormous cathedral. And then, abruptly, the avenue fell behind him and the house came into view, set four-square on the brow of the hill, with the whole panoramic vista of the glen spread out at its feet. The evening breeze had done its work, tearing the clouds to tatters, lifting the mist. The distant hills, the peaceful acres of farmland were washed in golden sunlight.

All at once, it became essential to have a moment or two to himself. This was selfish. He was already late, and Isobel was waiting for him, in need of his moral support. But he pushed guilt out of his mind, drew up out of earshot of the house, and switched off the engine.

It was very quiet, just the sough of the wind in the trees, the cry of curlews. He listened to the silence, from some distant field heard the bleat of sheep. And Violet's voice: *All of you young again. Coming and going . . . And Pandora there . . .*

She shouldn't have said that. He did not want his memories stirred. He did not wish to be consumed by this yearning nostalgia.

All of you young again.

He thought about Croy the way it had once been. He thought about coming home as a schoolboy, as a young soldier on leave. Roaring up the hill in his supercharged sports car with the roof down and the wind burning his cheeks. Knowing, with all the confidence of youth, that all would be just as he had left it. Drawing up with a screech of brakes at the front of the house; the family dogs spilling out of the open door, barking, coming to greet him, and their clamour alerting the household, so that by the time he was indoors, they were all converging. His mother and father, Harris the butler, and Mrs. Harris the cook, and any other housemaid or daily lady who happened to be helping out at the time.

"Archie. Oh, darling, welcome home."

And then, Pandora. *I always felt that when she left she took so much of the laughter with her.* His young sister. In memory, she was about thirteen and already beautiful. He saw her flying, long-legged, down the stairs, to leap into his waiting embrace. He saw her, with her full, curving mouth and her woman's provocative, slanting eyes. He felt the lightness of her body as he swung her around, off her feet. He heard her voice.

"You're back, you brute, and you've got a new car. I saw it out of the nursery window. Take me for a ride, Archie. Let's go a hundred miles an hour."

Pandora. He found himself smiling. Always, even as a child, she had been a life-enhancer, an injector of vitality and laughter to the most stuffy of occasions. Where she had sprung from he had never quite worked out. She was a Blair born and bred, yet so different in every way from the rest of them that she might have been a changeling.

He remembered her as a baby, as a little girl, as that delicious leggy teenager, for she had never suffered from puppy fat, spots, or lack of confidence. At sixteen, she looked twenty. Every friend he brought to the house had been, if not in love with her, then certainly mesmerized.

Life had hummed with activity for the young Blairs. House parties, shooting parties, tennis in the summer, August picnics on the sunlit, purple-heathered hills. He recalled one picnic when Pandora, complaining of the heat, had stripped off all her clothes and plunged naked, with no thought for astonished spectators, into the loch. He remembered dances, and Pandora in a white chiffon dress, with her brown shoulders bare, whirling from man to man through Strip the Willow and The Duke of Perth.

She was gone. Had been gone for over twenty years. At eighteen, a few months after Archie's wedding, she had eloped with an American, some other woman's husband, whom she had met in Scotland during the summer. With this man she flew to California, and in the fullness of time became his wife. Waves of shock and horror reverberated around the county, but the Balmerinos were so loved and respected that they were treated with much sympathy and understanding. Perhaps, said people hopefully, she will come back. But Pandora did not come back. She did not return even for her parents' funerals. Instead, as though engaged in an endless Strip the Willow, she flung herself, wayward as always, from one disastrous love affair to another. Divorced from her American husband, she moved to New York, and later to France, where she lived for some years in Paris. She kept in touch with Archie by means of rare and sporadic postcards, sending a scrawled address, a scrap of information, and a huge straggling cross for a kiss. Now she seemed to have ended up in a villa in Majorca. God knew who was her current companion.

Long since, Archie and Isobel had despaired of her, and yet, from time to time, he found himself missing her more than anybody else. For youth was over, and his father's household dispersed. Harris and Mrs. Harris had long retired, and domestic help was reduced to Agnes Cooper who, two days a week, climbed the hill from the village to give Isobel a hand in the kitchen.

As for the estate, matters were hardly better. Gordon Gillock, the keeper, was still in situ in his small stone house with the kennels at the back, but the grouse moor was let to a syndicate, and Edmund Aird paid the keeper's salary. The farm, as well, had gone, and the parkland was ploughed for crops. The old gardener—a weathered stick of a man and an important part of Archie's childhood—had finally died, and not been replaced. His precious walled garden was put down to grass; unpruned, the rhododendrons grew massive, and the hard tennis court was green with moss. Archie now was officially the gardener, with the sporadic assistance of Willy Snoddy, who lived in a grubby cottage at the end of the village, trapped rabbits and poached salmon, and was pleased from time to time to earn a little drinking money.

And he himself? Archie took stock. An ex-Lieutenant-Colonel in the Queen's Loyal Highlanders, invalided out with a tin leg, a sixty-per-cent disability pension, and too many nightmares. But still, thanks to Isobel, in possession of his inheritance. Croy was still his and would, God willing, belong to Hamish. Crippled, struggling to make ends meet, he was still Balmerino of Croy.

Suddenly, it was funny. Balmerino of Croy. Such a fine-sounding title, and such a ludicrous situation. It was no good trying to work out why everything had gone so wrong because there was nothing much he could do about it anyway. No more harking back. Duty called and the Lady Balmerino waited.

For some obscure reason he felt more cheerful. He started up the engine and drove the short distance across the gravel to the front of the house.

5

I T HAD DRIZZLED MOST OF THE DAY but now it was fine, so after his tea Henry went out into Edie's garden with her. This ran down to the river, and her washing line was strung between two apple trees. He helped her to unpeg the washing and put it into the wicker basket, and they folded the sheets together with a snap and a crack to get all the creases out of them. With this accomplished, they went back into the house and Edie set up the ironing board and began ironing her pillowcases and her pinafore and a blouse. Henry watched, liking the smell and the way the hot iron made the crunchy damp linen all smooth and shiny and crisp.

He said, "You're very good at ironing."

"I'd need to be after all these years at it."

"How many years, Edie?"

"Well . . ." She dumped the iron down on its end and folded the pillowcase with her dimpled red hands. "I'm sixty-eight now, and I was eighteen when I first went to work for Mrs. Aird. Work that one out."

Even Henry could do that sum. "Fifty years."

"Fifty years is a long way to look ahead, but looking back it doesn't seem any time at all. Makes you wonder what life's all about."

"Tell me about Alexa and London." Henry had never been to London, but Edie had lived there once.

"Oh, Henry, I've told you these stories a thousand times."

"I like to hear them *again*."

"Well . . ." She pressed a crease, sharp as a knife edge. "When your daddy was much younger, he was married to a lady called Caroline. They were married in London, at St. Margaret's, Westminster, and we all went down for the occasion, and stayed at a hotel called the Berkeley. And what a wedding that was! Ten lovely bridesmaids, all in white dresses, like a flock of swans. And after the wedding we all went to another very grand hotel called the Ritz, and there were waiters in tailcoats and so grand you'd have thought they were wedding guests themselves. And there was champagne and such a spread of food you didn't know where to start."

"Were there jellies?"

"Jellies in every colour. Yellow and red and green. And there was cold salmon and wee sandwiches you could eat with your fingers, and frosted grapes all sparkling with sugar. And Caroline wore a dress of wild silk with a great long train, and on her head was a diamond tiara that her father had given her for a wedding present, and she looked like a queen."

"Was she pretty?"

"Oh, Henry, all brides are beautiful."

"Was she as pretty as my mother?"

But Edie was not to be drawn. "She was good-looking in a different sort of way. Very tall, she was, with lovely black hair."

"Did you like her?"

"Of course I liked her. I wouldn't have gone to London to look after Alexa if I hadn't liked her."

"Tell me about that bit."

Edie set aside her pillowcases and started in on a blue-and-white-checked table-cloth.

"Well, it was just after your Grandfather Geordie died. I was still living at Balnaid, and working for your Granny Vi. It was just the two of us in the house, keeping each other company. We knew that Alexa was on the way, because Edmund had come up for his father's funeral and he told us then. 'Caroline is having a baby,' he told us, and it was a wonderful comfort to your Granny Vi to know that even if Geordie was with her no longer, there was a new wee life on the way. And then we heard that Caroline was looking for a Nanny to take care of the bairn. Your Granny Vi was up to high doh. The truth of the matter was that she couldn't bide the thought of some uninformed bisom having the care of her grandchild, filling her wee head with all the wrong ideas, and not taking the time to talk to the child, nor read to her. I never thought about going until your Granny Vi asked me to. I didn't want to leave Balnaid and Strathcroy. But . . . we talked it over and in the end decided that there was nothing else to be done. So I went to London. . . ."

"I bet Daddy was pleased to see you."

"Och, yes, he was pleased enough. And at the end of the day, it was a mercy I went. Alexa was born safe and sound, but after the baby arrived, Caroline became very, very ill."

"Did she have measles?"

"No, it wasn't measles."

"Whooping cough?"

"No. It wasn't that sort of illness. It was more nervous. Post-natal depression they call it, and it's a horrible thing to see. She had to go to hospital for treatment, and when she was allowed home she was really not good for anything, let alone take care of a baby. But eventually she recovered a wee bit and her mother, Lady Cheriton, took her off on a cruise to a lovely island called Madeira. And after a month or two there, she was better again."

"Were you left all alone in London?"

"Not *all* alone. There was a nice lady who came in every day to clean the house, and then your father was in and out."

"Why didn't you come back to Scotland and stay with Vi?"

"There was a time when we thought we might. Just for a visit. It was the week of Lord and Lady Balmerino's wedding . . . only then of course he was Archie Blair, and such a handsome young officer. Caroline was still in Madeira and Edmund said we'd all come north together for the occasion and stay at Balnaid. Your Granny Vi was so excited when she heard the news that we were coming to visit. She got the cot down from the attic and washed the baby blankets and dusted up the old pram. And then Alexa started teething . . . she was only a wee thing and what a time she had of it. Crying all night and not a mortal thing I could do to quieten her. I think I went two weeks without a proper night's sleep, and in the end Edmund said he thought the long journey north would be too much for the pair of us. He was right, of course, but I could have cried from disappointment."

"And Vi must have been disappointed too."

"Yes, I think she was."

"Did Daddy come to the wedding?"

"Oh, yes, he came. He and Archie were old, old friends. He had to be there. But he came on his own."

She had finished the table-cloth. Now she was onto her best blouse, easing the point of the iron into the gathered bit on the shoulder. That looked even more difficult than ironing pillowcases.

"Tell me about the house in London."

"Oh, Henry, do you not weary of all these old tales?"

"I like hearing about the house."

"All right. It was in Kensington, in a row. Very tall and thin, and what a work. The kitchens in the basement and the nurseries right up at the top of the house. It seemed to me that I never stopped climbing stairs. But it was a beautiful house, filled with precious things. And there was always something going on—people calling, or dinner parties, and guests arriving through the front door in their fine clothes. Alexa and I used to sit on the turn of the stairs and watch it all through the bannisters."

"But nobody saw you."

"No. Nobody saw us. It was like playing hide-and-seek."

"And you used to go to Buckingham Palace . . ."

"Yes, to watch the Changing of the Guard. And sometimes we took a taxi to Regent's Park Zoo and looked at the lions. And when Alexa was old enough, I walked her to school and dancing class. Some of the other children were little Lords and Ladies, and what a toffee-nosed lot *their* Nannies were!"

Little Lords and Ladies and a house filled with precious things. Edie, Henry decided, had had some marvellous experiences. "Were you sad to leave London?"

"Oh, Henry, I was sad because it was a sad time, and the reason for leaving was so sad. A terrible tragedy. Just think, one man driving his car far too fast and without thinking of any other body on the road, and in a single instant Edmund had lost his wife and Alexa her mother. And poor Lady Cheriton her only child, her only daughter. Dead."

Dead. It was a terrible word. Like the snap of a pair of scissors cutting a piece of string in two and knowing that you could never, ever put the piece of string together again.

"Did Alexa mind?"

" 'Mind' is not the word for such a time of bereavement."

"But it meant that you could come back to Scotland."

"Yes." Edie sighed and folded her blouse. "Yes, we came back. We all did. Your father to work in Edinburgh and Alexa and I to live at Balnaid. And things gradually got better. Grief is a funny thing because you don't have to carry it with you for the rest of your life. After a bit you set it down by the roadside and walk on and leave it resting there. As for Alexa, it was a new life. She went to Strathcroy Primary, just as you do, and made friends with all the village children. And your Granny Vi gave her a bicycle and a wee Shetland pony. Before very long you'd never have known she ever lived in London. And yet every holiday, when she was old enough to travel on her own, back she went to stay a little while with Lady Cheriton. It was the least we could do for the poor lady."

Her ironing was finished. She turned off the iron and set it in the grate to cool, and then folded up her ironing board. But Henry did not want to stop this fascinating conversation.

"Before Alexa, you looked after Daddy, didn't you?"

"That's what I did. Right up to the day when he was eight years old and went away to boarding-school."

Henry said, "I don't want to go to boarding-school."

"Oh, come away." Edie's voice turned brisk. She was not about to have any teary nonsense. "And why not? Lots of other boys your own age, and football and cricket and high jinks."

"I won't know anybody. I won't have a friend. And I shan't be able to take Moo with me."

Edie knew all about Moo. Moo was a piece of satin and wool, remains of Henry's cot blanket. It lived under his pillow and helped him to get to sleep at nights. Without Moo he would not sleep. Moo was very important to him.

"No," she admitted. "You won't be able to take Moo, that's for certain. But nobody would object if you took a teddy."

"Teddies don't work. And Hamish Blair says only babies take teddies."

"Hamish Blair talks a lot of nonsense."

"And you won't be there to give me my dinner."

Edie stopped being brisk. She put out a hand and ruffled his hair. "Wee man. We all have to grow up, move on. The world would come to a standstill if we all stayed in the same place. Now"—she looked at her clock—"it's time you were away home. I promised your mother you'd be back by six. Will you be all right on your own, or do you want me to come a bit of the way with you?"

"No," he told her. "I'll be all right on my own."

6

EDMUND AIRD WAS NEARLY FORTY when he married for the second time, and his new wife Virginia was twenty-three. She hailed not from Scotland but from Devon, the daughter of an officer in the Devon and Dorset Regiment who had retired from the Army in order to run an inherited farm, a considerable spread of land between Dartmoor and the sea. She had been brought up in Devon, but her mother was American, and every summer she and Virginia crossed the Atlantic in order to spend the hot months of July and August in her old family home. This was in Leesport on the south shore of Long Island, a village facing out over the blue waters of the Great South Bay to the dunes of Fire Island.

The grandparents' house was old, clapboard, large and airy. Sea breezes blew through it, stirring filmy curtains and bringing indoors the scents of the garden. This garden was spacious and separated from the quiet, tree-shaded street by a white picket fence. There were decks furnished for outdoor living, and wide porches screened for coolness and sanctuary from bugs. But its greatest charm was that it adjoined the country club, that hub of social activity with its restaurants and bars, golf course, tennis courts, and enormous turquoise swimming pool.

It was a world away from damp and misty Devon, and the annual experience gave the young Virginia a polish and sophistication that set her apart from her English contemporaries. Her clothes, purchased during mammoth Fifth Avenue shopping sprees, were both sleek and trendy. Her voice held a trace of her mother's charming drawl, and returning to school with her groomed blonde head and her long, slender American legs, she was a source of much wonder and admiration and, inevitably, on the receiving end of a good deal of malicious envy.

Early on she learned to cope with this.

Not particularly scholastic, her passion was the open air and any sort of outdoor activity. In Long Island she played tennis, sailed, and swam. In Devon she rode, hunting every winter with the local foxhounds. As she grew up, young men flocked to her side, pole-axed by the sight of her in hunting gear astride some enviable horse, or flying expertly about the tennis court in a white skirt that barely covered her bottom. At Christmas dances they clustered like bees around the proverbial honey-pot. When she was home, the telephone constantly rang, was constantly for her. Her father complained but secretly he was proud. In time, he stopped complaining, and installed a second telephone.

Leaving school, she went to London and learned to work an electric typewriter. This was extremely dull, but as she had no particular talent nor ambition, it seemed to be the only thing to do. She shared a flat in Fulham and did temporary jobs, because that way she was free to come and go whenever a pleasant invitation came her way. The men were still there but now they were different men: older, richer, and sometimes married to other women. She allowed them to spend enormous sums of money on her, take her out to dinner and give her expensive presents. And then, when they were at their wit's end with unrequited lust and devotion, she would without warning disappear from London—to spend another blissful summer with her grandparents, or head for a house party in Ibiza, or a yacht on the west coast of Scotland, or Christmas in Devon.

On one of these impetuous jaunts she had met Edmund Aird. It was September and at a house party in Relkirkshire for the Hunt Ball, where she was staying with the family of a girl with whom she had been at school. Before the ball, there was a lavish dinner party and all the guests —those staying in the house and others who had been invited—gathered in the great library.

Virginia was the last to make her entrance. She wore a dress of so pale a green that it was almost white, strapless but caught over one shoulder by a spray of ivy, the dark leaves fashioned of gleaming satin.

She saw him instantly. He was standing with his back to the fireplace, and he was tall. Across the room their eyes met and held. He had black hair streaked with white, like silver-fox fur. She was accustomed to men in all the peacock glory of Highland dress but she had never seen one who looked so easy and so well in his finery, the diced hose and the kilt, and the sombre bottle-green jacket sparked with silver buttons.

". . . Virginia dear, there you are." This was her hostess. "Now who do you know and who do you not know?" Unknown faces, new names. She scarcely heard them spoken. Finally, ". . . and this is Edmund Aird. Edmund, this is Virginia, who is staying with us. All the way from Devon. And you mustn't talk to her now because I've put you next to each other at dinner, and you can talk to her then. . . ."

She had never before fallen so instantly and totally in love. There had, of course, been affairs, mad infatuations in the high old days of the Leesport Country Club, but never anything that lasted longer than a few weeks. That evening was very different, and Virginia knew, without question, that she had met the only man with whom she had ever wanted to share the rest of her life. It did not take very long to realize that the incredible miracle was actually happening and that Edmund felt exactly the same way about her.

The world became brilliant and beautiful. Nothing could go wrong. Dazzled by happiness, she was ready to throw in her lot with Edmund, abandon all common sense and any tiresome principle. Give him her life. Live in the back of beyond if necessary; on the top of a mountain; in blatant sin. It didn't matter. Nothing mattered.

But Edmund, having lost his heart, kept a tight rein on his head. He went to some lengths to explain his position. He was, after all, head of the Scottish branch of Sanford Cubben, a man of some prominence and very much in the eye of the media. Edinburgh was a small city, and he had many friends and business colleagues, and their respect and trust he valued. To step too blatantly out of line and end up with his name plastered over the gossip columns of the tabloid newspapers would be not only foolish but possibly disastrous.

As well, he had to consider his family.

"Family?"

"Yes, family. I have been married before."

"I should think it very strange if you hadn't been."

"My wife was killed in a car accident. But I have Alexa. She's ten. She lives with my mother in Strathcroy."

"I like little girls. I would be very careful of her."

But there were still other hurdles to be faced.

"Virginia, I'm seventeen years older than you. Does forty seem so very decrepit?"

"Years don't matter."

"It would mean your living in the wilds of Relkirkshire."

"I shall drape myself in tartan and wear a hat with a feather."

He laughed, but wryly. "Unfortunately, it's not September all the year round. All our friends live miles apart and the winters are long and dark. Everybody hibernates. I am so afraid that you would find it very dull."

"Edmund, it sounds a little as though you're having second thoughts and are trying to put me off."

"It's not that. Never that. But you have to know all the truths. No illusions. You are so young, and so beautiful, and so vital, and you have all of life in front of you. . . ."

"To be with you."

"That's another thing. My job. It's demanding. I'm away so much. Abroad so often, sometimes for two or three weeks at a time."

"But you'll come back to me."

She was adamant, and he adored her. He sighed. "I wish for both our sakes that it could be different. I wish that I were young again, and without responsibilities. Free to behave any way I wanted. Then we could live together and have time to get to know each other. And be totally sure."

"I am totally sure."

She was. Undeviating. He took her in his arms and said, "Then there's nothing for it. I shall have to marry you."

"You poor man."

"You will be happy? I want so much to make you happy."

"Oh, Edmund. Darling Edmund. How could I be anything else?"

They were married two months later, at the end of November, in Devon. It was a quiet wedding in the tiny church where Virginia had been christened.

The end of her beginning. No regrets. The casual, indiscriminate affairs were over and she let them go without a backward glance. She was Mrs. Edmund Aird.

After their honeymoon they travelled north to Balnaid, Virginia's new home, and her new and ready-made family: Violet, Edie, and Alexa. Life in Scotland was a new and very different experience from anything that Virginia had previously known, but she made every effort to adjust, if only because others, very obviously, were doing the same thing. Violet had already moved firmly out and gone to Pennyburn. She proved a mistress of non-interference. Edie was equally tactful. The time had come, she announced, for her to leave as well and settle herself in the cottage in the village where she had been brought up and which she had inherited from her mother. She was retiring from resident work but instead would continue on a daily basis, sharing her time between Virginia and Violet.

Edie was, in those early days, a tower of strength, a source of excellent advice, and a fund of cosy gossip. It was she who, for Alexa's sake, filled in for Virginia some details of Edmund's previous marriage, but once this was done, never mentioned it again. It was over, finished. Water under the bridge. Virginia was grateful. Edie, the old servant who had seen and heard everything, could well have proved to be the fly in the ointment. Instead she became one of Virginia's closest friends.

Alexa took a little longer. Sweet-natured and self-contained, she was inclined to be shy and withdrawn. She was not a beautiful child, with a dumpy shape and pale-red hair and the white skin that goes with this colouring, and was at first uncertain of her position in the family, yet almost touchingly anxious to please. Virginia responded to the best of her ability. This little girl was, after all, Edmund's child and an important part of their marriage. She could never be a mother, but she could be a sister. Unobtrusively, she eased Alexa out of her shell, speaking to her as though they were the same age, taking much care not to tread on any tender toes. She showed interest in Alexa's ploys, her drawing and her dolls, and included her in every possible activity and occasion. This was not always convenient, but the most important thing was that Alexa should never feel abandoned.

It took about six months, but it was worth it. She was rewarded by Alexa's spontaneous confidences, and a touching admiration and devotion.

So there was family, but there were friends too. Liking her for her youth, for their affection for Edmund, for the fact that Edmund had chosen to marry her, they made her welcome. The Balmerinos, of course, but others too. Virginia was a gregarious girl who did not relish solitude and found herself surrounded by people who seemed to want her. When Edmund was away on business, which he was right from the start, more often than not, everybody was enormously kind and attentive, asking her out on her own, constantly phoning to be certain that she was neither lonely nor unhappy.

Which she was not. Secretly she almost relished Edmund's absences because, in some strange way, they enhanced everything; he was gone but she knew that he was coming back to her, and each time he came back, being married to him was even better than before. Occupied with Alexa, with her new house, and her new friends, she filled in the empty days and counted the hours until Edmund should return to her. From Hong Kong. From Frankfurt. Once he had taken her with him to New York, and afterwards had indulged in a week's leave. They had spent it at Leesport, and she remembered that time as one of the best in the whole of her life.

And then, Henry.

Henry changed everything, not for the worse, but for the better, if that was possible. After Henry, she didn't want to go away any more. She had never imagined herself capable of such selfless love. It was different from loving Edmund, but all the more precious because it was utterly unexpected. She had never thought of herself as maternal, and never analyzed the true meaning of the word. But this tiny human being, this little life reduced her to wordless wonder.

They all teased her, but she didn't mind. She shared him with Violet and Edie and Alexa, and relished in the sharing because, at the end of the day, Henry belonged to her. She watched him grow and savoured every moment of his progress. He stumbled and walked and spoke words, and she was enchanted. She played with him, drew pictures, watched Alexa push him in her old doll's pram across the lawn. They lay in the grass and watched ants, walked down to the river and threw pebbles into the swift-flowing brown stream. They sat by winter fires and read picture books.

He was two. He was three. He was five years old. She took him to his first day at the Strathcroy Primary School and stood at the gate watching him walk away from her up the path to the school-house door. There were children everywhere but none of them took any notice of him. He seemed, at that moment, especially small and very vulnerable, and she could scarcely bear to see him go.

Three years later, he was still small and vulnerable, and she felt more protective of him than ever. And this was the cause of the cloud that had gathered and now lay on the edge of her own personal horizon. She was afraid of it.

From time to time the subject of Henry's future had come up, but she had shied from discussing it through with Edmund. He knew, however, her opinion. Lately, nothing had been said. She was happy to leave it this way, on the principle that it was best to leave a sleeping tiger to lie. She did not want to have to fight Edmund. She had never stood up to him before because she had always been happy to leave important decisions to him. He was, after all, older, wiser, and infinitely more competent. But this was different. This was Henry.

Perhaps, if she did not look, if she paid no attention, the problem would go away.

When Archie and Violet had left, trundling away down the drive in the battered old Land Rover, Virginia stayed where she was, in front of the house, feeling unsatisfactorily aimless and at a loss for something to do. The church meeting had broken the day in half, and yet it was too early to go indoors and start thinking about dinner. The weather was improving by the moment, and the sun was about to appear. Perhaps she should attempt a little gardening. She considered this idea and then rejected it. In the end she went into the house, gathered up the tea-mugs from the dining-room table and carried them through to the kitchen. Edmund's spaniels were dozing in their baskets under the table. As soon as they heard her footsteps, however, they were awake, on their feet and anxious for exercise.

"I'll just put these in the dishwasher," she told them, "and then we'll go out for a bit." She always talked aloud to the dogs, and sometimes, like right now, it was comforting to hear the sound of her own voice. Mad old people talked to themselves. At times it was not difficult to understand why.

In the back kitchen, with the dogs milling around her, she took an old jacket off a hook and pushed her feet into rubber boots. Then they set off, the dogs racing ahead, down the wooded lane that ran along the south bank of the river. Two miles upstream another bridge crossed the water, leading back to the main road, and so to the village. But she left this behind her and walked on to where the trees stopped and the moor began, untrammelled miles of heather and grass and bracken, leaning up into the hills. Far away, the sheep grazed. There was only the sound of flowing water.

She came to the dam, the river sliding over its rim, the deep pool beyond. This was Henry's favourite swimming place. She sat on the bank where, in summer, they brought picnics. The dogs loved the river. They stood now knee-deep, and drank as though they had not seen water for months. When they had done this, they came out and shook themselves lustily all over her. The afternoon sun felt warm. She pulled off her jacket and would have sat on, revelling in the sun's warmth, but inevitably the midges appeared in droves and started biting, so she got to her feet, whistled the dogs, and went home.

She was in the kitchen preparing dinner when Edmund returned. They were having roast chicken and she was grating breadcrumbs for bread sauce. She heard the car, looked with surprise at the clock, and saw that it was only half past five. He was very early. Driving from Edinburgh, he did not usually arrive back at Balnaid until seven or even later. What could have happened?

Speculating, hoping there was nothing wrong, she finished the breadcrumbs and dumped them into the saucepan with the milk and the onion and the cloves. She stirred. She heard his footsteps coming down the long passage from the hall. The door opened and she turned, smiling but faintly anxious.

"I'm back," he announced unnecessarily.

Her husband's masculine appearance, as always, filled Virginia with satisfaction. He wore a navy-blue chalk-striped suit, a light-blue shirt with a white collar, and a Christian Dior silk tie that she had given him for Christmas. He carried his brief-case and looked a bit creased, as well he might after a day's work and a long drive, but not in the least weary. He never looked weary and he never complained of feeling tired. His mother swore he had never been tired in his life.

He was tall, his figure youthful as it had ever been, and his handsome face, with the quiet, hooded eyes, hardly lined. Only his hair had changed. Once so black, it was now silvery-white but thick and smooth as ever. For some reason the ageless face, in juxtaposition to that white hair, rendered him more distinguished and attractive than ever.

She said, "Why so early?"

"Reasons. I'll explain." He came to kiss her; looked at the saucepan. "Good smells. Bread sauce. Roast chicken?"

"Of course."

He dumped his brief-case on the kitchen table. "Where's Henry?"

"With Edie. He won't be back till after six. She's given him his tea."

"Good."

She frowned. "Why good?"

"I want to talk to you. Let's go into the library. Leave the sauce, you can cook it later. . . ."

He was already on his way out of the kitchen. Puzzled and apprehensive, Virginia put the saucepan aside and replaced the big lid on the hob. Then she followed him. She found him in the library, crouched by the fireplace, setting a match to the newspaper and kindling.

She felt faintly defensive, as though this were some sort of criticism. "Edmund, I was going to light the fire when I'd got the sauce made and the potatoes peeled. But it's a funny sort of day. We spent all afternoon in the dining-room, having the church meeting. We never came in here. . . ."

"Doesn't matter."

The paper had caught, the kindling snapped and crackled. He straightened, dusting his hands, and stood watching the rising flames. His profile gave nothing away.

"We're going to have this sale in July." She sat on the arm of one of the chairs. "I've got the worst job of all, collecting jumble. And Archie wanted some envelope from the Forestry Commission . . . he said you knew about it. We found it in your desk."

"Yes. That's right. I meant to give it to you."

". . . oh, and something frightfully exciting. The Steyntons are going to have a dance, for Katy, in September. . . ."

"I know."

"You know?"

"I had lunch with Angus Steynton in the New Club today. He told me then."

"They're going the whole hog. Marquees and bands and caterers and everything. I'm going to get a really sensational dress. . . ."

He turned his head and looked at her, and her chatter died. She wondered if he had even been listening. After a little, she asked, "What is it?"

He said, "I'm home early because I haven't been in the office this afternoon. I drove down to Templehall. I've been with Colin Henderson."

Templehall. Colin Henderson. She felt her heart drop into her stomach and her mouth was suddenly dry. "Why, Edmund?"

"I wanted to talk things over. I hadn't made up my mind about Henry, but now I feel sure it's the right thing to do."

"What is the right thing to do?"

"To send him there in September."

"As a boarder?"

"He could scarcely attend as a day-boy."

Apprehension by now had gone, overwhelmed by a slow, consuming anger. She had never experienced anger like this against Edmund. As well, she was shocked. She had known him to be overbearing, even dictatorial, but never underhanded. Now, behind her back, it seemed that he had betrayed her. She felt betrayed, without defences, destroyed before she had even time to fire a single gun.

"You had no right." Her own voice, but it did not sound like Virginia. "Edmund. You had *no* right."

He raised his eyebrows. "No right?"

"No right to go without me. No right to go without telling me. I should have been there, to talk things over, as you put it. Henry is my child just as much as he is yours. How dare you sneak off and organize everything behind my back, without saying a single word!"

"I didn't sneak off and I'm telling you now."

"Yes. As a fait accompli. I don't like being treated as a person who doesn't matter, someone who has no say. Why should *you* always make all the decisions?"

"I suppose because I always have."

"You were underhanded." She rose to her feet, her arms folded tightly across her breast, as though the only way to stop them from actually striking her husband was to keep them under control. Always so compliant, she was a tigress now, fighting for her cub. "You know, you've always known, that I don't want Henry to go to Templehall. He's too little. He's too young. I know you went when you were eight to boarding-school, and I know that Hamish Blair is there, but why should it have to be a rigid tradition that we all have to follow? It's archaic, Victorian, out of date, to send little children away from home. And what is worse is that it doesn't have to happen. Henry can perfectly well stay at Strathcroy until he's twelve. And then he can go to boarding-school. That's reasonable. But not before, Edmund. *Not now.*"

He gazed at her in genuine perplexity. "Why do you want to make Henry different from other boys? Why should he be marked out as an oddity, staying at home until he's twelve? Perhaps you're confusing him with American children who seem to rule the family household until they're practically adult. . . ."

Virginia was incensed. "It's nothing to do with America. How can you say such a thing? It's to do with what any sensible, normal mother feels about her children. It's you who are on the wrong tack, Edmund. But you won't ever consider the possibility that you might be wrong. You're behaving like a Victorian. Old-fashioned and pigheaded and chauvinistic."

She got no reaction from this outburst. Edmund's expression did not change. On such occasions, his was a poker-face, with sleepy eyes and an unsmiling mouth. She found herself longing for him to behave naturally, let himself go, lose his temper, raise his voice. But that was not Edmund Aird's way. In business, he was known as a cold fish. He stayed unmoved, controlled, unprovoked.

He said, "You are thinking only of yourself."

"I'm thinking of *Henry*."

"No. You want to keep him. And you want your own way. Life has been kind to you. You've always had your own way; spoiled and indulged by your parents. And perhaps I continued where they left off. But there comes a time when we all have to grow up. I suggest that you grow up now. Henry is not your possession and you must let him go."

She could scarcely believe that he was saying these things to her.

"I *don't* think of Henry as a possession. That is the most insulting accusation. He's a person in his own right, and I've made him that person. But he's eight years old. Scarcely out of the nursery. He needs his home. He needs *us*. He needs the security of surroundings he's known all his life, and he needs his Moo under the pillow. He *can't* be just sent away. I don't want him to be sent away."

"I know."

"He's too little."

"So he needs to grow."

"He'll grow away from me."

Edmund made no comment on this. Her bracing anger had dissolved and she was left hurt and defeated, and near to tears. To hide these, she turned away from her husband and walked to the window, and stood there with her forehead against the cool glass. She stared, hot-eyed, unseeing, at the garden.

There was a long silence. And then, reasonable as ever, Edmund began to speak again. "Templehall's a good school, Virginia, and Colin Henderson's a good headmaster. The boys are never pushed, but they're taught to work. Life is going to be hard for Henry. It's going to be hard for all these youngsters. Competitive and tough. The sooner they face up to this, and learn to take the rough with the smooth, the better. Accept the situation. For my sake. See it my way. Henry is too dependent on you."

"I'm his mother."

"You smother him." With that, he walked calmly from the room.

7

IN THE GOLDEN EVENING, Henry walked home. There were few people about because it was nearly six o'clock and they were all indoors eating their tea. He imagined this comforting meal. Soup perhaps, and then haddock or chops and then cakes and biscuits, all washed down with strong and scalding tea. He himself felt pleasantly full of sausages. But perhaps before he went to bed there would be space for a mug of cocoa.

He crossed the curving bridge that spanned the Croy between the two churches. At the top of the curve he stopped and leaned over the ancient stone parapet to gaze down at the river. There had been much rain, too much for the farmers, and it was running deeply, carrying on its spate stray scraps of flotsam gathered on its journey. Branches of trees and bits of straw. Once he had seen a poor little dead lamb swept away beneath the bridge. Farther down the glen the land flattened out and there the Croy changed character, to widen and wind through pasture land, between fields where the peaceful cattle came down at evening time to drink at the water's edge. But here it flowed steeply downhill, leaping and sliding over the rocks in a series of miniature waterfalls and deep pools.

The sound of the Croy was one of Henry's earliest memories. At night he could hear it from the open window of his bedroom, and he awoke to its voice every morning. Upstream was the pool where Alexa had taught him to swim. With his friends from school he played many wet, muddy games on its banks, building dams and making camps.

Behind him, the big clock on the Presbyterian church tower struck the hour with six solemn, donging tolls. Reluctantly he drew back from the parapet and went on his way, down the lane that bordered the south bank of the river. Tall elms towered overhead, their topmost branches noisy with a colony of cawing rooks.

Reaching the open gates of Balnaid and anxious all at once to be home, he began to run, his satchel bumping at his side. As he came around the house he saw his father's dark-blue BMW parked on the gravel. Which was splendid, and an unexpected treat. His father did not usually get home until after Henry was in bed. But now he would find them in the kitchen, comfortably chatting and exchanging news of the day, while his mother prepared dinner and his father had a cup of tea.

But they were not in the kitchen. He knew this the moment he went through the front door because he could hear voices from behind the closed library door. Just voices and the closed door, so why did he have this feeling that it was wrong; that nothing was as it should be?

His mouth had gone dry. He tiptoed down the wide passage and stood outside the door. He had truly meant to go in and surprise them, but instead he found himself listening.

". . . Scarcely out of the nursery. He needs his home. He needs *us*." His mother, speaking in a voice he had never heard before, high-pitched and sounding as though she was about to burst into tears. ". . . He *can't* be just sent away. I don't want him to be sent away."

"I know." That was his father.

"He's too little."

"So he needs to grow."

"He'll grow away from me."

They were quarrelling. They were having a row. The unbelievable had happened: his mother and father were fighting. Cold with horror, Henry waited for what was going to happen next. After a bit, his father spoke again.

"Templehall's a good school, Virginia, and Colin Henderson's a good headmaster. The boys are never pushed, but they're taught to work. Life is going to be hard for Henry. . . ."

So that was what the row was about. They were going to send him to Templehall. To boarding-school.

". . . and learn to take the rough with the smooth, the better."

Away from his friends, from Strathcroy, from Balnaid, from Edie and Vi. He thought of Hamish Blair, so much older, so superior, so cruel. *Only babies have teddies.*

". . . Henry is too dependent on you."

He could not bear to listen any more. Every fear that he had ever known crowded in on Henry. He backed away from the library door and then, reaching the safety of the hall, turned and ran. Across the floor, up the stairs and down the passage to his bedroom. Slamming the door shut behind him, he tore off his satchel and threw himself onto his bed, bundling the duvet around him. He reached under his pillow for Moo.

Henry is too dependent on you.

And so he was going to be sent away.

Plugging his mouth with his thumb, pressing Moo to his cheek, he was, for the moment, safe. Comforted, he would not cry. He closed his eyes.

8

HE DRAWING-ROOM AT CROY, used only for formal occasions, was of enormous size. The high ceiling and scrolled cornices were white, the walls lined with faded red damask, the carpet a vast Turkey rug, thread-bare in places but still warm with colour. There were sofas and chairs, some loose-covered, some in their original velvet upholstery. None of them matched. Small tables stood about, littered with Battersea boxes, silver-framed photographs, stacks of back numbers of *Country Life*. There were a great many dark oil-paintings, portraits and flower arrangements, and on the table behind the sofa stood a Chinese porcelain jar containing a flowering and scented rhododendron.

Behind the leather-seated club fender, a log fire burned brightly. The hearthrug was shaggy and white, and if wet dogs sat about upon it, smelled strongly of sheep. The fireplace was marble with an impressive mantelpiece, and on this stood a pair of gilt-and-enamel candelabra, two Dresden figures, and a florid Victorian clock.

This clock, chiming sweetly, now struck eleven o'clock.

It surprised everybody. Mrs. Franco, sleek in black silk trousers and creamy crêpe blouse, announced that she could not believe it was so late. They had all been talking so much that the evening had just flown by. She must get to bed, and her husband as well, if he was to be fit and ready for his golf game at Gleneagles. With that, the Francos gathered themselves and rose to their feet. So did Mrs. Hardwicke.

"It's been perfect, and such an elegant dinner. . . . Thank you both for your hospitality. . . ."

Good-nights were said. Isobel, in the two-year-old green silk dress that was her best, led them from the drawing-room to see them safely on their way upstairs. She closed the door behind her and did not return. Archie was left with Joe Hardwicke, apparently disinclined to retire so early. He had settled back in his chair again and looked good for at least another couple of hours.

Archie did not mind, and was content to be left in his company. Joe Hardwicke was one of their better guests, an intelligent man with liberal views and a dry sense of humour. Over dinner . . . often a sticky session . . . he had done his bit to keep the easy conversation going; he told, against himself, one or two extremely funny stories, and proved to be unexpectedly knowledgeable about wine. Discussing Archie's inherited cellar had taken up most of the second course.

Now Archie poured him a nightcap, which the American gratefully accepted. He then filled a tumbler for himself, threw a log or two on the fire, and sank deep into his own chair, his feet on the sheepskin rug. Joe Hardwicke began to question him about Croy. He found these old places fascinating. How long had his family lived here? From where had the title come? What was the history of the house?

He was not curious but interested, and Archie happily answered his questions. His grandfather, the first Lord Balmerino, had been an industrialist of some renown, who had made his fortune in heavy textiles. His elevation to the peerage had followed on from this, and he had bought Croy and its lands at the end of the nineteenth century.

"There wasn't a dwelling house here then. Just a fortified tower dating back to the sixteenth century. My grandfather built the house, incorporating the original tower. So, although bits at the back are ancient, it's basically Victorian."

"It seems large."

"Yes. They lived on a grand scale in those days. . . ."

"And the estate . . . ?"

"Mostly let out. The moor's gone to a syndicate for the grouse shooting. I have a friend, Edmund Aird, and he runs it, but I have a half-gun in the syndicate and I join them on days when they're driving. I've kept some stalking, but that's just for my friends. The farm is tenanted." He smiled. "So you see, I have no responsibilities."

"So what do you do?"

"I help Isobel. I feed the dogs and exercise them when I can. Deal with all the fallen timber, keep the house supplied with logs. We've got a circular saw in one of the outbuildings and an old villain comes up from the village every now and then and gives me a hand. I cut the grass." He stopped. It wasn't much of an answer but he couldn't think of anything more to tell.

"Do you fish?"

"Yes. I have a boat on the Croy, about two miles upstream from the village, and there's a loch up in the hills. It's good to go up there for the evening rise. Take the boat out. It's very peaceful. And when it's winter and dark at four, I have a workshop down in the basement. There's always something that needs repairing. I mend gates, renew skirtings, build cupboards for Isobel, put up shelves. And other things. I like to work with wood. It's basic, very therapeutic. Perhaps instead of joining the Army I should have been a joiner."

"Were you with a Scottish Regiment?"

"I was a Queen's Loyal Highlander for fifteen years. We spent two of those in Berlin with the American forces. . . ."

The conversation moved on, from Berlin to the Eastern Bloc, and so to politics and international affairs. They had another night cap, lost track of time. When they finally decided to call it a day, it was past one o'clock in the morning.

"I've kept you up." Joe Hardwicke was apologetic.

"Not at all." Archie took the empty glasses and went to place them on the tray that stood on the grand piano. "I'm not much of a sleeper. The shorter the night, the better."

"I . . ." Joe hesitated. "I hope you don't think I'm being impertinent, but I see that you're lame. Did you have an accident?"

"No. My leg was shot off in Northern Ireland."

"You have an artificial leg?"

"Yes. Aluminium. Marvellous piece of engineering. Now, what time do you want breakfast? Would eight-fifteen do you? That should give you time before the car comes to collect you and take you to Gleneagles. And shall I call you in the morning?"

"If you would. About eight o'clock. I sleep like the dead in this mountain air."

Archie moved to open the door. But Joe Hardwicke was offering to dispose of the tray of drinks. Could he perhaps carry it to the kitchen for Archie? Archie was grateful but firm. "Not at all. House rule. You're guests. Not allowed to lift a finger."

They went out into the hall. "Thank you," said Joe Hardwicke, standing at the foot of the staircase.

"Thank you. Good night. And sleep well."

He stayed at the foot of the stairs until the American had disappeared and Archie had heard the opening and the shutting of his bedroom door. Then he returned to the drawing-room, settled the fire, put on the fire-guard, drew back the heavy curtains. Outside, the garden lay washed in moonlight. He heard an owl. He went out of the room, leaving the drink tray where it was, switched off lights. He crossed the hall to the dining-room. The table had been cleared of all traces of dinner, and was now set for breakfast. He felt guilty, for this was, by tradition, his job, and Isobel had accomplished it all alone, while he had sat talking.

He went on to the kitchen. Here again, all was neat and orderly. His two black Labrador bitches slumbered by the Aga in their round baskets. Disturbed, they woke and raised their heads. Thump, thump, went their tails.

"Have you been out?" he asked them. "Did Isobel take you out before she went to bed?"

Thump, thump. They were content and comfortable. There was nothing left for him to do.

Bed. He found himself, all at once, very tired. He climbed the staircase, switching off lights as he went. In his dressing-room, he took off his clothes. His dinner jacket, his bow-tie, his studded white shirt. Shoes and socks. Trousers were the most complicated, but he had perfected a routine for their removal. The tall mirror in his wardrobe reflected his image, but he made a point of not looking at it, because he so hated to see himself unclothed; the livid stump of his thigh, the shining metal of the leg, the screws and hinges, the belts and strappings that kept it in place—all revealed, shameless and somehow obscene.

Quickly he reached for and pulled on his night-shirt, easier to deal with than pyjamas. He went to the adjoining bathroom, peed, and cleaned his teeth. In their vast bedroom, no lights burnt but moonlight flowed through the uncurtained window. On her side of the wide double bed, Isobel slept. But as he moved across the room, she stirred and woke.

"Archie?"

He sat down on his side of the bed.

"Yes."

"What time is it?"

"About twenty past one."

She thought about this. "Were you talking?"

"Yes. I'm sorry. I should have been helping you."

"It doesn't matter. They were nice."

He was unstrapping the harness, gently easing the padded leather cup away from his stump. When it was free, he bent to lay the hateful contraption on the floor beside the bed, the webbing arranged neatly, so that in the morning he could put it on again with the least possible inconvenience. Without it, he felt lopsided and strangely weightless, and his stump burnt and ached. It had been a long day.

He lay beside Isobel and pulled the cool sheets up to his shoulders.

"Are you all right?" Her voice was drowsy.

"Yes."

"Did you know that Verena Steynton's going to throw a dance for Katy? In September."

"Yes. Violet told me."

"I shall have to get a new dress."

"Yes."

"I haven't got anything to wear."

She drifted back to sleep.

As soon as it started, he knew what was going to happen. It was always the same. Forsaken, bleak streets, plastered with graffiti. Dark skies and rain. He wore a flak jacket and drove one of the armoured Land Rovers, but there was something amiss because he should have a companion and he was on his own.

All he had to do was to get to the safety of the barracks. The barracks was a requisitioned Ulster Constabulary police station, fortified to the hilt and bristling with armoury. If he could get there, without them coming, he would be safe. But they were there. They always came. Four figures, spread out across the road ahead, shrouded by the rain. They had no faces, only black hoods, and their weapons were trained upon him. He reached for his rifle, but it had gone. The Land Rover had stopped. He could not remember stopping it. The door was open and they were upon him, dragging him out. Perhaps this time they were going to beat him to death. But it was the same. It was the bomb. It looked like a brown paper parcel but it was a bomb, and they loaded it into the back of the Land Rover, and he stood and watched them. And then he was back behind the wheel and the nightmare had truly begun. Because he was going to drive it in through the open gates of the barracks, and it would explode and kill every man in the place.

He was driving like a lunatic and it was still raining, and he could see nothing, but would soon be there. All he had to do was to get through the gates, drive the explosive vehicle into the bomb pit, and somehow get out and run like Jesus before the bomb went off.

Panic was destroying him, and his ears roared with the sound of his own breathing. The gates swung up, he was through them, down the ramp, into the bomb pit. Its concrete walls rose on either side of him, shutting out the light. Escape. He tugged at the door handle but it was stuck. The door wouldn't open, he was trapped, the bomb was ticking like a clock, lethal and murderous, and he was trapped. He screamed. Nobody knew he was there. He went on screaming. . . .

He awoke, screaming like a woman, his mouth open, sweat streaming down his face . . . arms caught him. . . .

"Archie."

She was there, holding him. After a little, she drew him gently down onto the pillows. She comforted him like a child, with small sounds. She kissed his eyes. "It's all right. It was a dream. You're here. I'm here. It's all over. You're awake."

His heart banged like a hammer and he streamed with sweat. He lay still in her embrace and gradually his breathing calmed. He reached for a glass of water, but she was there before him, holding it for him to drink, setting the glass back on the table when he had had enough.

When he was quiet, she said, with a ghost of a smile in her voice, "I hope you haven't woken anybody up. They'll think I'm murdering you."

"I know. I'm sorry."

"Was it . . . the same?"

"Yes. Always the same. The rain, and the hoods and the bomb and that fucking pit. Why do I have nightmares about something that never happened to me?"

"I don't know, Archie."

"I want them to stop."

"I know."

He turned his head, burying his face in her soft shoulder. "If only they would stop, perhaps then I could make love to you again."

August

1

Monday the Fifteenth

THE ARRIVAL OF THE MORNING POST at Croy was a movable feast. Tom Drystone, the postman, driving his scarlet van, covered, during the day, an enormous area. Long, winding single-track roads led up into the glens, to remote sheep farms and distant crofts. Young wives, isolated with small children, would watch for his coming while hanging out lines of washing in the cold, fresh wind. Old people, living on their own, depended on him to deliver their prescriptions, pause for a chat, even sit down and drink a cup of tea with them. In winter-time, he swapped his van for a Land Rover, and only the worst of blizzards prevented him from somehow getting through and delivering the long-awaited letter from Australia, or a new blouse ordered from the Littlewoods catalogue, and when the howling north-west gales damaged telephone lines and power cables, he was very often the only source of communication with the outside world.

Because of this, even if he had been a dour-faced man with no small talk and a sharp tongue on him, Tom's daily appearance would always be welcome. But he was a cheerful fellow, born and bred in Tullochard, and so unfazed by anything that the wild country or the elements could throw at him. As well, when he was not being a postman, he was greatly admired for his ability to play the accordion, and was a kenspeckle figure at local ceilidhs, up on the platform with a glass of beer on the floor beside him, and leading the bank in an endless round of jigs and reels. This catchy music went with him everywhere, because, as he delivered the mail, he whistled.

*   *   *

It was now the middle of August. A Monday. A blowy day with a good deal of cloud. Not hot but, at least, not raining. Isobel Balmerino, tied up in an apron, sat at one end of the kitchen table at Croy and plucked three brace of grouse. They had been shot on Friday and hung in the game larder for three days. They should, perhaps, hang a little longer, but she wanted to be shed of the messy job and have the grouse safely in the deep-freeze before the next lot of Americans arrived.

The kitchen was vast and Victorian, filled with every evidence of her busy life. A dresser was stacked with a set of chipped ironstone dinnerware, a notice-board was pinned with postcards, addresses, scribbled reminders to ring the plumber. The dogs' baskets lay near the great four-oven Aga, and large bunches of drying flowers hung from hooks in the ceiling, once employed for curing hams. Over the Aga was a drying rack, on a pulley, where sodden tweeds were hoisted after a day on the hill, or ironed linen, still not quite dry, put to air. This was not a wholly satisfactory arrangement because if there were kippers for breakfast, then pillowcases smelt faintly of fish, but as Isobel had no airing cupboard, there was nothing to be done about it.

Once, a long time ago in old Lady Balmerino's day, this pulley had been the source of a long-standing family joke. Mrs. Harris was then resident cook, and a splendid cook but not one troubled by any silly prejudices concerning hygiene. Her habit had been to keep, on the Aga, an enormous black iron stock-pot simmering with bones and the remains of any vegetable she thought fit to scrape off a plate. With this, she made her famous soups. One year a house party stayed for the shooting. The weather was appalling, so the rack above the Aga constantly drooped with soaked jackets, knickerbockers, sweaters, and hairy stockings. The soup that fortnight got better and better, more and more tasty. Guests begged for recipes. "How do you do it, Mrs. Harris? The flavour! Quite delicious." But Mrs. Harris simply bridled and smugly said that it was just a wee knack she'd picked up from her mother. The week ended and the house party left, tucking large tips into Mrs. Harris's boiled red hand as they left. When they had gone, the stock-pot was finally emptied for scouring. At the bottom was found a felted and none-too-clean shooting stocking.

Four birds plucked and two to go. Feathers floated everywhere. Isobel gathered them cautiously, bundling them into newspaper, stowing the bundles into a black plastic dustbin bag. Spreading fresh newspaper and starting in on number five, she heard whistling.

The back door flew open, and Tom Drystone burst cheerfully in on her. The draught caused a cloud of feathers. Isobel let out a wail, and he hastily shut it behind him.

"I see the laird's keeping you busy." The feathers settled. Isobel sneezed. Tom slapped a pile of mail down on the dresser. "Can you not get young Hamish to give you a hand?"

"He's away. Gone to Argyll for a week with a school friend."

"What kind of day did they have at Croy on Friday?"

"Disappointing, I'm afraid."

"They got forty-three brace over at Glenshandra."

"They were probably all ours, flown over the march fence to call on their friends. Do you want a cup of coffee?"

"No, not today, thanks. I've a full load on board. Council circulars. Well, I'll be off. . . ."

And he was away, whistling before he had even banged the door shut behind him.

Isobel went on tearing feathers out of the grouse. She longed to go and inspect the letters, see if there was anything exciting, but was firm with herself. She would finish the plucking first. Then she would clear away all the feathers. Then she would wash her hands and look at the mail. And then she would embark upon the bloody job of cleaning the birds.

The post-van sped away. She heard footsteps approaching down the passage from the hall. Painful and uneven. Down the few stone steps, one at a time. The door opened and her husband appeared.

"Was that Tom?"

"Didn't you hear the whistle?"

"I'm waiting for that letter from the Forestry Commission."

"I haven't looked yet."

"Why didn't you tell me you were doing those grouse?" Archie sounded more accusing than guilty. "I'd have come to help."

"Perhaps you'd like to clean them for me?"

He made a distasteful face. He could shoot birds, and wring the neck of an injured runner. He could, if pressed, pluck them. But he was squeamish about cutting them open and pulling out their innards. This had always been a small cause of friction between himself and Isobel, and so he swiftly changed the subject. As she had known he would.

"Where is the mail?"

"He put it on the dresser."

He limped over to collect it, brought it back to the other end of the table, well out of reach of the general mess. He sat down and leafed through the envelopes.

"Hell. It's not here. I wish they'd put their skates on. But there's one from Lucilla . . ."

"Oh, good, I hoped there would be. . . ."

". . . and something very large and stiff and thick, which might be a summons from the Queen."

"Verena's writing?"

"Could be."

"That's our invitation."

"And two more, similar, to be forwarded on. One for Lucilla, and another for"—he hesitated—"Pandora."

Isobel's hands were still. Down the long, feather-strewn table, their eyes met. "Pandora? They've asked Pandora?"

"Apparently."

"How extraordinary. Verena never told me she was going to ask Pandora."

"No reason why she should."

"We'll have to send it on to her. Open ours and let's see what it looks like."

Mrs. Angus Steynton

At Home

For Katy

Friday, 16th September 1988

R S V P
Corriehill
Tullochard
Relkirkshire

Dancing 10 P.M.

Archie did so. "Very impressive." He raised his eyebrows. "Embossed, copperplate, and gold edges. The sixteenth of September. Verena's left it pretty late, hasn't she? I mean, that's scarcely a month away."

"There was a disaster. The printers made a mistake. They printed the first batch of invitations on the wrong side of the paper, and so she sent them all back and they had to be done again."

"How did she know they were printed on the wrong side of the paper?"

"Verena knows about things like that. She's a perfectionist. What does it say?"

"It says, 'Lord and Lady Balmerino. Mrs. Angus Steynton. At Home. For Katy. Blah Blah. Dancing at ten. R.S.V.P.'" He held it up. "Impressed?"

Without her glasses, Isobel screwed up her eyes and peered. "Very impressed. It'll look splendid on the mantelpiece. The Americans will think we've been invited to something Royal. Now, read me Lucilla's letter. That's much more important."

Archie slit the flimsy envelope with the French stamp and postmark and unfolded two sheets of cheap, lined, and very thin paper.

"Looks as though she's written it on lavatory paper."

"Read it."

" 'Paris. August sixth. Darling Mum and Dad. Sorry I've been such ages in writing. No time for news. This is just a short note to let you know my movements. Am leaving here in a couple of days and going down to the south. I am travelling by bus, so no need to anguish about hitch-hiking. Going with an Australian boy I've met called Jeff Howland. Not an art student but a sheep-farmer from Queensland, with a year off to bum round Europe. He has friends in Ibiza, so we might possibly go there. I don't know what we'll do when we get to Ibiza, but if there is the chance of getting over to Majorca, would you like me to go and see Pandora? And if you would, will you send me her address because I've lost it. And I'm a bit short of cash, so could you possibly float me a loan till my next allowance comes through? Send all c/o Hans Bergdorf, PO Box 73, Ibiza. Paris has been heaven but only tourists here just now. Everybody else has disappeared to beaches or mountains. Saw a blissful Matisse exhibition the other day. Lots of love, darlings, and DON'T WORRY. Lucilla. PS. Don't forget the money.' "

He folded the letter and put it back into the envelope.

Isobel said, "An Australian."

"A sheep-farmer."

"Bumming round Europe."

"At least they're travelling by bus."

"Oh well, I suppose it could be worse. But thinking that she might go and see Pandora . . . isn't that extraordinary? We don't mention Pandora's name for months and all at once it keeps popping up everywhere we turn. Is Ibiza very far from Majorca?"

"Not very."

"I wish Lucilla would come home."

"Isobel, she's having the time of her life."

"I hate her being short of money."

"I'll send her a cheque."

"I miss her so."

"I know."

She was done with plucking, the feathers all painfully collected and stowed in the black rubbish bag. The six small corpses lay in a pathetic row, their heads askew, their clawed feet pointed like dancers. Isobel reached for her lethally sharpened knife and without ado sliced into the first little flaccid body. Then she laid down the knife and plunged her hand into the bird. She withdrew it, red with blood, drawing out a long string of pearly, greyish entrails. These piled in surprising profusion onto the newspaper. The smell was overwhelming.

Archie sprang to his feet. "I'll go and write that cheque." He gathered the mail. "Before I forget." And he headed for his study, firmly closing the kitchen door behind him, shutting away the small scene of domestic carnage.

At his desk, he held Pandora's envelope for a moment or two. He thought about writing to her. Tucking a letter from himself in with Verena's invitation. It's a party, he would say. It'll be fun. Why not come home for it, and stay with us at Croy? We would so love to see you. Please, Pandora. Please.

But he had written thus before and she had scarcely bothered to reply. It was no good. He sighed and carefully readdressed the envelope. He added a few stamps for good measure and an airmail sticker, then laid it aside.

He wrote a cheque payable to Lucilla Blair, for a hundred and fifty pounds. He then began a letter to his daughter.

Croy, August 15th.

My darling Lucilla.

Thank you very much for your note which we received this morning. I hope you will have a good journey to the south of France, and are able to raise enough cash to get you to Ibiza, as I am sending this cheque there as you asked me to. As for Pandora, I am sure she would be delighted to see you but suggest that you telephone before you make any plans, and let her know that you propose to visit her.

Her address is Casa Rosa, Puerto del Fuego, Majorca. I haven't got her telephone number but I am sure you will be able to find it in the phone book in Palma.

As well, I am forwarding on an invitation to a party that the Steyntons are throwing for Katy. It's only a month off and you may have other and better things to do, but I know that your mother would be so happy if you could be there.

A good day on the twelfth. They were driving, and so I joined the guns for the morning only. Everybody was kind and I was allowed the bottom butt. Hamish came with me to carry my gun and my game bag, and help his old father up the hill. Edmund Aird shot exceptionally well, but at the end of the day the bag was only twenty-one and half brace, and two hares. Hamish went off yesterday for a week in Argyll with a school friend. He took his trout rod, but hopes for some deep-sea fishing. My love, my darling child. Dad.

He read this missive through, then folded it neatly. He found a large brown envelope and into this put the letter, the cheque, and Verena's invitation. He sealed and stamped it and addressed it to Lucilla at the Ibiza address that she had given them. He took both letters out into the hall and laid them on the chest that stood by the door. The next time that anyone went to the village they would be posted.

2

Wednesday the Seventeenth

THE STEYNTONS' INVITATION WAS DELIVERED to Ovington Street on the Wednesday of that week. It was early morning. Alexa, barefoot and wrapped in her bathrobe, stood in the kitchen, waiting for the kettle to boil. The door to the garden was open, and Larry was out there, having his routine sniff-around. Sometimes he found traces of cat and became very excited. It was a grey morning. Perhaps later the sun would come out and burn the mist away. She heard the rattle of the letter-box and, looking up through the window, saw the postman's legs as he strode on down the pavement.

She laid a tray, put tea-bags into the teapot. The kettle boiled and she made the tea, and then, leaving her little dog to his own devices, carried the tray up the basement stairs. The letters lay on the doormat. Juggling with the tray, she stooped to gather them up and push them into the capacious pocket of her robe. Up again, the thick carpet soft beneath her bare feet. Her bedroom door stood open, the curtains already drawn back. It was not a very large room, and almostly completely filled by the bed that Alexa had inherited from her grandmother. It was an impressive bed, wide and downy, with tall brass bedsteads at either end. She put the tray down and climbed back between the sheets.

She said, "Are you awake, because I've brought you a cup of tea?"

The hump on the other side of the bed did not instantly respond to this summons. Then it groaned and heaved. A bare brown arm appeared from the covers, and Noel turned to face her.

"What's the time?" His hair, so dark on the white linen pillow, was tousled, his chin rough with stubble.

"A quarter to eight."

He groaned again, ran his fingers through his hair. She said "Good morning," and bent to kiss his unshaven cheek. He put his hand on the back of her head and held her close. He said, mumbling, "You smell delicious."

"Lemon shampoo."

"No. Not lemon shampoo. Just you."

He took his hand away. Released, she kissed him again, and then turned to the domestic business of pouring his tea. He pummelled pillows, heaved himself up to lean against them. He was naked, brown-chested as though he had just returned from some tropical holiday. She handed him the steaming Wedgwood mug.

He drank slowly, in silence. He took a long time to come to in the mornings, and scarcely said a word before breakfast. It was something she had found out about him, one of his small routines of existence. Like the way he made coffee, or cleaned his shoes, or mixed a dry martini. At night he emptied his pockets, laying their contents in a neat row on the dressing-table, always in the same order. Wallet, credit cards, penknife, small change, the coins tidily stacked. The best of all was lying in bed and watching him do this; then watching him undress, waiting for him to be ready, to come to her.

Each day brought new knowledge; each night fresh, sweet discovery. All the good things piled up so that every moment, every hour was better than the moment and the hour before. Living with Noel, sharing this blissful blend of domesticity and passion, made her understand for the first time why people ever wanted to get married. It was so that it would go on for ever.

And once . . . only three months ago . . . she had thought herself perfectly satisfied. Alone in the house, with only Larry for company, occupied with her work, her little routine, occasional evenings out, or visits to friends. No more than half a life. How had she endured it?

You never miss what you've never had. Edie's voice, loud and clear. Thinking of Edie, Alexa smiled. She poured her own mug of tea, stood it beside her, and then reached into her pocket for the letters. She spread them on the eiderdown. A bill from Peter Jones, a circular for double glazing, a postcard from a woman who lived in Barnes and wanted some goodies concocted for her deep-freeze, and finally the huge, stiff, white envelope.

She looked at it. A Scottish postmark. An invitation? To a wedding, perhaps . . .

She ripped the envelope with her thumb and took out the card.

She said, "Goodness me."

"What is it?"

"An invitation to the ball. 'You *shall* go to the ball,' said the Fairy Godmother to Cinderella."

Noel reached out and took it from her.

"Who's Mrs. Angus Steynton?"

"They live near us in Scotland. About ten miles away."

"And who's Katy?"

"Their daughter, of course. She works in London. You've maybe met her. . . ." Alexa thought about this and then changed her mind. "No. I don't think you would have. She's inclined to go round with young men in the Guards . . . lots of race meetings."

"Sixteenth of September. Are you going to go?"

"I shouldn't think so."

"Why not?"

"Because I wouldn't want to go without you."

"I haven't been invited."

"I know."

"Will you say, 'I shall come if I can bring my lover with me'?"

"Nobody knows I've got a lover."

"You still haven't told your family that I've moved in with you?"

"Not yet."

"Any particular reason?"

"Oh, Noel . . . I don't know." But she did know. She wanted to keep it all to herself. With Noel, she inhabited a secret magic world of love and discovery, and she was afraid that if she let anybody in from the outside, then it would all dissolve and somehow be spoilt.

As well . . . and this was a pathetic admission . . . she lacked any form of moral courage. She was twenty-one but that didn't help, because she still felt, inside, about fifteen, and as anxious to please as she had ever been. The thought of possible family reactions filled her with agonized distress. She imagined her father's disapproval, Vi's horrified astonishment, and Virginia's concern. Then, the questions.

But who is he? Where did you meet him? You've been living together? At Ovington Street? But why is this the first we've heard of it? What does he do? What is his name?

And Edie. *Lady Cheriton must be turning in her grave.*

It wasn't that they wouldn't understand. It wasn't that they were strait-laced or hypocritical in any way. Nor was it that they didn't all love Alexa—she couldn't bear any of them to be upset.

She drank some tea.

Noel said, "You're not a little girl any longer."

"I know I'm not. I'm adult. I just wish I wasn't such a wet adult."

"Are you ashamed of our sinful cohabitation?"

"I'm not ashamed of anything. It's just . . . the family. I don't like hurting them."

"My sweet, they'll be much more hurt if they hear about us before you've got around to telling them."

Alexa knew that this was true. "But how could they find out?" she asked him.

"This is London. Everybody talks. I'm astonished your father hasn't got the buzz already. Take my advice and be a brave girl." He gave her his empty mug and a swift kiss on the cheek. Reaching for his bathrobe, he swung his legs over the side of the bed. "And then you can write to Mrs. Stiffden, or whatever her name is, and say yes, please, you'd love to come to the ball, and you're bringing Prince Charming with you."

Despite herself, Alexa smiled. "Would you come?"

"Probably not. Tribal dances are scarcely my scene." And with that he took himself off to the bathroom. Almost at once Alexa heard the gushing of the shower.

So what was all the fuss about? Alexa picked up the invitation again, and frowned at it. I wish you'd never come, she told it. You've just stirred up a lot of trouble.

3

Monday the Twenty-second

THAT AUGUST, THE ENTIRE ISLAND simmered in an unprecedented heat wave. The mornings started hot, and by midday the temperatures had risen to unbearable heights, driving any person with sense indoors for the afternoon, to loll breathless upon a bed, or sleep on some shady terrace. The old town, up in the hills, quiet and shuttered, slumbered through the hours of siesta. The streets were empty and the shops closed.

But, down in the port, it was a different story. There were too many people about, and too much money being spent, to respect this time-honoured custom. The tourists did not want to know about siestas. They did not want to waste a moment of their costly holiday in sleeping. And the day visitors had nowhere to go. So, instead, they sat about in droves, red and perspiring, in the pavement cafés; or wandered aimlessly in air-conditioned gift arcades. The beach was littered with palm-thatch umbrellas and half-naked, kippering bodies, and the Marina packed with seagoing craft of every description. Only the boat people seemed to know what was good for them. Usually bustling with activity, the yachts and launches dipped lazily in the swell of the oily water, and in the shade of canvas awnings supine bodies, brown as mahogany, lay about on the decks, as though already dead.

Pandora awoke late. She had tossed and turned her way through the night and finally, at four in the morning, taken a sleeping pill and fallen at last into a heavy, dream-troubled sleep. She would have slept on but the sound of Seraphina clattering away in the kitchen disturbed her. The clatter shattered the dream, and after a little, reluctantly, she opened her eyes.

The dream had been of rain, and brown rivers, and cold wet scents, and the sound of wind. Of deep lochs and dark hills with boggy paths leading to their snow-capped summits. But most important was the rain. Not falling straight, not thunderous and tropical as it was when it fell here, but gentle and misty. Rolling in on clouds, insidious as smoke . . .

She stirred. The images dissolved, were gone. Why should she dream of Scotland? Why, after all these years, did those old chilly memories come back to tug at her sleeve? Perhaps it was the heat of this cruel August, the endless days of relentless sunshine, the dust and the dryness, the hard-edged black shadows of noon. One yearned for that gentle, scented mist.

She turned her head on the pillow and saw, beyond the sliding glass doors that had stood open all night, the balustrade of the terrace, the glaring brilliance of geraniums, the sky. Blue, cloudless, already brazen with heat.

She propped herself up on an elbow and reached across the wide empty bed to the bedside table and her watch. Nine o'clock. More racket from the kitchen. The sound of the dishwasher churning. Seraphina was making her presence heard. And if she was here, that meant that Mario—her husband and Pandora's gardener—was already scratching away with his archaic hoe in the garden. Which precluded all possibilities of an early skinny-dip. Mario and Seraphina lived in the old town and came to work each morning on Mario's moped, roaring full throttle up the hill. Mario drove this noisy brute of a contraption with Seraphina perched behind him, riding, modestly, side-saddle, and with her strong brown arms wrapped around his waist. It was a wonder that the daily assault of din that proclaimed their arrival had not woken Pandora before this, but then the sleeping pills were very strong.

It was too hot to go on lying in this rumpled, messy bed. She had been here long enough. Pandora threw aside the thin sheet and, barefoot and naked, crossed the wide expanse of marbled floor and went into her bathroom. She collected her bikini—no more than two scraps of knotted handkerchief—climbed into it, and then walked back through her bedroom, out onto the terrace, and down the steps that led to the swimming pool.

She dived. It was cool, but not cool enough for true refreshment. She swam. She thought of diving into the loch at Croy and coming up screaming with agony because the cold bit into every painful pore of one's body; it was a numbing cold that took all breath away. How could she have swum in what was virtually snow-water? How could she and Archie and all the rest of them have indulged in such masochistic pleasures? But what fun it had been. And then coming out, and struggling damply into warm sweaters, and lighting a fire on the pebbly shore of the loch, and cooking the best trout in the world over the smoky embers. Trout, ever since, had never tasted so good as at those impromptu camp-fire meals.

She swam on. To and fro, up and down the long pool. Scotland again. Not dreams now but conscious memories. So what? She let them have their way. Let them lead her away from the loch, down the rough turfy track that followed the course of the burn, tumbling and spilling its way down the hill, finally to join the Croy. Peaty water brown and frothy as beer, spilling over rocks and splashing into deep pools where the trout lurked in the shadows. Over the centuries this stream had cut for itself a little valley, and the banks of this were green and verdant, sheltered from the north winds and bright with wild flowers. Foxgloves grew, and starwort, sweet green bracken and tall purple thistles. One particular spot was special. They called it the Corrie and it was the venue for many spring and winter picnics when the winds from the north were too cold to light camp-fires by the loch.

The Corrie. She did not let her memories linger there but hurried them on. The track steepened, winding between great rock formations, cliffs of granite older than time. A final turn and the glen lay spread far below, sunlit, rolling with cloud shadows, revealed in all its pastoral beauty. The Croy a glittering thread, its two arched bridges just visible through the trees; the village reduced by distance to a child's plaything, set out on some nursery carpet.

A pause for contemplation and then on again. The track levelled off. The deer-fence lay ahead and the tall gate. Now visible, the first of the trees. Scots pines, and beyond them the green of the beeches. Then Gordon Gillock's house, with Mrs. Gillock's washing line flying a bunting of laundry, and the gun dogs, disturbed, exploding into a cacophony of frenzied barking from their kennels.

Nearly home. The track a proper road now, Tarmacked, leading between farm buildings, stone steadings, and barns and byres. The smell was of cattle and dung. Another gate and past the farmhouse with its bright cottage garden and drystone wall smothered in honeysuckle. The cattle-grid. The drive lined with rhododendrons . . .

Croy.

Enough. Pandora jerked her wayward memories back into line as though they were over-eager children. She had no wish to go farther. Enough of self-indulgence. Enough of Scotland. She swam a final length and then climbed the shallow steps up and out of the pool. The stones beneath her bare feet were already hot. Dripping, she made her way back into the house. In her bathroom, she showered, washed her hair, put on a fresh dress, loose and sleeveless, the coolest garment she owned. She left her bedroom, crossed the hall, went into the kitchen.

"Seraphina."

Seraphina swung around from the sink where she was busily engaged in scrubbing a bucket of mussels. She was a small, squat, brown woman with sturdy bare legs thrust into espadrilles, and dark hair drawn back into a knot at the nape of her neck. She always wore black because she was perpetually in mourning. No sooner was she out of mourning for one old grandparent or distant relation than another of her clan passed on and she was back in mourning again. The black dresses all looked exactly the same, but as if to make up for their gloom, her pinafores and aprons were invariably brightly coloured and hectically patterned.

Seraphina went with the Casa Rosa. Previously, she had worked for fifteen years for the English couple who had originally built the villa. When, two years ago, due to family pressures and uncertain health, they reluctantly returned to England, Pandora, searching for some place to live, had bought the property from them. Doing this, she discovered that she had inherited Seraphina and Mario. At first Seraphina was not certain whether she wished to work for Pandora, and Pandora was in two minds about Seraphina. She was not exactly attractive and very often looked quite grumpy. But tentatively they tried out a month together, and then the month stretched to three months, and then to a year, and the arrangement, quite comfortably, settled itself, without anything actually being said.

"*Señora. Buenos días.* You are awake."

After fifteen years with her previous employers, Seraphina spoke reasonable English. Pandora was grateful for this small mercy. Her French was fluent but Spanish a closed book. People said it was easy because of having done Latin at school, but Pandora's education did not include Latin and she was not about to start now.

"Any breakfast?"

"Is on the table. I bring the coffee."

The table was set on the terrace, which faced out over the driveway. Here it was shady and cooled by any breeze that blew from the sea. Crossing the sitting-room, Pandora's eye was caught by a book that lay on the coffee-table. It was a large and lush volume, sent as a present from Archie for her birthday. *Wainwright in Scotland.* She knew why he had sent it. He never stopped, in his simple and transparent way, trying to lure her home. Because of this, she had not even opened it. But now she paused, her attention caught. *Wainwright in Scotland*. Scotland again. Was this a day to be drenched in nostalgia? She smiled at herself, at this weakness that had suddenly come upon her. Why not? She stooped and picked up the book and carried it out onto the terrace. Peeling an orange, she opened it on the table.

It was indeed a coffee-table book, built for browsing. Pen-and-ink drawings, beautifully executed maps, and a simple text. Coloured photographs sprang from every page. The silver sands of Morar. Ben Vorlich. The Falls of Dochart. The old names resounded satisfactorily, like a roll of drums.

She began to eat the orange. Juice dripped on the pages of the book, and she brushed them carelessly away, leaving stains. Seraphina brought her coffee but she never looked up, so engrossed was she.

Here the river, after a long and sedate journey, suddenly erupts into a furious rage, descending in a turbulent cataract of white foam along a wide and rocky channel in a remarkable display of thrashing waters. The flow of the rapids is interrupted by wooded islands, one of which was the burial place of the clan MacNab, and a bower of lovely trees enhances a scene of outstanding beauty. . . .

She poured coffee, turned a page and read on.

Wainwright in Scotland consumed her day. She carried it from the breakfast table to a long chair by the pool and then, after lunch, took it to bed with her. By five o'clock, she had read it from cover to cover. Closed at last, she let it drop to the floor.

It was cooler now, but for once she had scarcely been troubled by the heat. She got off her bed and went out of doors and swam once more, then dressed in white cotton trousers and a blue-and-white shirt. She did her hair, her eyes, found earrings, a gold bracelet. White sandals. She sprayed on scent. Her bottle was nearly finished. She would have to buy more. The prospect of this small luxurious purchase filled her with pleasure.

She said goodbye to Seraphina and went out of the front door and down the steps to where her car was parked in the garage. She got in and drove down the winding hill and so out onto the wide road that led to the port. She parked her car in the courtyard of the post office and went in to collect her mail. She put this in her leather-strapped basket and then left her car and walked slowly through the still-crowded streets, pausing to glance into shop windows, to assess a dress, to price a delectable lacy shawl. At the scent shop, she went in and bought a flagon of Poison, then went on, always walking in the direction of the sea. She came at last to the wide, palm-fringed boulevard that ran parallel to the beach. At the end of the day it seemed as busy as ever, the sands crowded and people still swimming. Far out, windsurfers' sails caught the evening breeze, dipping like birds' wings out across the surface of the water.

She came to a little café where a few tables stood empty on the pavement. The waiter came and she ordered coffee and cognac. Then, leaning back in the uncomfortable iron chair, pushing her sunglasses up onto the top of her head, she reached into the basket and took out her letters. One from Paris. One from her lawyer in New York. A postcard from Venice. She turned it over. Emily Richter, still staying at the Cipriani. A large stiff white envelope, addressed to Croy and readdressed in Archie's handwriting. She opened it and read, in disbelief and then with some amusement, Verena Steynton's invitation.

At Home

For Katy

Extraordinary. As though she were receiving a summons from another age, another world. And yet a world which, by some strange coincidence, like it or not, she had inhabited for the whole of the day. She knew uncertainty. Was it an omen of some sort? Should she pay heed? And if it was an omen, did she believe in omens in the first place?

At Home For Katy. She remembered other invitations, "stiffies" she and Archie had called them, propped on the mantelpiece of the library at Croy. Invitations to garden parties, cricket matches, dances. Dances galore. There had been a week in September when one scarcely slept, somehow surviving with the stolen naps in the backs of cars, or a doze in the sun while others played tennis. She remembered a wardrobe filled with ball dresses, and she herself perpetually complaining to her mother that she had nothing to wear. Everybody had seen the ice-blue satin because she'd worn it at the Northern Meetings, and anyway, some man had spilt champagne all down the front and the stain wouldn't come out. And the rose-pink? The hem was torn and one of the straps had come loose. Whereupon her mother, the most indulgent and patient of women, instead of suggesting that Pandora find a needle and thread and mend the rose-pink, would put her daughter into the car and drive to Relkirk or Edinburgh and there suffer the traumas of Pandora's capricious whims, trudging from shop to shop until the most beautiful—and inevitably most costly—dress was finally run to earth.

How spoilt Pandora had been, how adored, how cherished. And in return . . .

She laid down the card and looked up at the sea. The waiter came with her coffee and brandy on a little tray. She thanked him and paid. As she drank the bitter, black, scalding coffee, Pandora watched the windsurfers and the slow ambling flow of passers-by. The evening sun slipped down out of the sky and the sea became like molten gold.

She had never gone back. Her own decision. Nobody else's. They had not come chasing after her but they had never lost touch. Always letters, still filled with love. After her parents died, she thought the letters would stop but they didn't, because then Archie took over. Detailed descriptions of shoots, news of his children, scraps of village gossip. Always they ended in the same way. "We miss you. Why don't you come and stay for a few days? It is too long since we have seen you."

A yacht was moving out of the Marina, motoring gently until it was clear of the beach and able to fill its sails with wind. Idly, she watched its passage. She saw it, but her inner eye was filled with images of Croy. Her thoughts, once more, ran ahead and this time she did not pull them back, but let them go. To the house. Up the steps to the front door. The door stood open. Nothing to stop her. She could go. . . .

She set down her coffee-cup with some force. What was the point? The past was always golden because one recalled only the good times. But what about the darker side of memory? Happenings better left where they were, shut away, like sad mementoes stuffed in a trunk, the lid closed down, the key turned in the lock. Besides, the past was people, not places. Places without people were like railway stations where no trains ran. I am thirty-nine. Nostalgia drains all energy from the present, and I am too old for nostalgia.

She reached for her brandy. As she did this, a shadow came between herself and the sun, to lie across her table. Startled, she looked up and into the face of the man who stood beside her. He gave a little bow.

"Pandora."

"Oh, Carlos! What are you doing creeping up on me?"

"I have been to the Casa Rosa but found nobody there. You see, if you don't come to me, then I have to come to you."

"I *am* sorry."

"So I tried the port. I thought that I should find you somewhere here."

"I was shopping."

"May I join you?"

"Of course."

He drew out a chair and sat facing her. He was a tall man in his mid-forties, formally attired in collar and tie and a light jacket. His hair was dark, as were his eyes, and even on this sultry evening his appearance was cool and crisp. He spoke impeccable English and looked, Pandora always thought, like a Frenchman. But he was, in fact, a Spaniard.

As well, extremely attractive. She smiled. She said, "Let me order you a brandy."

4

Wednesday the Twenty-fourth

VIRGINIA AIRD SHOULDERED HER WAY through the swing-doors of Harrods and stepped out into the street. In the store, the heat and the hassle had become oppressive. Outside, it was scarcely better. The day was humid, the air heavy with petrol fumes and the claustrophobia of surging humanity. Brompton Road stood solid with traffic, and the pavements were choked with a slow-moving river of people. She had forgotten that city streets could contain so many people. Some had to be Londoners, one supposed, going about their daily business, but the general impression was of some global immigration from all points of the compass. Tourists and visitors. More visitors than one could have believed possible. Great blond students with backpacks passed by. Entire families of Italians or possibly Spaniards; two Indian ladies in brilliant saris. And, of course, Americans. My fellow countrymen, thought Virginia wryly. They were instantly recognizable by their clothes and the plethora of camera equipment slung about their necks. One huge man was even wearing his ten-gallon hat.

It was four-thirty in the afternoon. She had been shopping all day and was now laden with loot, carrier bags, and parcels. Her feet hurt. But still she stood there, because she had not yet made up her mind what she was going to do next.

There were two alternatives.

She could return forthwith, by any means of transport that made itself available, to Cadgewith Mews, where she was staying in great comfort with her friend Felicity Crowe. She had been given a latchkey, so even if the house was empty—Felicity out shopping, or taking her dachshund for a turn around the gardens—Virginia could let herself in, kick off her shoes, make a cup of tea, and fall, in a stupor of exhaustion, onto her bed. The prospect of such a course of action was immensely tempting.

Or she could go to Ovington Street and risk finding Alexa out. This was what she *ought* to do. Alexa was not exactly on her conscience, but there could be no question of returning to Scotland without having made contact with her stepdaughter. She had already tried to do this, telephoning last night from Felicity's, but there had been no answer to the call and she had finally replaced the receiver, deciding that, for once, Alexa was out on some spree. Then she had tried again this morning, and at lunch-time, and again from the hairdresser's, boiled with heat from the blow drier. Still no reply. Was Alexa perhaps out of London?

At that moment a small Japanese, gazing in the opposite direction, barged into her and knocked one of her parcels to the ground. He apologized profusely in his polite Japanese way, picked up the parcel, dusted it off, returned it to her, bowed, smiled, raised his hat, and went on his way. Enough. A taxi drew up to unload its cargo and, before anyone else could claim it, Virginia did so.

"Where to, love?"

She had made up her mind. "Ovington Street." If Alexa was not at home, she would keep the taxi and go on to Felicity's. With the small decision taken, she felt better. She opened the window, sat back, thought about taking off her shoes.

It was a short journey. As the taxi turned into Ovington Street, Virginia sat forward to search for Alexa's car. If her car was there, then, in all probability, Alexa would be at home. It was—a white minivan with a red stripe was parked at the pavement outside the blue front door. Relief. She directed the cab driver and he drew up in the middle of the street.

"Can you wait a moment? I just want to make sure somebody's in."

"Okay, love."

She gathered up her shopping and bundled out, climbed the steps and pressed the bell. She heard Larry barking, Alexa's voice telling him to be quiet. She dumped her parcels on the doorstep and, opening her bag, went back to pay off the taxi.

Alexa was in her kitchen, dealing bravely with the detritus of her day's work, all of which she had brought back from Chiswick in the back of her van. Saucepans, plastic containers, wooden salad bowls, knives, egg-whisk, and a cardboard wine crate filled with dirty glasses. When all was clean, dried, and put away, she planned to go upstairs, strip off her crumpled cotton skirt and shirt, take a shower, and then put on an entirely fresh set of clothes. After that, she would make a cup of tea . . . Lapsang souchong with a slice of lemon . . . and then she would take Larry for a little stroll, and later start thinking about dinner. On the way back from Chiswick, she had stopped off at the fishmonger and bought rainbow trout, Noel's favourite. Grilled, with almonds. And perhaps . . .

She heard the taxi approaching slowly down the street. Standing at the sink, visibility was limited. The taxi stopped. A woman's voice. High-heeled footsteps tapped across the pavement. Alexa, rinsing a wineglass under the tap, waited, listening. Then her doorbell rang.

Larry hated the doorbell and burst into an aria of barking. And Alexa, so occupied and busy, resented the interruption and was equally unenthusiastic. Who on earth could this be? "Oh, be quiet, you stupid creature." She set down the glass, untied her apron and went upstairs to find out. Hopefully, it would be no one of importance. She opened the door to a pile of expensive-looking parcels. The taxi made a U-turn and trundled away. And . . .

She gaped. Her stepmother. Dressed for London but still instantly recognizable. She wore a black dress and a scarlet jacket and patent pumps, and her hair, fresh from the hands of some exclusive expert, had been dressed in a new style, drawn back from her face and clasped in a huge black velvet bow.

Her stepmother. Looking fantastic but unannounced and entirely un-expected. The implications of this caused every thought but one to fly from Alexa's head.

Noel.

"Virginia."

"Don't die of shock. I kept the taxi waiting because I thought you might be out." She kissed Alexa. "I've been shopping," she explained unnecessarily, and stooped to gather up the parcels. Alexa, with an effort, pulled herself together and helped.

"But I didn't even know you were in London."

"Just for a day or two." They dumped it all on the hall table. "And don't say why didn't you ring me up, because I've been calling non-stop. I thought you must be away."

"No." Alexa shut the door. "We . . . I went out for dinner last night, though, and I've been out on a job all day. I was just washing up. That's why I'm looking such a mess. . . . "

"You look great." Virginia eyed her. "Have you lost weight?"

"I don't know. I never weigh myself."

"What was the job?"

"Oh, a lunch for an old man's ninetieth birthday. In Chiswick. A lovely house, right on the river. Twenty guests, and all relations. Two great-grandchildren."

"What did you give them?"

"Cold salmon and champagne. That's what he wanted. And a birth-day cake. But why didn't you tell me you were coming . . . ?"

"Oh, I don't know. It was all done on the spur of the moment. I just felt I wanted to get away for a day or two. I've been shopping all day."

"It looks like it. And I love your hair. You must be exhausted. Go on in and take the weight off your feet. . . . "

"That's all I want. . . ." Pulling off her jacket, Virginia went through the open door, tossed her jacket aside, headed for the largest armchair, collapsed into it, kicked off her shoes and placed her feet on a stool. "Heaven."

Alexa stood and looked at her. How long did she plan to stay? Why . . . ? "Why aren't you staying here with me?" Thank heavens she wasn't, but it was the obvious question to ask.

"I would have invited myself, of course, but I promised Felicity Crowe next time I came to London I'd stay with her. You know, she's my childhood friend. She'd have been my bridesmaid if I'd had brides- maids. And we never see much of each other, and when we do we talk and giggle non-stop."

So that was all right. "Where does she live?"

"A dear little house in Cadgewith Mews. But I must say, it's not as pretty as this."

"Would you . . . would you like a cup of tea?"

"No, don't bother. A cold drink would do."

"I've got a can of Coke in the fridge."

"Perfect."

"I . . . I'll just get it."

She left Virginia and went down to the kitchen. She opened the fridge and took out the can of cola. Virginia was here and it was necessary to be cool and objective. Being cool and objective was not Alexa's strong point. Downstairs, evidences of Noel were scarce. His Barbour jacket and a tweed cap hung in the downstairs loo. A *Financial Times* lay in the drawing-room. That was all. But upstairs was different. His personal belongings were everywhere, and the bed, very obviously, made up for the occupancy of two people. There could be no question of trying to hide it all away. If Virginia went upstairs . . .

She found herself overwhelmed with indecision. On the one hand, perhaps this was the best way to do it. She hadn't planned anything but it had happened; and Virginia was here. As well, Virginia was young and not even, strictly speaking, family. She would hopefully understand, and perhaps even approve. She, after all, had had strings of men in her life before she married Fa. Virginia could be Alexa's advocate, the best per- son of all to break the news gently that the shy and puddingy Alexa had not only found a man of her own at last but had taken him into her heart and her home, and was openly living with him.

On the other hand, if she did this, then the secret was out and Alexa would be expected to share Noel. Speak about him and allow them all to meet him. She imagined her father coming to London, ringing up. "I'll take you both to Claridges for dinner." The prospect caused her knees to shake, but in the end, she knew that she would be able to cope with such a situation. The unanswered question was how Noel would react. Would he, perhaps, feel that he was being pressurized in some way? Which would be disastrous because, after three months of living with him and learning all the capricious twists of another person's character, Alexa knew that this was the one thing in life that Noel could not stand.

At a loss, totally out of her depth, she made a huge effort to be rational. There is nothing you can do about it, she told herself in Edie's voice. You'll just need to take things the way they come. Thinking of Edie made her feel a bit stronger. She closed the door of the fridge, found a glass, and went back upstairs.

"Sorry I've been so long." Virginia was smoking. "I thought you'd given up cigarettes."

"I did but I started again. Don't tell your father."

Alexa opened the Coke and poured it, and handed Virginia the glass.

"Oh, marvellous. Delicious. I thought I was going to die of thirst. Why are all the shops so hot? Why are there so many people everywhere?"

Alexa curled up in the corner of the sofa.

"Visitors. It took me hours to get back from Chiswick. And you've got on the wrong sort of shoes for shopping. You should be wearing trainers."

"I know. It's crazy, isn't it? Dressing up to come to London. Habit, I suppose."

"What have you been buying?"

"Clothes. Basically something for the Steyntons' party. I see you've got your invitation."

"I haven't answered it yet."

"You're coming, of course."

"I . . . I don't know . . . I'm pretty busy round then."

"But of course you must come. We're counting on you. . . ."

Alexa diverted her. "What sort of a dress did you get?"

"It's dreamy. Sort of voile, white, in layers, with black spots everywhere. Tiny shoe-string straps. I'll have to try to step up my suntan."

"Where did you find it?"

"Caroline Charles. I'll show it to you before I go. But, Alexa, do try to come. It's September, so everybody will be there and it'll be a great do."

"I'll see. How's Fa?"

"He's fine." Virginia turned away to stub out her cigarette in the ashtray. Alexa waited for her to enlarge on this flat statement, but she didn't say any more.

"And Henry?"

"Henry's great too."

"Are they both at home?"

"No. Edmund's spending this week in the flat in Edinburgh, and Henry's taken his sleeping-bag and gone to stay at Pennyburn with Vi. I took him to Devon for his summer holidays. We had three weeks, and it was a success. I took him riding for the first time in his life, and he liked all the farm animals and going fishing with my father." Another pause, not entirely comfortable, or was that Alexa's imagination? Then Virginia went on. "I really wanted to take him out to the States. I suddenly got this yen for Leesport and Long Island. But Gramps and Grandma had taken themselves off for a long cruise, so there wasn't much point our going."

"No, I suppose not." A car started up and sped away down the street. "So what's happening at home?"

"Oh, not a lot. The usual. We had the church sale in July, to try to raise money for the electrics. It was more work than you can possibly imagine, and we ended up with around four hundred pounds. I thought it was scarcely worth the effort, but Archie and the rector seemed quite satisfied. Henry won a bottle of rhubarb wine in the raffle. He's going to give it to Vi for her birthday."

"Lucky Vi. How is she? And how's Edie?"

"Oh, *Edie*. That's a real problem. Haven't you heard?"

It sounded disastrous. "Heard what?"

"She's got this dreadful cousin come to stay with her. She arrived last week and Edie's already looking demented."

The idea of Edie looking demented was enough to fill Alexa's heart with chill. "*What* dreadful cousin?"

Virginia told her, in some detail, the saga of Lottie Carstairs. Alexa was horrified. "I remember the Carstairses. They were very old, and they lived in a croft up the hill from Tullochard. And sometimes on Sundays they used to come to Strathcroy to have their dinner with Edie."

"That's right."

"They used to drive a tiny, rattly car. The two little old people sitting in the front and the great gawky daughter in the back."

"Well, the two little old people are now dead and the gawky daughter has gone witless. Which is putting it mildly."

Alexa was indignant. "But why should Edie have to look after her? Edie's got enough to do without such a responsibility."

"That's what we all told her, but she wouldn't listen. She says there's nowhere else for the poor soul to go. Anyway, last week she arrived in an ambulance and she's been with Edie ever since."

"But not for ever? She'll surely go back to her own house?"

"Let's hope so."

"Have you seen her?"

"Have I? She wanders round the village and talks to everybody. And not just the village. I took the dogs up to the dam the other day, and I was just sitting there on the bank when, all of a sudden, I had this queer feeling and I turned around, and there was Lottie sneaking up behind me."

"How spooky."

"Spooky's the word. Edie can't keep track of her. And that's not the worst of it. She goes out at night too, and drifts around the place. I suppose she's quite harmless, but the thought of her peering through windows is enough to put the fear of God into anybody."

"What does she look like?"

"She doesn't *look* mad. Just a bit strange. With very pale skin and eyes like boot buttons. And she's always smiling, which makes her spookier than ever. Ingratiating. I think that's the word. Edmund and Archie Balmerino say she was always like that. She worked at Croy one year as a housemaid. I don't think Lady Balmerino could find anybody else. Vi said it was the year Archie and Isobel were married. Archie swears every time you opened a door, Lottie was always lurking behind it. And then she smashed so much china that Lady Balmerino sacked her. So all in all, as you can gather, it's something of a problem."

The telephone rang.

"Oh, bother." Alexa, engrossed in the drama of Strathcroy, resented the interruption. Reluctantly she got to her feet and went to her desk to answer the call.

"Hello?"

"Alexa Aird?"

"Speaking."

"You won't remember me—Moira Bradford—but I was a guest at the Thomsons' dinner party last week . . . and I wondered . . ."

Business. Alexa sat down, reached for her note pad, her Biro, her engagement diary.

". . . not until October, but thought it better to fix things right away . . ."

Four courses, for twelve people. Perhaps, Mrs. Bradford suggested delicately, Alexa could give her some idea of cost?

Alexa listened, answered questions, made notes. Behind her, she was aware that Virginia had got out of her chair and was making for the door. She looked up. Virginia made gestures, mouthed "Just going to the john . . ." and before Alexa had the opportunity to tell her to use the cloakroom and not go upstairs, was gone.

". . . of course, my husband will see to the wine . . ."

"I beg your pardon?"

"I said my *husband* will see to the *wine*."

". . . oh, yes, of course . . . look, shall I get back to you?"

"But can't we decide everything now? I'd rather do it that way. And another thing is serving. Do you have a colleague, or do you do the serving yourself?"

Virginia had gone upstairs. She would see everything, draw the obvious conclusions, guess the truth. In a strange way, Alexa felt a sort of resigned relief. There wasn't much point in feeling anything else because it was too late to do anything about it.

She took a deep breath. She said, in her most capable voice, "No. I don't have a colleague. But you don't have to worry, because I can manage it all very easily on my own."

*   *   *

Virginia, in stockinged feet, climbed the staircase, reflecting, as she always did, that this was one of the prettiest of small London houses. So fresh, with its wallpaper and shining white paint. And so comfortable, with thick carpets and extravagantly generous curtains. On the landing, the doors to the bedroom and the bathroom both stood open. She went into the bathroom and saw that Alexa had new curtains here, a quilted chintz patterned with leaves and birds. Admiring them, she looked around for other signs of refurbishment.

There were none, but other unexpected objects caught her eye and the implication of these drove all other thoughts from her head. Two tooth-brushes in the tooth-mug. Shaving-tackle on the glass shelf, a wooden bowl of soap and a shaving-brush. A bottle of aftershave—Antaeus by Chanel—the same that Edmund used. By the side of the bath was a huge Turkish sponge, and hanging from the tap a ball of soap on a cord. From hooks behind the door hung two towelling robes, one large, blue-and-white-striped, the other smaller and white.

By now she had totally forgotten her reason for coming upstairs. She went out of the bathroom, back onto the landing. Downstairs was silent. The telephone call apparently was finished, and Alexa's voice stilled. She looked at the bedroom door, then put out her hand, pushed it completely open and went in. Saw the bed, piled with double pillows; Alexa's night-gown neatly folded on one set, a man's sky-blue pyjamas on the other. On the bedside table a pigskin travelling clock softly ticked. That clock did not belong to Alexa. Her eyes moved around the room. Silver brushes on the dressing-table, silk ties slung on the mirror. A row of masculine shoes. A wardrobe door, perhaps faulty, hung open. She saw rows of suits on hangers, and on the chest of drawers a pile of immaculately ironed shirts.

A step on the stair behind her. She turned. Alexa stood there, in her crumpled cotton clothes looking much as she had always looked. Yet different. "Have you lost weight?" Virginia had asked, but she knew now no diet was responsible for that indefinable radiance about Alexa that she had noticed the moment she saw her.

Their eyes met, and Alexa's were steady. She did not look away. There was no guilt there, no shame, and Virginia was glad for her. Alexa was twenty-one. It had taken long enough, but now it seemed that, at last, she had grown up.

Standing there, she remembered Alexa as a child, as she had first known her, so shy, so unsure, so eager to please. Then, the newly married Virginia had trod with the greatest of care, chosen her words, always painfully aware of the pitfalls of impetuously saying or doing the wrong thing.

It was the same now.

In the end it was Alexa who spoke first. She said, "I was going to tell you to use the downstairs loo."

"I'm sorry. I didn't mean to pry."

"You didn't have to. It's pretty obvious."

"Do you mind me knowing?"

"No. You would have found out sometime."

"Want to talk about it?"

"If you like."

Virginia came out of the bedroom and closed the door behind her. Alexa said, "Let's go back downstairs and I'll tell you there."

"I haven't been to the john yet." And all at once they were both laughing.

"He's called Noel Keeling. I met him in the street. He'd come to dinner with some people called Pennington—they live a couple of doors down —but he'd got the wrong night, so he was at a loose end."

"Was that the first time you'd ever seen him?"

"Oh, no, we'd met before that, but not very memorably. At some cocktail party, and then I did a directors' lunch for his firm."

"What does he do?"

"He's in advertising. Wenborn and Weinburg."

"How old is he?"

"Thirty-four." Alexa's face became dreamy, the very picture of a girl able to talk at last about the man she loves. "He's . . . oh, I can't describe him. I was never any good at describing people."

A pause fell. Virginia waited. And then, in an effort to get Alexa back to the point of the story, said, "So, he'd come to dine in Ovington Street on the wrong night."

"Yes. And he was tired out. You could see how tired he was. He'd just flown in from New York and he hadn't had any sleep, and he looked so down in the mouth, I asked him in. And we had a drink, and then something to eat. Chops. And then he went to sleep on the sofa."

"You can't have been very entertaining."

"Oh, Virginia, I *told* you. He was tired."

"Sorry. Go on."

"And then the next evening was the night he was meant to have dinner with the Penningtons, so he dropped in for a moment first, and brought me a great bunch of roses. A sort of thank-you. And then a couple of nights later, we went out for dinner. And . . . well, it sort of snowballed from there."

Virginia wondered if 'snowballed' was, under the circumstances, an appropriate word. But she said, "I see."

"And then a weekend came along and we drove out into the country for a day. And it was very warm and blue-skyed, and we took Larry and walked for miles over the downs, and we had dinner on the way back to London, and then we went to his flat for coffee. And then . . . well . . . it was dreadfully late . . . and . . .''

"You spent the night with him."

"Yes."

Virginia reached for another cigarette and lit it. Snapping out her lighter, she said, "And the following morning, you had no regrets?"

"No. No regrets."

"Was it . . . the first time? For you?"

"Yes. But you didn't have to ask that, did you?"

"Oh, honey, I know you very well."

"It made everything a bit embarrassing to begin with. Because I couldn't just let him find out. I couldn't pretend. It would have been like pretending you can swim frightfully well, and then jumping into the deep end and drowning. I didn't want to drown. So I told him. I was sure he would think I was dreadfully schoolgirlish or prissy. But do you know what he said? He said it was like being given a really splendid and unexpected present. And the next morning he woke me up by opening a bottle of champagne with a tremendous pop and a flying cork. And we sat in bed and drank it together. And after that . . ."

She paused, having apparently run out of both breath and words.

"More snowballing . . . ?"

"Well, you know. We were always together, I mean when we weren't working. And after a bit, it seemed ludicrous, at the end of the evening, driving off in different directions or having to borrow the other person's tooth-brush. So we talked about it. He's got a very nice flat in Pembroke Gardens and I would happily have gone there, but I couldn't leave this house empty when it's so full of Granny Cheriton's precious things. And for the same reason I didn't feel very keen to let it. It was a bit of a dilemma but then Noel met up with these friends who'd just got married and wanted a place to rent until they'd found somewhere of their own. So he let them have his flat and moved in with me."

"How long has he been here?"

"About two months."

"And you never let on."

"It wasn't that I was ashamed or secretive. It was just that it was all so incredibly marvellous, I wanted to keep it to ourselves. Somehow that was part of the magic."

"Does he have family?"

"His parents are both dead but he's got two sisters. One's married and lives somewhere in Gloucestershire. The other's in London."

"Have you met her?"

"No, and I don't really want to. She's much older than Noel and she sounds rather frightening. She's Editor-in-Chief of *Venus,* and terribly high-powered."

"So when I get home, do you want me to say anything?"

"It's up to you."

Virginia thought about it. "It would surely be better to tell Edmund before he hears about it from some other person. He's in London a lot and you know how people talk. Especially men."

"That's what Noel says. Would you mind telling Fa? And Vi? Would it be very difficult to tell them?"

"Not difficult at all. Vi's amazing. She takes everything in her stride. And as for your father, at the moment I don't really care what I have to say to him."

Alexa frowned. "What *do* you mean?"

Virginia shrugged. She was frowning. When she frowned, all the fine lines on her face sprang into relief and she no longer looked so young. "I suppose you might as well know. We're not on the best of terms at the moment. We have a running row going on, no harsh words, but a certain frigid politeness."

"But . . ." Noel was forgotten and Alexa filled with apprehension. She had never heard Virginia speak about Fa in that cold tone of voice, could not remember them ever having quarrelled. Virginia adored him, fell in with all his plans, agreed with everything he suggested. There had never been anything but loving accord, every evidence of physical affection, and always—even from behind closed doors—much laughter and chat when they were together. They never seemed to run out of things to talk about, and the stability of their marriage was one of the reasons Alexa returned home to Balnaid whenever she could grab a holiday. She liked to be with them. The very thought of their falling out, not speaking, not loving, was unendurable. Perhaps they would never love again. Perhaps they would divorce. . . . "I can't *bear* it. What's happened?"

Virginia, seeing all the joy flow from Alexa's face, felt guilty and knew she had said too much. It was just that, talking about Noel, she had forgotten that Alexa was her stepdaughter and had allowed herself to speak bluntly and coldly about her problems, as though confiding in some old and intimate friend. A contemporary. But Alexa was not a contemporary.

She said quickly, "Don't look so horrified. It's not as bad as that. It's just that Edmund is insisting on sending Henry to boarding-school and I don't want him to go. He's only eight, and I think he's too young. Edmund has always known how I feel, but he settled it all without consulting me and I was very hurt. It's got to a pitch when we can't even talk about it. The subject is never mentioned. We've both dug our toes in and that seems to be it. Which is one of the reasons I took Henry away to Devon. He knows he's got to go away to school, and he knows that we're angry with each other. For his sake, I try to have fun with him, and do things with him the way I always have. And I would never dream of saying a word to him against Edmund. You know how he adores his father. But it's not easy."

"Oh, poor little Henry."

"I know. I thought maybe a day or two with Vi would make things better for him. You know what buddies they are. So I made the excuse of a new dress and seeing you, and came to London for a few days. I don't really need a new dress, but I've seen you, and the way things have turned out, that's made it worthwhile."

"But you've still got to go home to Balnaid."

"Yes. But perhaps things will be better."

"I am sorry. But I do understand. I know how Fa can be once he's made up his mind about something. Like a brick wall. It's the way he works. I suppose it's one of the reasons that he's been so successful. But it's not easy if you're on the other side of the fence and you've got a point of view of your own."

"That's right. I sometimes think he would be a little more human if, just once in his life, he'd made a real cock-up of something. Then he could admit to the possibility of being mistaken. But he never has and he never does."

In total agreement, they gazed at each other glumly. Then Alexa said, without much conviction, "Perhaps Henry will love school, once he gets there."

"Oh, I hope so much that he will. For all our sakes. For Henry's sake in particular, I'd be grateful to be proved wrong. But I'm terribly afraid that he'll hate it."

"And you . . . ? Oh, Virginia. I can't imagine you without Henry."

"That's the trouble. Neither can I."

She reached for another cigarette and Alexa decided that the time had come to take some positive action.

She said, "Let's have a drink. After all this, I think we could both do with one. What for you? A Scotch?"

Virginia looked at her watch. "I should go. Felicity's expecting me for dinner."

"There's heaps of time. And you must stay and meet Noel. He won't be long now. Now that you know about him, please don't go. And it'll make it much easier for you, telling Fa, if you've met Noel and can say how much you like him."

Virginia smiled. Alexa was twenty-one and now a woman of some experience but still wondrously naïve.

"All right. But don't make it too strong."

Noel had bought the flowers from a street vendor near the office. Carnations and sweet peas and a misting of gypsophila. He had not intended to buy flowers but had seen them as he passed, thought about Alexa, and then gone back to take a second look. The flower-lady was anxious to be home and let him have two bunches for the price of one. Two bunches made a good show.

Nowadays, living in Ovington Street, he walked home from the office each evening. It gave him the chance to stretch his legs and yet was not too great a distance to be tiring at the end of a day's work. It was pleasant to turn in at the end of the street and know that this was where he now belonged.

Domesticity with Alexa, he had discovered, had many advantages, for she had proved to be not only a charming, compliant lover but the most undemanding of companions. At first Noel had harboured fears that she might become possessive, and jealous of any time that he spent away from her. He had suffered such resentments before, and had ended up feeling as though he had a millstone hanging round his neck. But Alexa was different, generous and understanding about evenings when he was committed to giving dinner to some overseas client, or the regular twice-weekly games of squash at his club.

Now, he knew that when he opened the blue front door she would be there, waiting for the sound of his key in the door, running up the stairs from the basement to greet him. He would relax with a drink, take a shower, eat an excellent dinner; later, watch the news, perhaps, or listen to some music. And, finally, bear Alexa off to bed.

His pace quickened. He took the steps in a single stride, juggling with the flowers in order to reach into his trouser pocket for his latchkey. The door, well-oiled, swung silently inwards, and he heard at once the voices from beyond the open drawing-room door. Alexa apparently had a caller. Which was unusual because ever since Noel had moved into Ovington Street, she had firmly kept all visitors at bay.

". . . I wish you'd stay for dinner," she was saying. He closed the door, being careful to make no sound. "Can't you ring Felicity and make some excuse?"

The hall table was piled with some person's expensive-looking shopping. He put his brief-case down on the floor.

"No, it would be too rude." A female visitor. He paused for a second to check on his appearance, sagging at the knees in front of the oval mirror, smoothing back his hair with his hand.

"It's grilled trout and almonds. . . ."

He went through the open door. Alexa was on the sofa with her back to him, but her visitor saw him at once, and their eyes met across the room. She had the most astonishingly blue eyes that he had ever seen, and their bright glitter was cool as a challenge.

She said, "Hi!"

Alexa, alerted, sprang up. "Noel. I never heard you come in." She looked rosy and faintly grubby but very sweet. He gave her the flowers and stooped to kiss the top of her head.

"You were talking too hard," he told her, and turned to the guest, who was now on her feet; a tall and stunning blonde, wearing a slender black dress and a huge black velvet bow at the back of her head. "How do you do. I'm Noel Keeling."

"Virginia Aird." Her handshake was firm and friendly and, it occurred to him, at variance with the light in those brilliant eyes. He knew then that Alexa had been confiding, and that this glamorous creature was totally *au fait* with their situation. It was up to him to carry it off.

"And you're . . . ?"

"My stepmother, Noel." Alexa spoke quickly, which meant that she was a little agitated and somewhat out of her social depth. "She's just down from Scotland to do some shopping. She dropped in out of the blue. It was the most lovely surprise. Oh, what gorgeous flowers. You are dear." She buried her nose in them and sniffed luxuriously. "Why do carnations always make me think of bread sauce?"

Noel smiled at Virginia. "She's got a one-track mind. Food."

"I'll go quickly and put them in water. We're having a drink, Noel."

"So I see."

"Do you want one?"

"Yes, of course, but don't worry, I'll help myself."

She left them bearing her bouquet, headed for the kitchen. Alone with Virginia, Noel turned to her. "Do sit down again. I didn't mean to disturb you." She did so, arranging her long limbs with some grace. "Tell me, when did you come to London? And how long are you staying?"

She explained. A spur-of-the-moment decision, an invitation from an old friend. Her voice was deep, with the attractive trace of an American accent. She had tried to get in touch with Alexa by telephone but had not been successful. Finally, she had just come around and taken Alexa by surprise.

As she told him all this, Noel fixed his drink. Now he brought it back to where she sat, and settled himself in the chair facing her. She had, he noticed, exceptional legs.

"And when are you going back to Scotland?"

"Oh, tomorrow, maybe. Or the day after."

"I heard Alexa inviting you to dinner. I wish you'd stay."

"That's kind of you, but I'm already committed. I shall have to go very soon, but Alexa wanted me to be here when you got home." Her eyes were bright as sapphires, unblinking. "She wanted me to meet you." She was splendidly direct, with no beating about the bush. He decided to meet her challenge head-on.

"I imagine that she's explained the situation to you."

"Yes, she has. I am entirely in the picture."

"I'm glad. It will make things much easier for all of us."

"Have they been difficult?"

"Not at all. But I think her conscience was troubling her."

"Her conscience has always troubled her."

"She's been a little worried about her family."

"Her family means a lot to her. She's had a strange upbringing. It's left her in some ways quite mature, and in others still childlike."

Noel wondered at her saying this. She must realize, surely, that he had already found that out for himself. He said, "She didn't want anybody hurt."

"She's asked me to tell her father."

"I think that's a splendid idea. I have been urging her to do so." He smiled. "Do you imagine that he will appear at our door with a horse-whip?"

"I shouldn't think so." Virginia reached for her handbag, took a cigarette and lit it with a gold lighter. "He's not a man who gives way to his emotions. But I think that, as soon as possible, you should make his acquaintance."

"It was never I who balked at the idea."

She eyed him through the drifting smoke of her cigarette. "I think it would be best if you were to come to Balnaid. Then we would all be around you, and Alexa would have a little moral support."

He realized that he was being invited to stay. In that solid old Edwardian house with the dogs and the conservatory and the country all around. Alexa had spoken to him, with great enthusiasm and at some length, of the joys of Balnaid. The garden, the picnics, the small brother, the grandmother, the old Nanny. He had shown polite interest but not much more. It did not sound like a place where amusing things might happen, and Noel's greatest horror was to be trapped, a guest in another person's house, and bored.

But now, faced by Virginia Aird, he found his preconceptions of Balnaid doing a swift about turn. For this elegant and sophisticated woman, with her mesmerizing eyes and her charming suggestion of a transatlantic drawl, could never be dull. Perceptive enough to leave you alone with *The Times,* if that was what you wanted, but still the sort of hostess who could, on the spur of the moment, think up some new and amusing ploy or ask a party of entertaining friends around for an impromptu drink. His imagination moved on to other delights. There would probably be some fishing. And shooting, too. Although that wouldn't be much use to Noel because he had never shot. Nevertheless . . .

He said, "How very kind of you to invite me."

"It would be best if we kept it very casual . . . as though, for some reason, you were coming anyway." She thought about this, and then her face lit up with bright inspiration. "Of course. The Steyntons' dance. What could be more natural than that? I know Alexa is in two minds about coming, but . . ."

"She said she wouldn't go without me and of course I haven't had an invitation."

"That's no problem. I'll have a word with Verena Steynton. There are never enough men at these affairs. She'll be delighted."

"You may have to persuade Alexa."

As he said this, Alexa came back into the room, bearing a pink-and-white jug in which she had loosely arranged Noel's offering. "Are you talking about me behind my back?" She put the jug on the table behind the sofa. "Don't those look lovely? You are kind, Noel. It makes me feel special, being brought flowers." She fiddled with a stray carnation, and then abandoned the arrangement and returned to her seat in the corner of the sofa. "Persuade Alexa to do what?"

"Come to the Steyntons' dance," said Virginia, "and bring Noel with you. I'll fix an invitation for him. And stay with us at Balnaid."

"But perhaps Noel doesn't want to go."

"I never said I didn't want to go."

"You did so!" Alexa was indignant. "The morning the invitation came you said tribal dances were scarcely your scene. I thought that was the end of the matter."

"We never really discussed it."

"You mean you *would* come?"

"If you want me to, of course."

Alexa shook her head in disbelief. "But Noel, it *will* be tribal dances. Reels and things. Could you bear that? It's no fun if you can't do them."

"I'm not totally inexperienced. That year I fished in Sutherland, there was a hooley in the hotel one evening and we all leaped around like savages, and as far as I remember, I leaped with the best of them. A couple of whiskies are all I need to lose my inhibitions."

Virginia laughed. "Well, if it all becomes too much for the poor man, I'm sure there'll be a night-club or a disco, so he can go and smooch in there." She stubbed out her cigarette. "What do you say, Alexa?"

"There doesn't seem to be much for me to say. Between the two of you, you've fixed the whole thing up."

"In that case, that's our little dilemma solved."

"What little dilemma?"

"Noel casually meeting Edmund."

"Oh. I see."

"Don't look so miserable. It's the perfect plan." She glanced at the clock, laid down her glass. "I must go."

Noel got to his feet. "Can I drive you somewhere?"

"No. You're sweet, but if you could find me a taxi, that would be great. . . ."

While he was gone on this errand, Virginia put her shoes back on, checked on her beautiful hairdo, reached for her scarlet jacket. Fastening the buttons, she caught Alexa's anxious gaze and smiled encouragingly.

"Don't worry about a thing. I'll make it okay for you before you've even set foot in the house."

"But you and Fa. You won't still be having a row, will you? I couldn't bear it if there was a hateful atmosphere with the two of you being angry with each other."

"No, of course not. Forget that. I shouldn't have told you in the first place. We'll have a great time. And your being there will cheer me up after poor Henry's gone to school."

"Poor little boy. I can't bear to think about it."

"Like I said, neither can I. However, there doesn't seem to be much either of us can do about it." They kissed. "Thank you for the drink."

"Thank you for coming. And for being so marvellous. You . . . you do like him, don't you, Virginia?"

"I think he's dishy. You'll answer the invitation now?"

"Of course."

"And, Alexa, buy yourself a peachy new dress."

5

Thursday the Twenty-fifth

EDMUND AIRD DROVE HIS BMW into the car-park of Edinburgh Airport just as the seven-o'clock shuttle from London drifted down out of the clouds and lined up for landing. Unhurriedly, he found a slot for himself, got out of the car and locked the door, watching, as he did so, the approach of the plane. He had timed things exactly, and this gave him much satisfaction. Standing around and waiting, for any thing or anybody, filled him with impatience. Every moment of time was precious, and to fill in so much as five minutes kicking his heels and doing nothing caused him considerable frustration and anguish.

He walked through the car-park, crossed the road, entered the terminal. The aircraft, with Virginia on board, had landed. A number of people stood around, come to meet friends or relations. They were a mixed bunch and appeared to be either in a state of wild excitement or total unconcern. A young mother with three small children milling noisily around her knees lost her patience and slapped one of them. The child roared in indignation. The carousel began to move. Edmund stood jingling the loose change in his trouser pocket.

"Edmund."

He turned to see a man he met most days lunching at the New Club. "Hello, there."

"Who are you meeting?"

"Virginia."

"I've come to pick up my daughter and her two children. They're coming to stay for a week. There's some wedding on and the wee girl's going to be a bridesmaid. At least the plane's on time. I caught the three-o'clock shuttle from Heathrow last week and we didn't take off until half past five."

"I know. It's hell, isn't it?"

The doors at the top of the stairway had opened, the first trickle of passengers started to descend. Some searched for the one who had come to meet them; some looked lost and anxious, laden by too much hand-luggage. There was the usual proportion of businessmen returning from London conferences and meetings, complete with brief-cases, umbrellas, folded newspapers. One, quite unself-consciously, bore a sheaf of red roses.

Edmund watched them, waiting for Virginia. His appearance, tall and elegantly suited, his demeanour, the heavily lidded eyes and expressionless features gave nothing away, and a stranger observing him would glean no clue as to his inner uncertainties. For the truth was that Edmund could not be sure either of his welcome from Virginia, nor what her reactions would be when she saw him standing there.

Relations between them, ever since the evening he had broken the news of his plans for sending Henry away to school, had been painfully strained. They had never had a row before, never quarrelled, and although he was a man who could exist very well without other people's approval, he was bored by the whole business, longed for a truce, and for this chill politeness that lay between them to come to an end and be finally finished.

He was not hopeful. As soon as the Strathcroy Primary had broken up for the summer, Virginia had packed Henry up and taken him to Devon to stay there with her parents for three long weeks. Edmund had hoped that this extended separation would somehow heal the wounds and bring Virginia's sulks to an end, but the holiday, spent in the company of her beloved child, appeared only to have hardened her attitude, and she returned home to Balnaid as cool as ever.

For a limited time, Edmund could deal with this, but he knew that the chill atmosphere that existed between them did not go unnoticed by Henry. He had become uncommunicative, prone to easy tears, and more dependent than ever on his precious Moo. Edmund hated Moo. He found it offensive that his son was still unable to sleep without that disgusting old scrap of baby blanket. He had been suggesting for some months that Virginia should wean Henry from Moo, but Virginia, as far as he could see, had ignored his advice. Now, with only weeks to go before Henry left for Templehall, she was going to have her work cut out.

After the debacle of the Devon holiday, and becoming frustrated with Virginia's resolute non-communication, Edmund had considered precipitating another row with his young wife, so bringing matters to a head. But then he decided that this could do nothing but worsen the situation. In her present state of mind, she was quite capable of packing her bags and hightailing it off to Leesport, Long Island, to stay with her devoted grandparents, now returned from their cruise. There she would be petted and spoiled as she had always been, and vociferously reassured that she was in the right and Edmund a hard-hearted monster even to contemplate sending small Henry away from her.

And so Edmund had kept his counsel and decided to ride out the emotional storm. He was, after all, not about to change his mind nor make any compromises. It was, at the end of the day, up to Virginia.

When she announced that she was going to London by herself for a few days, Edmund greeted the news with nothing but relief. If a few days of fun and shopping did not put her in a more sensible frame of mind, then nothing would. Henry, she told him, was going to stay with Vi. He could do what he pleased. And so he put the dogs into kennels with Gordon Gillock, closed Balnaid, and spent the week in his flat in Moray Place.

The time alone had come as no hardship to him. He simply cleared his mind of all domestic problems, allowed himself to become absorbed in his work, and enjoyed being able to put in long and productive days at his office. As well, the word went swiftly around that Edmund Aird was in town and on his own. Extra attractive men were always at a premium, and the invitations to dinner had poured in. During Virginia's absence he had not once spent an evening at home.

But the hard truth was that he loved his wife and deeply resented this constraint that had lain for so long, like a fetid bog, between them. Standing waiting for her to appear, he hoped devoutly that the time spent enjoying herself in London had brought her to her senses.

For Virginia's sake. Because he had no intention of living under the cloud of her disapproval and umbrage for so much as one more day, and had already made the decision to stay in Edinburgh, and not return to Balnaid, if she had not relented.

Virginia was one of the last to appear. Through the door and down the stairs. He saw her at once. Her hair was different and she was dressed in unfamiliar and obviously brand-new clothes. Black trousers and a sapphire-blue shirt, and an immensely long raincoat that reached almost to her ankles. She was carrying, along with her flight bag, a number of shiny and extravagant-looking boxes and carriers, the very picture of an elegant woman fresh from a mammoth shopping spree. As well, she looked sensationally glamorous and about ten years younger.

And she was *his* wife. Despite everything, he realized all at once how dreadfully he had missed her. He did not move from where he stood, but he could feel the drum-beat of his own heart.

She saw him and paused. Their eyes met. Those blue and brilliant eyes of hers. For a long moment they simply looked at each other. Then she smiled, and came on down towards him.

Edmund took a long, deep breath in which relief, joy, and a surge of youthful well-being were all inextricably mingled. London, it appeared, had done the trick. Everything was going to be all right. He felt his face break into an answering, unstoppable smile, and went forward to greet her.

Ten minutes later, they were back in the car, Virginia's luggage stowed in the boot, doors closed, seat-belts fastened. Alone and together.

Edmund reached for the car keys, tossed them in his hand. "What do you want to do?" he asked.

"What suggestions do you have?"

"We can head straight back to Balnaid. Or we can go to the flat. Or we can go and have dinner in Edinburgh and then drive back to Balnaid. Henry is spending another night with Vi, so we are completely free."

"I should like to go out for dinner and then go home."

"Then that is what we shall do." He inserted the car key, switched on the ignition. "I have a table booked at Rafaelli's." He manoeuvred the crowded car-park, drove to the toll-gate, paid his dues. They moved out onto the road.

"How was London?"

"Hot and crowded. But *fun*. I saw masses of people, and went to about four parties, and Felicity had got tickets for *Phantom of the Opera*. I spent so much money, you're going to pass out when the bills come in."

"Did you get a dress for the Steyntons' dance?"

"Yes. At Caroline Charles. A really dreamy creation. And I got my hair done."

"I noticed."

"Do you like it?"

"Very elegant. And that coat is new."

"I felt such a country frump when I got to London, I went slightly mad. It's Italian. Not much use in Strathcroy, I admit, but I couldn't resist it."

She laughed. His own sweet-tempered Virginia. He was filled with grateful satisfaction, and swore to himself that he would remember this when the inevitable American Express account came in. She said, "I can see I shall have to go to London more often."

"Did you see Alexa?"

"Yes, and I've lots to tell you, but I'll save that up till we're having dinner. How's Henry?"

"I rang up a couple of evenings ago. He's having, as usual, the time of his life. Vi asked Kedejah Ishak to tea at Pennyburn, and she and Henry made a dam in the burn and sailed paper boats. He was quite happy to spend an extra night with Vi."

"And you? What have you been doing?"

"Working. Going out to dinner. I've had a social week."

She glanced at him wryly. "I'll bet," she said without rancour.

He drove into Edinburgh by the old Glasgow road, and as they approached, the Old City looked its most impressive, etched like a romantic engraving beneath the immense and steely sky. The wide streets were verdant with leafy trees, the skyline pierced by spires and towers, and the Castle on its rock brooded over all, with flag snapping at the mast-head. Coming to the New Town, they entered the gracefully proportioned purlieus of Georgian terraces and spacious crescents. All had been newly sandstoned, and the buildings, with their classic windows and porticoes and airy fanlights, stood honey-coloured in the evening light.

Circling the one-way system, Edmund made his way through a labyrinth of hidden lanes and turned at last into a narrow cobbled street to draw up at the pavement's edge outside the little Italian restaurant. On the opposite side of this street stood one of Edinburgh's many beautiful churches. High up on the tower, above the massive arched doorway, the hands of a golden clock moved to nine o'clock, and as they got out of the car, its chimes pealed out across the rooftops, striking the hours. Flocks of pigeons, disturbed from their airy roosts, exploded upwards in a flurry of flight. When the last chime had struck, they settled again, on sill and parapet, cooing to themselves, folding their wings, pretending nothing had happened, as though ashamed of their silly agitation.

"You'd think," said Virginia, "that they'd get used to the din. Become blasé."

"I never met a blasé pigeon. Did you?"

"Come to think of it, no."

He took her arm and led her across the pavement and through the door. Inside the restaurant was small, dimly lighted, smelling of fresh coffee and garlic and delicious Mediterranean food. The place was pleasantly busy and most of the tables were occupied, but the head waiter spied them at once and made his way across the floor to welcome them.

"Good evening, Mr. Aird. And Madame."

"Good evening, Luigi."

"I have your table ready."

The table Edmund had particularly asked for, in the corner, tucked under the window. A starched pink damask cloth, pink damask napkins, a single rose in a slender vase. Charming, intimate, seductive. The ultimate ambience for the ending of a feud.

"Perfect, Luigi. Thank you. And the Moët et Chandon?"

"No problem, Mr. Aird. I have it on ice."

They drank the chilled champagne. Virginia filled in the details of her social activities, the art exhibitions she had been to, the concert at the Wigmore Hall.

They ordered in a leisurely fashion. Eschewed the ravioli and tagliatelli, and went instead for duck pâté, and cold Tay salmon.

"Why do I bring you to Italian restaurants, when you can eat Tay salmon at home?"

"Because there is nothing in the world so delicious, and after my whirl in London I seem to have had my fill of ethnic food."

"I shall not ask with whom you have been dining."

She smiled. "Nor I you."

Without haste, they ate their way through the perfect meal, ending with fresh raspberries coated in thick cream, and a Brie of exactly the right consistency. She told him of the exhibition at Burlington House, Felicity Crowe's plans to buy a country cottage in Dorset, and tried to explain, with a certain amount of confusing detail, the plot of *Phantom of the Opera*. Edmund, who knew the plot anyway, listened with absorbed interest, simply because it was so marvellous to have her back, to listen to her voice, to have her sharing her pleasures with him.

Finally, their plates were cleared, and coffee brought, black and fragrant, steaming in the tiny cups. As well as a dish of chocolate peppermints thin as wafers.

By now most of the other tables had emptied, the diners gone home. Only one other couple sat, as they sat, but drinking brandy. The man smoked a cigar.

The Moët et Chandon was finished, up-ended in the ice-bucket. "Would you like a brandy?" Edmund asked.

"No. Not a thing more."

"I'd have one, but I have to drive."

"I could drive."

He shook his head. "I don't need a brandy." He leaned back in his chair. "You've told me everything, but you still haven't told me about Alexa."

"I was keeping it to the end."

"Does that mean it's good?"

"I think it's good. I'm not sure what you'll think."

"Try me."

"You won't become Victorian, will you?"

"I don't think I ever am."

"Because Alexa's got a man. He's moved in with her. He's living with her in the house in Ovington Street."

Edmund did not at once reply to this. Then he said, quite calmly, "When did this happen?"

"In June, I think. She didn't tell us because she was afraid we would all be upset or disapproving."

"Does she think we wouldn't like him?"

"No. I think she thinks you'd like him very much. It's just that she wasn't sure how you'd take it. So she gave me the job of telling you."

"Have you met him?"

"Yes. Just for a little while. We had a drink together. There wasn't time for more."

"Did you like him?"

"Yes, I did. He's very good-looking, very charming. He's called Noel Keeling."

Edmund's coffee-cup was empty. He caught Luigi's eye and asked for it to be refilled. When this was done, he stirred it thoughtfully, his eyes downcast, his handsome features giving nothing away.

"What do you think?" Virginia asked.

He looked up at her and smiled. "I think I'm thinking that I thought it would never happen."

"But you're pleased that it has?"

"I'm pleased that Alexa has found someone who is sufficiently fond of her to want to spend much time with her. It would be easier for every-body if it could have taken a less dramatic course, but I suppose nowa-days it's inevitable that they should shack up together and give it a try before making any momentous decision." He took a mouthful of the scalding coffee, set down the cup. "It's just that she's such an extraordi-narily unsophisticated child."

"She isn't a child any more, Edmund."

"It's hard to think of Alexa as anything else."

"We have to."

"I realize that."

"She was in rather a state about my telling you all. She *asked* me to tell you, but I know, in a funny way, she was dreading the secret coming out."

"What do you think I should do?"

"You don't have to do anything. She's going to bring him up to Balnaid in September for the weekend of the Steyntons' dance. And we'll all behave as casually as all-get-out . . . just as though he were an old childhood chum or a school friend. I don't think we can do more. After that, it's up to them."

"Was that your idea or Alexa's?"

"Mine," Virginia told him, not without pride.

"What a clever girl you are."

"I told her other things as well, Edmund. I told her that, over the last few weeks, we haven't exactly been the best of friends."

"That must be the understatement of the year."

She fixed him with her brilliant gaze. She said, "I haven't changed my mind. I haven't changed my attitude. I don't want Henry to go and I think he's too young, and I think you're making a dreadful mistake; but I know that Henry's been upset by all this ill feeling, and I've decided we've got to stop thinking about ourselves and think about the children instead. Think about Henry and Alexa. Because Alexa said that if we were still glowering at each other, then she wasn't going to come up with Noel because she couldn't stand the idea of any sort of bad atmosphere between us." She paused, waiting for Edmund to make some sort of comment. But he said nothing and so she continued. "I've been thinking about that. I tried to imagine going back to Leesport and finding my grandparents snapping each other's heads off, but it was unimaginable, and that's the way we've got to make it for Henry and Alexa. I'm not giving in, Edmund. I'll never come round to your way of thinking. But what can't be cured must be endured. Besides, I've missed you. I don't really like being on my own. In London I kept wishing you were there." She put her elbows on the table, her chin in her hands. "You see, I love you."

After a little, Edmund said, "I'm sorry."

"Sorry I love you?"

He shook his head. "No. Sorry I went to Templehall and settled the whole affair with Colin Henderson without consulting you. I should have had more consideration. It was overbearing."

"I've never heard you admit to being in the wrong before."

"I hope you never have to again. It's painful." He reached out and took her hand in his. "It's a truce then?"

"With one proviso?"

"What would that be?"

"That when the terrible day comes and poor Henry has to go to Templehall, I am not asked nor expected to take him. Because I don't think that I could physically bear to do that. Later on maybe, when I've got used to being without him. But not the first time."

"I'll be there," said Edmund. "I shall take him."

It was growing late. The other couple had departed, and the waiters were standing around trying not to look as though they were longing for Edmund and Virginia, too, to go home and let them close up for the night. Edmund called for the bill and, while this was coming, leaned back in his chair, put his hand in the pocket of his jacket and brought out a small package wrapped in thick white paper and sealed with red wax.

"It's for you." He put it on the table between them. "It's a welcome-home present."

6

*I*F HENRY COULD NOT BE AT HOME, at Balnaid, then the next best thing was staying with Vi. At Pennyburn, he had his own bedroom, a tiny room over what had once been the front door, with a narrow window looking out over the garden and the glen and the hills beyond. From this window, if he screwed his neck around a bit, he could even see Balnaid, half-hidden in trees beyond the river and the village. And in the mornings when he awoke and sat up, he could watch the rising sun stretching long fingers of early light across the fields, and listen to the song of the blackbird that had its nest in the top branches of the old elder tree by the burn. Vi did not like elder trees, but she had let this one stand, because it was a good tree for Henry to climb. That was how he had found out about the blackbird's nest.

The room was so small, it was a little like sleeping in a Wendy house, or even a cupboard, but that was part of its charm. There was space for his bed and a chest of drawers with a mirror hanging over it, but no more. A couple of hooks on the back of the door did duty as a wardrobe, and there was a neat little light over his bedhead, so that he could read in bed if he wanted to. The carpet was blue and the walls were white. There was a nice picture of a bluebell wood, and the curtains were white with bunches of field flowers spattered all over them.

This was his last night with Vi. Tomorrow, his mother was going to come and fetch him, and take him home. It had been a funny sort of few days, because the Strathcroy Primary had already opened for the winter term, and all his friends were back at their lessons. And so Henry, destined for Templehall, had nobody to play with. But somehow it hadn't mattered. Edie was there most mornings, and Vi was always full of bright ideas for a small boy's amusement and entertainment. They had gardened together, and she had taught him how to make fairy cakes, and for the evenings she had produced a mammoth jigsaw puzzle with which they had struggled together. One afternoon Kedejah Ishak had come for tea after school, and she and Henry had built a dam in the stream and become extremely wet. Another day he and Vi had taken a picnic lunch up to the loch and made a collection of twenty-four different wild flowers. She had shown him how to press them dry between leaves of blotting paper and thick books, and when they were ready he was going to stick them into an old exercise book with bits of Sellotape.

He had had his supper and his bath, and was now in bed in his sleeping-bag, and reading his library book, which was by Enid Blyton and called *The Famous Five*. He heard the clock in the hall strike eight o'clock, and then Vi's footsteps treading heavily up the staircase, which meant that she was coming to say good night to him.

His door was open. He laid down his book and waited for her to come through it. She appeared, tall and large and solid, and settled herself comfortably on the foot of his bed. The springs creaked. He was cosy in his own sleeping-bag, but she had tucked a blanket over the top of it, and he thought that it was one of the best feelings, having someone sit on your bed, with the blanket pulled tight over your legs. It made him feel very safe.

Vi wore a silk blouse with a cameo brooch at the collar, and a soft, heathery-blue cardigan, and she had brought her spectacles with her, which meant that she was quite prepared, if he wished, to read aloud a chapter or two from *The Famous Five*.

She said, "This time tomorrow, you'll be back in your own bed. We've had a good time, though, haven't we?"

"Yes." He thought of all the fun they had had. Perhaps it was wrong to want to go home and leave her, but at least he knew that she was safe and happy alone in her little house. He wished that he could feel the same about Edie.

Lately, Henry had stopped dropping in on Edie, because he was frightened of Lottie. There was something witchy about her, with her strange dark eyes that never blinked, and her ungainly, unaccountable movements, and her endless flood of chat that was too disjointed to be called conversation. Most of the time Henry hadn't the least idea what she was talking about, and he knew that it exhausted Edie. Edie had told him to be nice to Lottie, and he had done his best, but the truth was that he hated her, and could not bear to think of Edie closeted up with her scary cousin, and having to deal with her, day in and day out.

From time to time he had seen headlines in the newspapers about poor people being murdered with axes or carving knives, and felt certain that Lottie, if roused or thwarted, was perfectly capable of attacking darling Edie—perhaps late at night, in the dark—and leaving her, dead and blood-stained, on the kitchen floor.

He shivered at the thought. Vi noticed the shiver. "Is something worrying you? A ghost just went over your grave."

This observation was too close for comfort. "I was thinking about Edie's cousin. I don't like her."

"Oh, Henry."

"I don't think Edie is safe with her."

Vi made a little face. "To be honest, Henry, I'm not very happy either. But I think that it's just a great trial for Edie. We talk about her cousin in the mornings, over coffee. Lottie's certainly a very tiresome lady, but apart from driving Edie to distraction with her ways, I don't think Edie's in any real danger. Not the kind you're imagining."

He hadn't told her what he imagined, but she knew. Vi always knew things like that.

"You will take care of her, won't you, Vi? You won't let anything happen?"

"No, of course I won't. And I shall make a point of seeing Edie every day, and keeping an eye on the situation. And I'll ask Lottie for tea one day, and that'll give Edie a bit of a breather."

"When do you think Lottie will go away?"

"I don't know. When she's better. These things take time."

"Edie was so happy, on her own. And now she's not happy a bit. And she has to sleep on the Put-U-Up. It must be horrid not being in her own room."

"Edie is a very kind person. More kind than most of us. She is making a sacrifice for her cousin."

Henry thought of Abraham and Isaac. "I hope Lottie doesn't make a sacrifice of her."

Vi laughed. "You're letting your imagination run away with you. Don't go to sleep worrying about Edie. Think about seeing your mother again tomorrow."

"Yes." That was much better. "What time do you think she'll come?"

"Well, you've got a busy day tomorrow, out with Willy Snoddy and his ferrets. I should think about tea-time. When you get back, she'll be here."

"Do you think she'll bring me a present from London?"

"Sure to."

"Perhaps she'll bring you a present, too."

"Oh, I don't expect a present. Besides, it's my birthday soon, so I'll get one then. She always gives me something quite special, something that I never realized how much I wanted."

"What day is your birthday?" He had forgotten.

"The fifteenth of September. The day before the Steyntons' party."

"Are you going to have the picnic?"

Vi always arranged a picnic for her birthday. Everybody came, and they all met up at the loch and lit a fire and cooked sausages, and Vi brought her birthday cake in a big box, and when she cut it, the assembled party stood around and sang "Happy Birthday to You." Sometimes it was a chocolate cake, and sometimes it was an orange cake. Last year it had been an orange cake.

He remembered last year. Remembered the inclement day, the racing wind and the scattered showers that had dampened nobody's enthusiasm. Last year he had given Vi a picture that he had drawn with his felt pens, and which his mother had had framed and mounted, just like a proper picture. Vi had it hanging in her bedroom. This year he was giving her the bottle of rhubarb wine that he had won in the raffle at the church sale.

This year . . . He said, "This year, I shan't be there."

"No. This year, you'll be at boarding-school."

"Couldn't you have your birthday earlier, so that I could be there?"

"Oh, Henry, birthdays don't work that way. But it won't be the same without you."

"Will you write me a letter, and tell me all about it?"

"Of course I will. And you shall write to me. There'll be such a lot that I will want to hear."

He said, "I don't want to go."

"No. I don't suppose you do. But your father thinks that you should go, and he nearly always knows best."

"Mummy doesn't want me to go, either."

"That's because she loves you so. She knows that she'll miss you."

He realized then that this was the first time he and Vi had talked about his going away. This was because Henry did not even want to think about it, let alone discuss it, and Vi had never brought the subject up. But now they had started speaking about it, he discovered that he felt easier. He knew that he could say anything to Vi, and knew, too, that she would never repeat it.

He said, "They've been quarrelling. They've been cross with each other."

"Yes," said Vi. "I know."

"How do you know, Vi?"

"I may be old, but I'm not stupid. And your father is my son. Mothers know lots about their sons. The good bits and the not-so-good bits. It doesn't stop them loving them, but it makes them a little bit more understanding."

"It's been so horrid, with them so unkind to each other."

"It must have been."

"I don't want to go away to school, but I *hate* them being cross with each other. I simply *hate* it. It makes the house feel all headachy and ill."

Vi sighed. "If you want to know what I think, Henry, I think they've both been very short-sighted and selfish. But I haven't been able to say anything, because it's none of my business. That's another thing a mother mustn't do. She must never interfere."

"I really want to go home tomorrow, but . . ." He gazed at her, his sentence left unfinished, because he didn't really know what he was trying to say.

Vi smiled. When she smiled her face creased into a thousand wrinkles.

She laid her hand on his. It felt warm and dry, and rough from all the gardening she did.

She said, "There's an old saying, that parting makes the heart grow fonder. Your mother and father have had a few days apart, on their own, with time to think things over. I'm sure they'll both have realized how wrong they both have been. You see, they love each other very much, and if you love someone, you need to be with them, close to them. You need to be able to confide, to laugh together. It's just about as important as breathing. By now, I'm certain that they will have found this out. And I'm just as certain that everything will be just as it was before."

"Really certain, Vi?"

"Really certain."

She sounded so certain that Henry felt that way too. Such a relief. It was as though a huge weight had dropped from his shoulders. And this made everything much better. Even the prospect of leaving home and parents and being sent to board at Templehall had lost some of its fearfulness. Nothing could be as bad as thinking that his home would never be the same again. Reassured, and filled with grateful love for his grandmother, he held out his arms, and she leaned forward, and he embraced her, hugging her tight around her neck and pressing kisses on her cheek. When he drew back, he saw that her eyes were very shiny and bright.

She said, "It's time to sleep."

He was ready for it, now suddenly drowsy. He lay back on the pillow and felt beneath it for Moo.

Vi laughed at him, but gently, teasing him. "You don't need that old bit of baby blanket. You're a grown-up boy now. You can make fairy cakes, and do jigsaw puzzles, and remember the names of all those wild flowers. I think you can do without Moo."

Henry screwed up his nose. "But not tonight, Vi."

"All right. Not tonight. But tomorrow, maybe."

"Yes." He yawned. "Maybe."

She stooped to kiss him, and then got up off the bed. The springs creaked once more. "Good night, my lamb."

"Good night, Vi."

She turned out his light and went out of the room, but she left the door open. The darkness was soft and blowy and smelt of the hills. Henry turned on his side, curled up in a ball, and closed his eyes.

7

W<small>HEN, TEN YEARS AGO,</small> V<small>IOLET</small> A<small>IRD</small> bought Pennyburn from Archie Balmerino, she had become owner of a sad and drab little house with little to commend it save its view and the small stream that tumbled down the hill on the western march of its land. It was from this stream that the house took its name.

It stood in the heart of Archie's estate, on the face of the hill that sloped up from the village, and access was by the Croy back drive and then a rutted track overgrown by thistles and fenced by sagging posts and broken barbed wire.

The garden, such as it was, lay on the slope to the south of the house. This too was surrounded by rotting posts and straggling wire, and consisted of a small drying-green, a weedy vegetable patch, and dismal evidences of hen-keeping—leaning wooden sheds, much wire netting, and nettles grown waist-high.

The house was built of dull coloured stone, with a grey-tiled roof and maroon paintwork in a sad state of repair. Concrete stairs led up from the garden to the door, and inside were small and lightless rooms, hideous peeling wallpaper, the smell of damp, and the persistent drip of some faulty tap.

In fact, so unattractive was the entire property that Edmund Aird, viewing it for the first time, strongly recommended that his mother abandon the idea of ever living there and start to look for somewhere else.

But Violet, for reasons of her own, liked the house. It had stood empty for some years, which accounted for its dereliction, but despite the mould and the gloom, it had a pleasant feel to it. And it had that little burn within its lands, tumbling away down the hill. And, as well, the view. Inspecting the house, Violet would pause from time to time to glance out, rubbing a clear space on the dusty glass of the windows, seeing the village below, the river, the glen, the distant hills. She would never find another house with such a view. The view and the burn seduced her, and she disregarded her son's advice.

Doing it all up had been tremendous fun. It had taken six months to complete the work, and during that time Violet—politely spurning Edmund's invitation to remain at Balnaid until such time as she could move into her new abode—camped in a caravan that she had rented from a tourist park a few miles up the glen. She had never lived in a caravan before, but the idea had always appealed to her gypsy instincts and she leaped at the chance. The caravan was parked at the back of the house, along with the concrete mixers and barrows and shovels and daunting piles of rubble, and from the open door she could keep an eye on the workmen, and dash out to have a word with the long-suffering architect the moment she spied his car come bumping up the road. For the first month or two of this cheerfully vagabond existence, it was summer, and the only hazards were the midges and a leaky roof whenever it rained. But when the winter gales blew, the caravan trembled beneath their blast and rocked unsteadily at its temporary mooring, not unlike a small boat in a storm. Violet found this quite exciting and relished the dark and gusty nights. She could lie in her bunk, which was far too short and too narrow for such a sizy lady, listening to the keening wind and watching the clouds racing across the cold, moonlit skies.

But she did not spend all her time alternately bullying and cajoling the builders. To Violet, a garden was even more important than a house. Before the workmen had started in on their labours, she had already engaged a man with a tractor, who tore up all the old fence posts and broken wire. In their place she planted a beech hedge on either side of her driveway and all around her small plot of land. After ten years, this was still not high, but thick and firm, always leafy, and so providing good shelter for birds.

Within this hedge, on either side, she planted trees. To the east, conifers. Not her favourites, but quick-growing and good for keeping the worst of the coldest wind at bay. On the west, overhanging the stream, grew gnarled elder, willows, and double white cherries. At the foot of the garden she had kept her planting low, in order to conserve the view. Azaleas grew there, and potentillas, with drifts of spring bulbs in the rough grass.

There were two curving flower-beds, one herbaceous and one filled with roses, and between them a good-sized lawn. This was on the slope and tricky to cut. Violet had bought an electric lawn-mower, but Edmund—interfering again—decided that she was likely to sever the flex and electrocute herself, and so engaged the services of Willy Snoddy to come once a week and do the job for her. Violet knew perfectly well that Willy was a great deal less competent than she herself at handling complicated equipment, but she went along with the arrangement as being the line of least resistance. Every now and then Willy, being laid low with a killing hangover, did not turn up, and then Violet, quite happily and efficiently, cut the grass herself.

But she did not tell Edmund that she had done so.

As for the house, that she had transformed, turning it back to front and opening out all the poky and ill-proportioned rooms. Now the main entrance stood to the north and the old front door had become a glassed garden door, opening straight out of her sitting-room. The concrete stairs she had demolished, and in their place stood a semi-circular flight of steps built of old stone salvaged from a fallen dyke. Aubrietia and scented thyme grew from crannies between these rocks and smelt delicious when one trod upon them.

After some consideration, Violet decided that she could not bear the dull colour of the stone walls of Pennyburn, and so had them all harled and painted white. Windows and doorways were outlined in black, which gave the face of the house a crisp and down-to-earth appearance. To embellish it, she had planted a wistaria, but, after ten years, it had scarcely grown as high as her shoulder. By the time it reached the roof, she would probably be dead.

At seventy-seven one was perhaps better off sticking to hardy annuals.

All that was missing was a conservatory. The one at Balnaid had been built at the same time as the house. Its erection was due to the insistence of Violet's mother, Lady Primrose Akenside, a woman not addicted to the great outdoors. It was Lady Primrose's opinion that, if forced to live in the wilds of Scotland, a conservatory was absolutely essential. Quite apart from the fact that it was useful for keeping the house supplied with pot plants and grapes, it was somewhere to sit when the sun shone and yet the wind blew with an edge like ice to it. Such days, everybody knew, occurred with amazing frequency during the winter and spring and autumn months. But Lady Primrose spent a good deal of the summers in her conservatory as well, entertaining her friends and playing bridge.

Violet had loved the Balnaid conservatory for less social reasons, relishing the warmth, the peace, the smell of damp earth and ferns and freesias. When the weather was too inclement to garden, you could always potter about in the conservatory, and what better place to sit down after lunch and try to do *The Times* crossword?

Yes, she missed it, but after deliberation had decided that Pennyburn was too small and modest for such an extravagant addition. It would make the house look pretentious and foolish, and she was not about to inflict such an indignity upon her new home. And it was scarcely a hardship to sit in her sheltered and sunny garden and try to do the crossword there.

She was in her garden now, and had been out working all afternoon, staking clumps of Michaelmas daisies before the autumn winds arrived to fell them flat. It was a day to start thinking about autumn. Not cold but fresh, with a certain smell about the air, a briskness. The farmers were harvesting, and the distant rumble of combine harvesters working in tall fields of barley was seasonal and strangely reassuring. The sky was blue but sailing with clouds blown in from the west. A blinking day, the old country people called it, as the sun went in and out.

Unlike many people, Violet did not mourn the passing of the summer and the prospect of a long dark winter ahead. "How can you bear to live in Scotland?' she was sometimes asked. "The weather so unpredictable, so much rain, so cold." But Violet knew that she could not bear to live anywhere else, and never yearned to move away. When Geordie was alive they had travelled together extensively. They had explored Venice and Istanbul, paced the art galleries of Florence and Madrid. One year they had taken an archaeological cruise to Greece; another time had sailed the fjords of Norway, as far north as the Arctic Circle and the midnight sun. But without him, she knew no urge to journey abroad. She preferred to stay right here, where her roots were deep, surrounded by a countryside that she had known since she was a child. As for the weather, she disregarded it, caring not if it froze or snowed or blew or rained or scorched, provided she could be out of doors and part of it all.

Which was proved by her complexion, weather-beaten and lined as an old farm worker's. But again, at seventy-seven, what did a few wrinkles matter? A small price to pay for an energetic and active old age.

She drove in the last stake, twisted the last length of wire. Finished. She stepped back onto the grass to survey her work. The canes showed, but once the Michaelmas daisies had thickened out a bit, they would be concealed. She looked at her watch. Nearly half past three. She sighed, always reluctant to stop gardening and go indoors. But she stripped off her gloves and dropped them into her wheelbarrow, then collected her tools, the last of the canes, the drum of wire, and barrowed the lot around the house to her garage, where all was stowed neatly away until the next day's labour.

Then she went into the house by the kitchen door, toeing off her rubber boots and hanging her jacket on a hook. In the kitchen, she filled the kettle and switched it on to boil. She laid a tray with two cups and saucers, a milk jug, a sugar bowl, and a plate of chocolate digestive biscuits. (Virginia would not eat anything at teatime but Violet was never averse to a small snack.)

She went upstairs to her bedroom, washed her hands, found a pair of shoes, tidied her hair, slapped a bit of face powder onto her shining nose. As she did this, she heard the car come up the hill and turn into the lane. A moment later came the slam of its door, her own front door opening, and Virginia's voice.

"Vi!"

"Just coming."

She settled her pearls, fixed a stray wisp of hair, and went downstairs. Her daughter-in-law stood in the hall waiting for her; her long legs were in corduroys and a leather jacket was slung around her shoulders. She had a new hair-do, Violet noticed, drawn back from her brow and fastened at the nape of her neck with a ribbon bow. She looked, as always, casually elegant, and happier than Violet had seen her for a long time.

"Virginia. How lovely to have you home again. And how chic you look. I love the hair." They kissed. "Did you have it done in London?"

"Yes. I thought perhaps it was time I changed my image." She looked about her. "Where's Henry?"

"He's out ferreting with Willy Snoddy."

"Oh, *Vi*."

"It's all right. He'll be home in half an hour."

"I didn't mean that. I meant what's he doing spending his time with that old reprobate?"

"Well, there are no children to play with because they're all in school. And he got talking to Willy when he came to cut the grass this week, and Willy invited him to go ferreting. He seemed very keen to go, so I said he could. You don't disapprove, do you?"

Virginia laughed and shook her head. "No, of course not. It's just rather unexpected. Do you think Henry realizes what ferreting entails? It's quite a bloodthirsty business."

"I've no idea. We'll doubtless hear all about it when he gets back. Willy will see that he's on time, I know."

"I always thought you thought the old drunk was quite undependable."

"He wouldn't dare break his promise to me, and he never gets drunk in the afternoons. Now, how are you? Did you have a good time?"

"A great time. Here . . ." She thrust a flat package, impressively wrapped, into Violet's hands. "I brought you a present from the big city."

"My dear, you didn't need to."

"It's a thank-you for having Henry."

"I've loved having him. But he's longing to see you and go home to Balnaid. He was all packed up and ready long before breakfast this morning. Now, I want to hear all about everything. Come and watch me open my present."

She led the way into her sitting-room and settled herself in comfort in her own fireside chair. It was a relief to get the weight off her feet. Virginia perched herself on the arm of the sofa and watched. Violet undid the ribbon bow and unwrapped the paper. A flat box, orange and brown, was revealed. She removed the lid. Inside, folded and silken beneath the layers of tissue paper, was a Hermès scarf.

"Oh, Virginia. This is far too much."

"No more than you deserve."

"But having Henry was a *treat*."

"I've brought him a present, too. It's in the car. I thought he could open it here, before I take him home."

The scarf was all pinks and blues and greens. Just the thing for brightening up that grey woollen dress. "I can't thank you enough—I'm really delighted with it. And now . . ." She folded the scarf, returned it to its box, and set it aside. "Let's have a cup of tea, and you can tell me everything that's happened in London. I want to hear all the details. . . ."

"When did you get back?"

"Yesterday evening, on the shuttle. Edmund met me at Turnhouse and we went into Edinburgh and had dinner at Rafaelli's, and after that we drove home to Balnaid."

"I hope"—Violet fixed Virginia with a firm stare—"that you used the time together to sort out your differences."

Virginia had the grace to look abashed. "Oh, Vi. Did it show so much?"

"It was obvious to anyone but a blind man. I didn't say anything, but you must realize that it's very worrying for Henry if you and his father are not on good terms."

"Did Henry talk to you about it?"

"Yes, he did. He's much upset. I think he feels that going to Templehall is bad enough, but having you and Edmund at each other's throats is more than he can bear."

"We weren't exactly at each other's throats."

"Icy politeness is almost worse."

"I know. And I'm sorry. And Edmund and I have made it up. By that I don't mean anything's changed. Edmund won't budge from his decision, and I still think it's a dreadful mistake. But at least we've called a truce." She smiled and held out a slender wrist circled by a wide bracelet of gold. "Over dinner, he gave me this. It's a welcome-home present. So I'd be churlish to carry on sulking."

"That is a great relief to me. I managed to persuade Henry that you would both have come to your senses and would be friends again. And I'm grateful to you both, because now I don't feel that I am letting him down. He needs a lot of reassurance, Virginia. A lot of security."

"Oh, Vi, don't I know it?"

"And there's another thing. He's very bothered about Edie. He's frightened of Lottie. He thinks that Lottie might harm Edie in some way."

Virginia frowned. "Did he say so?"

"We talked about it."

"Do you think he's right?"

"Children are perceptive. Like dogs. They recognize evil where, perhaps, we adults don't see it."

"Evil is a strong word, Vi. I know she gives me the shivers, but I've always told myself she's just harmlessly dotty."

"I really don't know," said Violet. "But I've promised Henry that we will all keep a weather eye on the situation. And if he talks to you about it, you must listen to him, and try to set his mind at rest."

"Of course."

"Now." With that necessary exchange safely disposed of, Violet steered the conversation into a more cheerful direction. "Tell me about London. Did you get a dress? And what else did you do? And did you see Alexa?"

"Yes." Virginia leaned forward to refill her cup from the teapot. "Yes, I did get a dress, and yes, I did see Alexa. That's what I want to talk to you about. I've already told Edmund."

Violet's heart sank. What on earth was happening now?

"She's all right?"

"Never better." Virginia leaned back in her chair. "There is a man in her life."

"Alexa has a young man? But that's splendid news! I was beginning to think that nothing exciting was ever going to happen to the dear child."

"They're living together, Vi."

For an instant, Violet was silenced. Then: "*Living* together?"

"Yes. And I'm not telling tales out of school. She particularly asked me to let you know."

"And *where* are they living together?"

"At Ovington Street."

"But . . ." Violet, flustered, sought for words. "But . . . how long has this been going on?"

"About two months."

"Who is he?"

"He's called Noel Keeling."

"What does he do?"

"He's in advertising."

"How old is he?"

"About my age. Good-looking. Very charming."

About Virginia's age. A dreadful thought occurred to Violet. "I hope he's not already married."

"No. A very eligible bachelor."

"And Alexa . . . ?"

"Alexa is radiantly happy."

"Do you think they will marry?"

"I have no idea."

"Is he kind to her?"

"I think so. I only saw him for a little while. He came home from the office and we all had a drink together. He brought Alexa flowers. And he didn't know I was going to be there, so he didn't buy them to impress me."

Violet fell silent, trying to come to terms with this astonishing revelation. They were living together. Alexa was living with a man. Sharing a bed, sharing a life. Unmarried. She did not approve but her own opinions were best kept to herself. All that mattered was that Alexa should know that they all would support her, whatever might happen.

"What did Edmund say when you told him?"

Virginia shrugged. "Not a lot. He's certainly not about to fly to London with a loaded shotgun. But I think he is concerned, if only for the fact that Alexa is a girl of some wealth . . . she has that house and she has the money she inherited from Lady Cheriton. Which, as Edmund pointed out, is considerable."

"He's afraid this young man is after her money?"

"It's a possibility, Vi."

"You've met him. What do you think of him?"

"I liked him. . . ."

"But you have reservations?"

"He's so personable. Cool. Like I said, charming. I'm not *certain* if I trust him. . . ."

"Oh dear."

"But that's just me talking. I may be making a total misjudgement."

"What can we do?"

"We can't do anything. Alexa is twenty-one, she must make her own decisions."

Violet knew that this was true. But Alexa . . . so far away. In London.

"If only we could *meet* him. That would put everything on a much more normal footing."

"I entirely agree with you, and you will meet him." Violet glanced at her daughter-in-law and saw that she was smiling, looking as pleased with herself as the cat that got the cream. "I'm afraid I stuck my oar in and made noises like a mother. I talked to the two of them and they've agreed to come north together for the weekend of the Steyntons' dance. They're going to stay at Balnaid."

"Oh, what a clever idea!" Violet could have kissed Virginia, so delighted was she. "What a brilliant girl you are. Quite the best way of doing things, without making too much of an occasion of it."

"That's what I thought. And even Edmund approves. But we'll have to be very casual and tactful and matter-of-fact. No suggestive glances or meaningful remarks."

"You mean I'm not to say anything about their getting married?" Virginia nodded. Violet thought about this. "I wouldn't, you know. I'm sufficiently modern to know when to hold my tongue. But, by living together, young people create for themselves such difficult situations.

They make it so difficult for *us*. If we make too much of the young man, then he will think he is being pressurized and he'll back off and break Alexa's heart. And if we don't make enough of him, Alexa will think we disapprove and *that* will break her heart."

"I wouldn't be too sure about that. She's grown up a lot. She has much more confidence. She's changed."

"I couldn't bear her to be hurt. Not Alexa."

"I'm afraid we can't protect her any longer. The affair has already gone too far."

"Yes," said Violet, feeling in some way admonished. This was no time for apprehensive sentiment. If she was to be of any use to anybody, then she must remain sensible. "You are absolutely right. We must all—"

But there was no time for more. They heard the front door open and slam shut. *"Mummy!"*

Henry was back. Virginia laid down her teacup and sprang to her feet, Alexa forgotten. She made for the door but Henry was there first, bursting in on them, red-cheeked with excitement and the effort of running up the hill.

"Mummy!"

She held out her arms, and he flung himself, bodily, into them.

8

Saturday the Twenty-seventh

EDMUND WAS FREQUENTLY ASKED, by well-meaning fellow-guests at dinner parties, if he did not find the long commute between Edinburgh and Strathcroy an almost unbearable strain, every morning and evening each day of the week that he was working in Edinburgh. But the truth was that Edmund thought nothing of the miles that he covered. Getting home to Balnaid and his family was more important than the considerable effort that it involved, and only a late business dinner in Edinburgh, an early plane to catch, or impassable winter roads persuaded him to stay in town and spend the night in the flat in Moray Place.

As well, he enjoyed driving. His car was both powerful and safe, and the motorway, slicing over the Forth and through Fife to Relkirk, had become as familiar as the back of his hand. Once through Relkirk, he was onto country roads that necessitated slowing down to a more prudent speed, but even so the journey rarely took him more than an hour.

He used this time to switch off at the end of a day of stress and decision-making, and to let his mind concentrate instead upon the many other, but equally absorbing, facets of his busy life. In winter-time, he listened to the radio. Not the news nor political discussions . . . he had had enough of both by the time he finally cleared his desk and locked away all confidential documents . . . but Radio Three, classical concerts and erudite plays. For the rest of the year, as the hours of daylight lengthened and he no longer made the journey in the dark, he found much pleasure and solace in simply watching the unfolding seasons of the countryside. The ploughing, the sowing, the greening of the trees; the first young lambs in the fields, the crops turning gold, the raspberry pickers out in the long drills of canes, the harvest, the autumn leaves, the first of the snows.

They were harvesting now, on this fine, blowy evening. The scenery was both peaceful and spectacular. Fields and farmlands were washed in fitful sunlight, but the air was so clear that every crag and corrie on the distant hills presented itself with startling visibility. The light flowed over these hills, touching their summits with reflected radiance; the river running alongside the road glittered and sparkled; and the sky, skimming with clouds, was infinite.

He felt more content than he had for a long time. Virginia was back, restored to him. His gift to her was the nearest he could get to an apology for the things that he had said on the day of the original explosion: accusing her of smothering Henry; wanting to keep him by her side for selfish reasons; never thinking of any person but herself. She had accepted the bracelet with gratitude and love, and her unqualified pleasure was as good as forgiveness.

Last night, after their dinner at Rafaelli's, he had driven her home to Balnaid through a twilit countryside and beneath the banner of a spectacular skyscape, rose-pink to the west, and streaked as though by some gargantuan paintbrush with dark charcoal clouds.

They had returned to an empty house. He could not remember when this had last happened, and it made their homecoming even more special. No dogs, no children; just the two of them. He had dealt with the luggage, then taken two malt whiskies up to their bedroom and sat on the bed and watched her unpack. There was no sense of urgency, because the whole of the house, the night, the sweet darkness belonged to them. Later, he showered; Virginia took a bath. She came to him, scented and cool, and they made the most satisfying and blissful love.

He knew that the bone of contention still lay between them. Virginia did not want to lose Henry, and Edmund was determined that he should go. But for the time being they had ceased snarling over this particular bone and, with a bit of luck, it would stay buried and forgotten.

As well, there were other good things to look forward to. This evening, he would see his small son again after a week of separation. There would be much to tell and much to hear. And then, next month, in September, Alexa was bringing her young man to stay.

Virginia's bombshell about Alexa had caught Edmund unawares, rendering him confounded but not shocked nor disapproving. He was extremely fond of his daughter, and recognized her many sterling qualities; but during the last year or two he had privately wished, more than once, that she would take her finger out and start to grow up. At twenty-one, her lack of sophistication, her shyness, her dumpy shape had become an embarrassment to him. He was used to being surrounded by elegant and worldly women (even his secretary was a stunner) and disliked himself for his own impatience and irritation with Alexa. But now, all by herself, she had found a man, and a personable one, if Virginia was to be believed.

Possibly he should be taking a tougher line. But he had never relished the image of himself as a paterfamilias, and was more concerned with the human side of the situation rather than the moral.

As always, when faced with a dilemma, he planned to go by his own set of rules. Act positively, plan negatively, expect nothing. The worst that could happen would be Alexa's getting hurt. For her, it would be a frightening new experience, but at least she would come out of it more adult and, hopefully, stronger.

He drove into Strathcroy as the church clock was striking seven. He thought, in pleasant anticipation, of getting home. The dogs would be there, rescued from the kennels by Virginia; and Henry, in his bath or eating his tea in the kitchen. He would sit with Henry while he consumed his fish fingers or beefburgers or whatever horror he had chosen to eat, listening to all that Henry had been up to during the week, and drinking, meanwhile, a very long and strong gin and tonic.

Which reminded him that they were out of tonic. The drink cupboard had been allowed to run dry of this precious commodity, and Edmund had meant to stop off and buy a crate before he left Edinburgh, but had forgotten to do this. And so he passed the bridge that led to Balnaid and drove on into the village, drawing up outside the Pakistani supermarket.

All the other shops had long since shut their doors and closed their shutters, but the Pakistanis never seemed to close. Long after nine o'clock in the evening they were still selling cartons of milk and bread and pizzas and frozen curries to anybody who wanted to buy them.

He got out of the car and went into the shop. There were other customers but they were filling their own wire baskets from the shelves or being assisted by Mr. Ishak, and it was Mrs. Ishak who dimpled at Edmund from behind the counter. She was a comely lady, with huge dark eyes ringed in kohl, and this evening dressed in butter-yellow silk, with a paler yellow silk scarf draped around her head and shoulders.

"Good evening, Mr. Aird."

"Good evening, Mrs. Ishak. How are you?"

"I am very well, thank you for asking."

"How's Kedejah?"

"She is watching television."

"I hear she had an afternoon at Pennyburn with Henry."

"That is true, and my God, she came home soaking wet."

Edmund laughed. "They were building dams. I hope you weren't annoyed."

"Not at all. She has had a most lovely time."

"I want some tonic water, Mrs. Ishak. Have you got some?"

"But of course. How many bottles do you need?"

"Two dozen?"

"If you wait, I will fetch them for you from the store."

"Thank you."

She went. Edmund, unimpatient, stood waiting for her to return. A voice spoke from behind him.

"Mr. Aird."

It was so close, just behind his shoulder, that he was much startled. He swung around and found himself faced by Edie's cousin, Lottie Carstairs. Since she had come to stay with Edie, he had glimpsed her once or twice, pottering about the village, but had taken some pains and avoiding action, not wishing to be confronted by her. Now it seemed she had him cornered and there was no escape.

"Good evening."

"Remember me?" She spoke almost coyly. Edmund did not relish finding himself so close to her with her pallid, bloodless skin and the strong suggestion of a moustache upon her upper lip. Her hair was the colour—and roughly the texture—of steel wool, and under wildly arched eyebrows her eyes were brown as currants, and round and quite unwinking. Apart from all this, her appearance was reasonably normal. She wore a blouse and skirt, a long green cardigan perkily embellished with a sparkling brooch, and shoes with high heels upon which she tottered slightly as she engaged Edmund in conversation. "I used to be with Lady Balmerino, staying with Edie Findhorn right now I am. Seen you around the village, never had the chance of an old chin-wag . . ."

Lottie Carstairs. She must be nearly sixty now, and yet she had not changed so much since those days when she had worked at Croy and caused every person in the house untold annoyance and aggravation, with her stealthy tread and her habit of always appearing just when least wanted or expected. Archie always swore that she listened at keyholes, and he had been perpetually throwing doors open in the expectation of catching Lottie there, crouched and eavesdropping. In the afternoons, Edmund remembered, she had always worn a brown woollen dress with a muslin apron tied over it. The muslin apron was not Lady Balmerino's idea but Lottie's. Archie said it was because she wanted to appear servile. The brown dress had stains under the armpits, and one of the worst things about Lottie was her smell.

The family complained vociferously and Archie demanded that his mother take some step to rectify the situation. Either sack the bloody woman or do something to ensure a little personal daintiness. But poor Lady Balmerino, with Archie's wedding on her mind, every bed filled with guests and a party planned at Croy on the evening of the great day, did not feel strong enough to sack her housemaid. And she was far too kind-hearted actually to send for Lottie, face her fair and square, and tell her that she smelt.

Under attack, she fell back on feeble excuses.

"I must have someone to clean the rooms and make the beds."

"We'll make our own beds."

"Poor thing, she's only got one dress."

"Well, buy her another."

"Perhaps she's nervous."

"Not too nervous to wash. Give her a bar of Lifebuoy."

"I'm not certain that that would make much difference. Perhaps . . . for Christmas . . . I could give her some talcum powder . . . ?"

But even this timid notion came to nothing, for, soon after the wedding, Lottie dropped the tray and broke the Rockingham china, and Lady Balmerino was finally driven to firing her. By Christmas Lottie was gone from Croy. Now, trapped in Mr. Ishak's shop, Edmund wondered if she still smelt. He was not about to risk finding out. Trying not to make it too obvious, he moved a pace or two away from her.

"Yes," he said, sounding as pleasant and friendly as he could. "Of course, I remember you . . . ."

"Those days at Croy! The year Archie was wed to Isobel. Oh my, what times those were. I remember you coming up from London for the wedding and around the place all that week, helping Lady Balmerino with one thing and another."

"It seems a long time ago."

"Yes."

"And all of you so young. And old Lord and Lady Balmerino so good and kind. Croy's changed now, I hear, and not for the better. But then, hard times come to everybody. It was a sad day when Lady Balmerino died. She was always so good to me. She was good to my parents too. My mother and my father died. You knew that, didn't you? I've been wanting to talk to you, but somehow I missed you in the village. And all of you so young. And Archie with his two good legs . . . fancy getting his leg shot off! Never heard of anything so ridiculous . . ."

Oh, Mrs. Ishak, come back quickly. Please, Mrs. Ishak, come back to me.

". . . hear all your news from Edie, of course; very worried about Edie, she's grown so fat, can't be good for her heart. And all of you so young. And that Pandora! Flying around the place like a spinning top. Dreadful way she went, wasn't it? Funny she never came home. Always thought she might come back for Christmas, but no. And not to be there for Lady Balmerino's funeral, well, I'm sorry and I don't like to say such things, but in my view, it was downright un-Christian. But then, she always was a wee fly-by-night . . . in more ways than one . . . you and I know that, don't we?"

At this point she burst into a peal of manic laughter and actually struck Edmund a playful, but quite painful, blow on his arm. His immediate and instinctive reaction was to hit her right back, a good punch, bang, square on the end of her long, inquisitive nose. He imagined it crumpling, concertinaed, into her face. He imagined the headlines in the local newspapers: "Relkirkshire Landowner Assaults Strathcroy Lady In Village Supermarket." He thrust his hands, the fists balled, into his trouser pockets.

". . . and your wife's been in London? Nice. And the wee boy with his gran. Seen him sometimes around the place. He is peaky, isn't he?" Edmund could feel the blood rising to his cheeks. He wondered how long he could continue to control himself. He could not remember when any person had cast him into such a confusion of impotent rage. ". . . small for his age, I'd say . . . not strong . . ."

"I am sorry, Mr. Aird, to keep you so long." It was Mrs. Ishak's soft voice that finally stilled the flood of Lottie's mindless malice. Mrs. Ishak, bless her darling heart, come to his rescue with the cardboard crate of tonic water borne before her like a votive offering.

"Oh, thank you, Mrs. Ishak." And not a moment too soon. "Here, let me take that." He went to relieve her of the heavy load. "I wonder, can you put that down to my account?" He could easily pay in cash but did not wish to linger a moment longer than he had to.

"Of course, Mr. Aird."

"Thank you." The crate was transferred. With its weight safely in his arms, he turned to take his leave of Lottie and make his escape.

But Lottie had jumped the gun and was gone. Abruptly and disconcertingly, she had simply disappeared.

9

"*H*AS SHE ALWAYS LIVED IN MAJORCA, this aunt of yours?"

"No. She's only been here for about two years. She lived in Paris before that, and New York before that, and then California before that," Lucilla said.

"A rolling stone."

"Yes, I suppose you could call her that, except that she's gathered lots of lovely moss."

Jeff laughed. "What's she like?"

"I don't know because I've never seen her. By the time I was born, she was gone, married to an immensely wealthy American and living in Palm Springs. It seemed to me that she must be the most glamorous woman in the world. So wicked and sophisticated like someone out of those old 1930 plays, with men falling for her like ninepins, and always unashamedly outrageous. She eloped when she was eighteen. Such a frightfully brave thing to do. I'd never have had the nerve. *And* she was beautiful."

"Will she still be beautiful?"

"I don't see why not. After all, she's only about forty, not over the hill yet. There's a portrait of her at Croy in the dining-room. It was painted when she was about fourteen and even then she was a stunner. And photographs too, all over the place, in frames or the old albums that my grandfather used to fill with snapshots. I used to welcome wet afternoons because then I could spend them poring over those old albums. And when people talked about her, even if they started by being disapproving because she'd been so thoughtless and uncaring to her parents, they always ended up by remembering some funny anecdote about Pandora, and then of course there could be nothing but laughter."

"Was she surprised when you spoke to her on the telephone?"

"Of course she was. But pleased surprised, not horrified surprised. You can always tell. At first she could hardly believe it was me. But then she just said 'Of course you can come. As soon as possible. And stay for as long as you like.' And she gave me directions and hung up." Lucilla smiled. "So you see, we're good for at least a week."

They had hired a car, a little Seat, the cheapest they could get, and were now well on their way across the island, driving over flat, intensely cultivated countryside, dotted here and there with slow-moving windmills. It was afternoon and the road ahead of them shimmered in the heat. On their left, far-distant and hazy, marched a range of impassable-looking mountains. On the other side, somewhere out of sight, lay the sea. For air, they had opened all the windows of the car, but the wind was scorching and dusty and very dry. Jeff was driving and Lucilla sat beside him, holding the scrap of paper on which she had scribbled the directions that Pandora had given her over the telephone.

She had rung Pandora from Palma, having arrived with Jeff that morning in a boat from Ibiza. They had spent a week in Ibiza, staying with Jeff's friend, Hans Bergdorf. Hans was a painter and *his* house had taken some finding, being at the very top of the old town, within the ancient walls of the fortified city. Finally discovered, it had proved very picturesque. It was thick-walled and whitewashed, but primitive beyond belief. The views from its jutting stone balcony took in the whole panorama of the old town, the new town, the harbour, and the sea, but even this delight scarcely made up for the fact that any cooking had to be done on a miniature Calor gas stove and the only running water came from a single cold tap. Consequently, both Jeff and Lucilla were extremely dirty, if not to say smelly, and the bulging backpacks piled onto the back seat of the car were stuffed with unsavoury, soiled and sweaty clothes. Lucilla, never a girl to spend time worrying about her appearance, had started to have fantasies about washing her hair, and Jeff in desperation had allowed his beard to grow. It was blonde like his hair, but uneven and straggly and made him look more like a down-and-out than a Viking. In fact, the pair of them presented such a disreputable picture that it was a wonder that the hire-car man had agreed to rent them the Seat. Lucilla had noticed a certain suspicion on his face, but Jeff had produced a wad of pesetas and, with cash safely in hand, he could scarcely refuse.

She said, "I hope Pandora's got a washing-machine."

"I'd settle for a pool."

"You can't wash your clothes in a pool."

"Want a bet?"

Lucilla gazed through the open car window. She saw that the mountains had drawn closer and the countryside become more lush. There were pine trees, and the smell of warm resin blew in through the open windows along with the dust. They came to a junction joining another main road. They paused for traffic to pass. The road sign was marked "Puerto del Fuego."

"Well, we're on the right track. What happens now?"

"We take the Puerto del Fuego road, but we have to turn off to the left in another mile or so. It's a little road and it's signposted to 'Cala

San Torre.' " The traffic thinned. Taking his chance Jeff cautiously ne-
gotiated the junction. "If we find ourselves in the port, then we've gone
too far."

"That follows."

Now she could smell the sea. Houses appeared, a new apartment
block, a garage. They passed a riding stables with scrubby paddocks
where sad, bony horses tried to graze.

"Oh, poor creatures," said the tender-hearted Lucilla, but Jeff had
eyes only for the road ahead.

"There's a sign. 'Cala San Torre.' "

"That's it!"

They turned off the sun-baked dual carriageway and found themselves, abruptly, in a green and verdant countryside totally unlike the flat
and exposed land through which they had been travelling. Umbrella
pines threw shade across the road, speckled by sun splashes, and from
ramshackle farms came the contented cackle of hens and the bleat of
goats.

"It's suddenly gone pretty," Lucilla observed. "Oh, look at that
sweet little donkey."

"Keep your eyes on the map, girl. What happens next?"

Lucilla obediently consulted her notes. "Well, *next* is a very sharp turn
to the right, and then we go right up a hill to the last house at the very
top."

They came upon the turning around the next corner. Jeff changed
down and made the turn. The Seat, sounding as though at any moment
it might boil like a kettle, ground painfully up the steep and winding
lane. There were other houses, large villas scarcely glimpsed beyond
closed gates and burgeoning gardens.

"This," said Lucilla, "is what estate agents call a much-sought-after
neighbourhood."

"You mean snob."

"I think I mean expensive."

"I think you do too. Your aunt must be loaded."

"She's got a Californian divorce," Lucilla told him and her voice
implied that there was no need to say more.

Another hundred yards or so, another hairpin bend or two, and they
had reached their destination. Casa Rosa. The name, embellished on
decorated tiles, was set into a high stone wall and clearly visible despite a
cloak of pink-blossomed mesembryanthemum. Open gates lay ahead. A
driveway, deeply bordered, sloped up to a garage. The garage had a car
parked in it, and another car—an enviable silver BMW—was parked in
the shade of a gnarled olive tree. Jeff switched off the engine. It was very
quiet. Then Lucilla heard water splashing, as though from a fountain,
and the distant, gentle clangour of sheep bells. The mountains now were

close by, their summits bleached and barren, their lower slopes silvery with groves of olive.

They got slowly and gratefully out of the car, stretching their sweaty limbs. Up here, so high, there was a breeze blowing off the sea, cool and refreshing. Lucilla, looking about her, saw that the Casa Rosa stood on a rocky bluff above them, the main entrance reached by a flight of steps. The risers of these steps were set with blue-and-white tiles, and pots of geraniums stood sentry all the way to the top. As well, all was entwined by a torrent of purple bougainvillaea; and hibiscus grew, and plumbago, and a tangle of azure-blue morning glory. The air was sweet with flowery scents mingled with the damp smell of newly watered earth.

So amazing was it all, so unlike anything they had previously experienced, that for a moment neither of them could think of anything to say. Then Lucilla whispered, "I'd no *idea* it would be as grand as this!"

"Well, one thing's for sure, we can't stand here all day."

"No." He was right. Lucilla turned towards the first step, leading the way. But before she had mounted the first step, the silence was broken by the sound of sharp heel-taps, hurrying along the terrace above them.

"Darlings!" A figure appeared at the head of the stairs, arms outstretched in welcome. "I heard the car. You've come. And you've not lost the way. How clever you are and how perfect to see you."

Lucilla's first impression of Pandora was one of insubstantial thinness. She looked ethereal, as though at any moment she might blow away. Embracing her was like holding a little bird. You didn't want to hug too hard in case she snapped in two. Her hair was chestnut brown, swept back from her forehead and falling, in frondy curls, to her shoulders. Lucilla guessed that Pandora had worn her hair that way when she was eighteen and had never seen any reason to change the style. Her eyes were dark grey, shadowed by sooty black lashes, and her curving mouth full and sweet. On her right cheek, just above the corner of her upper lip, was a round dark beauty spot, too sexy to be called a mole. She was dressed in loose pyjamas of the brilliant pink of the hibiscus flowers, and there were gold chains around her neck and knots of gold in her ears. She smelled . . . Lucilla knew that scent. Poison. She had tried wearing it herself but could never decide whether she loved it or hated it. Smelling it on Pandora, she was still not certain.

"I'd have known you were Lucilla, even if nobody had told me. You look so like Archie. . . ." It seemed that she did not even notice their unsavoury appearance, their soiled cut-off shorts and grubby T-shirts. And if she did, she gave no indication of objecting. "And you must be Jeff. . . ." She held out a pink-tipped hand. "How wonderful that you could come with Lucilla."

He took it in his own enormous paw and, looking a bit overwhelmed by her welcome and her dazzling smile, said, "Pleased to meet you."

She picked up his accent at once. "You're an Australian! How heavenly. I don't think I've ever had an Australian here before. Did you have a hideous drive?"

"No. Not at all. Just hot."

"You must be longing for a drink. . . ."

"Shall we get our stuff out of the car . . . ?"

"You can do that later. A drink first. Come along, I've a friend here for you to meet."

Lucilla's heart sank. It didn't matter about Pandora, but they were certainly in no shape to be introduced to company. "Pandora, we're dreadfully dirty. . . ."

"Oh, heavens, that doesn't matter. He won't mind. . . ." She turned from them and led the way, and there was no alternative but to follow, down a long shaded and airy terrace furnished with white cane and butter-yellow cushions and great blue-and-white porcelain jars planted with palms. "He can't stay for very long and I want you to meet him. . . ."

They turned the corner of the house and, hard on Pandora's tapping heels, stepped out into blinding sunshine. Lucilla longed for her sunglasses, left in the car. In a dazzle, she saw the wide, open terrace, shaded by striped awnings and paved in marble. Shallow steps led down from this to a spacious garden, massed with flowering trees and shrubs. Grass paths were set with flagged stepping-stones, and these encircled a swimming pool, aquamarine and still as glass. Just seeing it made Lucilla feel cooler. An inflatable sun-bed floated upon the surface of the water, drifting with the undercurrent of the filter.

At the far end of the garden, half hidden by hibiscus, she saw another house, small and single-storied, but with its own little terrace facing out over the pool. This was shaded by a tall umbrella pine, and beyond the ridge of its roof there was nothing to be seen but the brazen blue sky.

"Here they are, Carlos, safely arrived. My directions can't have been as confusing as we'd feared." At the top of the steps, in the shade of the awning, stood a low table. On this was a tray with glasses and a tall jug. An ashtray, a pair of sunglasses, a paperback. More cane chairs, yellow-cushioned, stood about, and as they approached, a man rose from one of these and stood, smiling, waiting to be introduced. He was tall and dark-eyed and very handsome. "Lucilla, darling, this is my friend Carlos Macaya. Carlos, this is Lucilla Blair, my niece. And Jeff . . . ?"

"Howland," Jeff supplied for her.

"And he's Australian. Isn't that exciting? Now, let's all sit down and have a lovely drink. This is iced tea, but I can get Seraphina to bring something stronger if you'd like. Coke maybe? Or wine?" She began to laugh. "Or champagne? What a good idea. But perhaps a little early in the day. Let's save the champagne till later."

They told her that iced tea would be perfect. Carlos drew forward a chair for Lucilla and then settled himself beside her. But Jeff, who could soak up sun like a lizard, went to lean on the balustrade of the terrace, and Pandora perched herself beside him, legs swinging and one high-heeled sandal dangling from a toe.

Carlos Macaya poured iced tea and handed Lucilla her glass.

"You have come from Ibiza?"

"Yes, this morning, on the boat."

"How long were you there?" His English was perfect.

"A week. Staying with a friend of Jeff's. It was a lovely house but dreadfully primitive. Which is why we look so filthy. Because we are. I'm sorry."

He made no comment on this; simply smiled in an understanding way. "And before Ibiza?"

"I've been in Paris. That's where I met Jeff. I'm meant to be a painter, but there was so much to see and so much to do, I didn't achieve very much."

"Paris is a wonderful city. Was this your first visit?"

"No, I'd been once before. I spent some time as an au pair, to learn the language."

"And how did you get from Paris to Ibiza?"

"We thought of hitch-hiking but in the end we travelled by bus. We did the journey in stops and starts, staying in *gîtes*, and taking time to do some sightseeing. Cathedrals and wine châteaux—that sort of thing."

"You have not been wasting your time." He glanced at Pandora, chattering away to Jeff, who watched her intently as though she were some strange species of wildlife that he had never before observed. "Pandora tells me that this is the first time you have met each other."

"Yes." Lucilla hesitated. This man was probably Pandora's current lover, which meant that now was neither the time nor the place to en-large on Pandora's youthful elopement and subsequent life-style. "She was always abroad, you see. I mean, living abroad."

"And your home is in Scotland?"

"Yes. In Relkirkshire. That's where my parents live." A small pause fell. She took a mouthful of iced tea. "Have you ever been to Scotland?"

"No. I studied in Oxford for a couple of years" (that explained his English), "but I never found time to go to Scotland."

"We're always wanting Pandora to come back and see us, but she never will."

"Perhaps she doesn't like the cold and the rain."

"It isn't cold and rainy *all* the time. Only some of the time."

He laughed. "Whatever. It is a splendid thing that you have come to keep her company. And now . . ." He pushed back his silk cuff and glanced at his watch. It was a handsome and unusual watch, the numbers marked by tiny replicas of yachting pennants, and was strapped to his wrist by a heavy gold bracelet. Lucilla wondered if Pandora had given it to him. Perhaps the pennants spelt out "I Love You" in naval code. ". . . it is time for me to take my leave. I hope you will excuse me but I have work to do. . . ."

"Of course. . . ."

He rose once more to his feet. "Pandora, I must go."

"Oh dear, what a shame." She fixed her sandal and hopped down off the balustrade. "Never mind, you've had time to meet my guests. We'll come and see you off."

"Don't disturb everybody."

"They've got to get their luggage anyway. They're dying to unpack and have a swim. Come. . . ." She took his arm.

And so they all made their way back to where his car was waiting in the shade beneath the olive tree. Goodbyes were said, he sketched a kiss over the back of Pandora's hand, and then got in behind the wheel of the BMW.

He started up the engine, and Pandora stood back. But before he drove away, he said, "Pandora."

"Yes, Carlos?"

"You will let me know if you change your mind."

She did not answer immediately, and then shook her head. "I shan't change my mind," she told him.

He smiled, shrugged resignedly, as though good-naturedly accepting her decision. He put the car into gear and, with a final wave, left them, driving away, through the gates, down the hill, out of sight. They stood waiting until the sound of the BMW could be heard no longer. Only the splash of water from that unseen fountain, the tinkle of sheep bells.

You will let me know if you change your mind.

What had Carlos been asking of Pandora? For an instant Lucilla toyed with the idea that he had been proposing marriage, but almost at once put this notion out of her head. It was too prosaic for such a sophisticated and glamorous pair. More likely, he had been trying to persuade her to join him on some romantic trip, to the Seychelles or the palm-fringed beaches of Tahiti. Or perhaps he had simply asked her out for dinner and she didn't feel like going.

Whatever, Pandora was not about to enlighten them. Carlos was gone and now she sprang into practical activity, giving a little clap with her hands. "So. Down to business. Where's your luggage? Is that all? No suitcases or cabin trunks or hat-boxes? I take more than that if I go away for a single night. Now, come along. . . ."

She started up the steps once more, going at a great pace, and yet again they followed her, Lucilla carrying her leather satchel, and Jeff lugging the two bulging backpacks.

"I've put you in the guest-house. You can make yourselves at home, and then be quite independent. And I'm not frightfully good in the mornings, so you'll have to get your own breakfast. The fridge is full of goodies, and there's coffee and stuff in the cupboard." They were now back on the terrace. "You'll be all right?"

"Of course."

"And then I thought we'd have dinner about nine o'clock. Just something cold, because I can't cook to save my life, and Seraphina, my maid, goes home each evening. But she'll leave everything ready for us. Come over at half past eight and we'll have a drink. Now I'm going to have a little nap, so I'll leave you to find your own way and settle yourselves in. Later, I might swim before I change for dinner."

The prospect of Pandora, dressed in an even grander outfit than the pink silk pyjamas, brought up the vexing question of clothes.

"Pandora, we haven't got anything to change into. Nearly everything's dirty. Jeff's got one clean shirt, but it hasn't been ironed."

"Oh, darling, do you want to borrow something?"

"A clean T-shirt?"

"Of course, how stupid of me, I should have offered. Wait a moment."

They waited. She disappeared through wide sliding glass doors into what was presumably her bedroom, and returned almost at once bearing a midnight-blue silk shirt splashed with a rocket-fall of sequins. "Have this, it's frightfully vulgar but rather fun. You can keep it if you want, I never wear it." She tossed it over and Lucilla caught it. "And now, off you go and dig yourselves into your little nest. If you want anything, ring through on the house phone and Seraphina will bring it to you." She blew a kiss. "Half past eight. See you then."

And she was gone, leaving Lucilla and Jeff to their own devices. But still Lucilla hesitated, savouring the anticipation of what was about to happen next.

"Jeff, I can't believe it. We've got a whole house to ourselves."

"So what are we waiting for? If I don't get into that pool in two minutes flat, I'm going to explode."

Lucilla went first, leading the way down the steps and along the length of the garden. The little house awaited them. They crossed the terrace and opened the door into a living-room. Curtains had been drawn, and Lucilla went to pull them back. Light streamed in and she saw the little patio on the far side, the sheltered scrap of garden.

"We've even got our own place to sunbathe!"

There was an open fireplace, stacked with logs. There were a few comfortable chairs, a tray of drinks and glasses, a coffee-table stacked neatly with magazines, and a wall shelved with books. Opening other doors, they found two double bedrooms, and a bathroom of marvellously spacious proportions.

"I think *this* is the nicest bedroom. It's certainly the biggest." Jeff dumped the backpacks onto the tiled floor and Lucilla drew back more curtains. "We can see the sea from here. Just a little scrap, a triangle, but still a view of the sea." She opened cupboard doors, saw rows of padded hangers, smelled lavender. She put the borrowed shirt onto one of the hangers, where it hung in lonely style.

Jeff had toed off his trainers and was stripping off his T-shirt.

"You can play house as much as you like. I'm going to swim. You joining me?"

"I will in a moment."

He departed. An instant later she heard the splash as he took his running dive, and imagined the silken bliss of the cool water. But later. Just now she wanted to explore.

On detailed inspection Pandora's guest-house proved to be quite perfectly complete, and Lucilla was filled with admiration for such meticulous thought and planning. Someone . . . and who else but Pandora? . . . had somehow thought of anything that a visitor might want or need, from fresh flowers and lovely new books right down to spare blankets for chilly nights and hot-water bottles for possibly unsettled tummies. The bathroom was supplied with every sort of soap, scent, shampoo, aftershave, body-lotion, and bath-oil. There were thick white bath towels and bath-mats, and, hanging from the back of the door, a pair of voluminous and snowy-white towelling bathrobes.

Leaving all this luxury, she crossed the sitting-room and went in search of the kitchen, and found it sparkling neat, and lined with dark wooden cupboards filled with Spanish pottery, shining saucepans, casseroles, and a complete *batterie de cuisine*. If one wanted—which Lucilla didn't—it would be quite possible to concoct a dinner party for ten. There were an electric cooker and a gas cooker and a dishwasher and a fridge. She opened the fridge and discovered there, along with all the fixings for a robust breakfast, two bottles of Perrier water and a bottle of champagne. A second door led out of the kitchen. She opened this and found . . . joy of joys . . . a compact laundry with clothes washer, drying-lines, an ironing-board, and an iron. The sight of these homely items gave her more satisfaction than all the other luxuries put together. Because now, at last, they could be clean.

She set to work, losing no time. Went back to the bathroom, stripped off her clothes, put on one of the towelling robes and then started in on the unpacking. Which consisted of emptying the contents of the backpacks onto the bedroom floor. At the bottom of her own backpack were her wash-bag, her brush and comb, her sketch-pad, a book or two, and the envelope from her father, which had contained his cheque, his letter, and the invitation to a dance from Verena Steynton. She took this out of the envelope and propped it on the empty dressing-table. By now it was a bit dog-eared but bestowed, she decided, a personal note to the room, as though Lucilla had put her name to it and claimed it as her own.

Lucilla Blair

Mrs. Angus Steynton

At Home

For Katy

Why did it seem so ludicrous? She laughed. Another life, another world away. She gathered up armfuls of dirty socks, shorts, jeans, pants, and T-shirts and headed back to the laundry. Without bothering to sort any of these garments (her mother would have a fit if she could see red socks going in with white shirts, but her mother was not here to remonstrate so what did it matter?) Lucilla stuffed the open face of the washing-machine, poured in detergent, slammed the door, and switched it on. Water gushed and the drum revolved, and she stood back and observed this with as much delight as if it had been a longed-for programme on television.

Then she kicked aside the remainder of the dirty clothes, went to find her bikini, and joined Jeff in the pool.

She swam for a long time. After a bit Jeff got out and lay in the sun to dry off. Another two lengths and she saw he was gone, had taken himself indoors. She came out of the pool and wrung the water from her long dark hair. She went indoors. She found him in the bedroom, flat out on one of the beds. He looked as though he might be going to sleep. She did not want him to go to sleep. She said his name and took a running jump, and landed flat on top of him.

"Jeff."
"Yeah?"
"I told you she was beautiful."
"Who?"
"Pandora, of course." Jeff did not immediately reply to this. He was drowsy and on the edge of sleep, and not inclined to conversation. His arm, out-flung, pillowed Lucilla's head. His skin smelled of chlorine and swimming pool. "Don't you think she's beautiful?"
"She's certainly one sexy sheila."
"You think she's sexy?"
"But too old for me."
"She doesn't *look* old."
"And a bit too skinny as well."

"Don't you like skinny ladies?"

"No. I like my women with big tits and fat bums."

Lucilla, who had inherited her shape from her father and was tall and thin and almost breastless, gave Jeff a thump with her fist. "You do *not*."

He laughed. "Well, what do you want me to say?"

"You know what I want you to say."

He pulled her face towards his own and kissed her soundly. "Will that do?"

"I think you'll have to shave that beard off."

"Now why should I do that?"

"Because my face is going to start looking as though it's been cleaned off by sandpaper."

"I'll have to stop kissing you then. Or start kissing you someplace where it doesn't show."

They fell silent. The sun was dropping in the sky, and soon, quite suddenly, it would be dark. Lucilla thought of Scottish summer twilights that went on until midnight. She said, "Do you think they're lovers? Do you think they're having a raging affair?"

"Who?"

"Pandora and Carlos Macaya."

"I wouldn't know."

"He's terribly handsome."

"Yeah. A real smoothie."

"I thought he was nice. Rather cosy. Easy to talk to."

"I liked his car."

"You have a one-track mind. What do you think it was he asked her?"

"Come again?"

"He said, 'Let me know if you change your mind.' And she said, 'I won't change my mind.' He must have asked her something. He must have wanted her to do something with him."

"Well, whatever it was, she didn't look too bothered."

But Lucilla was not satisfied. "I'm certain it was something terribly significant. A turning-point in both their lives."

"You have a runaway imagination. More likely he was trying to fix a tennis game."

"Yes." But somehow, Lucilla did not feel that this was so. She sighed, and the sigh turned into a yawn. "Perhaps."

At half past eight they were ready to join Pandora, and Lucilla decided that, after all her anxiety, they didn't look too bad. Both of them had showered and scrubbed and now smelled sweetly of the gratuitous shampoo. Jeff had neatened up his beard with a pair of nail scissors, and Lucilla had ironed his one clean shirt and salvaged from the pile of clothes on the laundry floor his tidiest pair of jeans.

As for herself, she had washed her long dark hair and brushed it dry, pulled on a pair of black leggings, and now buttoned up the borrowed shirt. The heavy silk felt deliciously cool against her bare skin, and the sequined embroidery, viewed in the mirror through half-closed eyes, was not nearly as outrageous as she had first imagined. Perhaps it had something to do with these unaccustomed surroundings. Perhaps the ambience of enormous luxury helped absorb such small vulgarities. It was an interesting notion and one that she would have liked to discuss at length, but right now there was no time.

"Come on," Jeff told her. "Time to be off. I need a drink."

He made for the door and she followed him, first making sure that all the lights in the guest-house were switched off. She was fairly certain that Pandora would not give a damn if every light was left burning, but, brought up by a thrifty Scottish mother, such small housewifely economies were engrained in Lucilla, as though her subconscious were a programmed computer. She found this strange, because later strictures had left as little impression as water on a duck's back. Another interesting thought worth chewing over at a later date.

Out of doors, they stepped into a blue night, star-bright and soft and warm as velvet. The garden was headily fragrant, the swimming pool floodlit, and lamps lit the way along the stepping-stones of the path. Lucilla heard the incessant chirp of the cicadas, and there was music coming from Pandora's house.

Rachmaninoff. The Second Piano Concerto. Banal, maybe, but perfect for just such a Mediterranean night. Pandora had set the scene and now she was waiting for them on the terrace, lying in a long chair with a wineglass on the table beside her.

"There you are!" she called as they approached. "I've already opened the champagne. I couldn't wait any longer."

They went up the steps and into the pool of light that illuminated their hostess. She had changed into something black and cobwebby and wore gold sandals on her bare feet. The smell of Poison was even stronger than the scents of the garden.

"Don't you both look sleek! I can't think why you were so worried about yourselves. And Lucilla, the shirt is divine on you, you must keep it. Now, find chairs and settle down. Oh, blast, I've forgotten the glasses. Lucilla, darling, go and get some, will you? The little bar's just behind the door, you'll find everything there. There's a second bottle of bubbly in the fridge, but we'll leave it there till we've finished this one. Now, Jeff, you come and sit *here,* beside me. I want to hear all about what you and Lucilla have been up to. . . ."

Lucilla left them and obediently went in search of the wineglasses, stepping indoors through wide, curtained doors. The bar was immediately at hand, no more than a large closet fitted with everything that any human being could need to fix a drink. She took two wineglasses from the shelf but did not at once return to the terrace. This was the first time she had actually been inside Pandora's house, and she found herself in a room so spacious and spectacular that she was momentarily diverted from her errand. All was cool and creamy, sparked here and there with touches of brilliant colour. Sky-blue and turquoise cushions, and coral-pink lilies massed in a square glass vase. Alcoves, cunningly lit, displayed a collection of Dresden figures and Battersea enamel. A plate-glass coffee-table was stacked with books and magazines, more flowers, a silver cigarette box. There was an open fireplace faced with blue-and-white tiles, and above this hung a mirror-framed flower painting. At the other end of the room the dining-table—glass again—was set for dinner with candles and crystal and yet more flowers, and to Lucilla's bemused eyes it all seemed more like a stage set than a room designed for living in. And yet, she realized, there were homely touches too. An open paperback tossed onto a sofa; a half-finished tapestry lying close at hand for an empty moment. And there were photographs. Archie and Isobel on their wedding day. Lucilla's grandparents, sweet old things in their tweeds, standing in front of Croy with their dogs beside them.

Lucilla found these evidences of nostalgia immensely touching. For some reason, she had not expected them, perhaps not imagining Pandora capable of such sentiment. Now she pictured Pandora taking them everywhere with her, all through her wayward love affairs and her turbulent nomad's life. Saw her unpacking them from her suitcase in houses in California, hotel bedrooms, apartments in New York and Paris. And now, Majorca. Setting the seal of her past and her identity upon yet another temporary home.

(There did not seem to be any pictures of the men who had owned these apartments and occupied so much of Pandora's life, but perhaps she kept those in her bedroom.)

Warm dark breezes blew through the opened windows, and Rachmaninoff emanated from some unseen stereo, concealed by a gold-latticed trellis. The piano solo dripped its notes, pure as raindrops. From the terrace came the low murmur of comfortable conversation, Pandora and Jeff sounding peaceful and unimpatient.

There were other photographs on the mantelpiece, and Lucilla crossed the floor to inspect these more closely. Old Lady Balmerino, resplendent in a feathered tam-o'-shanter, apparently opening a village fête. A snapshot of Archie and Edmund Aird, two very young men sitting in the boat at the edge of the loch with their rods and their creels stowed on the thwarts. Finally, a studio portrait of herself and Hamish, Lucilla in smocked Liberty lawn and Hamish a fat baby on her knee. Archie must have sent that one to Pandora with one of his letters and she had framed it in silver and set it in the place of honour. Tucked into this silver frame was an invitation whose format was instantly familiar.

Pandora Blair

Mrs. Angus Steynton

At Home

For Katy

Lucilla's first thought was, how nice. And then, how ridiculous. A waste of a card, a waste of a stamp, because there was not the slightest possibility that Pandora would accept. She had gone from Croy when she was eighteen and never returned. Resisted all pleading, first from her parents, and then from her brother, and stayed resolutely away. It was scarcely likely that Verena Steynton, of all people, would achieve what Pandora's own family had so abjectly failed to do.

"Lucilla!"

"Coming . . ."

"What are you doing?"

Lucilla, bearing the wineglasses, joined them on the terrace. "Sorry. I've been snooping round that beautiful room. And listening to the music . . ."

"Oh, darling, don't you love Rachmaninoff? It's one of my most favourites. I know it's a bit hackneyed, but I seem to go for hackneyed things."

"I'm just the same," Lucilla admitted. "Songs like 'Oh, Lovely Moon' and 'The Barcarolle' leave me quite weak-kneed. And some of the old Beatles records. I've got them all at home at Croy. And if I'm feeling *really* blue, I've got a tape of a Fiddlers' Rally in Oban and I play it and I can feel my spirits rise visibly, like mercury in a thermometer when you've got a temperature. All those dear old men and little boys in their kilts and their shirt-sleeves, and an endless round of jigs and reels, as though they didn't know how to stop and didn't want to anyway. I usually end up dancing all by myself and leaping around the room like an idiot."

Jeff said, "I've never seen you do that."

"Well, if you hang around long enough, you probably will. But seriously, Pandora, this is the most beautiful place you've got. And our guest-house is perfection."

"It is rather sweet, isn't it? I was so lucky to snap it all up. The people who lived here before had to go back to England; I was looking for somewhere to live and it seemed that it was just waiting for me. Jeff, you're meant to be pouring champagne . . ."

"And the furniture? Is that all yours too?"

Pandora laughed. "Oh, darling, I haven't got any furniture, just little bits and pieces that I've gathered on my travels and cart about with me.

Most of the furniture here I took over with the house, but of course I've changed almost everything. The sofas were the most hideous blue, and there was a carpet with swirls on. Got rid of that pretty sharpish. I took Seraphina over with the house as well, and she's got a husband who does the garden. All I'm missing out on is a little doggie, but doggies in Majorca are inclined to get shot by youths with airguns, or else they get ticks, or they get stolen, or run over. So there's not really much point." All the glasses were now brimming full. Pandora raised hers.

"Here's to you both, and what heaven it is to have you here. Lucilla, Jeff's been telling me all about your journey down through France. How fascinating it must have been. And you got to see Chartres, such an experience. I'm longing to hear more, get all the details; but first, and most important, I want to be told all about home, and my precious Archie and Isobel and Hamish. Hamish must be enormous now. And Isobel, with those tedious Americans to stay. I hear all about them in Archie's letters, when he isn't telling me about the latest grouse-bag, or the size of the salmon he caught last week. It's a miracle he's able to do so much with that terrible leg. Tell me how the poor leg is."

"He can't actually do that much," Lucilla told her bluntly. "He just writes you positive letters because he doesn't want you to be upset. And his leg isn't anything. It's tin, full stop. It can't get any better, and we all pray it'll never get any worse."

"Poor darling. Beastly, beastly IRA. How they dare to do such things, and to Archie, of all people."

"They weren't necessarily gunning for *him*, Pandora. They were waiting, over the border, to blast off at a lot of British jocks, and he happened to be one of them."

"Did he know they were there? Or was it an ambush?"

"I don't know. And if I asked, he wouldn't tell me. He won't talk about it. He won't talk about it to anybody."

"Is that a good thing?"

"I don't suppose it is, but there's not much we can do about it."

"He was never a great talker. The most darling man, but even as a little boy he always kept everything to himself. We never even knew he was courting Isobel, and when he told our mother that he wanted to marry her, Mama nearly dropped dead with astonishment because she'd got him lined up for some entirely different female. Never mind, she made the best of it. Just as she always made the best of everything. . . ." Her voice faded. She fell silent, then swiftly emptied her glass. "Jeff, is there any more left in that bottle, or shall we open another?"

But the bottle was not yet empty and Jeff refilled Pandora's glass, and then topped up Lucilla's and his own. Lucilla was now beginning to feel not only light-hearted but light-headed as well. She wondered how much Pandora had already consumed before they joined her. Perhaps the champagne was why she seemed to be talking so much.

"Now tell me . . ." She was off again. "What are the two of you going to do next?"

Jeff and Lucilla looked at each other. Making plans was not one of their strong points. Doing things on the spur of the moment was half the fun.

It was Jeff who replied. "We don't really know. Only thing is, I have to go back to Australia at the beginning of October. I've a flight booked with Qantas on the third."

"Where do you fly from?"

"London."

"So, sometime, you'll have to go back to England."

"Right."

"Is Lucilla going with you?"

Again they looked at each other. "We haven't discussed it," Lucilla said.

"So you're free. Free as air. Free to come and go as you wish. The world is your oyster." She made an expansive gesture with her hand and spilled some of her champagne.

"Yes," Jeff agreed cautiously, "I suppose it is."

"Then let us make plans. Lucilla, would you like to make plans with me?"

"What sort of plans?"

"When you were snooping, as you put it, around my drawing-room, did you notice that large and pretentious copperplate invitation on my mantelpiece?"

"From Verena Steynton? Yes, I did."

"Have you been asked?"

"Yes. Dad sent my invitation on to me and I got it in Ibiza."

"Are you going?"

"I . . . I hadn't actually thought about it."

"*Might* you go?"

"I don't know. Why?"

"Because . . ." She laid down her glass. "I think that I shall go."

The shock of this announcement stunned Lucilla out of her delightful tipsiness and into a state of cold sobriety. She stared at Pandora in total disbelief, and Pandora stared back, her grey eyes with their huge black pupils bright with a strange elation, as though delighting in the expression of blank incredulity she had brought to Lucilla's face.

"You'd go?"

"Why not?"

"Back to Scotland?"

"Where else?"

"For Verena Steynton's *dance*?" It did not make sense.

"It's as good a reason as any."

"But you've never come before. Dad asked you and begged you, and you've never come. He told me."

"There has to be a first time. Perhaps now is the right time." All at once she stood up and walked away from them to stand looking out over the garden. She stayed there for an instant, quite still, silhouetted against the light that shone upwards from the pool. Her dress, her hair moved in the breeze. Then she turned to face them, leaning against the balustrade. She said, and she spoke now in quite a different voice, "I've been thinking so much about Croy. Just lately, I've been thinking so much about it. I'd dream about it, and wake up, and start remembering things I hadn't thought of in years. And then the invitation came. Like yours, Lucilla, forwarded on from Croy. And it brought back a million memories of the fun we used to have at those ridiculous dances and hunt balls. And house parties, and the hills ringing with the crack of guns, and every evening an enormous dinner party. How my poor mother coped with us all, I cannot imagine." She smiled at Lucilla, and then at Jeff. "And you two arriving. Phoning from Palma and turning up out of the blue, and Lucilla so like Archie. Omens. Do you believe in omens, Lucilla?"

"I don't know."

"Neither do I. But I'm certain, with the Highland blood that courses through our veins, that we should." She came back to her chair and sat on the foot-rest, her face close to Lucilla's. Beneath the beauty, Lucilla could discern the years stamped on Pandora's lovely features: the lines around her eyes and mouth, the papery skin, the sharp angle of her jaw-bone. "So, let us make plans. Will you both make plans with me? Would you mind if I asked you to do that thing?"

Lucilla looked across at Jeff. He shook his head. She said, "We wouldn't mind."

"Then this is what we'll do. We'll stay here for a week, just the three of us, and you shall have the time of your lives. And then we'll take my car, and we'll catch the ferry to Spain. And we'll drive through Spain and France, taking our time and making a pleasure of the journey. When we get to Calais, we'll cross over to England. And we'll head north, and we'll go to Scotland, and we'll go home. Back to Croy. Oh, Lucilla, say you think it's a wonderful idea."

"It's certainly totally unexpected," was all Lucilla could come up with, but if Pandora noticed a certain lack of enthusiasm in her voice, she gave no indication of doing so. Swept along on her own excitement, she turned to Jeff. "And you? How does it sound to you? Or do you think I'm out of my mind?"

"No."

"You wouldn't mind coming to Scotland with us?"

"If that's what you and Lucilla want, I'd be delighted."

"Then it's all settled!" She was triumphant. "We'll all stay at Croy with Isobel and Archie, and we'll all go to the Steyntons' lovely party."

"But Jeff hasn't been asked," Lucilla pointed out.

"Oh, that's no problem."

"And he won't have anything to wear."

Pandora dissolved into laughter. "Darling, you do disappoint me. I thought you were an unworldly artist, and all you seem to do is worry about clothes! Don't you see, clothes don't matter. Nothing matters. The only thing that matters is that we're going back home, together. Just think what fun we're going to have. And now we must celebrate!" She sprang to her feet. "The perfect moment to open that second bottle of champagne!"

September

1

*I*SOBEL BALMERINO, AT HER SEWING-MACHINE, stitched the last name-tape, HAMISH BLAIR, onto the last new handkerchief, cut the thread, folded the handkerchief, and laid it on top of the pile of clothes that stood on the table beside her. All done. All that remained were those garments which required that the name-tapes be hand-sewn . . . rugger stockings, an overcoat, and a grey polo-necked pullover, but these could be done at leisure, in the evening, and by the fireside.

She had not had such a session of name-tapes since Hamish first went to Templehall, four years ago, but he had grown during the summer holidays to such an alarming extent that she had been forced to wheel him into Relkirk, school-clothes list in hand, and start all over again. The expedition, as she had known it would be, had been both painful and expensive. Painful because Hamish did not want to think about going back to school, hated shopping, hated new clothes, and miserably resented being done out of a single day of his holiday freedom. And expensive because the regulation uniform could only be purchased at the most up-market and costly shop in the town. The overcoat, the polo-necked sweater, and the rugger stockings were bad enough, but five new pairs of enormous leather shoes were almost more than Isobel, and her bank balance, could take.

With some idea of cheering Hamish up, she had bought him an ice-cream, but he had devoured this morosely and without joy, and they had returned to Croy in an uncommunicative and mutually unfriendly silence. Once home, Hamish had immediately taken himself off, armed with his trout rod, and wearing an expression which implied that he had been grossly mistreated. Isobel was left to hump the parcels and boxes upstairs, where she had slung them into the foot of his wardrobe and firmly shut the door, then made her way to the kitchen to boil a kettle for a cup of tea and start preparing dinner.

The horrible experience of spending vast quantities of money that she could not afford left her feeling quite sick, and Hamish's patent ingratitude did not help. Peeling potatoes, she said a silent goodbye to any dreams of buying herself a new dress for the Steyntons' dance. The old navy taffeta would have to do. Letting herself feel martyred and ill done by, she toyed with the notion of freshening it up with a touch of white at the neck.

But that had all happened two weeks ago, and now September was here. That made everything better, and for a number of reasons. The most important was that, until next May, she was finished with the business of paying guests. Scottish Country Tours had shut up shop for the winter, and the last lot of Americans, complete with baggage, souvenirs, and tartan bonnets, had been waved away. The tiredness and depression that had dogged Isobel all summer was dissolved almost instantly by her sense of freedom and the knowledge that, once more, she and Archie had Croy to themselves.

But this was not all. Born and bred in Scotland, she experienced each year this lifting of the spirits as August slipped away, off the calendar, and one could stop pretending that it was summer. Some years, it was true, there came seasons like the old days, when the lawns grew dry from lack of rain and golden evenings were spent watering the roses and sweet peas and the rows of young lettuces in the vegetable garden. But too frequently the months of June, July, and August were nothing but a long and soggy endurance test of frustration and disappointment. Grey skies, chill winds, and dripping rain were enough to dampen the enthusiasm of a saint. The worst were those dark and muggy days when, in desperation, one eventually retreated indoors and lit a fire, whereupon the sky instantly cleared and the late afternoon sun dazzled out over the sodden garden, tantalizingly too late to be of use to anybody.

This summer, in particular, had been specially disappointing, and with hindsight Isobel realized that the weeks of dark clouds and sunlessness had done much to contribute to her low spirits and physical exhaustion. The first snap of frost was actually welcome, and she was able to put away her cotton skirts and shirts with some satisfaction and revert once more to friendly old tweeds and Shetland pullovers.

But even after splendid summers, September in Relkirkshire was special. Those first light frosts cleared the air, so that the colours of the countryside took on a stronger and richer hue. The deep blue of the skies was reflected in loch and river, and with the harvest safely in, the fields stood golden with stubble. Harebells grew in wayside ditches, and the scented heather, coming into full bloom, stained the hills with purple.

And then, most important of all, September meant fun. A packed season of socializing before the darkness of a long winter closed in on them all, when the bitter weather and snow-packed roads isolated scattered communities and precluded any form of contact. September meant people. Friends. For this was when Relkirkshire came truly into its own.

By the end of July, the last of the annual invasion of holiday-makers had, by and large, left; tents were packed up and caravans towed away, as the tourists headed for home. In their stead, August brought the vanguard of a secondary immigration from the south, regular visitors who returned each year to Scotland for the sport and the parties. Shooting lodges that had stood forlornly empty for most of the year were once more opened up, and their owners, driving north up the motorway in Range Rovers loaded to the gunwales with rods, guns, small children, teenagers, friends, relations, and dogs, took happy and grateful repossession.

As well, local households swelled, not with Americans nor paying guests but with the young families who belonged to these establishments and had, by necessity, moved south to London to live and work, saving their yearly vacations to return home at just this time. All bedrooms were occupied, attics turned into temporary accommodation for gangs of grandchildren, and sparse bathrooms worked overtime. Huge quantities of food were produced, cooked, and eaten every day at dining-room tables elongated by extra leaves.

And then, September. In September, all at once, everything came to life, as though some celestial stage-manager had made his countdown and pulled the switch. The Station Hotel in Relkirk was transformed from its customary Victorian gloom to a cheerful, crowded meeting-place for old friends, and the Strathcroy Arms, taken over by the syndicate of businessmen who paid Archie reassuring sums of money for the privilege of shooting grouse over his moor, fairly buzzed with activity and sporting talk.

At Croy, the invitations stood stacked on the mantelpiece in the library, and covering every type of convivial occasion. Isobel's contribution to the general jollity was an annual buffet lunch party before the Strathcroy Games. Archie was Chieftain of these Games and led the opening parade of village worthies, their stride tactfully slowed to match his halting gait. For this important ceremony, he wore his regimental balmoral and carried a drawn sword. He took his responsibilities with great solemnity and, at the end of the day, presented prizes, not only for piping and Highland dancing but also for the sweater most expertly knitted from hand-spun wool, the lightest of sponge cakes, and the winning pot of home-made strawberry jam.

* * *

Isobel kept her sewing-machine in the old linen room at Croy, mostly for reasons of convenience but also because it was her favourite and most private retreat. Not large, but quite spacious enough, it had windows facing west, out over the croquet lawn and the road that led up to the loch, and on bright days was always filled with sunshine. The curtains were white cotton, the floor brown linoleum, and the walls were lined with large white-painted cupboards in which were stowed all the household sheets and towels and spare blankets and fresh bed-covers. The solid table on which stood the sewing-machine was also useful for cutting out and dressmaking, and the ironing-board and the iron stood ready for instant use. As well, there was always a comforting nursery smell of laundered linen and the lavender bags that Isobel tucked in with her crisp piles of pillowcases, and this contributed in no small way to create an extraordinary aura of timelessness and tranquillity.

Which was why, with the name-tapes finished, she made no immediate effort to move but stayed, sitting on the hard chair, with her elbows on the table and her chin in her hands. The view beyond the open window led, up beyond the trees, to the first gentle summits of the hills. All was washed in golden sunlight. The curtains stirred in the breeze, and that same breath of air shivered through the branches of the silver birches that stood on the far side of the lawn.

A leaf dropped, drifting like a tiny kite.

It was half past three and she was alone in the house. Indoors all was still, but from the farmyard she heard distant hammering and the barking of one of the dogs. For once in her life she had time to herself, there being no commitment nor person urgently requiring her attention. She could scarcely remember when she had last found herself in such a situation, and her thoughts drifted back to childhood and youth and the lazy, aimless joys of empty days.

A floor creaked. Somewhere a door slammed shut. Croy. An old house with a heartbeat all its own. Her home. But she remembered the day, over twenty years ago, when Archie had first brought her here. She was nineteen and a tennis party had been arranged, with afternoon tea served in the dining-room. Isobel, the daughter of an Angus solicitor, and neither beautiful nor assured, had found herself overwhelmed by the size and grandeur of the place, and as well by the glamour and sophistication of Archie's other friends, all of whom seemed to know each other frighteningly well. Already hopelessly in love with Archie, she could not imagine why he had bothered to include her in the general invitation. Lady Balmerino appeared to be equally perplexed, but had been kind, making certain Isobel sat next to her at the tea-table, and taking pains to see that she was not left out of any conversation.

But there was another girl, long-legged and blonde, who seemed already to have claimed Archie for her own, and made this very clear to the assembled company, teasing him, and catching his eye across the table as though they shared a million private secrets. Archie, she was telling them all, belonged to her, and no other person would be permitted to take possession.

But, at the end of the day, Archie had made up his own mind to marry Isobel. His parents, once they had got over their astonishment, were patently delighted and welcomed Isobel into the family not as Archie's wife but as another daughter. She was fortunate. Gentle, funny, hospitable, unworldly, and totally charming, the Balmerinos were adored by everybody and Isobel was no exception.

From the farm, she heard one of the tractors starting up. Another leaf fluttered to the ground. It occurred to Isobel that now could be an afternoon that had happened long ago, as though time had slipped backwards. The sort of afternoon when dogs sought for shade, and cats basked on window-sills, their furry bellies turned to the sun. She thought of Mrs. Harris, with one of the younger maids in tow, emerging from the kitchen and headed for the walled garden, there to fill a bowl with the last of the raspberries, or reach for the bloomy Victoria plums, capturing their sweetness before the wasps got at them.

All of Croy the way it once had been. Nobody had gone away. Nobody had died. They were still alive, those two dear old people; Archie's mother out with her roses, snipping away at the dead heads and finding time to chat with one of the gardeners while he raked the dusty gravel; and Archie's father in the library, stealing a little snooze with his silk handkerchief spread across his face. Isobel only had to go and find them. She imagined doing this, making her way down the stairs, crossing the hall to stand at the open front door. She saw Lady Balmerino in her straw gardening hat coming in from the garden, carrying the basket filled with snippings and faded rose petals. But when she looked up and saw Isobel, she would frown and show some confusion because the middle-aged Isobel would be unfamiliar to her as a ghost. . . .

"Isobel!"

The voice, raised, impinged upon her daydreams. Isobel was aware that it had already called, more than once, but she had scarcely heard. Who was wanting her now? Reluctantly she collected herself, pushed back the chair and got to her feet. Perhaps to be left alone for more than five minutes was too much to expect. She went out of the room and down the nursery passage to the head of the stairs. Leaning over the bannister, she saw below her the foreshortened view of Verena Steynton standing in the middle of the hall, having walked into the house through the open front door.

"Isobel!"

"I'm here."

Verena tilted her head and looked up. "I was beginning to think there was nobody in."

"Only me." Isobel started down the stairs. "Archie's taken Hamish and the dogs to the Buchanan-Wrights' cricket match."

"Are you busy?" Verena did not look as though she had been busy. As usual, she was immaculately and suitably turned out, and surely had just been to the hairdresser.

"I've been sewing Hamish's name-tapes for school." Instinctively, Isobel put a hand to her hair, as though the casual gesture might improve her own tousled head. "But I've finished now."

"Can you spare me a moment?"

"Of course."

"I've got lots to tell you and two favours to ask. I meant to phone but I've been in Relkirk all day and then, driving home, I thought it much simpler and nicer just to call in."

"Do you want a cup of tea?"

"In a moment. No hurry."

"Let's go and be comfortable." Isobel led her visitor into the drawing-room, not with any intentions of grandeur but simply because it was full of sunlight, and the library and the kitchen, at this time of day, were inclined to be gloomy. The windows stood open, the room felt cool, and a mass of sweet peas, which Isobel had picked that morning and arranged in an old soup tureen, filled the air with their fragrance.

"Heaven." Verena sank into a corner of the sofa and stretched out her long and elegantly shod legs. "What a day for the cricket match. Last year it bucketed with rain and they had to pull stumps in the middle of the afternoon because the pitch was flooded. Are those your own sweet peas? What colours! Mine were a bit of a failure this year. Do you know I really hate Relkirk on a warm afternoon? The pavements were banked three deep with fat girls in jeans pushing babies in buggies. And all the babies seemed to be howling."

"I know the feeling. How's everything going?"

She had already made up her mind that Verena wanted to talk about the dance and she was not mistaken.

"Oh . . ." Verena, for a moment, became quite dramatic, groaning as though in pain and closing her eyes. "I'm beginning to wonder why I ever *thought* about throwing a party. Do you know half the invitations haven't even been answered yet? People are so thoughtless. I think they leave them curling on mantelpieces, waiting to die of old age. It makes trying to arrange dinner parties and find beds for everybody quite impossible."

"I wouldn't worry." Isobel tried to sound soothing. "I'd let them make their own arrangements."

"But that would mean utter chaos."

Isobel knew that it wouldn't, but Verena was a perfectionist. "Yes, I suppose so. It must be awful." She added, almost afraid to ask, "Has Lucilla replied yet?"

"No," Verena told her bluntly.

"We did send your invitation on, but she's travelling so she may not even have got it. She sent us a rather vague address in Ibiza, but we haven't heard from her since she was in Paris. She thought she might go and see Pandora."

"I haven't heard from Pandora either."

"I'll be surprised if you do. She never answers anything."

"But Alexa Aird's coming, and bringing a boyfriend. Did you know that Alexa has found herself a man?"

"Vi told me."

"Extraordinary. I wonder what he's like."

"Virginia says he's dishy."

"Can't wait to see him."

"When is Katy arriving?"

"Next week sometime. She called last night. Which is one of the favours that I have to ask you. Have you got a houseful of people staying over the dance?"

"So far, nobody. Hamish will be back at school and I don't know whether Lucilla will be here or not. . . ."

"Well, could you be an angel and have a stray man to stay? Katy told me about him last night. She met him at some dinner party, and liked him. He's an American—a lawyer, I think—but his wife's just died, and he's come over here for a bit of a holiday. He's coming to Scotland anyway to stay with some people who live in the Borders, and she thought it would be friendly to send him an invitation. We can't put him up at Corriehill because I'm full, with all Katy's friends, and Toddy Buchanan hasn't a room free at the Strathcroy Arms, so I thought you could give him a bed? Would you mind? I don't know anything about him except the bit about his wife dying, but if Katy liked him I don't suppose he'd be *dreadfully* heavy weather."

"Poor man. Of course he can come."

"And you'll bring him to the party? You are sweet. I'll ring Katy tonight, and tell her to tell him to get in touch with you."

"What's his name?"

"Something funny. Plucker. Or . . . Tucker. That's it. Conrad Tucker. Why do you suppose Americans always have such peculiar names?"

Isobel laughed. "They probably think Balmerino's pretty odd. What else is happening?"

"Nothing really. We've persuaded Toddy Buchanan to do the catering and run the bar, and produce some sort of a breakfast. For some reason, Katy's generation are always ravenously hungry around four in the morning. And darling Tom Drystone is organizing the band."

"Well, it wouldn't be a party without our whistling postman up on the platform. Are you having a disco?"

"Yes. A young man from Relkirk is doing that. He produces everything. A sort of job lot. Flashing lights and amplifiers. What the noise is going to be like, I dread to think. And we're going to have fairy lights all the way up the drive. I thought it would look festive, and if it's a miserably dark evening, it'll help people find the way."

"It'll look wonderful. You've thought of everything."

"Except flowers. That's the other favour I've got to ask you. Would you help with the flowers? Katy will be there, and I've press-ganged one or two others, but nobody does flowers the way you do, and I'd be endlessly grateful if you'd help."

Isobel felt flattered. It was nice to think that there was something that she could do better than Verena, and gratifying to be asked.

"The thing is," Verena went on before Isobel had a chance to speak, "I can't think how to decorate the marquee. The house isn't so difficult, but the marquee presents something of a problem because it's so enormous and ordinary flower arrangements would simply be dwarfed. What do you think? You're always full of bright ideas."

Isobel searched for a bright idea but drew a blank. "Hydrangeas?"

"They'll be over by then."

"Hire some potted palms."

"Too depressing. Like the ballroom of some provincial hotel."

"Well, why not make it really countrified and seasonal? Sheaves of ripe barley and branches of rowan. Lovely red berries and those pretty leaves. And the beeches will be turning as well. We can soak the stems in glycerine and simply cover the tent-poles, make them look like autumn trees. . . ."

"Oh, a brainwave. You're brilliant. We'll do it all the day before the party. The Thursday. Will you write it down in your diary?"

"It's Vi's birthday picnic that day, but I can give that a miss."

"You're a saint. What a weight off my mind. The relief of it." Verena stretched luxuriously, swallowed a yawn, fell silent.

The clock on the mantelpiece ticked gently, and the quiet of the room closed in on the two women. Yawns were catching. And it was a mistake ever to sit down in the middle of the afternoon because you didn't feel like ever getting up again. Summer afternoons and nothing in particular to do. Once more Isobel drifted back into that illusion of timelessness in which she had been lost before Verena's interruption. She thought again of old Lady Balmerino, who used to sit here, as she and Verena sat, reading a novel or peacefully sewing her tapestry. Everything now as once it had been. Perhaps in a moment there would come a discreet tap on the door and Harris the butler would enter, pushing before him the mahogany trolley laid with the silver teapot and the eggshell china cups; the covered dishes of scones, fresh from the oven, the bowl of cream, the strawberry jam, the lemon sponge-cake, and the dark, sticky ginger-bread.

The clock, with silvery notes, struck four, and the illusion dissolved. Harris was long gone and would never return. Isobel yawned again and then, with some effort, pulled herself to her feet. "I'll go and put the kettle on," she told Verena, "and we'll have that cup of tea."

2

Friday the Ninth

". . . THAT WAS THE YEAR my cousin Flora had her bairn. Did you know her parents? Uncle Hector was my father's brother, much younger, of course, and married to a girl from Rum. Met her when he was a police-man; she was always a shiftless creature, lost all her teeth when she was scarcely out of her twenties. When my granny heard, she was up to high doh, didn't want any candle-bearing Catholics in the family; she'd been brought up Wee Free. I knitted a matinee coat for the bairn. Pink silk with a fern pattern, but she put it in the boiler with the sheets, it just about broke my heart. . . ."

Violet stopped listening. It didn't seem necessary to listen. One just nodded, or said "Oh, yes," every time Lottie paused for breath, and then she was away again on some other confusing tack.

". . . went into service when I was fourteen, over in a big house in Fife; I cried buckets, but my mother said I had to go. I was the kitchen maid and the Cook was a bisom; I've never been so tired in my life, up at five o'clock in the morning and slept in the attic with a moose."

This at least caught Violet's attention. "A *moose*, Lottie?"

"I think it was a moose. One of those stuffed heads. On the wall. Too big for a stag. Mr. Gilfillan had been in Africa, a missionary. You wouldn't have thought a missionary would have gone round killing mooses, would you? Christmas they had roast goose, but all I got was a bit of cold mutton. Mean. Wouldn't give you the drippings off their noses. The attic was that damp, my clothes were wringing wet, caught pneumonia. The doctor came, Mrs. Gilfillan sent me home, never been so glad to get back. Had a cat at home. Tammy Puss. He was that quick. Open the larder door and in with the cream; once we found a dead mouse in the cream. And Ginger had a litter of kittens, half-wild, scratched the skin off my mother's hands . . . she was never good with animals. Hated my father's dog. . . ."

They sat, the two elderly ladies, on a bench in the big park in Relkirk. Before them, the river flowed, heavy with flood-water and stained brown with peat. A fisherman, up to his hips in water, flogged his salmon rod. So far he did not seem to have had so much as a nibble. Across the river stood large Victorian houses, deep in spacious gardens with lawns that ran down to the water. One or two had little boats moored. There were ducks on the water. A man, passing with his dog, threw crusts and the ducks came gobbling, squabbling, to snatch the crusts up.

". . . the doctor said it was a stroke, said she'd got nerves. I wanted to go and be a volunteer, with the war on and everything, but if I'd gone there'd be no one to stay with my mother. My father was a worker out of doors, he grew lovely turnips, but indoors, sit down and take off his boots and that was it . . . never seen a man who could eat so much. He was never a talker, some days never said a word. Trapped rabbits. Ate a lot of rabbits, we did. Course that was before mixamy-toasties. Filthy things now . . ."

Violet, having made her promise to Henry that she would take Lottie off Edie's hands for an afternoon, had suffered an uneasy conscience until she had finally decided to take the plunge and get it over, and had invited Lottie to come shopping with her in Relkirk and to have high tea. She had duly collected Lottie from Edie's cottage, packed her into the car, and driven her into the town. For the occasion Lottie had dressed in her best, a beige Crimplene coat and a hat the shape of a cottage loaf. She carried a huge handbag and wore her tottery high-heeled shoes. From the moment she got into the car, she had not stopped talking. She had talked as they made their way around Marks and Spencer, talked as they waited in the queue to buy fresh vegetables, talked as they searched the crowded streets for what Lottie insisted on calling a haberdasher's.

"I don't think there are any haberdasher's any longer, Lottie. . . ."

"Oh, yes, a little one down that street . . . or was it the next? Mother always came for her knitting wool."

Never believing they would find it, Violet allowed herself to be led around in circles, getting more hot and footsore by the moment, and was torn between annoyance and relief when Lottie finally ran the shop to earth. It was very old and dusty, and crammed with a collection of cardboard boxes containing crochet hooks, faded embroidery silks, and out-of-date knitting patterns. The old woman behind the counter looked as though she had just managed to make it out of a geriatric home, and it took her fifteen minutes to find what Lottie wanted, which was a yard of boiling knicker elastic. Finally, however, it was produced from a drawer filled with odd buttons, put shakily into a paper bag, and paid for. They stepped out onto the pavement, and Lottie was triumphant. "Told you so," she crowed to Violet. "Didn't believe me, did you?"

With their shopping over and it not yet being time for tea, Violet had suggested a walk in the park. They had made their way back to her car, dumped their purchases in the boot, and then crossed the wide sward of grass that led to the river. At the first bench, Violet had firmly sat down.

"We'll have a little rest," she told Lottie, and so here they were, side by side in the golden sunshine, and Lottie still with plenty to say.

"That's the Relkirk Royal, that's where I was, you can just see it through the trees. Nice enough place, but I couldn't stand the nurses. The doctor was good enough, but no more than a young student, don't imagine he knew anything, although he pretended he did. Lovely gardens, though, just as nice as the Cremmy. I wanted Mother cremated, but the minister said she wanted to lie by my father in the churchyard at Tullochard. Though I don't know how he should know more than me."

"I expect your mother told him. . . ."

"More likely made it up himself, always liked to interfere."

Violet looked across the river to where the Relkirk Royal stood high on the hill, its red stone turrets and gables scarcely visible through the leafy trees that surrounded it. She said, "The hospital certainly has a lovely position."

"That's doctors for you. They can pay for anything."

Casually, "What was he called, the young doctor who took care of you?"

"Dr. Martin. There was another, Dr. Faulkner, but he never came near me. It was Dr. Martin who said I could go and live with Edie. I wanted a taxi but it was an ambulance."

"Edie is very kind."

"*She's* had a good enough life, some people have all the luck. Different living in a village to being stuck away up the hill."

"Perhaps you could sell your parents' house and move into a village?"

But Lottie ignored this sensible suggestion and went on, full flood, as though Violet had never made it. It occurred to Violet then that Lottie was more astute than any of them suspected. "Worry about her being so fat, it's a heart attack she'll have one morning, carrying all that flab around with her. And always flying out of the house, off to your house or Virginia's, never sits down for a bit of peace or a chat or to watch the telly. Ought to think of herself sometimes. She told me that Alexa's coming up for Mrs. Steynton's party. Bringing a friend. That's nice, isn't it? But you'll need to watch, men are all the same, after what they can get their hands on. . . ."

"What do you mean, Lottie?" Violet was sharp.

Lottie turned dark round eyes upon her. "Well, she's no pauper, is Alexa. Old Lady Cheriton was never short of sixpence. I read the news-

papers, know all about *that* family. Nothing like a bit of cash to start a
man leering at a young girl."

Violet found herself assailed by a helpless rage that seemed to surge
up from the soles of her feet and, reaching her cheeks, burn them red.
Rage at Lottie's impertinence, and helplessness because Lottie was, after
all, only voicing what all Alexa's family, obscurely, feared.

She said, "Alexa is very pretty and very dear. The fact that she is also
independent has nothing to do with the friends she chooses."

But Lottie either ignored or missed the snub. She gave a little laugh,
tossing her head. "I wouldn't·be too sure about that. And coming from
London, too. Lot of money grubbers. Yuppies," she added with some
force, saying the word as though it were dirty.

"Lottie, I don't think you know what you're talking about."

"All these girls are the same. Always were, see a handsome man and
they're away like a bitch in heat." She shivered suddenly, as though the
excitement of the thought had reached every nerve-end of her gangling
frame. Then she put out a hand and closed it over Violet's wrist. "That's
another thing. Henry. See him about the place. He's small, isn't he?
Comes to Edie's and never says a word. Looks funny to me sometimes.
I'd worry if I were you. Not like other little boys . . ."

Her bony fingers were strangely strong, the grip viselike. Violet, re-
pelled, knew an instant of panic. Her immediate instinct was to prize the
fingers loose, get to her feet and escape, but just then a girl walked by
pushing a child in a buggy, and common sense came to Violet's rescue.
The panic, the annoyance faded. It was, after all, just poor Lottie Carstairs, to whom life had not been kind, letting her sad, sexual frustrations
and her rambling imagination run away with her. And if Edie could
stand having her cousin to live with her, surely Violet could cope calmly
for a single afternoon.

She smiled. She said, "It's good of you to be concerned, Lottie, but
Henry is a very ordinary little boy and sound as a bell. Now . . ." She
shifted slightly, glancing at her watch, and felt Lottie's fingers loosen
their manic grip and slip away. Violet, unhurried, reached for her handbag. ". . . I think it's time we went and found somewhere pleasant to
have our tea. I'm feeling quite peckish. I fancy fish and chips. How
about you?"

3

As Isobel, worn out with the daily demands of her busy life, retreated from time to time to the linen room, so her husband found solace in his workshop. This was in the basement of Croy, an area of stone-flagged passages and dimly lighted cellars. The old boiler lived down here, a brooding, smelly monster that looked large enough to drive a liner, and demanded constant and regular attention and enormous quantities of coke. As well, one or two other rooms were still employed—to store unused china, unwanted items of furniture, the coal and the logs, and a much-diminished wine cellar. But mostly, the basement stood deserted, hung with cobwebs and invaded each year by families of field mice.

The workshop was next door to the boiler room, which meant that it was always pleasantly warm, and it had large windows, barred like a jail's, which faced south and west and let in sufficient light for cheerfulness. Archie's father, neat with his hands, had set it all up, with heavy benches, racks for tools, vises, and clamps. And it was here that the old man had liked to potter, repairing his children's damaged toys, dealing with various inevitable breakages that occurred about the house, and concocting his own salmon flies.

After he died, the workshop had stood empty for some years, unused, neglected, and gathering dust. But when Archie came back to Croy after his eight months in hospital, he painfully made his way down the stone stairs, limped the length of the echoing passage, and took repossession. The first thing he saw as he entered the room was a broken balloon-back chair, its back legs shattered by the weight of some corpulent occupant. It had been brought down to the workshop before old Lord Balmerino died. He had made a start on its repair but never finished the job, and the chair had been left, forgotten and untended, ever since.

Archie stood and looked at the forlorn piece of furniture for some time. Then he shouted for Isobel. She came. She helped him sweep away the dirt and the cobwebs and the mouse droppings and the drifts of old sawdust. Scuttling spiders were sent packing, as were solidified pots of glue, piles of yellowed newspapers, ancient tins of paint. Isobel cleaned the windows and somehow forced them open, letting in the sweet fresh air.

Meanwhile Archie, having wiped and oiled all the fine old tools, the chisels and hammers, saws and planes, replaced them in orderly fashion in their racks. With that done, he sat down and wrote out a list of all that he needed, and Isobel went into Relkirk and bought it for him.

Only then was he able to get down to work and finish the job that his father had started.

Now he sat at that same bench, the afternoon sun slanting through the top half of the window, and finished priming the carving he had been working on, from time to time, over the last month or two. It was about ten inches high and depicted the figure of a girl sitting on a boulder with a small Jack Russell terrier leaning against her knee. The girl wore a sweater and a kilted skirt, and her hair was windblown. It was, in fact, Katy Steynton and her dog. Verena had given Archie a photograph of her daughter, taken up on the moor last year, and from this he had made the drawings for the carving. With the primer dry, he would paint it, reproducing as closely as possible the muted colours of the photograph. And then it would be given to Katy as a twenty-first birthday present.

It was done. He laid down the brush and leaned back in his chair to stretch the aches out of his limbs, and assess his creation over the top of his half-moon spectacles. He had never before attempted the complications of a sitting figure, and a female one at that, and was inordinately pleased with the way it had turned out. Girl and dog made a charming composition. Tomorrow he would paint it. He looked forward with some satisfaction to applying the final touches.

From upstairs, he heard the faint sound of the telephone ringing. It was only just audible, and for months he and Isobel had been talking about the sense of installing another bell in the basement so that he could hear the sound more easily, should he be alone in the house. But they had done nothing about this and he was alone in the house now, and wondered how long the telephone had been ringing, and if there was time for him to make his way upstairs and pick up the receiver before the caller, losing heart, hung up. He thought about ignoring it but the ringing continued. Perhaps it was important. He pushed back his chair and made his slow way down the passage and up the stairs to answer the wretched instrument. The nearest receiver was in the kitchen and it was still ringing shrilly as Archie crossed over to the dresser and picked it up.

"Croy."

"Dad!"

"Lucilla!" His heart leaped with joy. He reached for a chair.

"Where were you? The phone's been ringing for hours."

"Down in my workshop." He settled himself, taking the weight off his leg.

"Oh, I'm sorry. Is Mum not there?"

"No. She and Hamish have gone blackberrying. Lucilla, where are you?"

"I'm in *London*. And you'll never guess where I'm ringing from. You'll never guess in a thousand years."

"In that case you'd better tell me."

"The Ritz."

"What the hell are you doing there?"

"Staying the night. And then we're driving up tomorrow. We'll be home tomorrow night."

Archie took off his spectacles; he could feel the grin of delight spreading over his face. "Who's 'we'?"

"Jeff Howland and me. And . . . wait for it . . . *Pandora*."

"Pandora?"

"I thought that would surprise you. . . ."

"But what's Pandora doing with you?"

"She's coming home. She says it's for Verena Steynton's dance, but I suspect it's really to see Croy and all of you again."

"Is she there now?"

"No. She's having a toes-up. I'm phoning from my room. I'm all alone except for Jeff. I've got so much to tell you and Mum, but I won't do it now because it's all so complicated. . . ."

But Archie would not let her off with this excuse. "When did you get to London?"

"This morning. Just before lunch. We've all been driving through Spain and France in Pandora's car. We've had the most amazing time. Then we caught the ferry early this morning and came to London. I was all ready to head north right away, but Pandora wanted to draw breath, so she brought us here. Insisted. And don't worry about the bill because she's footing it. She footed the whole trip, ever since we left Palma. Paid for all the petrol, the hotels, everything."

"How . . ." His voice broke. It was ridiculous, unmanly, to be so emotional. He tried again. "How is she?"

"She's fine. Terribly pretty. Lots of fun. Oh, Dad, you are pleased I'm bringing her home, aren't you? It's not going to be too much for Mum? Pandora's not what you call madly domesticated and I don't suppose she'll ever raise a finger to do anything to help, but she's so excited about seeing you both again. It will be all right, won't it?"

"More than all right, my darling. It's like a miracle."

"And don't forget, I'm bringing Jeff as well."

"We look forward to meeting him."

"See you tomorrow then."

"What time?"

"About five? But don't worry if we're a little late."

"We won't."

"I can't wait."

"Nor me. Drive carefully, my darling."

"Of course." She sent him a kissing noise down the hundreds of miles of wire, and rang off.

Archie was left sitting on the hard kitchen chair and holding the buzzing receiver in his hand. Lucilla and Pandora. Coming home.

He replaced the receiver. The buzzing ceased. The old kitchen clock ticked slowly. For a few moments he sat where he was, and then got to his feet and went out of the kitchen and down the passage to his study. Sitting at his desk, he opened a drawer and took out a key. Using this key, he opened another, smaller drawer. From this he withdrew an envelope, yellowed with the years and addressed in Pandora's large and immature scrawl to himself, at the Headquarters of The Queen's Loyal Highlanders, in Berlin. The date of the postmark was 1967. It contained a letter, but he did not take this letter out to read because he knew it by heart. Which meant that there was no reason why he had never torn it to shreds, nor flung it on a fire, except that he could not bring himself to destroy it.

Pandora. Coming back to Croy.

From the distance came the sound of a car, growing louder, approaching the house, up the hill from the main road. The noise of its engine was unmistakable. Isobel and Hamish returning in the minibus from their blackberrying expedition. Archie put the envelope back into its drawer, locked it away, disposed once more of the key, and went to meet them.

Isobel had driven the minibus around the back of the house and parked it in the yard and, by the time Archie returned to the kitchen, they were there, his wife and his son, flinging open the door and staggering triumphantly through it, each weighed down by two huge baskets brimming with dark fruit. After a session in the bramble thickets they were both disreputable, dirty, and mud-stained, and looked, Archie decided fondly, no better than a pair of tinkers.

Every time he set eyes on Hamish, he knew a small shock of surprise, because the boy, these summer holidays, had grown like a young tree, getting taller and larger by the day. At twelve, he now topped his mother, and his out-at-elbow sweater was strained across a pair of muscular shoulders. His shirt hung out of his jeans, purple juice stained his hands and mouth, and his abundant corn-coloured hair was sorely in need of a cut. Archie, eyeing him, was filled with pride.

"Hi, Dad." Dumping the baskets onto the kitchen table, Hamish groaned. "I'm starving."

"You're always starving."

Isobel, too, set down her load. "Hamish, you've been eating blackberries all afternoon." She wore her baggy corduroys and a shirt that Archie had long since discarded. "You can't be hungry."

"I am. Blackberries don't fill you up." Hamish was headed for the dresser where the cake tins were stacked. He removed a lid with a clatter and reached for a knife.

Archie admired their harvest. "You've done frightfully well."

"We must have picked about thirty pounds. I've never seen so many. We went over to the other side of the river where Mr. Gladstone grows his turnips. The hedgerows around those fields are groaning with fruit." Isobel pulled out a chair and sat down. "I'd die for a cup of tea."

Archie said, "I have news for you."

She looked up quickly, always fearing the worst. "Good news?"

"The best," he told her.

"But when did she call? What did she say? Why didn't she let us know before?" Isobel, alight with excitement, gave Archie no time to answer any question. "Why didn't they call us from Palma, or France, and give us more notice? Not that I need a moment's notice, it doesn't matter; all that matters is that they're coming. And staying at the *Ritz*. I don't think that Lucilla's ever stayed in a hotel in the whole of her life. Pandora is ridiculous. They could easily have gone somewhere a little less grand. . . ."

"Pandora probably doesn't know anywhere else."

"And they're staying over the dance? And she's bringing the sheep-farmer? Do you suppose she actually persuaded Pandora to come? It's so extraordinary, after all these years, that it's taken *Lucilla* to persuade her. I'll have to get all the bedrooms ready. We'll be quite a house party because we've got that American friend of Katy's coming as well. And food. I think there are still some pheasants in the deep-freeze. . . ."

They were, by now, sitting around the table and drinking tea. Hamish, in famished desperation, had put the kettle on and made this. While his parents talked, he had set the table with three mugs, the tins that contained the cakes and biscuits, and a loaf of bread on its wooden board. As well, he had found butter and a jar of Branston Pickle. Hamish had, just now, a passion for Branston Pickle and spread it on everything. He was, at this moment, engaged in concocting a sandwich, the dark pickle oozing out between two enormous doorstops of bread.

". . . did she tell you about Pandora? Did she say anything at all about her?"

"Not very much. Just sounded pleased with life."

"Oh, I wish I'd been here to talk to her."

"You can talk to her tomorrow."

"Have you told anyone else they're coming?"

"No. Just you."

"I'll have to call Verena and tell her she's got three more people coming to her party. And I must tell Virginia. And Vi."

Archie reached for the teapot and refilled his mug.

"I was thinking. Perhaps it would be a good idea to ask all the Airds for lunch on Sunday? What do you say? After all, we don't know how long Pandora's going to be staying, and next week's going to be like a three-ring circus with one thing and another. Sunday might be a good day."

"That's a brilliant idea. I'll ring Virginia. And I'll order a sirloin from the butcher."

Hamish said "Yum yum" and reached for another slice of gingerbread.

". . . and if it's a fine day we can play croquet. We haven't played croquet all summer. You'll have to cut the grass, Archie." She set down her mug, businesslike. "Now. I've got to make bramble jelly, and I'll have to get all the bedrooms ready. But I mustn't forget to ring Virginia. . . ."

"I'll do that," said Archie. "You can leave that to me."

But Isobel, with the great jelly-pan set on the Aga and the blackberries simmering, knew that if she did not share her exciting news with somebody, she would burst, and so found time to call Violet. At first there was no reply from Pennyburn, so she hung up and called again half an hour later.

"Hello."

"Vi, it's Isobel."

"Oh, my dear."

"Are you busy?"

"No, I'm sitting down with a drink in my hand."

"But, Vi, it's only half past five. Have you taken to the bottle?"

"Temporarily. I've had the most exhausting day of my life, wheeling Lottie Carstairs around Relkirk and giving her tea. Never mind, it's all over now and I've done my good deed for the week. But I did feel I deserved a large whisky and soda."

"You certainly do. Or even *two* large whiskies and soda. Vi, something really exciting has happened. Lucilla rang from London and she's coming home tomorrow and she's bringing Pandora with her."

"She's bringing *who?*"

"Pandora. Archie's over the moon with delight. Just think. He's been trying to get her back to Croy for the past twenty-one years and now she's actually coming."

"I can't believe it."

"Incredible, isn't it? Come for lunch on Sunday and see them all. We're asking all the other Airds as well, you can come with them."

"I'd love to do that. But . . . Isobel, why did she suddenly decide to come? Pandora, I mean."

"No idea. Lucilla said something about the Steyntons' party, but it seems a fairly feeble excuse."

"How extraordinary. I . . . I . . . wonder what she will look like?"

"No idea. Probably smashing. Except that she's thirty-nine now, so there are bound to be a few wrinkles. Anyway, we'll soon see for ourselves. I must go, Vi. I'm making bramble jelly and it's just about to boil over. See you Sunday."

"So kind. And I'm thrilled about Lucilla . . ."

But the brambles claimed Isobel. " 'Bye, Vi." And she rang off.

Pandora.

Vi put down her receiver, took off her spectacles, and rubbed her aching eyes. She had been tired before, but Isobel's news, delivered with such joy, left her with the sensation that she was being beleaguered. As though impossible demands were about to be made of her, and vital decisions to be made.

She lay back in her chair and closed her eyes, wished that Edie were here, her oldest and dearest friend, so that she could confide, and discuss, and be comforted. But Edie was in her cottage, lumbered with Lottie, and even a telephone call was out of the question, with Lottie listening to every word and drawing her own dangerous conclusions.

Pandora. Now thirty-nine, but because Violet had not seen her since she was eighteen, she had stayed, in Violet's mind, perpetually that enchanting teenager. Like a person already dead. People who had died never aged, just stayed in the memory the way they had once been. Archie and Edmund had matured to middle age, but not Pandora.

Which was ridiculous. Everybody grew older at the same speed, like people at airports being carried along by those moving walkways. Pandora was thirty-nine and had lived a life, if all accounts were to be believed, that was anything but quiet and peaceful. Experience would have left its mark, drawing lines, wrinkling skin, dulling the bright lustre of that amazing hair.

But it was almost impossible to imagine. Violet sighed, opened her eyes, reached for her drink. This would not do. She must pull herself together. The implications of the situation had nothing to do with her. She would make no decision because there was none to be made. She would simply continue to do what she had always done, which was to observe, disregard, and keep her counsel.

Edmund Aird, returning home to Balnaid from Edinburgh at seven o'clock in the evening, walked through his front door just as the telephone started to ring. Standing in the hall, he paused, but when no one immediately answered the call, he laid his brief-case down on the table and went to the library, to sit at his desk and pick up the receiver.

"Edmund Aird."

"Edmund. Archie here."

"Yes, Archie."

"Isobel asked me to call you. She wants you and Virginia and Henry to come for lunch on Sunday. We've asked Vi as well. Can you make it?"

"How very kind of Isobel. I think so . . . just a moment . . ." He reached in his pocket for his diary, laid it on the blotter, turned the pages. "As far as I'm concerned, that would be fine, but I'm only just back and I haven't spoken to Virginia yet. Do you want me to go and find her?"

"No, don't bother. You can ring me if you can't come, and if we don't hear, we'll expect you all at about a quarter to one."

"We look forward to it." Edmund hesitated. "Is this for some occasion we should know about, or just a routine invitation?"

Archie said, "No." And then said, "Yes. I mean, it is an occasion. Lucilla's coming home tomorrow. . . ."

"That's great news."

"She's bringing some Australian with her."

"The sheep-farmer?"

"That's right. And she's bringing Pandora."

Edmund, with some deliberation, closed his diary. It was bound in navy-blue hide, with his initials in gold in one corner. It had been in his stocking last Christmas, a present from Virginia.

"Pandora?"

"Yes. Lucilla and the sheep-farmer went to stay with her in Majorca. They've all come back together, driving through Spain and France. Got to London this morning." Archie paused, as though waiting for some comment from Edmund. But Edmund did not speak and, after a bit, Archie went on. "I forwarded an invitation from Verena Steynton, so I suppose she thought it might be fun to come home for the party."

"It's as good a reason as any."

"Yes." Another pause. "Sunday then, Edmund?"

"Yes, of course."

"Unless we hear from you."

"We look forward to it. Thank you for calling."

He rang off. The library, the house were silent. It occurred to him that perhaps Virginia and Henry were out somewhere, and he was totally alone. This sense of solitude grew, became oppressive. He found himself straining his ears, needing the reassurance of a raised voice, the clatter of dishes, the bark of a dog. Nothing. Then, from beyond the open window, came the long, bubbling call of a curlew, flying low over the fields beyond the garden. A cloud covered the sun, and the cool air stirred. He put the diary back in his pocket, smoothed his hair with his hand, straightened his tie. He needed a drink. He got up from the chair, left the room, and went in search of his wife and his son.

4

Saturday the Tenth

LUCILLA SAID, "I'VE NEVER COME home in such style before."

"How did you come before?" Jeff was driving. He had been at the wheel the whole of their long journey north.

"In trains from school. Or driving a ratty little car from Edinburgh. Once I flew from London, but that was in the days when Dad was still a soldier and the War Office paid my fare."

It was half past three, a Saturday afternoon, and now there were only twenty miles to go. They had made good time. The motorway was behind them, Relkirk bypassed, and the winding road comfortingly familiar, leading them to Strathcroy and home. The river kept them company, and ahead lay the hills. The air was clear, the sky enormous, and the fresh breeze, sweeping in through opened windows, sweet and heady as young wine.

Lucilla could scarcely believe their good fortune. It had been raining in London and pouring in the Midlands, but as they crossed the Border, she had watched the clouds disintegrate, disperse, roll away to the east, and Scotland welcomed them with a blue sky and trees just on the point of turning gold. Lucilla thought that this was extremely obliging of her native country and felt as pleased as if she, personally, had stage-managed the miraculous transformation, but deliberately made no comment on either their luck or the stunning scenery. She had known Jeff for long enough to discover that he did not appreciate, and was even embarrassed by, over-effusion.

They had set off at ten o'clock this morning, checking out of the Ritz, and watching the majestic porters load Pandora's dark-red Mercedes with her impressive array of matched luggage, along with their own humble backpacks. Pandora had forgotten to tip the porters, so Lucilla had had to do it for her. She knew that she would never get it back, but after a night of total luxury with dinner and breakfast thrown in, she felt that it was the least she could do.

To begin with, Pandora had sat in the front of her magnificent car, cosy in her mink, because after the nailing heat of a Majorcan August, she felt in need of its opulent comfort. The cold and the rain were not what she had expected. While Jeff drove them out of the city, jousted with traffic, achieved the motorway, she kept up an endless stream of inconsequential chat. Later, she fell silent, gazing out of the window at the grey and dull countryside through which they swept, in the fast lane, at eighty miles an hour. The windscreen wipers worked flat out, immense juggernauts sent up blinding, muddy showers of spray, and even Lucilla had to admit that it was all thoroughly disagreeable.

"Goodness, it's ugly." Pandora snuggled deeper into her fur.

"I know. But it's just this bit."

For lunch, they stopped at a Motorway Service Station. Pandora wanted to leave the motorway and go in search of some wayside pub, preferably thatched, where they could sit by an open fire and drink cheering concoctions like whisky and ginger ale. But Lucilla knew that if they allowed themselves to be so diverted, they would never get back to Croy.

"There isn't time. This isn't Spain, Pandora. It isn't France. We've no time to waste on frivolities."

"Darling, hardly a *frivolity.*"

"Yes, it is. And you'd get talking to the barman and we'd be there forever."

So the Motorway Service Station it was, which proved just as unenjoyable as Lucilla feared it would be. Queuing with trays for sandwiches and coffee; and then sitting on orange plastic chairs at a Formica table, hemmed in by irritable families with fractious children, punky youths in pornographic T-shirts, and muscular truck drivers, all seemingly content to wrap themselves around mind-boggling platefuls of fish and chips, evilly coloured trifles, and cups of tea.

After lunch, Pandora and Lucilla had changed places; Pandora had made herself comfortable on the back seat and fallen instantly asleep. She had been asleep ever since, which meant that she had missed the dramatic crossing of the Border, the clearing of the sky, and the miraculous excitement of actually coming home.

They drove through a small country town. "Where's this?" Jeff asked.

"Kirkthornton."

The pavements were crammed with Saturday-afternoon shoppers, the municipal gardens bright with dahlias. Old men sat on benches enjoying the kindly warmth. Children licked ice-creams. A bridge curved high over a tumbling river. A man fished. The road led on up the hill. Pandora, bundled in mink, was curled up like a child, her head supported by Jeff's jacket rolled into a pillow. A lock of bright hair fell across her face, her lashes lay black on her jutting cheek-bones.

"Do you think I should wake her up?"

"Up to you."

This had been her pattern, her routine, all through the long journey from Palma, through Spain and France. Spurts of immense energy, activity, conversation, much laughter, and sudden impetuous suggestions.

We really should see that cathedral. It's only ten kilometers out of our way.

Look at that delicious river. Why don't we stop for a moment and have a skinny-dip? There's no one to see.

You know, we've just passed the most enchanting café. Let's turn round and go back and have a drink.

But the drink would spin out into a long and leisurely lunch, with Pandora falling into conversation with any person who happened to be within earshot. Another bottle of wine. Coffee and cognac. And then . . . out. Sleep. She could catnap anywhere, and though this was sometimes embarrassing, it meant, at least, that she stopped talking, and Lucilla and Jeff had learned to be grateful for these respites. Without them Lucilla was not certain whether they would have survived the passage. Travelling with Pandora was a little like travelling with an ebullient child, or a dog—entertaining and companionable but as well quite dauntingly draining.

The Mercedes crested the slope. At the summit, the countryside opened and the views were magnificent. Beeches, fields, scattered farms, grazing sheep, the river far below them, the far-away hills bloomy and purple as ripe plums.

"If I don't wake her now she'll still be asleep when we get home. It's only about ten minutes away."

"Then wake her."

Lucilla stretched out her arm, laid her hand on the soft fur of Pandora's shoulder and gave her a little shake.

"Pandora."

"Um."

"Pandora." Another shake. "Wake up. We're almost there. We're almost home."

"What?" Pandora's eyes fluttered open. They stared blankly, disorientated, confused. She closed them again, yawned, stirred, stretched. "What a lovely sleep. Where are we?"

"Heading for Caple Bridge. Almost home."

"Almost home? Almost at Croy?"

"Sit up and you'll see. You've missed the best bit of the drive, snoring away on the back seat."

"I wasn't snoring. I never snore." But after a bit she made an effort and did sit up, pushing her hair out of her eyes, gathering her furs around her as though chilled. She yawned again, stared from the window. Blinked. Her eyes brightened. "But . . . we're nearly *there!*"

"I told you."

"You should have woken me hours ago. And the rain's gone. It's all sunshiny. And the green. I'd forgotten such greenness. What a welcome. 'Caledonia, stern and wild, fit nurse for a poetic child.' Who wrote that? Some stupid old fool. It's not stern and wild, it's just utterly beautiful. How perfectly sweet of it to be looking so lovely." She groped for her bag, her comb; tidied her hair. A mirror, some lipstick. A generous splash of Poison. "I must smell good for Archie."

"Don't forget about his leg. Don't expect him to come running to sweep you up in his arms. If he sweeps you up in his arms, he'll probably fall flat on his back."

"As if I'd suggest such a thing." She looked at her tiny diamond watch. "We're early. We said we'd be there at five and it's not four o'clock yet."

"We've made fantastic time."

"Dear Jeff." Pandora gave his shoulder an appreciative thump, as though she were patting a dog. "What a clever driver."

Now they were running downhill. At the bottom of the incline, they took the steep hump of Caple Bridge, turned left, and were at the start of the glen. Pandora leaned forward in her seat. "But it's amazing. Absolutely nothing seems to have changed. Some people called Miller used to live in that cottage. They were terribly old. He'd been a shepherd. They must be dead by now. They used to keep bees and sell jars of heather honey. Oh dear, I'm getting so fraught, I think I might have to stop for a pee. No, of course I don't want to. Just imagination." She gave Jeff another thump on his shoulder. "Jeff, you're doing your silent act again. Can't you think up one small word of appreciation?"

"Sure," he grinned. "It's great."

"It's more than that. It's *our* country now. The Balmerinos of Croy. Really heart-stirring, like a roll of drums. And we're coming home. We should be wearing feathers in our bonnets, and there should be a piper playing somewhere. Why didn't you think of that, Lucilla? Why didn't you arrange it? After twenty years, surely it's the least you could have done for me."

Lucilla laughed. "I'm sorry."

Now the river once more ran alongside the road, its banks verdant with green rushes, the pastures on the other side grazed by peaceful herds of Friesian cows. Harvested fields were carpets of gold in the sunlight. The Mercedes swept around the curve of the road and the village of Strathcroy came into view. Lucilla saw the cluster of grey stone houses, smoke rising straight from chimney-pots, the tower of the church, the pleasing groups of ancient and shady beeches and oaks. Jeff slowed down to a prudent speed and they passed the War Memorial, the small Episcopal church, and were into the long, straight main street.

"The supermarket's new." Pandora sounded quite accusing.

"I know. It's run by people called Ishak. They're Pakistanis. Now, Jeff, it's here . . . turn right . . . up through the gates. . . ."

"But the park's gone! It's not parkland any more. It's all ploughed up."

"Pandora, you knew that happened. Dad wrote and told you."

"I suppose I forgot. But it does look strange."

Up the back drive. The hill reared ahead of them, the tumbling waters of the Pennyburn splashed and tumbled down under the little stone bridge. Then the avenue . . .

"We're here," said Lucilla, and leaned across Jeff to put the heel of her hand on the horn.

At Croy, Lucilla's family filled in the long waiting hours of the afternoon. Isobel was upstairs seeing to the final details of the visitors' bedrooms, checking clean towels and arranging flowers for dressing-tables and mantelpieces. Hamish had decided to take the dogs for a walk, disappeared after lunch and had not been seen since. And Archie, Lord Balmerino, was in the dining-room laying the table for dinner.

He had been finally forced into doing this. Waiting for anything or anybody was not his strong point, and as the day wore on, he had become increasingly restless, impatient, and anxious. He hated the thought of his loved ones belting up the murderous miles of the motorway, and his imagination had no difficulty at all in presenting hideously detailed pictures of pile-ups, mangled metal, and dead bodies. He had spent much time looking at his watch, going to the window at the faintest sound of a car engine, and was patently unable to settle for a moment. Isobel had suggested that he mow the croquet lawn but he had turned this down because he wanted to be certain of being on the spot when the car actually drew up in front of the house. Retreating to his study, he had sat down with *The Scotsman* but could not concentrate either on the news or the crossword. He tossed the paper aside and started prowling again.

At last Isobel, who had enough to do without her husband getting under her feet, lost her patience.

"Archie, if you can't sit still, then make yourself useful. You can lay the table for dinner. The clean mats and the napkins are on the sideboard." And she had gone upstairs quite crossly, and left him to it.

Not that he minded laying tables. In the old days, Harris used to perform the task, so there could be nothing unmanly about it. And when the American paying guests stayed, laying the table for dinner was always Archie's job, and he got certain pleasure from doing it with military thoroughness, knives and forks precisely aligned, and napkins folded into mitres.

The wineglasses looked slightly dusty, so he had found a tea-towel and was engaged in giving them a bit of a polish when he heard the car coming up the hill. His heart lurched. He looked at the clock, which told him four o'clock. Too early surely. He set down the glass and the cloth. It could not be. . . .

The blast of the car horn, a long continuous blare, tore the quiet afternoon and his own uncertainty into shreds.

Lucilla's traditional signal.

He could not move fast, but he moved as fast as he could. Down the length of the dining-room, through the door.

"Isobel!"

The front door stood open. He was crossing the hall as the car appeared, a thundering great Mercedes scattering gravel beneath its wheels.

"Isobel! They're here."

He got to the door but no farther. Pandora was quicker than he, out of the car almost before it had drawn to a halt, running across the gravel towards him. Pandora with that same bright hair flying all over the place and those same long spindly legs.

"Archie!"

She wore a fur coat that reached almost to her ankles but that did not stop her bounding two at a time up the steps, and if he could no longer lift her off her feet and whirl her around the way he used to when she was a child, there was nothing the matter with his arms, and his arms were ready and waiting for her.

Isobel . . . dear, uncomplicated, hospitable, unchanging Isobel . . . had allocated Pandora the best spare bedroom. This was in the front of the house, with tall sash windows facing south down the hill and over the glen and the river. It was furnished much as Pandora remembered it in her mother's day. Twin brass bedsteads, high off the ground, each wide as a small double bed. A faded carpet patterned with roses and an ornate dressing-table with many small drawers and a swing-mirror.

The old curtains, however, were gone, and heavy cream linen draperies hung in their place. The refurbishment had probably been planned with all the paying guests in mind. They would scarcely appreciate threadbare chintz with sun-rotted linings. For them as well, the adjoining dressing-room had been converted into a bathroom. Not that it looked very different, because Isobel had simply installed a bath and a basin and a lavatory, and left the rugs, the laden bookshelves, and the comfortable armchair where they were.

Pandora was meant to be unpacking. "Unpack and make yourself comfortable," Isobel had told her. She and Jeff, between them, had humped all Pandora's luggage upstairs. (Archie, of course, could not hump luggage on account of his leg. Pandora decided not to think about Archie. His grey hairs had shocked her, and she had never seen a man so thin.) "Have a bath if you want. There's gallons of hot water. Then come down and have a drink. We'll eat about eight o'clock."

But that was fifteen minutes ago and Pandora had got no farther than carrying her dressing-case into the bathroom and putting a few bottles out on the marble wash-stand. Her pills and potions, her Poison, bath-oil, creams and cleansers. Later she would have a bath. Not now.

Now, she still had to convince herself that she was really home. Back at Croy. But it was difficult because in this room she did not feel as though she belonged. She was a guest come to stay, a bird of passage. Abandoning her bottles, she went back to the bedroom, to the window, to lean out with her elbows on the sill, to gaze at the oft-remembered view and be quite, quite certain that it was not all a dream. This took some time. But what had happened to her own room, the room that had been Pandora's since babyhood? She decided to go and have a nose-around.

She went out of the room, went to the top of the stairs, paused. From the direction of the kitchen came cheerful domestic sounds and muted voices. Lucilla and Isobel busy with preparations for dinner and probably talking about Pandora. They were bound to talk. It did not matter; she did not mind. She crossed the landing and opened the door of what had been her parents' room, and was now Archie and Isobel's. She saw the huge double bed, the chaise longue at the foot of it with a sweater of Isobel's flung down, a pair of shoes, carelessly discarded. She saw the family photographs, the silver and crystal on the dressing-table, bedside books. There was the smell of face-powder and eau-de-cologne. Sweet and innocent scents. She closed the door and went on down the passage. She found the room that had been Archie's, swept and garnished with Jeff's backpack and his jacket set down in the middle of the carpet. The next room . . . Lucilla. Still filled with all the cherished flotsam of a schoolgirl . . . posters thumbtacked to the walls, china ornaments, a tape player, a guitar with a broken string.

And finally her own room. Her old room. Perhaps Hamish slept here? She had not yet met Hamish. Cautiously she turned the knob and pushed the door open. Not Hamish. Not anybody. Empty of any personal possession. New furniture, new curtains. No trace of Pandora.

What had they done with her books, her records, clothes, diaries, photographs . . . her *life*? All probably swept upstairs to some attic when the room was stripped and emptied, repainted, re-wallpapered, and given that beautiful new, blue, fitted carpet.

It was as though Pandora had ceased to exist, was already a ghost.

There was no point in asking why, because it was patently obvious. Croy belonged to Archie and Isobel, and to keep the place going as a viable proposition, every room must be put to good use. And Pandora had given up any claim to it by the simple act of going away and never coming back.

Standing there, she thought of those last miserable weeks when she had been beyond herself with an unhappiness that she was not allowed to talk about. Misery had made her cruel, and she was cruel to the two people she loved most in the world; snapping at her father, ignoring her mother, sulking for days on end and generally making their lives a misery.

In this room, she had spent hours lying face downwards on her bed with her record player churning out, over and over again, the saddest songs she knew. Matt Monro telling some female to "Walk Away." And Judy Garland tearing her guts out with "The Man That Got Away."

> *The road gets tougher,*
> *It's lonelier and rougher,*
> *With hope you burn up,*
> *Tomorrow he will turn up . . .*

Voices.
Darling, do come and eat some lunch.
I don't want any lunch.
I wish you'd tell me what's troubling you.
I just want to be left alone. It wouldn't be any good telling you. You'd never *understand. . . .*

She saw again her mother's face, confused and dreadfully hurt. And was ashamed. At eighteen, I should have known better. I thought that I was adult and sophisticated, but the truth was that I knew less about life than a child. And it took me too long to find out.

Too long, and too late. All over. She closed the door and went back to her unpacking.

Dinner was over. They had sat, the six of them, around the candle-lit table, and eaten their way through Isobel's lovingly prepared celebratory meal. If she had not exactly killed a fatted calf, she had gone to great pains to produce a suitable feast. Cold soup, roast pheasant, *crème brûlé,* and a splendid Stilton, all washed down by the best wine that Archie could bring up from his father's depleted cellar.

Now it was nearly ten o'clock, and Isobel, with Pandora in attendance, was in the kitchen dealing with the last of the washing-up—the pots and pans, the ivory-handled knives and vegetable dishes too large to fit into the dishwasher. Pandora was meant to be helping, but after drying up a knife or two and putting three saucepans into the wrong cupboard, she had laid aside the tea-towel, made herself a mug of Nescafé, and sat down to drink it.

Conversation during dinner had been non-stop, for there was much to hear and much to tell. The adventure of Lucilla and Jeff's bus journey down through France from Paris; their Bohemian sojourn in Ibiza; and at last the bliss of Majorca and the Casa Rosa. Isobel's mouth had watered, hearing Lucilla's description of the garden there.

"Oh, I would love to see it."

"You should come. Lie in the sun and do nothing."

Archie laughed at this. "Isobel lie in the sun and do nothing? You must be mad. Before you could blink, she'd be bottoms up in the flower-beds, tearing at weeds."

"I haven't got any weeds," said Pandora.

And then, home news. Pandora was avid for every scrap of gossip. The latest on Vi, the Airds, the Gillocks, Willy Snoddy. Did Archie still hear from Harris and Mrs. Harris? She listened with some dismay to the saga of Edie Findhorn and her cousin Lottie.

"Heavens! That ghoul. Don't say she's come back into our lives. I'm glad you warned me. I shall take pains to cross the road if I see her coming."

She was told about the Ishak family, exiled from Malawi and arriving in Strathcroy with scarcely a penny between them.

". . . but they had some relations in Glasgow who'd already managed to do quite well for themselves, and with a bit of financial help from them, they managed to take over Mrs. McTaggart's newsagent's shop. You wouldn't recognize the place. It's a proper supermarket. We didn't think they'd last, but we were all mistaken. They're as industrious as ants, never seem to close their shop, and business booms. As well, we like them. They're all so helpful and kind."

And so on to the Balmerinos' slightly grander neighbours, which meant anybody living within a radius of twenty miles: the Buchanan-Wrights, the Ferguson-Crombies, the new people who had come to live at Ardnamoy; whose daughter had married; whose unlikely son had become a money-broker in the City and was coining millions.

No detail was unimportant. The only topic that was never brought up, as though by tacit agreement, was Pandora and what she had been doing with herself for the past twenty-one years.

She did not mind. She was back at Croy and for the moment that was all that mattered. The wayward years faded into unreality, like a life that had happened to another person, and surrounded by family she was happy to consign them to oblivion.

Sitting at the kitchen table, she sipped coffee and watched Isobel at the sink, scouring the roasting pan. Isobel wore red rubber gloves and a blue-and-white apron tied over her tidy dress, and it occurred to Pandora that she was an exceptional woman, peacefully labouring away and quite unresentful of the fact that the rest of her family had taken themselves off, and she was left to clear up the detritus of the meal by herself.

For, after dinner, the others had all dispersed. Archie, excusing himself, had gone down to his workshop. Hamish, with the promise of financial reward, had agreed to take advantage of the long evening light and mow the croquet lawn. He had gone to do this with good grace, and Pandora was much impressed. What she did not realize was how impressed Hamish had been by her. An aunt to stay was not an exciting prospect. Hamish had visions of a Vi-type person with grey hair and laced-up shoes, and had received the shock of his life when he was introduced to Pandora. A stunner. Like a film star. Over his pheasant, he entertained fantasies of showing her off to the other seniors in his class at Templehall. Perhaps Dad would bring her over to watch some match or other. Hamish's stock with schoolmates would go sky-high. He wondered if she liked rugger.

"Isobel, I do love Hamish."

"I'm quite keen on him myself. I just hope he doesn't grow too enormous."

"He's going to be divinely handsome." She took another mouthful of coffee. "Do you like Jeff?"

Jeff, predictably sated by two weeks of female company and unaccustomed gracious living, had wheeled Lucilla down to the Strathcroy Arms for a restoring jar of Foster's lager downed in comfortably masculine surroundings.

"He seems really nice."

"Terribly kind. And all through that long drive, he never once lost his patience. A bit laconic, though. I suppose all Australians are strong and silent. I wouldn't really know. Never met any others."

"Do you think Lucilla's in love with him?"

"No, I don't think so. They're just . . . that awful phrase . . . very good friends. Besides, she's terribly young. You don't want to start thinking about permanent relationships when you're only nineteen."

"You mean marriage."

"No, darling. I don't mean marriage."

Isobel fell silent. Pandora decided that she had, perhaps, said the wrong thing and cast about for a more amusing and less touchy topic. "Isobel, I know who you haven't told me about. Dermot Honeycombe and Terence. Are they still running the antique shop?"

"Oh dear." Isobel turned from the sink. "Didn't Archie tell you in one of his letters? So sad. Terence died. About five years ago."

"I don't believe it. What did poor Dermot do? Find himself another nice young man?"

"No, never. He was heart-broken, but faithful. We all thought he might leave Strathcroy, but he stayed; all by himself. Still running the antique shop, still living in their little cottage. Every now and then he asks Archie and me over for a meal, and gives us tiny helpings of fright-fully dainty food with amusing sauces. Archie always comes home starv-ing and has to be given soup or cornflakes before he goes to bed."

"Poor Dermot. I must go and see him."

"He'd love that. He's always asking after you."

"I can buy some trinket from him to give Katy Steynton for her birthday. We haven't talked about that either. The dance, I mean." Isobel, finished at last, pulled off her rubber gloves, laid them on the draining-board, and came to sit down with her sister-in-law. "Are we going to be a huge house party?"

"No. Just us. No Hamish because he'll be back at school. And some sad American Katy met in London and took pity on. Verena hasn't got space for him, so he's coming here."

"Goodness! How nice. A man for me. Why is he sad?"

"His wife's just died."

"Oh dear, I hope he's not too gloomy. Where's he going to sleep?"

"In your old bedroom."

Which settled that question. "And what about the night of the party? Where are we having dinner?"

"Here, I think. We could ask the Airds to join us, and Vi. They're coming for lunch tomorrow; I thought I'd speak to Virginia then."

"You never said."

"What, that they're coming for lunch? Well, I've told you now. That's why Hamish is cutting the croquet lawn."

"Lovely afternoon entertainment, all laid on. What are you going to wear for the dance? Have you got a new dress?"

"No. I've run out of money. I had to buy Hamish five new pairs of shoes for school. . . ."

"But, Isobel, you *must* have a new dress. We'll go and find one for you. Where shall we go? To Relkirk. We'll have a day out . . ."

"Pandora, I told you . . . I really can't afford it."

"Oh, darling, the least I can do is stand you a little gift." The back door opened and Hamish appeared, having finished his mowing just before darkness fell, and once again in his usual state of ravenous hun-ger. "We'll talk about it later."

Hamish collected his snack. A bowl of Weetabix, a glass of milk, a handful of chocolate biscuits. Pandora finished her coffee, set down the mug. She yawned. "I think I must go to bed. I'm bushed." She got to her feet. "Good night, Hamish."

She did not attempt to kiss him and Hamish was torn between relief and disappointment.

"Will I find Archie in his workshop? I'll just pop down and have a word." She stooped and kissed Isobel. "And good night to you, darling. Heaven to be here. Delicious dinner. See you all in the morning."

*　*　*

In the basement, Archie, absorbed and concentrated, worked by a strong bulb with a wide shade that threw a bright circle onto his work-bench. Painting the carving of Katy and her dog was both tricky and fiddly. The muted check of the skirt, the texture of the sweater, the subtle, varying streaks of colour in the hair, each presented a challenge and took all his dexterity to accomplish.

He laid down one sable brush and took up another, then heard Pandora approach. Her step was unmistakable, descending the stone stair that led down from the kitchens, as was the sharp tap of her high heels down the ill-lighted stone-flagged passage. He paused in his work to look up and saw the door open and Pandora's head come around the edge of it.

"Am I interrupting?"

"No."

"Goodness, it's gloomy. I couldn't find the light switch. Like a dungeon. But I must say, you're quite cosy in here." She found a chair and sat beside him. "What are you doing?"

"Painting."

"I can see that. What a charming little statue. Where did you get it?"

He told her, not without pride. "I made it."

"You made it? Archie, you are brilliant. I never knew you were so handy."

"It's for Katy's birthday. It's her. With her dog."

"What a lovely idea. You didn't used to be able to make things. It was always Pa who glued our toys together and mended broken china. Did you go to classes or something?"

"I suppose I did. After I was wounded . . ." He corrected himself. "After my leg was shot off and when I was finally discharged from hospital, I got sent to Headley Court. That's the Forces rehabilitation centre for chaps who've been disabled. Dismembered in some way. That's where they fit the artificial limbs. Legs, arms, hands, feet. Anything that you are missing is supplied for you. Within, of course, reason. And then they give you months of bloody hell until you've learned to use it properly."

"It doesn't sound very nice."

"It was all right. And there was always some poor bugger worse off than yourself."

"But you were alive. You weren't dead."

"True."

"Is it very horrible, having a tin leg?"

"Better than none at all, which seems to be the alternative."

"I never heard how it happened."

"Better not."

"Was it a nightmare?"

"All violence is a nightmare."

Forbidden ground. She backed off. "I'm sorry . . . go on telling me."

"Well . . . once I . . ." He had lost the thread of what he had been saying. He took off his spectacles, rubbed his eyes with his fingers. "Once . . . I was more or less ambulant, they taught me how to use a treadle jigsaw. Occupational therapy and good exercise for the leg. And from that, it sort of snowballed. . . ."

It was all right. The dangerous moment was safely over. If Archie did not want to talk about Northern Ireland, then Pandora did not want to hear.

"Do you mend things, like Pa used to?"

"Yes."

"And that dear little figure. How do you start to make something like that? Where do you begin?"

"You start with a block of wood."

"What kind of wood?"

"For this one, I used beech. Beech from Croy, a windblown branch from years back. I squared it off into a block with the chainsaw. Then I made two drawings from the photograph, a front view and a side view. Then I transferred the front elevation onto the face of the block, and the side elevation onto the side of the block. Are you with me?"

"All the way."

"Then I cut it out on the band-saw."

"What's a band-saw?"

He pointed. "That's the band-saw. It's electrically operated and lethally sharp, so don't start fiddling."

"I wasn't going to. What do you do then?"

"Start carving. Whittling."

"What with?"

"Wood-carver's chisels. A penknife."

"I'm amazed. Is this the first you've done?"

"By no means, but this was more difficult because of the composition. The girl sitting and the dog. That was quite difficult. Before, they've been standing figures. Soldiers mostly, in various regimental uniforms. I get the details of the uniforms from a book of plates I found up in Pa's library. It was that book that gave me the idea. They make quite good wedding presents if the bridegroom happens to be in the Army."

"Have you got any to show me?"

"Yes. There's one here." He pulled himself out of his chair, went to a cupboard, took out a box. "I didn't actually give this one away because I wasn't quite satisfied with it, so I made another. But it'll give you an idea. . . ."

Pandora took the figure of the soldier from him and turned it in her hands. It was a replica of an officer in the Black Watch, every detail perfect—from brogues, to kilt, to the red hackle in his khaki bonnet. She thought it perfect and was filled with wordless admiration for Archie's unsuspected talent, his precision, his undeniable artistry.

Also incredulous. "Do you mean to say you *give* these away? Archie, you're dotty. They're beautiful. Unique. Visitors from overseas would snap up just such a souvenir. Have you ever tried selling them?"

"No." He seemed quite surprised at the idea.

"Have you ever thought of it?"

"No."

She knew a burst of sisterly irritation. "You are hopeless. You always were a laid-back old stick, but this is ridiculous. There's Isobel slaving away, trying to keep everything going by having strings of Americans to stay, and you could be churning these things out and making a fortune."

"I doubt that. Anyway, it's not a case of churning. They take a lot of time."

"Well, get someone to help you. Get two people to help you. Start a little home industry."

"I haven't the space down here."

"What about the stables? They're empty. Or one of the barns?"

"It would mean reconstruction, equipping, electricity laid on, safety regulations, fire precautions."

"So?"

"So it would cost money. Which is a commodity pretty thin on the ground."

"Could you get a grant?"

"Grants, as well, are thin on the ground just now."

"You could *try* for one. Oh, don't be so hopeless, Archie. Be a bit more enterprising. I think it's the most wonderful idea."

"Pandora, you were always full of wonderful ideas." He took the soldier from her and laid him back in his box. "But you're right about Isobel. I do what I can to help, but I know she's got far too much on her plate. Before Northern Ireland, I thought about trying to get some sort of a job . . . as a factor, or something. I don't know who'd have employed me but I didn't want to leave Croy, and it seemed the only sort of work I could do. . . ." His voice, ruminating, trailed to silence.

"But now you've learned a new trade. All this. Hidden talents have sprung to life. All you need is a little enterprise and a lot of determination."

"And a lot of money."

"Archie"—she spoke quite crossly—"whether you have one leg or two, you can't just shed responsibility."

"Are you speaking from experience?"

"*Touché.*" Pandora laughed and shook her head. "No. I'm the last to preach. Just talking off the top of my head." Abruptly, she abandoned the argument, yawned and stretched, reached upwards, spreading her fingers. "I'm tired. I came to say good night. I'm going to bed."

"I hope you have sweet dreams."

"What about you?"

"I want to get this finished and done with. Then, every spare moment I have I shall be able to spend with you."

"Dear man." On her feet, she stooped to kiss him. "I'm glad I came home."

"Me too."

She went to the door, opened it, hesitated, and turned back. "Archie?"

"What is it?"

"I've often wondered. Did you get that letter I sent you in Berlin?"

"Yes."

"You never replied."

"By the time I'd decided what I was going to say, you'd gone to America and it was too late."

"Did you tell Isobel?"

"No."

"Did you . . . speak to anybody?"

"No."

"I see." She smiled. "The Airds are coming for lunch tomorrow."

"I know. I asked them."

"Good night, Archie."

"Good night."

The evening slipped into night. The house settled as the momentum of another busy day wound itself down. Hamish watched television for a bit and then made his way upstairs. Isobel, in the kitchen, laid the table for breakfast—the last chore of the day—and then let the dogs out for their last sniff around the dark garden, alert for scents of marauding rabbit. Lights were turned off, and she too headed for bed. Later still Jeff and Lucilla returned from the village. They let themselves in through the back door. Archie heard their voices above him in the hall. And then silence.

Past midnight, and he was finally finished. Another day and the enamel would be dry. He tidied up, put lids on small paint-pots, cleaned his brushes, turned off the light and closed the door. Slowly he made his way down the shadowy passage and up the stairs to do his nightly rounds, which he called putting the house to bed. He checked locks on doors and snibs on windows, fire-guards and electrical plugs. In the kitchen, he found the dogs asleep. He filled a tumbler with water and drank it. Finally he trod up the stairs.

But he did not go immediately to his own bedroom. Instead he walked down the passage and saw the shaft of light, still burning, beneath the door of Lucilla's room. He tapped and opened the door and found her in bed, reading by lamplight.

"Lucilla."

She looked up, marked her page and laid her book aside. "I thought you'd gone to bed hours ago."

"No. I've been working." He came to sit on the edge of her bed. "Did you have a good evening?"

"Yes, it was fun. Toddy Buchanan in his usual good form."

"I wanted to say good night, and I wanted to say thank you."

"What for?"

"Coming home. Bringing Pandora."

His hand lay on her eiderdown. She laid her own on top of it. Isobel's night-gowns were white lawn trimmed with lace, but Lucilla slept in a green T-shirt with "Save the Rain Forests" printed across the chest. Her long dark hair was spread like silk on her pillow, and he was filled with love for her.

"You're not disappointed?" she asked him.

"Why should I be disappointed?"

"Often when you've looked forward to something for years, you feel a bit let down when it actually happens."

"I don't feel let down."

"She is beautiful."

"But dreadfully thin, don't you think?"

"I know. There's nothing of her. But she's so hyper that she burns everything up."

"What do you mean?"

"Just that. She sleeps a lot, but when she's awake she's charging on every cylinder. Super-charging, I would say. Being with her all the time is really quite exhausting. And then she passes out as though sleep is the only thing that's going to top up her batteries."

"She was always like that. Mrs. Harris used to say, 'That Pandora. Either up in the clouds or doon in the midden.' "

"Manic-depressive."

"Surely not as bad as that."

"Tending that way."

He frowned. And then asked the question that had been niggling around at the back of his mind all evening. "You don't think she's on drugs?"

"Oh, Dad."

He immediately wished that he had not mentioned his fears. "I only ask you because I imagine you know more about these things than I do."

"She's certainly not a junkie. But perhaps she does take something to bubble her along. A lot of people do."

"But she's not addicted?"

"Oh, Dad, I don't know. But worrying about Pandora isn't going to do any good. You've just got to accept her for what she is. The person she's turned into. Have fun with her. Lots of laughs."

"In Majorca . . . do you think she's happy?"

"She seems to be. And why not? A heavenly house, a garden, a pool, lots of money . . ."

"Does she have friends?"

"She has Seraphina and Mario, who take care of her . . ."

"That wasn't what I meant."

"I know. No, we didn't meet her friends, so I don't know if she has any or not. We didn't really meet anybody. Except one man. He was there the day we arrived, but after that we never saw him again."

"I thought she would have a resident lover."

"I think probably he was her lover and the reason he didn't come back was because we were there." He said nothing to this, and Lucilla smiled. "It's a different world out there, Dad."

"I know that. I know."

She put her arms around his neck and pulled him down and kissed him. She said, "You mustn't worry."

"I won't."

"Good night, Dad."

"Good night, my darling. God bless you."

5

Sunday the Eleventh

S UNDAY MORNING. OVERCAST, VERY STILL, very quiet, hushed with the weekly inertia of a Scottish Sabbath. It had rained during the night, leaving puddles by the roadside and gardens dripping with moisture. In Strathcroy, cottages slumbered, curtains stayed drawn. Slowly the occupants stirred, rose, opened doors, lit fires, made cups of tea. Plumes of peat-smoke rose, straight, from chimney-pots. Dogs were walked, hedges clipped, cars washed. Mr. Ishak opened up his shop for the sale of morning rolls, milk, cigarettes, Sunday newspapers, and any other commodity that a family might need to get through the empty day. From the tower of the Presbyterian church, the bell tolled.

At Croy, Hamish and Jeff were downstairs before anyone else and, between them, cooked their own breakfast. Bacon and eggs, sausages and tomatoes, racks of fresh toast, marmalade and honey, all washed down with large cups of very strong tea. Isobel, descending later, found their dirty breakfast dishes stacked by the sink, and a note from Hamish.

Dear Mum. Jeff and me have taken the dogs up to the loch. He wants to see it. Back about twelve-thirty. In time for beef.

Isobel made coffee, sat and drank it, thought about peeling potatoes, making a pudding. She wondered if there was enough cream for a fool. Lucilla appeared, and finally Archie, wearing his good tweed suit because it was his day to read the lesson in church. Neither his wife nor his daughter offered to accompany him. With ten people for lunch, they had more than enough to do.

Pandora slept the morning through and did not put in an appearance until a quarter past twelve, by which time all the hard work in the kitchen had been accomplished. It was instantly clear, however, that she had not been idle, but busy titivating: painting her nails, washing her hair, doing her face, splashing herself in Poison. She wore a jersey dress patterned in diamonds of brilliant colour; it was so fine and supple and elegant that it had to be Italian. Discovering Lucilla in the library, she swore that she had slept the night through, but seemed perfectly happy to sink into the depths of an armchair and gratefully accept the offer of a glass of sherry.

At Pennyburn, Vi sat up in her bed, drank her early morning tea, and planned her day. She should perhaps go to church. There was plenty to pray for. She thought about this and then decided against it. Instead, self-indulgence. She would stay where she was, conserving her energy. She'd finish her current book and then, after a late breakfast, sit at her desk to deal with overdue bills, pension funds, and that incomprehensible demand from the Inland Revenue. For lunch, she had been invited to Croy. Edmund, with Virginia and Henry, would pick her up and drive her on up the hill.

She thought about this with more disquiet than delight and gazed from the window and assessed the mood of the weather: rain all night but now damp and still and muggy. Perhaps later it would cheer up. It was the sort of day, in more ways than one, that needed to be cheered up. For comfort, she decided, she would wear her grey wool. For courage, the new Hermès scarf.

*   *   *

At Balnaid, Virginia went in search of Henry.

"Henry, come and change."

He was on the floor of his playroom, constructing Space Lego, and resented the interruption. "Why do I have to change?"

"Because we're going out for lunch and you can't go looking like that."

"Why can't I?"

"Because your jeans are dirty, and your T-shirt's dirty, and your shoes are dirty, and you are dirty."

"Do I have to *dress up?*"

"No, but you have to put on a clean T-shirt and a clean pair of jeans and a clean pair of sneakers."

"What about socks?"

"Clean socks."

He sighed, hard done by. "Do I have to put my Space Lego away?"

"No, of course you don't have to. Leave it where it is. Just come, or Daddy'll start getting impatient."

She led him, lagging, to his bedroom, then sat on his bed and stripped off his T-shirt.

"Will there be any other children there?"

"Hamish."

"He won't want to play with me."

"Henry, you're such a ninny about Hamish. If you don't behave like a ninny, he'll like playing with you. Take off your jeans and your trainers."

"Who's going to be there?"

"Us. And Vi. And the Balmerinos. And Lucilla because she's come home from France. And her friend. He's called Jeff. And Pandora."

"Who's Pandora?"

"Archie's sister."

"Do I know her?"

"No."

"Do you know her?"

"No."

"Does Daddy know her?"

"Yes. He knew her when she was a little girl. Vi knows her too."

"Why don't you know her?"

"Because she's been living abroad for a long, long time. She lived in America. This is the first time she's come back to Croy."

"Does Alexa know her?"

"No. Alexa was only a tiny baby when she went to America."

"Does Pandora know your gramps and grandma at Leesport?"

"No. They live in Long Island, and Pandora lived in California. That's right over the other side of the United States."

"Does Edie know her?"

"Yes. Edie knew her when she was a little girl as well."

"What does she look like?"

"Heavens above, Henry, I've never met her, so I can't tell you. But you know that picture in the dining-room at Croy? Of the pretty girl? Well, that's Pandora when she was young."

"I hope she's still pretty."

"You like pretty ladies."

"Well, I certainly don't like ugly ones." He screwed up his face, making a monster grimace. "Like that Lottie Carstairs."

Despite herself, Virginia had to laugh. "You know something, Henry Aird, you'll be the death of me. Now, hand me your hairbrush, and then go and wash your hands."

From the foot of the stairs, Edmund called, "Virginia."

"We're on our way!"

He waited for them, dressed for the occasion in grey flannels, a country shirt, a club tie, a blue cashmere pullover, his chestnut-polished Gucci loafers.

"We should go."

Reaching his side, Virginia kissed him. "You're looking handsome, Mr. Aird. Did you know that?"

"You're not looking so gruesome yourself. Come along, Henry."

They got into the BMW and drove. They stopped for a moment in the village, where Edmund went into Mr. Ishak's and emerged with the bulky wodge of the Sunday newspapers. Then on to Pennyburn.

Vi heard them coming and was ready for them, on the point of locking her front door. Edmund leaned over to open the door for her and she got in beside him. Henry thought she was looking very smart and told her so.

"Thank you, Henry. This is the pretty scarf your mother brought me from London."

"I know. She brought me a cricket bat and a ball."

"You showed me."

"And she brought Edie a cardigan. Edie loves it. She says she's keeping it for best. It's sort of pinky blue."

"Lilac," Virginia told him.

"Lilac." He said the word over to himself because it had a pleasant sound. Lilac.

The powerful car left Pennyburn behind and sped on up the hill.

Arriving, they found Archie's old Land Rover parked in front of the house. As Edmund drew up alongside and the Aird family disgorged from his car, Archie appeared at the open front door, come to greet them. They made their way up the steps.

"Well, here you are."

"You're looking very formal, Archie," Edmund told him. "I hope I'm not underdressed."

"Been to church. Read the lesson. I thought about changing into something a little less stuffy, but now you've arrived, so there isn't time. So you'll have to take me as I am. Vi. Virginia. Lovely to see you. Hello, Henry, good morning. How are you? Hamish is in his bedroom getting cleaned up. He's set his Scalectrix Road Race up on the floor of the playroom. If you want to go and have a look at it . . ."

The suggestion, casually made, was adroit and caught Henry's attention, as Archie knew it would. He had no qualms about his son, who had been warned that Henry was coming, and had it made clear to him that he was to behave towards this small guest in a hospitable fashion.

As for Henry, it took only an instant to remember that Hamish, provided there was nobody else around to claim his attention, could be quite good company, even though Henry was four years younger. And Henry hadn't got a Scalectrix Road Race. It was one of the things he was thinking of putting on his Christmas list.

His face brightened. He said "All right" and set off at a fast clip, up the stairs, leaving the grown-ups to their own devices.

"Brilliant," murmured Vi, as though to herself. And then: "What sort of a congregation did you have this morning?"

"Sixteen, including the rector."

"I should have been there to swell the throng. Now I'm going to have a conscience for the rest of the day. . . ."

"But it's not all bad news. The Bishop's come up trumps and ferreted out some obscure trust, set up years ago. He thinks he can wangle a sizy sum from that, which would pay off the balance of the bill for the electrics. . . ."

"Wouldn't that be splendid?"

"But," said Virginia, "I thought that was why we had the church sale. . . ."

"We can always divert funds. . . ."

Edmund made no comment. It had been a long morning, deliberately filled with small and insignificant tasks that nevertheless had been demanding his attention for some weeks. Letters written, accounts paid, a query from his chartered accountant clarified and answered. Now, he found himself dealing with a growing impatience. At the far end of the wide hallway, the double doors of the library stood invitingly open. He looked forward to a gin and tonic, but Archie, Virginia, and Vi, loosely grouped at the foot of the stairs, had become absorbed by churchly problems. In these Edmund had little interest, having always taken great pains never to become involved.

". . . of course, we do need new kneelers."

"Vi, paying for the coke for the boiler is more urgent than new kneelers. . . ."

The real reason for their coming to Croy appeared to have been forgotten by his wife and his mother. Stifling his irritation, Edmund listened. And then did not listen. Another sound caught his attention. From the library came the tap of high heels. He looked up, over the top of Virginia's head. Saw Pandora emerge.

Watching, assessing the situation, she paused, framed by the open doorway. Across the long space that divided them, her eyes met Edmund's. He forgot his impatience, and found words flowing through his brain as though he had been abruptly asked to produce some sort of a report and was frantically searching for, and then abandoning, suitable adjectives with which to state his case: older, thinner, attenuated, elegant, *mondaine*, amoral, experienced. Beautiful.

Pandora. He would have seen her, recognized her, known her anywhere in the world. Still those wide and watchful eyes, the curving mouth with its provocative mole at the corner of her upper lip. The features, the bone structure were untouched by the years that had passed, the profusion of chestnut hair still youthful.

He felt his face freeze. He could not smile. As though he were a gun dog pointing at a bird, the quality of his stillness, his silence, obscurely reached the others. Their attention wandered, their voices died away. Vi turned her head.

"Pandora."

The church and its affairs were abandoned. She moved away from Virginia's side, across the polished parquet, her back view erect, her arms outflung, her bulging leather handbag dangling by its strap from her elbow. "Pandora, my dearest child. What a joy. What a delight to see you again."

". . . but Isobel, you can't possibly have us all for dinner. That's far too many."

"No. If my counting's right, we'll be eleven. That's only one more than we are now."

"Has Verena not lumbered you with people to stay?"

"Just one man . . ."

Pandora chipped in. "He's known as 'The Sad American,' because Isobel can't remember what his name is."

"Poor chap," said Archie from the head of the table. "Sounds as though he's doomed before he's even arrived."

"Why is he sad?" asked Edmund, reaching for his glass of lager. At Croy, wine was never served at luncheon. This was not for any reason of parsimony but because of a family tradition, going back to Archie's parents, and his grandparents before that. Archie upheld it because he thought it a sound idea. Wine was apt to render guests both garrulous and comatose, and Sunday afternoons, in his opinion, were made to be spent in useful outdoor activities, not snoozing over the newspapers in some armchair.

"He probably isn't sad at all," Isobel told him. "He's probably a very sensible, cheerful fellow, but he's been recently widowed and he's taken a couple of months off, and has come over here for a bit of a break."

"Does Verena know him?"

"No. But Katy does. She felt sorry for him and asked Verena to send him an invitation."

Pandora said, "I do hope he's not dreadfully solemn and sincere. You know how they can be. Show them round a sewage works and they'll go into polite ecstasies. Swearing it was all very very interesting, and wanting to know when it was built."

Archie laughed. "Pandora, how many times have you shown an American around a sewage works?"

"Oh, darling, never. Just giving a tiny example."

They sat around the dining-room table. The tender roast beef, perfectly cooked and pink in the middle, had been appreciatively consumed, along with fresh beans, fresh peas, roasted potatoes, horseradish sauce, and dark gravy delicately laced with red wine. Now they were onto Isobel's blackberry fool and hot-syrup tart, drooling with fresh cream.

Out of doors, the day, like a fickle woman, had ceased to sulk and decided, for no obvious reason, to brighten up. A wind had risen, freshening the air. From time to time, lozenges of sunlight fell upon the polished table, sparking from silver and cut-glass tumblers.

"Well, if we all come to dinner," Virginia firmly led the conversation back to essentials, "you must let me help. I'll make a starter, or a pudding, or something."

"That would help," Isobel admitted. "Because the whole of the day before I'm going to be up at Corriehill helping Verena with the flowers."

"But that's my birthday." Vi was quite indignant. "That's the day of my picnic."

"I know, Vi, and I'm sorry, but for the first time in years I'm not going to be able to be there."

"Well, I hope nobody else is going to back out. You haven't got to go and do flowers, have you, Virginia?"

"No. I've just been asked to lend my biggest flowerpots and vases. But I can take them all up to Corriehill on Wednesday."

"When does Alexa arrive?" Lucilla asked.

"On Thursday morning. She and Noel are going to drive overnight. Noel can't get off before that. And of course they're bringing Alexa's dog. So *they'll* all be at the picnic, Vi."

"I shall have to start writing this all down," said Vi, "otherwise I shall lose count and produce far too much food or too little." She leaned forward and looked down the length of the table to catch Henry's eye. Henry's expression was gloomy. He did not like people talking about Vi's birthday when they all knew he would not be there. She said, "I shall post two huge slices of birthday cake over to Templehall. One for Henry and one for Hamish."

"Well, make sure it's a cake that doesn't go squishy." Hamish scraped the last spoonful of syrup tart out of his plate. "Mum sent me a cake once and all the cream oozed out through the parcel, and Matron was livid. She threw the whole lot into the Sick Bay dustbin."

"Mean old Matron," said Pandora sympathetically.

"She's a cow. Mum, can I have some more?"

"Yes, but hand it round first."

Hamish got to his feet and went to do this, a dish in either hand.

Lucilla said, *"We* have a small problem." Everybody looked at her, interested to know what it was but not particularly concerned. "Jeff hasn't got anything to wear. To the dance, I mean."

Eyes were now turned on Jeff, who had sat through the meal without taking much part in any conversation. He looked faintly abashed and seemed pleased for the diversion of Hamish arriving at his side with the offer of second helpings of pudding. He turned to dip the spoon into what remained of the blackberry fool.

He said, "When I left Australia I never thought I'd be asked to a formal do. Besides, there wasn't space in my backpack for a dinner jacket."

They all considered the problem.

Archie said, "I'd lend you mine, only I'm wearing it myself."

"Dad, yours wouldn't even go round Jeff."

"He could always hire one. There are places in Relkirk . . ."

"Oh, Dad, they're dreadfully expensive."

Archie was humbled. "Sorry. I wouldn't know."

Across the table, Edmund eyed the young Australian. "You're about the same size as I am. I'll lend you something if you like."

Violet, hearing this, was taken aback. Sitting next to her son, she turned her head to look at him. He seemed unaware of her piercing regard, and his profile, composed and unsmiling, gave nothing away. Trying to analyze her un-motherly astonishment, she realized that the truth of it was that she had never expected Edmund to come up with such a kindly and impetuous suggestion.

But why? He was her son, the child of Geordie. She knew that where important issues were concerned he would never be anything but gener-ous—with both time and money—concerned and considerate. Violet could turn to him—and had done so many times—knowing that he would go to endless trouble to sort out a problem or help her make a decision.

But little things . . . little things were different, the small gesture, the tender word, the trivial gift that had cost nothing but a few pence and a moment of time, but was significant because of the thought be-hind it. Her eyes strayed across the table to Virginia and the heavy gold bracelet that she wore around her wrist. Edmund had given her that bracelet—and Violet did not like to think what it had cost—like a tube of glue, to patch up their disagreement. But how much better had they not quarrelled in the first place, and so spared themselves weeks of unhappiness.

And now he was offering Lucilla's Jeff a favour. It would be no hardship to him, but the offer had been made so spontaneously that Violet was reminded of Geordie. Which should have filled her with pleasure, but instead left her sad because she could not remember when she had last looked at Edmund and recognized any characteristic inherited from his gentle father.

As for Jeff, he seemed as disconcerted as she was herself.

"No. I couldn't impose. I'll just hire something."

"No skin off my nose. I've some spare things at Balnaid. You can try them on, see how they fit."

"But won't you need them yourself?"

"I shall be decked out, like the man on a shortbread tin, in my kilt."

Lucilla, however, was deeply grateful. "You are a saint, Edmund. What a relief. Now all I have to do is find some garment to wear."

"Isobel and I are going shopping for finery in Relkirk," Pandora told her. "Why don't you come too?"

Lucilla, surprising everybody, said, "I'd love to." But their surprise was short-lived. "There's a wonderful market in Relkirk, and a stall stuffed with glorious nineteen-thirties tat. I'm sure I'll find something there."

"Yes," said her mother. "I am quite sure that you will."

"Dad, you are a brute! You've bashed me right into the rhododendrons."

"I wanted to get you out of the way."

"You didn't need to hit me *quite* so far."

"Yes, I did. You're far too cunning a player to be left jostling around the hoop. Now, Virginia, you need to come just *here.*"

"Which blade of grass did you have in mind?"

Isobel's lunch party, with coffee drunk, had amicably dispersed. The boys, abandoning Scalectrix, had gone to play in Hamish's tree-house, and swing on his trapeze. Isobel had taken Vi to look at her border . . . not as grand or imposing as it had been in the old days but still something that she was always quite proud to show off and have admired. Archie, Virginia, Lucilla, and Jeff had decided to take advantage of Hamish's labour and were engaged in a needle contest of croquet. Edmund and Pandora sat in the old swing-seat at the top of the grassy bank and watched them.

It had turned into a pleasant and blowy afternoon. Clouds, in layers, drifted across the sky, but there were wide patches of blue in between, and when the sun shone, it became very warm. Despite this, Pandora, on her way out into the garden, had collected from the cloakroom an old shooting jacket of Archie's, oiled khaki and lined with hairy tweed. Bundled in this garment, she sat with her legs tucked up beneath her. From time to time Edmund gave a push with his foot to set the old seat swinging. It needed to be oiled and made a hideous squeaking sound.

A wail from the middle of the rhododendrons. "I can't find the beastly ball and I've been scratched by a bramble."

"In a moment," Edmund observed, "family fur is going to fly."

"It always did. It's a lethal game."

They fell silent, rocking gently to and fro. Virginia took a swipe at her ball, which rolled placidly at least four yards beyond the spot that Archie had been indicating.

"Oh, sorry, Archie."

"You hit it too hard."

"Nothing," said Edmund, "is so obvious as the obvious remark."

Pandora made no comment. Squeak, squeak went the swing.

They watched in silence while Jeff played his shot. She said, "Do you hate me, Edmund?"

"No."

"But you despise me? Think little of me?"

"Why should I do that?"

"Because I made such a mess of everything. Running off with another woman's husband, and he old enough to be my father. Leaving no word of explanation, breaking my parents' hearts, never coming back. Sending waves of shock and horror to reverberate around the county."

"Is that what happened?"

"You know it is."

"I wasn't here at the time."

"Of course. You were in London."

"I never found out why you went flying off."

"I was miserable. I didn't know what to do with my life. Archie had gone and was married to Isobel, and I missed him. There didn't seem to be any way to turn. And then along came a little diversion, and it all seemed frightfully glamorous and grown-up. Exciting. My ego needed a boost and that's what he provided."

"How did you meet him?"

"Oh, at some party. He had a horse-faced wife called Gloria, but she scarpered pretty sharpish as soon as she saw the way the wind was blowing. Went off to Marbella and never returned. Which was another reason for eloping to California."

Lucilla, with bits of leaf in her hair, emerged from the rhododendrons and rejoined the game. "Who's been through the hoop, and who hasn't?"

The seat, gradually, stopped swinging. Edmund gave another push and started it up again. Squeak, squeak.

Pandora said, "Are you happy?"

"Yes."

"I don't think I was ever happy."

"I'm sorry."

"I liked being rich but I wasn't happy. I was homesick and I missed the dogs. Do you know what he was called, the man I ran away with?"

"I don't think I was ever told."

"Harold Hogg. Can you imagine anybody eloping with a man called Harold Hogg? After our divorce, the first thing I did was to change my name back to Blair. So I didn't keep his name, but I did keep much of his money. So lucky, to be divorced in California."

Edmund said nothing.

"And then, when it was all over, and after I'd changed my name back to Blair, do you know what I did?"

"I have no idea."

"I went to New York. I'd never been there before, didn't know anybody. But I checked in at the classiest hotel I could find and then I walked down Fifth Avenue and knew that anything I wanted I could buy. For myself. And then I didn't buy anything. That's a sort of happiness, isn't it, Edmund? Knowing that you can buy anything you want and then discovering that you don't want it."

"Are you happy now?"

"I'm home."

"Why did you come back?"

"Oh, I don't know. Reasons. Lucilla and Jeff were there to drive me. I wanted to see Archie again. And then, of course, the irresistible lure of Verena Steynton's party."

"I have a feeling that Verena Steynton has little to do with it."

"Perhaps. But it's a nice excuse."

"You never came home when your parents died."

"That was unforgivable, wasn't it?"

"You said it, Pandora. I didn't."

"I wasn't brave enough. I didn't have the nerve. I couldn't face funerals, graves, condolences. I couldn't face anybody. And death is so final, just as youth is so sweet. I couldn't bear to accept that it was all over."

"Are you happy in Majorca?"

"I'm home there too. All these years, and the Casa Rosa is the first home I've actually owned."

"Are you going back?"

All the time they had been talking, they had not looked at each other. Instead, they had watched, with patent intent, the croquet players. But now he turned to face her, and her head came around, and her remarkable eyes, fringed with thick black lashes, stared into his own. Perhaps it was because she had become so painfully thin, but they seemed to Edmund more enormous and lustrous than they had ever been.

She said, "Why do you ask?"

"I don't know."

"Perhaps I don't know either."

She laid her head back on the faded striped cushions and returned her attention to the croquet. Their conversation, such as it was, appeared to be over. Edmund watched his wife. She stood in the middle of the verdant lawn, leaning on her mallet, while Jeff lined up to play a tricky shot. She wore a checked shirt and a short blue denim skirt, and her legs were long and bare and brown, and her canvas sneakers very white. Fit, slender, bursting into laughter at Jeff's abortive attempt to get his ball through the hoop, she radiated the sort of vitality that Edmund associated with glossy magazine advertisements for sports clothes, Rolex watches, or sun-tan oil.

Virginia. My love, he told himself. My life. But for some reason the words were empty as incantations that were never going to work, and he found himself racked by despair. Pandora had fallen silent. He could not imagine what she thought about. He turned to look at her and it took him no time at all to realize that she was fast asleep.

So much for his entertaining company. He was torn between chagrin and amusement, and this healthy reaction to her perfidy served to fend off for the time being the deadly sensation that he had come to the end of his rope.

6

Monday the Twelfth

MONDAY WAS ONE OF EDIE'S MORNINGS for helping Virginia at Balnaid, and Virginia was grateful for this arrangement. She had never relished Mondays, with the weekend over and Edmund gone from her once more, dressed in his city suit, and leaving the house at eight o'clock in order to get into Edinburgh and his office before the worst of the rush-hour traffic. His departure left an emptiness, a flatness, a sense of anticlimax, and it was always something of an effort to get down to day-to-day living again and cope with all the tedious demands of simply keeping the house going. But hearing the bang of the back door as Edie let herself in always made everything, instantly, a bit more bearable. To know that Edie was *there*. There was someone to talk to, someone to laugh with, someone to dust the library and vacuum the dog hairs off the hall carpet. The clatter from the kitchen was comforting. Edie, dealing with the breakfast dishes, loading the washing-machine with a weekend's worth of dirty clothes, and talking to the dogs.

"Now don't you get under my feet, or you'll get your tail trodden on."

Virginia, in her bedroom, changed the sheets on their big double bed, her regular Monday-morning chore. Henry had gone shopping. His mother had given him five pounds, and he had set off to the village, to visit Mrs. Ishak, and buy the allotted amount of sweets, chocolates, and biscuits that he was permitted to take to Templehall in his tuck-box, and which were meant to last him for a full term. He had never before been given so much money to spend on sweets, and the novelty of this, for the moment, had diverted his attention from the fact that tomorrow he was leaving home for the first time. Eight years old and going away. Not for ever, it was true. But Virginia knew that when she saw him again, he would already be a different Henry because he would have seen things and done things and learned things totally dissociated from his mother's life. Tomorrow, he was going. The first day of ten years of regular separation from his parents and his home. The beginning of his growing up. Up and away from her.

She folded pillowcases. They had only another twenty-four hours. All through the weekend she had resolutely put his inevitable departure out of her mind; pretended to herself that Tuesday was never going to happen. Henry, she guessed, had done the same, and her heart bled for his innocence. Last night, saying good night to him, she had steeled herself for a dam-burst of tears and lamentations. *The weekend's over. Our last weekend. I don't want to go to school. I don't want to leave you.* But Henry had simply told her that he'd quite liked playing with Hamish, he'd hung by one leg from Hamish's trapeze; and then, worn out by the day's activity, had fallen almost instantly asleep.

She spread crisp, ironed sheets. I'll get through today and make it fun for him, she told herself. And then, somehow, I'll get through tomorrow. After Edmund has taken Henry, after they've driven away and I can't hear the car any longer, I'll think of something diverting or industrious to do. I'll go and see Dermot Honeycombe and spend hours looking for a present for Katy Steynton. A bit of china, or an antique lamp, or perhaps a little piece of Georgian silver. I'll write a long letter to Gramps and Grandma. I'll turn out the linen cupboard, sew buttons on Edmund's shirts. . . . And then Edmund will come home, and after that the worst will be over, and I can start counting the days until Henry's first weekend home.

She bundled up the soiled sheets and flung them out onto the landing, then put away a few random clothes and shoes, straightened a cushion. The telephone rang. She went to answer it, sitting on the edge of the freshly made bed.

"Balnaid."

"Virginia." It was Edmund. At a quarter past nine in the morning?

"Are you in the office?"

"Yes. Got here ten minutes ago. Virginia. Look. I have to go to New York."

She was not particularly perturbed. His flying off to New York was a regular occurrence.

"When?"

"Now. Today. I'm catching the first shuttle down to London. Flying out of Heathrow this afternoon."

"But—"

"I'll be back at Balnaid on Friday in time for the party. Probably about six in the evening. Earlier if I can make it."

"You mean . . ." It was difficult actually to take in what he was telling her. "You mean you'll be away all week?"

"That's right."

"But . . . packing . . . clothes . . ." Which was ridiculous because she knew that he kept a duplicate wardrobe in the flat at Moray Place, with suits, shirts, and underclothes suitable for any capital and any climate.

"I'll do that here."

"But . . ." The implication, the truth of what he was saying, broke at last. *He can't do this to me.* The bedroom window was open and the air that flowed through it was not cold, but Virginia, hunched over the telephone, shivered. She saw the knuckles of her hand, clenched around the receiver, grow white. "Tomorrow," she said. "Tuesday. You're taking Henry to Templehall."

"I can't do that."

"You promised."

"I have to go to New York."

"Somebody else can go. Not you."

"There's nobody else who can. There's a panic on and it has to be me."

"But you *promised*. You said that you would take Henry. I told you that it was the one thing that I wouldn't do. It was my condition and you accepted it."

"I know, and I'm sorry. But what's happened is beyond my control."

"Send somebody else to New York. You're the boss. Send some underling."

"It's because I am who I am that I have to go."

"You are who you are!" She heard her own voice, shrill with scathing. "Edmund Aird. You think of nobody but yourself and nothing but your hateful job. Sanford Cubben. I hate Sanford Cubben. I realize I come fairly low on your priority list, but I thought Henry rated a little higher. You didn't only promise me, you promised Henry. Does that mean nothing to you?"

"I didn't promise anything. I just said that I'd take him, and now I can't."

"I call that a commitment. If you made such a commitment in business, you'd kill yourself to see it through."

"Virginia, be reasonable."

"I will *not* be reasonable! I will not sit here and listen to you and be told to be reasonable. And I will not deliver my child to a boarding-school that I never wanted him to go to in the first place. It's like asking me to take one of the dogs to the vet to be put down. I won't do it!"

By now she was sounding like a fishwife, and did not care. But Edmund's voice remained, as always, infuriatingly cool and dispassionate.

"In that case, I suggest that you call Isobel Balmerino and ask her to take Henry. She's driving Hamish. She'll have plenty of space for Henry."

"If you think I'm going to palm Henry off onto Isobel—"

"Then you'll have to take him yourself."

"You're a bastard, Edmund. You know that, don't you? You're behaving like a selfish bastard."

"Where is Henry? I'd like to speak to him before I go."

"He's not here," Virginia told him with a certain malicious satisfaction. "He's buying his sweets from Mrs. Ishak."

"Well, when he comes home, tell him to ring me at the office."

"You can ring him yourself." And on this biting exit line, she slammed down the receiver and put an end to the miserable exchange.

Her raised voice had penetrated to the kitchen.

"What was that all about?" Edie asked, turning from the sink as Virginia stormed in with a face like thunder, and arms filled with rumpled linen, to stride across the kitchen towards the open door of the utility room and hurl her burden in the general direction of the washing-machine.

"Is something wrong?"

"Everything." Virginia pulled out a chair and sat, her arms folded and her expression mutinous. "That was Edmund, and he's going to New York *today. Now.* And he's going to be away a week, and he promised me . . . he *promised,* Edie . . . that he'd drive Henry to school to-morrow. I told him that it was the one thing I *wouldn't* do. I've hated the *whole* idea of Templehall from the very beginning, and the only reason I finally relented was because Edmund *promised* that he would take Henry tomorrow.''

Edie knew a nasty temper when she saw one. She said reasonably, ''Well, I suppose if you're an important business man these things are bound to happen.''

''Only to Edmund. Other men manage their lives without being so bloody selfish.''

''You don't want to take Henry yourself?''

''No, I do not. It's the last thing in the world I want to do. It's inhuman of Edmund to expect it of me.''

Edie, wringing out her dishcloth, considered the problem.

''Could you not ask Lady Balmerino to take him with Hamish?''

Virginia did not let on that Edmund had already made this sensible suggestion and got an earful for his pains.

''I don't know.'' She thought about it. ''I suppose I could,'' she admitted sulkily.

''Isobel's very understanding. And she's been through it herself.''

''No, she hasn't.'' It was obvious to Edie that she could say nothing right. ''Hamish was *never* like Henry. You could send Hamish to the moon, and all he'd worry about would be when he was going to get his next meal.''

''That's true enough. But if I were you, I'd have a word with Isobel. It's no good working yourself up into a state if there's nothing to be done. What—''

''I know, Edie. What can't be cured must be endured.''

''That's true enough,'' said Edie placidly, and went to get the kettle and fill it with water. A cup of tea seemed to be in order. There was nothing, in times of stress, like a good hot cup of tea.

They were drinking the tea when Henry returned, his carrier-bag bulging with goodies.

''Mummy, look what I got!'' He emptied the contents out onto the kitchen table. ''Look, Edie. Mars Bars, and Smarties, and Cadbury's Dairy Milk, and some Jellybabies, and Jaffa Cakes, and Chocolate Digestives, and treacle toffees, and Rolos; and Mrs. Ishak gave me a lollipop for going away. I didn't have to pay for the lollipop, so can I eat it now?''

Edie surveyed his loot. ''I hope you're not going to eat that lot all at once, otherwise you won't have a tooth left in your head.''

''No.'' He was already unwrapping the lollipop. ''It's got to last a long time.''

By now Virginia's fury had simmered down. She put her arm around Henry and said, in consciously cheerful tones, ''Daddy phoned.''

He licked. ''What about?''

''He has to go to America. Today. He's flying from London this afternoon. So he won't be able to take you to school tomorrow. But I thought I'd . . ."

Henry stopped licking. His pleasure flowed from his face, and he turned enormous, apprehensive eyes upon his mother.

She hesitated, and then started up again. ". . . I thought I'd ring Isobel and ask if she'd take you with Hamish . . ."

She got no further. His reaction to the news was even worse than she had dreaded. A wail of dismay and floods of instant tears . . .

"I don't want Isobel to take me. . . ."

"Henry . . ."

He jerked himself out of her embrace and flung his lollipop onto the floor. "I'm not going to go with Isobel and Hamish. I want my mother or my father to take me. How would you like it, if you were me and . . ."

"Henry . . ."

". . . you had to go away with people who weren't your own mother and father? I think you are being very unkind to me. . . ."

"I'll take you."

"And Hamish will be horrid and not talk because he's a senior. It's not *fair!*"

Furiously weeping, he turned and fled for the door.

"Henry, I'll *take* you. . . ."

But he was gone, his footsteps stamping up the stairs to the sanctuary of his bedroom. Virginia, gritting her teeth, closed her eyes and wished that she could close her ears as well. It came. The deadly slam of his bedroom door. Then silence.

She opened her eyes and met Edie's across the table. Edie gave a long sigh. She said, "Oh, dearie dear."

"So much for *that* bright idea."

"Poor wee soul. He's upset."

Virginia leaned her elbow on the table and ran a hand through her hair. All at once the situation had become more than she felt able to cope with.

She said, "This is the very last thing I wanted to happen." She knew, and Edie knew, that Henry's tantrums, though rare, left him vulnerable and touchy for hours. "I wanted this to be a *good* day, and not miserable. Our last day together. And now Henry's going to spend it bursting into tears and blaming me for everything. As if things weren't bad enough. Damn Edmund. What am I going to do, Edie?"

"How would it be," said Edie, "if I just came back this afternoon and took Henry off your hands? He's never so bad with me. Have you finished his packing yet? Well, I could finish his packing and do any wee bits that need to be done, and he can just be around the place and have time to collect himself. A quiet day, that's what he needs."

"Oh, Edie." Virginia was filled with grateful love. *"Would* you do that?"

"No trouble. Mind, I'll have to go home and see to Lottie, give her her dinner, but I'll be here again by two."

"Can't Lottie see to her own dinner?"

"Well, she can, but she makes such a hash of it, burns the pans, and leaves my kitchen in a midden, I'm better to do it myself."

Virginia was repentant. "Oh, Edie. You do so much. I'm sorry I shouted at you."

"Good thing I was here for you to shout at." She heaved herself onto her swollen legs. "Now, I must get on, or we won't get the baby bathed at this rate. Up you go and have a word with Henry. Tell him he can spend the afternoon with me, and what I'd really like would be one of his bonny pictures."

Virginia found Henry, as she knew she would, under his duvet with Moo.

She said, "I'm sorry, Henry."

Racked with huge sobs, he did not reply. She sat on his bed. "It was a silly thing to suggest. Daddy suggested it to me, and I thought it was silly then. I had no right even to mention it to you. Of course you won't go with Isobel. You'll come with me. I'll take you in the car."

She waited. After a bit, Henry rolled onto his back. His face was swollen and tear-stained, but he seemed to have stopped crying.

He said, "I don't mind so much about Hamish, but I want *you.*"

"I'll be there. Perhaps we'll take Hamish with *us.* It would be kind. Save Isobel a journey."

He sniffed. "All right."

"Edie's coming back after lunch. She said she'd like to spend the afternoon with you. She wants you to draw her a picture."

"Have you packed my felt pens?"

"Not yet."

He put out his arms, and she gathered him up and held him close, rocking him gently, pressing kisses onto the top of his head. After a bit, he emerged from beneath his duvet, and they found a handkerchief and he blew his nose.

It was not until then that she remembered Edmund's message. "Daddy wanted you to ring him up. He's at the office. You know the number."

Henry went to her bedroom to do this, but Virginia had left it too late and Edmund had already gone.

The playroom was peaceful and warm. Sun poured through the wide windows, and the breeze sent the wistaria branches tapping at the panes. Henry sat at the big table in the middle of the room, and drew. Edie was on the window-seat, stitching the last of the name-tapes onto his new socks. In the mornings, for work, Edie wore her oldest clothes and a pinafore, but this afternoon she had turned up looking quite smart, and had put on her new lilac cardigan. Henry felt flattered, because he knew that she was keeping it for best. As soon as she arrived, she had set up the ironing-board, and ironed the morning's load of washing, fresh from the line. This was now stacked, crisp and folded, on the other end of the table, and emanated a pleasant smell.

Henry laid down his felt pen and searched in his pen-box, making scrabbling sounds. He said, "Bother."

"What is it, pet?"

"I want a Biro. I've drawn people with balloons coming out of their mouths, and I want to write what they're saying."

"Look in Edie's bag. There's a pen in there."

Her bag was on the chair by the fireside. It was large, made of leather, and bulged with important things: her comb, her fat housekeeping purse, her Old Age Pension book, her Post Office Savings book, her rail-card, her bus pass. She didn't have a car, so she had to go everywhere by bus. Because of this she had a timetable, a little booklet, "Relkirkshire Bus Company." Henry, rooting for the pen, came upon this. It occurred to him, out of the blue, that it might be a sensible and useful thing to own. Edie probably had another at home.

He looked up at Edie. She was intent on her sewing, her white head bowed. He removed the booklet from her bag and slipped it into the pocket of his jeans. He found the Biro, closed her bag, and went back to his work.

Presently, Edie asked, "What would you like for your tea?"

He said, "Macaroni cheese."

Dermot Honeycombe's antique shop stood at the far end of the village street, beyond the main gates of Croy, and at the foot of a gentle slope that leaned between the road and the river. Once it had been the village smithy, and the cottage where Dermot lived, the blacksmith's house. Dermot's cottage was painfully picturesque. It had tubs of begonias at the door, latticed windows, and a thickly thatched roof. But the shop was much as it had always been, with walls of dark stone and blackened beams. Outside was a yard of cobbles where once the patient farm horses had stood, waiting to be shod, and here Dermot had set up his shop sign, an aged wooden cart, painted blue, with DERMOT HONEYCOMBE ANTIQUES emblazoned tastefully on its side. It was an eye-catching gimmick, and brought in much casual trade. It was also useful for tying dogs to. Virginia clipped the leads onto the spaniels' collars, and knotted the ends around one of the cartwheels. The dogs sat, looking reproachful.

"I shan't be long," she told them. They thumped their stumpy tails, and their eyes made her feel like a murderer, but she left them and went across the cobbles and in through the door of the old smithy. Here Dermot sat, in his paper-piled birdcage of an office. He was on the telephone but spied her through the glass, raised a hand, and then reached out to turn on a switch.

Within the shop, four dangling bulbs sprang to light, doing a little to alleviate the gloom, but not very much. The place bulged with every sort of junk. Chairs were piled on tables, on the tops of chests of drawers. Huge wardrobes towered. There were milk churns, jelly pans, stacks of unmatched china, brass fenders, corner cupboards, curtain rails, cushions, bundles of velvet, threadbare rugs. The smell was damp and musty, and Virginia knew a small frisson of anticipation. Visits to Dermot's were always something of a lottery because you never knew—and neither did Dermot—what you might, by chance, turn up.

She moved forward, edging her way between the tottering stacks of furniture, with the wary caution of a pot-holer. Already, she felt marginally more cheerful. Browsing was a comforting therapy, and Virginia allowed herself the self-indulgence of putting Edmund, the morning's traumas, and tomorrow, all out of her mind.

A present for Katy. Her eye wandered. She priced a chest of drawers, a wide-lapped chair. Searched for the silver mark on a battered spoon, poked through a box of old keys and brass doorknobs, turned the pages of a dignified old wreck of a book. Found a lustre cream jug, and wiped the dust from it, searching for chips or cracks. There were none.

She was joined by Dermot, finished with his telephone call.

"Hello, my dear."

"Dermot. Hello."

"Looking for something in particular?"

"A present for Katy Steynton." She held up the lustre jug. "This is sweet."

"It's a pet, isn't it? The Garden of Eden. I love that dark gentian blue." He was a rotund, smooth-faced man of mature years, but strangely ageless. His cheeks were pink, and his fluffy pale hair airy as dandelion down. He wore a faded green corduroy jacket, much adorned with drooping poachers' pockets, and had a red-spotted kerchief tied in a jaunty knot around his neck. "You're the second person I've had in today looking for something for Katy."

"Who else has been here?"

"Pandora Blair. Popped in this morning. Lovely to see her again. Couldn't believe it when she walked through the door. Just like old times. And after all these years!"

"We had lunch at Croy yesterday." Virginia thought about yesterday, and knew that it had been a good day, the sort they would all remember when they were old and there was nothing much left to do but reminisce. *It was the time when Pandora came home from Majorca, and*

Lucilla was there and some young Australian. Can't remember his name. And we played croquet. And Edmund and Pandora sat in the swing seat, and Pandora went to sleep, and we all teased Edmund for being such a boring companion. "That's the first time I'd met Pandora."

"Of *course*. Amazing. How the years fly by."

"What did she buy for Katy? I mustn't get the same."

"A lamp. Chinese porcelain, and I'd made the shade for it myself. White silk, lined in palest pink. Then we had a cup of coffee and caught up on all the news. She was ever so sad when I told her about Terence."

"I'm sure." Virginia was afraid that Dermot's eyes were about to swim with tears, and went on hurriedly, "Dermot, I think I'll have this jug. Katy can use it either for cream or flowers, yet it's pretty enough on its own."

"Don't think you could find anything nicer. But stay for a bit. Have a snoop around. . . ."

"I'd love to, but I'm taking the dogs for a walk. I'll pick the jug up on my way home, and write you a cheque for it then."

"Righty ho." He took the jug from her and led the devious way back towards the door. "Are you going to Vi's picnic on Thursday?"

"Yes. Alexa will be there too. She's bringing a friend up for the dance."

"Oh, lovely. Haven't seen Alexa for months. I'm going to see if I can get someone to mind the shop for me that day. If I can't, I'll shut it up. Wouldn't miss Vi's picnic for anything."

"I hope it's a good day."

They emerged and stepped out into the sunshine. The dogs, spying them, wheaked blissfully and leaped to their feet, tangling the leads. "How's Edmund?" asked Dermot.

"On his way to New York."

"I don't *believe* it! What a thing! I wouldn't have his job for all the tea in China."

"Don't waste your sympathy. He loves it."

She rescued the dogs, waved goodbye to Dermot, walked on, leaving the last straggling cottages of Strathcroy behind her. Another half mile and she had come to the bridge that spanned the river at the west end of the village. The bridge was ancient, steeply humpbacked, and once used by cattle-drovers. On the far side, a winding, tree-shaded lane followed the convolutions of the river, and led the way back to Balnaid.

On the crest of the bridge she paused to loosen the dogs and let them run free. They shot off at once, noses enticed by the smell of rabbits, to plunge into a thicket of bracken and brambles. Every now and then, as though to prove they were not wasting their time, they made hunting calls, or bounced high out of the tall bracken, with ears flying like furry wings.

Virginia let them go. They were Edmund's gun dogs, patiently

trained, intelligent and obedient. A single whistle and they would return
to her. The old bridge was a pleasant spot to loiter. The stone wall felt
warm in the sunshine, and she leaned her arms on this and gazed downwards at the flowing peat-brown water. Sometimes she and Henry
played Pooh-sticks from this bridge, flinging sticks upstream and then
racing back to watch for the first, the winning stick, to appear. Sometimes the sticks never did appear, having been caught up in some unseen
obstruction.

Like Edmund.

Alone, with only the river for company, she felt strong enough to
think about Edmund, by now probably winging his way over the Atlantic towards New York, drawn, as though by a magnet, away from his wife
and his son, just at a time when he was most needed at home. The
magnet was his work, and right now Virginia felt as jealous and resentful
and lonely as if he were gone to keep an assignation with a mistress.

Which was strange because she had never been jealous of other
women, never tortured herself with imaginings of infidelity during the
long periods when Edmund was away from her, in far-flung cities on the
other side of the world. Once, teasing, she had told him that she didn't
care what he did, provided she wasn't expected to watch. All that mattered was that he always came home. But today, she had slammed down
the telephone receiver and never said goodbye, and then forgotten, until
too late, to give Henry his father's message. Experiencing a twinge of
guilt, she gathered her hurt feelings about her. *It's his own fault. Let him
brood. Perhaps another time he'll*—

"Out for a walk, are you?"

The voice came from nowhere. Virginia thought, oh, God, let a few
seconds pass, and then slowly turned. Lottie stood only a few feet away.
She had come up the slope of the bridge from the village, the way that
Virginia had, soft-footed, unheard. Had she seen Virginia in the street,
watching from Edie's window, reached for her horrible beret, her green
cardigan, and followed? Had she been waiting while Virginia was with
Dermot, ducking out of sight and then dogging Virginia's footsteps,
always just out of earshot? The very idea was spooky. What did she want?
Why could she not leave people alone? And why, beyond Virginia's irritation, lurked, like a ghost, a sense of presentiment, a foreboding of fear?

Ridiculous. She pulled herself together. Imagination. It was only
Edie's cousin, avid for company. With some effort, Virginia put a
friendly expression on her face. "What are you doing here, Lottie?"

"Fresh air belongs to everybody, I always say. Looking at the water?"
She moved to Virginia's side, to lean over the wall as she had been
doing. But she was not as tall as Virginia and had to stand tiptoe, and
crane her neck. "Seen any fish?"

"I wasn't looking for fish."

"Been to Mr. Honeycombe's, haven't you? Lot of rubbish he's got in

there. Most of it only fit for a bonfire. But then, there's no accounting
for tastes. And as for what I'm doing, I'm out for a walk, same as you.
On your own, Edie tells me over dinner. Edmund gone to America."

"Just for a few days."

"That's not so nice. On business, is he?"

"He wouldn't go for any other reason."

"Oh, ho, ho, that's what you think. Saw Pandora Blair this morning.
Thin, isn't she? Like a scarecrow. And that hair! Looks like dyed to me.
Called out to her but she didn't see *me*. Had dark glasses on. Could have
had a good old chin-wag about the old days. I was up at Croy, you
know, resident housemaid. Old Lady Balmerino then. She was a lovely
lady. Felt sorry for her, with a daughter no better than she should be.
That was the time of the wedding. Lord and Lady Balmerino, but they
were Archie and Isobel then. There was a dance at Croy the evening of
the wedding. What a work. So many people staying you couldn't turn
round. Course, Mrs. Harris was cook, old Lady Balmerino didn't have to
cook. There were some fine goings-on, but no doubt you've been told."

"Yes," said Virginia, and tried to think of some way in which she
could escape this unwelcome flood of words.

"Scarcely out of school she was, Pandora, but she knew a thing or
two, I can tell you. Men. She'd eat them for breakfast, and leave them
chewed. A right wee whore."

She was smiling, her tones inconsequent and chatty, almost approving, so that the archaic word caught Virginia unawares and surprised her
into saying, quite sharply, "Lottie, I don't think you should say that
about Pandora."

"Oh, you *don't*?" Lottie was still smiling. "Not pleasant, is it, hearing
the truth? Nice Pandora's back, everybody is saying. But if I were you, I
wouldn't be too happy. Not with your husband. Not with her. Lovers
they were, Edmund and Pandora. That's why she's back, mark my
words. Come back for him. Eighteen years old, and Edmund a married
man and the father of a wee bairn, but that didn't stop them. That
didn't stop him, rutting in her own bed. Night of the wedding it was,
and everybody dancing. But *they* weren't dancing. Oh, no. They were up
the stair and thinking nobody noticed. But I noticed. Not much missed
me." Pink spots burned on Lottie's sallow cheeks, her boot-button eyes
were like a pair of nails, hammered into the sockets of her head. "I went
after them. Stood at the door. It was dark. I heard. Never heard anything like it. You didn't guess, did you? He's a cool fish, that Edmund.
Never let on. Never say a word. Just like the rest of them. They all knew.
Well, it was obvious, wasn't it? Edmund back in London and Pandora
sulking in her bedroom, face swollen with tears, wouldn't eat. And the
way she spoke to her mother! But, of course, they're all thick as thieves.
That's why Lady Balmerino gave me my notice. Didn't want *me* around.
I knew too much."

Still smiling. Hot with excitement. Mad. I must, Virginia told herself, keep very calm. She said, "Lottie, I think you are making all this up."

Lottie's demeanour, with quite startling suddenness, changed. "Oh, am I?" The smile was wiped from her face. She backed away from Virginia and stood, four-square, facing up to her as though they were about to engage in a contest of physical strength. "And why do you think your husband's suddenly taken himself off to America? You ask him when he comes home to you, and I'll doubt you'll enjoy his answer. I'm sorry for you, do you know that? Because he'll make a fool of you, same as he did his first wife, poor lady. There's no streak of decency in him."

And then, abruptly, it was over. Her venom spent, Lottie seemed to slump within herself. The colour seeped from her cheeks. She pursed her lips, brushed a scrap of lichen from the front of her cardigan, tucked a wisp of hair under her beret, patted it into place. Her expression became complacent, as though all were now well, and she was content to prink.

Virginia said, "You are lying."

Lottie tossed her head and gave a little laugh. "Ask any of them."

"You are lying."

"Say what you please. Sticks and stones may break my bones. . . ."

"I shall say nothing."

Lottie shrugged. "In that case, what's all the fuss about?"

"I shall say nothing and you are lying."

Her heart was banging in her chest, her knees trembling. But she turned her back on Lottie and began to walk away; walking steadily and without haste, knowing that Lottie watched, determined to give her no satisfaction. The worst was never looking back. Her scalp crawled with terrified apprehension, the fear that, at any moment, she would feel Lottie's weight leap upon her shoulders, dragging her to the ground with all the inhuman strength of a clawed monster from childhood nightmares.

This did not happen. She reached the far bank of the river, and felt a little safer. She remembered the dogs and pursed her lips to whistle for them, but her mouth and her lips were too dry for whistling, and she had to try again. A tiny piping sound, a pathetic effort, but Edmund's spaniels had had enough of abortive rabbiting, and almost immediately appeared, bounding through the bracken towards her, trailed with goose-grass and with twigs of thorny bramble entwined in their feathery fur.

She had never been so glad to see them, so grateful for their instant obedience. "Good dogs." She stopped to fondle them. "Good to come. Time to go home."

They ran ahead, down the lane. Leaving the bridge behind her, Virginia went after them, her pace still resolutely unhurried. She did not allow herself to look back until she reached the bend of the river, where the lane curved away beneath the trees. There, she stopped and turned. The bridge was still visible but there was no sign of Lottie.

She was gone. It was over. Virginia took a deep breath and let it all out in a whimpering sigh that was not far from panic. Then the panic took over, and, without shame, she bolted for home. Ran to Edie, to Henry, to the sanctuary of Balnaid.

Back to the beginning.
You are lying.
Two o'clock in the morning and Virginia was still awake, her eyes, scratchy with fatigue, wide open, staring out into the soft darkness. She had tossed and turned, been either too hot or too cold, fought with pillows lumpy with pummelling. From time to time, she got out of the bed, wandered about in her night-gown, fetched a glass of water, drank it, tried again to sleep.

It was no good.

On the far side of the bed, Edmund's side, Henry slumbered peacefully. Virginia, defiantly breaking one of Edmund's strictest rules, had taken her son to bed with her. Every now and then, as though for reassurance, she put out a hand to touch him, to feel his gentle breathing, his warmth through the flannel of his striped pyjamas. In the huge bed, he seemed small as a baby, scarcely alive.

She'd eat them for breakfast and leave them chewed. A right wee whore.

She could not get the appalling scene out of her mind. Lottie's words went on and on, round and round like some scratchy old gramophone record, worn with playing. Circles of torment, never ceasing, never coming to any sort of conclusion.

Lovers they were. Edmund a married man, and the father of a wee bairn.

Edmund and Pandora. If it was true, Virginia knew that she had never imagined nor suspected for a single instant. In her innocence, she had not watched for evidence, had read no inner meaning into Edmund's casual words, his easy demeanour. "Pandora's home," he had told her, pouring himself a drink and going to the refrigerator to search for ice. "We've been asked for lunch at Croy." And Virginia had said, "How nice," and gone on frying beefburgers for Henry's supper. Pandora was simply Archie's errant young sister, back from Majorca. And when the great reunion happened, she had paid little regard to the brotherly kiss Edmund had planted on Pandora's cheek, their laughter, and the understandable affection of this greeting. And as for the rest of the day, Virginia had been more interested in the croquet game than curious to know what it was that Edmund and Pandora, watching from the swing seat, were talking about.

And what did it matter what they talked about? Be sensible. So what if they had had a wild and impetuous affair and ended up in Pandora's bed? Pandora at eighteen must have been sensational, and Edmund at the height of his virility. This is today, and adultery is no longer called adultery but extra-marital sex. Besides, it was all a long time ago. Over twenty years. And Edmund had not been unfaithful to Virginia, but to his first wife, Caroline. And now Caroline was dead. So it didn't matter. There was nothing to agonize over. Nothing . . .

They all knew. All thick as thieves. Didn't want me around. I knew too much.

Who knew? Did Archie know? Did Isobel? Did Vi know? And Edie? Because if they knew, they would have been watching, fearing perhaps that it was all going to happen all over again. Watching Edmund and Pandora. Watching Virginia, their eyes filled with a pity that she had never seen. Did they worry for Virginia as they must have worried for Caroline? Did they talk amongst themselves, like conspirators, agreeing to keep the truth from Edmund's second wife? Because if they had, then Virginia had been betrayed, and by the very people she was closest to and most relied upon.

And why do you think your husband's suddenly taken himself off to America? He'll make a fool of you, same as he did his first wife, poor lady.

This was the worst. These were the most dreaded doubts. Edmund had gone. Had he really had to fly off like that, or was New York simply a trumped-up excuse to get away from Balnaid and Virginia and to give himself time to work out his problems? His problems being that he loved Pandora, had always loved her, and now she was back and as beautiful as ever, and Edmund was once more trapped in marriage with yet another woman.

Edmund was fifty, a vulnerable age for restlessness and mid-life crises. He was not a man for showing emotion, and most of the time Virginia had no idea what he was thinking about. Her own self-doubt grew to terrifying proportions. Perhaps this time he would cut his losses and run, leaving Virginia with her marriage and her life tumbling in ruins. Leaving her and Henry lost in the rubble of what she had once thought totally impregnable.

It did not bear thinking about. She rolled over, burying her face in her pillow, shutting out the ghastly prospect. She would not acknowledge it. Would not let it be true.

You are lying, Lottie.

This is where we came in. Back to the beginning.

7

Tuesday the Thirteenth

THE RAIN WAS CRUEL, RELENTLESS, and unwelcome. It had started before daybreak, and Virginia awoke to the sound of it, and had known a dreadful sinking of the heart. As if things weren't bad enough on this dreaded day, without the elements turning against her. Perhaps it would stop. But the gods were not on anybody's side and the downpour continued, monotonously streaming down from a charcoal-grey sky, right through the long morning and the early afternoon.

Now, it was half past four, and they were on their way to Templehall. Because she had the two boys with her, and all their clobber—trunks, tuck-boxes, duvets, rugger balls, and book-bags—Virginia had left her own little car in the garage, and instead drove Edmund's Subaru, a four-wheel-drive work-horse that he used when he went into rough country, or up the hill. She was not used to driving this vehicle, and its unfamiliarity and her own uncertainty only served to heighten the sense of doom and hopelessness that had dogged her for nearly twenty-four hours.

Conditions were miserable. What light there had been was already seeping from the sky, and she drove with headlights on and the windscreen wipers working full tilt. Tyres hissed on flooded patches of road, and oncoming cars and lorries sent up great waves of blinding mud. Visibility was almost nil, which was frustrating, because under normal conditions, the road that led from Relkirk to Templehall was an exceptionally scenic drive—through prosperous farmlands, alongside the banks of a wide and majestic river famous for its salmon, and past large estates, with distant glimpses of stately homes.

It would have eased the atmosphere had they been able to observe any of this. Remarking on beauty spots, pointing out some distant peak would have given Virginia something to talk about. As it was, she had tried engaging Hamish in lively conversation, hoping that this would divert Henry from his speechless misery, and that he might even join in. But Hamish was in a bad mood. Knowing that the freedom of summer holidays was over was bad enough, but worse was having to go back to school in the company of a new boy. A babe. That's what they called the little ones. The babes. Travelling with a babe was beneath Hamish's dignity, and he just prayed that none of his contemporaries would be around to witness his humiliating arrival. He was not going to be made responsible for Henry Aird, and had made this fact vociferously clear to his mother while she helped him lug his trunk down the stairs of Croy, and flattened, with a brush, his gruesome short haircut.

Accordingly, he had decided upon a course of non-communication, and had soon put a stop to Virginia's advances by answering her in a series of non-committal grunts. She got the message, and after that the three of them had lapsed into a stony and wordless silence.

Which made Virginia wish that she hadn't brought the wretched boy; had let Isobel drive her own sulky son. But without him there, Henry might well have succumbed to tears, sobbed throughout the journey and arrived at Templehall sodden with weeping and in no fit state to deal with the rigours of his new and daunting future.

The prospect she found almost unendurable. I am hating this, she told herself. It is even worse than I imagined it would be. It is inhuman, hellish, unnatural. And worse is to come, because the moment waits when I have to say goodbye to Henry and drive away, and leave him standing, alien and alone. I hate Templehall, and I hate the headmaster, and I could strangle Hamish Blair. I have never had to do anything in my life that I have hated so much. I am hating the rain, hating the entire educational system, hating Scotland, hating Edmund.

Hamish said, "There's a car behind us. It wants to get past."

"Well, it can bloody wait," Virginia told him, and Hamish was silenced.

An hour later, she was back on the same road, driving the empty vehicle in the opposite direction.

It was over. Henry was gone. She felt numb. Non-existent, as though the trauma of parting from him had robbed her of all identity. Just now, she would not think about Henry, because if she did she would weep, and the combination of tears, half-darkness, and relentless rain would most likely cause her to drive the Subaru off the road, or into the back of a ten-ton lorry. She imagined the crunch of metal, her own body flung like a broken doll to the side of the road, flashing lights, the howl of ambulances and police cars.

She would not think about Henry. That part of her life was over. But what was happening to her life? What was she doing here? Who was she? What was the reason for driving home to a house that stood dark and empty? She did not want to go home. She did not want to go back to Strathcroy. But where? Somewhere perfectly gorgeous, a million miles from Archie and Isobel and Edmund and Lottie and Pandora Blair. A place of sunlight and calmness and no responsibilities, where people would tell her she was marvellous, and she could be young again instead of about a hundred years old.

Leesport. That's it. She was driving to an airport to catch a jet to Kennedy, a limousine to Leesport. It wouldn't be raining there. It would be Long Island autumn weather, with blue skies and golden leaves and a crisp breeze blowing in over the Bay from the Atlantic. Leesport, unchanged. The wide streets, the crossroads, the hardware store and the drugstore, with the kids outside, wheeling about on their bicycles. Then, Harbor Road. Picket fences and shade trees and sprinklers out on lawns. The road sloping to the water, the yacht anchorage a coppice of masts. The gates of the country club, and then Grandma's house. And Grandma in the garden, pretending to rake leaves but in reality watching for the car, so that she could be out on the sidewalk the moment it drew up.

"Oh, honey, you're back." The soft, wrinkled cheek, the scent of White Linen. "It's been too long. Did you have a good journey? What a treat to see you!"

Indoors, and the other smells. Wood-smoke, sun oil, cedar, roses. Braided rugs and faded slip-covers. Cotton curtains blowing at open windows. And Grandpa coming in from the sundeck, with his glasses on top of his head and *The New York Times* under his arm. . . .

"Where's my sweetheart?"

Through the murky gloom, clusters of lights now shone ahead. Relkirk. Back to reality, and Virginia now realized that here she was going to have to stop for a little. She needed to go to the loo, freshen up. Find a bar, have a drink, be made to feel human again. She needed warmth and the syrupy comfort of Musak and low lights. No reason to hurry home because there was nobody there to hurry to. A sort of freedom, perhaps. Nobody to care how late she was, nobody to worry about what she was doing.

She drove into the old city. Cobbled streets were awash, rain shimmered in the street lights, pavements were crowded with shoppers and workers, booted, mackintoshed, carrying umbrellas and bags, all hurrying home to the comfort of their firesides and tea.

She made for the King's Hotel because it was familiar and she knew where to find the Ladies'. It was an old-fashioned edifice and in the middle of the town, and so had no car-park of its own. Instead, Virginia found a space on the opposite side of the road and parked the Subaru there, beneath a dripping tree. As she locked the door, a taxi drew up outside the hotel. A man got out, wearing a raincoat and a tweed hat. He paid the driver off, and, carrying a grip, went up the steps that led from the pavement to the revolving door. He disappeared. Virginia paused for traffic to pass, and then ran across the road and followed him inside.

The Ladies' was on the far side of the foyer, but the man had paused at the reception desk. He had taken off his hat and was shaking the rain from it.

"Yes?" The receptionist was a sulky-looking girl, with fat pink lips and frizzy straw-coloured hair.

"Good evening. I have a room booked. I called about a week ago, from London."

An American. His voice husky but lightly pitched. Something about it caught Virginia's attention, as though a hand had tugged at her sleeve. Half-way across the floor, she paused to glance at him. Saw a tall, broad-shouldered back view, dark hair streaked with grey.

"What name did you say?"

"I didn't, but it's Conrad Tucker."

"Oh, yes. If you'd like to sign here . . ."

Virginia said, "Conrad."

Startled, he swung around to face her. Across the space that divided them, they stared at each other. Conrad Tucker. Older, growing grey. But Conrad. The same heavy horn-rimmed spectacles, the same indelible tan. For a second his expression remained blank, then slowly, incredulously, he smiled.

"Virginia."

"I don't believe this. . . ."

"Well, I'll be god-damned."

"I thought I recognized your voice."

"What are you doing here . . . ?"

The boot-faced girl was not amused. "Excuse me, sir, but would you mind signing?"

"I live near here."

"I never knew . . ."

"And you . . . ?"

"I'm staying . . ."

"And how will you be paying, sir?" Boot face again. "By credit card or cheque?"

"Look," said Conrad to Virginia, "this is hopeless. Give me five minutes and I'll meet you in the bar and we'll have a drink. Can you do that? Have you time?"

"Yes, I have time."

"I'll get settled, wash up, and then join you. How's that?"

"Five minutes."

"No more.

The ladies' room, frilled and chintzy, was mercifully empty. Virginia had shed her grotty old Barbour, been to the loo, and now stood at the mirror gazing at her own reflection, and feeling more disorientated than ever by the astonishing unexpectedness of her encounter with Conrad.

Conrad Tucker, not seen nor thought of for twelve years or more. Here, in Relkirk. Come from London, and for what reason she could not imagine. She only knew that she had never been so glad to see a known face, because now, at least, she had someone to talk to.

She was not dressed for socializing. Blue jeans and an old grey cashmere sweater with a muffler of a collar. Her appearance was scarcely better. Hair lank with rain, her face clean of make-up. She saw the lines on her forehead and at the corners of her mouth, and the dark bruises beneath her eyes, evidence of her sleepless night. She reached for her bag, found a comb, fixed her hair, fastened it back from her face with an elastic band.

Conrad Tucker.

Twelve years. She had been twenty-one. So long ago, and so much, since, had taken place, that it took some effort to recall the details of that particular summer. But they had met at the country club in Leesport. Conrad was a lawyer, in business in New York with his uncle. He had an apartment in the East Fifties, but his father owned an old house in Southampton, and Conrad had come from there to Leesport to play in some tennis championships.

So far, so good. How had he played? That was lost in the mists of time. Virginia simply remembered that she had watched the match and cheered for him, and afterwards he had sought her out and bought her a drink, which was exactly what she had intended should happen.

She searched in her bag, in vain, for a lipstick, but found scent and splashed it on.

It had been a good summer. Conrad turned up in Leesport most weekends, and there were midnight barbecues and clambakes on the Fire Island beach. They played a lot of tennis, sailed Grandpa's old sloop out onto the blue waters of the Bay. She remembered Saturday nights at the club, and dancing with Conrad on the wide terrace with the sky full of stars and the band playing "The Look of Love."

Once, mid-week, she had driven up to the City with her grandmother, to stay at the Colony Club, do a bit of shopping, and take in a show. And Conrad had phoned, and taken her out to dinner at Lespleiades, and after that they had gone on to the Café Carlyle and stayed until the small hours listening to Bobby Short.

Twelve years. Light-years ago. She picked up her bag and her Barbour and went out of the room and up the stairs and into the bar. Conrad had not yet reappeared. She bought herself a whisky and soda, a packet of cigarettes, and carried her drink to an empty table in the corner of the room.

She drank half the whisky at a single go, felt at once warmed, comforted, and marginally stronger. The day was not yet over, but at least she was being offered a little respite, and she wasn't alone any longer.

* * *

She said, "You start, Conrad."

"Why me?"

"Because before I say a single word, I have to know what you're doing here. What has brought you to Scotland, to Relkirk? There has to be some logical explanation, but I can't think what it is."

He smiled. "I'm not in fact doing anything. I'm on a long vacation. Not exactly a sabbatical, just an extended break."

"Are you still a lawyer in New York?"

"I am."

"Working with your uncle?"

"No. I'm the top of the heap now."

"How impressive. Go on."

"Well . . . I've been away about six weeks. Travelling in England, staying with various acquaintances. Somerset, Berkshire, London. Then I came north and I've been in Kelso for a few days with some distant cousins of my mother's. It's a great place. Great fishing. Left them after lunch today. Caught the train up here."

"How long are you staying in Relkirk?"

"Just tonight. Tomorrow morning I'm hiring a car, and driving on north. I have to go to a party."

"And where is the party?"

"Some place called Corriehill. But I'm staying at another house called Croy. With—"

"I know." Virginia interrupted. "Archie and Isobel Balmerino."

"How do you know?"

"Because they're our closest friends. We all live in the same village, Strathcroy. And . . . you know Katy Steynton?"

"I met her in London."

"You're the Sad American." Virginia said this without thinking and could at once have bitten out her tongue.

"Sorry?"

"No, Conrad. *I'm* sorry. I shouldn't have said that. It's just that nobody could remember your name. That's why I didn't know it was you who was coming."

"You've lost me."

"We had lunch with the Balmerinos on Sunday. Isobel told me about you then."

Conrad shook his head. "I knew you'd married and I knew you'd married a Scotsman, but no more than that. I never imagined we'd meet up like this."

"Well, here I am, Mrs. Edmund Aird." *At least I think I am.* She hesitated. "Conrad, I didn't mean to say that. The Sad American bit, I mean. It's just that Isobel didn't seem to know anything about you. Except that Katy had met you in London. And that your wife had died."

Conrad was holding his whisky tumbler. He turned it in his hand, watching the amber liquid swirl. After a bit he said, "Yes. That's right."

"I am so very sorry."

He looked up at her. He said, "Yes."

"Can I ask? What happened?"

"She had leukemia. She was ill for a long time. That's why I came over. After the funeral."

"What was she called?"

"Mary."

"How long were you married?"

"Seven years."

"Do you have children?"

"A daughter. Emily. She's six. Right now she's with my mother in Southampton."

"Getting away . . . has that made things better for you?"

"I'll know when I get back."

"When are you going?"

"Next week sometime." He tossed back the last of his drink, got to his feet. "I'll get us the other half."

She watched him as he stood at the bar, ordering and paying for their second round of drinks, and tried to work out why he was so unmistakably American, when he didn't actually chew gum nor sport a crew cut. Perhaps it was his shape, the broad shoulders, narrow hips, long legs. Or his clothes. Polished loafers, chinos, a Brooks Brothers shirt, a blue Shetland sweater discreetly tagged with the Ralph Lauren logo.

She heard him ask the barman for some nuts. He did this quietly and politely, and the barman found a packet and emptied them into a little dish, and Virginia remembered that Conrad seldom raised his voice and was always mannerly to any person who happened to be doing a job for him. Gas-station attendants, barmen, waiters, cab drivers, doormen. The old black odd-job man who carried the trash and did all the dirty jobs down at the Leesport anchorage was much taken with Conrad, because Conrad had gone to the trouble to find out his Christian name, which was Clement, and always addressed him thus.

A kindly man. She thought about his dead wife, and was certain that the marriage must have been a happy one, and was angry for him. Why did tragedy always aim its venom at the couples who least deserved it while others were spared to make each other miserable and everybody else as well? Seven years. It wasn't very long. But at least he had his little daughter. She thought of Henry, and was glad that he had a child.

He was coming back to their table. She put a smile on her face. The whiskies looked very dark. She said, "I only meant to have one drink. I'm driving."

"How far?"

"About twenty miles."

"Do you want to call your husband?"

"He's not at home. He's in New York. He works for Sanford Cubben. I don't know if that got through to you on the grape-vine or not."

"I think I did know. How about your family?"

"If by family you mean kids, there's no family at home either. I have one child, a little boy, and I have just, this very afternoon, abandoned him to start his first term at boarding-school. That is how I have spent this gruesome day. The most ghastly day of my life. That's why I came in here. To go to the john and gather up my courage before travelling on." Even to herself, she sounded truculent.

"How old is your boy?"

"Eight."

"Oh, God!" His voice was despairing, which Virginia found comforting. Here at last was a twin soul, someone who thought the way she thought.

"He's just a baby. I never wanted him to go, and I fought every inch of the way. But his father was adamant. It's tradition. Good old British stiff-upper-lip tradition. He thinks it's the right thing to do, and he was all set to take Henry himself. But then he had to go to New York. So it had to be me. I don't know which of us was most miserable, Henry or myself. I don't know which of us I feel most sorry for."

"Was Henry okay? Being left, I mean. Saying goodbye."

"Conrad, I don't know. I honestly don't know. It was the fastest turn-round you could imagine. Split-second timing. Not a moment to stand, no time for a tear. I'd hardly stopped the car before two burly chaps were there, opening the back door and manhandling all the luggage onto trolleys. And then the Matron . . . quite young and quite pretty . . . took Henry by the hand and led him indoors. I don't think he even looked back. I was standing there with my mouth open, all set to have a scene, and suddenly the Headmaster appeared from nowhere, shook me by the hand and said, "Goodbye, Mrs. Aird." So I got back into the car and drove away. Do you know something? I felt like a dead chicken on a conveyor belt. Do you think I should have asserted myself?"

"No, I don't. I think you did the right thing."

"Nothing could have made it any better." She sighed, drank whisky, set down the glass. "At least neither of us had the chance to disgrace ourselves."

"I guess that's what it's all about." He smiled. "But you could still do with a bit of cheering. So why don't we have dinner together?"

* * *

". . . I never thought I'd live in Scotland. To me it was a place one came to at the end of the summer for a bit of jollity and the odd Hunt Ball or two; but never somewhere one would spend the rest of one's life. . . ."

The King's Hotel was not famous for its food, but it was warm and friendly, and the darkness and the streaming rain out of doors offered no inducement to tramp the windy streets in search of someplace a little more sophisticated. They had already eaten their Scotch broth, and were now ploughing their way through steaks, onions, chips, and mixed veg. For pudding, there was a choice of trifle or various ices. The waitress had already told them that the trifle was "offly guid."

Conrad had ordered wine, which was perhaps a mistake, and Virginia was drinking it, which was a bigger one, because she didn't usually talk as much as this, and, for the life of her, she couldn't think how to stop. Even if she'd wanted to. Because Conrad was a sympathetic listener, and so far had not started to look bored. On the contrary, he seemed to be fascinated.

She had already explained about Edmund, and his first wife, and Vi and Alexa. She had told him about Henry, about Balnaid, about the almost indescribable remoteness, and yet closeness, of their existence in Strathcroy.

"What goes on there?"

"Nothing, really. It's just a little place on the way to somewhere else. And yet everything. You know how small communities are. And we have a pub and a school, and shops, and two churches, and a dear queer who sells antiques. There always seems to be something going on. A jumble sale, or a garden opening, or a school play." It sounded dreadfully dull. She said, "It sounds dreadfully dull."

"Not a bit. Who lives there?"

"The village people, and the Balmerinos, and the minister and his wife, and the rector and his wife, and the Airds. Archie Balmerino is the Laird, which means that he owns the village and thousands of acres of land. Croy is enormous, but he's not in the least grand, and neither is Isobel. Isobel works harder than any woman I know, which is saying something in Scotland because all the women beaver away endlessly. If they're not running huge houses, or bringing up children, or gardening, then they're organizing enormous charity events or engaged in some home industry or other. Like running farm shops and selling all their own produce, or drying flowers, or keeping bees, or restoring antiques, or making the most beautiful curtains for people."

"Don't they ever have fun?"

"Yes, they have fun, but it's not Long Island fun, and it's not even Devon fun. In August and September, everything comes to a rising boil and there's a party most nights, and hunt balls and shooting and things. You've come at the right time, Conrad, though you'd never believe it on a dismal evening like this. But then the winter closes in and everybody hibernates."

"How do you see your girl-friends?"

"I don't know." She tried to work this one out. "It's not like any-where else. We all live such miles apart, and there's no club life. I mean, there aren't country clubs like there are in the States. And pubs aren't the same as they are in the south. Women don't really go into pubs. There are golf clubs, of course, but those are mostly male-orientated, and women are strictly personae non grata. You might go to Relkirk and meet a girl-friend there, but most of the socializing is done in people's private houses. Lunch parties for the girls, and dinner parties for the couples. We all get dressed up, and like I said, drive for forty miles or more. Which is one of the reasons that life more or less stops during the winter. That's when people escape. They go to Jamaica, if they can af-ford it, or Val d'Isère for the skiing."

"And what do you do?"

"I don't mind the winters. I hate the wet summers, but the winters are beautiful. And I go skiing up the glen. There's a ski-area only about ten miles on from Strathcroy, with a couple of tows and some good runs. The only thing is that if there's a lot of snow you can't get up the road. Which rather defeats the purpose."

"You used to ride."

"I used to hunt. For me, that was the whole purpose of riding. When I first came to Balnaid, Edmund said I could keep a couple of horses, but there didn't seem any point if there was to be no hunting."

"So how do you fill your days?"

"So far," she told him, "I've filled them with Henry." She gazed at Conrad, in glum hopelessness, across the table, because he had nailed with a single question the sum total of all her apprehension. Henry was gone, torn from her against her will. *You smother him,* Edmund had told her, and she had been furiously hurt and angry, but the smothering and the mothering had been her daily occupation and her greatest joy.

Bereft of Henry, there was only Edmund.

But Edmund was in New York, and if he wasn't in New York, then he was in Frankfurt or Tokyo or Hong Kong. Before, she had coped with these long separations, partly because there had always been Henry for comfort and companionship, but also because she had been totally confi-dent, wherever he might be, in Edmund's strength and constancy and love.

But now . . . the doubts and dreadful possibilities of last night's waking nightmares crowded in on her again. Lottie Carstairs, that mad-woman . . . but perhaps not so mad . . . telling Virginia things that she had never thought to hear. Edmund and Pandora Blair. *Why do you think he's taken himself off to America? He'll make a fool of you, same as he did his first wife, poor lady.*

Suddenly, it was all too much.

To her horror, she felt her mouth tremble, her eyes prick with tears. Across the table, Conrad watched her, and for a mad instant she thought about confiding in him, spilling out all the anguish of her miserable uncertainties. But then the tears swam into her eyes and his face dissolved into a watery mist, and Virginia thought, oh, bugger, I'm pissed. Just in time. The moment mercifully was over, and the dangerous temptation behind her. She must never speak about it to anybody, because if she did, then the words, said aloud, might make it all true. Might make it happen.

She said, "I'm sorry. So silly." She sniffed lustily, searched for a handkerchief, couldn't find one. Across the table, Conrad offered his own, white and clean and freshly ironed, and she took it thankfully and blew her nose. She said, "I'm tired and I'm miserable." She tried to make light of it. "I'm also slightly pissed."

He said, "You can't drive yourself home."

"I have to."

"Stay here the night and go back in the morning. We'll get a room for you."

"I can't."

"Why not?"

Tears poured again. "I have to get back for the dogs."

He did not laugh at her. He said, "Stay here for a moment. Order coffee. I just have to make a telephone call."

He laid down his napkin, pushed back his chair, and went. Virginia mopped her face, blew her nose again, glanced around the dining-room, anxious that no other person had noticed her sudden attack of weepy emotion. But the other diners were all absorbed in their dinners, munching stolidly at fried fish, or spooning their way through the "offly guid" trifle. The tears, mercifully, receded. The waitress approached to remove their plates.

"Did you enjoy your steak?"

"Yes, it was delicious."

"Are you taking sweet?"

"No. I don't think so, thank you. But if we could have some coffee?"

She had brought the coffee, and Virginia was already drinking the black and noxious stuff, which tasted as though it had been made out of a bottle, before Conrad returned to her. He drew back his chair and sat down. She looked at him inquiringly, and he said, "That's all settled."

"What have you settled?"

"I've cancelled my room, and cancelled the hire car for tomorrow. I'll drive you back to Strathcroy. I'll drive you home."

"Will you go to Croy?"

"No. They're not expecting me until tomorrow morning. I can go to the pub you mentioned."

"No, you can't, because they won't have a room. They're filled with grouse-shooting visitors who've taken Archie's moor." She sniffed away the last of her weeping, poured his coffee. "You can come to Balnaid. Stay the night there. The guest-room beds are all made up." She looked up, and caught the expression on his face. She said, "There's no problem," but even as she said this, knew that there was.

In the darkness, Conrad drove. It had stopped raining, as though the skies had run out of water, but the wind was from the south-west, and still damp, and the night stayed overcast. The road climbed and wound and dipped, and in the hollows lay pools of flood-water from the over-flowing ditches. Virginia, bundled in her Barbour, thought of the last time that she had made this journey; the evening Edmund had met her off the shuttle and they had had dinner together in Edinburgh. Then the sky had been an artist's wonder of rose-pink and grey. Now the darkness was sombre and menacing, and the lights that shone from the windows of farmhouses scattered over the surrounding braes of Strathcroy gave little relief, seeming distant and unreachable as stars.

Virginia yawned.

"You're sleepy," Conrad told her.

"Not really. Just too much wine." She reached out and rolled down the window, and felt the cold, wet, mossy air pour over her face. The tyres of the Subaru hissed on the wet Tarmac; out of the darkness came the long call of a curlew.

She said, "That's the sound of coming home."

"You certainly live a long way from anywhere."

"We're just about there."

The street of the village stood empty. Even Mr. Ishak had closed up his shop, and the only lights were those that burnt from behind drawn curtains. On such a night people stayed at home, watched television, made tea.

"We turn left, over this bridge."

They crossed the river, turned into the lane beneath the trees, came to the open gates, the drive that led to the house. All was, predictably, in darkness.

"Don't go around to the front, Conrad. Park just here, at the back. I don't use the front door when I'm on my own. I've got the back-door key."

He drew up, turned off the engine. While the headlights still burnt, she climbed down and went to unlock the back door, reach inside and switch on a light. The dogs had heard the car and were waiting, and showed gratifying excitement at her return, hurling themselves at her feet and uttering small welcoming noises in the back of their throats.

"Oh, what good doggies." She crouched to fondle them. "I'm sorry

I've been such a long time. You must have thought I was never coming home. Go on, out you both go and spend pennies, and I'll give you lovely biscuits before you go to bed."

They bundled happily out into the darkness, barked at the alien figure alighting from the Subaru, went to smell him, were patted and spoken to, and then, reassured, bounded off into the trees.

Virginia went on, switching on more lights. The big kitchen slumbered, the Aga was warm, the refrigerator gently hummed to itself. Conrad joined her, carrying his grip.

"Do you want me to put the car away?"

"No matter. We'll leave it in the yard for the night. Just take the keys out. . . ."

"I have. . . ." He laid them on the table.

In the uncompromising brightness, they regarded each other, and Virginia found herself overcome, quite suddenly, by a ridiculous shyness. To deal with this, she became businesslike and hostessy.

"Now. You'd like a drink? A nightcap. Edmund has some malt whisky he keeps for these occasions."

"I'm okay."

"But you'd like one?"

"Yes, I would."

"I'll get it. I won't be a moment."

When she came back bearing the bottle, he had taken off his coat and hat, and the dogs had returned from their nightly expedition and were already curled up on the beanbags by the Aga. Conrad, hunkered down, was making friends with them, talking softly, smoothing their high-domed well-bred heads with a gentle hand. As Virginia appeared, he stood up.

"I've closed the door, and locked it."

"How kind. Thank you. Actually, we often forget to lock doors. Thieves and robbers don't seem to be a problem in Strathcroy." She set the bottle down on the table, found a glass. "You'd better pour it yourself."

"You're not joining me?"

She shook her head, rueful. "No, Conrad, I've had enough for this evening."

He poured the malt and filled the tumbler from the cold tap. Virginia fed the dogs with biscuits. They took them politely, not snapping nor grabbing, and munched them appreciatively up.

"They're beautiful spaniels."

"Edmund's gun dogs, and very well behaved. With Edmund in charge, they don't dare be anything else." The biscuits were finished. She said, "If you'd like to bring your drink upstairs with you, I'll show you where you're sleeping." She gathered up his hat and coat, and Conrad collected his grip, and she led the way out of the kitchen, turning lights off and on as she went. Down the passage, across the big hall, and up the stairs.

"What a lovely house."

"It's big, but I like it that way."

He followed behind her. Below them, the old grandfather clock ticked the minutes away, but their feet made no sound on the thick carpets. The spare room faced over the front of the house. She opened the door and turned on the switch, and all was illuminated by the cold brilliance of the overhead chandelier. It was a large room, furnished with high brass bedsteads and a mahogany suite of Victorian furniture that Virginia had inherited from Vi. Taken unawares, it presented an impersonal face, without flowers or books. As well, the air was stuffy and unused.

"I'm afraid it doesn't look very welcoming." She dropped his hat and coat on a chair and went to fling open the tall sash window. The night wind flowed in, stirring the curtains. Conrad joined her and they leaned out, gazing into the velvety darkness. Light from the window drew a chequered pattern on the gravel beyond the front door, but all else was obscured.

He took a deep lungful of air. He said, "It all smells so clean and sweet. Like fresh spring water."

"You have to take my word for it, but we're looking at a wonderful view. You'll see it in the morning. Out over the garden to the fields and the hills."

From the trees by the church, an owl hooted. Virginia shivered and withdrew from the window. She said, "It's cold. Shall I close it again?"

"No. Leave it. It's too good to shut away."

She drew the heavy curtains, settling them so that there should be no chinks. "The bathroom's through that door." He went to investigate. "There should be towels, and the water's always hot if you want to take a bath." She turned on the small lights on the dressing table, and then the bedside light, and then went to switch off the cold brilliance of the chandelier. At once the high-ceilinged room was rendered cosier, even intimate. "I'm afraid there's no shower. This isn't a very modern establishment."

He emerged from the bathroom as Virginia turned back a heavy bedcover, revealing puffy square pillows encased in embroidered linen, a flowered eiderdown. "There's an electric blanket if you want to turn it on." She folded the cover, laid it aside. "Now."

There was nothing more to occupy her hands, her attention. She faced Conrad. For a moment neither of them spoke. His eyes, behind the heavy horn-rims, were sombre. She saw his rugged features, the deep lines on either side of his mouth. He was still holding his drink in his hand, but now moved to set it down on the table beside the bed. She watched him do this, and thought of that hand gently fondling the head of one of Edmund's dogs. A kindly man.

"Will you be all right, Conrad?" An innocently intended question, but as soon as the words were spoken she heard them as loaded.

He said, "I don't know."

There's no problem, she had told him, but knew that the problem had lurked between them all evening and now could no longer be pushed out of sight. It was no good prevaricating. They were two grown-up people, and life was hell.

She said, "I'm grateful to you. I needed comfort."

"I need you. . . ."

"I had fantasies about Leesport. Going back to Grandma and Gramps. I didn't tell you that."

"That summer, I fell in love with you. . . ."

"I imagined getting there. In a limousine from Kennedy. And it was all the same. The trees and the lawns, and the smell of the Atlantic blowing in over the Bay."

"You went back to England. . . ."

"I wanted someone to tell me I was great. That I was doing all right. I wanted not to be alone."

"I feel like shit . . ."

"It's two worlds, isn't it, Conrad? Bumping, and then moving apart. Light-years away from each other."

". . . because I want you."

"Why does everything have to happen when it's too late? Why does everything have to be so impossible?"

"It's not impossible."

"It is, because it's over. Being young is over. The moment you have a child of your own being young is over."

"I want you."

"I'm not young any more. A different person."

"I haven't slept with a woman. . . ."

"Don't say it, Conrad."

"That's what loneliness is all about."

She said, "I know."

Outside in the garden, nothing moved. Nothing stirred the dripping leaves of the rhododendrons. Eventually, a figure slipped away down the narrow paths of the shrubbery, leaving a trail of footmarks on the sodden grass, the indentations of high-heeled shoes.

8

Wednesday the Fourteenth

*I*SOBEL SAT AT HER KITCHEN TABLE, drank coffee and made lists. She was an inveterate list-maker, and these small inventories of things to be done, food to be bought, meals to be cooked, telephone calls to be made, as well as reminders to herself to split the polyanthus or dig up the gladioli, were constantly pinned to her kitchen notice-board, along with postcards from friends and children, and the address of a man prepared to clean the outside of the windows. At the moment she was working on three lists. Today, tomorrow, and then Friday. With one thing and another, life had suddenly become very complicated.

She wrote: "Dinner Tonight." There were some chicken joints in the deep-freeze. She could grill these or make some sort of a casserole.

She wrote: "Get chicken legs out. Peel potatoes. String beans."

Tomorrow was more complicated, with her house party committed in three different directions. Isobel herself would be at Corriehill for most of the day, helping Verena and her band of ladies to arrange flowers and somehow decorate that enormous marquee.

She wrote: "Secateurs. String. Wire. Wire-cutters. Beech-branches. Rowan-branches. Pick all the dahlias."

But, as well, there was Vi's birthday picnic by the loch to think about, and a day's shooting for Archie, because tomorrow they were driving grouse over Creagan Dubh, which meant that he would be joining the other guns.

She wrote: "Baps and cold ham for Archie's piece. Gingerbread. Apples. Hot soup?"

As for Vi's picnic, Lucilla, Jeff, Pandora, and the Sad American would probably want to go to that, which meant a hefty contribution of goodies from Croy.

She wrote: "Sausages for Vi's barbecue. Make some beefburgers. Sliced-tomato salad. French bread. Two bottles wine. Six cans lager."

She poured more coffee, went on to Friday. "Eleven people for dinner," she wrote, and then underlined the words and sat debating over grouse or pheasant. Pheasant Theodora was spectacular, cooked with celery and bacon and served with a sauce of egg yolks and cream. As well as being spectacular, Pheasant Theodora could be concocted in advance, which precluded a lot of last-minute labour while the dinner guests were drinking cocktails.

She wrote: "Pheasant Theodora." The door opened and Archie appeared.

Isobel scarcely raised her head. "You like Pheasant Theodora, don't you?"

"Not for breakfast."

"I didn't mean for breakfast, I meant for dinner the night of the party."

"Why can't we have roast grouse?"

"Because it's a fiddle to serve. Little last-minute bits and pieces, like scraps of toast to arrange and gravy to stir."

"Roast pheasant then?"

"Same objections."

"Is Pheasant Theodora the one that looks like sick?"

"It does, a bit, but I can cook it ahead."

"Why don't you just cook *a head*?"

"Ha ha."

"What's for breakfast?"

"It's in the bottom oven."

Archie went over to the Aga and opened the oven door. "A red-letter day! Bacon, sausages, and tomatoes. What's happened to the porridge and boiled eggs?"

"We have visitors staying. Bacon, sausages, and tomatoes are what we always give visitors." He brought his plate over to the table and settled himself beside her, pouring coffee, reaching for the toast and the butter.

"I thought," he said, "that Agnes Cooper was coming to help on Friday evening."

"So she is."

"Why can't she roast the pheasant?"

"Because she's not a cook. She's a washer-up."

"You could always ask her to cook."

"All right. I will. And we'll have mince and tatties for dinner because that's all the poor woman's capable of."

She wrote: "Clean silver candlesticks. Buy eight pink candles."

"I just wish Pheasant Theodora didn't look like sick."

"If you say it looks like sick in front of all our guests, I shall cut your throat, there and then, with a fruit knife."

"What are we going to have for starters?"

"Smoked trout?"

Archie put half a sausage into his mouth and chewed it thoughtfully. "And pudding?"

"Orange sorbet."

"White or red wine?"

"A couple of bottles of both, I think. Or champagne. We'll be drinking champagne for the rest of the evening. Perhaps we'd better stick to that."

"I haven't got any champagne."

"I shall order a crate today, in Relkirk."

"Are you going to Relkirk?"

"Oh, Archie!" Isobel laid down her Biro and gazed at her husband in hopeless exasperation. "Do you never listen to anything I tell you? And why do you think I'm all dressed up in my posh clothes? Yes, I am going to Relkirk today. With Pandora and Lucilla and Jeff. We're going shopping."

"What are you going to buy?"

"Lots of things for Friday night." She did not say "A new dress," because she still hadn't made up her mind about this extravagance. "And then we're going to lunch in the Wine Bar, and then we're coming home again."

"Will you get me some cartridges?"

"I'll get you anything you need if you'll write me a list."

"So I'm not expected to come." He sounded pleased. He hated shopping.

"You *can't* come because you've got to be here when the Sad American arrives. He's driving a hired car from Relkirk, and he's due sometime this morning. And you're not to go wandering off, otherwise he'll be faced by a deserted house and think he's not expected and go away again."

"Might be as well. What shall I give him for lunch?"

"There's soup and pâté in the larder."

"Which room's he sleeping in?"

"Pandora's old room."

"What's his name?"

"I can't remember."

"So how am I supposed to greet him? Hail, Sad American." Archie seemed to find this funny. He made his voice enormously deep. "Big Chief Running Nose Speaks with Forked Tongue."

"You've been watching too much television." But luckily she found it funny too. "He'll think he's come to a madhouse."

"Wouldn't be all that far off the mark. What time are you setting off for Relkirk?"

"About half past ten."

"Lucilla and Jeff seem to be on the move, but you'd better prize Pandora out of bed or you'll still be waiting for her at four o'clock in the afternoon."

"I already did," Isobel told him. "Half an hour ago."

"She's probably climbed back into bed and gone to sleep again."

But Pandora had not done this thing. The words were scarcely out of

Archie's mouth when they heard the tap of her high heels coming down the passage from the hall. The door opened and she burst into the kitchen, her profusion of hair bright as a flame, and face filled with laughter.

"Good morning, good morning, here I am, and I bet you thought I'd gone back to bed." She kissed the top of Archie's head and settled herself beside him. She was wearing dark-grey flannel trousers and a pale-grey sweater patterned with pink knitted sheep, and was carrying a magazine. This, it appeared, was the root cause of her amusement. "I'd forgotten this marvellous mag. Papa used to take it every month. *The Country Landowner's Journal.*"

"We still take it. I never got around to cancelling the subscription."

"I found this copy in my bedroom. It's simply fascinating, full of mind-boggling articles about something called Flea-Beetle Dust, and how we've all got to be terribly kind to badgers." She began to riffle through the pages. Isobel poured her a cup of coffee. "Oh, thank you darling, heaven. But the best are the ads at the back. Do listen to this one: 'For Sale. Titled Lady Wishes to Dispose of Underclothes. Peach-Pink Directoire Knickers and Silk Opera-Top Vests. Hardly Worn. Offers.' "

Archie finished munching his bit of toast. "Who do we write to?"

"Box number. Do you suppose that because she's titled, she's simply *stopped* wearing underclothes?"

"Perhaps somebody's died," Isobel suggested. "An old aunt. And she's cashing in on the loot."

"Some loot. *I* think she's having a mid-life crisis and has changed her image. Gone on a diet and lost stones of weight and become all flighty. She's into satin camiknickers now with lace round the legs, and His Lordship doesn't know what's hit him. And here's another marvellous one. Do listen, Archie. 'Work Wanted. Personable Farmer's Son. (Does that mean the farmer's personable or the son is?) Thirty Years Old. Some Experience in Draining. Driver. Fond of Shooting and Fishing.' Just *think!*" Pandora's eyes became enormous. "He's only *thirty* and he's able to drive a car. I'm sure he'd be frightfully useful to you, Archie. 'Some Experience in Draining.' He'd be able to take care of all the plumbing. Ballcocks and such. Why don't you drop him a line and offer to take him on?"

"No. I don't think so."

"Why ever not?"

Archie thought about it. "He's over-qualified?"

Simultaneously, their shared sense of the ridiculous bubbled to the surface and brother and sister dissolved into giggles. Isobel, observing them, shaking her head at their idiotic paroxysms of mirth, was nevertheless filled with grateful wonder. Since Pandora's arrival, Archie had been in better spirits than Isobel had seen for years, and now, sitting at her own breakfast table, she recognized once more that attractive and blissfully funny man she had fallen in love with over twenty years ago.

Pandora was not the perfect guest. Domestically speaking, she was a dead loss, and Isobel spent much time clearing up after her—making her bed, cleaning her bath, tidying away her clothes, and doing her laundry. But Isobel would forgive her anything, because she knew that it was his sister who had brought about the miraculous change in Archie, and for this she could be nothing but grateful, for somehow Pandora had rekindled Archie's youth and brought, like a gust of fresh wind, laughter back to Croy.

The shopping party, one by one, mustered. Jeff, having eaten his way through Isobel's enormous breakfast, went to collect Pandora's Mercedes from the garage, and drive it around to the front of the house. Isobel, armed with shopping baskets and the inevitable lists, joined him. Pandora was the next to appear, wearing her mink coat and her dark glasses and reeking of Poison.

It was another windy day with flashes of sunshine, and they all stood around in the breeze and waited for Lucilla. She came at last, shouted for by her father, and then shooed out through the door by him, just as he shooed his dogs. But she turned back to say goodbye, embracing and kissing him as though she were never going to see him again, before running down the steps with her dark hair flying.

"Sorry, I didn't know you were waiting."

Lucilla was dressed in old and faded jeans with slits at the knees that had been ineptly patched with some red-spotted material. With these, she wore a crumpled cotton shirt with much embroidery and drooping sleeves. The tails of this hung down below a very small leather waistcoat, dangling with fringe. She looked, thought her mother, as though she had just been raped by a Sioux.

"Darling, aren't you going to change?" She spoke rashly.

"Mum, I *am* changed. These are my best jeans. I bought them in Majorca when I was staying with Pandora."

"Oh, yes, of course." They all got into the car. "I am sorry, Lucilla. How silly of me."

Having reached Relkirk and found a place to park, the shoppers split up, because Lucilla and Jeff wanted to case the antique shops and browse around the famous street market.

"We'll meet you for lunch in the Wine Bar," Isobel told them. "At one o'clock."

"Have you booked a table?"

"No, but we should get one."

"Right. We'll be off then." They walked away across the cobbled square. As Isobel watched them go, she saw Jeff put his arm around Lucilla's thin shoulders. Which surprised her, because he had struck her as a most undemonstrative young man.

"That's got rid of them," said Pandora, sounding like a wicked child who, having disposed of the grown-ups, was ripe and ready for mischief. "Now, where are all the dress shops?"

"Pandora, I haven't quite made up my mind . . ."

"We're going to get you a dress for the dance, and that's it. And stop looking agonized because it's going to be my present to you. I owe it. I'm paying a debt."

"But . . . shouldn't we do all the important shopping first? The food for Friday, and . . ."

"What could be more important than a new dress? We can leave all the boring stuff until the afternoon. Now, stop standing around and dithering, or we'll waste the day away. Head us in the right direction. . . ."

"Well . . . there's McKay's . . ." said Isobel doubtfully.

"Not a dreary department store. Isn't there somewhere exclusive and expensive?"

"Yes, there is, but I've never been into it."

"Well, now is the time to start. Come on."

And Isobel, feeling all at once carefree and pleasantly sinful, abandoned her Calvinistic tendencies and followed.

The shop was narrow and deep, thickly carpeted, lined with mirrors, and sweetly scented like a glamorous woman. They were the only customers, and as they came through the plate-glass door, a woman rose from behind an enviable little marquetry desk and came to meet them. Dressed for work, she wore the sort of outfit that Isobel would have happily gone out to dinner in.

"Good morning."

She was told what they searched for.

"What size are you, madam?"

"Oh." Isobel, already, was flustered. "I think a twelve. Or maybe a fourteen."

"Oh, no." A professional eye was cast over Isobel, gauging. Isobel hoped that her tights hadn't laddered. "I'm sure a twelve. The ball gowns are through here, if you'd like to come."

They followed her into the back of the shop. She swept aside a curtain and revealed open wardrobes bulging with racks of evening dresses. Some short, some long; silk and velvet, glimmering satin, chiffon, and voile; and every beautiful colour under the sun. She rattled the hangers along the rail.

"These are twelves, here. But of course, if you find something you like in another size, I could always get it altered for you."

"We haven't time," Isobel told her. Her eyes moved to the darker gowns. Dark colours didn't date, and you could always add bits to them to make them look different. There was a brown satin. Or a navy-blue ribbed silk. Or maybe black. She took down a black crepe with jet buttons, and moved to the mirror to hold it in front of her . . . a bit governessy perhaps, but she saw it standing her in good stead for years. . . . She tried squinting at the price ticket but was not wearing her glasses.

"This is nice."

Pandora scarcely gave it a glance. "Not black, Isobel. And not red." She pushed more hangers aside, and then pounced. "Now, *this.*"

Isobel, still listlessly holding the black crepe, looked—at the most beautiful dress she had ever imagined. Sapphire-blue Thai silk shot with black, so that as the light moved over the material, it shimmered like the wings of some exotic insect. The skirt was huge, puffed out with petticoats, and it had a low neck. The sleeves were finished at the elbow with narrow ruffles of the same silk, and an identical ruffle bordered the hem.

Scarcely daring to imagine herself owning such a garment, Isobel eyed the tiny waist. "I'll never get into that."

"Try."

It was as though she had lost all will of her own. Bundled into a curtained changing-room, stripped, like some votive sacrifice, of all her outer clothes. "Now." She stood in her bra and tights, and the profusion of whispering silk was lowered cautiously over her head; sleeves pulled up over her arms; the zip . . .

She sucked in her breath, but there was no problem. The waistline hugged her snugly, but she could breathe. The saleslady settled the shoulders, bouffed out the skirt, stepped back to admire.

Isobel saw herself full-length in the mirror, and it was like seeing another person. A woman from another age, stepped down from the frame of an eighteenth-century portrait. The hem of the dress swept the floor, the stiff silk arranging itself in gleaming folds. The sleeves were infinitely flattering, and the deep neckline revealed Isobel's best points, which were her pretty plump shoulders and the swelling curve of her breasts.

Overwhelmed with desire, she tried to remain practical. "It's too long."

"It won't be with high heels," Pandora pointed out. "And the colour makes your eyes as blue as ink."

Isobel looked and saw that this was true. But she put her hands to her tanned and weathered cheeks. "My face is all wrong."

"Darling, you're wearing no make-up."

"And my hair."

"I'll do your hair for you." Pandora narrowed her eyes. "You need jewellery."

"I could wear the Balmerino earrings. The diamond drops with the pearls and sapphires."

"Of course. Perfection. And Mamma's pearl choker? Have you got that as well?"

"It's in the bank."

"We'll get it out this afternoon. You're beautiful in it, Isobel. Every man in the room will be in love with you. We couldn't have found anything more becoming." She turned to smile at the silent but satisfied saleslady. "We'll have it."

The dress was unzipped, gently removed, and taken away to be parcelled up.

"Pandora!" Isobel whispered urgently, reaching for her Marks and Spencer's petticoat. "You never even asked the price."

"If you have to ask the price, you can't afford it," Pandora whispered back and disappeared. Isobel, torn between excitement and guilt, was left to put on her blouse and skirt, button up her jacket and lace up her shoes. By the time she had done this, the cheque had been written, the price-tag removed, and the ravishing dress packed into a huge box.

The saleslady went to open the door for them.

"Thank you so much," said Isobel.

"I'm glad you found something you liked."

The whole transaction had taken no more than ten minutes. Pandora and Isobel stood on the pavement in the sunshine.

"I can't thank you . . ."

"Don't thank me. . . ."

"I've never in my life owned such a dress. . . ."

"Then it's about time you did. You deserve it. . . ."

"Pandora . . ."

But Pandora did not want to hear any more. She looked at her watch. "It's only a quarter to twelve. What shall we go and buy now?"

"But haven't you spent enough money?"

"Heavens no, I've only just started. What's Archie going to wear to the party? His kilt?"

They began slowly to walk down the pavement.

"No. He hasn't worn his kilt since his leg was shot off. He says a horrible tin knee sticking out is an obscenity. He'll just wear his dinner jacket."

Pandora stopped dead. "But Lord Balmerino can't go to a Highland dance in his dinner jacket."

"Well, he's been doing it for years."

A fat lady with a basket, annoyed by the obstruction they were causing, said "Excuse *me*," and pushed her way between them. Pandora ignored her.

"Why doesn't he wear tartan trews?"

"He hasn't got any."

"Why ever not?"

Isobel tried to think why this obvious solution had not solved the problem years ago, and realized that, along with his leg, Archie had lost all pride and pleasure in his appearance. It was as though it didn't matter any longer. As well, luxury clothes cost money, and there always seemed to be something else more essential to spend it on.

"I don't know."

"But he always used to look so yummy at dances. And what's more, knew he did. In a boring old dinner jacket, he'll look like an undertaker, or a part-time waiter. Or worse, a Sassenach. Come on, let's go and buy him something brilliant. Do you know what size he is?"

"Not offhand. But his tailor will."

"Where's his tailor?"

"In the next street."

"Would he have tartan trews? Off the peg?"

"I should think so."

"Then what are we waiting for?" And Pandora was off again, striding away with her mink coat open and flying. Isobel, lugging her parcel, had to run to keep up with her.

"But even if we find some trews, what's he going to wear with them? He can't wear a dinner jacket."

"Papa had a very handsome velvet smoking jacket. Faded bottle green. What's happened to that?"

"It's up in the attic."

"Well, we'll go and find it. Oh, how exciting. Just imagine how majestic the dear man is going to look."

They found the old tailor working away at his table in the back regions of the shop, a Gentleman's Outfitters Specializing in Highland Dress for All Occasions. Disturbed, he raised his head from an unrolled bolt of tweed, saw Isobel, laid down his scissors and favoured her with a beaming smile.

"Lady Balmerino."

"Good morning, Mr. Pittendriech. Mr. Pittendriech, do you remember my sister-in-law, Pandora Blair?"

The old man looked at Pandora over the top of his spectacles. "Yes, I remember. But it's a long time ago. You couldn't have been more than a wee girl." Across the table, he and Pandora shook hands. "Very pleased to see you again. And how is His Lordship, Lady Balmerino?"

"He's very well."

"Is he able to get up the hill?"

"Not very far, but . . ."

Pandora, impatient, interrupted. "We've come to buy him a present, Mr. Pittendriech. A pair of tartan trews. You know his measurements. Would you come and help us choose a pair?"

"Most certainly. It would be a pleasure." He abandoned his cutting and emerged from behind his table to lead them back to the main shop, where a plethora of tartans, leather sporrans, skean dhus, diced hose, lace jabots, silver-buckled shoes, and cairngorm brooches fairly dazzled the eye.

Mr. Pittendriech obviously felt that all this was a little beneath his dignity.

"Would it not be better if I were to tailor His Lordship a pair of trews? He's never been a gentleman to buy his clothes off-the-peg."

"We haven't time," Isobel said for the second time that morning.

"In that case, would it be regimental tartan, or family tartan?"

"Oh, family tartan," said Pandora firmly. "Anyway, it's such a pretty one."

It took a little time to find the right tartan, and then more time fiddling with a tape measure to ensure that the inside leg was the correct length. Finally, Mr. Pittendriech made his choice.

"This pair should do His Lordship very nicely."

Isobel considered them. "They aren't going to be too narrow, are they? Otherwise he won't be able to get them over his tin leg."

"No, I think they should be amply comfortable."

"In that case," said Pandora, "we'll have them."

"And how about a cummerbund, Miss Blair?"

"He can wear his father's, Mr. Pittendriech." She turned her dazzling smile upon him. "But perhaps a really lovely new white cotton shirt?"

More parcels, more cheques. Out on the pavement again. "Time for lunch," said Pandora, and they headed, mutually delighted with themselves, in the direction of the Wine Bar. Propelled into this popular rendezvous by the revolving door, they came up against the first obstacle of the day. There was no sign of Lucilla and Jeff, most of the tables were occupied, and those that weren't had "Reserved" notices placed upon them.

"We want a table for four," Pandora told the superior-looking woman behind the high desk.

"Have you resairved?"

"No, but we still want a table for four."

"I'm afraid if you haven't resairved, then you will have to await your turn."

Pandora opened her mouth to argue, but before she could say anything the telephone on the desk began fortuitously to ring and the woman turned aside to pick up the receiver. "This is the Waine Bar."

Behind her back, Pandora dug Isobel in the ribs, and then, looking unconcerned, stalked over to where an empty and reserved table stood by the window. Reaching it, she unobtrusively whisked the "Reserved" sign up and pushed this deep into the pocket of her coat. A brilliant and professional piece of sleight of hand. She then settled herself gracefully, disposed of her bag and parcels, spread the mink over the back of the chair, and reached for the menu.

Isobel, horrified, hovered. "Pandora, you *can't*. . . ."

"I have. Bloody woman. Sit down."

"But someone's *reserved* it."

"But we've got it. Possession is nine-tenths of the law." Isobel, who dreaded any sort of a scene, continued to hesitate, but Pandora took no notice of her waffling, and after a bit, with no alternative, she sat down as well, facing her blatantly criminal sister-in-law. "Oh, look, we can have a cocktail. And we can eat quiche and salad, or an omelette aux fines herbes."

"That woman's going to be *livid*."

"I hate cocktails, don't you? Do you suppose they have any champagne? Let's ask when she comes gunning for us."

Which she did, almost immediately.

"Excuse me, madam, but this table is resairved."

"Oh, *is* it?" Pandora's eyes were bland and innocent orbs. "But there's no sign."

"This table is resairved, and there was a sign upon it."

"Where can it be?" Pandora craned her neck to look under the table. "It's not on the floor."

"I'm sorry, but I'm afraid you will have to move and await your turn."

"I'm sorry, but I'm afraid we're not going to. Will you take our order, or would you rather send one of the waitresses?"

The woman's neck was growing red, like turkey wattles. Her mouth worked. Isobel felt rather sorry for her.

"You know perfectly well that there was a resairved notice upon this table. The manager put it there himself this morning."

Pandora raised her eyebrows. "Oh, there's a manager, is there? Then perhaps you would like to go and find him, and tell him that Lady Balmerino is here and wishes to order lunch."

Isobel, hot with embarrassment, felt her cheeks burn. Pandora's adversary by now looked as though she was about to burst into tears. Humiliation stared her in the face. "The manager is not in this afternoon," she admitted.

"In that case, you are obviously in charge, and you have done all you can. Now, perhaps you will send a waitress over and we can order."

The poor woman, reduced to pulp by such nerveless authority, dithered for a moment, but finally collapsed, her ire deflating like a pricked balloon. In silence, gathering her tattered dignity about her, and with lips pressed together, she turned to go. But Pandora was remorseless. "Just one more thing. Would you be very kind and tell the barman that we'd like a bottle of his best champagne." Her smile dazzled. "Iced."

No more objections, no more argument. It was over. Isobel stopped blushing. She said, "Pandora, you are shameless."

"I know, darling."

"Poor female. She's practically in blubs."

"Silly old cow."

"And the Lady Balmerino bit . . ."

"That's what did the trick. These sort of people are the most appalling snobs."

It wasn't any good trying to scold her. She was Pandora, generous, loving, laughing . . . and ruthless if she didn't get her own way. Isobel shook her head. "I despair of you."

"Oh, darling, don't be cross. We've had such a heavenly morning, and I'll be good for the rest of the day and hump all your grocery boxes. Oh, look, there are Lucilla and Jeff. Laden with rather tatty carrier bags. What could they have been buying?" She waved, flapping a red-nailed hand. "Here we are!" They saw her, and came over. "We've ordered champagne, Jeff, so you're not to be boring and say you'd rather have a can of Foster's."

Over the champagne, Lucilla and Jeff were told, in lowered tones and with a certain amount of muffled mirth, the saga of the resairved table.

Lucilla was amused, but at the same time almost as shocked as her mother, and Isobel was glad to see this. "Pandora, that's dreadful. What's going to happen to the poor people who *did* reserve the table?"

"That's the old bag's problem. Oh, don't worry, she'll tuck them in somewhere."

"But it's frightfully dishonest."

"I think you're being very ungrateful. If it wasn't for my quick-thinking enterprise, we'd all be standing in a queue with aching shoppers' feet. Anyway, she was offhand and rude to me. And I don't like being told I can't have anything I really want."

Archie, left on his own and forbidden by his wife to leave the purlieus of the house, decided to fill in the time before their guest arrived by clearing up the first of the fallen leaves that littered the lawn beyond the gravel sweep. He would then perhaps find time to cut it, and all would look orderly for the party on Friday night. With only his dogs for company, he duly drove his garden tractor out of the garage and set to work. The Labradors, who had imagined that he was about to take them for a small walk, sat about and looked bored, but diversion was on its way, for Archie had only completed a couple of runs before a Land Rover came spinning up the front drive, turned in over the cattle-grid, and came to a halt a few yards from where he laboured.

It was Gordon Gillock, the Croy keeper, with his two spaniels penned into the back of the vehicle. A cacophony of barking instantly erupted, from both inside and outside the Land Rover, but all four dogs were swiftly silenced by a stream of routine abuse from Gordon, and quiet was once more achieved.

Archie stopped his machine and switched off the engine, but stayed where he was, seated, because that was as good a place as any to engage in conversation.

"Hello, Gordon."

"Good morning, milord."

Gordon was a lithe and stringy Highlander in his early fifties but looking, with his black hair and dark eyes, a good deal younger. He had come to Croy as an under-keeper in the days of Archie's father, and had been in the family's employ ever since. Today he wore his working clothes, which meant an open-necked shirt and a tweed hat stuck with fishing flies that had seen many years of windy weather. But on shooting days, he wore a collar and tie and a knickerbocker suit with a deerstalker of the same tweed, and was a good deal better-dressed than most of the other gentlemen out on the moor.

"Where have you come from?"

"Kirkthornton, sir. I took thirty brace of birds down to the game dealer."

"Did you get a good price?"

"Not so bad."

"What's happening tomorrow?"

"That's why I'm here, sir. Wanted a word. Mr. Aird's not going to be with us. He's away in America."

"I know. He rang me before he left. We're shooting Creagan Dubh?"

"That's right, the main glen. I thought, first thing we'd drive the Clash, and then come in the other way over Rabbie's Naup."

"What about the afternoon? Should we try the Mid Hill?"

"It's up to you, sir. But mind, the birds are getting pretty wild. They'll be coming in fast over the butts and the guns will need to keep their wits about them."

"They know they're responsible for seeing that all the shot birds are picked up and brought down the hill? No runners abandoned. I don't want any wounded birds left to die."

"Oh aye, they know that. Mind, there are some good dogs this year."

"You were walking on Monday. How did you get on?"

"There was a fair wind and a lot of water about. Then an eagle and a buzzard started working overhead, and that scared the daylights out of the grouse. They either wouldn't get up or they flew in all directions. But there was some good shooting. We finished with thirty-two brace."

"Any deer?"

"Oh aye, a big herd. Saw them on the skyline sticking their heads up over the Sneck of Balquhidder."

"And how about that damaged bridge over the Taitnie burn?"

"I've seen to that, sir. It was just about down, with the rain we've been having and the water in spate."

"Good. We don't want any of the London gentlemen suffering a ducking. How about beaters for tomorrow?"

"I've got sixteen."

"And flankers? The last time we drove, a lot of the birds slipped away because of poor flanking."

"Aye, they were a useless pair of buggers. But tomorrow I've got the schoolmaster's son and Willy Snoddy." The keeper caught Archie's eye and the two of them grinned. "He's an unreliable old villain but a rare flanker." Gordon shifted his weight, took off his hat, scratched the back of his neck, and then put his hat on again. "I was up at the loch early yesterday morning. Caught him there with that old lurcher of his, lifting your trout out of the water. He's there evenings forbye, making full use of the late rise."

"Do you see him?"

"He sneaks up the back lane from the village, but, aye, I've spied him more than once."

"I know he poaches, Gordon, and so does the local bobby. But he's done it all his life, and he's not going to stop now. I don't say anything. Besides"—Archie smiled—"if he's flung into jail, we're short of a flanker."

"True enough, sir."

"What about the beaters' money?"

"Went to the bank this morning, sir, collected it then."

"You seem to have got it all well organized, Gordon. Thank you very much for dropping. And I'll see you tomorrow. . . ."

Gordon and his dogs departed, and Archie continued with his leaf-sweeping. He had just about completed the task when he heard a second car coming up the back drive from the village, and decided that this time, in all likelihood, it would be the Sad American in his hired car. He wished to hell he knew what the bloody man was called. In preparation, he once more stopped the tractor and switched off the engine, and as he eased himself cautiously onto his two feet, the car came down the avenue towards him and he realized that it was Edmund's Subaru, and so not the Sad American after all. Virginia was at the wheel, but a man sat beside her. The Subaru drew to a halt, and as Archie, awkwardly stiff, limped forward, they got out of the car and came to meet him.

"Virginia."

"Hello, Archie. I've brought your guest to stay with you." Archie, at a loss, turned to the stranger. Tall, well built, quite handsome in a weathered sort of way. Not young, and wearing heavy horn-rimmed spectacles. "Conrad Tucker; Archie Balmerino."

The two men shook hands. Archie said, "I'm sorry . . . I thought you were coming under your own steam, in a hired car. . . ."

"I intended doing that, but . . ."

Virginia interrupted. "I'll explain. It's the most extraordinary

coincidence, Archie. I met Conrad yesterday evening in the King's Hotel, in Relkirk. Out of the blue. And of course we're very old friends. We
knew each other in Long Island when we were young. So instead of
spending the night at the hotel as he'd planned, he came back to Balnaid
with me and stayed there."

So all was clear. "But what a fortuitous meeting, and what a good
idea." And then added, for Conrad's benefit, "The ridiculous thing is
that my wife was either never told, or forgot, your name, and so Virginia
would never have known that our house guest was yourself. I'm afraid
sometimes we're dreadfully vague."

"It's very good of you to have me."

"Anyway . . ." Archie hesitated, wishing that Isobel were here.
". . . this is all splendid. Come along. Let's go indoors. There's nobody here but me because the others have all gone shopping. Have you
got a bag, Conrad? What's the time? A quarter to twelve. The sun's not
over the yardarm yet, but I think we could have a gin and tonic. . . ."

Virginia said, "No, Archie," and she sounded jumpy and unlike herself. Archie looked at her with closer attention and saw the pallor beneath her tan and the dark rings under her eyes. She seemed upset and
he was concerned for her, and then remembered that only yesterday she
had had to take Henry to Templehall and leave him there. Which explained everything.

He felt very sympathetic and said kindly, "Why not? It'll do you
good."

"It's not that I don't want to stay, but I have to take some stuff up to
Corriehill for Verena. Flower vases. Things like that. If you don't mind, I
think I'd better get home."

"Whatever you want."

"We'll all see each other tomorrow at Vi's picnic."

"Not me. I'm shooting. But Lucilla and Jeff and Pandora will take
Conrad along with them."

Conrad had retrieved his bag from Virginia's car and was standing
waiting for what was going to happen next. Virginia went to him and
gave him a kiss. "See you tomorrow, Conrad."

"Thanks for everything."

"It's been great."

She got back into the Subaru and drove away, back under the trees
and down the hill. When she had gone, Archie turned to his guest.
"How very nice that you already know Virginia. Now, come along and
I'll show you where you're sleeping. . . ."

He led the way up to the door and into the house, and Conrad,
slowing his pace down to his host's halting step, followed him.

* * *

Back at Balnaid, in her flower pantry, searching for jugs, urns, bowls, old soup tureens, Virginia was grateful for domestic occupation. At the moment she needed neither idle hands nor an empty mind. Especially an empty mind. She assembled her loot and then collected pin-holders and screwed-up pieces of chicken wire, essential for keeping top-heavy flower arrangements in place. Making two or three trips, she carried everything out to the Subaru and stowed it all neatly into the back of the car.

Meanwhile, she made plans. Tomorrow morning early, Alexa and Noel and Alexa's dog would be arriving, having driven up from London overnight. They would be at Balnaid for breakfast. When I come back from Corriehill, she told herself, I shall get the bedrooms ready for Alexa and Noel. Bedrooms. Not a bedroom. In London they slept together, in a double bed, but Virginia knew that if she were to put them in a double bed at Balnaid, Alexa would be embarrassed, and even more put out than her father.

Tomorrow. She would think about tomorrow. She would not think about yesterday, nor the day before. Nor last night. They were over. Finished with. Done. Nothing could be changed and nothing could be altered.

When the bedrooms were finished, she would emulate Isobel and make lists, visit Mrs. Ishak and do an enormous shop. The dogs would have to be walked. After that she might do some cooking, make a cake or a pot of soup. Or brownies for tomorrow's picnic. By then it would be evening, and then night, and the long lonely, soul-searching day would be over. She would sleep in her empty bed, in her empty house. Without Edmund, without Henry. But the morning would bring Alexa and Noel, and with them for company surely things must get better; life would seem less impossible and easier to bear.

She drove to Corriehill and found the place in a turmoil. Alien vans and lorries were parked on the gravel outside, and inside, the house appeared to have been taken over by armies of workmen, as though the family were on the point of moving out, or moving in. In the hall, most of the furniture and the rugs had already been shunted aside, electric cables snaked in all directions, and the open doors of the dining-room revealed that this, by means of festoons of darkly striped material, had been transformed into a lightless cave. The night-club. She paused to admire but was almost instantly asked to move aside by a young man with long hair who staggered, with bent knees, beneath the weight of some piece of audio equipment.

"Do you know where I can find Mrs. Steynton?"

"Try the marquee."

Picking her way through the confusion, Virginia made for the library and saw, for the first time, the gargantuan tent that had been erected on the lawn the day before. It was very tall and very wide, and took most of the daylight from the rooms inside. The French doors of the library had been removed, and house and marquee were joined by the umbilical cord of a wide, tented passageway. She went down this and stepped into the aqueous, filtered gloom that was the interior of the marquee, saw the soaring tent-poles, tall as masts, the yellow-and-white-striped lining. On the top of tall ladders, more electricians were perched fixing the overhead lights, and at the far end a couple of burly men were constructing, with trestles and planks, a platform for the band. There was the smell of trodden grass and canvas, rather like an agricultural show, and in the middle of it all she found Verena with Mr. Abberley, who was in charge of the entire operation, and apparently being given a piece of Verena's mind.

". . . but it's ridiculous to say we've got the measurements wrong. You *took* the measurements."

"The thing is, Mrs. Steynton, that the floor comes in prefabricated units. Six by three. I explained when you ordered my largest tent."

"I never imagined there would be a problem."

"And there's another thing. Your lawn's not level."

"Of course it's level. It used to be a tennis court."

"I'm sorry, but it's not. Sinks down in that corner a foot or more. That means wedges."

"Well, use wedges. Just be certain the floor doesn't collapse."

Mr. Abberley looked hurt. "My floors never collapse," he told her, and took himself off to mull over the situation.

Virginia said, "Verena." Verena turned. "I don't seem to have come at a very good time."

"Oh, Virginia." Verena ran fingers through her hair in a most uncharacteristic fashion. "I'm going demented. Have you ever seen such a mess?"

"I think it looks fantastic. Terribly impressive."

"But it's so *huge*."

"Well, you're having a huge party. When it's full of flowers and people and the band and everything, it'll be quite different."

"You don't think it's all going to be the most dreadful flop?"

"Of course not. It'll be the dance of the century. Look, I've brought the flower vases. If you tell me where to put them, I'll bring them into the house and then get out of your way."

"You are a dear. If you go into the kitchen, you'll find Katy and some friends of hers. They're making silver stars, or streamers, or something, to decorate the night-club. She'll show you where to put them."

"If there's anything else you're needing . . ."

But Verena's attention was already wandering. "If I think of anything, I'll call you. . . ." She had too much on her mind. "Mr. Abberley! I've just remembered. There's something else I want to ask you. . . ."

Virginia drove home. By the time she reached Balnaid again, it was nearly two o'clock. She was beginning to feel ravenously hungry, and decided that before she did anything else, she must have something to eat. A cold beef sandwich, perhaps, some biscuits and cheese, and a cup of coffee. She parked the Subaru at the back door and walked indoors and into her kitchen.

All thoughts of food instantly flew out of her head. She stopped dead, her empty stomach contracting in a spasm of shock and outrage.

For Lottie was there. Waiting. Sitting at the kitchen table. She did not look abashed in the very least, but smiled as though Virginia had asked her to drop by, and Lottie, graciously, had taken up the invitation.

"What are you doing here?" This time Virginia made no effort to keep the irritation out of her voice. She was startled but she was as well enraged. "What do you want?"

"Just waiting for you. And I wanted a wee word."

"You have no right to walk into my house."

"You should learn to lock your doors."

Across the kitchen table, they faced each other.

"How long have you been here?"

"Ooh, about half an hour." Where else had she been? What had she been doing? Had she been snooping around Virginia's house, gone upstairs, opened cupboards, opened drawers, touched Virginia's clothes? "I thought you'd not be long, leaving the doors open like that. Course, the dogs barked, but I soon quieted them down. They can always tell a friend."

A friend.

"I think that you should go at once, Lottie. And please don't ever come back unless you are asked."

"Oh, Miss Hoity-Toity, is it? Am I not good enough for the likes of you?"

"Please go."

"I'll go in my own time when I've said what I have to say."

"You have nothing to say to me."

"But that's where you're wrong, Mrs. Edmund Aird. I have plenty to say to you. Up to high doh you were, when I met you out a walk on the bridge. Didn't like what I had to say, did you? I could tell. I'm not stupid."

"You were telling lies."

"And why should I tell lies? I have no reason to tell lies because the truth is black enough. 'Whore' was what I called Pandora Blair, and you buttoned up your lips as though I'd said a dirty word, pretending to be so pure yourself, and high and mighty."

"What do you want?"

"I want to see no evil and fornicating," Lottie droned, and she sounded like a Wee Free minister promising his congregation Eternal Damnation. "The vileness of men and women. Lustful practices . . ."

Infuriated, Virginia cut her short. "You're talking drivel."

"Oh, drivel, is it?" Lottie became herself again. "And is it drivel that when your man's away, and you're rid of your wee boy, you bring your fancy men home with you and take them to your bed?" It was impossible. She was making it up. Letting her crazy twisted imagination feast on her own carnal fantasies. "Aha, I thought that would silence you. Mrs. Edmund Aird indeed. You're no better than a street-walker."

Virginia took hold of the edge of the table. She said, and kept her voice quite cold and quite calm, "I don't know what you're talking about."

"And who's lying now, may I ask?" Lottie, with her hands clasped in her lap, leaned forward, her strange eyes fixed on Virginia's face. Her skin was waxy as a candle and the faint shadow of her moustache darkened her upper lip. "I was there, Mrs. Edmund Aird." Her voice dropped, and now she spoke in the hushed tones of a person telling a ghost story, and making it as scary as possible. "I was outside your house when you came home last night. I saw you coming back. I saw you, switching on all the lights and making your way up the stair with your fancy man. I saw you at the bedroom window, leaning out like a pair of lovers and whispering between the two of you. I saw you draw the curtains, and shut yourselves away, with your lust and your adultery."

"You had no right to be in my garden. Just as you have no right to be in my house. It's called trespass, and if I wanted I could call the police."

"The police." Lottie gave a cackle of laughter. "Fat lot of good they are. And wouldn't they be interested to know what goes on when Mr. Aird is in America. Missing him, were you? Thinking of him and Pandora? Told you about them, didn't I? Makes you wonder, doesn't it? Makes you wonder who you can trust."

"I want you to go now, Lottie."

"And *he's* not going to be too pleased when he knows what's been going on."

"Go. Now."

"One thing's for certain. You're no better than the rest of them, and don't try to convince me you're not guilty, because your face gives you away. . . ."

Virginia finally lost her cool. Through clenched teeth she screamed at Lottie. "GET OUT!" She flung out an arm, pointing at the open door. "Get out and stay out and never come back, you creeping old bag."

Lottie was silenced. She did not budge. Across the table, she stared at Virginia, her eyes hot with hatred. Virginia, dreading what might happen next, stood, tense as strung wire. If Lottie made one move to touch her, she would turn the heavy table on top of the old lunatic and squash her flat as a beetle. But, far from becoming physically violent, Lottie's face assumed an expression of deep complacency. The glitter went out of her eyes. She had said her piece, achieved what she'd set out to do. Without hurry, in her own time, she got to her feet and neatly buttoned up her cardigan. "Well," she announced, "I'll be off then. Bye-bye, doggies, nice to have met you."

Virginia watched her go. Lottie, on her high heels, tapping jauntily across the kitchen. At the open door she paused to look back. "That's been very nice. No doubt I'll see you around."

And then she was gone, quietly closing the door behind her.

Violet, in her own little kitchen at Pennyburn, stood, aproned, at the table, and iced her birthday cake. Edie had made the cake, which was large and had three tiers, but Violet had been left to do the decorating. She had made chocolate-butter icing and with this had stuck the three tiers together. Now she was engaged in spreading what remained of the sticky goo over the outside of the cake. She was not an expert at cake decorating and, when it was completed, it had a fairly rough-and-ready appearance, more like a newly ploughed field than anything else, but by the time she had stuck a few brightly coloured Smarties into the icing and added the single candle that was all she allowed herself, it would be quite festive enough.

She stood back to eye the finished cake, licking a few gobs of icing off her fingers. At that moment she heard a car coming up the hill and then turning into her own driveway. She looked up and through the window and saw that her visitor was Virginia, and was pleased. Virginia was on her own, and Violet was always gratified when her daughter-in-law unexpectedly dropped in, uninvited, because it meant that she wanted to come. And today was specially important, because they would have time to sit down and talk, and Violet would be able to hear all about Henry.

She went to wash her hands. Heard the front door open and close.

"Vi!"

"I'm in the kitchen." She dried her hands, reached to untie her apron.

"Vi!"

Violet tossed her apron aside and went out into the hall. Her daughter-in-law stood there at the foot of the stairs, and it was immediately obvious to Violet that something was very wrong. Virginia was as pale as paper, and her brilliant eyes were hard and bright, as though they burnt with unshed tears.

She was filled with apprehension. "My dear. What is it?"

"I have to see you, Vi." Her voice was controlled, but there was unsteadiness there. She was not far from weeping. "I have to talk."

"But of course. Come along. Come and sit down. . . ." She put her arm around Virginia and led her into the sitting-room. "There. Sit down. Be quiet for a moment. There's nothing to disturb us." Virginia sank into Vi's deep armchair, laid her head back on the cushion, closed her lovely eyes, and then, almost immediately, opened them again.

She said, "Henry was right. Lottie Carstairs is evil. She can't stay. She can't stay with Edie. She must go away again."

Vi lowered herself into her own wide-lapped fireside chair. "Virginia, what has happened?"

Virginia said, "I'm frightened."

"That she will do Edie some harm?"

"Not Edie. Me."

"Tell me."

"I . . . I don't quite know how to start."

"Everything from the beginning."

Her quiet tones had effect. Virginia gathered herself, visibly making some effort to keep control and stay sensible and objective. She sat up, smoothing back her hair, pressing her fingers to her cheeks as though she had already wept and was wiping tears away.

She said, "I've never liked her. Just as none of us has ever liked her, or been happy with the fact that she's living with Edie. But, like the rest of us, I told myself that she was harmless."

Violet remembered her own reservations about Lottie. And the frisson of panic she had experienced, sitting with Lottie by the river in Relkirk, with Lottie's hand closed around her wrist, the fingers strong and steely as a vise.

"But now you believe that we were all wrong?"

"The day before I took Henry to school . . . Monday . . . I took a walk with the dogs. I went to Dermot's to buy something for Katy, and then on and over the west bridge. Lottie appeared out of nowhere. She'd been following me. She told me that you all knew—all of you— you and Archie and Isobel and Edie. She said that you knew."

Violet thought, oh, dear God. She said, "Knew what, Virginia?"

"Knew that Edmund and Pandora Blair had been in love with each other. Had been lovers."

"And how did Lottie know this?"

"Because she was working at Croy at the time of Archie and Isobel's wedding. There was a dance that night, wasn't there? She said that she followed them upstairs in the middle of the party, and listened at Pandora's bedroom door. She said that Edmund was married and had a child, but that made no difference, because he was in love with Pandora. She said that everybody knew because it was so blatantly obvious. She said that they are still in love with each other, and that is why Pandora has come back."

It was even worse than Violet had dreaded, and for once in her life she found herself at a total loss for words. What could one say? What could one do to comfort? How to salvage a single grain of comfort from those muddy depths of scandal, stirred up by a madwoman who had nothing to do with her pathetic life but make trouble?

Across the small space that divided them, her eyes met Virginia's. And Virginia's were filled with pleading, because all she wanted was for Violet to assure her that the whole fabrication was a pack of lies.

Violet sighed. She said, with total inadequacy, "Oh dear."

"It's true then. And you did know."

"No, Virginia, we didn't know. We all had a pretty shrewd idea, but we didn't know, and we never spoke about it to each other, and we all went on behaving as though it had never happened."

"But *why?*" It was a cry of despair. "Why did you all shut *me* out? I'm married to Edmund. I'm his wife. How did you imagine that I wouldn't find out? And from that dreadful woman, of all people. It's a sort of betrayal, as though you didn't trust me. As though you thought I was some sort of innocent child, not old enough nor mature enough to deal with the truth."

"Virginia, how could we tell you? We didn't even know for certain. We simply suspected, and being the people that we are, we brushed it all away under the carpet and hoped that it would stay there. She was eighteen, and Edmund had known her since she was a child. But he'd been in London, and he'd married and had Alexa, and he hadn't seen Pandora for years. And then he came north for Archie's wedding, and there she was again. Not a child any longer but the most ravishing, wicked, delicious creature you've ever seen in your life. And I have an idea that she had always been in love with Edmund. When they met again, it was like an explosion of fireworks. We all saw the fireworks but we turned away and did not watch. There was nothing we could do except hope that the fireworks would burn themselves out. And it wasn't as though there was any chance of it going on for ever. Edmund had commitments in London. His wife, his child, his job. When the wedding was over, he went away, back to his own responsibilities."

"Did he go willingly?"

Violet shrugged. "With Edmund it's impossible to know. But I remember seeing him off, in his car, from Balnaid, and saying goodbye, and very nearly saying something more. Something ridiculous. Like 'I'm sorry' or 'Time is a great healer' or 'You'll forget Pandora,' but at the end of the day I lost my nerve and I never said anything."

"And Pandora?"

"She went into a sort of teen-age decline. Tears, sulks, misery. Her mother confided in me, and was in the greatest distress about it all, but truly, Virginia, what could we say? What could any of us do? I suggested sending Pandora away for a little . . . to do some sort of a course, or perhaps go to Paris or to Switzerland. At eighteen she was still very young in many ways, and some worthwhile project . . . learning a language or working with children . . . might have diverted her misery.

Given her the chance to meet other young people and the chance to get over Edmund. But I'm afraid she'd always been most dreadfully spoilt, and in a strange way her mother was frightened of Pandora's tantrums. Whether anything was ever said, I don't know. All I do know is that Pandora simply hung around Croy for a month or two, making everybody's lives utterly miserable, and the next thing was she'd run off with that dreadful Harold Hogg, rich as Croesus and old enough to be her father. And that, tragically enough, was the end of Pandora."

"Until now."

"Yes. Until now."

"Were you concerned when you knew she was coming back?"

"Yes. A little."

"Do you think they are still in love with each other?"

"Virginia, Edmund *loves* you." Virginia said nothing to this. Violet frowned. "You *surely* know that."

"There are so many different sorts of love. And sometimes, when I really need it, Edmund doesn't seem to have it to give."

"I don't understand."

"He took Henry away from me. He said I smothered him. He said I only wanted to keep Henry because he was some sort of a possession, a toy I wanted to go on playing with. I begged and pleaded and finally had that dreadful row with Edmund, but nothing made any difference. It was like arguing with a brick wall. Brick walls don't love, Vi. That isn't love."

"I shouldn't say this, but I am on your side as far as Henry is concerned. However, he *is* Edmund's child, and I truly believe that Edmund is doing what he thinks best for Henry."

"And then this week he swanned off to New York, just when I really needed him here. Taking Henry to Templehall and leaving the poor little scrap was the worst thing I've ever had to do in the whole of my life."

"Yes," said Vi inadequately. "Yes, I know." They fell silent. Violet considered the miserable situation, went back in her mind on all they had been saying. And then realized that there was a small discrepancy. She said, "Virginia, all this happened on *Monday*. But you came to see me today. Has something else occurred?"

"Oh." Virginia bit her lip. "Yes. Yes, it has."

"Lottie again?" Violet scarcely dared to ask.

"Yes. Lottie. You see . . . Vi, you remember last Sunday, having lunch at Croy and all of us teasing Isobel about her house guest, the Sad American? Well, on my way back from Templehall, I stopped off at the King's Hotel to go to the loo, and I met him there. And I know him. I know him quite well. He's called Conrad Tucker and we used to play tennis together in Leesport, about twelve years ago."

This was about the most cheerful thing Violet had been told since Virginia appeared. She said, "But how very nice."

"Anyway, we had dinner together, and then it seemed silly, his staying in Relkirk when he was coming to Croy the next day, so he came back to Balnaid with me, and stayed there. I took him up to Croy this morning and left him with Archie. And then I went to Corriehill with some flower vases for Verena. And then I came home and I found Lottie in the kitchen."

"In the kitchen at Balnaid?"

"Yes. She was waiting for me. She told me . . . that last night she'd been at Balnaid, standing in the garden, in the dark and the rain, when Conrad and I came back. She watched us. Through the windows. None of the curtains were drawn. She watched us going upstairs. . . ." Virginia met Violet's horrified gaze, opened her mouth and shut it again. Finally, she said, "She called me a whore. Called Conrad a fancy man. Raved on about lust and fornication . . ."

"She is obsessed."

"She must go, or she will tell Edmund." Before Violet's eyes, Virginia all at once went to pieces, her face crumpling like a child's, tears brimming into her blue eyes and overflowing, streaming down her cheeks. "I can't bear any more, Vi. I can't bear everything being so horrible. She's like a witch, and she hates me so much . . . I don't know why she hates me. . . ."

She groped for a handkerchief but could not find one, so Violet handed over her own, lawn and lace-trimmed and little use for damming such a flood of misery.

"She is jealous of you. Jealous of all normal happiness. . . . As for telling Edmund, he will know, as we all know, that it is nothing but a pack of lies."

"But that's just it," Virginia wailed. "It's true. That's what's so ghastly. It's true."

"True?"

"I did sleep with Conrad. I went to bed with him because I wanted to, and I wanted him to make love to me."

"But *why?*"

"Oh, *Vi.* I suppose we needed each other."

It was a desperate admission, and watching her weeping daughter-in-law, Violet found herself flooded with compassion. That Virginia, of all people, should have been driven to such lengths was a clear indication of the state that her marriage had been allowed to reach. But, thinking it over, it was perfectly understandable. The man, Conrad Tucker or whatever he was called, had just lost his wife. Virginia, in a turmoil over Edmund's motivations, had just lost her beloved son. They were old friends. For comfort, people turned to old friends. She was a desirable woman, sexual and attractive, and the American was in all probability a personable man. But still, Violet wished, beyond all else, that it had never happened. More than that, she wished that she had never been told.

Only one essential stood out, crystal-clear.

She said, "You must never tell Edmund."

Virginia blew her nose on the sodden handkerchief. "Is that all you have to say?"

"It's the only important thing to say."

"No reproaches? No recriminations?"

"What took place is none of my affair."

"It was wrong."

"But, under the circumstances, understandable."

"Oh, Vi." Virginia slipped out of the chair, onto her knees, put her arms around Violet and buried her face in Violet's considerable bosom. "I'm sorry."

Violet laid a hand on her hair. She said sadly, "We are all of us human."

For a little, they stayed as they were, comforted by closeness. Virginia's sobs gradually stilled. Presently, she drew away from Violet and sat back on her heels. She blew her nose in a final sort of fashion.

She said, "There's just one more thing, Vi. When Edmund's back, and the dance is all over, I'm thinking of going back to Long Island for a little. To stay with Gramps and Grandma. I need to get away. I've been wanting to go for some months but it never worked out, and now that I have no Henry, it seems a good time."

"And Edmund?"

"I thought . . . Edmund could stay with you?"

"When did you think of leaving?"

"Next week?"

"Is that wise?"

"You tell me."

"Just remember that you can't run away from reality any more than you can run away from guilt."

"Reality being Edmund and Pandora?"

"I didn't say that."

"But that's what you're thinking, isn't it? You just told me she'd always been in love with him. And I'm certain that she's no less beautiful now than she was at eighteen. And they share something that I can't share with Edmund, which is a thousand memories of youth. And in a funny way, those are always the most enduring and the most important."

"You are important, and I don't think you should leave Edmund just now."

"I've never minded before. All the times he has to go away and leave me, I've never known jealousy or worried about what he was up to. I tell him I don't care what he does provided I don't have to watch him doing it. A joke. But it's not a joke now. If anything's going to happen, I don't want to be a witness."

"You underestimate your friends, Virginia. Do you imagine that Archie would stand by and watch, and do nothing?"

"If Edmund wants his own way, then Archie would be no match for him."

"Pandora will not stay at Croy for ever."

"But she's there *now*. And *now* is going to be my problem."

"Do you dislike her?"

"I think she's charming."

"But you don't trust her?"

"At the moment I don't trust anybody, least of all myself. I need to stand back, make a re-appraisal, get things in perspective. That's why I'm going back to the States."

"I still think that you shouldn't go."

"I think I have to."

There did not seem to be anything more to be said. Violet sighed. "In that case, we'll talk no more about it. Instead, we must be practical and take steps. One thing, very clear, is that Lottie must go. Back to hospital. She is a deadly mischief-maker and I fear for Edie. I shall see to that immediately. And while I'm making my telephone call, I suggest that you go and wash your face and tidy your hair, and then find my brandy bottle, which is in the dining-room sideboard, and a couple of glasses. We shall both have a cheering medicinal tot and then we shall feel much stronger and much better."

Virginia did as she was told. While she was out of the room, Violet heaved herself out of her chair and went to her desk. She looked up the number of the Relkirk Royal, dialled, and asked to be put through to Dr. Martin. A little wait while the telephonist bleeped him, and then he came on the line.

"Dr. Martin?"

Violet, at some length, explained who she was, and her connection with Lottie Carstairs.

"You know who I'm talking about, Dr. Martin?"

"Yes, of course."

"I'm afraid that she is really not fit to be out of hospital. She behaves in a most irrational fashion, and is distressing and upsetting a lot of people. As for Miss Findhorn, with whom she is staying, I think it is really all too much for her. She's not a young woman, and Lottie is too much of a responsibility for her."

"Yes." The doctor sounded thoughtful. "I see."

"You don't seem surprised."

"No, I'm not surprised. I discharged her into the care of Miss Findhorn because I thought that maybe going back into ordinary life and living in a regular household would help to restore her to some sort of normality. But it was always a risk."

"It seems that the risk has not paid off."

"No. I realize that."

"Will you take her back into your care?"

"Yes, of course. I'll speak to my Ward Sister. Will you be able to drive Miss Carstairs into the hospital? It might be better than sending an ambulance. And bring Miss Findhorn with you. It's important that she is there, as she is the patient's next of kin."

"Of course. We'll be with you some time this afternoon."

"If there's any trouble, let me know."

"I certainly will," Violet promised him, and put down her receiver.

Knowing that the dilemma of Edie's cousin had been dealt with and that Lottie was probably being returned to the Relkirk Royal that very afternoon did more than the slug of Violet's best brandy to restore Virginia's equilibrium.

"When are you taking her?"

"Now," Violet told her. She had already changed her shoes and was buttoning herself into her jacket.

"Supposing Lottie refuses to go?"

"She won't."

"Supposing she has a tantrum in the car and tries to strangle you?"

"I shall have Edie with me, and she will stop her. I know this will be a great relief to dear Edie. She can't object."

"I'd come with you, only . . ."

"No. I think *you* must keep well out of the way."

"You'll give me a ring when it's all safely over?"

"Of course."

"Just take care." Virginia put her arms around Violet and kissed her. "And thank you. I love you, and I never get around to telling you."

Violet was touched, but had other things now on her mind. "Dear girl." Absently, she patted Virginia's shoulder, as she laid her plans for dealing with Lottie and Edie. "I'll see you tomorrow at the picnic."

"Of course. And Alexa and Noel will be there too."

Alexa and Noel. More family, more friends arriving. So many people, so many demands, so many decisions, so much to be resolved. I am seventy-eight tomorrow, Violet reminded herself and wondered why she was not sitting peacefully in a wheelchair with a lace cap on her head. She reached for her handbag, found her car keys, opened the front door. Alexa and Noel.

"I know," she told Virginia. "I hadn't forgotten."

She had feared a terrible scene with Lottie, but at the end of the day it was all quite painless. She found Lottie sitting in Edie's armchair watching television and looking as though butter wouldn't melt in her mouth. Violet paused to exchange a few pleasantries with her, but Lottie was far more interested in the fat lady on the screen who was demonstrating how to make a pleated lampshade out of an old piece of wallpaper. Through the kitchen window, Violet spied Edie in her garden, pegging out her daily line of washing. She went to join her and tell her, quietly and out of earshot of her cousin, all that had been decided and all that had been arranged.

Edie, who had been, of late, looking tireder by the day, now looked as though she was about to cry.

She said, "I'm no' wanting to send her away."

"Edie, it's getting too much for all of us. It's always been too much for you, and now she's started persecuting Virginia and spreading the most distressing rumours. You know what I'm talking about."

Of course Edie knew, but between them nothing needed to be spoken.

"I was afraid," Edie admitted.

"She's sick, Edie."

"Have you told her?"

"Not yet."

"What will you say?"

"Just that Dr. Martin wants to see her again. To keep her in the Relkirk Royal for a day or two."

"She'll be furious."

"I don't think so."

Edie pegged out the last of her washing, stopped to pick up the empty laundry basket. She did this as though it weighed a ton, as though Edie were hefting all the worries of the world.

She said, "I should have kept an eye on her."

"How could you?"

"I blame myself."

"Nobody could have done more." Violet smiled. "Come. We'll all have a cup of tea, and then I'll tell her what's happening while you put her belongings into a suitcase."

Together they made their way up the long garden and back to the cottage.

"I feel," said Edie, "like a murderer. She's my cousin and I've failed her."

"It's she who's failed you, Edie. You haven't failed her. Just as you've never failed any of us."

By six o'clock in the evening, the whole distasteful episode was over, and Lottie was once more incarcerated in the Relkirk Royal under the care of a kindly Ward Sister, and the incredibly youthful Dr. Martin. Mercifully, she had made no objections when Violet told her what was about to happen, simply announced that she hoped that Dr. Faulkner would take a bit more notice of her, and then raised her voice to remind Edie not to forget to pack her best green cardigan.

She had even come to the door of the hospital, with Ward Sister in attendance, and waved them a cheerful goodbye as Violet drove Edie away down the road between the dismally formal gardens that Lottie had thought so beautiful.

"You mustn't worry about her, Edie."

"I can't help it."

"You have done all you can. Been a saint. You can always visit Lottie. It's not the end."

"She's such a poor soul."

"She needs professional care. And you have more than enough to do. Now you must put it all behind you and enjoy yourself again. It's my picnic tomorrow. No long faces for my birthday."

Edie, for a little, sat silent. And then, "Have you iced your cake?" she asked, and they made plans for the picnic, and by the time Violet dropped her back at her cottage, she knew that they were over the worst.

She drove back to Pennyburn, let herself indoors through the back door and heaved a sigh of relief because she was safely home again. The birthday cake still sat on the table where she had left it. Seventy-eight years old. No wonder she was feeling utterly drained. The icing had become too hard for Smarties, so it would have to do just the way it was. She put it in a tin, then went into her sitting-room, poured herself a large, strong whisky and soda, sat at her desk, and made the last, but vitally important, telephone call of the day.

"Templehall School."

"Good evening. This is Mrs. Geordie Aird speaking. I am Henry Aird's grandmother, and I would like to speak to the Headmaster."

"This is the Headmaster's secretary speaking. Can I take a message?"

"No, I'm afraid you can't."

"Well, the Headmaster's busy at the moment. Perhaps I could ask him to ring you?"

"No. I should like to speak to him now. If you would go and find him, and tell him that I am waiting."

The secretary hesitated, and then said reluctantly, "Oh. Very well. But it may take some minutes."

"I shall wait," Violet told her majestically.

She waited. After a long time, she heard, from some distant uncarpeted passageway, the approaching tread of footsteps.

"Headmaster speaking."

"Mr. Henderson?"

"Yes."

"It's Mrs. Geordie Aird, Henry Aird's grandmother. I'm sorry to bother you, but it's important that you give Henry a message from me. Will you do that?"

"What is the message?" He sounded rather impatient, or cross.

"Just tell him that Lottie Carstairs is back in hospital, and no longer living with Edie Findhorn."

"Is that all?" He sounded disbelieving.

"Yes, that's all."

"And it's important?"

"Vitally important. Henry was very worried about Miss Findhorn. He will be most relieved to know that Lottie Carstairs is no longer living with her. It will be a weight off his mind."

"In that case, I'd better write it down."

"Yes, I think you had better. I shall repeat it." Which she did, raising her voice and enunciating clearly, as though the Headmaster might be stone-deaf. "LOTTIE CARSTAIRS IS BACK IN HOSPITAL. AND NO LONGER LIVING WITH EDIE FINDHORN. Have you got that?"

"Loud and clear," said the Headmaster, revealing a thin vein of humour.

"And you'll tell Henry, won't you?"

"I'll go at once and find him."

"You're very kind. I'm sorry I bothered you." She thought about asking for Henry, inquiring as to his well-being, and then decided against it. She didn't want to be labelled as an old fuss-pot. "Goodbye, Mr. Henderson."

"Goodbye, Mrs. Aird."

At the top of the long climb where the roughly bulldozed road crested the summit of Creagan Dubh, Archie halted the Land Rover and the two men climbed down and stood to survey the wondrous view.

They had come, that afternoon, from Croy by way of the track that led through the farmstead and the deer-fence, alongside the loch, and so up into the wilderness of the hills. Now, the Wester Glen lay far behind and below them, the waters of the loch blue as a jewel. Ahead, the main glen of Creagan plunged down in a succession of corries and spurs to where the purling waters of a narrow burn glittered like a bright thread in the spasmodic sunshine. To the north, ramparts of empty countryside folded away into infinity. The light was fitful, constantly changing, so that distant peaks were shadowed with a blue bloom, and cloud lay upon them like a blanket of smoke.

In the gardens of Croy, it had felt pleasantly warm, with sunlight streaming down through golden trees and only a faint breeze to cool the air. But here, so high had they come, that same air blew pure and clear as iced water, and the north-west wind had a cutting edge to it, buffeting across the open moorland with no tree nor any sort of obstruction to stand in its way.

Archie opened the back of the Land Rover and his two dogs, who had been waiting for some time for just this moment, leaped down. He reached in and pulled out two disreputable old weatherproof coats, much dirtied and torn, but with thick woollen linings.

"Here." He tossed one over to Conrad, and then, propping his stick against the rear of the Land Rover, pulled on the other. Its pockets were ripped and there were blood-stains down the front of it, witness to some long-since slaughtered hare or rabbit.

"We'll sit down for a bit. There's a spot a few yards in . . . we can get out of the wind. . . ."

He led the way, stepping off the stony surface of the road and into the high heather, using his stick as a third leg to get him through the thick of it. Conrad followed, observing his host's painful progress but making no offer to assist. After a little, they came to an outcrop of granite, weathered by a million years of exposure, crusted with lichen and jutting like some ancient monolith from its deep bed of heather. Its natural shape provided a place to sit and a not-very-comfortable back rest against which to lean but, settled, they achieved some shelter from the worst of the wind.

The dogs had been ordered to heel, but the younger one was not as disciplined as her mother, and as Archie made himself as comfortable as he could, and reached for his field-glasses, she scented game, bolted off in high excitement and put up a covey of grouse. Eight birds exploded out of the heather only yards from where they sat. *Go-Back Go-Back* they called, sailing down into the depths of the glen, jinking beneath the skyline, settling far below, disappearing.

Conrad, in amazed delight, watched their flight. But Archie snarled at the dog, and, drooping with shame, she returned to his side, leaning her head against his shoulder and apologizing profusely. He put his arm around her and drew her close, forgiving her small misdemeanour.

"Did you mark them?" he asked Conrad.

"I think so."

Archie handed over his glasses. "See if you can find them."

With the field-glasses to his eyes, Conrad searched. Distance sprang into detail. In the deep clumps of heather at the foot of the glen, he scanned painfully for the vanished birds, but could see no trace, mark no movement. They had gone. He gave the glasses back to Archie.

"I never imagined I'd see grouse so close."

"After a lifetime, they never fail to amaze me. So wily and brave. They can fly at eighty miles an hour, and use every trick to outwit a man with a gun. They're the most demanding adversaries, which is why they provide such incomparable sport."

"But you shoot them . . ."

"I've shot grouse all my life. And yet, as I grow older, I shoot less frequently and, I must admit, with some reservation. My son Hamish, so far, has shown no qualms, but Lucilla hates the whole business and refuses to come out with me." He sat hunched in his ragged old coat, with his good leg drawn up and his elbow resting on his knee. His worn tweed cap was pulled low over his forehead, shading his eyes against the fitful blasts of sunlight. "She feels very strongly that they are wild birds, and so part of God's creation. By wild, I mean that they are self-perpetuating. It is impossible to rear them as one might rear pheasants, because to put chicks from a hatchery out onto these moors would mean instant and certain death from predators."

"What do they feed on?"

"Heather. Blaeberries. But mostly heather. Because of that, a well-keepered moor is regularly burnt in strips. By law, burning is controlled. It's only allowed during a few weeks in April, and if you haven't burnt by then, it has to be left for another year."

"Why do you burn?"

"To encourage new growth." He pointed with his stick. "You can see the black strips on the Mid Hill where we burnt this year. The longer heather is left to give the birds good protective cover."

Conrad gazed in some bewilderment at the rolling miles all about him. "It's a hell of a lot of land for what seems to me an awfully few birds."

Archie smiled. "It does appear to be a bit of an anachronism, in this day and age. But if it wasn't for the great sporting estates in Scotland, enormous tracts of land would become neglected, or decimated either by intensive farming of some sort or other, or else commercial forestry."

"Is planting trees such a bad thing?"

"It's a touchy subject. The Scots pine is our indigenous tree, not Sitka spruce from Norway, nor lodge-pole pine from North America. And it depends on how well the woodland is husbanded. But a tightly packed stand of Sitka spruce destroys the breeding ground of upland birds because they won't nest within nine hundred yards of it. It harbours too many predators—foxes and crows. And I'm not simply talking about grouse but redshank and golden plover and curlews as well. And other forms of wildlife. Bugs, insects, frogs, adders. And plantlife. Harebells, cotton-grass, rare mosses and fungi, bog asphodel. Properly cared for, the moor is a power-house of rational ecology."

"But isn't the image of the rich guy on the grouse moor blasting away at the birds the subject of some ridicule?"

"Of course it is. The chinless aristocrat loading his gun with ten-pound notes. But I believe that image is fading, as even the greenest of politicians becomes aware that the link between country sports and conservation is of immense importance if the basic ecosystem of the Highlands is going to survive."

They fell silent. Stealthily, that silence was filled with small sounds, as seeping water will fill a void. The faint piping and drumming of the wind. The whisper of the distant burn, running in spate. Across the glen, scattered over the side of the hill, sheep grazed, moved, bleated. And as these sounds filled the quiet, so Conrad, at ease with his companion, found himself pervaded by tranquillity, a peace of mind that he had forgotten even existed.

Maybe this was wrong. Maybe after what had taken place last night, he should be suffering agonies of remorse and guilt. But his conscience was dormant, even self-satisfied.

"I feel like shit," he had told Virginia, "because I want you."

And he *had* felt guilty, aching with the physical need to make love to another man's wife, behind that other man's back, and in that other man's house. But he could do little to quench his desire, and even less when it became perfectly clear that Virginia's need for comfort and love was just as great as his own. It had been, for him, a night of joyous release after months of enforced celibacy. And for her, perhaps an assuagement of loneliness and a last impetuous taste of lost youth.

Last night, coming to Balnaid, she had become shy, keeping Conrad at arm's length with her hostessy busy-ness, aware as a young animal of potential danger. But this morning, she was composed. He had woken late, having slept more deeply than he had for months, and found her gone. Dressed, he made his way downstairs and discovered Virginia in the kitchen cooking breakfast, perking coffee, talking to the two spaniels. She still looked pale, but far less strained, and greeted him with a smile. Over bacon and eggs, they talked of trivial matters, and he respected her reticence. Perhaps it was better that way, with neither of them indulging in heart-searching analysis, nor trying to rationalize the events of the previous evening.

A one-night stand. For Virginia, perhaps, that was it. Conrad could not be sure. For himself, he simply felt deeply grateful to the fates that had flung them together at a time when both were vulnerable, bereft, and deeply in need of each other. Matters had taken their own course in a natural progression as basic as breathing.

No regrets. For Virginia he had no real worry. For himself, he only knew that twelve years ago he had been in love with her, and now he could not be too certain that anything had changed.

A movement caught his eye. A buzzard appeared, floating in the sky, then began its descent, spiralling in flight. A second later, another covey of grouse burst from the heather half-way down the hill and flew southward, at amazing speed, with the wind on their tails. The two men watched them go.

Archie said, "I hoped we'd see more birds. We're shooting this glen tomorrow. Driving over the butts."

"Will you be there?"

"Yes. It's about all I can manage, provided I can get myself to the bottom butt. It's one of the things I really regret, not being able to walk the hill any longer. Those were the best days; walking up with a few friends and half a dozen dogs. Now just a thing of the past."

Conrad hesitated. The two men had spent most of the day in each other's company, but Conrad, not wishing to appear curious or impertinent, had deliberately not brought up the subject of Archie's obvious disability. Now, however, it seemed a sensible opportunity. "How did you lose your leg?" he asked casually.

Archie watched the buzzard. "It was shot off."

"An accident?"

"No. Not an accident." The buzzard hovered, dived, swept back up into the sky, its prey, a small rabbit, dangling from its beak. "An incident in Northern Ireland."

"What were you doing there?"

"I was a regular soldier. I was there with my Regiment."

"When was this?"

"Seven, eight years ago." The buzzard had gone. Archie turned his head to look at Conrad. "The Army has been in Northern Ireland now for twenty years. Sometimes I think the rest of the world forgets how long that bloody conflict has been going on."

"Twenty years is a long time."

"We went to stop the violence, to keep the peace. But we haven't stopped the violence, and peace still seems a long way off." He shifted his position, laid down his glasses, leaned on his elbow. He said, "During the summers, we have Americans to stay, as paying guests. We give them beds, arrange diversions for them, wine them and dine them, and make conversation. During these conversations, the subject of Northern Ireland is frequently raised, and inevitably, some joker comes out with the opinion that Northern Ireland is Great Britain's Vietnam. I have learned swiftly to change the subject and talk about something else."

"I wasn't going to say that. About Vietnam, I mean. I wouldn't be so presumptuous."

"And I didn't mean to sound aggressive." He eyed Conrad. "Were you in Vietnam?"

"No. I've worn glasses since I was eight years old, so I was labelled medically unfit."

"Would you have fought, without that legitimate let-out?"

Conrad shook his head. "I don't know. But my brother went. He joined the Marines. He flew a gunship. He was killed."

"What a flaming, bloody, useless war. But then, all war is flaming and bloody and useless. And Northern Ireland most useless of all because the troubles have their roots in the past, and nobody is willing to pull those roots up and throw them away, and start planting something decent and new."

"By the past, you mean Cromwell?"

"I mean Cromwell, and William of Orange, and the Battle of the Boyne, and the Black-and-Tans, and the young men who went on hunger strike and died of starvation. And I mean long and bitter memories, and unemployment, and segregation and no-go areas and religious intolerance. And worst of all, the impossibility of being able to apply logic to the situation."

"How long were you there?"

"Three months. It should have been four, but I was in hospital when the Battalion came home."

"What happened?"

"To me, or to the Battalion?"

"To you."

Archie's response to this was a deep and reluctant telling silence. Looking at him, Conrad saw that once again his attention had been caught by some distant movement, far away out on the opposite hill. His profile was gaunt, seemingly frozen in concentration. Conrad sensed the other man's reluctance to talk, and swiftly retracted from his question.

"I'm sorry."

"Why sorry?"

"I sound curious. I don't mean to be."

"That's all right. It was an incident. That's the euphemistic term for bombings, murders, ambushes, general mayhem. You hear the word every other day over the evening news. An incident in Northern Ireland. And I was involved."

"You were operational?"

"Everybody was operational, but my actual job was Officer Commanding H.Q. company."

"One reads of such incidents, but, still, it's hard to imagine how it must be out there . . . I hear it's a very pretty country." Conrad was on the point of saying, "I didn't mean that," and then thought better of it, and let Archie continue.

"Parts of Northern Ireland are very beautiful. Sometimes my job took me out of H.Q. for the best part of the day, visiting units in their posts all over the countryside. Some of those on the border were in beleaguered forts made from old police stations which one could only get to by helicopter for fear of ambush on the roads. It was great, flying over that country. Some of it I saw in spring and early summer. Fermanagh with all its lakes, and the Mountains of Mourne." He stopped, and grinned wryly, shaking his head. "Although one had to realize that they not only swept down to the sea, but to the badlands as well. The border."

"Is that where you were?"

"Yes. Right in the thick of it. And different country again. Very green, small fields, winding country roads, lachans and streams. Sparsely populated. Tiny farms dotted about the place, grotty little homesteads surrounded by dead and broken machinery; old cars and tractors left to rot. But all quite pastoral. Peaceful. I found it impossible, sometimes, to relate such surroundings with what was going on."

"It must have been rough."

"It was all right. We were all in it together. Being with your own Regiment is a little like being with your own family. You can cope with most things if you have your family around you."

Archie fell silent again. The granite boulder made a painful resting place, and he had become uncomfortable. He shifted his position slightly, easing the strain on his leg. The younger dog, alert, moved in beside him, and Archie fondled her head with a gentle hand.

"Did you have your own barracks?" Conrad asked.

"Yes. If you can call a requisitioned clothing factory a barracks. It was all fairly rough and ready. We lived behind barbed wire, corrugated iron and sandbags, seldom saw daylight, and had little chance of exercise. We worked on one floor, went downstairs to eat, and upstairs to sleep. Scarcely the Ritz. I had a batman cum bodyguard who went everywhere with me, and even in plain clothes, we were never unarmed.

"One existed in a state of siege. We were never actually attacked, but there was always the threat of some sort of ambush or assault, so one was prepared for any of the various ploys for blowing a police or military establishment off the face of the earth. One of these was to hijack an armed Land Rover, load it with high explosives and then get the poor bugger at the wheel to drive it through the open gates of the barracks, park it and set it off from a distance. This actually happened once or twice, whereupon a device was conceived to deal with such a contingency. A solid concrete pit with a steep ramp. The idea was to drive the vehicle into the pit, and then run, shit-for-ginger and screaming warning like a maniac, before the whole caboodle blew up. The resultant devastation was still pretty formidable, but by and large, lives were saved."

"Did that happen to you?"

"No, that didn't happen to me. I have nightmares about those bloody bomb pits, and yet it was never an experience that I had to endure. Strange, isn't it? But then there can be no explanation for the workings of one's own subconscious."

By now Conrad had abandoned his inhibitions about curiosity. "So what *did* happen?"

Archie put his arm around his young dog, and she settled, to lie with her head on her master's tweeded knee.

"It was June. Early summer. Sunshine and blossom everywhere. Then an incident on the border at the crossroads near Keady. A bomb buried beneath the road, in a culvert. Two armoured vehicles—we call them Pigs—were out on border patrol, four men in each Pig. The bomb was detonated by remote control from over the border. One Pig was blown to smithereens and all four men with it. The other was badly damaged. Two men dead and two wounded. One of the wounded was the Sergeant in charge, and it was he who radioed back to H.Q. to report. I was in the Operations Room when the message and the details came through. On such occasions, for security reasons, no names are ever mentioned over the radio, but every man in the Battalion has his own Zap code, a number for identification purposes. So, as the Sergeant gave us the numbers, I knew exactly who had been killed and who was still alive. And they were all my men."

"*Your* men?"

"I told you, I was Officer Commanding the Administrative company rather than a rifle company. That meant I was in charge of the Signals, the Quartermaster, the Pay Office and the Pipes and Drums."

"Pipes and Drums?" Conrad could scarcely keep the disbelief out of his voice. "You mean you had a *band* out there?"

"But of course. The Pipes and Drums are an important part of any Highland Regiment. They play Reveille and the Last Post, beat retreat on ceremonial occasions, provide the music for dancing and smoking concerts, and guest nights in the Officers' and Sergeants' Messes. And pipe the lament at funerals. 'The Flowers of the Forest.' The saddest sound on earth. But apart from being an integral part of the Battalion, every Piper and Drummer is, as well, an active service soldier and trained as a machine gunner. It was some of these men who were trapped in that ambush. I knew them all. One of them was a boy called Neil MacDonald, who was twenty-two years old and the son of the head keeper at Ardnamore—that's up at the head of our glen, beyond Tullochard. I first heard him piping at the Strathcroy Games, when he was about fifteen. That year he walked away with all the prizes, and I suggested that when he was old enough, he should join the Regiment. And that day, I listened to those Zap codes coming in, and I knew that he was dead."

Conrad could think of no suitable comment to make, and so sensibly said nothing. A pause fell, not uncompanionable, and after a little, Archie, unprompted, went on.

"To deal with such emergencies there is always an Air Reaction Force at full alert. Two bricks of men . . ."

"Bricks?"

"You'd call them squads, and a Lynx helicopter ready and waiting for take-off. That day, I told the Sergeant to stand down, and I took his place and went with them. There were eight of us in the helicopter, the pilot and a crewman, five Jocks, and myself. It took less than ten minutes to get to the scene. When we reached the area, we circled to suss out exactly what had happened. The explosive, which had totally destroyed the first Pig, had left a hole in the road the size of a crater, and the second Pig was arse-over-tit in this. All around was littered with scraps of metal, clothing, mess tins, bits of camouflage netting, bodies, clothing, burning tyres. A lot of smoke, flames, the stench of burning rubber and fuel and paint. But no sign of movement. No sign of anything or anybody."

Once more Conrad found himself astonished by what he thought of as an obvious discrepancy.

"You mean no local people, farmers, or ploughmen, hearing the explosion and running to investigate?"

"No. Nothing. In that part of the world no person goes within an arm's length of that sort of trouble, unless of course he wishes to be dead or kneecapped within the week. There was nobody, just the smoke and the carnage.

"There was a patch of grass, like a layby, alongside the road. The helicopter landed and we all piled out. Our immediate task was to stake out the area, and get out the wounded while the helicopter flew back to base to bring in the M.O.—the Medical Officer—and his boys. But the helicopter had scarcely taken off, and before we had time to shake out, we were caught in a hail of machine-gun fire from across the border. They were waiting for us, you see. Watching and waiting. Three of my Jocks were killed instantly, another was wounded in the chest, and I caught it in the leg. Shot to pieces.

"When the helicopter returned with the M.O. on board, myself and the worst of the wounded were flown straight to hospital in Belfast. The Sergeant didn't make it, he died on the way. In the hospital my leg was amputated above the knee. I stayed there a few weeks, and then was flown back to England to begin the long business of rehabilitation. Finally I returned to Croy, pensioned off with the rank of Lieutenant Colonel."

Conrad endeavoured to make a mental tally of the casualties, but lost count and gave up. "So what did that particular incident achieve?" he asked.

"Nothing. A hole in the road. A few more British soldiers dead. The next morning, the IRA officially claimed responsibility."

"Do you feel bitter about it? Angry?"

"Why? Because I've lost my leg? Because I have to hump myself around on this aluminium contraption? No. I was a Regular soldier, Conrad. Being shot to ribbons by an implacable enemy is one of the occupational hazards of being a soldier. But I could just as easily have been an ordinary civilian, a run of the mill guy, trying to get peacefully on with his own life. An old father, perhaps, gone to Enniskillen to mourn his dead son on Armistice Day, and ending up dying beneath a pile of rubble. A young boy, taking his girl-friend to a Belfast pub for a drink, and seeing her blown to kingdom come by a booby-trap bomb. I could have been an off-duty serviceman, in the wrong car, at the wrong place, at the wrong time; dragged by a mob into a patch of waste ground, stripped, clubbed nigh to death, and finally shot."

Conrad shuddered. He chewed his lip, shamed by his own queasiness. He said, "I read about that. It made me want to vomit."

"Mindless, pointless, bloody violence. And there are other outrages that never reach the papers, are never made public. Do you know, one time a man went into a pub for a few beers. Just an ordinary young man, except that he happened to be a member of the IRA. One of the lads he was drinking with suggested it might be a laugh if he shot off somebody's kneecaps. Which was something he had never actually done, but after three beers he was ready to have a go. He was given a gun, and left the pub, and walked up to the local housing estate. He saw a young girl who was walking home from a friend's house. He hid in a passageway, and as the young girl came past, he grabbed hold of her and pushed her to the ground. He then shot off both her knees. That girl will never walk again.

"Just another incident. But it haunts me because it could have been any man's daughter, and more personally, it could have been my Lucilla. So you see I don't feel bitter and I don't feel angry. Just desperately sad for the people of Northern Ireland, the ordinary, decent people who are trying to make a life for themselves, and bring up their children under this terrible, perpetual shadow of blood and revenge and fear. And I feel sad for the whole human race, because if such senseless cruelty is accepted as the norm, then I can see no future for us all. It is frightening. And I am frightened for myself because, like a child, I still get nightmares that terrify me, and leave me screaming. And there is still worse. Guilt and remorse for that young man I told you about. Neil MacDonald. Twenty-two years old and dead as a doornail. Nothing left of his body, nothing to bury. His parents left without even the consolation of a funeral, or a grave to visit. I knew Neil as a soldier, and a good one, too, but I remember him as a boy, standing on the platform at the Strathcroy Games, piping his Pibroch. I remember the day, the sun shining down on the grass, and the river, and hills, and he and his Pibroch part of it all. Just a boy. With all his life before him, and standing there making that marvellous music."

"You can't blame yourself for his death."

"It was because of me that he became a soldier. If I hadn't shoved my oar in, he would still be alive now."

"No way, Archie. If he was meant to join your Regiment, he'd have done it, with no prompting from you."

"You think that? I find it hard to be a fatalist. I wish I could be, because then I might be able to lay his ghost and leave him in peace, and stop asking myself, why? Why should I be here, on the top of Creagan Dubh, seeing, breathing, touching, feeling, when Neil MacDonald is dead?"

"It is always worst for the one who is left to carry on."

Archie turned his head and looked at Conrad. Across the small space which divided them, the eyes of the two men met. Then Archie said, "Your wife died."

"Yes. Of leukemia. I watched her die and it took a long time. And all that time I was resentful and bitter, because it wasn't me who was dying. And when she died, I hated myself because I was alive."

"You too."

"I think, probably, it's an inevitable reaction. One simply has to come to terms with it. It takes time. But at the end of the day, all those self-accusing and soul-searching questions are unanswerable. And so, as you Brits would say, it's bloody silly even to ask them."

There was a long pause. Then Archie grinned. "Yes. You are right. Bloody silly." He turned his face up and surveyed the sky. "You are right, Conrad." The sky was darkening. They had sat for too long, and it was becoming cold. "Perhaps we should make tracks for home. And I must apologize. For a moment, I admit, I forgot that you had tragedies of your own to deal with. I hope you will believe me when I tell you that I didn't bring you up here in order to unload my troubles onto your shoulders."

Conrad smiled. "I asked for them," he reminded Archie. He realized then that he was chilled and stiff with sitting, tucked into that hard and inhospitable perch. He rose painfully to his feet, stretching the cramps out of his legs. Out of the shelter of the rock, the wind pounced upon him, stinging his cheeks, sneaking down the back of his collar. He shivered slightly. The dogs, stirring at this promise of activity, and already thinking of their dinners, sat up and gazed with hopeful eyes into Archie's face.

"So you did. But now let us both forget it all and not speak of it again. All right, you greedy bitches, I'll take you home and feed you." He held out an arm. "Give me a hand, would you, Conrad, old boy, and heave me to my feet?"

They left the hills at last, and trundled slowly homewards, down the main glen and so back to Croy. As they came through the front door, the grandfather clock by the staircase chimed the half-hour. Half past six. The dogs were ravenous. It was long past their dinner-time and they headed straight for the kitchen. Archie glanced into the library but there did not seem to be anybody about.

"What would you like to do?" he asked his guest. "We usually eat about half past eight."

"If it's okay with you, I think I'll go up and unpack my bag. Maybe take a shower."

"Fine. Use any bathroom that doesn't happen to be occupied. And come downstairs when you're ready. If there's still nobody around, you'll find a tray of drinks in the library. Help yourself. Make yourself at home."

"That's very kind." Conrad started up the stairs and then turned back. "And thanks for today. It was special."

"Perhaps it is I who should thank you."

Conrad continued on his way. Archie followed the dogs, and in the kitchen found Lucilla and Jeff, at sink and stove, both aproned and looking industrious and companionable. Lucilla turned from some pot she was stirring.

"Dad. You're back. Where've you been?"

"Up on the moor. What are you two up to?"

"We're cooking dinner."

"Where's Mum?"

"She went to have a bath."

"Would you feed the dogs for me?"

"Of course. No problem . . ." She returned to her stirring. "But they've got to wait a moment, otherwise this sauce is going to end up in lumps."

He left them to their cooking, shut the door, went back to the library, poured himself a whisky and soda and, carrying the glass, climbed the stairs in search of his wife.

He found her in the bath, soaking in scented steam and looking as comic as she always did in her blue-and-white-spotted shower-cap.

"Archie." He made himself comfortable on the lavatory seat. "Where have you been?"

"To the top of Creagan Dubh."

"It must have been heavenly. Did the Sad American turn up all right?"

"Yes, and he's not sad. He's very good company. And he's called Conrad Tucker, and he happens to be an old chum of Virginia's."

"I don't believe it! You mean they know each other? What an extraordinary coincidence. But what a lucky one. It'll make him feel not so strange, dumped in this alien household." She sat up and reached for the soap. "You obviously like him?"

"Delightful man. Exceptionally nice."

"What a relief. What's he doing now?"

"Same as you, I think."

"Has he ever been to Scotland before?"

"I don't think so."

"Because I've been thinking. Neither he nor Jeff are going to be able to do any of the dances on Friday night. Do you think it would be a good idea to have a bit of instruction after dinner this evening? Provided they can get themselves through an eightsome reel and one or two others, they can at least join in some of the fun."

"Why not? Good idea. I'll look for some tapes. Where's Pandora?"

"Crashed out, I think. We didn't get home till five. Archie, would you mind if she came up the hill with you tomorrow? I told her about Vi's picnic but she said she'd rather spend the day with you. She wants to sit in your butt and chat."

"No, that's all right, provided she doesn't make too much noise. You'd better see she's got some warm clothes."

"I'll lend her my green wellies and my Barbour."

He drank whisky. Yawned. He was tired.

"How was the shopping? Did you get my cartridges?"

"Yes. And the champagne, and the candles, and enough food to feed a starving army. And I got a new dress for the dance."

"You bought a new dress?"

"No, I didn't buy it. Pandora bought it for me. And it's perfectly beautiful, and I wasn't allowed to know how much it cost, but I think probably an arm and a leg. She seems to be dreadfully rich. Do you think I should have allowed her to be so extravagant and generous?"

"If she wanted to give you a dress, there's no way you could have stopped her. She always loved giving presents. But it was kind. Am I allowed to see it?"

"No, not until Friday, when I shall astonish you with my beauty."

"What else did you do?"

"We had lunch in the Wine Bar. . . ." Isobel, squeezing water from her sponge, considered telling Archie about Pandora and the reserved table, and then decided against it because she knew that he would disapprove. "And Lucilla bought a dress off a stall in the market."

"Oh God, it's probably full of fleas."

"I made her leave it at the cleaner's. Somebody will have to go to Relkirk on Friday morning to pick it up. But the most exciting bit of news I've kept to the end. Because Pandora bought *you* a present as well, and if you hand me my towel I shall get out of the bath and show it to you."

He did this. "A present for me?" He tried to imagine what on earth his sister had brought back for him. He hoped not a gold watch, a cigar cutter, nor a tie-pin, none of which he would use. What he really needed was a new cartridge belt. . . .

Isobel finished drying herself, pulled off the bath-cap, shook out her hair, reached for her silk dressing-gown, knotted the sash around her waist. "Come and look." He pulled himself off the lavatory and followed her through to their bedroom. "There."

It was all laid out on the bed. Tartan trews, a new white shirt still in its cellophane wrapper, black satin cummerbund, and his father's remembered green velvet smoking jacket, which Archie hadn't set eyes on since the old man died.

"Where did that come from?"

"It's been in the attic, in moth-balls. I hung it over the bath to get the wrinkles out. And the trews and the shirt are from Pandora. And I've polished your evening shoes."

He gaped. "But what's all this for?"

"Friday night, you goop. When I told Pandora you wouldn't wear your kilt, and you'd go to Verena's party in a dinner jacket, she was horrified. She said you'd look like a part-time waiter. So we visited Mr.

Pittendriech and he helped us choose these." She held up the trews. "Aren't they heaven? Oh, do try it all on, Archie, I can't wait to see how you look."

The last thing Archie wanted to do, at this particular moment, was to try on a lot of new clothes, but Isobel seemed so excited that he hadn't the heart to refuse her. And so he put his glass down on her dressing-table and obediently began to shed his old tweeds.

"Leave your shirt on. We don't want to open the new one in case you get it dirty. Take off your brogues and those smelly old stockings. Now . . ."

With her help, he pulled on the new trousers. Isobel dealt with zips and buttons, tucking in the tails of his blue country shirt and generally fussing around as if she were dressing a child for a tea-party. She fixed the cummerbund, laced his evening shoes for him, held out the velvet smoking jacket. He put his arms into the silk-lined sleeves, and she turned him around and did up the frogged fastenings.

"Now." She smoothed his hair with her hands. "Go and look in the mirror."

For some reason, he felt like an idiot. His stump ached and he yearned for a hot bath, but he limped obediently over to Isobel's ward-robe, where her full-length mirror was set in the centre panel. Observing himself in mirrors was not his favourite occupation, because his reflec-tion nowadays seemed such a travesty of his former handsome self, so thin and grey had he become, so graceless in his shabby clothes, so awkward with his lumbering, hated aluminium leg.

Even now, with Isobel's proud eyes upon him, it took some effort actually to face himself. But he did so, and it wasn't as bad as he thought it would be. It wasn't bad at all. He looked all right. Great, in fact. The trews, long and slim-legged, immaculately cut and sharply creased, had a crisp and almost military dash about them. And the marvellously rich and lustrous velvet of the jacket provided exactly the right touch of worn and gentlemanly elegance, the faded green picking up the thread of green in the tartan.

Isobel had smoothed his hair, but now he smoothed it again, for himself; turned to see other aspects of his reflected finery. Undid the jacket to admire the satiny sheen of the cummerbund, sleek around his skinny middle. Did the jacket up again. Caught his own eye and smiled wryly, seeing himself preen like a bloody peacock.

He turned to his wife. "What do you think?"

"You look amazing."

He held out his arms. "Lady Balmerino, will you waltz with me?"

She came to him, and he held her close, his cheek resting on the top of her head, the way they used to dance long ago, smooching in night-clubs. Through the thin silk of her gown his hands felt her skin, still warm from the bath-water, the curve of her hips, her neat waist. Her breasts, soft, unrestricted, pressed against him, and she smelt sweetly of soap.

They shifted gently from foot to foot, rocking in each others' arms, dancing, as best they could, to music which only the two of them could hear.

He said, "Have you, at this moment, got anything pressing that you have to go and do?"

"Not that I can think of."

"No dinner to cook, no dog to feed, no bird to pluck, no border to weed?"

"No."

He pressed a kiss on her hair. "Then come to bed with me."

She was still, but Archie's hand moved on, stroking her back. After a little, she drew away from him, looked up into his face, and he saw that her deep-blue eyes were bright with unshed tears.

"Archie . . ."

"Please."

"The others?"

"All occupied. We'll lock the door. Hang up a 'Do Not Disturb' sign."

"But . . . the nightmare?"

"Nightmares are for children. We are too old to allow dreams to stop us loving each other."

"You are different." She frowned, her sweet face filled with puzzlement. "What has happened to you?"

"Pandora bought me a present?"

"Not that. Something else."

"I found a guy who would listen. At the top of Creagan Dubh, with only the wind and the heather and the birds for company, and no person to obtrude. And so I talked."

"About Northern Ireland?"

"Yes."

"All of it?"

"All of it."

"The bomb blast, and the bits of body and the dead Jocks?"

"Yes."

"And Neil MacDonald? And the nightmare?"

"Yes."

"But you told *me*. You talked to *me*. And that didn't do us any good."

"That's because you are part of me. A stranger is different. Objective. There was never anybody like that before. Only relations and old friends who had known me all my life. Too close."

"The nightmare's still there, Archie. That won't go away."

"Maybe not. But maybe its fangs have been drawn."

"What makes you so sure?"

"My mother had a saying. Fear knocked at the door, Faith went to answer it, and no one was there. We'll have to see. I love you more than life itself, and that's all that's important."

"Oh, Archie." Her tears overflowed and he kissed them away, unloosened the sash of her gown and slid his hand beneath the soft silk, caressing her nakedness. His lips moved to her mouth, the lips opening for him . . .

"Shall we give it a try?"

"Now?"

"Yes. Now. Right away. Just as soon as you can get me out of these damned trousers."

9

Thursday the Fifteenth

VIRGINIA, AWAKE AT FIVE O'CLOCK, waited for the dawn. It was Thursday, Vi's seventy-eighth birthday.

Vi, as she had promised, had rung in the evening just before the nine-o'clock news. Lottie was back in the Relkirk Royal, she had told Virginia. Not at all upset, she seemed to take it in her stride. Edie had been distressed, but after some persuasion, had accepted the inevitable. And Vi had telephoned Templehall and instructed the headmaster to reassure Henry that he no longer needed to agonize over his beloved Edie. The horrendous episode was over at last. Virginia must put it out of her mind.

The conversation left Virginia in a state of confused emotions. The most important was one of thankfulness and overwhelming relief. Now she could face the darkness of the night, go to bed by herself in the large and empty house; sleep, in the certain knowledge that no ghoul haunted the shadows of the garden, hovering, watching, waiting to pounce. Lottie would not return; she was shut away with her dangerous secrets. Virginia was free of her.

However, she knew a certain uneasiness. It was hateful to imagine Edie's distress at having to admit failure, her reluctance to commit her cousin once more to the professional, but impersonal, care of the hospital. But surely, deep down, Edie must know some relief, if only for the fact that she was shed of that almost untenable responsibility and no longer had to endure listening to the seemingly endless spate of Lottie's conversation.

Finally, there was Henry, and here Virginia was filled with guilt. She knew how Henry felt about Lottie, and how he feared for Edie, and yet the sensible idea of making a telephone call to his school had never even occurred to her, and she realized that the shameful reason for this was that Henry had slipped out of her mind, so absorbed had she become in herself and the events of the last few days.

First, Edmund and Pandora. Now, Conrad.

Conrad Tucker. Here, in Scotland, in Strathcroy, already part of the Balmerino household and an important character in the dramatis personae of the next few days, his presence changed the shape of everything. Mostly herself, as though some unsuspected and hidden facet of her own personality had been, by him, revealed. She had slept with Conrad. They had made love with a mutual desire that had more to do with comfort than passion, and she had stayed with him, and spent the night in his arms. An act of infidelity; adultery. Call it the worst name in the world, and still Virginia regretted nothing.

Whatever you do, you must never tell Edmund.

Vi was a wise old lady, and confession was not a penance but a self-indulgence. It was unloading your so-called sin onto another person, and thus shedding guilt. But her own total lack of remorse had taken Virginia by surprise, and she felt that in the last twenty-four hours she had somehow grown, not physically, but within herself. It was as though she had been struggling up some precipitous hillside, and now had time to pause for breath, to rest, to appreciate the widened prospects that her efforts had achieved.

For so long she had been content to be simply Henry's mother, Edmund's wife, one of the Airds, her existence shaped by clan, and all her time and energy and love channelled into making a home for the family. But now Alexa was grown, Henry was gone, and Edmund . . . ? For the moment, she seemed to have lost sight of Edmund. Which left only herself. Virginia. An individual, an entity with a past and a future, bridged by the fleeting years of marriage. Henry's going had not only ended an era, but freed her as well. There was nothing to stop her stretching her wings, flying. All the world was hers.

The visit to Long Island, which for months had been simply a dream, edging around at the back of her mind, was now possible, positive, even imperative. Whatever Vi said, it was time to go, and if excuses were needed she would plead her grandparents' advancing age and her own burning need to see them again before they grew too old to enjoy her company; before they became ill or infirm; before they died. That was the excuse. But the true reason had much to do with Conrad.

He would be there. He would be around. In the City, or

Southampton, but never more than a telephone call away. They could be together. A man whom her grandparents had always known and liked. A kindly man. He was not one to leave abruptly, nor break promises, nor let you down just when you needed him most; nor love another woman. It occurred to her then that perhaps trust was more important than love if a relationship was to be truly enduring. In order to deal with these uncertainties, she needed time and space, some sort of an interlude in which to stand back and review the situation. She needed solace, and knew that she would find it in the company of one who had always been her friend and was now her lover. Her lover. An ambivalent word, loaded with meanings. Once more, she searched her conscience for that mandatory twinge of guilt, but found nothing but a sort of assurance, a comforting strength, as though Conrad had brought to her some sort of a second chance, another taste of youth, a whole new freedom. Whatever. She only knew that she was going to grab at it, before it eluded her forever. Leesport was there, just a jet flight away. Unchanged, because it was a place that never changed. She smelt the crisp autumn air, saw the wide streets scattered with fallen scarlet leaves, the smoke from the first fires rising from the chimneys of the stately white clapboard houses drifting sweetly upwards into the deep-blue sky of a Long Island Indian summer.

Recalling other years, she took stock. Labor Day was past, the kids back at school, the ferry no longer running to Fire Island, the shore bars closed. But Gramps would not yet have pulled his small motor boat out of the water, and the great Atlantic beaches were there, only a short trip distant. The dunes, combed by the wind; the endless sands littered with clam shells, and laced by the surf of the thundering rollers. She felt that blown spume on her cheeks. Saw herself, as though from a great distance, walking through the shallows, silhouetted against the evening sky, with Conrad at her side. . . .

And then, despite everything, Virginia found herself smiling, not with romantic delight, but with healthy self-ridicule. For this was a teenager's image, culled from some television ad. She heard the soupy music, the deeply sincere masculine voice urging her to use some shampoo, or deodorant, or biodegradable washing powder. Too easy, it would be, to drift through this day on a cloud of fantasy. It was not that day-dreams were the sole right of the young, it was just that their elders did not have the time to lose themselves in fantasy. They had too much to do, too much to see to, too much to organize. Like herself. Right now. Life, immediate and demanding, claimed her attention. Resolutely, she put Leesport and Conrad out of her mind and thought about Alexa. The first priority was Alexa. Alexa was due to arrive at Balnaid in an hour or two, and a month ago, in London, Virginia had made Alexa a promise.

". . . you and Fa," Alexa had pleaded. "You won't still be having a row, will you? I couldn't bear it if there was a hateful atmosphere. . . ."

And, "No, of course not," Virginia had assured her. "Forget that. . . . We'll have a great time. . . ."

Promises were not made to be broken, and she had enough pride to know that this one was no exception. By Friday, Edmund would be home again. She wondered if he would bring her another gold bracelet and hoped that he would not, for now it was not only Henry who lay between them, like a bone to be snarled over, but Virginia's new knowledge, both of herself and her husband. She felt that nothing would be either simple or straightforward again, but somehow, for Alexa's sake, she would make it seem that way. It was basically a question of getting through the next few days. She imagined a series of hurdles. Alexa's arrival, Vi's picnic, Edmund's home-coming, Isobel's dinner party, Verena's dance, all to be taken, one by one, without betraying a single base emotion. No doubt, no lust, no suspicion, no jealousy. Eventually, it would be all over. And when the September visitors were gone, and life was back to normal, Virginia, freed of commitments, would make plans for departure.

She waited for the dawn, from time to time turning on her bedside light to check the hour, but by seven o'clock she had had enough of this pointless occupation and was grateful to abandon her bed with its twisted sheets.

She drew back the curtains and was met by a pale-blue sky, a garden streaked with long, early shadows, and a thin ground mist hanging over the fields. All these were potential signs of a fine day. As the sun rose, the mist would be burnt away, and with a bit of luck, it might become really warm.

She knew a certain relief. To have been met by cold, grey, and rain, today of all days, would have been almost more than she could bear. Not simply because her spirits were low enough without extra depressions, but, as well, whatever the elements threw at them, Vi's birthday picnic, willy-nilly, would take place. For Vi was a stickler for traditions, and cared not if all her guests had to crouch beneath golf umbrellas, paddle about in rubber boots, and cook their damp sausages over a smoking, rain-sizzled barbecue. This year, it seemed, they were to be spared such masochistic pleasures.

Virginia went downstairs, dealt with the dogs, and made a cup of tea. She thought about starting to cook breakfast, abandoned this idea, and went back upstairs to dress and make her bed. She heard a car, dashed to the window, saw nothing. Just some person passing the gates as they headed down the lane.

She returned to the kitchen and made a pot of coffee. At nine o'clock the telephone rang, and she sprang for it, expecting some explanation of Alexa, stuck in a motorway telephone kiosk. But it was Verena Steynton.

"Virginia. Sorry to ring so early. Are you out of bed?"

"Of course."

"Heavenly day. You haven't got any damask table-cloths, have you? White ones, and huge. It's the one thing we never thought of, and of course Toddy Buchanan can't produce them."

"I think I've got about half a dozen, but I'll have to take a look at them. They were Vi's; she left them behind when she moved out."

"Are they really long?"

"Banquet-sized. She had them for parties."

"You couldn't be an absolute saint and bring them up to Corriehill this morning, could you? I'd come and fetch them, only we're all going to be doing flowers, and I simply haven't got a moment to spare."

Virginia was glad that Verena could not see her face. "Yes. Yes, I could do that," she said, sounding as obliging as possible. "But I can't come until Alexa and Noel have arrived, and they aren't here yet. And then I've got to go to Vi's picnic. . . ."

"That's all right . . . if you could just drop them in. Endlessly grateful. You are a love. Find Toddy and give them to him . . . and see you tomorrow if not before. Bye-eee . . ."

She rang off. Virginia sighed in some exasperation, because this morning the last thing she wanted to do was to drive the ten miles to Corriehill and then back again. However, after years of living in Scotland, she had become programmed to the local customs, and one of these was that in times of stress it was a case of all hands to the wheel—even if it was somebody else's—and putting a cheerful face on inconvenience. She supposed throwing a dance counted as a time of stress, but even so wished that Verena had thought of table-cloths before the last moment.

She wrote "Table-cloths" on the telephone pad. She thought about the picnic and put a large chicken into the oven to roast. By the time it had cooked and cooled, hopefully Alexa would be here, and she would get her to carve it into handy chunks.

The telephone rang again. This time it was Edie.

"Would you be able to give me a lift to the picnic?"

"Yes, of course. I'll come and pick you up. Edie, I'm so sorry about Lottie."

"Yes." Edie sounded curt, which was the way she always sounded when she had been much upset but didn't want to talk about it. "I felt bad." Which left Virginia uncertain as to whether Edie felt bad because Lottie had had to go, or because of Virginia's involvement in the whole sorry affair. "What time should I be ready?"

"I have to go to Corriehill with some table-cloths, but I'll try to be with you around twelve."

"Has Alexa come yet?"

"No, not yet."

Edie, imagining death and destruction, was instantly anxious. "Oh my, I hope they're safe."

"I'm sure. Perhaps heavy traffic."

"Those roads scare the life out of me."

"Don't worry. I'll see you at midday, and they'll be here by then."

Virginia poured another mug of coffee. The telephone rang.

"Balnaid."

"Virginia."

It was Vi. "Happy birthday."

"Aren't I lucky with the weather? Has Alexa come?"

"Not yet."

"I thought they'd have arrived by now."

"So did I, but they haven't shown up yet."

"I can't wait to see the darling child. Why don't you all come to Pennyburn early, and we'll have a cup of coffee and a chat before we head off up the hill?"

"I can't." Virginia explained about the table-cloths. "I'm not even certain where to find them."

"They're on the top shelf of your linen cupboard, wrapped in blue tissue paper. Verena is a nuisance. Why didn't she think of asking you earlier?"

"I suppose she's got a lot on her mind."

"So when will you all be here?"

Virginia made calculations and laid plans. "I'll send Noel and Alexa up to Pennyburn in the Subaru. And then I'll go to Corriehill in the small car, and on the way back I'll pick up Edie and bring her to Pennyburn. And then we'll pack all of us and all the picnic gear into the Subaru and go on from there."

"What a splendid organizer you are. It must have something to do with having an American mother. And you'll bring rugs, won't you? And wineglasses for yourselves." Under "Table-cloths," Virginia wrote "Rugs, Wineglasses." "And I'll expect Noel and Alexa at about eleven o'clock."

"I hope they're not too exhausted."

"Oh, they won't be exhausted," Vi assured her breezily. "They're young."

Noel Keeling was an urban creature, born and raised in London, his habitat the city streets and weekend forays into the diminishing country-side of the Home Counties. From time to time his pleasures took him farther afield, and he'd fly to the Costa Smeralda on Sardinia, or the Algarve in southern Portugal, invited to join some house party, where he would play golf or tennis or indulge in a bit of yachting. Sightseeing, gazing at churches or châteaux, admiring great tracts of vineyards did not enter his plans for enjoyment, and if such an outing was suggested, he usually found good reason to opt out, and instead spend the time either lying by the swimming pool, or drifting down to the nearest town to sit beneath the awning of a pavement bar and watch the world go by.

Once, some years ago, he had come to Scotland to join a few friends in a week of salmon fishing. That time he had flown to Wick from London, there been met by another member of the party, and driven to Oykel Bridge. It had been raining. It rained the whole way to the hotel, and continued to rain for the remainder of their stay, the downpour interrupted at infrequent intervals by a slight clearing of the mist, which revealed a great deal of brown and treeless moorland and very little else.

His memories of that week were mixed. Each day was spent thigh-deep in the flood of the river, flogging the swollen waters for the elusive fish. And each evening was passed in a cheerful blur of conviviality, eating quantities of delicious Scottish food and drinking even larger quantities of malt whisky. The surrounding scenery had left no impression whatsoever.

But now, at the wheel of his Volkswagen Golf, and driving the last few miles of their long journey, he realized that he was not only on familiar ground, but also in unexpected territory.

The familiar ground was metaphorical. He was an experienced guest, with long years of country weekend house parties behind him, and this was by no means the first time he had approached an unknown house to stay with strangers. In years gone by, he had devised a rating for weekends, awarding stars for comfort and pleasure. But that was when he had been much younger and poorer, and in no position to turn down any invitation. Now, older and more prosperous, with friends and acquaintances to match, he could afford to be more selective, and was seldom disappointed.

But the game, if it was to be properly played, had its own appointed rituals. And so, in his suitcase stowed in the boot were not only his dinner jacket and a selection of suitably countrified clothes, but a bottle of The Famous Grouse for his host, and a generously large box of Bendick's handmade chocolates for his hostess. As well, this weekend involved birthday presents. For Alexa's grandmother, celebrating her seventy-eighth year this very day, there were shiny boxes of soap and bath-oil from Floris—Noel's standard offering to elderly ladies, both known and unknown; and for Katy Steynton, whom he had never met, a framed sporting print depicting a sad-eyed spaniel with a dead pheasant in its mouth.

Thus, bearing gifts, he abided by the rules.

The unexpected territory was a physical thing, the astonishingly beautiful county of Relkirkshire. He had never imagined such rich and prosperous estates, such verdant farmlands, immaculately fenced and grazed by herds of handsome cattle. He had not expected avenues of beech, roadside gardens filled with flowers in such profusion and such colour. Driving overnight, he had watched the light creep into an overcast and misty dawn, but now the sun had done its work, and the greyness was dissolved into a morning of brilliant clarity. With Relkirk behind them, the road was clear, fields gold with stubble, rivers sparkling, bracken turning to saffron-yellow, the skies enormous, the air crystal-clear, unpolluted by smoke or smog or any horror that the hand of man could produce. It was like going back in time to a world that one had thought gone for ever. Had he ever known such a world? Or had he known it once and simply forgotten that it had existed?

Caple Bridge. They crossed a river, deep in a ravine far below them, and then took the turning signposted "Strathcroy." The hills, still bloomy with heather, folded away on either side of the narrow winding road. He saw scattered farmsteads, a man driving a flock of sheep up through green pasture fields to the rough grazing beyond. Alexa, with Larry on her knee, sat beside him. Larry slept, but Alexa was palpably tense with the scarcely suppressed excitement of coming home. In truth, she had been in a state of happy anticipation for weeks, counting the days off on her calendar, searching the shops for a new dress, getting her hair cut, buying presents. For the last two days, she had been spinning like a top with last-minute arrangements; packing for the pair of them, ironing all Noel's shirts, emptying the refrigerator, and leaving with a neighbour the spare keys of her house in case it should be invaded by vandalizing bandits. All this was accomplished with the transparent enthusiasm and energy of a child, and Noel had witnessed her furious activity with fond tolerance, while refusing to pretend that he felt the same way.

Now, however, with the long journey behind him, with the sunlight streaming down from that vast and pristine sky, the clean air blowing through the opened window, the fresh prospects revealed at each bend of the road, her excitement suddenly became contagious, and he was filled with ridiculous elation—not happiness, exactly, but a surge of physical well-being that was perhaps the next-best thing. Impulsively, he took his hand off the wheel and laid it on Alexa's knee, and at once she covered it with her own.

She said, "I'm not saying 'Isn't it beautiful' all the time, because if I do, it'll just sound too banal for words."

"I know."

"And coming back is always special, but it's more special this time because you're with me. That's what I've been thinking." Her fingers twined with his. "It's never been quite like this before."

He smiled. "I'll be on my best behaviour and try to keep it that way."

Alexa leaned over and kissed his cheek. She said, "I love you."

Five minutes later, they had arrived. Reaching the little village, they crossed another bridge, through open gates and up a drive. He saw the lawns, the banks of rhododendrons and azaleas, glimpsed the open view through to the hills that lay to the south. He drew up in front of the house, the house familiar from Alexa's photograph, but now reality, standing before him, solid and substantial, with the towering conservatory jutting out at one side. Virginia creeper, now turning crimson, framed the open front door, and before Noel had even switched off the ignition the two spaniels were there, not posed obediently at the top of the steps, but racing down them, in full cry and with ears flying, come to investigate the new arrivals. Larry, rudely awoken, gave as good as he got, yapping from Alexa's arms as she got out of the car.

Almost at once, right behind the dogs, Virginia appeared, wearing jeans and an open-necked white shirt and looking just as toothsome as she had in her sophisticated London clothes, that first and only time that Noel had met her.

"Alexa. Darling. I thought you were never coming." Hugs and kisses. Stretching the aches out of his arms and legs, Noel watched the loving reunion. "And Noel"—Virginia turned to him—"how lovely to see you." He was kissed as well, which was pleasurable. "Did you have a frightful drive? Alexa, I can't stand the din. Put Larry down and let them make friends right here in the garden, otherwise he'll pee all over my carpets. Why are you so late? I've been expecting you for hours."

Alexa explained. "We stopped in Edinburgh for breakfast. Noel's got some friends there called Delia and Calum Robertson. They live in the dearest little mews house just at the back of Moray Place. We woke them up by throwing stones at their window and they came down, let us in and cooked us bacon and eggs and weren't a bit cross at being woken up. I should have phoned you, but I never thought. I am sorry."

"It doesn't matter. All that does is that you're here. But there's not a moment to spare because you've got to be with Vi at eleven, and have coffee with her before we all head up the hill for the picnic." She looked at Noel with some sympathy. "Poor man, you're really being thrown in at the deep end, but Vi's longing to see you both. Can you bear it? You're not too exhausted after the long drive?"

"Not a bit," he assured her. "We shared the driving and the one who wasn't at the wheel was able to have a kip. . . ." He opened the boot of his car, and Virginia raised her eyebrows.

"Heavens, what a lot of luggage. Come on, let's hump it all in. . . ."

He was in his bedroom, left with his bags to settle himself in. The door stood open, and from down the passage, he could hear the voices of Alexa and Virginia, still with plenty to talk about. From time to time there was a burst of laughter. He went to close the door, finding himself in need of a moment of privacy before the next lot of demands were made upon him. He was to drive the Subaru, he had been told. There was some complication about table-cloths, but he and Alexa would have coffee with her grandmother, and later Virginia and Edie would join them, whereupon the entire party would drive up the hill for the celebratory picnic.

He was not dismayed by the prospect; on the contrary, he found himself quite looking forward to anything that the day might bring. He opened his suitcase and began in a desultory fashion to unpack. He hung up his dinner jacket in the towering Victorian wardrobe, dug around for Vi's birthday present, his hairbrushes, his wash-bag. He put the brushes on the dressing-table and went to inspect the bathroom. There he was confronted by a seven-foot bath with gargantuan brass taps, a marbled floor, tall mirrors, fluffy white bath-sheets neatly folded over a heated rail. He felt worn and grubby after his overnight drive, and, on an impulse, turned on the taps, tore off his clothes, and took the quickest, hottest bath of his life. Much refreshed, he dressed again, and, buttoning his clean shirt, walked to the window to observe the pleasing view beyond the boundary of the garden. Fields, sheep, hills. Out of the quiet came the liquid call of a curlew. It rose and died away, and he tried to remember when he had last heard that haunting, evocative sound, but could not.

Virginia Aird was half-American; young, vital, and chic. Once, on a business trip to the United States, Noel had stayed in the home of a colleague who lived in New York State. The house was ranch-type, set in lawns that ran into the lawns of the next-door property, and had been designed with convenience and ease of maintenance as first priorities. Centrally heated, marvellously thought out, and equipped with every sort of modern appliance, it should have been the most comfortable place in the world in which to spend a winter weekend. But somehow, none of it added up, because his hostess, although delightful, hadn't the first idea about having guests to stay. Despite the fact that she was possessed of an all-singing, all-dancing kitchen, she never cooked a single meal. Each evening, they dressed up and went out to the local country club for dinner, and the only food that emerged from that kitchen was fried eggs or micro-waved beefburgers. But that was not all. In the living room was an open fireplace, but the grate was filled with pot plants, and instead of a comfortingly blazing log fire, the sinfully comfortable couches and armchairs were arranged around the focal point of the television, and Sunday afternoon was spent gazing at a football match, the rules and shibboleths of which Noel found incomprehensible. There was another television set in his bedroom, and the bathroom off this was meticulously equipped with shower, shaving sockets, and even a bidet, but the largest of the navy-blue matched towels was so small that it barely covered his private parts, and this small inconvenience caused Noel to yearn wistfully for the comfort of his own, immense, white, thirsty bath-sheets. But worst of all was the discomfort and pain of shocked sinuses, caused by sleeping in a heated room, the window of which refused to open.

It was churlish and ungrateful to find fault, because they had been immensely kind, but he had never, in his life, been so glad to get away from anywhere.

The curlew called again. Peace. And . . . he turned back to the bedroom, stuffing his shirt-tails into his jeans . . . a marvellous, Edwardian opulence. As opulent as Ovington Street, but all on a massive and masculine scale. The great bath, built for the largest of men. The monster towels, the heavy curtains, swagged back with ropes of silk. He thought again about Virginia, and knew that although he had harboured no fears of a repeat of that sojourn in suburban America, he had scarcely expected her to be the mistress of a house that seemed to have been decorated and furnished fifty years ago and never altered since.

But he approved. He felt very much at home. He liked the feeling of the place, the solid comfort, the pleasant country-house smell, the gleam of polish on well-tended furniture, the crispness of fresh linen, the sense of family. Pulling on clean socks, a thick sweater, brushing his hair, he found himself whistling. He caught his own eye in the mirror and grinned at his reflection. Already, he had started to enjoy himself.

Finally ready, and bearing Vi's birthday present, he left his bedroom and went downstairs and, following the sound of feminine voices, found himself in Virginia's kitchen. Not all-singing, all-dancing, but large and homely, and filled, not only with sunshine, but with the fragrant smell of fresh coffee. Alexa professionally had carved a cold chicken and was packing the pieces into a plastic box, and Virginia was filling a vacuum flask with coffee. As Noel appeared, she set down the jug and screwed on the stopper.

"Everything all right?" she asked him.

"More than all right. I had a bath, and now I'm ready for anything."

"Is that a present for Vi? Put it in this big box, with all of ours. . . ." It was a grocery carton already crammed with oddly shaped and brightly wrapped packages.

He added his own. "Somebody's given her a bottle."

"Henry. It's rhubarb wine. He won it at the church sale. Noel, the Subaru's out at the back. Perhaps you could put the box in with all the other stuff, and then you can give it to Vi when you and Alexa get to Pennyburn."

Noel picked up the birthday box and carried it across the kitchen and out through the open back door. In the yard beyond, the Subaru, a sturdy four-wheel-drive vehicle, was parked, waiting, its rear compartment already half filled with assorted clobber. To Noel a picnic meant a sandwich eaten in a field, or perhaps a well-chosen hamper from Fortnum's, complete with champagne, to be ceremoniously opened on the lawns of Glyndebourne. Preparations for today, however, seemed to be more on the scale of an Army manoeuvre. Rugs, umbrellas; fishing rods, creels, and bags; a paper sack of charcoal, another of kindling; grids and tongs; dogs' bowls; a bottle of water, cans of beer; a basket filled with brightly coloured plastic plates and a number of plastic wineglasses. There were a roll of paper towel, a bundle of rainproof gear, Alexa's camera, a pair of field-glasses.

He loaded the box of presents, and as he did this was joined by Alexa with yet another basket containing the coffee flask and the box of cold chicken, some mugs, dog-leads, and a whistle.

"It looks," he told her, "as though we were going camping for at least two weeks."

"We have to be prepared for all eventualities." He took the basket from her and found a corner for it. "And we should go. We're late already."

"What about the dogs?"

"They all come with us. We'll have to squash them in with all this stuff."

"Can't they sit on the back seat?"

"No, because there are five of us going up the hill, and neither Vi nor Edie is noticeably slender."

"We could take my car as well."

"We could, but we wouldn't get very far. Wait till you see the track. It's precipitous and very rough. This is the only car that will make it."

Noel was protective of his Volkswagen, and so this ended the argument. The three dogs were rounded up, bundled aboard, and the doors shut in their faces. Their expressions were resigned. Alexa and Noel climbed up into the front seats, Noel at the wheel. Virginia, still in her apron, came to wave them away. "I'll be with you about twelve-fifteen," she told them. "Have a good time with Vi."

They set off, around the back of the house, through the gates, over the bridge. As he drove, Alexa gave him all the up-to-date local news. "Fa's in New York. I heard all about it while I was carving the chicken. But he's meant to be getting back sometime tomorrow, so he'll be there for the party. And Lucilla Blair's at Croy . . . she's come back from France . . . and Pandora Blair. She's Archie Balmerino's sister, so you'll meet both of them."

"Will they all be at the picnic?"

"I expect so. Not sure about Pandora, though. I'm longing to see her because I never have. Just heard about her. She's the black ewe of the Balmerino family, with a wonderfully risqué reputation."

"Sounds interesting."

"Well, don't get too excited. She's quite older than you."

"I always did go for the more mature lady."

"I don't think 'mature' is quite the right word for Pandora. And there's another man staying at Croy called Conrad Tucker. He's an American, and an old friend of Virginia's. Isn't that extraordinary? And poor Virginia had to take Henry to school herself, on account of Fa not being here. She said it was really horrible and she doesn't want to talk about it. And she hasn't yet heard from darling Henry, so we don't know how he's getting on. She says she doesn't want to ring the headmaster and ask in case he thinks she's a fussing parent." By now they were trundling down the village street. "I don't know why she shouldn't telephone. I don't see why she shouldn't talk to Henry if she wants to. Turn left here, Noel, through these gates and up the hill. This is Croy now. Archie Balmerino's land. I think he's shooting today, but we're all going to dinner with them tomorrow, before the dance, so you'll meet him then. . . ."

The road climbed steeply, through farmland that had once been parkland. The leaves of stately beeches were turning gold, and ahead the hills thrust their summits into the sparkling autumn sky. Despite the warmth of the sun, there was a nippy breeze, and Noel was glad of his thick sweater.

"Now we turn down this lane. It used to be really grotty, a brokendown track leading to an old gardener's cottage, but Vi did it all up when she bought the place from Archie. She's a manic gardener. I've told you that already. But just look at her view. Of course, she's in the teeth of the wind, but it's better now that the beech hedge has grown. . . ."

The little house stood blinding white in the sunshine, set in a garden of green lawns and bright flower-beds. As Noel drew up at the front door, this opened and a large and well-built lady emerged to greet them, her arms outstretched, and the brisk breeze playing havoc with her grey hair. She wore a very old tweed skirt, a cardigan, ankle socks, and sturdy brogues, and Alexa, jumping down from the car, was almost instantly swept up into her grandmother's mammoth embrace.

"Alexa. My darling child, what a joy to see you."

"Happy birthday."

"Seventy-eight, my darling. Isn't it terrible? Old as Methuselah." She kissed Alexa, and then, looking over her granddaughter's head, watched as Noel came around the front of the Subaru. Their eyes met, and held. Violet's gaze was steady and bright; sharp, but not unkindly. I am, Noel told himself, being summed up. He put on his most open smile. "How do you do? I'm Noel Keeling."

Violet released Alexa and held out her hand. He took it in his own, a healthy handshake, the palm warm and dry, the fingers strong. She was not a beautiful old lady, and probably had never been so, but he saw much liveliness and wisdom in her weather-beaten features, and all the lines on her face looked as though they had been put there by laughter. His liking for her, his immediate and wordless rapport with her, was instinctive, and he knew that she was the sort of person who, although quite capable of implacable enmity, could as well become the truest and staunchest of friends. All at once he wanted her on his side.

And then she said an odd thing. "We've never met?"

"I don't think so."

"Your name. Keeling. It rings a bell." She shrugged, let loose his hand. "No matter." She smiled, and he realized that if she had never been beautiful, then she had once been possessed of a great physical attraction. "How very nice of you to come and see us all."

"I must wish you a happy birthday. We've a box of presents for you."

"Bring them inside. I'll open them later."

He returned to the car, opened the doors, calmed the dogs, retrieved the birthday box, closed the doors again. By the time he had achieved all this, Alexa and her grandmother had disappeared into the house, and Noel followed them into a small hallway, and so through to an airy sitting-room filled with light, and with a glassed door giving out onto the old lady's delectable garden.

"Put the box down there! I won't open them yet, because I want to hear all your news. Alexa, the coffee and the cups are in the kitchen. Would you fetch the tray in for me?" Alexa disappeared to do this. "Now, Noel . . . I can't call you Mr. Keeling because nobody does these days, and you must call me Violet . . . where would you like to sit?"

But he did not want to sit. As always in new surroundings, he wanted to prowl, nose, get the feel of things. It was a charming room, with pale-yellow walls, bright rose-chintzed curtains, and cream carpets, fitted snug to the wainscot. Violet Aird had not lived here for many years, he knew, and there was a freshness and a lightness about everything, evidence of recent refurbishment; but her furniture, her pictures, her bibelots, her books, and her china had obviously all moved with her from some previous abode, presumably Balnaid. The chairs and sofa were loose-covered in coral linen, and an ebony cabinet, its doors standing open, was lined in that same coral, and contained a collection of Famille Rose porcelain. Everywhere he looked, Noel's eye fell upon a clutter of either enviable or practical objects, the squirrel hoard of an elderly lady, gathering about her, like a store of nuts, the comforting possessions of a lifetime. Here were hand-worked cushions, a wicker basket filled with logs, a brass fender, a pair of bellows, her sewing box, her little television set, stacks of magazines, bowls of pot-pourri. As well, every horizontal surface was cluttered with small and decorative objects. Enamel boxes, jugs of fresh flowers, a copper bowl filled with purple heather, silver-framed photographs, small arrangements of Dresden china.

She was watching him. He looked at her and smiled. He said, "You follow the rules of William Morris."

"And what do you mean by that?"

"You have nothing in your house that you don't know to be useful nor think to be beautiful."

She was amused. "Who taught you that?"

"My mother."

"It's an outmoded concept."

"But still viable."

In her grate, she had lighted a little fire. On the mantelshelf were a pair of Staffordshire dogs, and over the mantelpiece . . .

He frowned, moving to inspect the picture more closely. It was an oil-painting of a child in a field of buttercups. The field was in shadow, but, beyond the field, the sun shone on rocks and sea and the distant figures of two older girls. The illusionary effect of light and colour had caught his attention, not simply because it hummed with warmth but because the technique, the factual rendering of the three-dimensional form, sprang at him with all the familiarity of a face remembered from childhood.

It had to be. Noel scarcely needed to read the signature to know who it was.

He said, in wonder, "This is a Lawrence Stern."

"How clever of you to know. I love it more than anything."

He turned to face her. "How did you come to possess it?"

"You seem astonished."

"I am. There are so few about."

"My husband gave it to me many years ago. He was in London. He saw it in the window of a gallery, and went in and bought it for me, not minding that he had to pay a great deal more than he could afford."

Noel said, "Lawrence Stern was my grandfather."

She frowned. "Your grandfather?"

"Yes. My mother's father."

"Your mother's . . . ?" She paused, still frowning, and then all at once smiled, the puzzlement gone, and her face filled with pleasure. "So *that* is how I knew your name! Noel Keeling. But I knew her . . . I met her. . . . Oh, what has happened to Penelope?"

"She died about four years ago."

"I can't bear it. Such a lovely person. We only met once, but . . ."

They were interrupted by Alexa's reappearance from Violet's kitchen, bearing the tray with the coffee jug and cups and saucers upon it.

"Alexa, this is the most extraordinary thing! Just imagine, Noel isn't a stranger at all to me, because I once met his mother . . . and we made such friends. And I always hoped so much that we would meet again, but somehow we never did. . . ."

This discovery, this revelation, the extraordinary small-world coincidence, claimed all attention. The picnic and the birthday were, for the moment, forgotten, and Alexa and Noel sat and drank scalding coffee and listened with fascination to Vi's story.

"It was all through Roger Wimbush, the portrait painter. When

Geordie came back from the war, from prison camp, and went back to Relkirk to work, it was decided that, as chairman of the firm, he should have his portrait painted for posterity. And Roger Wimbush was given the commission. He came to Balnaid and stayed with us, and the portrait was accomplished in the conservatory, and duly hung, with some ceremony, in the Board Room at the office. As far as I know, it's still there. We made great friends, and when Geordie died, Roger wrote me such a dear letter, and sent me an invitation to the Portrait Painters' Exhibition at Burlington House. I didn't very often travel to London, but I felt the occasion deserved the long journey, so I went, and Roger met me there and showed me around. And all at once, he spied these two ladies. One was your mother, Noel, and the other, I think, an old aunt of hers whom she had brought to the exhibition as a little treat. A very old lady; tiny and wrinkled, but humming with vitality. . . ."

"Great-Aunt Ethel," said Noel, because it could have been no one else.

"That's it. Of course. Ethel Stern, and Lawrence Stern's sister."

"She died some years ago, but while she was alive she afforded us all an enormous amount of amusement."

"I can imagine it. Anyway, Roger and your mother were obviously old friends of long standing. I think she had taken him in as a lodger years before when he was a penniless young student, struggling to make his way. There was a great reunion between them, and then introductions, and I was told about the relationship with Lawrence Stern, and I was able to tell your mother about that picture. By now we were all on the best of terms, and we'd all seen all the portraits anyway, so we decided that we would have lunch together. I had a restaurant in mind, but your mother insisted that we all go back to her house and have lunch with her."

"Oakley Street."

"Absolutely. Oakley Street. We made noises about it being too much trouble, but she overrode all our objections, and the next thing we knew, all four of us were in a taxi and on our way to Chelsea. It was a beautiful day. I remember it so clearly. Very warm and sunny, and you know how pretty London can be on an early-summer day. And we had lunch in the garden, and the garden was big, and so leafy, and so sweet with the scent of lilac that it felt like being in another country, the south of France perhaps, or Paris, with the city sound of traffic muffled by trees, and everything spattered with sunlight and shadow. There was a terrace, nicely shaded, with a table and garden chairs, and we all sat and drank chilled wine, while your mother busied herself in that big basement kitchen, from time to time appearing to chat or pour more wine, or lay a cloth on the table, and set out the knives and forks."

"What did you eat?" asked Alexa, fascinated by the picture that Vi drew for them.

"Let me see. I have to think. It was delicious, I remember that. It was exactly right, and delicious. Cold soup—gazpacho, I think—and crusty home-made bread. And a salad. And pâté. And French cheese. And there was a bowl of peaches, which she had picked that morning from the tree that grew against the wall at the far end of the garden. We stayed all afternoon. We had no other engagement, or if we did, we forgot it. The hours just slid away, like an afternoon in a hazy, delicious dream. And then, I remember, Penelope and I left Ethel and Roger at the table, drinking coffee and cognac and smoking Gauloise cigarettes, and your mother took me around the garden and showed me all its delights. And as we walked, we talked, and never drew breath, and yet it is difficult to tell you what we talked about. I think she told me about Cornwall and her childhood there, and the house that they used to own, and the life that they led before the war. And it all sounded so different to my own. And when the time came to leave at last, I didn't want it to end. I didn't want to say goodbye. But when I finally came home again, back to Balnaid and Strathcroy, that picture, which I always loved, took on an even deeper meaning, because once I had met Lawrence Stern's daughter."

"Didn't you ever see her again?" Alexa asked.

"No. So sad. I so seldom went to London, and then, I believe, she moved to the country. We lost touch. So silly and careless of me to lose touch with someone I liked so much, felt so close to."

"What did she look like?" Alexa, naturally fascinated by this unexpected insight into Noel's family life, was avid for detail. Vi looked at Noel. "You tell her," she said.

But he couldn't. Features, eyes, lips, smile, hair eluded him. He could not have drawn them had some man put a gun to his head. What stayed, and remained with him, after four years of living without his mother, was her presence, her warmth, her laughter, her generosity, her contrariness, and her maddening ways, her endless cornucopia of hospitality and giving. Vi's recalling of that long-ago luncheon party, spontaneous and informal but infused with such style that she had not forgotten a single detail of the occasion, brought back the old days at Oakley Street so vividly that he found himself pierced with nostalgia for everything that he had taken so for granted and never found time to appreciate.

He shook his head. "I can't."

Vi met his eyes. And then, as though accepting and acknowledging his dilemma, did not press him further. She turned to Alexa. "She was tall and very good-looking—I thought beautiful. She had dark-grey hair, drawn back from her face into a chignon pierced with tortoiseshell pins. Her eyes were dark, very large and lustrous, and her skin smooth and brown, as though she had always lived out of doors, like a gypsy. She wasn't in the least fashionable or chic, but she held herself so proudly, and that endowed her with a great elegance. She gave off an enormous charge of . . . enjoyment. An unforgettable woman." She turned back to Noel. "And you are her son. Imagine it. How strange life can be. At seventy-eight, you'd think that you'd stop being surprised, and something like this happens, and it's as though the world had only just begun."

The loch at Croy lay hidden in the hills, three miles north of the house, and accessible only by a primitive track of great steepness that wound up onto the moor in a series of precipitous hairpin bends.

It was not a natural stretch of water. Long ago, this glen, encircled by the northern hills and the towering hulk of Creagan Dubh, had been a place of remote solitude, the habitat of eagles and deer, wild cat, grouse and curlew. At Croy, there were still to be seen old sepia photographs of the glen the way it had once looked, with a burn running through it, flanked by steep banks where the rushes grew, and by the burnside the ruins of a small dwelling-house, with byres and sheep-folds reduced to roofless desolation and tumbled granite walls. But then the first Lord Balmerino, Archie's grandfather, with a fortune to spend and trout fishing in mind, decided to create for himself a loch. Accordingly, a dam was built, sturdy as a bastion, twelve feet high or more, and wide enough to allow passage for a carriage to drive along the top of it. Sluice-gates were integrated to deal with any overflow, and when the dam was completed, these sluice-gates were closed, and the burn was trapped. Slowly, the waters rose, and the abandoned croft was drowned forever. Because of the bulk of the dam wall, any person approaching it for the first time did not see the water until the last rise was crested, when the huge expanse of the loch—two miles long and a mile wide—all at once was there. Depending on the hour and the season, it glittered blue in sunshine, was tossed with leaded grey waves, or lay still as glass in the evening light, with a pale moon reflected in its mirror surface, broken from time to time by the disturbance of rising fish.

A boat-house was built, strongly constructed, and large enough to shelter two boats, with an extra apartment to one side where picnics could be enjoyed in inclement weather. But it was not only fishermen who made their way to the loch. Generations of children had claimed it as their special place. Sheep grazed on the surrounding hills, and the closely cropped grass that sloped to the water's edge made splendid places for setting up tents, playing ball games, organizing cricket matches. Blairs and Airds, with attendant young friends, had learned to cast for trout from the shores of the loch, and mastered their first swimming strokes in its icy waters; and long happy days had been spent in building rafts, or makeshift canoes, which, paddled intrepidly out into the deep water, inevitably sank.

*   *   *

The overloaded Subaru, in four-wheel drive, and with Virginia at the wheel, thumped and bumped up the last stretch of the track, its bonnet pointing skywards. Noel, after half an hour of total discomfort, decided that, going back, he would make the journey on foot. Virginia had opted to drive because she said, quite rightly, that she knew the way, which he did not, and Violet—also quite rightly—had been given the seat next to Virginia, with her birthday cake, in its large box, to hold on her knee. In the back, things were not so easy. Edie Findhorn, about whom Noel had heard so much, proved to be a lady of ample girth, and took up so much space that Noel was forced to take Alexa upon his knee. There she crouched, her weight growing heavier by the moment and threatening his thighs with incipient cramp, but as every bump in the road caused her to clout her head on the roof of the car, he felt that it would be churlish to add his complaints to hers.

They had made two stops. One at the great house of Croy, where Virginia had alighted to see whether the Balmerino party had already left. But the door was locked and they obviously had. The second stop was to open and shut the deer gate, and here Alexa had let out the two spaniels, who had run the rest of the way behind the slowly moving car. Noel wished that he had been let out to run with them, but by now it was a little too late to make such a suggestion.

For, it seemed, they were nearly there. Violet peered through the windscreen. "They've lit the fire!" she announced.

Alexa screwed herself around to look, causing Noel even more discomfort. "How do you know?"

"I can see smoke."

"They must have brought their own kindling," said Edie.

"Probably used burnt leather," said Alexa. "Or rubbed two Boy Scouts together. I hope Lucilla's remembered the boat-house key. You can go fishing, Noel."

"At the moment, all I want to do is get a little feeling back into my legs."

"I'm sorry. Am I frightfully heavy?"

"No, not heavy at all. It's just that my feet have gone numb."

"Perhaps you're getting gangrene."

"Probably."

"It can happen in the wink of an eye, and then it spreads like wildfire, all through your body."

Edie was indignant. "For heaven's sake, Alexa, what a thing to say."

"Oh, he'll survive," Alexa told her airily. "Besides, we're very nearly there."

Which they were. The fiendish track levelled off, there were no more jolts, and the Subaru rolled onto smooth, sloping grass, coming to a halt. Virginia switched off the ignition. At once Noel opened the door, bundled Alexa gently out, and gratefully followed her. Standing, stretching his aching legs, he found himself assaulted by a blast of light, air, brightness, blueness, water, space, scents, wind. It was cold . . . colder than it had been down in the shelter of the valley, but so dazzled was he by all that he saw that he scarcely noticed the chill. As well he was impressed, as he had been impressed by the grandeur and apparent magnificence of Croy. He had not thought that the loch would be so large, so beautiful, and found it hard to come to terms with the fact that this immense tract of countryside, the hills and the moors, all belonged to one man. Everything was on such a huge scale, so lavish, so rich. Looking about him, he saw the boat-house, intricately gabled and windowed, the Land Rover already parked only a few yards away, the roughly constructed barbecue fireplace where smoke already rose into the clear air.

He saw two men down on the pebbly shore, searching for driftwood. He heard a grouse call high on the hill above him, and then, far distant, from some farther glen, the crack of guns.

The others were now all out of the car. Alexa had opened the back door and let out her little dog. Virginia's two spaniels had not yet turned up, but probably would in a moment or two. Violet was already making her way down towards the boat-house, and as she did a girl emerged from its open doors.

"Hello," she called. "You've got here. Happy birthday, Vi!"

Introductions were made all round, and as soon as this small chore was accomplished, everybody set to work, and it became clear to Noel that there was a well-ordered pattern for these traditional occasions. The Subaru was unloaded, the fire built up with sticks and charcoal. Two large folding tables were manhandled from the boat-house and set up nearby, spread with large checkered cloths. Food, plates, salads, glasses were arranged on these. Rugs were spread on beds of leather. The two spaniels, out of breath and with tongues hanging, lolloped over the crest of the hill and headed straight for the water, where they cooled their feet, drank lustily, and then collapsed, exhausted. Edie Findhorn, tied up in a large white apron, unpacked sausages and beefburgers and, when the charcoal began to turn to ash, commenced her cooking. The smoke thickened. Her rosy cheeks grew rosier in the heat, and the wind blew her white hair into an aureole.

One by one, other cars appeared, disgorging yet more guests. The wine was opened, and they stood about with glasses in their hands, or made themselves comfortable on the spread tartan rugs. The sun continued to shine. Then Julian Gloxby, the rector of Strathcroy, appeared over the brow of the hill with his wife and Dermot Honeycombe. Because none of them owned a vehicle tough enough to deal with the road from Croy, they had made the journey on foot, and turned up looking distinctly puffed, despite the fact that they all wore walking boots and carried sticks. Dermot had a rucksack on his back, and from this he produced his contribution to the feast, which proved to be six quail eggs and a bottle of elderberry wine.

Lucilla and Alexa stood at the table and buttered baps, those sweet white bread rolls mandatory for any Scottish picnic. Violet chased wasps away from her cake, and Alexa's dog stole a red-hot sausage and burnt his mouth.

The party was on its way.

Virginia said, "I shall make you a present." She pulled rushes, one by one, from a clump of reeds that grew on the bank.

"What will you make me?" asked Conrad.

"Wait, and watch, and see."

With the picnic consumed, and the coffee drunk, they had walked away from the others, along the length of the dam wall, and then made their way up the eastern shore of the loch where, over the years, the winds and high waters had eroded away the peaty bank and formed a narrow beach of shingly pebbles. No one else had followed them, and save for the two Balnaid spaniels, they were quite alone.

He stood, without impatience, and watched her. From the pocket of her corduroy trousers she took a scrap of sheep wool gleaned from a barbed-wire fence. She twisted this into a thread, and with it tied the rushes together into a bunch. Then she spread them, and started plaiting and folding, the rushes revolving like the spokes of a wheel. In her fingers, a little basket formed, which, finished, was about the size of a teacup.

He was fascinated. "Who taught you to do that?"

"Vi. And she was taught as a child by an old tinker woman. There." She tucked in the last of the rush ends, and held it up for him to admire.

"That's neat."

"Now I shall fill it with moss and flowers, and you will have an arrangement to put on your dressing-table."

She looked about her, spied moss growing on a rock, tore it loose with her finger-nails and crammed it into the little basket. They strolled on, Virginia pausing every now and then to pick a harebell, or a sprig of heather, or a stem of cotton-grass, which were added to her miniature creation. Finally satisfied, she held it out to him. "Here you are. A memento, Conrad. A souvenir of Scotland."

He took it. "That's really neat. Thank you. But I don't need a souvenir, because I'm not ever going to forget. Any of it."

"In that case," she said lightly, "you can throw it away."

"I wouldn't do that."

"So, put it in a tooth-mug of water, then it will neither wither nor die. You can take it back to America with you. But you'll have to hide it in your sponge-bag, or the customs man will get you for importing germs."

"Perhaps I could dry it, and then it would last for ever."

"Yes, perhaps you could."

They walked on, into the wind. Small brown waves ran up upon the shore, and out on the water, two fishing boats drifted gently, the fishers silent, absorbed, casting their rods. Virginia paused, stooped for a flat stone and chucked it expertly, causing it to bounce half a dozen times before it finally sank and disappeared for ever.

She said, "When are you going?"

"Sorry?"

"When are you going back to the States?"

"I've a flight booked next Thursday."

She searched for another stone. She said, "I'll maybe come with you." She found one, threw it. A failure. It disappeared at once. She straightened, turned to face him. The wind blew her hair across her cheeks. He looked down into her amazing eyes.

He said, "Why should you do that?"

"I just feel a need to get away."

"When did you decide?"

"I've been thinking about it for some months."

"That doesn't answer my question."

"All right. Yesterday. I decided yesterday."

"How much have I got to do with this decision?"

"I don't know. But it's not just you. It's Edmund and Henry as well. Everything. Everything's on top of me. I need time on my own. I need to stand back, and take the long view and get things into perspective."

"Where will you go?"

"To Leesport. To the old house. To Gramps and Grandma."

"Will I be around?"

"If you want to be. I hope you will be."

"I'm not sure if you appreciate the implications."

"Don't I, Conrad?"

"We'll be skating on pretty thin ice."

"We don't need to go out onto the middle of the ice. We can stay around the edge."

"I don't think I'll want to do that."

"I'm not sure about me, either."

"With your husband and your family an ocean away, I won't just feel like shit, but probably start behaving like one."

"That's a risk I'm prepared to take."

"In that case, I'll say no more."

"That's what I want you to say."

"Except that I'm flying Pan Am, eleven o'clock in the morning, out of Heathrow."

"I'll see if I can get on the same plane."

The worst part of growing old, Violet decided, was that happiness, at the most inappropriate of times, eluded one. She should feel happy now, but did not.

Now was the afternoon of her birthday, and to all intents and purposes everything was perfect. No woman could ask for more. She sat, cushioned in heather, high above the loch, and, despite a sinister-looking bruise of cloud that gathered in the west, the sun continued to shine, streaming down from a pristine autumn sky. Far below, but clearly visible, as though viewed through the wrong end of a telescope, the picnic party went about its business; small groups had dispersed to engage in their own activities. The two boats were out on the water. Julian Gloxby and Charles Ferguson-Crombie fished from one of them, Lucilla and her young Australian friend from the other. Dermot had drifted off on his own to search for wild flowers. Virginia and Conrad Tucker had made their way out along the top of the dam wall, and now could be seen walking, side by side, along the narrow shore on the far side of the loch. Edmund's two spaniels accompanied them. From time to time they paused, as though deep in conversation, or stooped to pick up some small flat pebble and send it skimming and jumping out over the glittering water. The others had chosen to stay where they were, gathered about the remains of the fire, lazing in the sunshine. Edie and Alexa sat together. Mrs. Gloxby, seldom seen off her feet, had brought her knitting and a book and was enjoying a spot of peace.

Small sounds reached Violet's ears. The buffet of the wind, a raised voice, the splash of oars, a bird-call. Every now and then the crack of guns from the far glen was carried towards them, borne on the wind across the summit of Creagan Dubh.

Everything just as it should be, and yet her heart lay heavy. It is because, she told herself, I know too much. I am the recipient of too many confidences. I should like to be ignorant, and so, blissful. I should like to be unaware of the fact that Virginia and Conrad Tucker . . . that personable and attractive American . . . are lovers. That Virginia has come to a certain crisis in her life; that, with Henry gone, she is capable of making some disastrous decision. I should like not to know that Edie is still agonizing over poor Lottie.

And at the same time, there were uncertainties that she would prefer resolved. I should like to feel confident that Alexa is not about to have her heart broken, that Henry is not eating *his* heart out for his mother. I should like to know exactly what is going on in Edmund's unfathomable mind.

Her family. Edmund, Virginia, Alexa, Henry, and Edie. Love and involvement brought joy, but as well could become a hideously heavy millstone slung about one's neck. And the worst was that she felt useless because there was not a mortal thing she could do to help resolve their problems.

She sighed. The sigh was clearly audible, and realizing this, Violet, with some effort, pulled herself together, assumed a cheerful expression, and turned to the man who lay propped on one elbow beside her.

She said the first thing that came into her mind. "I love the colours of the moor because they remind me of the most beautiful tweed. All russets and purple, and larch-green and peat-brown. And I love the beautiful tweeds because they remind me of the moor. How clever people are to be able to emulate nature so perfectly."

"Is that what you've been thinking?"

He was no fool. She shook her head. "No," she admitted. "I was thinking . . . that it's not the same."

"What isn't the same?" asked Noel.

Violet was not certain why he had come with her. She had not invited him to join her on her walk, and he had not suggested that he might accompany her. She had simply started out, up the hill, and he had fallen into step beside her, as though without words they had made some prearranged assignment. And they had climbed together, Violet leading the way up the narrow sheep-track, pausing every now and then to admire the expanding view, to watch the flight of a grouse, to pick a sprig of white heather. Reaching the summit, she had settled herself down for a small breather, and he had made himself comfortable beside her. She was touched that he had chosen to be with her, and a little more of her reserve towards him melted away.

For, meeting him for the first time, she had been wary. Though prepared to like the young man whom Alexa had chosen to love, she kept her defences well up, determined not to be taken in by any brittle veneer of too-obvious charm. His dark good looks, his tall frame, his bright and intelligent blue eyes had caught her slightly off-balance, and the fact that he was the son of Penelope Keeling had further taken the wind from her sails. That was another thing that had occurred to cloud her day, for Noel had told her that Penelope was dead, and for some reason she found it painful to come to terms with this. Filled with the regrets of hindsight, she knew that she had no person but herself to blame for the fact that she had never again got in touch with that vital and fascinating woman. And now it was too late.

"What isn't the same?" he prompted gently.

She gathered her flying thoughts. "My picnic."

"It's a splendid picnic."

"But different. Missing out. Henry is not here, nor Edmund, nor Isobel Balmerino. This is the first time she's missed my birthday celebration, but she had to go to Corriehill to help Verena Steynton arrange the flowers for the dance tomorrow evening. And as for my darling little Henry, he is now committed to boarding-schools for at least ten years, and by the time he is free to come again, I shall probably be six feet under the turf. I hope I shall be. Eighty-eight scarcely bears thinking about. Too old. Perhaps dependent on one's children. My only fear."

"I can't imagine you being dependent on anybody."

"Senility comes to us all eventually."

They fell silent. Out of this silence another spatter of distant and sporadic gun-fire echoed towards them over the hills.

Violet smiled. "They, at least, seem to be having a successful day."

"Who's shooting?"

"I suppose the members of the syndicate who happen to be here just now. And Archie Balmerino is with them." She turned to smile at Noel. "Do you shoot?"

"No. I never even owned a gun. I didn't have that sort of an upbringing. I lived in London all my life."

"In that wonderful house in Oakley Street?"

"That's right."

"What a fortunate young man you were."

He shook his head. "The shaming thing is that I didn't consider myself fortunate. I was sent to a day-school and thought myself very hard done by, because my mother couldn't afford to send me to Eton or Harrow. As well, my father had taken off by the time I was ready for school, and married some other female. I didn't exactly miss him, because I'd hardly known him, but in some strange way it rankled."

She did not waste her sympathy on him. Instead, thinking of Penelope Keeling, she said, "It is not easy for a woman to bring up a family on her own."

"Growing up, I don't think that ever occurred to me."

Violet laughed, appreciating his honesty. "Youth is wasted on the young. But you enjoyed your mother's company?"

"Yes, I did. But from time to time we had the most stupendous rows. Usually about money."

"That's what most family rows are about. And I don't imagine that she suffered from materialism."

"The very opposite. She had her own philosophy for living, and a selection of homespun truisms which she would come out with in times of stress, or in the middle of some really acrimonious argument. One of them was that happiness is making the most of what you have and riches is making the most of what you've got. It sounded plausible, but I never quite worked out the logic."

"Perhaps you needed more than wise words."

"Yes. I needed more. I needed not to feel an outsider. I wanted to be part of a different sort of life, to have a different background. The Establishment. Old houses, old families, old names, old money. We were brought up to believe that money didn't matter, but I knew that it only didn't matter provided you had plenty of it."

Violet said, "I disapprove, but understand. The grass is always greener on the other side of the hill, and it is human nature to yearn for what you cannot have." She thought of Alexa's little jewel of a house in Ovington Street, and the financial security she had inherited from her maternal grandmother, and knew a small stirring of disquiet. "The worst is," she went on, "that when you achieve that green grass, you often discover that you never really wanted it at all." He stayed silent, and she frowned. "Tell me," she said abruptly, coming straight to the point, "what do you think of us all?"

Noel was taken aback by her bluntness. "I . . . I've scarcely had time to form an opinion."

"Rubbish. Of course you have. Do you think, for instance, that we are Establishment, as you term it? Do you think that we are all very *grand*?"

He laughed. Perhaps his amusement disguised a certain embarrassment. She could not be sure. "I don't know about grand. But you must admit that you live on a fairly lavish scale. To achieve such a life-style in the south, one would need to be a millionaire ten times over."

"But this is Scotland."

"Precisely so."

"So you *do* think we're grand?"

"No. Just different."

"Not different, Noel. Ordinary. The most ordinary of folk, who have been blessed with the good fortune to be raised and to live in this incomparable country. There are, I admit, titles, lands, huge houses, and a certain feudalism, but scratch the surface of any one of us, go back a generation or two, and you'll find humble crofters, mill workers, shepherds, small farmers. The Scottish clan system was an extraordinary thing. No man was any man's servant, but part of a family. Which is why your average Highlander does not walk through life with a chip on his shoulder. He is proud. He knows he is as good as you are, and probably a good deal better. As well, the Industrial Revolution and Victorian money created an enormous and wealthy middle class out of a lot of hard-working artisans. Archie is the third Lord Balmerino, but his grandfather made his pile in heavy textiles, and he was raised in the city streets. As for my own father, he started life as the barefoot son of a crofter from the Isle of Lewis. But he was blessed with brains and a talent for book-learning, and his ambitions led him to scholarships, and eventually to study medicine. He became a surgeon and prospered and attained great heights—the Chair of Anatomy at Edinburgh University and a knighthood. Sir Hector Akenside. A resounding name, don't you think? But he always remained a man without pride or pretension, and for this reason was not only respected but loved."

"And your mother?"

"My mother came from an entirely different background. I have to admit that she *was* rather grand. Lady Primrose Marr, the daughter of an ancient and well-connected family from the Borders, who had, through nobody's fault but their own, become totally impoverished. She was very beautiful. Famously so. Small and elegant and with silvery-blonde hair, piled up on her head, so that it looked as though her slender neck might break with the weight of it. My father set eyes on her at some ball or reception in the Assembly Rooms, and fell instantly in love. I don't think she was ever in love with him, but by then he was something of a personage, and well-to-do to boot, and she was intelligent enough to realize on which side her bread had been buttered. Her family, although they could scarcely approve of the match, raised no objections . . . they were probably only too glad to get the girl off their hands."

"Were they happy?"

"I think so. I think they suited each other very well. They lived in a tall and draughty house in Heriot Row, and that is where I was born. My mother relished Edinburgh, with all its social life, the coming and going of friends, the theatre and the concerts, the balls and receptions. But my father remained a countryman with his heart in the hills. He had always loved Strathcroy, and had come every summer for his annual fishing holiday. When I was about five, he bought the land south of the river and built Balnaid. He was still working, and I was at school in Edinburgh, so to begin with, Balnaid was simply a holiday home, a sort of shooting lodge. To me it was paradise, and I lived for the summer months. When he finally retired, he retired to Balnaid. My mother thought it a rotten idea, but he had a stubborn streak to him, and in the end, she simply made the best of it. She filled the house with guests, thus ensuring a fourth for bridge, and a dinner party every night. But we kept the house in Heriot Row, and when the rain fell with unceasing venom, or the bitter winds of winter blew, she invariably found some excuse to return to Edinburgh, or take herself off to Italy, or the south of France."

"And you?"

"I told you. For me it was paradise. I was an only child, and a great disappointment to my mother because I was not only dreadfully large and fat, but plain as well. I towered over all my contemporaries, and was a total failure at dancing class because no boy ever wanted to be my partner. In Edinburgh society, I stuck out like a sore thumb, but at Balnaid it didn't seem to matter how I looked, and at Balnaid I could be just myself."

"And your husband?"

"My husband?" Violet's warm smile transformed her weathered features. "My husband was Geordie Aird. You see, I married my dearest

SEPTEMBER 🏵 *321*

friend, and at the end of over thirty years of marriage, he was still my dearest friend. Not many women can say that."

"How did you meet him?"

"At a shooting party, up on the moors of Creagan Dubh. My father had been asked to shoot with Lord Balmerino, and because my mother was away on some Mediterranean cruise, he asked me to accompany him. Going shooting with my father was always the greatest of treats, and I went to great pains to be useful, carrying his cartridge bag, and sitting, quiet and still as a mouse, in his butt."

"Was Geordie one of the guns?" asked Noel.

"No, Noel. Geordie was one of the beaters. His father, Jamie Aird, was Lord Balmerino's head keeper."

"You married the gamekeeper's son?" Noel could scarcely keep the astonishment out of his voice, but there was admiration there as well.

"I did. It smacks a little of Lady Chatterley, doesn't it, but I can assure you it was not like that at all."

"But when did this happen?"

"The early 1920s. I was ten and Geordie was fifteen. I decided he was the most beautiful boy I had ever seen, and when it was time for the luncheon picnic, I took my sandwiches over to where the keepers and the beaters sat, and ate them with him. You could say that I set my cap for him. After that, he was my friend; I was his shadow, he took me under his wing. I wasn't alone any more. I was with Geordie. We spent whole days together, always out of doors. He taught me to cast for salmon and guddle for trout. Some days we walked for miles, and he showed me the hidden corries where the deer grazed, and the high peaks where the eagles nested. And after a day on the moor, he would take me home to the little house where his parents lived . . . where Gordon Gillock, Archie's keeper, lives now . . . and Mrs. Aird would feed me bannocks and scones and pour me strong black tea from her best lustre teapot."

"Did your mother not object to this friendship?"

"I think she was quite glad to have me out of the way. She knew that I would come to no harm."

"And did Geordie follow in his father's footsteps?"

"No. Like my own father, he was a clever and academic boy and he did well at school. My father encouraged him in his ambitions. I think he recognized something of himself in Geordie. Because of this, Geordie won a place at the Grammar School in Relkirk, and after that was apprenticed to a firm of chartered accountants."

"And you?"

"Sadly, I had to grow up. All at once, I was eighteen, and my mother realized that her Ugly Duckling had become an Ugly Duck. Despite my size and my lack of social graces, she decided that I must Come Out—do a season in Edinburgh and be presented to Royalty at Holyroodhouse. It was the last thing I wanted to do, but Geordie had gone from me and was living in lodgings in Relkirk, and I worked it out in my own mind that if I was complaisant about this dreadful scheme of hers, then perhaps she would in time accept the fact that Geordie Aird was the only man in the world I would think of marrying. The Season and the Coming Out were, as you can imagine, a total failure. A charade. Dressed in enormous evening gowns, all satin and glitter, I looked like a youthful Pantomime Dame. At the end of the season I remained unsought, unwanted, and unengaged. My mother, deeply ashamed, brought me home to Balnaid, and I did the flowers and walked the dogs . . . and waited for Geordie."

"How long did you have to wait?"

"Four years. Until he had qualified and was in a position to support a wife. I had money of my own, of course. A trust, which came to me when I was twenty-one, and we could quite easily have managed on that, but Geordie would not hear of it. So I went on waiting. Until the great day came and he passed all his final examinations. I remember I was in the wash-house at Balnaid, giving the dog a bath. I'd taken him out for a walk, and he'd rolled in something disgusting, and there I was wrapped in an apron and soaking wet and smelling of carbolic. And the wash-house door was flung open, and there stood Geordie, come to ask me to marry him. It was the most romantic moment. And since then, I've always had a soft spot for the smell of carbolic."

"What was the reaction of your parents?"

"Oh, they'd seen it coming for years. My father was delighted and my mother resigned. Once she'd got over agonizing over what her smart friends would say, I think she decided that it was better for me to marry Geordie Aird than stay a spinster daughter, getting under her feet and interfering with her butterfly life. So, on an early summer day in 1933, Geordie and I finally wed. And for my mother's sake, I submitted to being laced into stays, and buttoned into white satin so stiff and gleaming that it was like being encased in cardboard. And after the reception, Geordie and I got into his little Baby Austin and we trundled all the way to Edinburgh, where we spent our wedding night in the Caledonian Hotel. And I remember undressing in the bathroom and taking off my going-away dress, and unlacing my stays, and dropping them, with great ceremony, into the waste-paper bin. And I made a vow. No person is ever going to make me wear a corset again. And no person ever has." She burst into lusty laughter and struck Noel a thump on his knee. "So you see, on my wedding night, I said goodbye, not only to my virginity, but my stays as well. It's hard to say which gave me the most satisfaction."

He was laughing. "And you lived happily ever after?"

"Oh, so happily. Such happy years in a little terraced house in Relkirk. Then Edmund was born, and Edie came into our lives. Eighteen years old and the daughter of the Strathcroy joiner, she came to me as a nursery maid, and we've been together ever since. It was a good time. So good that I pretended not to notice the gathering clouds of war looming up over our horizon. But the war came. Geordie joined up with the Highland Division and went to France. In May 1940, he was taken prisoner at Saint-Valéry, and I didn't see him again for five and a half years. Edie and Edmund and I moved back to Balnaid and sat out the war with my parents, but they were growing old, and by the time peace was declared, they had both died. So when Geordie finally came back to us, it was to Balnaid that he came, and it was there that we spent the rest of our life together."

"When did he die?"

"About three years after Edmund was married—for the first time, you understand, to Alexa's mother. It all happened with astonishing suddenness. We had such a good life. I made plans—for the garden, for the house, for holidays and trips that we would take together—as though both of us were going to live forever. And so I was quite taken by surprise when I realized that, quite suddenly, Geordie was failing. He lost his appetite, lost weight, complained of vague discomforts and pains. At first, refusing to be frightened, I told myself that it was simply some digestive disorder, legacy of his long years in prisoner-of-war camps. But a doctor was finally consulted and then a specialist. Geordie was wheeled into Relkirk General for what was, at that stage, euphemistically known as "tests." The result of these tests was conveyed to me by the specialist. He sat across a desk from me in a sun-filled office, and he was very kind, and when he had finished telling me, I thanked him very much, and I got up, and went out of the room, and down the long rubber-floored corridors to where Geordie lay in a side ward, propped up by pillows in the high hospital bed. I had brought him daffodils from Balnaid, and I arranged them for him in a jug, with plenty of water so that they should not wilt and die. But Geordie died two weeks later. Edmund was there with me, but not Caroline, his wife. She had started a baby, and was suffering from sickness. Knowing that Alexa was coming was one of the things I hung onto during those dreadful, dark days. Geordie was gone, but another new little life was on its way, to set the seal on the bonds of continuity. Which is one of the reasons that Alexa has always been so special to me."

After a little, Noel said, "You're special to her as well. She's talked to me so much about you."

Violet fell silent. A wind sprang up, shuddering through the grass. It carried with it the smell of rain. She looked, and saw the clouds rolling in from the west, blurring the hills and darkening their lower slopes with shadow.

She said, "We've had the best of the day. I hope you don't feel it has been wasted. I hope I haven't bored you."

"Not for a moment."

"I began by trying to prove a point to you, and ended up by telling you my life story."

"I feel privileged."

She said, "Alexa is coming."

He sat up, dusting scraps of grass from the sleeves of his sweater. "So she is."

They watched her approach, making her way up the steep path with youthful speed and energy. She wore her jeans and a dark-blue sweater, and her dark-golden hair was tousled and her cheeks were rosy with the wind and the sun and the effort of the climb. She looked, thought Violet, quite absurdly young. And, all at once, knew that she had to speak.

"I was so fortunate. I married the man I loved. I only hope that the same thing will happen to Alexa." Noel, slowly, turned his head, and their eyes met. "Virginia told me that I must keep my counsel and not interfere. But I think you know already how much she loves you and I cannot bear to see her hurt. I am not pressuring you, but I want you to be careful. And if you have to hurt her, then you must do it now, before it is too late. You are surely fond enough of her to be able to do that?"

His face was expressionless, but his gaze steady. After a bit, he said, "Yes. Yes, I am."

There was, perhaps mercifully, no time for more. Alexa was there, within earshot, pounding up the last few yards towards them, collapsing into the heather at Noel's side.

"What have you two been talking about? You've been up here for *ages*."

"Oh, this and that," her grandmother told her airily.

"I've been sent to come and tell you that perhaps it's time we thought about packing up. The Ferguson-Crombies have got to go to some dinner party, and they've offered to give the Gloxbys and Dermot Honeycombe a lift back to Croy. Anyway, before very long, it's going to start to rain; the sky's beginning to look really black."

"Yes," said Violet. She looked, and saw that the boats were coming in off the water. Someone had damped down the fire, and her guests were already on their feet, folding rugs, reloading the cars. "Yes, it is time to go."

She began to heave herself up, but Noel was on his feet before her and ready with a helping hand.

"Thank you, Noel." She dusted scraps of heather from her heavy tweed skirt, took a last lingering look. All over. All over for another year. "Come."

She led the way, down the path, off the hill.

*   *   *

Noel awoke to darkness and a raging thirst. And something more urgent. Analyzed, this proved to be a rising physical longing for love and Alexa. He lay for a bit, dry-mouthed and lonely and frustrated, in the strange bed, in the unfamiliar bedroom, with the windows wide open onto a dark and blowy night, where no lights shone, and no cars passed, and the only sound was the soughing of the wind in the topmost branches of the trees. He thought nostalgically of London, of Ovington Street, where he had existed for the last few months, lapped in comfort and care. If he awoke thirsty in London, he only had to reach out a hand to find the tumbler of spring water which Alexa set out for him each night, spiked with a slice of lemon. If, in the small dark hours of the morning, he found himself desiring her, he only had to turn to the downy bed, reach out and draw her towards him. Awakened, she was never resentful nor too sleepy for his ardour, but responded with the gentle passion that he had taught her, glorying in her own new-found knowledge, confident in her own desirability.

These reflections helped not at all. At last, unable to bear his thirst a moment longer, he turned on the bedside light and climbed out of bed. Went into the bathroom, ran the cold tap and filled a tooth-mug with water. The water was ice-cold and had a sweet and clean taste to it. He drained the tumbler and refilled it, and then went back to the bedroom and stood in the howling draught, gazing out into the bloomy darkness.

He drank some more. His thirst was assuaged, but his other need stayed with him. Fresh water and Alexa. It occurred to him that these two basic necessities, which, immediately, were more urgent than anything else in life, were in some strange way a reflection of each other. Adjectives flowed through his mind. Clean, sweet, pure, transparent, good, innocent, unsullied. They applied to both the element and the girl. And then, the final accolade. Life-giving.

Alexa.

He prided himself that it was he who was responsible for her flowering from gawky youngster to confident woman—finding out that she was a virgin had been one of the most astonishingly disarming experiences of his life—but as well he knew that it had been a two-way deal, and he had been on the receiving end of a great cornucopia of love and companionship and undemanding acceptance, for although she had been blessed with worldly riches, her gifts had not all been material. Being with Alexa had been a good interlude in his life, one of the best, and whatever happened in the future, he knew that he would always remember it with gratitude.

And what *was* going to happen? But he did not, at the moment, wish to consider this. More pressing to concentrate on now. Alexa. She slept in her own bed, in her childhood bedroom, only a few yards distant, across the landing and down a passage. He thought about going in search of her, silently opening and closing her door, slipping in between the sheets beside her. She would make space for him, turn to him, her arms ready for him, her body waking for him. . . .

He considered this course of action for a bit and then decided against it, for, he assured himself, practical rather than high-minded reasons. He knew from experience that it was all too easy to lose one's way in the unlit corridors of other people's country houses, and did not relish being discovered in some broom cupboard, along with the Hoover and a lot of old dusters. And here, at Balnaid, he had not even got the water-tight excuse of going to the loo, because he had a perfectly good bathroom of his own.

And yet, even without these excuses, and putting more worthy reasons out of his mind, he still found himself wondering if he could pluck up the nerve to go in search of her. It had something to do with this house. There was an atmosphere he had sensed as soon as he walked through the door, a feeling of family, which rendered the notion of clandestine corridor-creeping simply out of the question. His long conversation with Vi, out on the hill during the afternoon, had further strengthened his conception of Balnaid. It was as though all the generations who had lived here were still around the place, in residence, living and breathing, going about their daily occupations, watching, and perhaps judging. Not just Alexa and Virginia, but Violet and her stalwart and much-loved Geordie. And before them, the old people, Sir Hector and Lady Primrose Akenside, solidly entrenched, highly principled, and still in charge of a house brimming with individuals; children in the nurseries, guests in the spare rooms, and housemaids and parlourmaids snoring away in the attics upstairs. This was the sort of enduring household that, as a boy, trapped in London, Noel had longed to be part of. A well-ordered and lavish life-style with all the attendant delights of the outdoors. Tennis parties and picnics, on an even more elaborate scale than the one that had taken place this afternoon. Ponies, and guns and fishing rods, and devoted gillies and keepers only too eager and ready to give the young gentleman a guiding hand.

This morning, driving up to Strathcroy with Alexa beside him, dazzled by the countryside and the colours and the sparkling air, he had been overwhelmed by the sensation that in some way he was driving back to the past, to a world that he had once known and yet forgotten. Now, he accepted that he had never known that world but, having found it, was reluctant to let it go. For the first time in his life, he felt that he belonged.

And Alexa?

He heard Violet's voice. *If you have to hurt her, then you must do it now, before it is too late.*

The words had an ominous ring to them. It was possible that it was already too late, in which case he had reached the watershed of his relationship with Alexa, and with Vi's warning ringing in his ears, knew that the time had come to take stock. Before the weekend was over, some sort of a decision had to be made.

He saw himself, as though from some great distance, teetering on that watershed, endeavouring to make the vital choice as to which path he would follow. He could go back the way he had come, which meant leaving Alexa, saying goodbye, trying to explain, packing his bags, moving out of Ovington Street; returning to the basement flat in Pembroke Gardens, placating his tenants, informing them that they must find some other place to roost. It meant going back to the old life, somehow getting himself back into social circulation. Calling up friends, meeting in bars, eating in restaurants, trying to find the telephone numbers of all those emaciated and beautiful women, feeding them, listening to their conversation. It meant driving to the country on Friday evenings, and then struggling back to London, on roads choked with traffic, the following Sunday night.

He sighed. But he'd done it all before, and there was no reason why he should not do it again.

The other alternative, the other path, led the way to commitment. And for Alexa, and everything she represented, he knew that this time it had to be total. A lifetime of assumed responsibility—marriage and probably children.

Perhaps it was time. He was thirty-four, but still devilled by the uncertainties of immaturity. Basic and deep-rooted insecurities rattled their bones at him, like a lot of gruesome skeletons lurking in a forgotten cupboard. Perhaps it was time, but the prospect filled him with terror.

He shivered. Enough. The wind was rising. A gust rattled the open window-frame. He discovered that he was chilled to the bone, but, like an icy shower, the cold air had finally stilled his unrequited ardour. Which settled at least one problem. He got back into bed, bundled in blankets, and turned off the light. For a long time he lay awake, but when he finally turned and slept again, he had still made no decision.

10

Friday the Sixteenth

THE RAIN STARTED SOON AFTER he left Relkirk. As the country road climbed, heading north, mist drifted down from the hilltops, and his windscreen was beaded with damp. He switched on the wipers. It was the first rain he had seen for over a week, for New York had sparkled in the warmth of an Indian summer, sunshine reflected from towers of glass, flags snapping in the breeze outside Rockefeller Center, vagrants enjoying the last of the seasonal warmth, stretched out on the benches of Central Park, with their bags and bundles of meagre possessions gathered all about them.

Edmund had spanned two worlds in a single day. New York, Kennedy, Concorde, Heathrow, Turnhouse, and now back to Strathcroy. Under normal circumstances, he would have taken time to drop in at the office in Edinburgh, but this evening was the night of the Steyntons' dance, and for this reason he had elected to drive directly home. Getting out his Highland finery was apt to take some time, and there was the possibility that neither Virginia nor Edie had remembered to clean the silver buttons on his jacket and his waistcoat, in which case he would have to buckle down to the task himself.

A dance. They would, very likely, not get to bed until four o'clock in the morning. By now he had lost track of his own time-clock, and knew a certain weariness. Nothing, however, that a slug of whisky would not dispel. His wrist-watch still stood at New York time, but the clock on his dashboard told him that it was half past five. The day was not yet dead, but the low clouds rendered visibility murky. He switched on his side-lights.

Caple Bridge. The powerful car hummed along the winding curves of the narrow glen road. Tarmac glistened in the damp, whins and gorse were wreathed in mist. He opened the window and smelt the cool and incomparable air. He thought about seeing Alexa again. Thought about not seeing Henry. Thought about Virginia . . .

Their tenuous truce, he feared, had collapsed, and their final exchange, as he was on the point of leaving for New York, had been acrimonious. She had blasted her temper at him down the telephone, accusing him of selfishness, thoughtlessness, broken promises. Refusing to listen to his perfectly reasonable explanations, she had finally slammed down the receiver. He had wanted to speak to Henry, but she had either forgotten, or deliberately refrained from giving Henry his father's message. Perhaps, after a week without him, she had cooled down, but Edmund did not feel hopeful. Lately, she had taken to nursing grievances as though they were babies.

His saving grace would be Alexa. For Alexa, he knew Virginia would put on her best face, if necessary play-act her way through the weekend, performing a charade of enjoyment and affection. For this small mercy, at least, he would be grateful.

The road sign came up at him out of the mist. "Strathcroy." He slowed, changed down, crossed the bridge by the Presbyterian church, drove beneath the high branches of the elms, clattering with rooks, and through the open gates of Balnaid.

Home. He did not go around to the front of the house, but turned into the old stable-yard and parked the BMW there. Only one car, Virginia's, stood in the garage, and the back door, which led into the kitchen, was open. But this, he knew, did not necessarily mean that anybody was at home.

He switched off the ignition and waited, expecting, if not a delighted family spilling out of that door to greet him, then at least some sort of a welcome from his dogs. But he was met by silence. There did not appear to be anybody about.

He climbed wearily from his car, went to open the boot and collect his baggage. His suitcase, his bulging leather brief-case, his raincoat, the yellow plastic bag of Duty-Free. It was heavy with bottles, Scotch and Gordon's Gin, and generous packages containing French perfume for his wife, his daughter, his mother. He carried these indoors, out of the rain. He found a kitchen warm, swept, orderly but empty, the only sign of his dogs their unoccupied baskets. The Aga hummed to itself. Into the sink, a tap dripped gently. He put his suitcase and his raincoat on the floor, the bag of Duty-Free on the table, and went to the sink to tighten off the faulty tap. The dripping ceased. He listened for other sounds, but none disturbed the ensuing quiet.

Carrying his brief-case, he went out of the kitchen, down the passage, through the hall. There he paused for a moment, waiting for an opened door, footsteps, a voice, another person. The old clock ticked. Nothing more. He went on, his footsteps muffled by the thick carpet, past the drawing-room, to open the door of the library.

Nobody here either. He saw cushions, smooth and fat, on the sofa, an empty fireplace, a neat pile of *Country Life* magazines, an arrangement of dried flowers, their colours faded, smoky, and rusty. The window was open and let in a great draught of damp and chilly air. He set down his brief-case and went to close it, and then returned to his desk, where a week's mail was tidily stacked, awaiting his attention. He turned over an envelope or two, but knew that there was nothing there that could not wait for another day.

The telephone rang. He picked up the receiver.

"Balnaid."

It clicked, buzzed, and then went dead. Probably some person dialling the wrong number. He put the receiver back, and all at once could not bear the gloom of the empty room for a moment longer. The library at Balnaid, without a fire for companionship, was like a person without a heart, and only on the hottest days of summer was it ever allowed to go out. He found matches, lit the paper in the hearth, waited until the kindling crackled, added logs. The flames leaped up the chimney, warming and lighting, bringing the room alive. Thus he contrived his own welcome and felt marginally cheered.

He watched the flames for a bit, then put on the fire-guard and made his way back to the kitchen. He unloaded the whisky and the gin and put them in the cupboard, and then carried his suitcase and the Duty-Free bag upstairs. The ticking of the grandfather clock accompanied his tread. He crossed the landing and opened the door of their bedroom.

"Edmund."

She was there, had been in the house all the time. She sat at her dressing-table and was engaged in painting her nails. The room, so spacious and feminine—dominated by the enormous king-size double bed draped in antique-white linen and lace—was, uncharacteristically, in a state of some disarray. Shoes lay about, a pile of folded clothes stood stacked on a chair, wardrobe doors hung open. On one of these doors, from a padded hanger, was suspended Virginia's new evening dress, the one she had bought in London especially for the occasion tonight. The skirt, flaring out in layers of some filmy material, was spattered with a confetti of black spots. Without her inside it, it looked a bit sad and empty.

Across the room, they eyed each other. He said, "Hi."

She wore her white towelling robe and had washed her hair and set it on the huge rollers that Henry always told her made her look like some monster from outer space.

"You're back. I never heard the car."

"I parked it by the garage. I thought there was nobody around."

He carried the suitcase through to his dressing-room and set it down on the floor. All his evening clothes were laid out on the single bed. His kilt, stockings, skean dhu, evening shirt, jacket, and waistcoat. The buttons of these shone like stars, as did the silver buckles on his shoes.

He went back into the bedroom. "You cleaned my buttons."

"Edie did."

"That was kind." He went over to her side and stooped to give her a kiss. "A present for you." He put the box on her dressing-table.

"Oh, lovely. Thank you." She had finished painting her nails, but the varnish had not yet dried. She sat with fingers outspread, from time to time blowing on them to speed the process up. "How was New York?"

"Okay."

"I didn't expect you back so soon."

"I caught the early shuttle."

"Are you tired?"

"I won't be when I've had a drink." He lowered himself onto the edge of the bed. "Is there anything wrong with the telephone?"

"I don't know. It rang about five minutes ago, but only once, and then it stopped."

"I answered it downstairs, but it went dead."

"It's done that once or twice today. But it's working for outgoing calls."

"Have you reported it?"

"No. Do you think we should?"

"I'll do it later." He leaned back on the piles of pillows, his head against the quilted bedhead. "How have things been with you?"

She inspected her nails. "All right."

"And Henry?"

"I don't know about Henry. I haven't heard and I haven't telephoned." She looked at him, and her brilliant blue gaze was cool. "I thought that perhaps telephoning was not *quite* the right thing to do. Untraditional, perhaps."

Which made it abundantly clear that he was not forgiven. But this was not the time to pick up the gauntlet and precipitate yet another row.

"Did you get him to Templehall?"

"Yes. I drove him. He didn't want to go with Isobel, so we took Hamish with us. Hamish was in one of his most disagreeable moods, Henry never said a single word the entire journey, and it peed with rain the whole way. Apart from that, it was a picnic."

"He didn't take Moo with him, did he?"

"No, he didn't take Moo."

"Thank God for that. And Alexa?"

"She arrived yesterday morning, with Noel."

"Where are they now?"

"I think they took the dogs out for a walk. After lunch they had to go to Relkirk to pick up Lucilla's dress from the cleaner's. We had an SOS from Croy. The dress had been forgotten, and they're all so busy getting the dinner party together that nobody had time to go."

"So what else has been happening?"

"What else has been happening? Vi had her picnic. Verena's had us all at her beck and call like slaves, and Edie's cousin has gone back to hospital."

Edmund raised his head a fraction, as an alert dog will prick its ears.

Virginia, her nails now satisfactorily dry and hard, took up the package that he had brought her, and began to tear off the cellophane wrapping.

"She's gone back?"

"Yes." She opened the box and drew out the bottle, square-cut and opulent, the stopper ringed with a bow of velvet ribbon. She unscrewed the stopper and dabbed a little on her neck. "Delicious. Fendi. How kind. I've been wanting this scent, but it's too expensive to buy for oneself."

"When did this happen?"

"Lottie, you mean? Oh, a couple of days ago. She became so impossible that Vi insisted. She should never have been discharged in the first place. She's insane."

"What did she do?"

"Oh, talked. Meddled. Made mischief. She wouldn't leave me alone. She's evil."

"What did she say?"

Virginia, turned back to the mirror, began, slowly, to take the pins out of her rollers. One by one, she laid them on the plate glass of the dressing table. He watched her profile, the line of her jaw, the curve of her lovely neck.

"Do you really want to know?"

"I shouldn't ask if I didn't."

"All right. She said that you and Pandora Blair were lovers. Years ago, the time of Archie and Isobel's wedding, when Lottie was a housemaid at Croy. You always said that she listened at doors. She doesn't seem to have missed a trick. Describing it all to me, she made it quite vivid. She became quite excited. Turned on, one might say. She said that it was because of *you* that Pandora ran off with her married man and never came home again. That it was all your fault. And now . . ." One of the rollers was being stubborn, and Virginia jerked at it, trying to free it, tugging at and tangling her corn-coloured hair. ". . . now she is saying that *you* are the reason that Pandora has come back to Croy. Nothing to do with the party tonight. Nothing to do with Archie. Just you. She wants to start it up all over again. To get you back."

Another jerk and the roller was loose, and Virginia's eyes were watering with agony. Edmund watched her, scarcely able to bear the pain that she was inflicting upon herself.

He remembered the evening when he had encountered Lottie in Mrs. Ishak's supermarket, and how she had buttonholed him. He had recoiled from her distasteful presence. He remembered her eyes, her pallid skin, her moustache, and the useless fury that she had kindled within him, so that he had come very close to losing his temper and inflicting upon her grievous bodily harm. He recalled the stirring of a dreadful apprehension. An apprehension well-founded, for now it seemed it had come to this.

He said coldly, "She is lying."

"Is she, Edmund?"

"Do you believe her?"

"I don't know. . . ."

"Virginia . . ."

"Oh . . ." In a burst of exasperation, she jerked another roller free, flung it at her own reflection in the mirror, and then rounded on him. "I don't know. I don't know. I can't think straight any longer. And I don't care. Why should I care? What does it matter to me that you and Pandora Blair once had a raging love affair? As far as I'm concerned, it's all lost in the mists of time and absolutely nothing to do with me. I only know that it happened when you were already a married man—married to Caroline—and that you were the father of a child. The simple fact is that that doesn't make me feel very secure."

"You don't trust me?"

"Sometimes I think I don't even know you."

"That is a ludicrous statement."

"All right, so it's ludicrous. But unfortunately we can't all be as cold and objective as you. And if it is ludicrous, you can put it down to human frailty, except that I don't suppose you even know what that means."

"I'm beginning to realize I know only too well."

"It's *us* I'm talking about, Edmund. You and me."

"In that case, perhaps it would be better to postpone this conversation until you are a little less overwrought."

"I am *not* overwrought. And I am not a child any longer, I am not your *little* wife. And I think perhaps that this is as good a time as any to tell you that I'm going away for a bit. I'm going back to Long Island, to Leesport, to spend some time with my grandparents. I've told Vi. She says you can stay with her. We'll close the house."

Edmund said nothing. She looked at him and saw his poker-face empty of expression, the handsome features still, the hooded eyes giving nothing away. No hurt showed, no anger. She let the silence lengthen, waiting for him to react to her announcement. For a mad moment, she imagined him flinging reserve to the wind, coming to her side, taking her in his arms, covering her with kisses, loving her, making love to her. . . .

"When did you plan all this?"

Tears pricked behind her eyes, but she set her teeth and willed them away.

"I've been thinking about going for months. I finally made up my mind after Henry went. Without Henry, there is no reason not to go."

"When are you leaving?"

"I've got a seat on a Pan Am flight out of Heathrow next Thursday morning."

"Thursday? That's less than a week away."

"I know." She turned back to her mirror, pulled free the last of the rollers, reached for her comb, began to draw it through the tangled curls, smoothing out the snarls. "But there is a reason, and you may as well be told that reason now, because if I don't tell you, some other person will. A strange thing has happened. You remember last Sunday Isobel telling us that she had some unknown American coming to stay? It turned out that he's a man called Conrad Tucker, and we knew each other years ago, in Leesport."

"The Sad American."

"Yes. And he is sad. His wife has just died of leukemia and he's been left with a little daughter. He's been over here for a month or more, but he's returning to the States on Thursday." She laid down the comb, tossing the shining, clean hair away from her face, turned back to face him. "It seemed," she said, "a good idea to make the journey together."

"Was that his idea or your idea?"

"Does it matter?"

"No. I don't suppose it makes any difference at all. When are you planning to return?"

"I don't know. I have an open-ended ticket."

"I don't think you should go."

"That has an ominous ring to it, Edmund. It wouldn't be a warning?"

"You're running away."

"No. I am simply taking advantage of a freedom that has been forced upon me. Without Henry, I am in a sort of limbo, and I've got to come to terms with being bereft of him, and I can't do that here. I need time to sort myself out. To be on my own. To be my own person. You have to try, just for once in your life, to see a situation from another person's point of view. In this case, mine. And perhaps, as well, you could try to give me some credit for being honest with you."

"I would have been astonished had you done anything else."

After that, there did not seem to be anything else to say. Beyond the open windows, the misty autumn evening sank into an early dusk. Virginia switched on the lights of her dressing-table, and then stood up and moved to close the heavy chintz curtains. From downstairs, sounds reached their ears. A door opening and shutting, dogs barking, voices raised.

She said, "Noel and Alexa. They're back from their walk."

"I'll go down." He got to his feet, stretched his arms, swallowed a yawn. "I need a drink. Do you want one?"

"Later."

He made for the door. "What time are we expected at Croy?"

"Half past eight."

"You can have your drink in the library before we leave."

"There's no fire."

"I lit it."

He went out of the room. Listening, Virginia heard him traverse the landing, start down the stairs. And then Alexa's voice. "Fa!"

"*Hello,* my darling."

He had left the door open. She went to shut it and then returned to her dressing-table, with some idea of starting to do something about her face. But tears, so long controlled, rose in her eyes, overflowed, streamed down her cheeks.

She sat and watched her own weeping reflection.

The country bus, stopping and starting and taking its time, trundled through the twilit countryside. Leaving Relkirk, it had been full, with every seat occupied, and one or two passengers standing. Some of the people were returning home from work, others had been shopping. A lot of them seemed to know each other, smiling and chatting as they climbed on board. Probably they travelled together every day. There was a man with a sheep-dog. The dog sat between his knees and gazed without ceasing into the man's eyes. The man didn't have to buy a ticket for the dog.

Henry sat at the front, just behind the driver. He was squashed in by the window, because a hugely fat lady had chosen to sit beside him.

"Hello, pet," she'd said, as she settled herself, her massive bottom shunting him sideways and her bulging thighs taking up most of the space. She had two laden message bags with her, one of which she put at her feet, and the other on her lap. From the top of this bag stuck out a head of celery and a bright pink celluloid windmill. Henry decided that she was taking it home for her grandchild.

She had a round, kind face, not unlike Edie, and beneath the brim of her sensible hat, her eyes screwed up in a friendly way. But when she spoke to him, Henry did not answer her; he simply turned away and gazed from the window, although there was nothing to be seen except rain.

He wore his school stockings and shoes, his new tweed overcoat, which was much too big for him, and his Balaclava helmet. The Balaclava helmet had been a good idea, and he was proud of himself for thinking of it. It was navy-blue and very thick, and he had pulled it right down over his face, like a terrorist, so that only his eyes showed. It was his disguise, because he did not want anybody to recognize him.

The bus made slow progress, and they had already been travelling for nearly an hour. Every mile or so, they drew to a halt at some crossroad, or lonely cottage, to allow people to get off. Henry watched as the seats emptied; passengers gathered up their possessions and alighted one by

336 ◈ Rosamunde Pilcher

one, to set off on foot, to walk the last bit of their journey home. The fat
lady beside him got out at Kirkthornton, but she didn't have to walk,
because her husband had come to meet her in his little farm truck. As
she struggled to her feet, she said, "Goodbye, pet," to Henry. He
thought this very nice of her but, once more, made no reply. It wasn't
easy to say something with a Balaclava over your mouth.

Once more, they set off. Now, there were only half a dozen people on
board. The engine of the bus made a grinding sound as they climbed the
hill out of the little market town, and at the top of the hill it became
quite foggy. The driver turned on his headlights, and thorn hedges and
wind-bent beeches raced towards them out of the gloom, wreathed in
mist and looking ghostly. Henry thought about the five empty miles
between Caple Bridge and Strathcroy, which he was going to have to
walk because Caple Bridge was where he had to get off the bus. The
prospect scared him a bit, but not all that much, because he knew the
road, and the difficult bit was over, and he was nearly there.

At Pennyburn, Violet prepared herself for the rigours of the evening that
lay ahead.

She had not been invited to a proper dance for longer than she could
remember, and, at seventy-eight, it was unlikely that she would ever be
invited to another. For this reason, she had decided to make the most of
the occasion. Accordingly, this afternoon, she had driven to Relkirk, and
there had her hair professionally washed and waved. As well, she had
indulged in a manicure, and the nice girl, with her cushion, had spent
some time digging earth out of Violet's nails and pushing back her neglected cuticles.

After this little beautifying session, she had called in at the bank, and
withdrawn from its vaults the battered leather box that contained Lady
Primrose's diamond tiara. It was not very large, and had to be held
together at the back with a loop of elastic, but she had brought it home
and cleaned it up with an old tooth-brush dipped in neat gin. This was a
household tip that she had gleaned, long ago, from Mrs. Harris, who
had once been cook at Croy. It worked well, but still seemed to Violet a
terrible waste of gin.

Then, from her wardrobe, she had taken down her ball-dress, black
velvet and at least fifteen years old. The frill of black lace at the neck had
come away a little, and needed the attention of a needle and thread, and
her evening shoes, black satin with diamanté buckles, proved, on inspection, to have grown a few whiskers around the toes, so she took up her
nail scissors and gave them a trim.

When all was ready, she allowed herself a little relaxation. She was not
due at Croy until half past eight. So, there was time to pour a restoring
whisky and soda and settle down by the fire to watch the news on

television and then "Wogan." She enjoyed Wogan. She liked his cheerful Irish charm, his blarney. This evening, he was interviewing a young pop star, who, for some reason, had become deeply involved in the preservation of rural hedgerows. People were really quite extraordinary, Violet decided, watching the young man, with his punk hair and his earring, burbling on about nesting yellowhammers.

Then Wogan finished, and a quiz-show came on. Four people were meant to guess the value of various bits of antique junk which were set before them. Violet, all on her own, joined in the guessing game, and became certain that her assessments were far more accurate than anybody else's. She was beginning to enjoy herself when the telephone rang.

How tiresome. Why did the wretched thing always ring at the least opportune moment? She set down her glass, heaved herself out of her comfortable chair, turned down the television, and picked up the receiver.

"Hello?"

"Mrs. Aird?"

"Yes."

"This is Dr. Martin. From the Relkirk Royal."

"Oh, yes."

"Mrs. Aird, I'm afraid we have a little trouble on our hands. Miss Carstairs has disappeared."

"She's *disappeared?*" It sounded like some sort of a dreadful conjuring trick, bringing visions of an explosion, a puff of smoke, and Lottie fading into nothing. "How could she *possibly* have disappeared?"

"She's gone. She went out of doors for a walk in the garden with another patient. She never returned."

"But that's perfectly terrible."

"We think she must have simply walked out through the gates. We've alerted the police, of course, and I'm certain that she cannot be far away. She'll probably come back here of her own accord. She's been quite content, responding to treatment, and not troublesome in any sort of way. There is no reason why she shouldn't return. But I felt I should let you know. . . ."

Violet thought that he was being very feeble.

"Surely you should have taken more care of her?"

"Mrs. Aird, we are overcrowded here and understaffed. Under the circumstances, we do the best we can, but ambulant patients, whom we consider able, up to a point, to take care of themselves, have always been allowed a certain amount of freedom."

"So what do we do now?"

"There is nothing to be done. But, as I said, I thought you should know what has happened."

"Have you spoken to Miss Findhorn, her next of kin?"

"Not yet. I thought it better to have a word with you first."

"In that case, *I* shall tell Miss Findhorn."

"I'd be very grateful if you would."

"Dr. Martin . . ." Violet hesitated. "Do you think that Lottie Carstairs will try to make her way back to Strathcroy?"

"It's possible, of course."

"She would go to Miss Findhorn's house?"

"Possibly."

"I shall be honest with you. I don't like the prospect at all. I fear for Miss Findhorn."

"I appreciate your fears but consider them groundless."

"I wish," Violet told him drily, "that I could be so certain, but thank you, Dr. Martin, for calling."

"If I have any news, I'll ring you."

"I shan't be here. But you will be able to reach me at Croy, because I shall be dining with Lord Balmerino."

"I'll make a note. Thank you. Goodbye, Mrs. Aird. And I'm sorry to have bothered you."

"Yes," said Violet. "You have bothered me. Goodbye."

And she was more than bothered. All peace of mind had been shot to ribbons. She was not only bothered but filled with fear. The same reasonless panic she had experienced sitting by the river with Lottie that day in Relkirk, and with Lottie's fingers clenched, viselike, around her wrist. Then, she had been tempted to leap to her feet and run. Now, she felt the same way, her heart pounding in her chest. It was the fear of the unknown, the unimaginable, some lurking danger.

Analyzed, she realized that this fear was not for herself, but for Edie. Her imagination leaped ahead. A knock on Edie's cottage door, Edie going to answer it, and Lottie, with her hands outstretched like claws, leaping upon her . . .

It didn't bear thinking about. On the television screen, a woman, presented with a flowered chamber-pot, dissolved into silent, embarrassed laughter, her mouth open, her hand over her eyes. Violet turned her off, picked up the receiver, and dialled Balnaid. Edmund must be back from New York by now. Edmund would know exactly what to do.

She heard the ringing sound. It continued to ring. She waited, became impatient. Why did none of them answer her call? What were they all doing?

Finally, exasperated, and by now in a state of fluster, she slammed the receiver down, and then picked it up again and dialled Edie.

Edie, too, was watching television. A nice Scottish programme, country dancing, and a comic in a kilt, telling rare stories. She sat with her supper tray on her lap, grilled chicken legs and chips and mushy peas. For afters, there was some left-over Apple Betty in the fridge. This evening, she was eating late. One of the good things about being on her own again was that she could eat when it suited her, without Lottie on at her all the time about when was the next meal coming. There were other good things. Quiet was one of them. And being able to get a good night's rest in her own bed, instead of tossing and turning on the inadequate Put-U-Up. Getting a good night's rest had done more than anything to restore her energy and good spirits. She still felt guilty about poor Lottie, back in the hospital, but there could be no doubt that life was a great deal easier without her.

The telephone rang. She set aside her tray and got up to answer it.

"Yes?"

"Edie."

She smiled. "Hello, Mrs. Aird."

"Edie . . ." There was something wrong. Edie could tell at once, just by the way Mrs. Aird said her name. "Edie, I've just been speaking to Dr. Martin from the hospital. Lottie's walked out. They don't know where she is."

Edie felt her heart sink into her boots. After a bit she said, "Oh dear, goodness," which was all she could think of to say.

"They've notified the police, and they are pretty certain she's not gone far, but Dr. Martin agrees with me that there is a strong possibility that she'll make her way back to Strathcroy."

"Has she got money with her?" asked Edie, ever practical.

"I don't know. I hadn't thought about that. But I'm certain that she wouldn't have gone far without her handbag."

"No. That's true enough." Lottie was devoted to her handbag, and kept it by her side even when she was just sitting by the fire. "Poor soul. Something must have upset her."

"Yes. Maybe. But, Edie, I'm concerned for *you*. If she does come back to Strathcroy, I don't want you to be alone in your house."

"But I must be here. If she comes, I must be here."

"No. No, Edie, listen. You must listen. You must be sensible. We don't know what is going on in Lottie's mind. She may have got it into her head that you have let her down in some way. Done her some hurt, rejected her. If she is in one of her states, you cannot possibly deal with her on your own."

"And what harm could she do to me?"

"I don't know. I only know that you must get out of your house . . . come to me for the night, or go to Balnaid until such time as she has been located and is safely back in hospital."

"But . . ."

Her protest was overridden. "No, Edie. I will not take no for an answer, otherwise I shall not have a moment's peace. You must pack a night-dress and go to Balnaid. Or come here. I don't mind which. And if you don't agree, then I shall be forced to get into my car and come and fetch you myself. And as I have to be at Croy at half past eight, and am not yet bathed nor dressed, this will be extremely inconvenient for me. It's up to you."

Edie hesitated. The last thing she wanted was to cause a lot of inconvenience. Besides, she knew of old that Violet, once she had set her mind, was immovable. And yet . . .

"I should stay here, Mrs. Aird. I'm her next of kin. She's my responsibility."

"You are also responsible to yourself. If you were to be distressed or threatened or hurt in any way, I should never forgive myself."

"And what will happen if she does come and finds the house empty?"

"The police have been alerted. I am certain that a patrol car will be around the place. It won't be difficult for them to pick her up."

Edie could think of no more arguments. She was defeated, her fate sealed. She sighed, and said quite crossly, "Oh, very well. But in my opinion, you're making a mountain out of a molehill."

"Maybe so. I hope I am."

"Do they know at Balnaid that I'm coming?"

"No. I can't get through to them on the telephone. I think something must be wrong with the wires."

"Have you reported it to Faults?"

"Not yet. I called you right away."

"Well, I'll give Faults a ring, and let them know the number's not answering. They must be there. All getting ready for the party."

"Yes, Edie. You ring Faults. And when you've done that, you must promise me that you'll go to Balnaid. Your room there is always ready, and Virginia will understand. Explain to her what has happened. If there is any inconvenience, you can put the blame on me. I'm sorry, Edie, to be so dictatorial. But I really wouldn't enjoy myself in the very least if I knew that you were on your own."

"It seems to me a lot of fuss about nothing, but I suppose a night at Balnaid won't kill me."

"Thank you, Edie dear. Goodbye."

"Have a good party."

Edie rang off. And then, before she should forget, she lifted the receiver again and called to report the dead line. She was answered by a helpful man, who said that he would investigate the trouble and ring her back.

Lottie gone. What was going to happen next? It was terrible to think of Lottie wandering around somewhere all on her own, perhaps frightened, lost. What was the stupid creature thinking about? Why could she not have stayed where she was, cared for by kindly folk? What wild idea had got into her head this time?

Edie would go to Balnaid, but not immediately. Her tray waited, with the cooling remains of her supper. She would finish it, then do her dishes, tidy the kitchen, and bank up the Rayburn with coke. After that, she would put a nightie into her leatherette message bag, and set off down the road.

She sighed in exasperation. That Lottie was a real nuisance, and no mistake, turning everybody's lives upside down. She settled herself once more with her supper tray on her lap, but the chicken had cooled and lost its tastiness, and even the Scottish programme could not claim her attention.

Once more the telephone rang. Once more she set aside the tray and got up to answer the call. The man from Faults told her that the Balnaid number did not seem to be ringing out, but that an engineer would be around to see to it tomorrow morning.

Edie thanked him. Nothing more could be done. She picked up her supper tray and carried it through to the kitchen. Scraping the remains on her plate into the rubbish bin, she washed up the few bits and pieces and stacked them on the draining-board, all the time trying to work out where on earth her sad, half-witted cousin could have got to.

Archie Balmerino, bathed, shaved, groomed, dressed in his evening clothes, and, given a kiss of approval by his wife, left Isobel at her dressing-table, doing something complicated to her eyelashes, and emerged onto the landing from their bedroom.

For a moment he paused, listening for other signs of activity, but nobody but himself appeared to be about, and so he set off down the stairs, one step at a time, with a hand on the bannister rail. All through the day, each occupant of Croy had been hard at it, with jobs allotted and tasks to be accomplished. Which was just as well, for there had been a hell of a lot to do. Now the house was ready, dressed for the party, a stage set for action, awaiting the raising of the curtain, the entrance of the dramatis personae.

He was the first. At the turn of the stair he paused, to stand, admiring with some satisfaction, the scene below him. The great entrance hall, cleared and tidied of all its normal day-to-day clobber, presented a face both impressive and welcoming. In the huge fireplace, with its carved overmantel, logs flamed, and the table that stood in the centre of the worn Turkey rug reflected, in its highly polished surface, the considerable arrangement of white chrysanthemums and scarlet rose-hip berries which Isobel had concocted sometime during the course of the afternoon.

Croy dressed for entertaining. An excitement in the air, a promise of pleasures to come. For once austerity and necessary economies had been tossed overboard, and the old house could be sensed revelling in the indulgence of rare extravagance.

He thought of other evenings. His own twenty-first; and the evening when he and Isobel had celebrated their engagement. Birthdays, Christmases, hunt balls, his parents' silver wedding . . .

And then, frowning at himself, he shut the memories away. Nostalgia was his greatest weakness. One could look back forever, but looking back was an old person's ploy and he was not old. He was not yet fifty. Croy was his and yet not his. It had come to him, through his father and his grandfather, to hold in trust for Hamish. And the strength of a chain was the strength of its weakest link.

He himself. The horrors of Northern Ireland would remain with him until the day he died, but the haunting ghosts and dreams had finally been laid to rest, and with them disposed of, he knew that there were no longer excuses to be made to himself. The time had come to stop vacillating and start constructing some practical plans for his inheritance and his family and their future. He had marked time for too long, and there were no more years to be wasted. He wasn't quite sure what he would do, but he would do something. Borrow money and start that factory that Pandora thought such a brilliant idea. Or grow soft fruit, raspberries and strawberries, on a huge commercial scale. Or go in for fish-farming. There were opportunities and possibilities all about him. All he had to do was make up his mind and go for it.

Go for it. The words had a heartening ring to them. He knew again some of his old, youthful confidence. Knew that the worst was over, and nothing could ever be quite so bad again.

He went on, down the stairs, into the dining-room. He and Pandora had laid the table together, just the way it had always been arranged for important occasions, when Harris was in charge, and pleased to instruct the youthful Blairs on correct and time-honoured procedure. It had taken them most of the afternoon, with Archie polishing up the bubble-thin wineglasses, and Pandora folding the starched white napkins into mitres, each tipped with the embroidered coronet and the letter *B*.

Now he observed, with a critical eye, their work. The effect was splendid. The four heavy silver candlesticks marched down the centre of the table, and firelight shone and sparkled from gleaming silver and glass, for here, as well, the logs flamed, and Jeff Howland had been given the job of filling all the wood-baskets. The scent of dry and crackling pine was warm and spicy. Archie walked the length of the room, checking on the placement, straightening a fork, altering, very slightly, the position of a salt-cellar. Satisfied, he went on into the kitchen.

Here he found Agnes Cooper, up from the village for the evening. Agnes normally came to work in her track suit and a pair of trainers, but this evening she wore beneath her pinafore her best turquoise Crimplene dress, and she had had her hair done.

She was at the sink, dealing with the odd saucepan or two, but turned at his footstep.

"Agnes. Everything all right?"

"All under control. I've just got to keep my eye on the casserole, and put the wee bits of smoked trout onto the plates when Lady Balmerino says."

"It's good of you to come and help us."

"That's what I'm here for." She eyed him in some admiration. "I hope you don't mind my saying, but you're looking *fantaastic.*"

"Oh, thank you, Agnes." He found himself a little embarrassèd, and to cover his confusion, offered her a drink. "A glass of sherry. How would that be?"

Agnes was also a little taken aback. "Oh. Well. That would be very nice."

She reached for a towel and dried her hands. Archie found a glass, and the bottle of Harvey's Bristol Cream. He poured her a generous tot. "Here you are. . . .'"

"Thanks a lot, Lord Balmerino. . . ." She raised the glass in a convivial fashion, saying, "Here's to having a good time," and then took a ladylike sip, folding her lips appreciatively around the rich taste. "Sherry's lovely," she said. "Like I say, it always gives you a beautiful glow."

He left her and went back, through the dining-room, across the hall, and into the drawing-room. Another fire, more flowers, soft lights, but no guests. His house party, it seemed, were taking their time. The drinks tray had been set out, and placed on top of the grand piano. He considered the situation. They would be on champagne for the remainder of the evening, but he needed a Scotch. He poured himself a drink, and then poured a second one, and, carrying the two glasses with a certain amount of care, painfully made his way upstairs again.

On the landing he came upon his daughter, who, for some reason, was wandering around in her underclothes.

"Lucilla!" he reproached her.

But she was more concerned over his appearance than her own.

"Goodness, Dad, you look *gorgeous.* Really romantic and distinguished. The Lord Balmerino in full fig. Are those new trousers? They're heaven. I wouldn't mind a pair of those. And Grandpa's old smoking jacket. Quite perfect." She put her naked arms around his neck and pressed a kiss on his newly shaved cheek. "And you smell delicious as well. All sleek and barbered and yummy. Who are the drinks for?"

"I thought I'd better make sure that Pandora's awake. Why haven't you got any clothes on?"

"Just on my way to borrow a petticoat from Mum. My new dress is a bit flimsy."

"You'd better get a move on. It's twenty-five past eight."

"I'm ready now." She went to throw open the door of her parents' bedroom. "Mum! I'm going to *have* to wear a petticoat. . . ."

Archie crossed the landing to the door of the guest-room. From within came faint strains of music, which meant that Pandora had turned on her radio, but did not necessarily mean that she was awake. He juggled the two glasses into one hand, gave a cursory thump on the panel, and opened the door.

"Pandora?"

She was not in bed, but she was on it, lying draped in a silk-and-lace wrapper. Clothes were scattered about all over the place, and the room was heavy with the smell of that strange scent that had become so much part of her presence.

"Pandora."

She opened her beautiful grey eyes. She had put on her make-up, and her thick lashes were heavy with mascara. She saw him and smiled. She said, "I'm not asleep."

"I've brought you a drink."

He went to sit on the edge of the bed, to set the glass down on her table, alongside the little lamp. Her radio crooned softly away to itself, a programme of dance music that sounded as though it came from a long way back.

She said, "How kind."

"It's almost time to come downstairs." Her shining hair spilled over the pillow, almost as though it had a life of its own, but lying there she looked so thin, so insubstantial, so weightless that, all at once, he felt concern. "Are you tired?"

"No. Just lazy. Where is everybody?"

"Isobel's dealing with her face, and Lucilla's wandering about in her knickers wanting to borrow a petticoat from her mother. So far, there's no sign of either of the men."

"It's always a good moment, isn't it? Just before a party. Time to have a toes-up and listen to nostalgic tunes. Do you remember this one? It's so pretty. Rather sad. I can't remember the words."

Together they listened. The tenor saxophone carried the melody. Archie frowned, trying to capture the elusive lyric. The music carried him back twenty years, to Berlin and some regimental ball. Berlin was the clue.

"Something about a long long time from May to December."

"Yes, of course. Kurt Weill. 'But the days grow short when you reach September.' And then autumn leaves, and the days running out, and there not being time for the waiting game. So dreadfully poignant."

She sat up, bunching her pillows behind her. She reached for her drink, and he saw her narrow wrist, and her red-tipped hand, so fine and pale and blue-veined that it seemed to Archie almost transparent.

He said, "Are you nearly ready?"

"Nearly. I've only got to slip my dress on and zip up the zip." She took a mouthful of whisky. "Oh, delicious. This will get me going."

Over the rim of the glass her eyes appeared enormous. "You look amazing, Archie. Just as dashing as you ever did."

"Agnes Cooper said I looked *fantaastic*."

"What a compliment. Darling, I wasn't asleep. I was just having a little quiet think about yesterday. It was all so perfect. Just like it used to be. The two of us. Sitting in the butt, and having time to chat. Or not chat, as the case might be. Perhaps I talked too much, but twenty years is a long time to tell. Was it dreadfully boring?"

"No. You made me laugh. You always made me laugh."

"And the sun and the blue sky and the heather linties cheeping away, and the guns going *crack,* and the poor little grouse tumbling out of the sky. And all those clever doggies. Weren't we lucky to have such a day? Like being given the most gorgeous present."

He said, "I know."

"It's nice to think those sort of days come back again. That they haven't gone forever."

"We must reform. Kick this invidious family habit of dwelling in the past."

"It was such a good past, it's difficult not to. Besides, what else is there to think about?"

"Now. Yesterday is dead and tomorrow not yet born. We only have today."

"Yes."

She took another sip from her glass. They fell silent. From beyond the closed door came sounds of activity. A door opened and closed. And then Lucilla's voice. "Conrad. How smart you look. I don't know where Dad is, but go downstairs and we'll all be with you in a moment. . . ."

"I hope," said Archie, "that she's wearing Isobel's petticoat."

"Conrad is such a gentleman that even if Lucilla is stark-naked, he'll pay no regard. Such a nice man. It would have been too awful for all of us if he'd been a crashing bore."

"You must make a point of dancing with him."

"I'll twirl him through a Dashing White Sergeant and introduce him to all the nobs as we move around the room. That's the only thing about this evening that makes me a little unhappy. You won't be able to dance."

"Don't worry about that. Over the years, I've perfected the art of sparkling conversation. . . ."

They were interrupted at last by Lucilla opening the door and putting her head around the edge of it.

"Sorry to barge in, but there's a crisis. Dad, Jeff can't tie Edmund's bow-tie. He's only worn a bow-tie once in his life, and that was a made-up one on an elastic. I tried to help, but it was a total failure. Can you come and assist?"

"Of course."

Duty called. He was needed. The quiet moments were over. He gave Pandora a kiss. "See you." And then got to his feet and followed Lucilla out of the room. Pandora, left alone, slowly finished her drink.

These precious days I'll spend with you.

The song was ended.

Violet, with Highland blood coursing through her veins, always stoutly averred that she was not superstitious. She walked under ladders, disregarded Friday the thirteenth, and never touched wood. If some sort of an omen presented itself, she usually told herself firmly that it was probably for the best, and looked for good news. She was grateful that she had not been blessed—or cursed—with second sight. It was better not to know what the future held.

Having dealt with Edie, and bullied that promise out of her, she expected her anxieties to be resolved, and her mind once more at rest. But this did not happen, and she returned to her fireside chair in a state of grave apprehension. What was amiss? Why did she feel all at once haunted by nameless, lurking fears? Bundled in her old dressing-gown, she sat forward, staring into the flames, searching for the root cause of her sudden chill, the unease that, like a weight, lay deep in her being.

Hearing that Lottie was on the loose, wandering about, up to Heaven knew what, was bad enough; but, ridiculously, the fact that she could not get through to Balnaid and speak to Edmund disturbed her a good deal more. It wasn't just the frustration of non-communication. Often, during the winter blizzards, Violet was cut off at Pennyburn for a day or more, and isolation did not worry her in the very least. It was just that the breakdown had occurred at such a startlingly inappropriate time. As though some uncontrollable and malevolent force were at work.

She was not superstitious. But misfortunes invariably happened in threes. First Lottie, then the faulty telephone. What next?

She let her imagination move forward to the evening ahead, and knew that there lay a veritable minefield of potential disaster. For the first time, the players in the drama that had been boiling up over the last week would all come together, gathered around the dining-room table at Croy. Edmund, Virginia, Pandora, Conrad, Alexa, and Noel. All, in their various ways, confused and restless, searching for some elusive happiness, as though it could be found, like a pot of gold, at the end of a fairy-tale rainbow. But in their efforts all they seemed to have unearthed was a useless cache of destructive emotion. Resentment, distrust, selfishness, greed, and disloyalty. Adultery, too. Only Alexa, it seemed, stayed unsullied. For Alexa, there was only the pain of love.

A log, burning through, collapsed with a whisper into the bed of ashes. An interruption. Violet looked up at her clock, and was horrified to see that she had sat, brooding, for too long, for it was already a quarter past eight. She would be late arriving at Croy. Under usual circumstances, this would have bothered her, for she was a stickler for punctuality, but this evening, with so much else on her mind, it scarcely seemed to matter. For fifteen minutes or so, she would not be missed, and Isobel would not lead them into the dining-room until at least nine o'clock.

She realized, too, that the last thing she wanted to do was go out. Smile, chat, conceal her apprehensions. She did not want to leave the safe haven of her house, her fireside. Something, somewhere, was lying in wait, and her frail human instinct was to bolt herself indoors, in safety, sit by the telephone, and keep watch.

But she was *not* superstitious.

She pulled herself together, got out of her chair, put the guard on the dying fire, and went upstairs. Swiftly, she bathed, and then dressed herself for the party. Silk underclothes and black silk stockings, the venerable black velvet gown, the satin court shoes. She dressed her hair, and then took up her diamond tiara and settled it on her head, fixing, with a bit of difficulty, the loop of elastic at the back. She powdered her nose, found a lacy handkerchief, sprayed a little eau-de-cologne about her person. Moving to her long mirror, she gauged, with critical eyes, the general effect. Saw a large and stout dowager for whom the word "dignified" seemed the kindest description.

Large and stout. And old. All at once, she felt very tired. Tiredness did funny things to one's imagination, for, staring into the mirror, she saw beyond her own reflection the cloudy image of another woman. Never beautiful, but unlined, and brown-haired and filled with a raging energy for life. Herself, wearing the crimson satin ball gown that had been her most favourite. And beside that other woman, stood Geordie. For an instant the mirage stayed, so real that she could have touched it. And then it faded and was gone, and she was left alone. For years, she had not felt so alone. But there was no time to stand and feel sorry for herself. Others were waiting for her, as always, demanding her company, her attention. She turned from the mirror, reached for her fur coat and pulled it on, picking up her evening bag and switching off the lights. Downstairs, she went out through the kitchen door, locking it behind her. The night was dark, and damp with a drizzling mist. She crossed over to the garage and got into her car. Lifts had been offered by all and sundry, but she had chosen to drive herself to Croy, and after dinner, she would drive herself to Corriehill. That way she would be totally independent of any person and able to return home whenever she chose.

You should always leave a party just when you are most enjoying yourself.

That had been one of Geordie's maxims. Thinking of Geordie, hearing his dear voice in her head filled her with a certain comfort. On such occasions, she never felt that he was very far away. How amused he would be by her now, seventy-eight years old, dolled up in velvet and diamonds and fur, and driving herself in her mud-stained motor car to . . . of all things . . . a ball.

Headed up the hill, watching the road ahead contained by the beam of her own headlights, she made Geordie a promise.

I know this is a ludicrous situation, my darling, but it is the last time. After this evening, if any person is kind enough to ask me to a dance, I shall tell them no. And my excuse will be that I am really far too old.

Henry walked. Darkness had fallen and a thin rain drifted into his face. The river, the Croy, kept him company, flowing alongside the winding road. He could not see it, but was aware all the time of the presence of moving water, the rippling sound as the shallows tumbled downhill in a series of little pools and waterfalls. It was comforting to know that the Croy was there. The only other noises to reach his ears were familiar, but strangely magnified by his own solitude. The wind, stirring the branches of trees, and the curlew's lonely call. His footsteps sounded enormous. Sometimes he imagined other footsteps, following some way behind him, but it was probably just an echo of his own tread. Any alternative was too scary to contemplate.

He had been passed by only three cars, driving from Caple Bridge and heading, as he was headed, up the glen. On each occasion, aware of the approaching headlights, he had bundled himself down into the ditch, hiding until the car was gone, zipping past with a hiss of tyres on the wet road. He did not wish to be observed, and as well, he did not wish to be offered a lift. Accepting lifts from strangers was not only dreadfully dangerous, but totally forbidden, and at this stage of his long journey, Henry was not about to risk being driven somewhere he did not want to go, and murdered.

However, when he was less than a mile from Strathcroy, and could actually see the lights of the village pricking like welcome stars through the gloom, he did get a lift. A massive double-deckered sheep-float came grinding up the road behind him, and Henry somehow hadn't the energy to jump for the ditch before being caught in its headlights. Even as it passed Henry, the sheep-float was already slowing down. It drew to a throbbing halt, and the driver opened the door of his high cab and waited for Henry to catch up with him. He squinted down into the murky dusk and saw Henry's Balaclava-ed face staring up at him.

"Hello, sonny." He was a great burly man in a tweed bonnet. A familiar sort of person. Not a stranger. As well, Henry's legs were beginning to feel wobbly, like cooked spaghetti, and he was not certain whether he was going to be able to make that last bit of the road to Strathcroy.

"Hello."

"Where are you off to?"

"Strathcroy."

"Did you miss the bus?"

This seemed a good excuse. "Yes," fibbed Henry.

"Want a ride?"

"Yes, please."

"Up you come, then."

The man reached down a horny hand. Henry put his own hand into it and was heaved upwards, as though he weighed no more than a fly, onto the big man's knee, and then over and onto the other seat. The cab was warm and snug and very dirty. It smelt fuggy, of old cigarettes and sheep, and there were sweetie papers and match-ends littered around the floor, but Henry didn't mind this, because it was good to be there, with another person for company, and to know that he didn't have to walk any farther.

The driver slammed his door shut, shoved his engine into gear, and they moved forward.

"Where have you walked from?"

"Caple Bridge."

"That's a long walk on a wet night."

"Yes."

"Do you live in Strathcroy?"

"I'm going to see someone there." Before he could be asked any more questions, Henry decided to ask one himself. "Where have you been?"

"To the market in Relkirk."

"Did you have a lot of sheep?"

"Aye."

"Were they your own?"

"No, I've no sheep. I'm just the driver."

"Where do you live?"

"Inverness."

"Are you going there tonight?"

"Oh, aye."

"It's a long way."

"Maybe so, but I like to sleep in my own bed."

The windscreen wipers swung to and fro. Through the clean fan of glass, Henry watched as the lights of Strathcroy came closer. Then they passed the thirty-miles-an-hour sign, and then the War Memorial. Around the last curve of the road, and the long main street of the village stretched ahead into the darkness.

"Where do you want me to drop you off?"

"Just here will do very nicely, thank you."

Once more, the sheep-float ground to a juddering halt.

"You'll be all right, now?" The man reached over to open Henry's door.

"Yes, of course. Thank you very much indeed. You've been very kind."

"You mind yourself, now."

"I will." He clambered down the great height to the road. "Goodbye."

"Goodbye, sonny."

The door slammed shut. The massive vehicle went on its way, and Henry stood and watched it go, its red tail-light winking like a friendly eye. The sound of the engine faded into the darkness, and after it was gone, everything seemed very quiet.

He started off again, walking down the middle of the deserted street. He felt extremely tired, but that didn't matter, because he was almost there. He knew exactly where he was going and what he was going to do, because he had laid his secret plans with the greatest possible thought and care. He'd mulled over every eventuality, and left nothing to chance. He was not going to Balnaid, nor Pennyburn, but to Edie's. He was not going to Balnaid because there would be nobody there. His mother, his father, Alexa and her friend were all at Croy, having dinner with the Balmerinos before going to Mrs. Steynton's party. And he was not going to Pennyburn because Vi was at Croy too. And even if they had all been at home, he would still have made for Edie's cottage because Edie would be there.

Without Lottie. Horrible Lottie was back in hospital. The news had been relayed to Henry by Mr. Henderson, and the relief of knowing that Edie was safely on her own again had filled Henry with courage and finally precipitated his illegal flight. It made all the difference, knowing that he had somewhere safe to go. Edie would take him in her arms, ask no questions, make him hot cocoa. Edie would listen to him. She would understand. She would be on his side. And with Edie on his side, surely everybody else would take notice of what she had to say and would not be angry with him.

The lights still burned in Mrs. Ishak's supermarket, but he kept to the far side of the road, so that Mrs. Ishak, by chance, would not see him as he passed by. The rest of the street was dark, lit only by the curtained windows of the wayside houses. From behind these windows Henry could hear muffled voices or music from people's television sets. Edie would be sitting in her armchair, watching television, busy with her knitting.

He came to her little cottage with its thatch, crouched down between its neighbours. The window of her sitting-room was dark, which meant she wasn't watching television. But from her bedroom window, light streamed brightly out, and it seemed that she had forgotten to draw her curtains.

She had other curtains, lace ones, for privacy, but it was perfectly possible to see through these. Henry went close to the window and peered inside, cupping his hands to the sides of his face as he had seen grown-ups do. The lace curtains veiled the interior a bit, but he saw Edie at once. She was standing at her dressing-table, with her back to him. She was wearing her new lilac cardigan and looked as though she was putting powder on her face. Perhaps she was going out. Dressed in her best lilac cardigan . . .

He balled his fist and rapped on the glass to catch her attention. She turned from the mirror with a start and came towards him. The overhead light shone down on her face, and his heart leaped in a spasm of horror, because something dreadful had happened to her. She had got a different face, with staring black eyes and a mouth red with lipstick, all smeared as though it were blood. And her hair was wrong, and her cheeks pale as paper. . . .

It was Lottie.

Those staring eyes. A revulsion, stronger than fear, jerked him away from the window. He backed off across the street, out of the patch of yellow light that lay across the wet pavement. Every exhausted limb in his body was shaking, and his heart thumped against his chest as though it were trying to fight its way out. Petrified with terror, he thought he would probably never be able to move again. The terror was for himself, but mostly it was for Edie.

Lottie had done something to her. His very worst nightmare was true, was happening. Somehow, Lottie had come creeping secretly back to Strathcroy and burst in on Edie when Edie wasn't looking. Somewhere in the cottage Edie lay. On the kitchen floor perhaps, with a meat chopper in the back of her neck and blood all over the place.

He opened his mouth to scream for help, but the only sound that emerged was a trembling, faint whisper.

And now Lottie was there, at the window, raising the lace curtain to peer out into the street, her horrible face pressed against the glass. In a moment, she would go to the door, she would be after him.

He forced his legs to move, backed away up the road, and then turned and ran. It was like running in a dreadful, treacly dream, but this time he knew that he would never wake up. His ears were filled with the thud of his own footsteps and the rasping of his breath. It was difficult to breathe. He tore the Balaclava helmet from his head, and the cold air streamed down on his head and cheeks. His brain cleared, and ahead, he saw his refuge. The bright windows of Mrs. Ishak's shop, stacked with the usual colourful display of soap powders and cereal packets and cut-price bargains.

He ran to Mrs. Ishak.

* * *

Mrs. Ishak's long day was winding itself down. Her husband, having emptied the till of the day's takings, had disappeared into the stock-room, where each evening he totted up all the cash, and then locked it away in his safe. Mrs. Ishak had been around the shelves, replacing tins and goods, and filling up the gaps left by the day's customers. She was now busy with her broom, sweeping the floor.

When the door burst open so suddenly and with such force, she was a little startled. She looked up from her sweeping, her brows raised over her kohl-rimmed eyes, and was even more startled than ever when she saw who it was.

"Henree."

He looked terrible, wearing a mud-stained tweed coat sizes too big for him, and with his socks falling down and his shoes covered with dirt. But Mrs. Ishak was less concerned by his clothes than the state of Henry himself. Gasping for breath, ashen-white, he stood there for a second, before slamming the door shut and setting his back against it.

"Henree." Mrs. Ishak laid down her broom. "What has happened?" But he had no breath for words. "Why are you not at school?"

His mouth worked. "Edie's dead." She could scarcely hear him. And then again, only this time he shouted it at her. "Edie's *dead.*"

"But . . ."

Henry burst into tears. Mrs. Ishak held out her arms and Henry fled into them. She knelt to his height, holding him close to her silken breast, her hand cupped around the back of his head. "No," she murmured. "No. It is not true." And when he went on crying, hysterically asserting that it *was,* she tried to soothe him, speaking to him in *katchi,* that intimate and unwritable dialect that all the Ishak family used when they spoke among themselves. Henry had heard the soft sounds before, when Mrs. Ishak comforted Kedejah, or sat her on her knee to pet her. He could not understand a word but he was comforted too, and Mrs. Ishak smelt musky and delicious, and her lovely rose-pink tunic was cool against his face.

And yet he had to make her understand. He pulled away from her embrace and stared into her confused and troubled face.

"Edie is dead."

"No, Henry."

"Yes, she *is.*" He gave her a little thump on her shoulder, maddened that she was being so stupid.

"Why do you say this?"

"Lottie's in her house. She's killed her. She's stealing her cardigan."

Mrs. Ishak stopped looking confused. Her face sharpened. She frowned.

"Did you see Lottie?"

"Yes. She's in Edie's bedroom, and . . ."

Mrs. Ishak got to her feet. "Shamsh!" she called to her husband, and her voice was strong and urgent.

"What is it?"

"Come quickly." He appeared. Mrs. Ishak, in a long stream of *katchi*, gave him instructions. He asked questions; she answered them. He went back to his stock-room, and Henry heard the sound as he dialled a number on his telephone.

Mrs. Ishak fetched a chair and made Henry sit on it. She knelt beside him and held his hands.

She said, "Henree, I do not know what you are doing here but you must listen to me. Mr. Ishak is telephoning the police now. They will come in a patrol car and fetch Lottie and take her back to hospital. They have been warned that she left the hospital without permission, and have been told to watch out for her. Now, do you understand that?"

"Yes, but Edie . . ."

With her gentle fingers, Mrs. Ishak wiped away the tears that dribbled down Henry's cheeks. With the end of her rose-pink chiffon scarf, which she wore draped around her shining black hair, she dabbed at his snivelling nose.

She told him, "Edie is at Balnaid. She is staying there for the night. She is safe."

Henry stared in silence at Mrs. Ishak, terrified that she was not telling him the truth.

"How do you know?" he asked her at last.

"Because on her way there, she dropped in to see me, to buy an evening newspaper. She told me that your granny, Mrs. Aird, had told her about Lottie, and also that Mrs. Aird did not want her to stay alone in her own cottage."

"Vi was frightened for Edie too?"

"Not frightened. Mrs. Aird would not be frightened, I think. But concerned for your dear Edie. So you see, it is all right. You are safe."

From the back of the shop, they could hear Mr. Ishak speaking on the telephone. Henry turned his head to listen, but could not catch the words. Then Mr. Ishak stopped speaking and rang off. Henry waited. Mr. Ishak came through the door.

"All right?" asked Mrs. Ishak.

"Yes. I have spoken to the police. They will send a patrol car. It should be in the village in about five minutes."

"Do they know where to go?"

"Yes. They know." He looked at Henry, and smiled reassuringly. "Poor boy. You have had a bad fright. But it is over now."

They were being very kind. Mrs. Ishak still knelt, holding Henry's hands, and he had stopped shaking. After a bit, he asked, "Can I ring Edie up?"

"No. It is not possible to do that because your telephone at Balnaid is out of order. Edie reported it to Faults before she left her home, but they said that they could not attend to the matter before tomorrow morning. But we will wait a little, and I will make you a hot drink, and then I will walk with you to Balnaid and you will be with your Edie."

It was only then that Henry was truly convinced that Edie was not dead. She was at Balnaid, waiting for him, and the knowledge that soon he would be with her was almost more than he could bear. He felt his mouth trembling like a baby's and the tears filling his eyes, but he was too tired to do anything about them. Mrs. Ishak said his name and once more gathered him into her silk and scented embrace and he wept for a long time.

Finally, it was all over, except for a few troublesome sobs. Mr. Ishak brought him a mug of hot chocolate, very sweet and brown and bubbly, and Mrs. Ishak made him a sandwich with jam in the middle.

"Tell me," said Mrs. Ishak, when Henry was feeling much stronger and more composed, "because you still have not answered my first question. Why are you here and not at school?"

Henry, with his fingers locked around the hot mug, gazed into her dark and liquid eyes.

"I didn't like it," he told her. "I ran away. I've come home."

The clock on the mantelpiece stood at twenty to nine as Edmund walked into the drawing-room at Croy. He had expected to find it filled with people, but instead discovered Archie and an unknown man, who by the simple process of elimination, he assumed to be the Sad American, Conrad Tucker, and the root cause of Edmund's immediate disagreement with Virginia.

Both men were resplendent in their evening gear, Archie looking better than Edmund had seen him look in years. They sat by the fire, companionably, glasses in their hands. Conrad Tucker occupied an armchair, and Archie perched, with his back to the fire, on the club fender. As the door opened, they stopped talking, looked up, saw Edmund, and got to their feet.

"Edmund."

"We're late, I'm sorry. We've had dramas."

"As you can see, not late at all. Nobody else, yet, has appeared. Where's Virginia?"

"Gone upstairs to shed her coat. And Alexa and Noel will be here in a moment. At the last minute Alexa decided to wash her hair, and she was still drying it when we left. God knows why she didn't think of doing it before."

"They never do," said Archie bleakly, speaking from years of experience. "Edmund, you've not met Conrad Tucker."

"No, I don't think I have. How do you do."

They shook hands. The American was as tall as Edmund, and heftily built. His eyes, behind the heavy horn-rims, met Edmund's in a steady gaze, and Edmund found himself torn by an uncharacteristic uncertainty.

For, deep within him, concealed by a civilized veneer of good manners, burnt a smouldering rage and resentment against this man, this American, who appeared to have taken over while Edmund's back was turned, rekindled Virginia's remembered youth, and was now calmly planning to fly back to the States with her—Edmund's wife—in tow. Smiling politely into Conrad Tucker's open face, Edmund toyed with the lovely idea of balling his fist and smashing it into that craggy and sun-tanned nose. Imagining the consequent mayhem, the blood and the bruising, filled him with shameful relish.

And yet, on the other hand he knew that, under different circumstances, this was the sort of person that it would be perfectly possible to like instantly.

Conrad Tucker's friendly expression mirrored Edmund's own. "How very nice to meet you." Damn his eyes.

Archie was headed for the tray of bottles.

"Edmund. A small whisky?"

"Thank you. I could do with one."

His host reached for The Famous Grouse. "When did you get back from New York?"

"About five-thirty."

Conrad asked, "Did you have a good trip?"

"More or less. A bit of trouble-shooting, a few well-chosen words. I believe you're an old friend of my wife's?"

If he had hoped to throw the other man off-balance, he did not succeed. Conrad Tucker gave nothing away, showed no discomfiture.

"That's right. We were dancing partners in our long-ago and misspent youth."

"She tells me you're travelling back to the States together."

Still no reaction. If the American guessed that he was being needled, he betrayed no sign. "She got a seat on that plane?" was all that he said.

"Apparently so."

"I hadn't heard. But that'll be great. It's a long trip on your own. I'll be going to the city straight from Kennedy, but I can see her through immigration and baggage claim, and then be certain that she has transportation to Leesport."

"That's more than kind of you."

Archie handed Edmund his drink. "Conrad, I didn't know you'd planned all this. I didn't even know Virginia was thinking of going to the States. . . ."

"She's going to visit her grandparents."

"And when are *you* off?"

"I'm staying here until Sunday, if that's all right by you, and then flying out of Heathrow on Thursday. I need a day or two in London to see to some business."

"How long have you been in this country?" Edmund asked him.

"A couple of months."

"I hope you've enjoyed your visit."

"Thank you. I've had a fine time."

"I'm glad." Edmund raised his glass. "Cheers."

At this point they were interrupted by the appearance of Jeff Howland who, having finally solved the problem of the bow-tie, had completed his dressing and come downstairs. He obviously felt ill at ease and self-conscious in his unaccustomed gear, and his face wore a faintly abashed expression as he walked into the room, but indeed he looked more than presentable in the outfit that he and Lucilla had gleaned from Edmund's wardrobe. Edmund was amused to see that Jeff had picked out a cream hopsack jacket, purchased in a moment of crisis in Hong Kong. It had proved to be a mistaken buy, for Edmund had worn it only once.

"Jeff."

The young man craned his neck and ran a finger around the restricting collar of the starched evening shirt. He said, "I'm not used to this sort of thing. I feel a real berk."

"You look splendid. Come and have a drink. We're onto the whisky before the women turn up and demand champagne."

Jeff relaxed a little. He was always happier in purely masculine company. "There wouldn't be a can of Foster's?"

"There most certainly would. On the tray. Help yourself."

Jeff relaxed a bit more, reached for the can, poured the long glass. He said to Edmund, "It was good of you to kit me out. I'm grateful."

"A pleasure. The jacket is perfect. Dressy, but with just the right touch of outback informality."

"That's what Lucilla said."

"She was quite right. And you look a great deal better in it than I did. Wearing it, I resembled an elderly barman . . . the useless variety that doesn't even know how to fix a dry Martini."

Jeff smiled, took a heartening swallow, and then looked about him. "Where are all the girls?"

"Good question," said Archie. "God knows." He had settled himself once more on the fender, seeing no reason to stand about for a moment longer than he had to. "Buttoning themselves into their evening gowns, I suppose. Lucilla was searching for underclothes, Pandora decided to go to bed, and Isobel's in a state of panic about her evening shoes." He turned to Edmund. "But you said that you had dramas. What's been happening at Balnaid?"

Edmund told him.

"Our phone's on the blink, which is one thing. We can make calls, but nobody can get through to us. However, it's been reported, and some guy's coming to see to it tomorrow morning. And that's the least of our worries. Edie turned up out of the blue, with her nightie in a bag, and the news that Lottie Carstairs is on the loose again. She walked out of the Relkirk Royal and hasn't been seen since."

Archie shook his head in exasperation. "That bloody woman is more trouble than a bitch in heat. When did this happen?"

"I don't know. Sometime this afternoon, I suppose. The doctor rang Vi to let her know. Then Vi tried to ring me, but couldn't get through. So she called Edie, and proceeded to order her out of her cottage for the night, and come to us. Which is what Edie has done."

"Vi surely doesn't think that lunatic is dangerous?"

"I don't know. Personally, I think she's capable of almost anything, and if Vi hadn't told Edie to come to Balnaid, then I should have done so myself. Anyway, Alexa will leave her bolted in with the dogs for company. But as you can imagine, it's all taken a bit of time."

"No matter." Archie, with domestic problems dealt with, changed the subject to more absorbing and important matters. "We missed you yesterday, Edmund. We had a great day. Thirty-three and a half brace, and the birds flying like the wind. . . ."

Violet was the last to arrive. She knew that she was the last, because as she drew up on the gravel sweep in front of Croy, she saw five other vehicles already parked there. Archie's Land Rover, Isobel's minibus, Edmund's BMW, Pandora's Mercedes, and Noel's Volkswagen. A bit, she decided, like the car-park at a Point-to-Point, and an awful lot of traffic for just two families.

She got out of her car, bundled her long skirts up out of the damp, and made for the front door. As she went up the steps, this was opened, and she saw that Edmund waited for her, standing in the bright light of the hall. With his silver hair, and wearing kilt, doublet, and diced hose, he looked even more distinguished than usual, and despite all her dratted anxieties, Violet found time to experience a dart of motherly pride, and the relief of having him actually around again filled her with gratitude.

"Oh, Edmund."

"I heard your car." He gave her a kiss.

"What a time I've had." She went indoors, he closed the door behind her, and came to help her off with her fur coat. "Your telephone. It's not working. . . ."

"It's all right, Vi. All under control. It's being fixed tomorrow morning. . . ."

He laid the coat on a chair while Vi shook out her ample velvet skirts and readjusted the lace frill at her shoulders. "Thank heavens for that. And my darling Edie? She's at Balnaid?"

"Yes. Safe and sound. You look trachled. Stop worrying now, or you're not going to enjoy yourself."

"It's impossible not to. That wretched Lottie. Just one thing after another. But you're home and safe, and that's all that matters. I am dreadfully late, aren't I?"

"This evening, everybody is. Isobel's only just appeared. Now, come and have a glass of champagne, and then you'll feel much better."

"Is my tiara straight?"

"Perfect." He took her arm and led her into the drawing-room.

"*I* think," said Pandora, "that Verena's missed out. We should all have been issued with darling little dance programmes, and tiny pencils hanging off them. . . ."

"That just shows," Archie told her, "how long you've been away. Dance programmes are a thing of the past. . . ."

"That's a *shame*. They were always half the fun. And then you kept them, all tied up in ribbon, and brooded over your lost beaux."

"It was all right," Isobel pointed out, "if one was a social butterfly, with lots of admirers. Not so much fun if nobody wanted to dance with you."

"I'm certain," said Conrad, with a certain transatlantic gallantry, "that that never happened to *you*."

"Oh, Conrad, how kind of you. But every now and then there did occur a disastrous evening when one had a spot on one's nose, or a horrid dress."

"So what did you do?"

"Hid in shame in the Ladies' Cloakroom. The Ladies' was always filled with sad wallflowers. . . ."

"Like Daphne Brownfield," Pandora chipped in. "Archie, you have to remember Daphne Brownfield. She was the size of a house and her mother always dressed her in white net . . . she was madly in love with you and blushed like a lobster whenever you came within spitting distance. . . ."

But Archie was more charitable. "She played a splendid game of tennis."

"Oh, jolly hockey sticks," Pandora scoffed.

The room rang with voices, and now, laughter. Violet, sitting at Archie's right hand, and with a glass of champagne inside her, was already feeling a little less edgy. She listened to Pandora's teasing, but with only half an ear, because it was far more fascinating to watch than to listen. The dining-room at Croy this evening presented a splendid spectacle. The long table was dressed overall, like a battleship, for ceremony, laden with gleaming silver, starched linen, green-and-gold china, sparkling crystal. Silver pheasants stood as a centre-piece, and all was illuminated by the flames of fire and candles.

"It wasn't just the girls who suffered," Noel pointed out. "For a young man, dance programmes could be dreadfully limiting. No chance to play the field, and by the time you'd spied some dishy chick, it was too late to do very much about her. . . ."

"How did you become so experienced?" Edmund asked him.

"Doing my circuit as a Debs' Delight, but those days, thank God, are over. . . ."

They ate smoked trout, with wedges of lemon and thin brown bread and butter. Lucilla moved around the table pouring white wine. Lucilla appeared, to Violet, to have raided the dressing-up box. Her flea-market dress was gun-metal-grey voile, sleeveless and hanging straight from her bony shoulders, with a skirt that drooped below her knees in a series of handkerchief points. It was so dreadful that she should have looked hideous, but for some reason she looked perfectly sweet.

And the others? Violet sat back in her chair and observed them covertly over her spectacles. Close family, old friends, new friends come together for this long-anticipated celebration. She disregarded the undercurrents of tension that she could feel charging the atmosphere like electric wires, and kept her gaze objective. Saw the five men; two of them come from the other sides of the world. Different ages, different cultures, but all groomed and barbered and dressed up to the nines. She saw the five women, each, in her own way, beautiful.

Colour assaulted her eye. Ball gowns of dark silk or flower-garden chintz. Virginia cool and sophisticated in black and white, Pandora ethereal as a dryad in sea-green chiffon. She saw jewels. Isobel's inherited pearls and diamonds, the silver-and-turquoise chain that encircled Pandora's slender neck, the gleam of gold that shone from Virginia's ears and at her wrist. She saw Alexa's face, laughing across the table at some remark of Noel's. Alexa wore no jewel but her pale-red hair shone like a flame, and her peachy face was alight with love. . . .

All at once, it wasn't any good. Violet was too involved with all of them to remain objective, to continue to observe them with a stranger's dispassionate eye. Her heart agonized for Alexa, so vulnerable and transparent. And Virginia? Across the table she faced her daughter-in-law, and knew that although Edmund was home again, nothing had been resolved between the two of them. For Virginia, this evening, was at her most animated. There was a brilliant and brittle sheen about her, and a dangerous brightness in her blue eyes.

I mustn't imagine the worst, Violet told herself. I must simply hope for the best. She reached for her glass and drank a little wine.

The first course was over. Jeff rose to his feet to act as butler and clear the plates. As he did this, Archie turned to Virginia.

"Virginia, Edmund tells me that you're going back to the States to see your grandparents?"

"That's right!" Her smile was too swift, her eyes too wide. "Such fun. I can't wait to see the darling old things."

So, despite Violet's warnings, she had done it. It was definite, official. Knowing that the worst of her fears was confirmed, Violet felt her heart sink.

"So you are going?" She did not try to keep the disapproval from her voice.

"Yes, Vi. I am. I told you I was. And now it's all fixed. I leave on Thursday. Conrad and I are travelling together."

For an instant Vi said nothing. Across the table their eyes met. Virginia's gaze was defiant and did not waver.

"How long will you be away?" Violet asked her.

Virginia shrugged her bare brown shoulders. "Not certain yet. I've got an open-ended ticket." She turned back to Archie. "I always wanted to take Henry, but now that he is no longer with us, I decided that I might as well go on my own. Such a funny feeling, being able to do things on the spur of the moment. No responsibilities. No ties."

"And Edmund?" Archie asked.

"Oh, Vi will take care of Edmund for me," Virginia told him airily. "Won't you, Vi?"

"Of course." She repressed an impulse to take her daughter-in-law by the shoulders and shake her until her teeth rattled. "It will be no trouble at all."

And with that Violet turned away from them both, and talked instead to Noel.

". . . my grandfather had a young under-keeper by the name of Donald Buist. Twenty years old and a fine, lusty lad . . ."

They were now onto the second course, Isobel's Pheasant Theodora. Jeff had handed round the vegetable dishes, and Conrad Tucker refilled the wineglasses. Archie, primed and prompted by Pandora, was engaged in telling a classic family anecdote, which, like the saga of Mrs. Harris and the shooting stocking, had become, over the years, an oft-repeated family joke. Blairs and Airds had heard it many times before, but for the sake of the newcomers Archie had been persuaded to recount it again.

". . . he was an excellent under-keeper, but he had one failing, and the net result of this was that every girl within twenty miles became, unfortuitously, pregnant. The shepherd's daughter at Ardnamore, the butcher's daughter in Strathcroy; even my grandmother's parlourmaid fainted clean away one lunch-time while serving the chocolate soufflé."

He paused. From beyond the closed door that led through the pantry and into the kitchen could be clearly heard the ringing of the telephone.

It rang twice, and then ceased. Agnes Cooper was dealing with the interruption. Archie continued with his story.

"Finally, my grandmother put her foot down and insisted that grandfather take Donald Buist to task. So he was sent for and duly wheeled into my grandfather's office for the distasteful interview. My grandfather named half a dozen of the ladies who were bearing, or had borne, the young man's little bastards, and finally demanded to know what Donald had to say for himself, and what possible excuse he could give for his behaviour. There was a long silence while Donald thought about this, and finally he came up with his defence. 'Well, you see, sir, I've got a bicycle!' "

As the laughter died, there sounded a cursory thump on the pantry door. It was at once opened, and Agnes Cooper put her head around the edge of it.

"Sorry to disturb you, but that's Edie Findhorn on the telephone; wants to speak to Mrs. Geordie Aird."

Misfortunes always came in threes.

Violet instantly felt very cold, as though the opened door had admitted not only Agnes, but a freezing, icy draught as well. She rose to her feet so abruptly that she would have knocked over her chair had not Noel put out a hand to steady it.

Nobody spoke. They were all looking at her, their faces mirroring her own concern. She said, "If you will excuse me . . ." and was ashamed of the shake in her voice. ". . . I won't be a moment."

She turned and left the table. Agnes held the door open for her, and she went through it, through to Isobel's big kitchen. Agnes followed her, but that didn't matter . . . privacy was, at the moment, the last thing to worry about. The telephone stood on the dresser. She picked up the receiver.

"Edie."

"Oh, Mrs. Aird . . ."

"Edie, what is it?"

"I'm sorry to get you out of your dinner party . . ."

"Is Lottie there?"

"It's all right about Lottie, Mrs. Aird. You were right. She did make her way to Strathcroy. Caught a bus. She went to my cottage. She got in through the back door. . . ."

"You weren't there?"

"No, I was no' there. I was here at Balnaid."

"Thank God for that. Where is she now?"

"Mr. Ishak telephoned the police and in five minutes they were there in a wee Panda car and picked her up."

"So where is she now?"

"Safely back in the hospital. . . ."

Relief made Violet feel quite weak. Her knees shook. She glanced about for a chair, but there was none within reach. However, Agnes Cooper, seeing her need, came forward with one, and Violet was able to take the weight off her legs.

"And you're all right, Edie?"

"I'm fine, Mrs. Aird." She stopped. Violet waited. There was something else. She frowned. "How did Mr. Ishak know about Lottie? Did he see her?"

"No. Not exactly." Another long pause. "You see, that's not all. You'll need to tell Edmund. He and Virginia must come back. Henry's here. He's run away from school, Mrs. Aird. He's come home."

Edmund drove, too fast, in the rain and the darkness, away from Croy and down the hill to the village. Virginia, her chin buried in the fur collar of her coat, sat beside him, staring ahead at the swinging windscreen wiper. She did not speak. Not because there was nothing to say, but because so distanced had they become from each other, so shocking was the situation in which they found themselves, that there was no way of saying it.

The short journey took only moments. They sped through the gates of Croy and out into the village street. Another hundred yards or so, and then over the bridge. The trees; the open gates; Balnaid.

Virginia spoke at last. She said, "You mustn't be angry with him."

"Angry?" He could scarcely believe that she could be so unperceptive.

She said no more. He turned the BMW into the backyard, slammed on the brakes, switched off the engine. He was out of the car before she was, leading the way to the house, flinging open the door.

They were in the kitchen, Edie and Henry, sitting at the table. Waiting. Henry faced the door. His face was very white, and his eyes round with apprehension. He wore his grey school sweater and looked pathetically small and defenceless.

How the hell had he managed that long and solitary journey? The thought flashed through Edmund's mind, and was gone.

He said, "Hello, Henry."

Henry hesitated for only an instant, and then slipped off the chair and bolted for his father. Edmund scooped him up into his arms, and the boy, it seemed, weighed nothing, no more than a baby. Henry's arms were locked about his neck, and he could feel Henry's tears wet on his own cheek.

"Henry." Virginia was there, beside him. After a bit, gently, Edmund set Henry down on his feet. Henry's stranglehold loosened. He turned to his mother, and Virginia, in one graceful fluid movement, dropped to her knees, with no regard for her evening gown, and gathered him into her soft and furry embrace. He buried his face into her collar.

"Darling. Darling. It's all right. Don't cry. Don't cry. . . ."

Edmund turned to Edie. She had risen to her feet, and down the length of the scrubbed kitchen table she and Edmund faced each other in silence. She had known him all his life, and he was grateful to her because there was no reproach in her eyes.

Instead she said, "I'm sorry."

"What for, Edie?"

"Spoiling your party."

"Don't be ridiculous. As if it could possibly matter. When did he get here?"

"About fifteen minutes ago. Mrs. Ishak brought him."

"Has anybody phoned from the school?"

"The phone's broken. Nobody can call."

He had forgotten. "Of course." So there were things to be seen to, practical matters of the utmost urgency. "In that case, I must go and do some telephoning."

He left them, Henry still weeping. Made his way through the quiet house to the library, switched on the lights, sat at his desk, dialled the number for Templehall.

The ringing sounded only once before the receiver was snatched up.

"Templehall."

"Headmaster?"

"Speaking."

"Colin, it's Edmund Aird."

"Oh . . ." The sound came down the line on a sigh of audible relief. Edmund found time to wonder how long the poor man had been trying to make some sort of contact. "I've been going insane trying to get in touch with you."

"Henry's here. He's safe."

"Thank God for that. When did he turn up?"

"About a quarter of an hour ago. I haven't heard the details. We're only just back ourselves. We were out for dinner. The message came through there."

"He disappeared just after bedtime. Seven o'clock. I've been trying to get hold of you ever since."

"Our phone's on the blink. No incoming calls."

"I finally found that out. When I did, I rang your mother, but there was no reply from her number either."

"She was at the same dinner party."

"Is Henry all right?"

"He seems to be."

"How the devil did he get home?"

"I've no idea. Like I told you, I've only just this minute got here myself. I've hardly spoken to him. I wanted to talk to you first."

"I'm grateful."

"I'm sorry you've been put to so much trouble."

"It's I who should apologize. Henry's your son, and I was responsible for him."

"You"—Edmund leaned back in his chair—"you don't know if anything in particular precipitated his flight?"

"No, I don't. Nor do any of my senior boys. Nor do any of my staff. He didn't seem either happy or unhappy. And it always takes a week or two for a new boy to settle down and get used to his new life, accept the change, and the unfamiliar environment. I kept an eye on him, of course, but he showed no signs of taking such dramatic action."

He sounded as upset and as puzzled as Edmund himself. Edmund said, "Yes. Yes, I see."

The Headmaster hesitated, and then he asked, "Will you send him back to us?"

"Why do you say that?"

"I just wondered if you wanted him to return."

"Is there any reason why he shouldn't?"

"From my point of view, absolutely no reason at all. He's a very nice boy, and I know I could make something of him. I, personally, would like to welcome him back at any time, but . . ." He paused, and Edmund got the impression that he was choosing his words with the utmost tact. ". . . but, you know, Edmund, every now and then a boy comes to Templehall who really shouldn't be away from home in the first place. I haven't had Henry long enough to be perfectly certain, but I think he is one of those children. It isn't just that he's young for his age; it's that he is not ready for the demands of boarding-school life."

"Yes. Yes, I see."

"Why don't you take a day or two to think it over? Keep Henry there till you've made up your mind. Remember, I really want him back. I'm not trying to shed my responsibilities, nor renege on my commitments, but I would seriously suggest that you reconsider the situation."

"And do what?"

"Return him to his local primary. It's obviously a good school, and he's been well-grounded. By the time he's twelve you can think again."

"You're saying exactly what my wife has been telling me for the past year."

"I am sorry. But with hindsight, I think she is right. And I think that you and I are to blame and that we have both been mistaken. . . ."

They talked a little more, agreed to be in touch in a couple of days, and finally rang off.

He is one of those children. He is not ready for the demands of boarding-school life. We have both been mistaken.

Mistaken. That was the word that hammered home, like a nail driven into a block of wood. Your wife is right, and you are mistaken. It took a bit of time to accept the word, to accept the implications. He sat at his desk, slowly coming to terms with the fact that he had been almost disastrously wrong. It was not an exercise that he was accustomed to, and it took a little time.

But after a bit, he got to his feet. The fire had, he saw, died. He crossed the room and fed it with logs, as he had already done earlier in the evening. When the dry wood had caught and the comforting flames were once more leaping, he left the library and returned to the kitchen.

Here, he found things more or less back to normal. Once more, they were all sitting around the table, Henry on his mother's knee. Edie had made a pot of tea, and cocoa for Henry. Virginia still wore her fur coat. As he came in, they all looked towards him, and he saw Henry's tears had dried and a little colour had come back into his cheeks.

Edmund put a cheerful expression on his face.

"That's done then. . . ." He tousled his son's hair and pulled out a chair. "Is there a cup of tea for me?"

"What have you been doing?" Henry asked.

"Speaking to Mr. Henderson."

"Was he very cross?"

"No, not cross. Just a bit worried."

Henry said, "I'm very sorry."

"Are you going to tell us about it?"

"Yes. I suppose so."

"How did you get home?"

Henry took another mouthful of the steaming, sweet cocoa, and then laid his mug on the table. He said, "I caught a bus."

"But how did you get out of school?"

Henry explained. He made it all sound ridiculously simple. At bedtime, he'd dressed under the bedclothes, and then put his dressing-gown on. And then when the lights went out, he'd pretended he wanted to go to the lavatory. In the bathroom there was a large airing cupboard, and at the back of this he had hidden his overcoat. He'd swapped his dressing-gown for his overcoat and then climbed out of the window onto the fire escape. After that, he'd made his way down the back drive, and so onto the main road where the buses ran.

"But how long did you have to wait for a bus?" Virginia asked him.

"Only a little bit. I knew there was one coming."

"How did you know?"

"I had a bus timetable." He looked at Edie. "I took it out of your bag one day. I kept it."

"I *wondered* what had happened to my wee timetable."

"I took it. I looked up the bus to Relkirk, and I knew it would come. And it did."

"But didn't anybody ask you what you were doing all on your own?"

"No. I had on my Balaclava helmet and it was my disguise and only my eyes showed. I didn't look like a schoolboy because I didn't wear my school cap."

"How did you pay the fare?" Edmund asked.

"Vi had given me two pounds when she said goodbye to me. I didn't hand it in. I kept it in the inside pocket of my overcoat. I put the timetable there too, so that nobody would find it."

"And then you got to Relkirk?"

"Yes. I got to the bus station. And it was getting dark, and I had to find the other bus, the one that goes past Caple Bridge. There was a Strathcroy bus too, but I didn't want to catch that one in case somebody saw me, somebody who knew me. And it was quite difficult to find that bus because there were lots of buses and I had to read the names on all the fronts of them. But I did find it, but we had to wait for quite a long time before it started."

"Where did you get off that bus?"

"I told you. Caple Bridge. And then I walked."

"You walked from Caple Bridge?" Virginia looked at her small son in wonder. "But, Henry, that's five miles. . . ."

"I didn't walk the whole of the way," he admitted. "I know I'm not allowed to get lifts, but I did get one at the very end from a very nice man in a sheep-float. And he took me to Strathcroy. And then . . ." His voice, which had sounded so clear and confident, began to shake again. "And then . . ." His eyes turned to Edie.

Edie took over. "Don't cry, pet. We won't talk about it if you don't want to. . . ."

"I want *you* to tell them."

So Edie did, in her most practical and down-to-earth fashion, but even this did not assuage the horror of Henry's terrible experience. At mention of Lottie, the colour seeped from Virginia's cheeks, and she drew Henry close and pressed her face to the top of his head and laid her hands across his eyes, as though she could shut out for ever the sight of Lottie Carstairs coming across Edie's bedroom floor to find out who stood beyond the window.

"Oh, Henry." She rocked him like a baby. "I can't bear it. . . . What a thing to happen. What a thing to happen to you."

Edmund, equally shaken, kept his voice calm.

"So what did you do, Henry?"

His father's level tones restored, a little, Henry's courage. He emerged, ruffled, from Virginia's embrace. He said, "I went to Mrs. Ishak. Her shop was still open and she was sweeping the floor. And she was very kind. And Mr. Ishak telephoned the police, and they came with the sirens going and a blue light flashing. We saw it from the shop. And then, when it had gone again, back to Relkirk, Mrs. Ishak put on her coat, and she and me walked here. And she rang the bell because the door was locked, and then the dogs barked, and Edie came." He reached for his cocoa and drained the mug, and then set the empty mug down on the table. He said, "I thought she was *murdered*! Lottie had put on her lilac cardigan and her mouth was all red, and I thought that she had killed Edie. . . ."

His face crumpled. It was all too much for him. He wept again, and they let him cry, and Edmund did not tell him to be a man but simply sat there, regarding his small and sobbing son with a growing admiration and pride. For Henry, at eight years old, had not only run away from school, but accomplished his flight in certain style. He'd planned the whole operation with undreamt-of courage, good sense, and forethought. He appeared to have been prepared for any contingency, and it was only the disastrous and unfortuitous reappearance of the wretched Lottie Carstairs that had finally defeated him.

Eventually, the tears ceased. Henry had cried himself dry. Edmund gave him his clean linen handkerchief, and Henry sat up and blew his nose. He said, "I think I should like to go to bed now."

"Of course." Virginia smiled down at him. "Do you want a bath first? You must be feeling very cold and dirty."

"Yes, all right."

He got off her knee. He blew his nose again, went to his father to return the handkerchief. Edmund took it, and drew Henry close, and bent to kiss the top of his head.

He said, "There's just one thing you haven't told us." Henry looked up. "Why did you run away?"

Henry thought. And then he said, "I didn't like it. It felt all wrong. Like being ill. Headachy."

"Yes," said Edmund after a bit. "Yes, I see." He hesitated, and then went on. "Look, old boy, why don't you go up with Edie and get into that bath. Mummy and I have got to go to this party, but I'll ring Vi first and tell her you're in great shape, and we'll come up and say good night before you go to sleep."

"All right." Henry put his hand into Edie's and they made for the door. But he turned back. "You will come, won't you?"

"Promise."

The door closed behind him. Edmund and Virginia were left alone.

With Henry gone, she sat slumped in the hard kitchen chair. There was no longer need to conceal the trauma of shock and strain, and beneath her make-up he saw her face pale and drawn, and her eyes shadowed, no longer bright with the evening's laughter.

She looked drained. He stood up and took her hand and pulled her to her feet. "Come," he said, and he led her out of the kitchen and along the passage to the empty library. The fire that he had rekindled still blazed, and the big, shadowy room was warm. She was grateful for the warmth. She went towards it, sank down on the fireside stool, and spread her hands to the flames. Her long, many-layered skirts flowed about her, and the collar of her fur coat supported her head, her clear-cut profile.

"You look like a particularly well-heeled Cinderella." She glanced up and sent him the ghost of a smile. "Would you like a drink?"

She shook her head. "No. I'm all right."

He went to his desk, switched on the lamp, and dialled the number for Croy. It was Archie who answered his call.

"Archie. Edmund here."

"Is Henry all right?"

"Yes, he's fine. Had a bit of an experience, but don't say anything to Vi. Just tell her that Edie's with him, and he's on his way to bed."

"Are you coming back here?"

Edmund watched his wife, sitting with her back to him, silhouetted against the firelight. He said, "No, I think not. We'll go straight to Corriehill and meet you all there."

"Right. I'll tell everyone. See you later, Edmund."

"Goodbye."

He put down the phone, went back to the fire, and stood, with one foot on the fender and a hand on the mantelpiece, gazing, as his wife gazed, at the flames. But the silence that lay between them was no longer one of enmity, but the peaceful communion of two people who, having together survived a crisis, felt no need for words.

It was Virginia who broke that silence. She said, "I'm sorry."

"What are you sorry about?"

"I'm sorry I said that. In the car. Telling you not to be angry. It was stupid. I should have known that you would never be angry with Henry."

"On the contrary, I feel proud of him. He did very well."

"He must have been so miserable."

"I think he just felt lost. I was wrong. You were right. Colin Henderson said as much. He's not ready, yet, for boarding-school."

"You mustn't blame yourself."

"That's a generous thing to say."

"No, it's not generous. I'm grateful. Because now we can stop arguing and quarrelling and destroying each other. And you had only the best intentions in mind. You thought it would be best for Henry. Everybody makes mistakes, sooner or later. A man who never made a mistake never made anything. It's over now. Let's leave it behind. Just be thankful that nothing dreadful happened to Henry, and that he's safe."

"Lottie happened to him. I should think that experience would be enough to give him nightmares for the rest of his life. . . ."

"But he dealt with it. Very sensibly. He got himself to Mrs. Ishak. Took care of himself, gave the alarm. It's no good brooding about it, Edmund."

He said nothing to this. After a bit, he moved away from the fire and sank down at one end of the great sofa, his long legs, in their red-and-white tartan stockings and silver-buckled shoes, stretched out in front of him. The firelight winked on polished buttons and the jewelled hilt of his sporran.

She said, "You must be exhausted."

"Yes. It's been a long day." He rubbed his eyes. "But I think we have to talk."

"We can talk tomorrow."

"No. It has to be now. Before it's too late. I should have told you this evening, when I got back and you started telling me about Lottie. Lottie and her talk, her gossip. I said she was lying but that wasn't strictly true."

"You are going to tell me about Pandora." Virginia's voice was cool, resigned.

"It has to be done."

"You were in love with her."

"Yes."

"I'm frightened of her."

"Why?"

"Because she is so beautiful. Mysterious. Under that flood of chat, you never know what she's thinking. I can't begin to imagine what goes on inside her head. And because she knew you for ever, when I didn't know you, and that makes me feel left out and insecure. Why did she come back to Croy, Edmund? Do you know why she came?"

He shook his head. "No."

"I'm afraid of her still being in love with you. She still wants you."

"No."

"How can you be so sure?"

"Pandora's motives, whatever they are, have no importance. To me, all that matters is you. And Alexa. And Henry. You seem to have lost sight of that basic priority."

"You were married when you loved Pandora. You were married to Caroline. You had a baby. Was that so different?"

It was an accusation, and he accepted it.

"Yes. And I was unfaithful to both of them. But Caroline wasn't like you. If I tried to explain to you why I married her in the first place, I don't suppose you'd understand. It was something to do with the way things were at that time, the swinging sixties, and all of us young, and a certain restless materialism in the air. I was making my way, making money, making my mark on London society. She was part of my ambitions, part of what I wanted. Her parents were immensely wealthy and she was an only child, and I craved the security of being established, and the reflected dazzle of success."

"But you *loved* her?"

Edmund shook his head. "I don't know. I didn't think about it all that much. I only know that she was wonderful to look at, immensely elegant, the sort of woman that would always turn heads, excite a certain envy. I liked being seen around with her. I was very proud of her. The sexual, loving part of our relationship wasn't quite so smooth. I don't quite know when it all started to go wrong. I'm sure it was as much my fault as Caroline's, but she was a strange girl. She used sex as a weapon and frigidity as a punishment. Before the first year was over, I was sleeping as often as not in my dressing-room, and when she realized that she was pregnant with Alexa, there was no joy, only tears and recriminations. She didn't want a baby, because she was frightened of childbirth, and as things turned out, she had every reason to be afraid. Because after Alexa was born, she went into a post-natal depression that lasted for months. She was in hospital for a long time, and when she was fit to travel, her mother took her off to Madeira to spend the winter there. In the early summer of that year, Archie and Isobel were married. He was my oldest, closest friend. I'd seen little of him after I went to London, but I knew that I had to be at his wedding. I took a week's leave and came home. I was twenty-nine. I came back to Strathcroy on my own. I stayed here, at Balnaid, with Vi, but Croy was filled with house guests and spinning like a three-ring circus, and on my first day home I went up to see Archie and become involved in all the fun.

"And Pandora was there. I hadn't seen her for five years. She was eighteen, finished with schools, finished with childhood. I'd known her for ever. She was part of my life, always there. A baby in a pram, a little girl tagging along with Archie and me, never missing a trick. Spoiled as hell, wayward, wicked, but utterly enchanting and endearing. I saw her again, and knew that she hadn't changed. All that had happened was that she had grown up. I saw her coming towards me across the hall at Croy, and I saw her eyes and her smile, and her long legs, and an aura of sexuality about her, so potent, almost visible. And she put her arms around my neck and kissed my mouth and said, 'Edmund, you horrible man. Why didn't you wait for me?' And that was all she said. And I felt as though I was drowning, and the deep waters had already closed over the top of my head."

"You were lovers."

"I didn't seduce her. She was only eighteen, but somewhere along the line, she had already lost her virginity. It wasn't difficult to be together. There was so much going on, so many people in the house, that nobody missed us if we went off on our own."

"She was in love with you."

"She said. She said she always had been, ever since she was a small girl. The fact that I was married only made her more obdurate. She'd never been denied anything that she wanted, and when I tried to talk reason to her, she put her hands over her ears and closed her eyes and refused to listen. She couldn't believe that I would leave her. She couldn't believe that I wouldn't come back.

"The wedding was on a Saturday. I had to drive back to London on the Sunday afternoon. On the Sunday morning, Pandora and I walked up the hill, on the road to the loch. But we stopped at the Corrie and lay on the grass, with the sound of the burn trickling at our feet. And I finally convinced her that I had to go, and she wept and protested and clung to me, and finally, to quieten her, I promised that I would come back, that I would write, that I did love her. All the stupid bloody things you say when you haven't the courage to end something. When you haven't the courage to be strong. When you can't bring yourself to destroy another person's dream."

"Oh, Edmund."

"I made such a fucking cock-up of it all. I was such a bloody coward. I went back to London, and as the miles lengthened behind me, I started to hate myself for what I'd done to Caroline and Alexa, and for what I was doing to Pandora. By the time I got back to London, I determined I would write to Pandora and try to explain that the whole episode had been a sort of fantasy; stolen days that had no more substance, no more future, than a soap bubble. But I didn't write. Because the next morning I went into the office, and by that evening I was in an aeroplane with my chairman, flying to Hong Kong. A huge financial deal was on the stocks, and I'd been picked to handle it. I was away for three weeks. By the time I returned to London, that time at Croy had dissolved into a sort of distant unlikelihood, like days stolen from another person's life. I could scarcely believe that it had happened to *me*. I was my own hard-headed business man, not that indecisive romantic, swept off his feet by a fleeting sexual infatuation. And there was too much at stake. My job, I suppose. A way of life that I'd worked my guts out to achieve. Alexa. Losing Alexa did not bear thinking about. And Caroline. My wife, for better, for worse. Back from Madeira, sun-tanned, well, recovered. We'd gone through a bad time together, but we'd come out on the other side. We were together again, and it wasn't the right time to blow it all apart. We picked up the threads of life, the warp and woof of a convenient marriage."

"And Pandora?"

"Nothing. Finished. I never wrote that letter."

"Oh, Edmund. That was cruel."

"Yes. A sin of omission. Do you know that dreadful feeling, when there is something immensely important that you should do, and you haven't done. And with each day that passes, it becomes more and more difficult to accomplish, until finally it passes the bounds of possibility and becomes impossible. It was over. Archie and Isobel went to Berlin, and immediate ties with Croy were severed. I heard nothing more. Until that day that Vi called from Balnaid to say that Pandora had gone. Run away, eloped to the other side of the world with a rich American old enough to be her father."

"You blame yourself?"

"Of course."

"Did you ever tell Caroline?"

"Never."

"Were you happy with her?"

"No. She wasn't a woman who engendered happiness. It worked all right, because we made it work, we were those sort of people. But love, of every sort, was always thin on the ground. I wish we had been happy. It would have been easier to accept her death if we'd had a good life, and I could have been certain that it hadn't all been just a"—he searched for words—"waste of ten good years."

There did not seem to be anything more to say. Across the distance that divided them, husband and wife regarded each other, and Virginia saw Edmund's hooded eyes filled with despair and sadness. She got up then, off the low stool, and went to sit beside him. She touched his mouth with her fingers. She kissed him. He reached out his arm and pulled her close.

She said, "And us?"

"I never knew how it could be, until I met you."

"I wish you'd told me all this before."

"I was ashamed. I didn't want you to know. I'd give my right arm to be able to change things. But I can't, because they happened. They become part of you, stay with you forever."

"Have you spoken to Pandora about all this?"

"No. I've scarcely seen her. There's been no opportunity."

"You must make it right with her."

"Yes."

"She is, I think, still very precious to you."

"Yes. But she's part of life the way it used to be. Not the way it is now."

"You know, I've always loved you. I suppose if I hadn't loved you so much, you wouldn't have been able to make me so miserable. But now I realize that you are human and frail and make the same idiotic blunders as the rest of us, it's even better. I never thought you needed me, you see. I thought you were quite self-sufficient. Being needed's more important than anything."

"I need you now. Don't go away. Don't leave me. Don't go to America with Conrad Tucker."

"I wasn't running *away* with him."

"I thought you were."

"No, you didn't. He's actually a very nice man."

"I wanted to kill him."

You must never tell Edmund. Still untouched by guilt, she felt protective of her husband, holding her secret like a proud and private trophy. She said lightly, "That would have been a dreadful waste."

"Will your grandparents be very disappointed?"

"We'll go some other time. You and me together. We'll leave Henry with Vi and Edie and we'll go and see them on our own."

He kissed her and leaned his head back on the deep cushions of the sofa and sighed. "I wish we didn't have to go to this bloody dance."

"I know. But we must. Just for a little."

"I would very, very much rather take you to bed."

"Oh, Edmund. We've lots of time for love. Years and years. The rest of our lives."

Presently Edie came to find them, knocking on the door before she opened it. The light from the hall shone from behind her and turned her white hair into an aureole.

"Just to say Henry's in bed and waiting for you. . . ."

"Oh, thank you, Edie. . . ."

They went upstairs. In his own room, Henry lay in his own bed. His night-lamp burnt dimly, and the room lay in shadows. Virginia sat on the edge of the bed and bent to kiss him. He was already half asleep.

"Good night, my darling."

"Good night, Mummy."

"You'll be all right."

"Yes. I'll be all right."

"No dreams."

"I don't think so."

"If dreams come, Edie's downstairs."

"Yes. I know."

"I'll leave you with Daddy."

She stood up and moved towards the door.

"Have a good party," Henry told her.

"Thank you, my darling. We will." She went through the door. Edmund took her place.

"Well, Henry, you're home again."

"I'm sorry about the school. It really wasn't right."

"No. I know. I realize that. Mr. Henderson does as well."

"I don't have to go back to it, do I?"

"I don't think so. We'll have to see if the Strathcroy Primary will take you on again."

"Do you think they'll say no?"

"I shouldn't think so. You'll be back with Kedejah."

"That'll be good."

"Good night, old boy. You did well. I'm proud of you."

Henry's eyes were closing. Edmund stood up and moved away. But at the open door, he turned back, and realized, with some surprise, that his own eyes were moist.

"Henry?"

"Yes?"

"Have you got Moo in there with you?"

"No," Henry told him. "I don't need Moo any more."

Out of doors, Virginia realized that the rain had stopped. From some-where a wind had sprung up, chill and fresh as snow, stirring the dark-ness, causing the high elms of Balnaid to rustle and creak and toss their heads. Looking up, she saw stars, for this wind was blowing all clouds away to the east, and in their wake the sky was clear and infinite, pricked with the jewel glitter of a million constellations. Sweet and cold, the clean air struck her cheeks. She took deep breaths of it and was revital-ized. No longer tired. No longer miserable, angry, resentful, lost. Henry was home and staying home, and Edmund, in more ways than one, returned to her. She was young and knew that she looked beautiful. Dressed to the nines and off to a party, she was ready to dance all night.

They drove into the beam of the headlights, the narrow country roads twisting away behind them. As they approached Corriehill, the night sky was bathed in reflected brilliance from the spotlights which had been directed onto the front of the house. Drawing closer, they saw Verena's strings of fairy lights looped from tree to tree all the way up the long drive, and as well, every twenty yards or so, the bright flares of Roman candles that grew from the grass verges.

The BMW swung around the last bend, and the house was revealed in its full glory, towering up against the dark backdrop of the sky. It looked enormously impressive and proud.

Virginia said, "It must be feeling really good tonight."

"What must?"

"Corriehill. Like a monument. In memory of all the dinner parties, and wedding feasts and dances and balls that it must have known in the course of its history. And christenings. And funerals too, I suppose. But mostly parties."

Three brilliant searchlights were beamed upwards, lighting Corriehill from basements to chimneys. Beyond stood the marquee, lit from inside, like a shadow theatre. Distorted silhouettes moved and turned against the white canvas. They heard the beat of music. The dancing, clearly, was already well under way.

Another spotlight hung from a tree to the left of the drive, illuminat-ing the big paddock. Here, cars were parked, in long, well-ordered rows, as far as the eye could see. A figure approached through the gloom, flashing a torch. Edmund stopped the car and rolled down his window. The torch-bearer stopped to peer in. Hughie McKinnon, the Steyntons' old handyman, press-ganged for the evening into the role of car-park attendant, and already reeking of whisky.

"Good evening, sir."

"Good evening, Hughie."

"Oh, it's yourself, Mr. Aird! I'm sorry, I didna' recognize the car. How are you, sir?" He craned a little farther in order to cock his eye at Virginia, and the whisky fumes flowed afresh. "And Mrs. Aird. How are you keeping yourself?"

"Very well, thank you, Hughie."

"Very good, very good," said Hughie. "You're awfully late. The rest of your party were all here an hour ago."

"I'm afraid we were unavoidably detained."

"Oh, well, no matter. The night's long enough. Now, sir"—with pleasantries over, he steadied his legs—"if you would just like to take your good lady to the front of the house, and drop her off there, you can come back here, and I'll be here, and I'll help you park the car over *there*." His torchbeam wavered haphazardly in the direction of the field, and he belched discreetly. "And see that you both enjoy yourselves, and have a rare time."

He stepped back. Edmund rolled up the window.

"I doubt that Hughie is going to last the evening."

"At least he's well centrally heated. He won't die of hypothermia."

The car moved forward to pull up at the front door behind a large Audi with a personalized number plate, disgorging its load of very young men and girls, all flushed and laughing from some extended and lavish dinner party. Virginia followed them up the steps while Edmund drove off to find Hughie again and park his car.

She entered the house and was assailed by light, warmth, music, the smell of flowers, greenery, wood-smoke; the sound of voices, raised in greeting, laughter, and high-pitched conversation. As she slowly made her way up the stairs, she looked down over the bannisters at the carnival scene. People everywhere. Many she knew, and others strangers, come from all parts of the country especially for the occasion. A log fire blazed in the huge fireplace, and around this, young men in kilts and evening dress stood talking to each other, drinks in hand. Two of them were officers from the Relkirk barracks, flamboyant in their scarlet regimental mess-jackets.

From the dining-room, its doors festooned in draperies of deep-blue silk, came the powerful beat of the disco music. A steady flow of two-way traffic passed through these doors. Eager boys, their partners in tow, disappeared into the darkness, while others emerged, the young men as hot and sweaty as if they had just completed a fast game of squash, while the girls, casual with assumed sophistication, raked their fingers through tousled hair, and reached for cigarettes. The lowered lights and the din were clearly engendering a certain sexual excitement.

On one of the sofas that guarded the entrance to the library sat old General Grant-Palmer, kilted, and with his knees indecently wide apart.

He talked to a formidable lady with a huge bosom, whom Virginia did not recognize. Past them, others made their way through to the library, and so to the marquee at the front of the house. "Virginia!" Some man, spying her, called her name.

She waved, smiled, continued on up the stairs. She went into the bedroom that had the sign LADIES on the door, shed her fur and laid it on top of the coats already piled on the bed. She went to the mirror to comb her hair. Behind her the bathroom door burst open and a girl appeared. She had hair pale as an aureole of dandelion fluff, and eyes blackened like a panda's. Virginia was about to tell her kindly that she'd inadvertently got her dress tucked up into her knickers, and then realized that she was wearing a puffball skirt. Wishing that Edmund were with her so that they could share the joke together, she did a quick turn to spin the creases out of her skirt, put her comb back in her bag, and went out of the room.

Edmund was waiting for her at the bottom of the stairs. He took her hand. "All right?"

"I've got something lovely and funny to tell you. Did you get the car parked?"

"Hughie found a place for me. Come on, let's go and see what's going on."

She had seen it all before, the morning that she had delivered her flower vases, when the marquee stood empty and unfinished, and there had been workmen everywhere. Now all was transformed, and Verena's months of planning, agonizing, and sheer hard labour had paid off. Corriehill, Virginia decided, might have been especially designed for just this occasion. From the library, the lead-out to the tent took in the stone garden steps. The urns that stood at the top and the bottom of these contained great masses of greenery and white chrysanthemums, and the lamps illuminating them swayed in the thin draught that blew beneath the enclosed awning.

At the top of the steps, a natural vantage spot, they paused to regard in some wonder and admiration the scene before them.

The tall tent-poles had been transformed into veritable trees of barley sheaves, beech branches, and rowan bright with scarlet berries. High overhead hung four sparkling chandeliers. At the far end, a platform had been erected and strung with silver helium balloons, and on this sat Tom Drystone and his band, thumping out an eightsome reel, "The Soldiers' Dance." Tom with the accordion sat, as leader, in the middle, and around him were grouped the others. A pianist, two fiddlers, and a young boy with a drum set. In white jackets and tartan trews, they presented a fine sight, and Tom caught Virginia's eye and sent her a wink and a crack of his head. His long tumbler of beer stood brimming on the floor beside him.

The sets of dancers, some in eightsome, some in sixteensome, circled and swung, linking arms, changing partners, clapping hands and stamping feet in time to the hypnotic pulse of the music. In the middle of one set was a huge young man making a fine exhibition of himself. He looked strong enough to be a shot-putter or caber-tosser, but this evening was putting all his energy into his dancing. Kilt flying, arms held high over his massive shoulders, shirt bursting from his scarlet waistcoat, he was giving it his all, and his muscled legs flailed as he leaped, uttering manic cries, high off the floor.

"If he doesn't watch out," remarked Edmund, "he's going to do himself an injury."

"More likely kill off one of the girls."

But the girls loved him, they screamed with glee, were lifted off their feet, or spun like tops. Virginia half-expected to see one of them tossed, like a doll, high up into the roof of the tent.

Edmund nudged her. "Look at Noel."

Virginia followed his pointing finger, saw Noel, and dissolved into laughter. He stood, with a bemused expression on his handsome face, in the centre of one of the sets, having clearly lost his bearings and any idea of what he was meant to do next. Alexa, quite undeterred, and in a state of giggles, was trying to point him in the direction of his next partner, while she, in her turn, was being deliberately non-co-operative and wore a look of mock boredom.

They searched for the others. Found Vi, Conrad and Pandora, and Jeff and Lucilla, all dancing in a big sixteensome together. Vi's partner was a retired Law Lord from Edinburgh, about half her size and perhaps the only person in the room older than she was. Vi, so large and so stout, moved, when she danced, lightly as a feather, gracefully swinging from man to man and never a step out of beat. As they watched, she took her place in the ring again, and two other ladies moved to dance together in the centre. Vi looked up, over their heads, and caught sight of Edmund and Virginia, standing hand in hand at the head of the stone steps.

For an instant, her cheerful, flushed face clouded. She raised her brows in fearful question. In answer, Edmund held their clasped hands up, as if in triumph. She got the message. A smile lit her homely features. The tempo of the catchy music quickened, she and the old Judge linked arms to swing again, and Violet gave him such an almighty spin that he was nearly sent flying off his spindly legs.

At last the Grand Chain, a final turn, a long chord from the band, and the eightsome reel was over. Applause for the musicians instantly broke out, clapping, cheering, and stamping. The dancers, hot, breathless, sweating, wanted more. There were noisy demands for an encore, another round.

But Violet had had enough. Excusing herself, she had abandoned her partner and was already on her way across the dance floor to where

Edmund and Virginia waited. They went down the stone steps to meet her, and Violet embraced her daughter-in-law.

"You're here at last. I've been so worried. Is everything all right?"

"Everything, Vi."

"Henry?"

"Safe and well."

Violet fixed her son with a beady stare.

"Edmund. You're not going to send him back?"

"With that look in your eye, I don't think I'd dare. No, we're going to keep him at home for a little while longer."

"Oh, thank heavens for that. You've come to your senses. And in more ways than one, if I'm not mistaken. I can tell, just by the look of the pair of you." She opened her bag, took out her handkerchief, mopped her beaded forehead. "I," she announced, "have now had enough. I shall take myself home."

"But, Vi," Edmund protested, "I haven't danced with you."

"Then you must be disappointed, because I'm on my way. I've had a splendid evening, a splendid dinner, and I've danced an eightsome reel. Done the hat trick. I'm enjoying myself thoroughly, and this is the moment to call it a day."

She was obdurate. "If you like," Edmund offered, "I'll fetch your car and bring it to the door."

"That would be kind. I'll go upstairs and rescue my coat." She kissed Virginia again. "We have so much to talk about, but this is neither the time nor the place. But I am so happy for you both. Good night, my dear. Enjoy yourselves."

"Good night, Vi."

Edmund, after some searching, finally ran Pandora to earth in the drawing-room, where a long bar had been set up down one side of the room, and sofas and chairs disposed in convenient conversational groups. Here, it was comparatively quiet, although impossible to escape totally from the pervasive beat of music from both marquee and disco. Standing in the door, he saw that a number of Verena's guests had chosen to sit out a dance or two, take a breather and have a drink. Very young girls sat on the floor . . . a good position for gazing up into the eyes of attendant young men. One of them had already caught Edmund's attention, for she wore the smallest black sequin dress he had ever seen in his life, its minimal skirt barely concealing her crotch. Inquiring as to her identity, he had been told she was an old school friend of Katy's, which was hard to believe. The provocative sequins and the endless black silk legs didn't seem to go with hockey sticks.

He spied Pandora at last, tucked into the corner of the sofa near the fire, and deep in conversation with some man. Edmund picked his way across the floor towards them, and she sensed his coming and turned her head at his approach.

"Edmund."

"Come and dance."

"Oh, darling, I'm exhausted. I've been leaping up and down like a yo-yo."

"The disco, then. They're playing 'Lady in Red.' "

"Heavenly tune. Edmund, you know Robert Bramwell, don't you? Yes, of course you do, because he's one of the guns in your syndicate. Silly me."

"Sorry, Robert. You don't mind if I steal her away?"

"No, of course not . . ." He had some difficulty in heaving himself out of the sofa, being both well-built and portly. ". . . Anyway, it's time I went in search of my wife. Said I'd do something called Hamilton House with her. Don't know how the hell to do it, but suppose I'd better report for duty. . . ."

"Such a lovely drink . . ." Pandora thanked him vaguely.

"A pleasure."

They watched him go. Across the crowded room, out through the door. Then Edmund, shamelessly, took his place.

"Oh, darling, you are naughty. I thought you wanted to dance."

"Poor chap. It probably took much sneaky manoeuvring to get you to himself, and now I've spoilt it all."

"You haven't spoiled it for *me*. You haven't got a drink."

"I'm laying off for the moment. I've already consumed far too much this evening."

"Poor darling, you've had such a horrid time. How is Henry?"

"Considering what he's been through, in great shape."

"Terribly brave to run away from school. Terribly brave, actually, to run anywhere."

"You did."

"Oh, darling, are we back to that? I thought we'd stopped talking about that."

"I'm sorry."

"Sorry for talking about it?"

"No. Sorry for everything that happened. For the way I behaved. I never explained to you, and I suppose it's too late to start explaining now."

"Yes," she told him, "I think it is a little late."

"You've never forgiven me?"

"Oh, Edmund, I don't forgive people. I'm not good enough to forgive people. 'Forgive' is a non-word in my vocabulary. How could I forgive, when during the course of my life *I* have made so many people desperately unhappy?"

"That's not the point."

"If you want to talk about it, let's be objective. You said you would write, be in touch, love me for ever, and you didn't do any of those things. It wasn't like you to break your word, and I could never under- stand . . ."

"If I had written it would have been to tell you that my promises were empty and I was backing out. And I left it too long, and when I finally plucked up the nerve, it was too late. . . . So I took the easy way out."

"That was the bad bit. I thought you never took the easy way out of anything. I thought I knew you so well, and that was why I loved you so much. And I couldn't believe that you didn't love me. I wanted you. So stupid. But all my life, everything I'd wanted I'd been allowed to have, I'd been given. To be denied anything I wanted was a new and cruel experience. And I wouldn't accept it. I couldn't believe that some mira- cle wouldn't happen, and everything that you'd done—going to Lon- don, and marrying Caroline, and having Alexa—couldn't be magically absolved, dissolved, swept under the carpet. So stupid. But then, I was only eighteen, and I never had much brain."

"I'm sorry."

She smiled at him, touched his cheek with her fingers. "Do you blame yourself for the mess I made of everything? Don't. I was born disaster material. We both know that. If it hadn't been you, it would have been somebody else. And if Harold Hogg hadn't been there, stinking-rich and panting with lust, then I'm certain I would have found some other equally impossible man to elope with. I would never have made you happy. I don't think Caroline made you happy. But now, I think, with Virginia, you are happy at last. So that makes me happy."

"What else makes you happy?"

"Even if I knew, I wouldn't tell you."

"Why did you come back to Croy?"

"Oh, a whim. An impulse. To see you all again."

"Will you stay?"

"I think not. Too restless, darling."

"That makes me feel guilty."

"Why?"

"I don't know. We all have so much."

"Me too. But mine are different things."

"I hate you being alone."

"Better that way."

"You are part of us all. You know that?"

"Thank you. That's the nicest thing you could say to me. That's just the way I want it to be. Just the way I want it to stay." She leaned forward and kissed his cheek, and his senses were assaulted by her close- ness, the touch of her lips, the scent of her perfume.

"Pandora . . ."

"And now, darling, we've sat here long enough. . . . Don't you think we should go and find the others?"

It was past one o'clock in the morning, with festivities at their peak, when Noel Keeling, unable and unwilling to deal with the complexities of a dance called the Duke of Perth, found himself abandoned and alone, decided that he was in need of liquid refreshment, and headed for the bar. He was offered champagne, but his mouth was dry and he settled instead for a glass of ice-cold lager. He had just set the glass to his lips and taken a long and refreshing swig when, all at once, Pandora Blair appeared at his elbow.

Since the dinner party, he had scarcely seen her all evening, which was a shame, because he thought her good news, and quite the most decorative and amusing female he had met for a long time.

"Noel."

It was gratifying to be sought out. He instantly laid down his glass and made space for her, and she settled herself beside him on an empty bar-stool and, having made herself comfortable, smiled conspiratorially into his face.

She said, "I have a favour to ask."

"But of course. Have a drink?"

She reached for a brimming glass of champagne and drank it like water.

He laughed. "Have you been on that the whole evening?"

"Of course."

"What's the favour?"

"I think it's time I went home. Would you take me?"

Noel was, in truth, a little taken aback. It was the last thing he had expected.

"But why do you want to go home?"

"I think I've stayed long enough. Danced with everybody, said all the right things, and now I'm longing for my beddy-byes. I'd ask Archie to take me, but he's having such a jolly time, closeted in Angus Steynton's office with old General Grant-Palmer and a bottle of Glen Morangie; it seems a shame to spoil his fun. And everybody else is leaping about in the tent, doing tribal dances. Even Conrad, our not-so-sad Sad American."

"I'm surprised he knows how to do them."

"Archie and Isobel organized a little class at Croy on Wednesday evening and gave us lessons, but I never imagined he'd become totally hooked. Will you take me, Noel? Is it a perfectly horrid thing to ask?"

"No, of course not. Of course I'll take you."

"I've got my car, but I'm truly not fit to drive and I'm sure I'd fall asleep on the way back and end up in a ditch. And the others will need to get home. So perhaps I should leave it behind for them. . . ."

"I'll drive you in my car."

"You're an angel." She finished her champagne. "I'll go and get my coat. Meet you at the front door."

He thought about telling somebody what he was about to do, and then decided against it, because the drive to Croy wouldn't take longer than half an hour, and most likely he would never be missed. At the foot of the staircase he waited for her and was amused to find himself in a pleasant state of anticipation, as though he and Pandora were embarking on a small, shared, and secret assignation, one with possible romantic connotations. Which, on analysis, he realized had much to do with her, and he guessed that she had probably always had this effect on any man on whom she chose to beam her attention.

"Ready." She ran down the stairs, wrapped in her long, voluptuous mink. He took her arm and they went out, down the steps and across the gravel. The grass of the paddock was cold and wet, and the ground muddy, and he offered to sweep her up into his arms and carry her to his car, but she only laughed at him and pulled off her fragile sandals and walked beside him in her bare feet.

Old Hughie had disappeared, but they finally located Noel's Golf. He turned up the heater to warm her toes. "Do you want music?"

"Not particularly. It might interfere with the stars."

He backed, turned, drove away from Corriehill, down the fairy-lit driveway, and into the dark countryside. The warm interior of the car was pervaded with the scent of her perfume, and he had a strange feeling that in the future, whenever he smelt it again he would remember *now,* this journey, this woman.

She began to talk. "It was a lovely party. Exactly right from beginning to end. Just the way they used to be, only even better. We used to have dances like that at Croy, ages ago, when we were all young. Christmas and birthdays. Magic. You'll have to come back to Croy, because things will get better now. They won't be gloomy any longer. Archie's better. He's his own man again. He's had a horrible, nightmare time, but he's over that. Come to terms with it."

For a little, she was silent. She sat, with her head turned away from him, her hair spilling over the soft fur of her coat. She stared from the window, as the lightless, empty road streamed away behind them.

After a bit, she said, "*Will* you come back to Croy, Noel?"

"Why do you ask that?"

"Perhaps I'm asking something else. Perhaps I'm asking you about Alexa."

He was cautious. "What are you asking me?"

"I think you're wavering, dithering. You don't know what to do."

He was surprised by her perception. "Have you been talking to Vi?"

"Darling, I never talk to anyone. Not about things that matter."

"Alexa matters."

"That's what I thought. You see, I have a funny feeling that you and I are rather alike. I never really knew what I wanted, and then when I got it, I discovered I'd never really wanted it at all. And that's because I was looking for something that didn't exist."

"Are you talking about a particular man, or a way of life?"

"Both, I think. Don't they go together? And perfection. The ultimate. But it never happens, because it doesn't exist. Loving isn't finding perfection, but forgiving horrible faults. I suppose it's all a matter of compromise. And recognizing the moment when it's time to decide whether you're going to fish or cut bait."

Noel said, "I love Alexa, but I am not in love with her." He thought about this statement and then smiled. "You know, I've never said those words aloud before. Not to myself. Not to anybody. Not about anybody."

"How does it feel, saying them aloud?"

"Frightening. I'm afraid of making promises, because I've never been much good at keeping them."

"Fear is the worst reason for doing anything, or for doing nothing. It's negative. Like not doing something because of what people will say. Pandora, you can't behave like that! *Whatever* will people *say*? As if it mattered. No, that won't do. You'll have to think of a better excuse."

"All right, how about this one? Uncommitted, I stay in charge of my own life."

"That's all right when you're young. But the unattached men about town very often end up as lonely and pathetic old bachelors, if they're not very careful. The sort that hostesses invite to dinner parties to make up the numbers. And afterwards, they drive themselves home to an empty flat and only a faithful doggie to take to bed."

"That's a jolly prospect."

"You only have one life. You don't get second chances. Let something really good slip through your fingers and it's gone forever. And then you spend the rest of your life trying to find it again . . . lurching from one unsatisfactory affair to another. And after a bit the day comes when you know it's all for nothing. Useless. Just a waste of time and effort."

"So what is the answer?"

"I don't know. I'm not you. I suppose a little courage and a lot of faith." She thought about this. "I sound just like a headmistress on Speech Day. Or a politician. 'Let us put our hands to the plough, and look forward, for there lies the way ahead.'" She began to laugh. "'Vote for Blair, and get free corn plasters.'"

He said, "You are advocating compromise."

Her laughter died. "There are worse things. This evening is the first time I ever met Alexa, but I watched her at dinner . . . watching you, and her face filled with love. She is a giver. She is gold."

"I know all that."

"So, I rest my case."

Silence once more, and now just a little way left to go. Down the long glen, and the lights of Strathcroy were dimmed; only the sparse street lamps shed their glow. The interior of the car had become very warm. Noel lowered the window a little and felt the fresh cold air on his face and heard the sound of the river running alongside the road.

They reached the first of the cottages, the gates of Croy, the front drive. He changed down, sped up the hill. The house awaited them, its windows dark. Only Archie's Land Rover stood parked in solitary state outside the front door. Noel drew up, switched off the ignition. The night was quiet; only the wind moved.

"There you are. Safely home."

She turned to him, her smile full of gratitude. "You've been really sweet. I hope I haven't ruined your fun. And I'm sorry if I've interfered."

"I can't quite work out why you said all those things."

"Probably because I've drunk too much champagne." She leaned over and kissed his cheek. "Good night, Noel."

"Will the door be open?"

"Of course. It's never locked."

"I'll see you in."

"No." She restrained him with a hand on his arm. "I'll be all right. Don't come. Go back to Alexa."

She got out of the car and slammed shut the door. In the beam of his headlamps she walked away from him across the gravel and up the steps. He watched her go. The big door opened, she turned to wave, slipped inside. The door closed. She was gone.

Even Tom Drystone could not play forever. At the end of two rousing rounds of "The Duke of Perth," finishing off with the distinctly non-Scottish strains of "The Girl I Left Behind Me," he pulled a long and breathless chord from his accordion, laid it on the floor, rose to his feet, and announced, over the microphone, that he and his colleagues were away for their supper. Despite exaggerated groans of despair and a good deal of derogatory badinage, he stuck to his guns and led his perspiring team of musicians across the dance floor and in the general direction of well-earned refreshment.

In the resultant lull the abandoned dancers, for a moment, stood about in aimless fashion, but almost at once were assailed by mouth-watering smells of frying bacon and fresh coffee drifting through from the house. These reminded the assembled company that it was some hours since they had last eaten, and there started a general exodus, headed for sustenance. However, as the marquee slowly emptied, a young man—spontaneously, or perhaps previously instructed by Verena —stepped up onto the platform, took his place at the piano, and began to play.

"Virginia . . ." She was already half-way up the stone steps that led into the house. She turned and saw Conrad behind her. "Come and dance with me."

"Don't you want bacon and eggs?"

"Later. This is too good to miss."

It was good. The sort of soft, pervasive mood music that went back a long way, a long time, to expensive, sophisticated restaurants and dark-ened night-clubs and sentimental movies that left you with tear-filled eyes and a wad of damp Kleenex.

Bewitched. "I'm wild again, beguiled again . . ."

She gave in. "All right."

She turned back, stepped into his arms. Conrad drew her close, laid his cheek against her hair. They danced, scarcely moving, hardly aware of other couples, who, succumbing to the seduction of the plangent piano, had taken once more to the floor.

He said, "Do you think this guy knows how to play 'The Look of Love'?"

She smiled to herself. "I don't know. You could ask him."

"It's been a good party."

"I'm impressed by your reeling."

"If you can do a square dance, I guess you can do anything."

"Just needs guts."

"Do they still have Saturday-night dances at the Leesport Country Club?"

"I expect so. A whole new generation smooching around the terrace under the stars."

"We're not doing too badly right now."

She said, "I'm not coming back, Conrad. I'm not coming back with you."

She felt his hand, against her rib-cage, moving, gentle as a caress. She looked up into his face. "You knew already, didn't you?"

"Yeah," he admitted. "I guessed."

"Everything's changed. Henry's home. We've talked. It's different now. We're together again, Edmund and I. It's all right again."

"I'm glad."

"Edmund's my life. I lost sight of him, but he's back and we're to-gether."

"For you, I'm really glad."

"Right now isn't the time to go away and leave him."

"He's a lucky man."

"No, not lucky. Just special."

"He's also a nice guy."

"I am sorry, Conrad. Whatever you feel, I don't want you to think that I was just using you."

"I think we used each other. We levelled off with our mutual need. At exactly the right time, the right person was there. At least, for me it was the right person. It was you."

"You're a special man, too. You know that, don't you? And one day, sooner or later, you'll meet someone. Someone just as special as you are. She won't fill Mary's place, because she'll have a place of her own. And she'll fill it for all the right reasons. You've got to remember that. For your own sake, and for the sake of your little daughter."

"Okay. A positive approach."

"I don't want you to be sad any longer."

"No longer the Sad American."

"Oh, don't *remind* me! How crass I was to blurt that out."

"When will I see you again?"

"Oh, soon. We'll come out to the States, Edmund and I. Sometime. We'll all get together then."

She laid her head on his shoulder. "Bewitched, bothered, and bewildered, am I." The last notes of the song trickled away off the piano.

He said, "I love you."

"Me too," Virginia told him. "It's been great."

Noel drove back to Corriehill. With the wind pouring in through the open window, the Golf headed back into the hills, and he took his time and did not speed. Being on his own was strangely peaceful, a small breathing space in which to collect some of his thoughts and let others wander. Leaving Croy, he had toyed with the idea of putting on a tape for company, and then decided against it because, for once, quiet was what he craved. Besides, it seemed almost blasphemous to intrude on the infinite darkness of the night by letting loose a blast of rock.

The countryside, all about him, was obscured, desolate, and scarcely habited, and yet he felt that his passage, in some inexplicable way, was being observed. This was an ancient land. The hilltops thrusting up into the sky had held those shapes since the beginning of time, and his immediate surroundings had probably looked for hundreds of years much as they looked now.

Ahead, the narrow road twisted away from him. Long ago, when its course was first laid, it would have followed the boundaries of a farmer's land, circumvented the drystone dykes of a crofter's small holding. Now, others owned these lands, and tractors and milk-floats and buses came this way, but yet the road wound and climbed and dipped, to no apparent purpose, just the way it had always done.

Unable to shrug off the sensation that he was being watched, he thought about those long-gone crofters pitting their energies against the cruel climate, the stubborn land, the barren soil. Ploughing the thin soil behind a horse, harvesting, with sickles, the meagre crops; braving blizzards in search of sheep, cutting peat to stack for fuel. He imagined just such a man making his way home, as Noel was now, headed up the empty glen, on horseback maybe, but more likely on foot. Slogging up the hill, bent against the wind that blew from the west. The road, then, would have seemed very long, and the labours of survival endless.

He found it impossible to imagine such hardships, such a tenuous existence. Safe in the twentieth century, taking both necessities and luxuries for granted, the problem of surviving was not one that Noel had ever contemplated, let alone had to deal with, and in comparison his own uncertainties seemed so unimportant that he felt diminished by their triviality.

And yet, it was his life. *You only have one life,* Pandora had told him. *You don't get second chances. Let something really good slip through your fingers and it's gone forever.*

Which brought him back to Alexa. *Alexa was gold.* Pandora was right, and he knew she was right. *If you have to hurt her, then you must do it now. . . .* That was old Vi, sitting on the hill above the loch and opening her heart to him.

He thought about Vi, and Pandora, and the Balmerinos and the Airds. Together they constituted a way of life that he had never before truly experienced. Family, friends, neighbours; involved and interdependent. He thought about Balnaid and once more was assailed by the reasonless conviction that here was where he belonged.

Alexa was the key.

Now, taking him by surprise, his mother joined in the argument. *Happiness is making the most of what you have.* Penelope's robust and certain tones rang clear in his head, brooking no argument, laying down the law as she always had when she felt strongly about some issue.

So what had he got?

The answer was painfully straightforward. A girl. Unsophisticated and not particularly beautiful. In fact, the very antithesis of every woman who had gone before. A girl who loved him. Not to distraction; never nagging him with demands. But with a constancy that burnt bright as a steady flame. He thought about the last few months, during which he had lived with Alexa in her little house in Ovington Street, and a series of random images floated, unsummoned, into his mind. And these took him by surprise, because for some reason his subconscious did not come up with any of those rich and material possessions which had first caught his attention that evening, so long ago, when Alexa had invited him in for a drink. The pictures, the furniture, the books and the porcelain; the handsome coasters on the sideboard, and the two silver pheasants which stood in the middle of her dining-room table. Instead, he saw delicious and domestic objects. A bowl of fresh apples, a loaf of newly baked bread, a jug crammed with tulips, the gleam of evening sunshine on the copper pans that hung in the kitchen.

And then the other good things which they had shared together. Kiri te Kanawa at Covent Garden, the Tate Gallery on a Sunday morning. Lunching at San Lorenzo. Making love. He thought of the peaceful feeling of walking home in the evenings, back from the office, turning into Ovington Street and knowing that she was there, waiting for him.

That was what he'd got. Alexa. There. Waiting for him. That was all he wanted. That was all that mattered. So what the hell was he dithering about? What the hell was he looking for? All at once the questions were of so little importance that he didn't even bother to attempt to think up the answers.

Because the prospect of a future without her was unimaginable.

He knew then that he was over the watershed and on the path to commitment. For better, for worse. Till death us do part. But the daunting words no longer rendered him shit-scared. Instead, he found himself filled with an unaccustomed and unexpected sense of purpose and elation.

And urgency. No more reason to linger. Instead, a new impatience. He had wasted enough time. He took a deep breath, accelerated. The engine responded and the car sped up the hill. Along the road that led to Corriehill.

His mother was still around somewhere. "All right," he said, "I heard you. You've made your point. I'm on my way." And he said the words aloud, and the wind snatched the words from his mouth and tossed them away behind him. He shouted, "I'm coming!" And the reassurance was for the two of them, his dead mother and his living love.

The first of the guests were on their way home from the dance. The headlights of their cars could be seen from far off, moving away from Corriehill, down between the trees and out of the imposing gates. Driving up the hill towards the house, Noel passed a couple of these cars, but there was plenty of space on the wide driveway and time, as well, for a certain amount of badinage; derisive remarks about Noel's apparently tardy arrival at the party, and assurances that it was better to be late than never.

The home-goers had clearly been enjoying themselves.

As the exodus had already begun, Noel did not bother to park the car in the field, but instead took it to the side of the gravel sweep at the front door. As he went up the steps, an old couple emerged, and he stood aside, to hold the door open for them and let them by. The husband thanked him courteously, and bade him good night, and then tucked his arm solicitously into his wife's, and helped her on her way. He watched them go, stepping cautiously, and deep in conversation. He heard their laughter. Elderly, perhaps, but they too had enjoyed themselves, had a fine time, and now together were going home. He thought again, till death us do part. But death, after all, was simply a part of life, and it was the living bit that was important.

He went through the doors and in search of Alexa. She was not in the disco, nor the drawing-room. Emerging from the drawing-room, he heard his name being spoken.

"Noel."

He stopped and turned, and saw a girl to whom he had not been formally introduced, but whom he knew to be Katy Steynton, because Alexa had pointed her out to him. She was blonde and very slender, with features the quintessence of Englishness; a beautiful complexion, a long face, pale blue eyes, and a tiny mouth. She wore a dress of slipper satin in exactly the same shade as her eyes, and held the hand of a man who was obviously impatient to get her into the throbbing, strobe-lit den of the disco.

"Hello, there."

"You are Noel Keeling, aren't you? Alexa's friend?"

For some reason, Noel felt faintly foolish. "That's right."

"She's in the marquee. I'm Katy Steynton."

"Yes, I know."

"She's dancing with Torquil Hamilton-Scott."

"Oh, thanks." Which sounded a bit abrupt, so Noel added tactfully, "Wonderful party. You must be thrilled. So kind of you to ask me."

"Not a bit. It was super . . ." She was already being towed away from him. ". . . that you could come."

A waiter bustled by with a trayful of brimming champagne glasses. As he passed, Noel adroitly lifted one off the tray, and then made his way through the library towards the marquee. The beat of the music there had reached a crescendo, for the band was on its second run through the dance, and the pace seemed to quicken with every moment that passed. At the top of the steps, he paused, to search for Alexa, but then, despite his anxiety to find her, and his impatience, found himself diverted, captivated by the sight before him. He had no great love of dancing, let alone Scottish country dancing, but the atmosphere had become electric, with a charge that could not be ignored. As well, his professional, creative instincts automatically responded to this visual assault on his senses, the whirling circles of colour and movement, and he wished, more than anything, that he were able to capture it on camera. For this dancing had about it an aggressive symmetry that reminded him of the precision of some oft-rehearsed military tattoo. The false floor of the marquee audibly groaned as one hundred pairs of feet banged down on it in perfect rhythm, and the centre of each ring was a vortex, sucking a dancer from the side of the set, and then throwing him out a second later with the full impact of centrifugal force. Bare-armed girls wryly displayed bruises inflicted by the silver cuff-buttons of a partner's kilt-jacket, but to all intents and purposes, they were mesmerized by the intricacies of the Reel, concentrating and waiting for their next turn to be pulled into the spinning inferno.

He saw Alexa at last, in her flower-splashed dress, with her cheeks rosy and her hair flying. She was unaware of his presence, and dancing with one of the young soldiers, a handsome figure with his raven black hair and his scarlet mess-jacket. Noel saw her engrossed, excited, blissfully happy, her face tilted up to her partner's, and filled with laughter.

Alexa.

"It's a hell of a dance, isn't it?"

Startled, Noel looked around and saw the man who stood beside him, come, presumably, to enjoy the spectacle, as he was.

He said, "It certainly is. What is it they're doing?"

"The Reel of the Fifty-first Highland Division."

"Never heard of it."

"It was devised in a German prison camp during the war."

"It looks extremely complicated."

"Well, why not? They had five and a half years to make the bloody thing up."

Noel smiled politely, and went back to watching Alexa. But now his patience was wearing thin, and he longed for it all to be over. Which, in a moment or two, it was. A rousing last few bars, and then a final, shattering roll of drums. Applause, clapping, and cheers took the place of the music, but Noel wasted not a moment. He laid down his glass in a handy plant pot, and shouldered his way across the crowded floor to her side, where he found her being gratefully and robustly embraced by her over-heated partner.

"Alexa."

She looked and saw him, and her flushed face lighted up, and she disentangled herself, reaching out her hand to him.

"Noel. Where have you been?"

"I'll explain. Come and have a drink. . . ." And he took her hand, and pulled her firmly off the dance floor, Alexa meanwhile calling her thanks to the young soldier over her shoulder, but doing nothing to resist Noel's masterful progress. He led her out of the tent, through the library; he searched for a peaceful spot, and decided that half-way up the staircase was as good a place as any.

"But, Noel, I thought we were going to have a drink."

"We will in a moment."

"You're taking me to the Ladies'."

"No, I'm not."

On the half landing it was quiet, and softly lit. He sat on the wide,

Turkey-carpeted stair and drew her down beside him, and took her head between his hands and kissed her warm, flushed cheeks, and her brow, and her eyes, and then her sweet and open mouth, thus stilling her laughing protests.

It took a long time. They drew apart at last. After a bit, he said, "I watched you dancing, yet that was all I wanted to do."

"I don't understand, Noel."

He smiled. "Nor do I."

"What has happened?"

"I took Pandora home to Croy."

"I didn't know where you'd gone."

"I love you."

"I looked for you, but . . ."

"I want you for always."

"You have me."

"Till death us do part."

She looked, quite suddenly, almost frightened. "Oh, Noel . . ."

"Please."

"But that's for ever."

He thought of the old couple, arm-in-arm, setting off in the darkness for home. Together. "I know." He had never felt so confident, so unafraid, so certain in the whole of his life. "You see, my darling Alexa, I am asking you to marry me."

Pandora shut the door behind her. Inside the house, with curtains drawn and doors closed, it was very dark, the great hall illuminated only by the glow of red ashes from the dying fire. She was alone. It was the first time in her life that she had had Croy to herself. Always, there had been others around the place. Archie, Isobel, Lucilla, Conrad, Jeff. And long before them, her parents, their servants, the constant stream of visitors and friends; always somebody, coming or going. Distant voices, distant laughter.

She switched on the light and went upstairs, down the upper passage to her room. She found it all just as she had left it, flung with clothes, the bed crumpled, the empty whisky glass still on the bedside table, along with her radio and a dog-eared paperback. The dressing-table was littered with bottles and jars, dusted with spilled face-powder; the wardrobe door hung open, and random shoes lay about the floor.

She tossed her bag onto the bed, and went over to the bombé desk. Here lay the letter that she had been writing before succumbing to exhaustion and taking to her bed to have one of her little toes-ups. She picked it up and read it through. It did not take very long. She folded it and put it into an envelope and licked the flap and pressed it down. She left the envelope on the blotter.

She went into the bathroom. This, too, was in its habitual state of disorder, with damp bath-mat and towels on the floor, and the soap lying, forgotten and soggy, in the bottom of the bath. At the basin, she filled a glass with water and drank it down, watching her own reflection in the tall plate-glass mirror. Her jars of pills stood on the shelf below this, and she reached for one of them, but clumsily, or perhaps her hand was shaking, because, inadvertently, she knocked over the bottle of Poison that stood alongside. It tipped and fell, and she watched this happen, and it all seemed to happen quite gradually, like watching a slow-motion film. It wasn't until it hit the basin and had smashed into smithereens that she put out her hand as though to save it.

Too late. All gone. The basin filled with shards of glass, and she herself, almost anaesthetized by the concentrated scent of the precious golden perfume. . . .

Bugger.

No matter. No good trying to clean it up, because she'd only cut her fingers to ribbons. Isobel would deal with it. In the morning. Tomorrow morning, Isobel would deal with it.

She stowed the jar of pills safely away, deep into the pocket of her mink coat, and then, carefully switching off all the lights, and closing her bedroom door, went back downstairs and into the drawing-room. She turned on the main switch, and the huge chandelier, suspended from the centre of the ceiling, sprang into a thousand facets of glittering crystal light. Here again, the fire was nearly dead, but the room was still warm and comfortingly shabby and familiar with its crimson damask walls hung with the old portraits and oil-paintings that Pandora had known all her life. It was all so dear. The battered armchairs and sofas, the mismatched cushions, the little green velvet footstool where she had sat, as a child, while her father read aloud to her before she went to bed. And the piano. Mamma used to play the piano in the evenings, and Pandora and Archie would sing the old songs. Scottish songs. Songs of loyalty and love and death . . . nearly all of them quite dreadfully sad.

> *Ye banks and braes of bonnie Doon,*
> *How can ye bloom sae fresh and fair . . .*

How lovely to be able to play as Mamma had. But then, being given lessons, the young Pandora had swiftly tired of them, and her gentle mother, as always, had allowed her to have her own way. And so she had never learned.

Another regret to add to all the others. Another missed opportunity of joy.

She went to the piano and lifted the lid and haltingly picked out the notes with a single finger.

It's a long long time
From May to December
But the days grow short . . .

Wrong note, try again.

. . . short
When you reach September.

Not much of a performance.

She shut the piano lid, went out of the room, across the hall and into the dining-room. Here, more detritus. The table uncleared, empty coffee-cups, port glasses, crumpled napkins, chocolate wrappings, the scent of cigar smoke. The sideboard was laden with decanters, and she found an open bottle of champagne, still three-quarters full, which Archie had capped for future consumption with some patent stopper. Carrying this, she went back across the hall and out through the front door.

Archie's Land Rover waited for her. She climbed up behind the wheel, into its smelly and battered interior. She had never driven it before, and it took a moment or two to work out the complexities of ignition, gear, and lights. But finally, she got the hang of them. With only sidelights burning, the old engine chuntered into life, and she was off.

Down the drive between the dark masses of the rhododendrons, across the cattle-grid, up to the right, headed for the hills. She drove very slowly, with immense care, feeling her way by the dim lights, as though she walked on tiptoe. Past the farmhouse, through the steadings. And then, Gordon Gillock's house. She had been afraid that the sound of the car engine would disturb Gordon's dogs, and they would start raging and barking and waking their master. But this did not happen.

Now she switched on the full beam of the headlights and was able to pick up a little speed. The road wound and twisted, but she knew every inch of the way. After a bit she reached the deer-fence with its tall gates. The last obstacle. She drew to a halt, pulled on the handbrake, and, leaving the engine throbbing, climbed down and went to open the gates. The bolt was rusted and awkward to pull free, but she finally achieved this, and the gates, weighted, swung open of their own accord. Back into the Land Rover, through the gap in the fence, and then the whole procedure all over again—pulling the gates shut, and bolting them closed behind her.

Free. Now she was free. Nothing more to be afraid of. Nothing more to worry about. Lurching and bumping, the Land Rover crawled its way up the unmade track, headlights pointing to the sky, and the sweet damp air pouring through the ill-fitting windows cool upon her cheeks.

Behind, the world dropped away, became smaller, infinitesimal, unimportant. The hills closed ranks, drew her close, like comforting arms. This was Pandora's country. She had carried it all through the wasted years in her heart, and now she was back for good. This was reality. The darkness, the feeling of belonging. Warm and safe and comforting as the womb.

You are my womb, she told the hills. I am returning to the womb. She began to sing.

> *Ye banks and braes of bonnie Doon,*
> *How can ye bloom sae fresh and fair . . .*

Her voice, thin and cracked and out of tune, sounded lonely as a curlew's cry. Too banal. Something cheerful.

> *Oh, the black cat piddled in the white cat's eye*
> *And the white cat said "Gorblimey."*
> *"I'm sorry, sir, if I piddled in your eye*
> *But I didn't know you were behind me."*

It was some time before she reached the loch, but time didn't matter, because there was no hurry now, no stress, no urgency, no panic. All had been attended to, nothing forgotten. Familiar landmarks came and went. The Corrie was one of them. She thought of Edmund, and then did not think of him.

She knew at last that she was drawing close to the loch when the bumping ceased and the land levelled out, and the wheels of the Land Rover ran smoothly over close-cropped grass.

In the beam of the headlights the dark waters lay revealed, the farther shores invisible, melding into the moors. She saw the black shape of the boat-house, the pale sickle of the pebbled beach.

She switched off the engine and the lights, reached for the bottle of champagne, and climbed out onto the grass. The heels of her sandals sank into the soft turf and the high air was very cold. She pulled her mink close about her and stood for a moment listening to the silence. Then she heard the piping of the wind, the ripple of water on shingle, the distant soughing of the tall pines that stood at the far end of the dam.

She smiled, because it felt just as it had always felt. She walked down to the water and sat on the turfy bank above the little beach. She set the champagne bottle beside her, then took the jar of sleeping pills from her coat pocket, unscrewed the cap and shook the lot out into her palm. There seemed to be an awful lot of them. She put her hand to her mouth and shovelled them in.

Their taste and texture caused her to shudder and gag. Impossible to chew or to swallow. She reached for the champagne bottle, tore off the stopper, tilted it to her lips, and washed the noxious mouthful down. The wine still fizzed and bubbled. It was important not to start vomiting. She drank more champagne, rinsing out her mouth as though she'd just endured a tiresome session at the dentist.

An amusing thought came to mind. How smart to do it with champagne. Like being poisoned by an oyster or run over with a Rolls-Royce. What else was smart? She'd once heard of somebody's mother who'd died of a heart attack in the Food Hall at Fortnum and Mason. Presumably she'd been laid out . . .

Her mind wandered. There really wasn't time to sit here, remembering that poor dead lady.

. . . laid out by some kindly swallow-tailed gentleman; stowed away behind the jars of Larks' Tongues in Aspic. . . .

She stopped to jerk off her high-heeled sandals and, straightening, felt her head reel as though some person had struck her a blow on the back of the neck. There is, she told herself with some deliberation, no time to lose. She shed her coat, left it lying, got to her feet, and walked the little distance that separated her from the loch. The stones were agony beneath her bare feet, but somehow it was a detached sort of agony, as though it were happening to another person.

The loch was cold, but no colder than other times, other remembered summers, other midnight swims. Here, the shore shelved steeply. A step and she was ankle-deep, another, and she was up to her knees. The filmy skirts of her dress dragged heavily with the weight of the water. Another step. And another, and that was it.

She plunged forward, out of her depth, and the water closed over the top of her head. She surfaced, gasping and spluttering for air. Her long wet hair clung to her naked shoulders, and she began to swim, but her arms felt feeble, and her legs were shrouded and tangled in layers of sodden chiffon. She could perhaps kick them free, but she was too tired . . . always too tired . . . to make the effort.

More restful, surely, just to float with the tide.

The hills were blurred now, but they were there, and that was comforting.

Always tired. I'll just have a little toes-up.

She saw, with grateful wonder, the night sky filled with stars. She laid back her head to gaze at these, and the dark water flowed over her face.

11

*I*T WAS FIVE-THIRTY IN THE MORNING when Archie Balmerino looked at his watch, realized the time, and heaved himself reluctantly out of the armchair in which he had been sitting, placidly sipping the last of the malt whisky, and having a crack with young Jamie Ferguson-Crombie.

The party was over. There was no sign of Isobel nor the rest of his house guests, the band had gone home, and the marquee was deserted. Only from the disco did the music still emanate and, glancing in, he observed two or three couples drooping around in the darkness, and looking as though they had fallen asleep on their feet. Nor was there any evidence of his hosts. From the kitchen could be heard voices, and he debated as to whether he should go and search for Verena, and then decided against it. It was time to head for home, and he would write his heartfelt thanks in a bread-and-butter letter the following morning.

He went out of the house, down the steps, set off in the direction of the car-park. The night had lightened, and the sky faded to grey. Dawn was not far off. It occurred to him then that perhaps he would find no form of transport waiting. The others, maybe returning to Croy in dribs and drabs, might well have forgotten all about Archie, and left nothing for him to drive. But then he saw Isobel's minibus standing in the middle of the field in lonely state, and knew that she had not forgotten him, and was filled with loving gratitude for her thoughtfulness.

He drove away from Corriehill. The Roman candles had burned themselves out, and the fairy lights had been extinguished. He knew that he was mildly tipsy, but, for some reason, felt totally clear-headed. He drove slowly, with concentrated care, only too aware that in the unlikely event of being stopped by the police, he hadn't a hope in hell of cheating the breathalyser. On the other hand, if he did meet a policeman, it would probably be young Bob McCrae from Strathcroy, and the last thing Bob would want to do would be to wheel the Laird in on a drunk-and-driving charge.

Dreadfully wrong; but one of the perks and privileges, he reflected wryly, of local gentry.

It had been a good party. He had enjoyed every moment of it. Seen a lot of old friends, made a lot of new ones. Drunk some excellent whisky, and eaten a splendid breakfast of bacon and eggs and sausages and black pudding and mushrooms and tomatoes and toast. Black coffee, too. Which was probably why he was feeling so wakeful and sparky.

All he had had to miss out on was the dancing. But he had taken great pleasure in watching some of the reels and listening to the toe-tapping music. The only time he had felt a little wistful was during the Duke of Perth. The Duke of Perth was the dance when, by tradition, your wife was your partner, and it had been a little galling to see Isobel being whirled off her feet by another man. No matter, she and Archie had shunted their way a couple of times around the floor of the disco, and very romantic and satisfactory it had been too, cheek to cheek, just like the old days.

The sun was edging its way over the eastern horizon as he turned into the front drive of Croy and mounted the hill. The sweep in front of the house was empty of cars. No Land Rover. Jeff, good fellow that he was, must have put it away in the garage.

He climbed out of the minibus and went indoors. Physically, he was very tired, and his stump hurt like hell, as it always did when he had spent too much time standing about on it. Haltingly, holding the bannister, he climbed the stairs. In their bedroom, he found Isobel, fast asleep. Evidence of her evening's finery lay across the floor in a little trail. Shoes, tights; the beautiful dark blue dress abandoned on the sofa which stood at the foot of the bed. Her jewels on the dressing-table, her evening bag on a chair. He sat on the edge of the bed and watched her sleep. There was still mascara on her eyelashes, and her hair was tousled. After a bit, he stooped and kissed her, and she did not stir.

He left her sleeping, went into his dressing-room, and slowly took off his clothes. In the bathroom, he turned on the taps, and the boiling water filled the air with steam. He sat on the lavatory seat and unbuckled his harness and his tin leg, and laid the awkward contraption out on the bathmat. Then, with a cunning expertise perfected over the years, he lowered himself into the scalding bath-water.

He soaked for a long time, turning on the hot tap whenever the water threatened to turn chill. He soaped himself, shaved, washed his hair. He thought about going to bed, and then decided against it. The new day had begun, and he might just as well see it through.

Later, dressed in old corduroys and a polo-necked sweater of great age and thickness, he went back downstairs and into the kitchen. The dogs were waiting for him, ready for their morning outing. He put on the kettle. When he came indoors again he would make a cup of tea. He led the dogs across the hall and out through the front door. They raced ahead of him, over the gravel and off onto the grass, scenting the rabbits who had played there during the night hours. He stood at the top of the steps and watched them go. Seven o'clock and the sun was on its way up the sky. A pearly morning with only a little light cloud drifting about in the west. Birds were singing, and so still was it that he could hear the sound of a car, far below in the glen, starting up, and driving away through the village.

Another sound. Footsteps on the gravel, approaching from the direction of the cattle-grid. He looked and saw, in some surprise, the unmistakable figure of Willy Snoddy, his lurcher at his heels, walking towards him. Willy, as disreputable as ever in his tinker's cap and muffler and his old jacket with its bulging poacher's pockets.

"Willy," Archie went down the steps to meet him. "What are you up to?" A ridiculous question, because he knew perfectly well that Willy Snoddy, at this hour of the day, was up to only one thing, and that was no good.

"I . . ." The old man opened his mouth and then shut it again. His eyes met Archie's and veered away. "I . . . I was up at the loch . . . me and the dog . . . I . . ."

He stopped.

Archie waited. Willy put his hands in his pockets and took them out again. And then the dog, sensing something, began to whine. Willy swore at it and slapped its head, but a frisson ran down Archie's spine and he tensed, consumed by a dreadful apprehension.

"Well, what is it?" he demanded sharply.

"I was up at the loch. . . ."

"You told me. . . ."

"Just a wee troot or twa, ken. . . ." But that wasn't what Willy had come to say. "Your Land Rover. It's there. And the lady's furry coat . . ."

And then Willy did a strange thing. He took off his cap, an instinctive and touching gesture of respect. He held it, twisted in his hands. Archie had never seen him bareheaded before. Willy's cap was part of his image, and rumour had it that he even slept in it. But now he saw that Willy's head was balding, and his sparse white hair lay thin over the defenceless scalp. Without the rakish slant of his bonnet it was as though the graceless poacher had been disarmed; no longer the well-kent villain, slouching about the place with his pockets full of ferrets, but simply an old countryman, uneducated and at a total loss, struggling to find the words to tell the untellable.

"Lucilla."

The voice came from a long way off. Lucilla decided to ignore it.

"Lucilla."

A hand on her shoulder, gently shaking.

"Lucilla, darling."

Her mother. Lucilla groaned, buried her head in the pillow and slowly awoke. She lay for a moment and then rolled onto her back and opened her eyes. Isobel was sitting on the edge of her bed, her hand on Lucilla's T-shirted shoulder.

"Darling. Wake up."

"I am awake," Lucilla mumbled. She yawned and stretched. Blinked once or twice. "Why did you wake me up?" she asked resentfully.

"I'm sorry."

"What time is it?"

"Ten o'clock."

"Ten o'clock. Oh, Mum, I wanted to sleep until lunch."

"I know. I'm sorry."

Lucilla slowly came to. The curtains had been drawn back, and morning sunlight slanted into the far corner of her room. She looked at her mother with sleepy eyes. Isobel was dressed, wearing a pullover and a husky, but her hair was untidy, as if she had not found time to do more than run a comb through it, and her expression seemed strained. But then, she would be tired. Lacking sleep. They had none of them got to bed before four o'clock.

But she was not smiling.

Lucilla frowned. "Is something wrong?"

"Darling, I had to wake you. And yes, something is wrong. Something's happened. It's very sad. I have to tell you. You've got to try to be brave." Lucilla's eyes widened in apprehension. "It's Pandora. . . ." Her voice faltered. "Oh, Lucilla, Pandora is dead. . . ."

Dead. Pandora *dead*? "No." The instinctive reaction was one of denial. "She can't be."

"Sweetheart, she is."

Lucilla was now awake, all trace of drowsiness shattered by shock. "But when?" Noel Keeling had driven Pandora home from the dance. "How?" She imagined Pandora, like a wraith, not breathing, still, on her bed. A heart attack, perhaps.

But not dead. Not Pandora.

"She drowned herself, Lucilla. We think she drowned herself. . . ."

"Drowned herself?" The implications were too horrifying to take in.

"In the loch. She took Dad's Land Rover. She must have driven herself up the road. Right past Gordon Gillock's house, but the Gillocks never heard a thing. The gates of the deer-fence were bolted shut. She must have shut them behind her."

Pandora drowned. Lucilla thought of Pandora somewhere in France, skinny-dipping in a deep and fast-flowing river, swimming against the current, calling to Jeff and Lucilla that it was lovely, the water was lovely, why didn't they come in?

Pandora drowned. Bolting the heavy gates behind her. Surely that in itself was proof that she had not taken her own life? Surely no one, under such circumstances, would painstakingly trouble to close the deer gates.

No.

"It must have been an accident. She would never, never have killed herself. Oh, Mum, not *Pandora* . . ."

"It wasn't an accident. We hoped it was. That she'd come home from the dance, and taken it into her head to go for a swim. It was just the sort of dotty decision that she was quite capable of taking. An impulsive whim. But by the loch they found her mink coat and her sandals; and an empty sleeping-pill jar, and the last of a bottle of champagne."

And the last of a bottle of champagne. The last of the wine. Like a final, terrible celebration.

". . . and when we went to her room, there was a letter for Dad."

Lucilla knew then that it was true. She was dead. Pandora had drowned herself. She shivered. An old cardigan lay on a chair beside her bed. She sat up, reached for it, wrapped it around her shoulders. She said, "Tell me what happened."

Isobel took Lucilla's hands in her own. "Willy Snoddy was up at the loch early, all set to lift a few trout out with the first rise. He'd walked up from the village with his dog. He saw the Land Rover parked by the boat-house. And then her coat, lying on the bank. He thought, like us, that perhaps someone had just gone for a midnight swim. And then he saw her body, washed up against the sluice-gates."

"I can't *bear* it for him. Poor old man."

"Yes. Poor Willy. But for once in his life he did the right thing, and came straight to Croy to find Archie. By then it was seven o'clock, and Dad was out with the dogs. He never went to bed after the dance. Just took a bath and dressed again. And he was out with the dogs, and he saw Willy coming, and Willy told him what he'd found."

Only too clearly, Lucilla could imagine the scene. She thought about her father, and then could not think about him, because Pandora was his sister, and he had loved her, and longed for her to come home to Croy. And she had come, and now she was gone for ever.

She said, "What did Dad do?"

"I was still sleeping. He woke me. We went along to Pandora's room, and she'd broken her bottle of scent in the bathroom basin. She must have knocked it over. The basin was filled with broken glass, and the smell filled the room, overpowering, like a sort of drug. So we drew back the curtains and threw open all the windows, and then we thought we must look for some sort of clue. We didn't have to look very far because she'd left an envelope on the desk, and there was a letter for Dad inside."

"What did it say?"

"Not very much. Just that she was sorry. And . . . something about money. Her house in Majorca. She said she was tired and she couldn't go on fighting any longer. But she didn't give any reason. She must have been so unhappy, and none of us knew. None of us had the slightest suspicion, the least idea of what was going on in her mind. If only I'd known. I should have been more perceptive, more sympathetic. I might have been able to talk to her . . . to help. . . ."

"How could you? You mustn't for a moment blame yourself. Of course you didn't know what Pandora was thinking. Nobody could ever know what she was thinking."

"I thought we were close. I thought that I was close to her. . . ."

"And you *were*. Just as close as any woman could be to Pandora. She loved you, I know. But I don't think she ever wanted to get too near to people. I think that was her defence."

"I don't know." Isobel, clearly, was distraught and bewildered. "I suppose so." Her grip on Lucilla's hands tightened. "I have to tell you the rest." She took a deep and steadying breath. "After we found the letter, Dad rang the police in Relkirk. He explained what had happened, and the difficulties of the location, the road to the loch. They sent, not an ambulance, but a police Land Rover, with a four-wheel drive. And the police doctor came with it. Then they drove on up to the loch. . . ."

"Who went?"

"Willy. And Dad. And Conrad Tucker. Conrad went with them. He was up and about by then, and he offered to go with Dad. So kind of him, such a kind man, because Archie didn't want me to go, and I couldn't bear the thought of his being on his own."

"So where are they now?"

"They're not yet back from Relkirk. They were going to take her— the body—there, to the Relkirk General. I suppose to the mortuary."

"Will there have to be an inquest?"

"Yes. A fatal-accident inquiry."

A fatal accident. The words had the chilling ring of officialdom about them. Lucilla imagined the courtroom, the cold and objective words of evidence and conclusion. Then newspapers, with accounts of the incident. Some old, blurred photograph of Pandora's lovely face. The headlines. "Death of Lord Balmerino's Sister."

The inevitable publicity, she knew, would be the final horror. "Oh, poor Dad."

Isobel said, "People always tell you, 'This will pass. Time will heal.' But at times like this one doesn't seem to be able to think more than a moment ahead. This is now. And it feels insupportable. There are no words of comfort."

"I can't take it in. It's all so *pointless*."

"I know, my darling. I know."

Isobel's voice was soothing, but Lucilla was not soothed. Instead, her distress blew up in an outburst of indignation. "It's all such a *waste*. *Why* did she have to? What on earth drove her to take such a step?"

"We don't know. We have no idea."

The little explosion of anger flickered and then died. Lucilla sighed. She said, "Does anybody else know? Has anybody been told?"

"There's really nobody to tell. Except Edmund. And Vi. I expect Dad will ring Edmund when he gets back from Relkirk. But Vi mustn't be told over the telephone. Somebody will have to go and see her and break the news. Too great a shock for an old lady. . . ."

"What about Jeff?"

"Jeff's downstairs in the kitchen. He appeared about five minutes ago. I'm afraid I'd forgotten all about him, and the poor man didn't get much of a welcome. Coming down to breakfast and being faced with such news. And there wasn't even any breakfast, because I hadn't got around to cooking anything. I think he's frying something up for himself right now."

"I must go and be with him."

"Yes. I think he could do with a little company."

"When will Dad and Conrad be back?"

"I suppose about half past ten or eleven. They'll be ravenous too, because there wasn't time to feed them before they left. I'll make them something when they come. And meantime . . ." She got to her feet. "I'm going to start clearing the dining-room. The table's still laden with all the remains of dinner last night."

"It seems a lifetime ago, doesn't it? Why don't you leave it? Jeff and I will do it later, or we'll get Agnes back from the village. . . ."

"No, I want something to do. Women are so much luckier than men. At ghastly times like this, they can always find something to occupy their hands, even if it's only scrubbing the kitchen floor. Washing glasses and polishing silver will fit the bill very nicely. . . ."

Lucilla was alone. She got out of bed and dressed, pulling on jeans and a sweater. Brushed her hair, went to the bathroom to clean her teeth and wash her face. A flannel soaked in scalding water, pressed to her eyes and cheeks. The heat cleansed, refreshed, cleared her head. She ran downstairs.

Jeff sat at one end of the kitchen table, with a mug of coffee and a plateful of bacon and sausages. He looked up as she came in, swallowed his mouthful, laid down his knife and fork, and got to his feet. She went to him, and he took her in his arms, and for a little while they just stood there. It felt warm and safe in his strong embrace, and the thick sheepy wool of his sweater smelt friendly and familiar. From the pantry came the sound of running water, the clink of glass. Isobel was already hard at work.

He didn't say anything. After a little they drew apart. She smiled her gratitude for his comfort, and reached for a chair and sat, leaning her elbows on the scrubbed table.

"Do you want something to eat?" he asked.

"No."

"You'd feel better with something inside you."

"I couldn't eat."

"A cup of coffee then." He went to the Aga and filled a mug, and brought it over and set it down before her. Then he sat down again and went on with his sausages.

She drank a little coffee. She said, "I'm glad we had that time with her."

"Yeah."

"I'm glad she came home with us."

"It was good." He reached over and took her hand. He said, "Lucilla, I think I should go."

"Go?" She stared at him in some dismay. "Go where?"

"Well, this isn't a very good time for your mother and father to have a stranger around the place. . . ."

"But you're not a stranger. . . ."

"You know what I mean. I think I should pack my bag and take myself off. . . ."

"Oh, but you *can't*. . . ." The very suggestion filled Lucilla with panic. "You can't leave us all. . . ." Her voice rose, and he shushed her gently, aware of Isobel's presence beyond the open door, and not wishing his hostess to overhear the conversation. Lucilla dropped her voice to a furious whisper. "You can't leave me. Not now. I need you, Jeff. I can't cope with everything being so utterly awful. Not on my own."

"I feel I'm intruding."

"You're not. You're *not*. Oh, please, don't go."

He looked into her beseeching face and relented.

"Okay. If I can be any help, I'll certainly stay around. But whatever happens, I can't stay for long, because the beginning of October I have to go back to Australia."

"Yes. I know. But don't talk about leaving us just yet."

He said, "If you like, you could come with me."

"Sorry?"

"I said, if you like you could come with me. To Australia, I mean."

Lucilla's fingers closed around her coffee mug. "What would I do there?"

"We could be together. Go on being together. There's plenty of room in my parents' house. And I know they'd make you very welcome."

"Why are you asking me now?"

"Seems a good idea."

"And what would I do in Australia?"

"Whatever you wanted. Get a job. Paint. Be with me. We could find some place of our own."

"Jeff . . . I don't quite know what you're asking of me."

"I'm not asking anything. Just extending an invitation."

"But . . . it . . . it isn't like that, is it? You and me. Not for ever."

"I thought we could maybe find out."

"Oh, *Jeff.*" A lump grew in her throat, and she felt her eyes swim with tears, which was ridiculous because she hadn't cried for Pandora, but now she was in floods just because Jeff was being so sweet, and asking her to go back to Australia with him, and because she wasn't going to go, because she wasn't in love with him, and knew that he was not in love with her.

"Come on, now, don't cry."

She reached for a tea-towel and unhygienically blew her nose on it.

"It's just that you're being so dear. And I would love to come. But not just now. Just now I have to stay here. Besides, I don't think you really want me hanging around when you go home. You're going to have enough to think about without me under your feet. Going back to work, getting on with your life, settling down. . . ." She blew her nose again and managed a watery smile. ". . . and, somehow, I don't think I'm quite the right person for you. When you do settle down, and you will, it will be with some lovely Australian girl. A sun-tanned sheila with a fat bum and big tits. . . ."

He cuffed her gently over the ear. He said, "That's not funny." But he was smiling.

She said, "It was the nicest invitation I've ever had in my life. And you are the dearest man I've ever met. And we've had just the best time ever since that day we met in Paris. And one day I *will* come to Australia, and I shall expect a huge welcome from you, red carpets, ticker tapes, the full treatment. But right now . . . and for ever . . . I can't come."

"Well, if you change your mind, the offer's open. . . ."

He had finished his breakfast, laid the knife and fork together on the plate, and carried it over to the sink. From the dining-room now could be heard the sounds of Hoovering. Jeff crossed the kitchen and closed the pantry door. He returned to the table and sat facing Lucilla.

He said, "I don't like to ask this and it's none of my business, but did Pandora leave any sort of a letter?"

"Yes, she did. For Dad. On the desk in her room."

"Did she say why she was going to kill herself?"

"No. Apparently not."

"What does your mother think?"

"At the moment she's too distressed even to try to think."

"So there's no obvious reason?"

"None."

"How about you?"

"I have no opinion, Jeff." His silence caught her attention. "Why? Have you?"

"I just thought. I was thinking. Remember that guy we met our first day at the villa? Carlos Macaya?"

"Carlos?" That suave and handsome man with his charming manners and his notable wrist-watch. "But of course." She could not imagine why she had not thought of him before. "Jeff. Do you think he might know something?"

"Probably not. But he was obviously very close to Pandora. Perhaps she confided. Told him something that we don't know. . . ."

Lucilla remembered that puzzling remark that Carlos had made to Pandora as he drove away from the villa. . . . *Let me know if you change your mind,* he had said. And she had replied, *I won't change my mind.* And Lucilla and Jeff had discussed the exchange, and decided that Carlos and Pandora had probably been referring to something quite trivial— a cancelled tennis match, or a rejected invitation.

"Yes. You're right. I think they were very close. Lovers, probably. Maybe he does know something. . . ."

"Even if he doesn't, if they were so close, perhaps he should be told what's happened."

"Yes." It was a perfectly viable suggestion. "But how can we tell him?"

"Ring him up."

"We don't know his number."

"Pandora must have had an address book . . . what's the betting we'll find Carlos Macaya's number in it?"

"Yes. You're right. Of course."

"If we're going to put a call through, we'd better do it now, before your father and Conrad get back, and while your mother's occupied. Is there a telephone where we won't be disturbed?"

"Nowhere. Except, perhaps, Mum's bedroom. We'll use the phone by her bed. . . ."

"Come on then." He got to his feet. "We'll do it now."

Isobel was still Hoovering. They went out of the kitchen and soft-footed up the carpeted stairs. Lucilla led the way along the passage to Pandora's bedroom. They went inside and she closed the door behind them.

The room, with its unmade bed and litter of feminine possessions, was cold. Every window was open, and the curtains ballooned in the breeze. And yet that perfume still hung like a pall; the smell of Poison.

Lucilla said, "I never knew, I could never make up my mind if I loved that scent or if I hated it."

"Why is it so strong?"

"She broke the bottle in her basin." She looked around her, saw the filmy dressing-gown tossed on the bed, Pandora's evening bag, the wardrobe full of her clothes, the brimming waste-paper basket, the crowded dressing-table, the odd shoes that lay about on the carpet.

The shoes, expensive Spanish leather, high-heeled, impractical, were somehow the most personal and poignant of reminders, because they could never have belonged to anybody but Pandora.

Lucilla closed her mind to them.

She said, "Her address book. Where would we find her address book?"

They found it on the desk, alongside the blotter. It was large and leather-bound, with Pandora's initials in gold, and endpapers of Florentine paper. Lucilla sat, ran her finger down the index, and opened it at the letter *M*.

Mademoiselle, Dress Shop.
Maitland, Lady Letitia.
Mendoza, Philip and Lucia.
Macaya . . .

Carlos Macaya. She sat very still, staring at the page. She did not speak.

After a bit, Jeff said, "Have you found it?"

"Yes."

"What's wrong?"

"Jeff." She looked up at him. "Jeff, he's a doctor."

"A doctor?" He frowned. "Let's see."

She pointed. "Here. 'Macaya, Dr. Carlos and Lisa.' Lisa must be his wife. Jeff, do you think he was Pandora's doctor?"

"Most probably. We'll find out." He looked at his watch. "It's ten-thirty. It'll be about eight-thirty in Majorca. We'll call him at home. It's a Saturday morning. Most likely we'll get him at home."

With the address book in her hand, Lucilla got to her feet. They went out of Pandora's room and along to her parents' bedroom where, on this unreal and disorientated morning, yet another bed had not been made. The telephone sat on the bedside table. Jeff found the phone book and looked up the international code for Spain, and carefully, digit by digit, Lucilla dialled the long and complicated number.

A wait. Various clickings and buzzings. And then the ringing sound. She thought about the Majorca morning, the Mediterranean sunlight already warm, the sky clear with the promise of yet another hot and cloudless day.

"*Hola?*" A woman's voice.

"Mrs. . . ." Something had gone wrong with Lucilla's throat. She cleared it and started again. "Mrs. Macaya? Señora Macaya?"

"*Sí?*"

"I'm so sorry, but do you speak English?"

"Yes, a little. Who is this?"

"My name is Lucilla Blair." She willed herself to calmness,

deliberately spoke slowly and clearly. "I am calling from Scotland. I want to talk to your husband. Is he there?"

"Yes, he is here. *Un momento . . .*"

The phone was put down. Footsteps receded, tapping across a polished tiled floor. From a distance, Lucilla heard her call. "Carlos!" And then a few unintelligible sentences in Spanish.

She waited. She reached out her hand, and Jeff took it in his own.

He came. "Dr. Macaya."

"Oh, Carlos, this is Lucilla Blair. Pandora Blair's niece. I met you at her house in August. I came with a friend from Palma and you were there drinking tea. Do you remember?"

"But of course I remember you. How are you?"

"I'm all right. I'm calling from my home in Scotland. Carlos, please forgive me, but were you Pandora's doctor?"

"Yes, I was. Why?"

"Because . . . I'm terribly sorry, but I'm afraid it's very sad news. Because she is dead."

He did not speak immediately. And then he said, "How did she die?"

"She drowned. She drowned herself. She took all her sleeping pills and then drowned herself. Last night . . ."

Another pause. And then Carlos Macaya said, "I see." Was that all he had to say?

"You don't seem very surprised."

"Lucilla, I am devastated by your news. But I am not completely surprised. I was very afraid that something like this might happen."

"Why?"

He told her.

Over the roar of the Hoover, Isobel heard Archie's Land Rover returning from Relkirk, the familiar sound of its old engine grinding up the hill from the village and then turning down into the avenue. She turned off the Hoover, and its din slowly died. Glancing through the tall window, she saw the Land Rover trundle past, with Conrad at the wheel.

She left the Hoover standing in the middle of the floor and went to meet them. Out through the front door, and down the steps onto the gravel. The two men were already alighting from the Land Rover, Archie limping badly, which was never a good sign. She went to him and put her arms around him and kissed him. His face was cadaverous, grey with fatigue, and felt very cold.

She said, "You're back. Come."

She took his arm and Conrad followed them and they mounted the steps and went indoors. Looking at the American, Isobel saw that he too showed signs of strain. She put questions aside, and concentrated on practicalities.

"You must be exhausted, and hungry as well. I didn't cook anything because I was waiting for you to come, but it won't take a moment. You'll both feel better when you've got something inside you."

Conrad said, "That sounds like a fine idea," but Archie shook his head.

"Isobel, in a moment. I must telephone first. I must ring Edmund Aird."

"Darling, that can surely wait. . . ."

"No." He raised his hand. "I'd rather get it over. You two go ahead. I'll be with you in a moment."

Isobel opened her mouth to argue, and then thought better of it and stayed silent. Archie turned and slowly, painfully, walked away from them, down the hall, headed for his study. In silence, Conrad and Isobel watched him go, and heard the door close behind him.

They looked at each other. Isobel said, "I think he probably wants to be alone for a moment."

"That's understandable." Conrad wore a borrowed pair of green rubber boots and an old jacket of Archie's. His head was bare, his eyes, behind the heavy glasses, filled with sympathy.

"Was it *very* awful?" she asked.

"Yes," he told her, and his voice was gentle. "Yes. It was very sad."

"Where did you find her?"

"Just where Willy said she'd be. By the sluice-gate."

"Did she . . . ?" She tried again. "I mean, how long had she been there?"

"Only a few hours."

"Yes." Only a few hours. Not long enough to change, swell, putrefy. "I'm glad Willy found her so soon. It was good of you to go with Archie, and bring him back again. I can't tell you how grateful I am. . . ."

"It was the least I could do."

"Yes. There isn't really very much anybody can do, is there?"

"Not very much."

"No. Well . . ." The subject, for the moment, had run its course. Breakfast. "I'm sure you must be ravenous."

"I am. But first, if I may, I'll shed these boots and wash my hands."

"Of course. I'll be in the kitchen."

Lucilla and Jeff had disappeared, taken themselves off somewhere. Isobel found frying pan, more sausages, bacon, tomatoes, and eggs. She put bread in the toaster, made a fresh pot of coffee, laid two places at the table. By the time Conrad joined her, his breakfast was just about ready. She poured a cup of coffee and set it by his place.

"Drink it while it's hot. I just have to fry you an egg. How do you like it? Sunny side up? Isn't that what they say in America?"

"That's what they say. Isobel . . ."

She turned from the Aga. "Yes?"

"I think I should leave you this afternoon. You have enough to think about without extraneous guests hanging around the place."

She was horrified. "But I thought you weren't leaving until tomorrow!"

"I can call a taxi, get myself to Turnhouse . . ."

"Oh, Conrad, please don't feel you have to go. . . ."

"This is not a time for visitors. . . ."

"I don't think of you as a mere visitor. I think of you as a friend. And I would be very distressed if you felt you had to leave us a day early. But if *you* would prefer to do that, I shall quite understand."

"It isn't that I would prefer it. . . ."

"I know. You're thinking of us. But you know, at the moment, it's good for us to have friends around. This morning, for instance. What would we have done without you? And I am certain that Archie will want you to stay. At least for one more night."

"If you really mean that, I would like to stay."

"I do really mean it. And when I said I think of you as a friend, I really meant that as well. You came as a stranger to Croy, and we none of us knew you or knew anything about you. But now, after just a few days, I feel as though we'd known you all our lives. I hope you'll come back again and visit us some other time."

"I'd like that. Thank you."

Isobel smiled. "And you can bring your little daughter. This is a good place for children."

"Watch out. I may take you up on that."

Isobel professionally broke the egg into the pan.

"When are you flying back to your little daughter?"

"On Thursday."

"And Virginia's coming with you?"

"No. Not now that Henry's home again. She's cancelling her flight, and calling her grandparents to explain. She and Edmund will maybe come out next spring, and we're all going to get together then."

"That's disappointing for her. But perhaps better. More fun to go on holidays with your husband." She stooped to take his plate out of the low oven, added the egg to the pile of goodies already on it, and then set the lot in front of him. "Now you wrap yourself around that, as my son Hamish always says." She glanced at the clock. "What *is* Archie doing? I think I'll take him a cup of coffee. You don't mind being left on your own, do you?"

"No, I'm perfectly all right. And this looks like the best breakfast I've ever eaten."

"You've earned it," Isobel told him.

* * *

Archie sat at his desk, in his study, in his father's chair, and surrounded by his father's possessions. The room faced west, and so, on this bright morning, was sunless. For the moment, he was grateful for quiet and solitude. Deadened by fatigue and his own despair, he waited until such time as he could muster enough moral courage to pick up the telphone, dial the Balnaid number, and speak to Edmund Aird.

From the moment that Willy Snoddy had finally managed to find the words with which to relay his dreadful tidings, Archie had experienced the grip of a mental numbness that precluded all intelligent incentive. Somehow, like a sleep-walker in the throes of a nightmare, he had got through the motions of doing what he knew had to be done.

Waking Isobel, having her there beside him, had been the first priority. Only with Isobel could he share his grief. Then, together, they had gone to Pandora's bedroom, disordered in characteristic fashion, as though she had, just that moment, gone from the room. It was Isobel who had drawn back the heavy curtains and opened all the windows to set free the suffocating odour of the spilled and wasted perfume. It was Isobel who had spied the envelope on the desk, and handed it to Archie.

And, together, they had read Pandora's final letter.

After that the inevitable, painful procedures. Ringing the police, and the seemingly endless wait until the official vehicle, with the police doctor on board, arrived. The long drive to the loch, crawling with agonizing slowness up the steep and bumpy track. The gruesome and heart-breaking operation of retrieving from the loch his dead sister's body.

The irony of the situation was his own hopelessness. No sooner, it seemed, had he come to terms with his memories of Northern Ireland than he was fated to be burdened by this new horror. The sight of Pandora, like a sodden doll, washed up beneath the sluice-gates. Her face bloodless, her wet hair wound, like silken cords, around her neck. Her white arms, thin and bleached as drifting twigs, the skirts of her dress tangled in a flotsam of broken branches and broken reeds.

How great it would be if the impossible were rendered possible, and he could blank the image from his mind's eye for ever.

He sighed, and drew her letter towards him. The thick blue paper embossed with the Croy address, and Pandora's scrawly handwriting, unformed as a child's. A ghost of a smile touched his lips, because he remembered how she had never bothered to learn to do anything properly, and at the end of the day, she still could scarcely write.

Friday evening.

My darling Archie. I once went to a funeral and a man got up and read something so nice, about dead people having just slipped away into the next room, and not being miserable nor sorry, but going on laughing at the same old jokes. If, by chance, you give me a lovely Christian funeral (and who knows, you may be so cross, you'll just toss me onto Isobel's compost heap), then it would be nice if somebody coud read that about me.

He laid the letter down, and gazed unseeing, over his spectacles, at the opposite wall. The strange thing was that he knew exactly the passage that Pandora referred to. He knew it because he had read it aloud in church during the course of his own father's funeral service. (But Pandora did not know that, because Pandora had not been there.) And moreover, wishing to be word-perfect and not make a hash of his emotional duty, he had privately rehearsed the reading a number of times, and ended up knowing it by heart.

Death is nothing at all. It does not count. I have only slipped away into the next room. Nothing has happened. Everything remains exactly as it was. I am I, and you are you, and the old life that we lived so fondly together is untouched, unchanged. Whatever we were to each other, that we are still. Call me by the old familiar name. Speak of me in the easy way which you always used. Put no difference into your tone. Wear no forced air of solemnity or sorrow. Laugh as we always laughed at the little jokes that we enjoyed together. Play, smile, think of me, pray for me. Let my name be ever the household word that it always was. Let it be spoken without an effort, without the ghost of a shadow upon it. Life means all that it ever meant. It is the same as it ever was. There is absolute and unbroken continuity. What is this death but a negligible accident? Why should I be out of mind because I am out of sight? I am but waiting for you, for an interval, somewhere very near, just round the corner. All is well.

All is well.
But then old Lord Balmerino had not taken his own life.

Archie, I have been very practical and sensible and made a will, and left all my worldly goods to you. Perhaps you should get in touch with my New York lawyer. He is called Ryan Tyndall and you'll find his address and telephone number in my address book. (He's terribly nice.) I know I've seemed to spend money like water, but there ought to be lots left in the Bank, as well as various Stocks and Bonds and even a little California Real Estate. And of course, the house in Majorca. You can do what you want with this, sell it or keep it. (Lovely hols. for you and Isobel) but whatever you do, just be sure that dear Seraphina and Mario are all right.

I like to think that you will use some of this money to turn the stables or the barn into a workshop, start manufacturing your clever little wooden people, and sell them all over the world at a socking profit. I know you can do it. It just needs a bit of get-up-and-go. And if the business side of it seems a bit daunting, I am sure that Edmund would help and advise.

Darling, I'm so dreadfully sorry about all this. It's just that everything's suddenly become so complicated and such an effort and I haven't the energy to fight any longer. I was never much use at being steadfast and brave.

It's been a funny old life.

I adore you both and I leave you my love.

Pandora.

I am sure that Edmund would help and advise.
Back to Edmund.
He thought of the other letter, safe in the drawer of this desk. He found the key, and unlocked the drawer, and took out that letter. The airmail envelope, creased and dog-eared, addressed to himself in Berlin; the postmark 1967.

He withdrew the two flimsy sheets, scrawled with the same immature handwriting. Unfolded them.

My darling Archie. It was such a lovely wedding and I hope you and Isobel are happy, had a lovely honeymoon and are happy in Berlin, but oh, I miss you so much. Everything is horrible, because everybody I love has gone away. I have got nobody to talk to. I can't talk to Mamma and Pa because it's about Edmund. This doesn't surprise you, does it, because you must have known. I don't know how I never knew it, but I must have loved him for ever, because when I saw him again, the few days before the wedding, I suddenly realized that there never had been, nor could be, anyone else, ever again. And the ghastly, tragic, unbearable thing is that he's married somebody else. But we love each other. I can write it in big letters. WE LOVE EACH OTHER. But I'm not allowed to tell anybody because of him being married to Caroline and having the baby and everything. He has gone back to her, but he doesn't love her, Archie. He loves me, and I am without him, stuck here, and I need you so badly and you're in Berlin. He said that he would write but he's been gone for a month and I haven't heard a word, and I can't bear it and I don't know what to do. I know it's wrong to break up a marriage, but I'm not doing that, because I had Edmund long before she did. I know you can't do anything to help but I just had to tell someone. I never knew Croy could be so lonely and I'm horrible to Mamma and Pa, and I can't help it. I can't stay here for ever, I think I shall go mad. There's only you I can tell. With lots of love and tears, Pandora.

Before he had always found the adolescent despair immeasurably poignant. Now, in the light of the morning's tragedy, it took on an even graver significance. He covered his eyes with his hand. Behind him, the door opened.

"Archie."

It was Isobel. "I've brought you some coffee." He did not turn. She reached over his shoulder and laid the steaming, fragrant cup on the desk in front of him, and then put her arms around his neck, and stooped to press her warm cheek against his own.

"Why are you taking so long? What are you doing?"

"Just reading." He laid the letter down.

She hesitated and then said, "That's the letter Pandora sent you just after we were married."

"Yes."

"I didn't know you'd kept it. Why did you, Archie?"

"I didn't have the heart to tear it up and throw it away."

"So sad. Poor little girl. Have you telephoned Edmund yet?"

"No. Not yet."

"You don't know what to say, do you?"

"I don't know what to think."

"Perhaps she *was* still in love with him. Perhaps that's why she came home. And then she saw him again, with Virginia and Alexa and Henry, and she realized it was hopeless."

She was voicing his own fears, his own unspoken dreads. He could not have spoken them, and hearing Isobel say the words aloud, bringing their shared suspicions out into the open, filled him with loving gratitude for her fearless good sense. Because now they could talk about it.

"Yes," he admitted. "That's what I'm afraid of."

"She was such a little sorceress. Always enchanting. Generous and funny. But you know, Archie, she could be ruthless. If she wanted something, she could be ruthless to get it. If she set her heart on something, other people didn't matter."

"I know. It was our fault. We all spoiled her, indulged her. . . ."

"I think it would have been impossible not to. . . ."

"She was only eighteen when they had that affair. Edmund was twenty-nine. He was married and he had a child. I know Pandora flung herself at him, but instead of backing off, he reneged on his responsibilities, threw them to the wind. She was like a fire, and he added his own potent fuel to that fire; the result was an explosion."

"Have you ever talked to Edmund about it?"

"No. Once, I could have. But not after that. He was the reason she ran away. He was the reason she never came back."

"You've never forgiven him, have you, Archie?"

"No. Not really." It was a bleak admission.

"Is that why you're hesitating now? Is that why you haven't rung him?"

"If all our conjectures are true, I would be unwilling to unload such a burden of guilt onto my worst enemy."

"Archie, that's not your—"

She stopped abruptly, raised her head to listen. From beyond the closed door could be heard footsteps coming down the hall.

"Mum!" It was Lucilla.

"We're in the study."

The door opened a crack. "Can I come in? I'm not disturbing you, am I?"

"No, of course not, darling. Come in."

Lucilla closed the door behind her. She looked as though she had been crying, but had dried her tears. Archie held out his arm to her, and she took his hand and bent to kiss his cheek. She said, "I am so dreadfully sorry." She sat on the edge of the desk, facing her parents. She said, "I've got something to tell you. And it's very sad, and I hope you won't be too distressed. . . ."

"Is it about Pandora?"

"Yes. I've found out why she did it." Waiting, they watched their daughter. "You see . . . she had terminal cancer."

Her voice was quiet, but quite calm and firm. Isobel looked into Lucilla's face and saw there, behind the youthful features, a great inner strength, and knew that, at nineteen, she had quite suddenly grown up. The child was gone forever. Lucilla would never be her child again.

"Cancer?"

"Yes."

"How do you know?"

"When Jeff and I went to stay with her in Majorca, the afternoon we arrived, there was a man with her called Carlos Macaya. I told you about him, Dad. He was very attractive, and Jeff and I were convinced he was her current lover. But he wasn't. He was her doctor. It was Jeff who remembered him, and suggested that we ring him up, just in case he knew something that we didn't know. We found his name and his telephone number in her address book, and it was then that we realized that he was a doctor, and not just a friend. So we put the call through, to Majorca, and spoke to him. And he told us everything."

"Had he been taking care of her?"

"Yes. But I think he found it a fairly difficult and thankless task. He realized that something was wrong when she started getting so thin, but he had a hard time of it getting her to agree to a consultation. And even then, she wouldn't face up to reality or keep appointments. By the time he finally managed to get her into his surgery, she had sat on her illness for a long time. As well, he discovered a carcinoma on one of her breasts. He did a needle biopsy, and sent it off to the hospital in Palma for a pathology report. It was malignant, and may well have spread. So he went to see Pandora and tell her that she would have to have surgery, a mastectomy, and then a course of chemotherapy. That was what he was telling her the day Jeff and I turned up. But she flatly refused. She said that nothing would induce her to have surgery, and nothing would induce her to endure the subsequent treatment, radiation, chemotherapy. He could give her no real hope of a total cure . . . the disease was too far along, I suppose . . . but he did tell her that if she went her own way, her expectation of life was not very long."

"Was she in pain?"

"Some. She was taking medication. Quite strong drugs. That's why she was always so tired. I don't think she suffered a great deal, but of course, in time, it would have got very bad."

"Cancer." Archie said the word, and it had about it the toll of finality. The end. The double line drawn at the foot of a column of figures. "I never thought. I never had the faintest suspicion. But we should have guessed. There was nothing of her. We should have known. . . ."

"Oh, Dad . . ."

"Why didn't she *tell* us. . . . We could have helped. . . ."

"No, you couldn't have helped. And she would never have told you. Don't you see, the last thing she wanted was for you and Mum to know. She just wanted to be back at Croy, and everything just the way it used to be. September. And parties, and little shopping sprees to Relkirk, and people coming and going and the house full of guests. No sadness. No talk of dying. And that's what you gave her. Verena's dance was the perfect, timely excuse for Pandora to come home and to accomplish what I think she had planned all along."

"Did the doctor know this?"

"Not for certain. But he did say that he would never have allowed her to make that journey through Spain and France if Jeff and I had not been with her."

"But he guessed what she had in mind?"

"I don't know. I couldn't ask. But I expect that he did. He knew her very well. And I think that he was very fond of her."

Archie said, "How could he have let her simply go away?"

"You mustn't blame Carlos, Dad. He did everything he could to persuade her to go to hospital, to try to make her grasp her only chance, however slight. But she was simply adamant."

"So she came home to die?"

"Not just that. She came home to be with you, to be at Croy. To give us all a good time, and lovely presents, and to make us laugh. She came back to her childhood and the places she remembered and loved. The house, the glen, the hills, the loch. If you think about it, it was a very brave thing to do. But that doesn't make it any easier for you. I'm sorry. I've hated telling you. I just hope it makes it all a bit easier to understand." Lucilla fell silent, thinking about this. Then she said, and her voice, which had been so strong, suddenly wavered. "Not that understanding helps very much." Isobel saw her face crumple like a child's and tears fill her eyes and overflow and stream down her cheeks. "She was so sweet to Jeff and me . . . we had such a good time together . . . and now it feels as though a light has gone out of all our lives. . . ."

"Oh, darling." Isobel could not bear it. She went to Lucilla, put her arms around her daughter's thin and heaving shoulders. "I know. I'm so sorry. And you've been so brave . . . but you're not alone, because we're all going to miss her. And I think we must be grateful that she did come home. How awful if we had never seen her again. You brought her back to us, even if it was only for just a little time. . . ."

After a bit, Lucilla calmed down and stopped crying. Isobel gave her a handkerchief, and she blew her nose. She said, "I've already had one blub, and I'd hoped that was the last of it. You see, Jeff asked me to go back to Australia with him, and I'm not going to go. For some idiotic reason that made me cry as well. . . ."

"Oh, Lucilla . . ."

"I'm going to stay home for a bit. If you and Dad can stand having me under your feet."

"I can't think of anything we would love more."

"Nor me."

Lucilla gave her mother a watery smile, blew her nose in a final sort of way, and got to her feet. She said, "I'll leave you two together. But, Dad, please come soon and eat some breakfast. You'll feel better then."

"I'll come," he promised her.

She went to the door. "I'll make certain those two greedy men haven't helped themselves to all the bacon." She smiled. "Don't be too long."

"I won't, my darling. And thank you."

She was gone, leaving Isobel and Archie with only each other. After a bit, Isobel left Archie's side and went over to the long window. Beyond lay the garden, the croquet lawn, and the squeaky old swing-seat. The sun had not yet reached the grass, and it was still damp with the night's dew. She saw the silver birches, their leaves turned to gold. Soon the leaves would drop, and the branches be stripped bare for the winter.

She said, "Poor Pandora. But I think I understand."

She looked up at the hills, the sky, and saw the rain-clouds looming, blowing in from the west. Sun at seven, rain at eleven. They had had the best of the day.

"Archie."

"Yes."

"This exonerates Edmund, doesn't it?"

"Yes."

She turned from the window. He was watching her. She smiled. "I think you should ring him now. And I think now is the time to forgive. It's all over, Archie."

Edie, breathless after her climb up the hill, hurried on her way along the lane that led to Pennyburn.

It seemed a funny thing to be doing on a Saturday. Saturday was one of the few days of the week that Edie kept to herself, seeing to her own little house, doing a bit of gardening if it was fine, clearing out cupboards, baking. This morning, because the sun had shone, she had pegged out a long line of washing, and then walked down the street to Mrs. Ishak's, to get a few groceries and the daily newspaper. As well, she had bought a *People's Friend* and a box of chocolates for Lottie, because she had planned to catch the afternoon bus into Relkirk and go to visit her poor cousin. She felt bad about Lottie, but also a little annoyed, because Lottie had nicked her new lilac cardigan. The police couldn't have known, of course, that it wasn't hers, but Edie was determined to get it back. She'd give it a good wash before she wore it again. Poor Lottie. Maybe, as well as the magazine and the box of chocolates, Edie would pick a few Michaelmas daisies out of her garden to liven up the impersonal ward. Not that she'd get any thanks for her pains, but still, her own conscience would be eased. Just because things had gone so wrong for Lottie, one couldn't simply abandon the poor soul.

Everything nicely organized.

But then, just as she was heating up a pot of broth for her dinner, Edmund had stopped by to see her. He had come straight to Edie's from Pennyburn, and before that, from Croy. He'd brought with him terrible tidings, and after hearing these, all thoughts of Lottie had flown from Edie's head, and she was left with her day fallen to pieces. She had picked up the bits and put them together again; only now everything was a different shape. A strange feeling. Upsetting.

From time to time she read in the papers of some family, setting out on an innocent and enjoyable outing in the car, perhaps to see friends, or simply to enjoy the countryside, only to have their lives blown apart for ever by an accident; a pile-up on the motorway, with dead drivers at the wheel, and shattered vehicles this way and that, all over the road. She felt now as though she had been, if not involved, then witness to such a disaster, and was standing there surrounded by wreckage, knowing only that there had to be something that she could do to help.

"I've told my mother," Edmund had said, "but she's alone. I asked her to come back to Balnaid for lunch, and to spend the day with us all, but she declined. She said that she just wanted to be on her own."

"I'll go to her."

"I would be grateful. If there is one person in the world she will want to be with, it's you."

So Edie had taken the pot of soup off the hob, and put on her coat and her walking shoes. Into her capacious bag she had put her spectacles and her knitting, then locked her house and set off for Pennyburn.

Now, she was there. She went in through the kitchen door. All was neat and tidy. Mrs. Aird had washed her own breakfast dishes this morning, and put them all away. Even swept the floor.

"Mrs. Aird!" She laid her bag on the table and, still wearing her coat, went through the hall and opened the sitting-room door.

She was there. Sitting motionless in her chair, staring at the unlit fire. Not knitting, not doing her tapestry, not reading the paper—just sitting. And the room, as well, felt chill. The morning, which had started so brightly, had clouded over, and without the warmth of the sun pouring through the windows, felt strangely comfortless.

"Mrs. Aird."

Disturbed, Violet turned her head, and Edie was shocked, because for the first time in her life she saw Vi as old, lost, confused; even infirm. For a moment her expression remained blank, as if she scarcely recognized Edie. And then, at last, her eyes brightened, and an expression of immeasurable relief filled her face.

"Oh, *Edie*."

Edie shut the door behind her. "Yes, it's me."

"But why are you here?"

"Edmund dropped by to see me. To tell me about Pandora. What a thing to do. He said you were on your own. Could maybe do with a bit of company. . . ."

"Only you, Edie. Nobody else. He wanted me to go back to Balnaid with him. So kind. But somehow I didn't feel quite up to it. I didn't feel strong enough. With one's children one always has to put on a brave face, and be the person who does the comforting. And somehow, I think I've just run out of the energy to comfort anybody. Just for the moment. I shall be better tomorrow."

Edie glanced about her. "It's awful cold in here."

"I suppose it is. I really hadn't noticed." Violet looked at the fireplace. "I was up quite early this morning. I got everything done. Cleaned out the ashes myself, and relaid the fire and everything. I've just not got around to lighting it."

"Won't take a moment." Edie unbuttoned her coat and laid it over a chair, then knelt on the hearthrug, lowering her bulk onto her well-padded knees, and reached for the box of matches. The paper caught. The sticks, the little pile of coals. The flames flickered.

Violet said, "I am sitting here filled with shame, Edie. We should have been more perceptive. We should have realized that Pandora was ill, perhaps dying. She was so dreadfully thin. Just skin and bone. We should have seen for ourselves that something was wrong. But I, for one, have been so taken up with my own family that I never gave Pandora a passing thought. Perhaps if I had been a little less self-absorbed, I would have sensed that all was not well." She sighed, and shrugged. "And yet, she was just the way she had always been. Beautiful, flirtatious, funny. Bewitching."

"She was always a wee character."

Edie reached for a couple of logs and set them on the brightly burning coals. Then, with some effort, she pulled herself up off her knees and settled down in the chair facing Violet. She was wearing her best tweed skirt and her Shetland cardigan with the bright colours around the neck, and her dear face was rosy from the effort of the long walk up the hill. With the fire burning, and Edie there, sitting on the other side of the hearthrug, Violet was warmed, and felt no longer quite so desolate.

"I hear," said Edie, in her gossiping voice, "it was Willy Snoddy who found her?"

"Yes. Poor Willy. I don't doubt he'll be drunk for days after such an experience."

"Cancer's a terrible thing. But to take your own life . . ." Edie shook her head. "I cannot understand a body doing such a thing."

"I think we have to understand, Edie, otherwise we shall never forgive her. . . ."

". . . but the Balmerinos. And wee Lucilla. Did she not think of them?"

"I am sure that she did. And yet, perhaps, she never thought very much about anybody except herself. And she was so pretty, so attractive to men. Little love affairs were always the excitement of her life. To understand, we have to try to imagine her future as she obviously saw it. Ill, maimed by surgery, fighting the disease, losing all her lovely hair, rendered unappealing." The fire now was crackling up the chimney. Violet spread her hands to its comfort. "No. She couldn't have coped with all of that, Edie. Not on her own, the way she was."

"And Edmund?" Edie asked.

They had no secrets from each other. It was a good feeling.

"You saw Edmund, Edie."

"But he didn't say very much."

"He said a great deal to me. He is naturally devastated about Pandora, as we all are, but, I think, no more than the rest of us. And I believe that now he will be all right, because he has Virginia and Alexa and Henry. Darling little Henry. And, who knows, perhaps even Noel Keeling as well. I have a feeling that, very soon, Noel is going to be a member of the family."

"Is that right?"

"Just a feeling, Edie. We'll have to wait and see. As well, Edmund told me that he is going to take a bit of a holiday. He wants to spend some time with Virginia and Henry, and of course he must be around to support Archie Balmerino through the next few days. There will be so much to be seen to. A fatal-accident inquiry is inevitable, and then, after that hurdle has been taken, the funeral, and all the sad and heart-rending tying-up of the loose ends. Afterwards, when it is all over, he and Archie plan to go fishing together, to Sutherland, perhaps, for a little while. And you know, that fills me with satisfaction. I have always loved Edmund, Edie, but just lately I have found myself not liking him very much. But I think that everything has changed. Perhaps he's realized at last that the little things in life are sometimes infinitely more important than the big ones. And it's a comfort to know that out of this appalling and unnecessary tragedy has come at least one good thing. Which is that Archie and Edmund are good friends again, just the way they used to be."

"It's taken a long-enough time," Edie pointed out, down-to-earth as ever, and not afraid to speak her mind. "Over twenty years."

"Yes. But then Edmund behaved very badly. We both, I think, know that."

Edie was silent for a little, and then made her only comment. "Alexa's mother. She was a very cold lady."

It was not much of an excuse, but her loyalty to Edmund filled Violet with gratitude. "Well, you should know, Edie. You lived with them in London. You knew them both, perhaps better than any of us."

"A nice-enough girl, but cold."

On the mantelpiece, Violet's little gilt clock struck the hour. One o'clock. Edie glanced up at it in some surprise. The time had flown by.

"Just look at that," she said. "One o'clock already. You must be needing something to eat. I'll go into the kitchen and see what I can find. There was a pot of beef stew I left in the larder yesterday. I'll give it a heat-up. There's plenty for the two of us. So what do you say? We'll have it here, on a tray, by the fire."

"I can't think of anything I'd like more. And perhaps a glass of sherry to cheer ourselves up?" Edie clicked her tongue in disapproval, but she was smiling. She rose to her feet and made for the door. "Oh, and Edie, you will stay with me, won't you? We'll spend the afternoon together, and talk about the old days."

"I'd like that," Edie told her. "I've no mind to be on my own today. And I've brought my knitting."

She went. A moment later Violet heard her clattering dishes in the kitchen, opening and shutting the larder door. Comforting and companionable sounds. She stood up, holding on to the mantelpiece until the stiffness left her knees. Behind the clock, she saw the invitation, which had stood there for so many weeks. Curling now, and a bit dusty from the smoke that rose from the fire.

Mrs. Angus Steynton

At Home

For Katy

She took it out from behind the clock, and read it for the last time, then tore it into pieces and dropped the scraps onto the flames. They flared, burnt, shrivelled to ashes, were gone.

She went to the door that led out into the garden, opened it, descended the steps and walked out onto the sloping lawn. With the sun gone, and the sky filled with sailing grey clouds, it felt very cold. Colder than it had been all autumn. September was passing, and soon the winter gales would begin.

She made her way to the foot of the garden, to stand by the gap in the hedge, looking out to the south, over the incomparable view. The glen, the river, the distant hills: sunless today, sombre, but beautiful. Always so beautiful. Never would she tire of them. Never would she tire of life.

She thought about Pandora. And Geordie. Geordie, wherever he was, would keep an eye on Pandora. She thought about Edie, and for the first time the dreadful possibility occurred to her that perhaps her dearest friend would die before she herself died, and she would be left with no contemporary, no person to turn to, to give her comfort; no person to talk to, remembering together the days that were gone.

She said a prayer. "I know I am a dreadfully selfish woman, but please let me go before Edie goes, because without her I don't think I could cope with living. I don't think I could cope with growing old."

A sound caught her ear. High up, far beyond the blowing clouds. A distant honking and gabbling, both haunting and familiar. The wild geese, returning. The first she had heard since they had flown away north at the end of the spring. She gazed up into the sky, screwing up her eyes, searching for them. And then the clouds momentarily parted, and she glimpsed the birds, a single skein, beating their way south, the vanguard of the many thousands already on their way.

They were early. They had left late, and were returning early. Perhaps it was going to be very cold. Perhaps it was going to be a hard winter.

But she had survived hard winters before, and this one would be no worse. In fact, it would be better, because she felt, in some strange way, that her family had been restored to her, and she knew that, together, the Airds were strong enough to withstand whatever the fates chose to hurl in their direction. That was the most important thing. Togetherness. There lay the greatest strength. Her family, putting the past behind them, and never losing sight of the fact that, beyond the winter, a new spring was already on its way.

"Mrs. Aird."

She turned, saw Edie standing there at the open door. She had tied one of Violet's aprons on over her good skirt, and her white hair blew in the breeze. "Come away in and get your dinner."

Violet smiled, raised a hand. "Coming, Edie." She walked . . . slowly at first and then briskly . . . back up the sloping lawn towards her house. "I'm coming."

VOICES IN SUMMER

For Mark
for reasons that will be obvious to him

CONTENTS

1

HAMPSTEAD

❦

HE DOCTOR'S RECEPTIONIST, a pretty girl in horn-rimmed spectacles, saw Laura to the door, opened it for her, and stood aside, smiling, as though the visit had been a social one that they had both enjoyed. Beyond the open door, scrubbed steps led down into Harley Street, sliced by the houses opposite into bright sunlight and dark shadow.

"It's a lovely afternoon," the receptionist remarked, and indeed it was; the end of July now, and fine and bright. She wore a crisp skirt and blouse and nylon tights on her well-rounded legs, and businesslike black court shoes, but Laura wore a cotton dress and her legs were bare. There was, however, a freshness to the brisk breeze that swept the summer streets, and she had tied a pale cashmere cardigan, by its sleeves, around her shoulders.

Laura said yes, but couldn't think of anything else to say about the weather. She said thank you, although the receptionist hadn't done anything very much except announce her arrival for her appointment with Dr. Hickley and then, fifteen minutes later, appear to take her away again.

"Not at all. Goodbye, Mrs. Haverstock."

"Goodbye."

The shiny, black painted door closed behind her. Laura turned her back on the façade of the handsome, imposing house and walked a little way down the pavement of the terrace, where she had found, by some miracle, an empty parking meter and had been able to leave her car. She stooped to unlock the door, and there was a stir from the back seat, and as she got in behind the wheel, Lucy leaped lightly over the back of the seat into her lap, stood on her back legs with plumy tail waving full tilt, and gave Laura's face a quick and affectionate wash with her long pink tongue.

"Oh, poor little Lucy, you must be boiling." She had left a bit of window open, but still the inside of the car was like an oven. She reached up and opened the sun roof, and at once everything felt a bit better. Cool air circulated, and hot sunshine struck the top of her head.

Lucy panted obligingly for a moment or two, as proof of her own personal doggy discomfort, her forgiveness, and her love. Her love was all for Laura. Despite this, she was a polite little creature, with charming manners, and made a point of greeting Alec each evening when he came back from work. Alec always told people that when he married Laura he got a sort of job lot, like a man at an auction sale: a new wife, with a dog thrown in.

When she was desperate for a confidant, Laura told Lucy things, secrets that she could safely divulge to no other person. Not even Alec. Especially Alec, because the secret thoughts were usually about him. Sometimes she wondered about other married women. Did they have secret thoughts from their husbands? Marjorie Anstey, for instance, who had been married to George for sixteen years and organized his entire life, from clean socks to airplane tickets. And Daphne Boulderstone, who flirted outrageously with every man she met and was constantly being spied in discreet restaurants lunching intimately with some other woman's husband. Did Daphne take Tom into her confidence, laughing, perhaps, at her own foolishness? Or was Tom cool and detached—disinterested, even—as he usually appeared? Perhaps he simply didn't care. Perhaps next week when they were all in Scotland together, at Glenshandra, for the long-planned fishing holiday, Laura would have time to observe these marriages and come to some sort of a conclusion . . .

She took a deep breath, maddened by her own stupidity. What was the point of sitting here fabricating these random possibilities, when, now, she wasn't even going to Scotland. Dr. Hickley had minced no words about this. "Let's get it over as soon as possible, waste no time. A couple of days in hospital and then a good rest."

What Laura had dreaded had happened. She put Daphne and Marjorie out of her head. Alec. She must concentrate on Alec. She must be dynamic and decisive, and work out a plan of action. Because whatever happened, Alec must go to Glenshandra with the others. Laura would have to be left behind. This, she knew, would take some persuasion. It was necessary to think up some convincing and foolproof plan, and nobody could do this but herself. Now.

Slumped in the seat behind the wheel of her car, Laura did not feel capable of being dynamic or decisive.

Her head ached, her back ached, her whole body ached. She thought about getting home, which was a tall, thin house in Islington, not very far, but far enough when you were tired and despondent on a hot afternoon in July. She thought about getting home and going upstairs and lying on her cool bed and sleeping away the remainder of the afternoon. Alec was a great believer in emptying one's mind and giving the subconscious a chance to solve apparently unsolvable problems. Perhaps Laura's subconscious would come up trumps and, beavering away while she slumbered, would present her, on waking, with some brilliant and obvious plan. She considered this and sighed again. She hadn't that much faith in her subconscious. To be truthful, she hadn't that much faith in herself.

"I've never seen you look so pale," Dr. Hickley had said, which was disturbing in itself, because Dr. Hickley was a cool and professional lady and seldom moved to make such impulsive remarks. "Better take a little blood test just to be sure."

Did it really show so much?

Laura pulled down the sunshield and inspected herself in the mirror set in its back. After a bit, without much enthusiasm, she took a comb from her bag and tried to do something with her hair. And then a lipstick. The lipstick was too bright, the color wrong for the pallor of her skin.

She looked into her own eyes, which were a very dark brown and fringed with long, bristly lashes. They gave the impression, she decided, of being too large for her face, like two holes cut in a sheet of paper. She met her gaze sternly. *Going home and going to sleep isn't going to solve anything. You know that, don't you?* There had to be somebody who could help, some person to talk to. At home there was nobody, because Mrs. Abney, who lived in the basement, took firmly to her bed every afternoon between two and four. She objected strongly to disturbance, even if it was something important like the man come to read the meter.

Someone to talk to.

Phyllis.

Brilliant. *When I come out of hospital, I could stay with Phyllis. If I was with Phyllis, then Alec could go to Scotland.*

She could not think why this obvious scheme had not occurred to her before. Delighted with herself, Laura began to smile, but at that moment a short toot on a car horn jerked her back to reality. A big blue Rover was drawn up alongside her car, the driver a red-faced man who made it clear that he wished to know whether she was about to vacate the parking space or if she intended sitting there, primping and preening in the mirror, for the rest of the day.

Embarrassed, Laura pushed the sunshield out of the way, started the engine, smiled more charmingly than was necessary, and, a little flustered, manoeuvred herself out into the street without actually hitting anything. She made her way out into the Euston Road, edged along as far as Eversholt Street, in the three-deep stream of traffic, and there turned north and headed up the hill, toward Hampstead.

At once she felt marginally better. She had had an idea and she was doing something about it. The traffic was thinner, the car picked up a little speed, air poured through the open roof. The road was friendly and familiar, because when she was young and living with Phyllis, she had traveled this way each day by bus—first to school, and then to college. Stopped at traffic lights, she remembered well the houses on either side, shabby and tree-shaded, some of them coming up in the world, with freshly painted faces and brightly colored front doors. The sunny pavements were crowded with people in flimsy clothes: bare-armed girls and mothers with half-naked children. As well, small shops had put up awnings and spilled their wares out onto the pavement. She saw vegetables, piled artistically, a set of scrubbed pine chairs, and green buckets packed with roses and carnations. There were even a couple of tables set up outside a little restaurant with striped umbrellas and white iron chairs. *Like Paris,* thought Laura. *I wish we lived in Hampstead.* And then the car behind her blared its horn and she realized that the light had gone green.

It wasn't until she was actually driving up Hampstead High Street that the thought occurred to her that perhaps Phyllis wouldn't be in. Laura should have stopped to telephone. She tried to imagine what Phyllis could be doing on a fine summer afternoon, but it wasn't difficult because the possibilities were endless. Shopping for clothes or antiques; prowling around her favorite art galleries; sitting on a committee dedicated to bringing music to the masses; or raising money to preserve some crumbling Hampstead mansion.

It was too late now to do anything about it, however, because Laura was almost there. A moment later, she turned out of the main road and into a lane that narrowed, curving uphill, and then straightened, and she saw the terrace of Georgian houses that climbed with it, each just a step higher than its neighbor. Front doors stood flush with the cobbled pavement, and in front of Phyllis' house was parked her car, which was at least a hopeful sign, although it didn't necessarily mean that Phyllis was in, because she was an indefatigable walker and only took the car when she had to go "down to London."

Laura parked her own car behind it, closed the sun roof, gathered Lucy up, and got out. There were tubs of hydrangeas on either side of Phyllis' front door. Laura banged the knocker and crossed her fingers. *If she's not in, I shall simply go back down the hill, go home, and telephone her.* But almost at once came the sound of Phyllis' busy tapping footsteps (she always wore the highest of heels), and the next moment the door opened, and everything was all right.

"Darling."

It was the best of welcomes. They embraced, Lucy getting in the way, and as always, hugging Phyllis felt like hugging a bird. A tiny-boned, bright-feathered bird. Today Phyllis was dressed in apricot pink, with cool, glassy beads at her neck and earrings that jangled like Christmas tree decorations. Her child-size hands were laden with rings, her face, as always, perfectly made up. Only her hair looked a little unruly, springing from her brow. It was graying now, but that detracted in no way from the youthful enthusiasm of her face.

"You should have called!"

"I've come on an impulse."

"Oh, darling, that does sound exciting. Come along!"

Laura followed her indoors, and Phyllis shut the door behind her. But it was not dark, because the narrow hall stretched straight through the house to another door, which led out into the garden, and this stood open. Framed within the aperture, Laura could see the sunny, paved yard, hung about with glossy greenery, and at the far end the white trellis summerhouse.

She stooped and set Lucy down on the ruby-red carpet. Lucy panted, and Laura dropped her handbag at the foot of the stair and went through to the kitchen to fill Lucy a bowl of water. Phyllis watched from the doorway.

"I was sitting in the garden," she said, "but it's almost too hot. Let's go into the sitting room. It's cool there and the French windows are open. Darling, you look terribly thin. Have you been losing weight?"

"I don't know. I suppose I might. I haven't been trying to."

"Would you like a drink? I've just made some proper lemonade. It's in the fridge."

"I'd love some."

Phyllis went to collect glasses. "You go and make yourself comfortable. Put your feet up, and we'll have a gorgeous chat. It's years since I saw you. How's that handsome Alec?"

"He's all right."

"You'll have to tell me everything."

It was heaven to be told to make yourself comfortable and put up your feet. Just like old times. Laura did as she was told, lying back in the corner of Phyllis' great downy sofa. Beyond the open glass doors, the garden stirred in the breeze with a faint rustling sound. There was the smell of wallflowers. It was very serene. Which was funny, really, because Phyllis wasn't a serene person. More like a little gnat, always on the go, her spindly legs carrying her up and down the stairs a hundred times a day.

She was her aunt, the younger sister of Laura's father. Their father was an impoverished Anglican clergyman, and many small economies and penny-pinching had been necessary to raise sufficient cash to send Laura's father to university to study medicine.

There was nothing left over for Phyllis.

Although the era, happily, was past when rectors' daughters were expected to stay meekly at home, helping Mother do the church flowers and run the Sunday School, the brightest prospect for Phyllis might well have been marriage to some solid and suitable man. But Phyllis, from an early age, had ideas of her own. Somehow, she got herself through a secretarial course and set off for London—not without a certain amount of parental opposition—where she found herself, in record time, not only a place to live, but also a job. Junior typist with Hay Macdonalds, an old-established firm of publishers. Before long her enthusiasm and enterprise had been noted. She became secretary to the fiction editor, and then, at the age of twenty-four, was made personal assistant to the chairman, Maurice Hay.

He was a bachelor of fifty-three, and everybody thought that he would remain in this happy state for the rest of his life. But he didn't, because he fell head over heels in love with Phyllis, married her, and bore her off—not exactly on a white charger, but at least in a very large and impressive Bentley—to live in state in his little jewel of a house in Hampstead. She made him very happy, never wasting a day of their time together, which was just as well, because three years later he had a heart attack and died.

To Phyllis he left his house, his furniture, and all his money. He was not a mean nor a jealous man, and there were no nasty codicils attached to his will ruling that she should have to relinquish the lot should she remarry. But even so, Phyllis never did again. The fact that she didn't was a conundrum to all who knew her. It was not that there was a shortage of gentlemen admirers; in fact, the very opposite. A constant stream was almost at once in attendance, telephoning, sending flowers, taking her out for dinner, abroad for holidays, to the theater in the winter, and to Ascot in the summer.

"But darlings," she protested when taxed with her independent lifestyle. "I don't want to marry again. I'd never find anyone as sweet as Maurice. Anyway, it's much more fun being single. Specially if you're single and rich."

When Laura was small, Phyllis had been something of a legend, and no wonder. Sometimes, at Christmas, Laura's parents brought her up to London, to see the decorations in Regent Street, and the shops, and to go perhaps to the Palladium or the ballet. Then, they had always stayed with Phyllis, and to Laura, brought up in the busy, humdrum establishment of a country doctor, it was like being suddenly magicked into a dream. Everything was so pretty, so bright, so scented. And Phyllis . . .

"She's just a fly-by-night," Laura's mother said goodnaturedly on the way home to Dorset, while Laura sat pole-axed in the back seat of the car, stunned by the memories of so much glamor. "One can't imagine her ever getting to grips with life, doing anything practical . . . and indeed, why should she?"

But there Laura's mother was wrong. Because, when Laura was twelve, her parents were both killed, driving home from a harmless dinner party, down a road they had both known all their lives. The pile-up was the direct result of a number of unimagined circumstances: a T-junction, a long distance lorry, a speeding car with inefficient brakes, all met together in a disaster of hideous finality. Almost, it seemed, before the dust of this horror had settled, Phyllis was there.

She didn't *tell* Laura anything. She didn't tell her to be brave, she didn't tell her not to cry, she didn't say anything about it being God's will. She simply hugged her and asked her very humbly if, just for a little, Laura would be absolutely sweet and come to Hampstead and live with her, just to keep her company.

Laura went, and stayed. Phyllis looked after everything: the funeral, the lawyers, the disposal of the practice, the selling of the furniture. One or two precious and personal things she kept for Laura, and these were installed in the bedroom that was to become Laura's own. A desk of her father's, her dollhouse, her books, and her mother's silver-backed dressing table set.

"Who do you live with, then?" girls at her new London school would ask when their blunt questions evinced the sad truth that Laura was an orphan.

"My aunt Phyllis."

"Gosh, I wouldn't like to live with an aunt. Has she got a husband?"

"No, she's a widow."

"Sounds fairly dreary."

But Laura said nothing, because she knew that if she couldn't be living in Dorset with her own darling mother and father, she would want above everything else in the world to be with Phyllis.

Theirs was, by any standards, an extraordinary relationship. The quiet and studious young girl and her extroverted, gregarious aunt became the closest of friends, never quarrelling or getting on each other's nerves. It was not until Laura was finished with college and qualified to go out and earn her own living that she and Phyllis had their very first difference of opinion. Phyllis had wanted Laura to go into Hay Macdonalds; to her it seemed the obvious and natural thing to do.

Laura jibbed at this scheme. She believed that if she did so, it would be a form of nepotism, as well as undermining her determination to be independent.

Phyllis said that she would be independent. She'd be earning her living.

Laura pointed out that she already owed Phyllis enough. She wanted to start her career—whatever it was going to be—under an obligation to nobody.

But nobody was *talking* about obligations. Why turn down a wonderful opportunity, simply because she was Phyllis' niece?

Laura said that she wanted to stand on her own two feet.

Phyllis sighed and explained patiently that she *would* be standing on her own feet. There was no question of nepotism. If she wasn't good at her job and couldn't do the work, there would be no delicate compunctions about sacking her.

This was scarcely comforting. Laura muttered something about needing a challenge.

But Hay Macdonalds *was* a challenge. Laura might just as well take up this challenge as another.

The argument continued, spasmodically, for three days, and Laura finally gave in. But at the same time, she broke the news to Phyllis that she had found herself a small, two-room flat in Fulham and that she was leaving Hampstead and going there to live. This decision had been made long ago; it had nothing to do with the argument about the job. It did not mean that she no longer *wanted* to live with Phyllis. She could have stayed forever in that warm and luxurious little house high on the hill above London, but she knew that it could not work. Their circumstances, subtly, had altered. They were no longer aunt and niece, but two adult women, and the unique relationship that they had achieved was too delicate and precious to risk putting into jeopardy.

Phyllis had a life of her own to lead—still full and exciting, despite the fact that she was now well into her fifties. And at nineteen, Laura had a life to *make,* and this could never be achieved unless she had the willpower to fly Phyllis' cozy nest.

After her initial dismay, Phyllis understood this. But, "It won't be for long," she prophesied. "You'll get married."

"Why should I get married?"

"Because you're the marrying kind. You're the sort of girl who needs a husband."

"That's what people said to you after Maurice died."

"You're not me, darling. I'll give you three years as a career girl. Not a moment longer."

But Phyllis, for once, was wrong. Because it was nine years before Laura set eyes on Alec Haverstock, and another six—by which time Laura was thirty-three—before she married him.

"Here we are. . . ." The tinkle of ice against glass, the tap of high heels. Laura opened her eyes, saw Phyllis beside her, setting down the tray on a low coffee table. "Were you asleep?"

"No. Just thinking. Remembering, I suppose."

Phyllis lowered herself into the other sofa. She did not lean back because to relax in any way was totally foreign to her character. She perched, looking as though at any moment she might spring to her feet and dart away on some vital errand.

"Tell me all. What have you been doing? Shopping, I hope."

She poured a tall tumbler of lemonade and handed it to Laura. The glass was frosty with cold and agony to hold. Laura took a sip and then put the glass on the floor beside her.

"No, not shopping. I've been to see Doctor Hickley." Phyllis cocked her head, her face at once assuming an expression of alert interest, her eyebrow raised, her eyes wide. "No," said Laura, "I'm not having a baby."

"Why did you go and see her, then?"

"Same old trouble."

"Oh, *darling.*" There wasn't any need to say more. They gazed at each other dolefully. From the garden where she had been having a little necessary visit, Lucy appeared, through the open windows. Her claws made a scratching sound on the parquet as she crossed the floor and leaped lightly up into Laura's lap, where she curled herself into a comfortable ball and proceeded to go to sleep.

"When did this happen?"

"Oh, it's been going on for a bit, but I've been putting off going to see Dr. Hickley because I didn't want to think about it. You know, if you don't take any notice and don't look, perhaps it will go away."

"That was very silly of you."

"That's what she said. It didn't make any difference. I've got to go into the hospital again."

"When?"

"As soon as possible. Maybe a couple of days."

"But darling, you're going to Scotland."

"Doctor Hickley says I can't go."

"I can't *bear* it for you." Phyllis' voice sank to match the total despair of the situation. "You've been looking forward to it so much, your first holiday in Scotland with Alec . . . and what's he going to do? He isn't going to want to go without you."

"That's really why I came to see you. To ask you a favor. Would you mind?"

"I don't know yet what the favor is."

"Well, can I come and stay with you when I come out of hospital? If Alec knows I'm here with you, he'll go to Glenshandra with the others. It means so much to him. And everything's been planned for months. He's booked the hotel rooms and rented a stretch of the river for fishing. To say nothing of the Boulderstones and the Ansteys."

"When would that be?"

"Next week. I'll be in the hospital for a couple of days and I don't need nursing or anything. . . ."

"Darling, it's too *awful,* but I'm going away."

"You're . . ." It was unthinkable. Laura stared at Phyllis and hoped that she was not going to burst into tears. "You're . . . not going to be here?"

"I'm going to Florence for a month. With Laurance Haddon and the Birleys. We only arranged it last week. Oh, if you're desperate. I *could* put if off."

"Of course you mustn't put it off."

"What about Alec's brother and his wife? The brother who lives in Devon. Couldn't they take care of you?"

"Go to Chagwell, you mean?"

"You don't sound very enthusiastic. I thought you liked them when you stayed with them at Easter."

"I did like them. They're perfectly sweet. But they've got five children, and it's holiday time, and Janey will have quite enough to do without me arriving, all pale and wan, and expecting breakfast in bed. Besides, I know how one feels after these operations. Absolutely drained. I think it's something to do with the anaesthetic. And the noise at Chagwell is never below about a million decibels. I suppose it's inevitable with five children around the place."

Phyllis saw her point, abandoned the idea of Chagwell, and sought for other solutions.

"There's always Mrs. Abney."

"Alec would never leave me with Mrs. Abney. She's getting on now, and she can't cope with the stairs."

"Would Doctor Hickley consider postponing the operation?"

"No. I asked her, and she said no." Laura sighed. "It's one of those occasions, Phyllis, that I long to be part of some enormous family. To have brothers and sisters and cousins and grandparents and a mother and a father . . ."

Phyllis said, "Oh, *darling,*" and Laura was instantly repentant.

"That was a silly thing to say. I'm sorry."

"Perhaps," said Phyllis, "if you got a nurse to look after you, then she and Mrs. Abney could cope between them. . . ."

"Or I could just stay in hospital?"

"That's a ridiculous suggestion. In fact this whole conversation is ridiculous. I don't think Alec will want to go to Scotland and leave you behind. After all, you're practically still on your honeymoon!"

"We've been married for nine months."

"Why doesn't he call the whole thing off and take you to Madeira when you're better?"

"He can't. He can't just take holidays when he wants. He's too horribly important. And Glenshandra is . . . a sort of tradition. He's been going there forever, every July, with the Ansteys and the Boulderstones. He looks forward to it for the whole year. Nothing ever changes. He's told me that, and that's what he loves about it. The same hotel, the river, the same ghillie, the same friends. It's Alec's safety valve, his breath of fresh air, the one thing that keeps him going, slaving away in the City for the rest of the year."

"You know he loves what you call slaving away. He loves being busy and successful, and chairman of this and that."

"And he can't let the others down at the last moment. If he doesn't go, they'll think it's my fault, and my stock will go down to subzero, if I spoil it for them."

"I don't think," said Phyllis, "that your stock with the Ansteys and the Boulderstones matters all that much. You have only to think about Alec."

"That's just it. I feel I'm letting him down."

"Oh, don't be ridiculous. You can't help it if your wretched insides suddenly go mad. And you were looking forward to going to Scotland just as much as he was. Or weren't you?"

"Oh, Phyllis, I don't know. If it was just Alec I was going with, it would be so different. When we're together, just the two of us, I can cope. We can be happy. I can make him laugh. It's like being with the other half of myself. But when the others are there too, I feel as though I'd strayed by mistake into some club or other and I know that however hard I try, I can never be a member."

"Do you want to?"

"I don't know. It's just that they all know one another so well . . . for years and years, and for most of the time Alec was married to Erica. Daphne was Erica's best friend, she's Gabriel's godmother. Erica and Alec had this house called Deepbrook down in the New Forest, and they all used to go there for weekends. Everything they've ever done, everything they remember together, goes back fifteen years or more."

Phyllis sighed. "It is fairly daunting. Other people's memories are hard to take, I know. But you must have realized all this when you married Alec."

"I didn't think about anything like that. I only knew that I wanted to marry him. I didn't want to think about Erica and I didn't want to think about Gabriel. I simply pretended that they didn't exist, which was quite easy, considering that they were both safely miles away, living in America."

"You wouldn't want Alec to drop all his old friends. Old friends are part of a man. Part of the person that he is. It can't always be easy for them either. You have to see it their way."

"No, I don't suppose it is."

"Do they mention Erica and Gabriel?"

"Sometimes. But then there's an ugly silence, and somebody quickly starts another conversation."

"Perhaps you should bring up the subject by yourself."

"Phyllis, how can I bring the subject up? How can I chat away about the glamorous Erica, who left Alec for another man? How can I talk about Gabriel, when Alec hasn't set eyes on her since the split-up?"

"Does she write to him?"

"No, but he writes to her. From the office. Once, his secretary forgot to put the letter in the post, and he brought it home with him. I saw the address, typewritten. I guessed then that he writes to her every week. But he doesn't ever seem to get one back. There are no photographs of Erica in the house, but there's one of Gabriel on his dressing table and a drawing she did for him when she was about five. It's in a silver frame, from Asprey's. I think if the house caught fire and he had to salvage one precious possession from the flames, that picture would be it."

"What he needs is another child," said Phyllis firmly.

"I know. But I may never have one."

"Of course you will."

"No." Laura turned her head on the blue silk cushion and looked at Phyllis. "I may not. After all, I'm nearly thirty-four."

"That's nothing."

"And if this business with my insides blows up again, then Doctor Hickley says I'll have to have a hysterectomy."

"Laura, don't think about it."

"I do want a baby. I really do want one."

"It will be all right. This time, everything will be all right. Don't be depressed. Think positively. And as for the Ansteys and the Boulder-stones, they'll understand. They're perfectly nice, ordinary people. I thought they were all charming when I met them at that lovely dinner party you gave for me."

Laura's smile was wry. "Daphne, too?"

"Of course, Daphne too," said Phyllis stoutly. "I know she spent the evening flirting with Alec, but some women can't help behaving that way. Even if they are old enough to know better. You *surely* don't think there was ever anything between them?"

"Sometimes, when I'm feeling blue, I wonder. . . . After Erica left him, Alec was on his own for five years."

"You must be mad. Can you see a man of Alec's integrity having an affair with his best friend's wife? I can't. You're underestimating yourself, Laura. And, which is infinitely more dangerous, you're underestimating Alec."

Laura put her head back on the sofa cushion and closed her eyes. It was cooler now, but Lucy's weight lay like a hot-water bottle upon her lap. She said, "What shall I do?"

"Go home," said Phyllis. "Have a shower and put on the prettiest garment you own, and when Alec comes home, give him an iced martini and talk to him. And if he wants to give up his holiday and stay with you, then let him."

"But I want him to go. I really want him to go."

"Then tell him so. And tell him that if the worst comes to the worst, I'll cancel Florence, and you can come and stay with me."

"Oh, Phyllis . . ."

"But I'm certain he'll come up with some brilliant brain wave, and all this heart-searching will have been for nothing, so don't let's waste time talking any more about it." She glanced at her watch. "And now it's nearly four. What would you say to a delicious cup of China tea?"

2

DEEPBROOK

ALEC HAVERSTOCK, EX-WINCHESTER AND CAMBRIDGE, investment analyst, manager of the Forbright Northern Investment Trust, and a director of the Merchant Bank, Sandberg Harpers, hailed—and some people found this surprising—from the heart of the West Country.

He was born at Chagwell, the second son of a family that for three generations had farmed a thousand acres or so of land that lay on the western slopes of Dartmoor. The farmhouse was built of stone, long and low, with large rooms made to accommodate large families. Solid and comforting, it faced southwest, over sloping green pastures where the dairy herds of Guernsey grazed, and down to lush, arable fields and the reedy margins of the little river Chag. Farther still lay the horizon of the English Channel, often veiled in a curtain of mist and rain, but on clear days blue as silk in the sunshine.

The Haverstocks were a prolific family, sprouting various branches all over Devon and Cornwall. Some of these offshoots veered toward the professions and produced a string of lawyers, doctors, and accountants, but on the whole the male members of the clan stayed stubbornly close to the land: building up pedigree herds, raising sheep and ponies on the moor, fishing in the summer, and hunting during the winter months with the local foxhounds. There was usually a youthful Haverstock riding in the yearly Hunt Steeplechase, and broken collarbones were treated as lightly as the common cold.

With the inheritance of land passing from the father to the eldest boy, younger sons were forced to look elsewhere for their livelihood and, following the tradition of Devon men, usually went to sea. Just as there had always been Haverstocks in the farming community of the country, the Navy Lists, for a hundred years or more, were never without their quota of Haverstocks, ranging from junior midshipmen to full captains, and sometimes even an admiral or two.

Alec's uncle Gerald had followed this tradition and joined the Royal Navy. With Chagwell entailed to his older brother Brian, Alec was expected to follow the same course. But he was born beneath a different star than his bluff, seagoing forebears, and it led him in a totally different direction. It became very clear after his first term at the local preparation school, that although tough and resourceful, he was also very bright. With the encouragement of the headmaster of this small school, Alec sat for and won a scholarship to Winchester. From Winchester he went to Cambridge, where he rowed, played rugger, and read economics, to emerge at the end of his last year with an honors degree. Before he had even left Cambridge, he had been spotted by a talent scout from Sandberg Harpers and was offered a job with them, in the City of London.

Alec was twenty-two. He bought himself two dark City suits, a furled umbrella, and a briefcase and flung himself into this exciting new world with the reckless enthusiasm of some previous Haverstock riding his hunter straight for a five-barred gate. He was installed in the department of the bank that specialized in investment analysis, and it was at this time that he first met Tom Boulderstone. Tom had already been with Sandberg Harpers for six months, but the two young men had much in common, and when Tom asked Alec to move into his flat with him, Alec accepted with alacrity.

It was a good time. Although they were both kept with their noses firmly pressed to the Harper Sandberg grindstone, there was still plenty of opportunity for the sort of irresponsible enjoyment that only occurs once in most people's lifetime. The little flat bulged with a constant stream of bright young things. Impromptu parties grew out of nothing, with spaghetti boiling up in a saucepan and crates of lager piled on the draining board. Alec bought his first car, and on weekends he and Tom would rustle up a couple of girls and go down to the country to other people's houses, or summer cricket matches, or winter shoots.

It was Alec who introduced Daphne to Tom. Alec had been at Cambridge with Daphne's brother and was asked to be a good fellow and keep his eye on this innocent creature who had just come to work in

London. Without much enthusiasm Alec did as he had been asked and was delighted to discover that she was as pretty as paint and marvelously entertaining. He took her out once or twice on his own and then, one Sunday evening, took her back to the flat, where she made him and Tom the worst scrambled eggs he had ever tasted.

Despite this disaster, and somewhat to Alec's surprize, Tom instantly fell in love with Daphne. For a long time she resisted his blandishments and continued to play her own extensive field, but Tom was a dogged fellow and regularly begged her to marry him, only to be fobbed off yet again with endless excuses and procrastinations. His moods, consequently, varied from euphoric elation to the deepest gloom, but, just as he finally put Daphne out of his life forever, she, perhaps sensing this, suddenly did a *volte-face,* threw over all the other young men, and told Tom that she would marry him after all. Alec was their best man, and Daphne duly moved into Tom's flat, as a very young and very inexperienced Mrs. Boulderstone.

It was necessary for Alec to move out, and it was at this early stage in his career that he bought the house in Islington. Nobody else that he knew lived in Islington, but when he first saw it, it seemed to him larger and more attractive than any of the poky mews and cottages that belonged to his friends. It had the added inducement of costing a great deal less than property in other parts of London. And it was only minutes from the City.

The bank helped him with his mortgage and he moved in. The house was tall and thin, but it had a good basement, which he did not really need, so he put an advertisement in the local paper, which was answered by Mrs. Abney. She was a widowed lady in early middle age. Her husband had been a builder; she had no children. Only Dicky, her canary. She would have to bring Dicky with her. Alec said that he had no objection to canaries, and it was agreed that Mrs. Abney should move in. It was an arrangement to their mutual satisfaction, for now Mrs. Abney had a home and Alec a live-in caretaker and someone to iron his shirts.

When Alec had been with Sandberg Harpers for five years, he was transferred to Hong Kong.

Tom was staying in London, and Daphne was wildly jealous. "I can't think why you're going and Tom isn't."

"He's brighter than I am," said the good-natured Tom.

"He's nothing of the sort. He's just bigger and better looking."

"Now, that's enough of that."

Daphne giggled. She loved it when Tom became masterful. "Anyway, Alec darling, you'll have the most wonderful time and I'm going to give you the address of my best girlfriend, because she's out there just now, staying with her brother."

"Does he work in Hong Kong?"

"Probably Chinese," said Tom.

"Oh, don't be silly."

"Mr. Hoo Flung Dung."

"You know perfectly well that Erica's brother isn't Chinese; he's a captain in the Queen's Loyals."

"Erica," said Alec.

"Yes. Erica Douglas. She's frightfully glamorous and good at games and everything."

"Hearty," murmured Tom, who was in a maddening mood.

"Oh, all right, *hearty,* if you want to spoil everything." She turned back to Alec. "She isn't hearty; she's just the most marvelous person, frightfully attractive."

Alec said that he was sure that she was. A week later he flew to Hong Kong, and once he had settled himself in, he went in search of Erica. He found her, living with friends, in a beautiful house up on the Peak. A Chinese houseboy answered the door and led him through the house and out onto the shady terrace. Below was a sunbaked garden and a blue, kidney-shaped swimming pool. Missy Ellica was swimming, the houseboy told him with a gentle gesture of his hand, and Alec thanked him and set off down the steps. There were six or seven people around the pool. As he approached, an older man observed him and got out of his long chair to come and meet him. Alec introduced himself and explained the reason for his call, and the man smiled and turned toward the swimming pool.

A girl, alone, was swimming there, moving up and down its length with a smooth, expert crawl.

"Erica!" She lolled onto her back, sleek as a seal, her black hair clinging to her head. "Someone to see you!" She swam to the side of the pool, pulled herself effortlessly out of the water, and came to meet him. She was very beautiful. Tall, long-legged, copper brown, her face and body running with droplets of water.

"Hello." She smiled and her smile was wide and open, her teeth even and shining white. "You're Alec Haverstock. Daphne wrote and told me. I got a letter yesterday. Come and have a drink."

He could scarcely believe his good fortune. He asked her out for dinner that very evening, and after that they were seldom apart. After murky London, Hong Kong was a positive fairground of pleasures to be enjoyed: a crowded, teeming fairground, to be sure, where poverty and riches rubbed shoulders on every corner; a world of contrasts that both shocked and delighted; a world of heat and sunshine and blue skies.

There was, all at once, so much to do. Together they swam and played tennis, went riding in the early mornings, sailed her brother's little dinghy on the breezy blue waters of Repulse Bay. At night they were inundated with all the glitter and glamor of Hong Kong's considerable social life. There were dinner parties in establishments more luxurious than he had ever dreamed existed in this day and age. Cocktail parties on board visiting cruisers; regimental occasions—the Queen's Birthday and Beating Retreat; naval occasions. Life for young people on the brink of falling in love seemed to have no limit to the good things it had to offer, and it finally sank through to Alec that the best thing of all was Erica herself. One evening, as he drove her home after a party, he asked her to marry him, and she gave a typical shout of pure pleasure and flung her arms around his neck, very nearly causing him to run the car off the road.

The next day they went shopping and bought her the biggest star sapphire engagement ring that he could afford. Her brother gave a party for them in the Mess, and there was more champagne drunk that evening than Alec had ever seen consumed in such a relatively short time.

They were married in the cathedral in Hong Kong by the bishop. Erica's parents flew out from England for the ceremony, and Erica wore a dress of fine white cotton lawn, encrusted with white embroidery. They spent their honeymoon in Singapore and then returned to Hong Kong.

And so the first year of their married life was passed in the Far East, but the idyll finally had to end. Alec's term of duty was over, and he was recalled to London. They returned in November, a gloomy enough month at the best of times, and when they came to the house in Islington, he picked her up and carried her over the doorstep, which meant, at least, that she didn't get her feet wet, because it was pouring with rain at the time.

Erica didn't think much of the house. Seen through her eyes, Alec had to admit that the décor was fairly uninspired, and he told her to do what she wanted to do with it, and he would foot the bill. This delightful ploy kept her happy and busy for some months, and by the time the house had been reconstructed, redecorated, and refurnished to Erica's exacting standards, Gabriel was born.

Holding his daughter for the first time was one of the most astonishing experiences in Alec's life. Nothing had prepared him for the humbleness, the tenderness, the pride he experienced as he pushed aside the baby's shawl and looked for the first time into her small, downy face. He saw the brilliant blue of her open eyes, the high forehead, the crest of spiky, silky, black hair.

"She's yellow," said Erica. "She looks like a Chinese."

"She isn't really yellow."

Some months after Gabriel's birth he was sent east again, this time to Japan. But now everything was different, and he was almost ashamed of his reluctance to leave his little daughter, even for three months. He admitted this to nobody, not even Erica.

Least of all Erica. Because Erica was not a natural mother. She had always been more interested in horses than children and had shown a sad lack of enthusiasm when she had realized that she was pregnant. The physical manifestations of child-bearing revolted her . . . she hated her swollen breasts, her ballooning abdomen. The long wait bored her, and even the interest of doing up the old house could not make up for morning sickness, lassitude, and occasional fatigue.

And now, she hated Alec going back to the Far East without her. She resented his going on his own, while she stayed behind, moldering in London, just because of Gabriel.

"You can't blame Gabriel. Even if we didn't have Gabriel, you couldn't come with me because it's not that sort of a trip."

"And what am I supposed to do with myself? While you're galli-vanting around with the geisha girls?"

"You could go and stay with your mother."

"I don't want to go and stay with my mother. She fusses over Gabriel until I could scream."

"Well, I tell you what . . ." She was lying on their bed during this particular exchange, and now he sat beside her and laid his hand on the sulky curve of her hip. "Tom Boulderstone's been on to me about an idea he's had. He and Daphne want to go to Scotland in July . . . for the fishing. The Anstey's are going as well, and they thought that we might go too and make up a party."

After a bit, "Whereabouts in Scotland?" Erica asked. She still sounded sulky, but he knew that he had caught her attention.

"Sutherland. It's called Glenshandra. There's a very special hotel, with marvelous food, and you wouldn't have to do anything but enjoy yourself."

"I know. Daphne told me about it. She and Tom went last year."

"You'd like fishing."

"What about Gabriel?"

"Perhaps your mother could have her? What do you think?"

Erica turned over onto her back and pushed her hair out of her eyes and gazed at her husband. She began to smile. She said, "I'd rather go to Japan."

He leaned over and kissed her open, smiling mouth. "Next best thing."

"All right. Next best thing."

And so the pattern of their lives evolved, and as the years slipped by, Alec's career broadened and became more involved and more responsi-ble as he climbed his own particular ladder of success. Gabriel was four. Then she was five and starting school. When Alec had time to stop and stand and look at his family life, he supposed that they were as happy as any of his friends. There were ups and downs, of course, but these were only to be expected, and always—like a glittering prize waiting to be grasped at the end of a long run—there was the holiday in Scotland, which had now become an annual event. Even Erica loved this and looked forward to it as much as Alec. A natural athlete, with an athlete's sense of timing and quick observant eye, she had taken to fly-fishing like a duck to water. Her first salmon had reduced her to a mixture of laughter and tears, and her childlike delight and excitement had almost caused Alec to fall in love with her all over again.

They were happy in Scotland, the carefree days as refreshing as a gust of clean wind blown through a stuffy house, dispersing resentments, clearing the air.

When Gabriel was old enough, they started taking her with them.

"She'll be a nuisance," said Erica, but she wasn't a nuisance, because she wasn't that sort of a child. She was charming, and it was at Glenshandra that Alec really got to know his little daughter—to talk to her, to listen to her, or simply to enjoy her companionable silence as she sat on the bank of the river and watched him casting over the brown, peaty water.

But even Glenshandra was not enough, and Erica was restless. She still resented Alec's overseas commitments, his constantly leaving her for glamorous foreign parts. Every time he went, there was a row, and he would fly off, miserable, with the sound of her angry, unforgiving words ringing in his ears. Now, she decided that she hated their house. Initially she had enthused over it, but now it was too small. She was bored with it. Bored with London. He wondered if she was going to tell him that she was bored with him, too.

He could be stubborn. At the end of a long, tiring day, faced with a moody wife, he could be more stubborn than usual. He told her that he had no intention of relinquishing his convenient house for something larger out at the smart end of London, which would cost an arm and a leg and involved even more traveling.

Erica lost her temper. "You never think about anybody but yourself. You don't have to spend your days in this beastly house, cooped up, surrounded by Islington pavements. What about Tom and Daphne? They've bought a house on Campden Hill."

It was at this point, listening to her, that Alec first came to realize that there was a chance, a possibility, that one day his marriage to Erica would end up on the rocks. She accused him of thinking about nobody but himself, and although this was not strictly true, what *was* true was that most of his waking hours were spent totally absorbed in his work, with no thought for anything else. But for Erica it was different. Domesticity and motherhood were not enough for her, and although their evenings were packed with social engagements—it seemed to Alec that they were scarcely ever in for dinner—it was natural that Erica's boundless energy yearned for more.

When she had run out of things to complain about and had fallen silent, he asked her what she really wanted.

She told him. "I want space. A bigger garden, space for Gabriel. That's what I want. Space and freedom. Trees. Somewhere to ride. Do you know, I haven't ridden since we were in Hong Kong. And before that I rode every single day of my life. I want somewhere to be when you're abroad all the time. I want to be able to have people to stay. I want . . ."

What she wanted, of course, was a house in the country.

Alec bought her one. In the New Forest. Erica found it, after three months of frantic searching, and Alec took a deep breath and wrote the enormous check demanded of him.

It was a compromise, of course, but he had recognized the danger signals of her desperation and was now in a financial position where he was able to shoulder the added expense of such a luxury. But was it such a luxury? It would mean country weekends and holidays for Gabriel, and property, with looming inflation, was always a good investment.

The house was called Deepbrook. Early Victorian, soundly built, with many rooms, a conservatory, an acre of garden, stabling for four horses, and three acres of paddock. The face of the house was smothered in an enormous, mauve-blossomed wisteria, and there was a big lawn with a cedar tree in the middle and various rather charming, old-fashioned, overgrown rosebushes.

Erica was happy at last. She furnished the house, found a gardener, and acquired for herself a couple of horses and a little pony for Gabriel. Gabriel was now seven and she did not much like the pony, preferring to play for hours on the monkey swing Alec had fixed up in the cedar tree.

Although they seemed to get on well enough, Gabriel and her mother never had very much in common. When she was eight, Erica began to make noises about sending Gabriel to boarding school. Alec was appalled. He did not approve of sending small boys to boarding school at such a tender age, let alone little girls. This argument continued for some time, without coming to any conclusion, but was ended abruptly by Alec having to go to New York for three months.

This time there were no recriminations, no complaints. Erica was schooling a young horse for showing, and she saw him off with scarcely a backward glance, having no thoughts in her head for anything but the job in hand. At least Alec assumed that she had no other thoughts, but when he returned from New York, he was told that she had found the perfect little boarding school for Gabriel, had put her name down, and the child would start there the following term.

It was a Sunday. He had flown into Heathrow that morning and driven straight down to Deepbrook. Erica presented him with her *fait accompli* in the drawing room, while he was pouring her a drink, and it was there, facing each other like antagonists across the hearthrug, that they had their most resounding row.

"You had no business . . ."

"I told you I was going to do it."

"I told you that you weren't to. I won't have Gabriel being packed off to some boarding school. . . ."

"I'm not packing her off. I'm sending her. For her own good . . ."

"Who are you to decide what's good for her?"

"I know what isn't good for her, and that is staying at the crummy little day school in London. She's an intelligent child—"

"She's only ten."

"And she's an only child. She needs companionship."

"You could give her that if you weren't too busy with your bloody horses. . . ."

"That's a lie . . . and why shouldn't I have my horses? God knows I've given up enough of my time taking care of Gabriel. . . . It's not as though I've ever had any help from you . . . you're away half the time." She began to pace up and down the room. "And I've tried to interest her in the things I do . . . heaven knows I've tried. I bought her that little pony, but she's more interested in watching television or reading books. How is she ever going to make friends with anybody if she never does anything but that?"

"I don't want her to go to boarding school. . . ."

"Oh, for heaven's sake stop being so selfish. . . ."

"I'm thinking about her. Don't you understand that? I'm thinking about *Gabriel*. . . ."

He was cold with rage, he could feel his anger like a physical thing, knotted hard against his chest. Erica said nothing. Turning at the far end of the room, she stopped, suddenly still, staring not at Alec but beyond him. Her expression did not change; pale and cold she stood there, her hands clenched, taut and bloodless around the scarlet wool of her sweater.

In the silence that followed, Alec laid down his glass and slowly turned. Behind him, in the open doorway, stood Gabriel. She wore old jeans and a sweat shirt with Snoopy on the front. Her feet were bare, her long dark hair like a curtain of silk falling down her shoulders.

For a long moment he looked into her eyes, and then her gaze fell and she stood there, fiddling with the door handle, waiting to be told something. Waiting to be told anything.

He took a deep breath. He said, "What's wrong?"

"Nothing." She shrugged, her thin shoulders hunched. "I just heard you."

"I'm sorry."

Erica said, "I've just told Daddy about the school, Gabriel. He doesn't want you to go, because he thinks you're too young."

"How do you feel about it?" Alec asked gently.

Gabriel went on fiddling with the doorknob.

"I don't mind," she said at last.

He knew that she would say anything to stop them quarrelling; and it occurred to him then, as anger died and sadness took its place, that he had two alternatives. Either he had to make an issue of the situation, which would inevitably involve Gabriel in the subsequent recriminations, or else he had to let the whole thing ride and go quietly along with it. Whatever he decided he knew that Gabriel was going to be the loser.

Later, after he had had a bath and changed, he went along to Gabriel's room to say good night to her. She was in her nightdress and bedroom slippers, kneeling in the twilight gloom and watching television. He sat on the bed and watched her face, her profile lifted to the screen, her features illuminated by its light. At ten she was neither as pretty as she had been or as beautiful as she would become, but to Alec she seemed so precious, so vulnerable, that his heart turned over at the thought of what might lie ahead for her.

After the program ended, she got up and switched off the television, then turned on her bedside light and went to draw the curtains. She was an extremely orderly child. When she had done this, he reached out and took her by the arm and drew her gently toward him, holding her between his knees. He kissed her. He said, "The quarrel's over. I'm sorry. We had no right to make so much noise. I hope you aren't upset."

She laid her head against his shoulder. He took his hand and touched her hair.

She said, "Most people go to boarding school sooner or later."

"Will you mind?"

"Will you come and see me?"

"Of course. Whenever I'm allowed. And there'll be half-terms and things. And holidays."

"Mummy took me to see the school."

"What did you think of it?"

"It smelled of polish. But the headmistress had a kind face. And she's quite young. And she doesn't mind if you take teddies and things."

"Look—if you really *don't* want to go . . ."

She drew away from him and shrugged. "I don't mind," she said again.

It was all he could do. He kissed her and left her and went downstairs.

So once again Erica had won, and three weeks later, Gabriel, wearing a gray school uniform and clutching her teddy, entered her new school. Leaving her was like leaving part of himself, and it took some time to get used to returning home to an empty house.

For now the pattern of life was totally changed. Freed from the responsibility of Gabriel, Erica found endless excuses not to come to London, but to stay on her own in the country. There was a new horse to be schooled, some coming event to train for, a Pony Club gymkhana to organize. After a little, it seemed to Alec that they were never together. Sometimes, if there was a party on in London, or she needed to go to the hairdresser or buy some new clothes, she would drive up to town in the middle of the week, and he would get back to the house in Islington to find it full of the fresh flowers she had brought with her from Deepbrook, and smelling of her scent. He would see her fur coat tossed over the banister, hear her voice talking to some girlfriend—probably Daphne —over the telephone.

"Just for a day or two. Are you going to the Ramseys' this evening? Well, let's lunch tomorrow. The Caprice? All right. About one o'clock. I'll book a table."

When she was not there, Mrs. Abney agreed to keep an eye on Alec. Heavy-footed she would tread up from the basement and produce a shepherd's pie or a stew from the oven. And in the evenings he often sat alone, with a whiskey and soda at hand, watching television or reading the paper.

If only for Gabriel's sake, however, it was important to keep up the façade of a sound and lasting marriage. Perhaps the charade convinced no person but himself, but if Alec was in London—for his overseas commitments now were more pressing than ever—he would dutifully drive himself down to Deepbrook on Friday evenings.

But here again things were no longer the same, for lately Erica had taken to filling the house with weekend guests. It was as though she were setting up some sort of a defense against Alec, as though she were reluctant even to spend a few hours alone with him. No sooner had he climbed tiredly out of his car than, it seemed, he was welcoming new arrivals, carrying suitcases, pouring drinks, opening wine. In the old days he had enjoyed the therapy of a little amateur gardening: trimming a hedge or mowing the lawn. There had been time to potter, plant bulbs or prune the roses, saw up a few logs, mend a sagging gate.

But now there were so many people to be taken care of that he never had a moment to himself, and he was too conscientious and courteous a host ever to lose his patience with these demanding hordes and tell them to drive themselves to the Point-to-Point; to find their own way to the National Trust Garden; to fetch their own garden chairs and pour their own bloody drinks.

One Friday evening at the beginning of September, in that blistering summer of 1976, Alec climbed into his car, slammed the door, and set off for Deepbrook. He loved London, it was his home, and like Samuel Pepys, he never tired of it. But for once he felt nothing but relief at the prospect of getting away from the city. The relentless heat, the drought, the dust, and the dirt had become enemies. The parks, usually so green, wilted, dry as deserts. Trodden grass lay dead and brown, and here and there sprouted sinister, unknown weeds, never seen before. The very air was stale and used, doors stood open to the breezeless evening, and the sinking sun, orange in the hazy sky, promised nothing but another scorcher the next day.

Driving, he deliberately put the problems of the week away into the back of his mind. His responsibilities were now so great that he had a long time ago schooled himself to do this, and had discovered that the discipline was a worthwhile one, for when he returned to the office on Monday morning his brain was clear and refreshed, and very often his subconscious mind was ready and waiting to present him with a solution or an idea that previously had eluded him.

Instead, heading south through the sweltering suburbs, he thought about the two days that lay ahead. He did not dread this particular weekend. On the contrary, he was actually looking forward to it. For once, there would not be a houseful of strangers. They had returned, only a month previously, from Glenshandra, and Erica had planned the weekend then, inviting the Ansteys and the Boulderstones to stay.

"We'll have a lovely time," she told them, "talking about Glenshandra and exchanging fishing stories."

As well, Gabriel was home. She was thirteen now. This summer, Alec had bought her a little trout rod of her own, and she had had a happy time with Jamie Rudd, the ghillie, learning to use this new toy. The school about which Alec had had such heart-searching reservations had proved, maddeningly enough, to be a success. Erica was not a fool and had gone to some trouble to find an establishment that would match up to Gabriel's needs, and after a term or so of homesickness, Gabriel seemed to have shaken down quite happily and made friends for herself. Having the Boulderstones and the Anstey's was like having family to stay —they had been so often, they knew how to take care of themselves. Alec would maybe take Gabriel off by himself one afternoon. Perhaps they would go swimming. The very idea filled him with pleasure. The traffic was thinning. He had reached the motorway and was able to pick up speed, to change up into overdrive. The powerful car surged forward.

In the New Forest it was just as hot, but now it was country heat. Deepbrook drowsed. The shadow of the cedar tree lay black across the lawn, and full-blown roses scented the cooling evening air. The awning was up over the terrace, shading a group of garden chairs, and indoors Erica, for coolness, had drawn all the curtains. This gave the house a blank look, as though the windows were the eyes of a sightless man.

He parked the car beneath the dappled shade of a young silver birch and got out, glad to stretch his legs and get the sweaty cramp out of his shoulders. As he stood there, he heard Gabriel calling him. "Daddy!" and saw her coming up the lawn toward him. She wore only the skimpiest of bikinis and an old pair of rubber sandals, and she had tied her hair up in a bundle on the top of her head. For some reason this made her look very grown up. In her hand she carried a bunch of yellow flowers.

"Look," she said, holding them out to show him. "Kingcups."

"Where did you find those?"

"Down by the brook. Mummy said she wanted some flowers for her dinner table and everything in the garden's wilting away, because we're not allowed to water *anything*. Every now and then of course we cheat, and do, but there's not much to pick. How are you?" She reached up, and he stooped down and they kissed. "Isn't it boiling? Isn't it absolutely boiling?"

He agreed that it was boiling. He opened the car door and pulled his suitcase off the back seat, and together they walked slowly across the gravel and into the house.

"Where's Mummy?" he asked, following her into the kitchen.

"She's up at the stables, I think." She filled a mug with water and put the kingcups into it. Alec opened the fridge and poured himself a glass of fresh orange juice. "She asked me to lay the table for her because she said she wouldn't have time. The others haven't come yet. I mean the Boulderstones and the Ansteys. Come and see the dinner table and tell me if you think it's all right. Mummy's so fussy, she's bound to say I've forgotten something."

The dining room, with the curtains drawn, was dim and shadowed, smelling vaguely of other dinner parties, cigars, wine. Gabriel went to draw back the curtains. "It's cooler now, Mummy won't mind." Yellow sunlight poured through the windows in dust-moted shafts, glancing off polished silver, crystal, and glass. He looked at the table and said he thought it looked perfect, which it did. Gabriel had used white linen mats and pale yellow napkins. The candles, in their ornate silver candlesticks, were yellow as well. "That's why I thought of the kingcups, to go with everything else. . . . I thought if I put them in a silver bowl they'd look all right. . . . Mummy's so *good* at doing flowers. . . ." She looked at him. "What's wrong?"

Alec frowned. "You've laid for eight. I thought there were only six of us."

"Seven with me. I'm coming down for dinner. And a man called Strickland Whiteside."

"Strickland Whiteside?" He almost laughed at the absurdity of the name. "Who on earth is . . . Strickland Whiteside?" But even as he repeated himself, a chord of familiarity rang like an echo in the back of his mind somewhere. He had heard that man's name before.

"Oh, Daddy, he's Mummy's new chum, and he's terribly famous. He's a frightfully rich American from Virginia and he rides."

Memory struck. Alec clicked his fingers. "That's it. I knew I'd heard of him. There was an article in *The Field* about him and his horses. There's one horse in particular. A great beast the height of an elephant."

"That's right. He's called White Samba."

"What does he do when he isn't riding?"

"He doesn't do anything else. He doesn't go to an office or anything like that. He just rides. He's got an enormous house on the James River and acres of land—he showed me some photographs—and he wins show jumping events all over America, and now he's come over here to train for some of ours."

"He sounds fairly formidable."

Gabriel giggled. "You know Mummy's horsey friends. But actually he's quite nice . . . in a rather overwhelming sort of way."

"Is he staying?"

"Oh, no, he doesn't have to stay, because he's taken a house over at Tickleigh."

Alec was intrigued. "Where did Mummy meet him?"

"At the Alverton Horse Show, I think. I'm not quite sure. Look, have I got the right wineglasses? I always get in a muddle with sherry and port."

"No. Yes, it's fine. You've got it quite right." He began to smile. "Do we have to call him Strickland? If I have to call him Strickland, I don't think I'm going to be able to keep a straight face."

"Everybody calls him Strick."

"That's even worse."

"Oh, he's not so bad. And just think what fun Daphne Boulderstone will have making eyes at him. There's nothing she likes more than a new man. It'll make a lovely change from boring old George Anstey."

"How about boring old me?"

Gabriel put her arms around his waist and pressed her cheek against his chest.

"*Never* boring old you. Just super, gorgeous, kind you." She pulled away, responsible and busy. "Now I must go and do something about the kingcups."

He was in a cold bath when he heard Erica come upstairs and into their bedroom. He called her name, and she appeared in the open doorway, her arms crossed, a shoulder propped against the wall. She was looking very tanned, very hot, and rather tired. She had tied back her dark hair with a cotton handkerchief and wore old, dirty jeans, riding boots, and a shirt that had once belonged to him. He thought of these as her horse-fangling clothes.

He said, "Hi."

"Hello there. You're early. I wasn't expecting you so soon."

"I wanted to freshen up before the others get here."

"How was London?"

"Like an oven."

"It's been hot here too. We're short of water."

"I hear we have a new acquaintance coming for dinner tonight." She met his gaze and smiled. "Gabriel tell you?"

"He sounds interesting."

"I don't know if you'll find him particularly interesting, but I thought it would be friendly to ask him along this evening to meet you all."

"I'm glad you did. Perhaps I shall find that we have American friends in common, and we'll be able to gas about them. What are we eating?"

"Smoked salmon and then grouse."

"Very smart. White wine or red?"

"I think some bottles of both, don't you? Don't be too long, will you, Alec? I'd like to have a bath myself and it's too hot to hurry." And she turned and went back into the bedroom. He heard her opening the sliding mirrored doors of her wardrobe. Imagined her standing there, trying to decide what she would put on. Thoughtfully, he squeezed dry the sponge and reached for his towel.

Alec, with his guests and his wife already seated, moved around the table pouring the wine. The windows of the dining room were wide open. Outside, it was still light, and very warm. There was not the faintest breeze and the garden drowsed in the scented evening air. On the table the candle flames glowed palely, striking soft reflections on crystal and silver. The kingcups, brilliant butter yellow, seemed to shine with a light all their own.

He put the bottle of wine back on the sideboard and went to take his place at the head of the table.

". . . of course, you would probably think it was terribly boring after fishing in those wilderness rivers in the United States, but there is something very special about Glenshandra. We all adore it . . . we're like children there."

That was Daphne, in full cry, monopolizing all conversation.

Strickland, Strick—Alec couldn't decide which was worse—assumed a modest expression. "I'm not actually much of a fisherman myself."

"No, of course you aren't, how silly of me, you wouldn't have time."

"Why wouldn't he have time?" asked Tom.

"Well, darling, of course he wouldn't have time if he's in training for some world-shaking equestrian event."

"Equestrian." That was George. "Daphne, I never realized you knew such long words."

She pouted at him, and Alec was reminded of the young girl she no longer was.

"But it is the right word, isn't it?"

"Sure," said Strickland. "It's the right word."

"Oh, thank you. You are sweet to be on my side." She picked up her fork and speared a delicate sliver of rosy-pink smoked salmon.

Erica had placed her guests as she normally did when there were eight people present. Alec was in his normal chair, at the head of the table, but Erica had moved around to the side and relinquished her place to Strickland Whiteside, in his capacity as guest of honor, so that he and Alec faced each other down the length of the table. In fact, although they sat thus they didn't have a particularly good view of each other because the tall silver candelabra got in the way. When Erica was sitting there, Alec sometimes found this irritating, because if he wanted to say something to her, or to catch her eye, it involved some maneuvering, but this evening he decided that it was probably a good thing.

He wanted to enjoy his dinner without being conscious the whole time of Strickland Whiteside's disconcertingly pale blue eyes.

Daphne and Erica sat on either side of Strickland and Marjorie Anstey and Gabriel on either side of Alec. Tom and George faced each other across the middle of the table.

Strickland Whiteside also took up his fork. "Do you ride?" he asked Marjorie.

"Oh, heavens no. I never rode, even at school. I was always far too terrified."

"She doesn't know a horse's arse from its elbow," said George, and his wife said *"George"* in tones of extreme disapproval, and glanced toward Gabriel.

"Sorry, Gabriel, forgot you were there."

Gabriel looked embarrassed, but Erica put back her head and laughed, as much at George's discomfort as at his joke.

Watching her, Alec decided that the time spent pondering over her wardrobe had not been wasted. She wore a caftan of the palest blue Thai silk, with the earrings he had once given her for some long-forgotten birthday and gold bracelets on her slender brown wrists. She looked amazingly young this evening. Her face still beautiful, her jawline firm, her hair without a thread of gray. Of all of them, he decided, she had aged and changed the least. Because, although not old, not even middle-aged, they, who had been young together, no longer were.

He wondered what Strickland thought of them all. What was his impression of them, as they sat there, dressed up and festive, around the formal dinner table? They were Alec's oldest friends; he had known them for so long that their individual appearances he took totally for granted. But now he let his eyes move around the table deliberately observing each of his guests with the eyes of the stranger who sat in Erica's chair. Daphne, tiny and slender as ever, but with her blond hair now silvery white. George Anstey ponderous and red-faced, his shirt buttons straining over his considerable waistline. Marjorie, who of all of them seemed happy to mature into full solid middle age, without any tiresome backward glances over her ample shoulder.

And Tom. Tom Boulderstone. Affection filled Alec's heart for the man who had been his closest friend for so many years. But this was an objective appraisal, not a sentimental one. So what did Alec see? A man of forty-three, balding, bespectacled, pale, clever. A man who looked more like a priest than a banker. A man whose somber expression could gleam with hidden laughter. A man who, when called upon, could make an after dinner speech so witty that it would be quoted in the City for months to come.

Daphne ran out of words at last, and George Anstey took advantage of the subsequent lull to lean forward and ask Strickland what had decided him to come to this country.

"Well"—the American glanced around the table and grinned depreciatingly—"I seem to have done most everything I could in the States, and I felt there was real new challenge over here."

"It must have meant the most awful lot of organization," Marjorie remarked. She was interested in organization. She organized her local Meals on Wheels. "I mean, renting a house for yourself and getting your horses over . . . what do you do for grooms?"

"I flew them over as well, and a couple of stable lads."

"Are they black or white?" Daphne wanted to know.

Strickland grinned. "Both."

"And what about a housekeeper?" Marjorie persisted. "Don't say you flew a housekeeper over as well?"

"Yes, I did. There wasn't any point taking Tickleigh Manor if I didn't have some person to look after me."

Marjorie sat back with a sigh. "Well, I don't know, but it all sounds like pure heaven to me. I've only got a daily two mornings a week, and she's never even been in an airplane."

"For that you should be thankful," said Tom dryly. "Ours flew to Majorca for a holiday and married a waiter and never came back."

Everybody laughed, but Tom did not even smile. Alec wondered what Tom was making of Strickland Whiteside, but that pale and clever face gave nothing away.

The American had arrived after they were all gathered with their drinks, bathed and shaved and changed and scented and expectant. When they heard the sound of his car drawing up outside the house, Erica went to greet him, and bring him indoors. They returned together, and there was no reason to imagine they had embraced, but Erica brought with her, out of the fragrant evening, a nervous glitter, like a nimbus of light. Formally she introduced Strickland Whiteside to her husband and her friends. He did not seem in the least put out by being suddenly faced with a roomful of people he had never met before, and all of whom, obviously, knew one another very well. On the contrary, his manner was almost benign, satisfied, as though he knew that the boot was on the other foot, and it was he who must put them at their ease.

He had, Alec guessed, taken some trouble with his dress. He wore a maroon gabardine jacket, brass buttoned, smoothly tailored; a pale blue polo-necked sweater; and a pair of maroon and pale blue plaid slacks. His shoes were white. There was a thick gold watch on one sinewy wrist and a heavy gold signet ring on his left hand. He was a tall man, lean and muscled and obviously immensely strong, but it was hard to guess his age, for while his features were formidable, hawk-nosed, big-jawed, intensely brown with eyes as pale as sixpences, his hair was corn colored, thick as the hair of a boy, growing springily from his forehead in a deep wave.

"Glad to meet you," he said when Alec welcomed him and gripped his hand. It was like shaking hands with a steel spring. "Erica's spoken so much about you, and it's a real privilege to make your acquaintance at last."

He continued to be charming. He kissed Gabriel—"My little girl-friend," allowed himself to be given a martini, sat in the middle of the sofa with one long ankle hitched up onto a hard-muscled plaid knee. He began at once to ask about Glenshandra, as though knowing that this topic would naturally bring everybody into the conversation and so break the ice. Marjorie was disarmed by this, and Daphne could scarcely keep her eyes off him and for the first five minutes was rendered speechless. After that she scarcely drew breath.

"What's Tickleigh Manor House like? Didn't the Gerrards used to live there?"

"They still do," Erica said. They were eating grouse now, and Alec poured the red wine.

"Well, they can't live there if Strick's living there."

"No, they've gone up to London for a couple of months."

"Were they going away, or did Strickland chase them out?"

"I chased them out," said Strickland.

"He offered them money," Erica explained to Daphne. "You know that old-fashioned stuff you keep in your wallet."

"You mean he *bribed* them . . . !"

"Oh, *Daphne* . . ."

Erica was laughing at Daphne, but there was exasperation in her amusement. Alec sometimes wondered how the friendship of two such totally different women had lasted for so long. They had known each other since school days, and it was doubtful that there was a single secret they did not share, and yet, on analysis, they had nothing in common. It could be that this was the glue that cemented their friendship. Their interests had never overlapped, and so the relationship was not in danger from the destructive touch of jealousy.

Daphne was interested only in men. That was the way she had been made, that was the way she would be even if she lived to be ninety. She came to life only if there was a man in the room, and if she did not have some current admirer tucked up her sleeve, to take her out for little luncheons or to telephone her in the mornings after Tom had gone to work, then life had lost all meaning and she became snappish and despondent.

Tom knew about this and accepted it. Once, very late at night, he had talked to Alec. "I know she's a fool," he had said, "but she's a very sweet fool, and I wouldn't want to lose her."

Whereas Erica . . . Erica was not really interested in men. Alec knew this. For the last few years he and Erica had lived more or less apart, but agonized conjectures as to how she spent her time had been the least of his worries; in fact, had scarcely entered his mind.

She had always been if not exactly frigid then sexually very cool. The emotions that other women needed—passion and excitement and challenge and affection—were apparently fulfillled by her obsession with her horses. Sometimes Alec was reminded of the small girls who haunted the Pony Club circuit. Pigtailed, single-minded, cleaning tack, mucking out their ponies. "It's a sex substitute," some person had once assured him, when he remarked upon this phenomenon. "Let them reach fourteen or fifteen, and it'll not be horses they'll be interested in, but men. It's a well-known fact. A natural development."

Erica must once have been just such a child. *I rode every day of my life until I went to Hong Kong.* But Erica, for some reason, had never grown up. For a little, perhaps, she had loved Alec, but she had never wanted a child, had never experienced the accepted maternal instincts of other young mothers. As soon as humanly possible, she had returned to her original love. That was why she had made him buy Deepbrook. That was, basically, why Gabriel had been sent away to school.

Now, her life revolved around horses. They were the center of her life, all she truly cared about. And the people who became her new friends were the people who rode them.

Two months after this weekend, on a dark, wet evening in November, Alec drove back to Islington from the City at the end of the day, expecting as usual to find his house empty. He had made no plans for the night and was glad of this, because his briefcase bulged with reading matter that he had had no time to deal with during the day, and there was a directors' meeting planned for the next day, during which he would be expected to make some well-studied pronouncements. He would have his meal early, then light the fire, put on his spectacles, and settle down to work.

He turned at last out of the City Road and into his own street, Abigail

Crescent. His house stood at the far end, and he saw the light shining from its windows. Erica, for some reason, had come up to London.

He was puzzled by this. The weather was bad and he knew that her social diary was empty for most of the week. A dentist's appointment perhaps, or a yearly check-up with her doctor in Harley Street?

He parked the car and sat, staring at the lighted house. He had grown accustomed to being alone, but he had never truly come to terms with it. He remembered when they had first come to live here, fresh from Hong Kong, before Gabriel was born. He remembered Erica arranging furniture and hanging curtains and struggling with huge books of carpet samples, but always finding some time to come and greet him as he let himself in through the door. That was how it had been. For only a little time, maybe, but that was how it had been. For a moment he let himself imagine that the years between had never happened, that everything was unchanged. Perhaps this time she would come to greet him, kiss him, go into the kitchen to fix him a drink. They would sit with their drinks and exchange the small gossip and doings of their day, and then he would ring some restaurant and take her out for dinner. . . .

The shining windows stared back at him. He was suddenly tired. He closed his eyes, covered them with his hand, as though to wipe fatigue away. After a little he collected his briefcase off the back seat and got out of the car, locked it, and walked across the rain-soaked pavement, with his bulky briefcase bumping against his knee. He got out his key and opened the door.

He saw her coat, slung across the hall chair, a silk Hermes scarf. He smelled her perfume. He closed the door and put down his briefcase.

"Erica."

He went into the sitting room, and she was there, sitting in an armchair, facing him. She had been reading a paper, but now she folded this and dropped it on the floor beside her. She was wearing a yellow sweater, a gray wool skirt, and long brown leather boots. Her hair, illuminated by the reading lamp that she had lighted, shone like a polished chestnut. She said, "Hi."

"This is a surprise. I didn't know you were coming up."

"I thought about telephoning your office, but there didn't seem much point. I knew you'd be here."

"For a moment I thought I'd forgotten about some dinner party or other. I haven't, have I?"

"No. There's nothing on. I just wanted to talk to you."

This was unusual. "Would you like a drink?" he asked her.

"Yes. If you're having one."

"What would you like?"

"A whiskey would be fine."

He left her and went into the kitchen and poured the drinks and manhandled ice cubes out of the tray, then carried the two glasses back to where she waited. He handed her the glass. "There's not much food in the fridge, I'm afraid, but if you like we could go out for dinner. . . ."

"I shan't be staying for dinner." He raised his eyebrows, and she went on smoothly, "I shan't even be staying the night, so you don't need to worry about entertaining me."

He reached for a chair and pulled it forward and sat facing her across the hearthrug.

"Then why have you come?"

Erica took a mouthful of the whiskey, and then laid the glass delicately down on the small marble-topped table that stood by her chair.

"I've come to tell you that I'm leaving you, Alec."

He did not at once say anything to this. Across the space that divided them, her gaze met his, her eyes unblinking, somber, quite cold.

After a bit, he said mildly. "Why?"

"I don't want to live with you anymore."

"We scarcely live together anyway."

"Strickland Whiteside has asked me to go to America with him."

Strickland Whiteside. He said, "You're going to go and live with *him?*" and he could not keep the appalled incredulity out of his voice.

"You find it astonishing?"

He remembered how they had come indoors together that warm, scented September evening. He remembered the way she had looked, not simply beautiful, but radiant in a way that he had never seen before.

"Are you in love with him?"

She said, "I don't think I've ever exactly known what being in love means. But I feel about Strick as I've never felt about anyone else. It's not just infatuation. It's doing things together, sharing interests. It's been like that from the moment we met. I can't live away from him."

"You can't live away from Strickland Whiteside?" The name still sounded absurd. The whole sentence sounded absurd, like a line from some ludicrous farce, and Erica exploded into irritation.

"Oh, stop repeating everything I say. I can't make it any plainer, I can't make it any simpler. Repeating everything I say isn't going to change what I'm trying to tell you."

He said ridiculously, "He's younger than you are."

For a moment she looked a little put out. "Yes, he is, but what difference does that make?"

"Is he married?"

"No. He's never been married."

"Does he want to marry you?"

"Yes."

"So you want a divorce?"

"Yes. Whether or not you agree to a divorce, I'm leaving you. I'm going out to Virginia to be with him. I shall simply live with him. I'm long past the age of minding about what people say. Conventions really don't matter anymore."

"When are you going?"

"I'm booked on a flight to New York next week."

"Is Strickland flying with you?"

"No." For the first time, her gaze faltered. She looked down, her hand reached for her drink. "He's already gone back to the States. He's in Virginia, waiting for me."

"What about all these big events he was booked in for?"

"He's given them up . . . canceled everything."

"I wonder why he did that?"

Erica raised her eyes. "He thought it would be better."

"You mean, he's chickened out. He hadn't the guts to face me and tell me himself."

"That's not true."

"He left it for you to do."

"It's better for me to do it. I wouldn't let him stay. I made him go. I didn't want there to be rows, unpleasantness, things said that are better left unsaid."

"You could hardly expect me to be delighted."

"I'm going, Alec. And I'm not coming back."

"You'd leave Deepbrook?"

"Yes."

This astonished him almost more than the fact that she was leaving him.

"I always thought that house meant more to you than anything."

"Not now it doesn't. Anyway, it's your house."

"And your horses?"

"I'm taking my horses with me. Strickland's arranged for them to be flown to Virginia."

She was, as usual, presenting him with a totally conceived plan, her usual method when she was utterly determined to have her own way. Strickland, Deepbrook, her horses, all had been neatly dealt with, but to Alec none of these things mattered a damn. There was only one real issue at stake. Erica had never been a moral coward. He waited in silence for her to continue, but she simply sat there, watching him with gray eyes unblinking and defiant, and he realized that she was waiting for him to fire the opening shot of the battle for the only thing that really mattered.

"Gabriel?"

Erica said, "I'm taking Gabriel with me."

The fight was on. "Oh no you're not!"

"Now we're not going to start shouting about this. You're going to have to listen to me. I'm her mother, and I've as much right as you— and more—to make plans for our daughter. I'm going to America. I'm going there to live, and nothing is going to change that. If I take Gabriel with me, then she can live with us. Strickland has a beautiful home, with space and land all around it. There are tennis courts, a swimming pool. It's a wonderful opportunity for a girl of Gabriel's age—young people have such a good time in America—life is geared to them. Let her have this chance. Let her take it."

He said quietly, "What about her school?"

"I'll take her out of school. She can go to school there. There's a particularly good one in Maryland. . . ."

"I won't let her go. I won't lose her."

"Oh, Alec, you won't lose her. We'll share her. You can have access to her whenever you want. She can fly back to this country and stay with you. You can take her to Glenshandra with the others. Nothing's going to change that much."

"I won't let her go to America."

"Don't you see, you have no alternative. Even if we drag this thing through the divorce courts and you fight me every inch of the way, ten to one the custody of Gabriel will be given to *me*, because they only separate a child from its mother under the most extreme of circumstances. I'd need to be a drug addict or proved in some way to be totally unfit to bring my daughter up, before they even considered giving her to you. And think what that sort of hideous, public tug-of-war would do to Gabriel. She's sensitive enough as it is, without you and me inflicting that sort of horror on her."

"Is it any worse than the horror of having her parents divorcing? Is it any worse than the horror of having to go and live in a strange country, in a strange house, under the roof of a man she scarcely knows?"

"And what is the alternative? We have to make a decision now, Alec. There can be no question of putting it off. That's why I came to see you this evening. She has to know what is going to happen to her."

"I won't let her go."

"All right, so what do you want? To keep her for yourself. You couldn't look after her, Alec. You haven't the time to give her. Even if she stayed at boarding school in this country, there are still the holidays. What would happen then, when you're working all day? And don't tell me you could leave her with Mrs. Abney. Gabriel's an intelligent child, and nobody could say that Mrs. Abney's the most stimulating company. She's only got two topics of conversation: one is last week's installment of 'Crossroads' and the other is that damned canary of hers. And what would you do with Gabriel when you have to leave on business for Tokyo or Hong Kong? You can hardly take her with you."

He said, "I can't just give her to you, Erica. Like some material possession I no longer have any use for."

"But don't you see, if we do it my way, you *aren't* giving her to me. All right, so we are splitting up and it's a terrible thing to do to a child, but it's happened before and it will happen again, and we have somehow to decide on a course of action that will hurt her the least. I think that my plan is that one. She comes with me next week. That way the cut will be quick, the break clean, and before she's had time to turn round, she'll be caught up in a whole new life, going to a new school, making new friends." She smiled, and for the first time he saw a glimpse of the old Erica at her most charming, sympathetic, and persuasive. "Don't let's fight over her, Alec. I know how you feel about Gabriel, but she's my child too, and it's I who brought her up. I don't think I've done such a bad job, and I do think I deserve a little credit for that. Just because you're not going to be there doesn't mean I won't go on bringing her up. And Strick is devoted to her. With us, she'll have the best of everything. A good life."

He said, "I thought that was what I was giving her."

"Oh, Alec, you are. You have. And you can go on doing it. Whenever you want, she can come and see you. We've agreed on that. You can have her all to yourself. You'll love that. Agree to it. For all our sakes. Let her come with me. It's the very best you can do for her. I know it is. Make the sacrifice . . . for Gabriel's sake."

He said, "I know your mother's told you what's happened, what's going to happen. But I wanted to talk to you myself, so that if there was anything you were worried about . . ."

Even as he said this, he knew that it was ridiculous. Gabriel's world was falling apart, and he was speaking as though it were some small domestic difficulty that, in a matter of seconds, he could put straight for her.

"I mean . . . it has happened fairly suddenly. There hasn't been time to talk anything over, and you'll be leaving in a week. I didn't want you to go without thinking that I hadn't . . . made some effort to see you. I would like to have had more time to talk things over . . . with *you*. Were you hurt that we didn't discuss it with you?"

Gabriel shrugged. "It wouldn't have made much difference."

"Were you surprised when your mother told you about herself and Strickland?"

"I knew she liked him. But she's liked lots of horsey people. I never thought she'd want to go and live with him in America."

"She's going to marry him."

"I know."

They walked, together but apart, slowly around a deserted games field. It was a horrible day, English winter weather at its worst. Cold, still, raw, misty. No breeze stirred the empty trees, and only the cawing of the rooks broke the foggy silence. In the distance stood the school buildings. Once they had been an elegant country house, with wings and stables, but these had been converted into gymnasiums and classrooms. Indoors, lessons were in progress, but Gabriel had been allowed to miss a biology lesson in order to speak to her father. Later, no doubt a bell would ring, and the place would erupt with girls dressed for hockey or netball, bundled into sweaters and striped scarves, running and calling to one another and complaining of the cold. Now, except for a few lighted windows that shone through the murk, the place looked deserted, stripped of life.

"It could be an adventure, going to America."

"That's what Mummy says."

"At least you won't have to play games in weather like this. It makes a difference if you play games in the sunshine. You might even become a tennis champion."

Gabriel, with her head drooping and her hands deep in the pocket of her coat, kicked at a stick. So much for tennis. Alec was chilled, disorientated by her lack of response, because it was so out of character. He liked to think that he had always been able to talk to her. But now he was not so sure.

He said, "I wouldn't have had this happen for anything in the world. You must realize that. But there's nothing I can do to keep your mother with me. You know what she's like once she's made up her mind about something. Wild horses couldn't make her change tracks."

She said, "I never never even thought about you and Mummy divorcing."

"I'm afraid it happens to a lot of children. You must have a lot of friends with divorced parents."

"But this is *me.*"

Once more, he was lost for words. In silence they paced on, around the corner of the field, passing a pole with a sodden red flag.

He said, "Whatever happens, you know, you're still my daughter. I shall pay your school fees and give you an allowance. You won't have to ask Strickland for anything. You won't ever have to be beholden to him. You . . . like him, don't you? You don't dislike him?"

"He's all right."

"Your mother says he's very fond of you."

"He's so young. He's much younger than Mummy."

Alec took a deep breath. "I suppose," he said carefully, "if you fall in love with a person, their age doesn't matter."

Abruptly, Gabriel stopped walking. Alec stopped too, and they stood facing each other, two solitary figures in the middle of nowhere. Not once during this afternoon's encounter had her eyes met his, and now she looked angrily straight ahead, at his coat buttons.

She said, "Couldn't I have stayed with you?"

He was invaded by an impulse to embrace her, pull his child into his arms, break down her reserve with a demonstration of love that would somehow convince her that this ghastly separation that they spoke of was as abhorrent to him as it was to her. But he had promised himself on the way down to the school to see her that he would not do this. *You mustn't upset her,* Erica had begged him. *Go and see her and talk things over, but don't upset her. She's accepted the situation. If you start getting emotional, then we're all back where we started and you're going to break Gabriel into little pieces.*

He tried to smile. He said evenly, "There's nothing I wanted more. But it wouldn't work. I couldn't look after you. I have too many commitments. I'd be away so much. You need your mother. For the time being, you should be with her. It's better that way."

She set her mouth as though, faced with the inevitable, she was gathering courage to accept it. She turned from him, and once more they walked.

"You'll come back to see me," Alec told her. "We'll go to Glenshandra again next summer. You could maybe try your luck with the salmon this year."

"What's going to happen to Deepbrook?"

"I suppose I shall sell it. There's not much point hanging on to it if your mother isn't there."

"And you?"

"I shall stay in Islington."

She said painfully, "My bedroom in London . . ."

"It's still your room. It always will be. . . ."

"It isn't that. It's just some books I'd like to take with me. I've . . . I've written down the names." She took her hand from her pocket and brought out a piece of lined paper torn from an exercise book. He took it from her and unfolded it. He read,

> *The Secret Garden*
> *Adventure of the World*
> *Gone with the Wind*

There were other titles, but for some reason he couldn't go on reading them.

"Of course." He spoke gruffly, pushing the piece of paper deep into the pocket of his own overcoat. "Is . . . is there anything else?"

"No, just the books."

"I don't know if your mother told you, but I'm going to drive you both to the airport to catch your plane. I'll bring the books with me then. So if you do think of any more things, let me know."

She shook her head. "There's nothing else."

Now, the mist had turned to rain. It beaded her hair and the rough surface of her navy-blue coat. They had rounded the field and were headed back toward the school buildings. They left the grass and walked on gravel, their footsteps crunching. There did not seem to be anything else to talk about. At the foot of the steps that led up to the imposing front door, she stopped and turned once more to face him.

She said, "I have to go and get ready for games. You'd better not come in."

He said, "I'll say goodbye now. I won't say goodbye at the airport."

"Goodbye, then."

Her hands remained firmly deep in her coat pockets. He put his hand under her chin and lifted up her face.

"Gabriel."

"Goodbye."

He stooped and kissed her cheek. For the first time that afternoon she looked straight at him. For an instant their eyes met, and hers were filled with neither tears nor reproach. Then she was gone, walking away from him up the steps, beneath the pretentious colonnade, through the door.

They left for America the following Thursday, his wife and his child, on the evening flight to New York. As he had promised, Alec drove them to the airport, and after their flight had been called, and he had said good-bye, he made his way up to the observation lounge. It was a wet, dark evening, with much low cloud, and he stood, staring through the streaming glass, waiting for their plane to take off. On time the great jet thundered down the runway, lights flashing through the gloom. He watched it lift off, but seconds later it was lost to sight, swallowed into the clouds. He stayed until the sound of the engines died into the darkness. Only then did he turn away, making the long walk across the polished floor toward the head of the escalator. There were people everywhere, but he did not see them, and no head turned to watch him go. For the first time in his life he knew how it felt to be a nonentity, a failure.

He drove himself back to his empty house. Bad news travels with the speed of light and by now it was common knowledge that his marriage was finished, that Erica had left him for a rich American and had taken Gabriel with her. This, in some measure, was a relief, because it meant that Alec didn't have to tell people, but he shied from social contact and sympathy, and although Tom Boulderstone had asked him around to Campden Hill for supper this evening, he had refused the invitation, and Tom had understood.

He was used to being alone, but now his solitude had a new dimension. He went upstairs, and the bedroom, stripped of Erica's possessions, seemed empty, unfamiliar. He had a shower and changed, and then went downstairs again, poured himself a drink, and took it into the sitting room. Without Erica's pretty ornaments, without any flowers, it looked desolate, and he drew the curtains and told himself that tomorrow he would stop off at the florist and buy himself a potted plant.

It was nearly half past eight, but he was not hungry. He was too exhausted, too drained, for hunger. Later, he would go and investigate, and see what Mrs. Abney had concocted and left in the oven for his supper. Later. Now, he switched on the television and collapsed in front of it, his drink in his hand, his chin sunk on his chest.

He stared at the flickering screen. After a moment or two he realized that he was watching a documentary, a program dealing with the problems of marginal farming. To illustrate the problem, the presenters had chosen a farm in Devon. There was a shot of sheep grazing the rocky slopes of Dartmoor . . . the camera panned down the hill to the farmhouse . . . the lush green slopes of the lower land . . .

It was not Chagwell, but it was a place very similar. The film had been shot in summertime. He saw the blue skies, the high white clouds, their shadows racing down the hillside, to where sunlight sparkled on the waters of a bubbling trout river.

Chagwell.

The past is another country. A long time ago Alec had been conceived, born, brought up in that country; his roots lay deep in that rich red Devon soil. But over the years, diverted by his own success, his own ambitions, and the demands of family life, he had almost totally lost touch.

Chagwell. His father had died, and Brian and his wife, Jenny, now ran the farm between them. In the space of seven years Jenny had borne Brian five blond, freckle-faced children, and the old house bulged with their pets and prams and bicycles and toys.

Erica had no time for Brian and Jenny. They were not her sort of people. Only twice during the whole of their married life had Alec taken her to Chagwell, but the two occasions had been so uncomfortable and so little fun for everybody concerned that, as if by mutual consent, they had never been repeated. Communication dwindled to an exchange of cards at Christmas and the odd letter, but Alec had not seen Brian for five years or more.

Five years. It was too long. Bad news travels with the speed of light, but it would not yet have reached Chagwell. Brian would have to be told about the pending divorce. Alec would write tomorrow, losing no time, for it was unthinkable that Brian should hear about the break-up of his brother's marriage from some other person.

Or he could telephone . . .

The telephone, at his side, began to ring. Alec reached out and picked up the receiver.

"Yes?"

"Alec."

"Brian here."

Brian. He was visited by a sense of blinding unreality, as though his imagination had reached out beyond the limits of his own despair. For a moment he wondered if he was going out of his mind. Automatically, he leaned forward and switched off the television.

"Brian."

"Who else?" He sounded his usual cheerful, breezy self, his voice as clear as a bell. For whatever reason he was calling, it was plainly not to impart bad news.

"Where are you ringing from?"

"Chagwell, of course, where else?"

Alec saw him sitting at the battered, roll-top desk in the old study at Chagwell, that dusty, book-lined room that had always been used as the farm office. He saw the piles of government forms and dog-eared files, the proud photographs of prizewinning pedigree Guernsey cows.

"You sound astonished," said Brian.

"It's been five years."

"I know. Far too long. But I thought you'd like to hear a fairly surprising piece of family news. Uncle Gerald's getting married."

Gerald. Gerald Haverstock of Tremenheere. Adm. G. J. Haverstock, C.B.E., D.S.O., D.S.C., R.N., once known as the most eligible bachelor in the Royal Navy.

"When did you hear this?"

"This morning. He rang up to tell us. Sounds over the moon. Wants us all to go to the wedding."

"When's that?"

"Weekend after next. In Hampshire."

Gerald, finally, getting married. "He must be sixty now."

"Well, you know what they say, the best wine comes from old bottles."

"Who's the bride?"

"She's called Eve Ashby. The widow of an old shipmate. It's all very suitable."

Still, Alec found it hard to believe, for it was indeed an astounding piece of news. Gerald, of all people, the career sailor, the perpetual bachelor, yearned after by countless lovelorn ladies. Gerald, with whom Brian and Alec had spent one blissful summer holiday, the only youngsters in a wholly adult house party. Running wild on the Cornish beaches and playing cricket on the lawn in front of the house, they had yet been treated—for the first time in their lives—as grown-ups. Allowed to stay up for dinner, drink wine, take the sailing dinghy on their own. Gerald became their hero, and they followed his meteoric career with proprietary pride.

Gerald had been best man at so many weddings that it took some imagination to see him as the bridegroom.

"Are you going to the wedding?" Alec asked.

"Yes, we all are. Kids and all. Gerald wants the lot of us. And you as well. It's not that far from Deepbrook. You could drive over in the afternoon. I don't suppose Erica would particularly want to come, but perhaps you and Gabriel . . . ?"

He paused, waiting for a reaction to this suggestion. Alec's mouth was suddenly dry. He saw again the transatlantic jet, taking off, lifting, disappearing into the darkness of night and cloud. She's gone. Gabriel's gone.

After a bit, in a totally different voice, Brian said, "Is everything all right, old boy?"

"Why do you ask?"

"Well, to tell you the truth, the last few days, I've been thinking about you . . . had the feeling you were a bit under the weather. In fact, I've been meaning to ring you. Had this urge to have a word. Telling you about Gerald's wedding was just a good excuse to pick up the telephone."

Had this urge to have a word.

They had, as boys, been very close. The barriers of distance, the passing years, the two incompatible wives, the lack of communication had not destroyed their closeness. They had always been in touch, linked by a strong, invisible cord of blood and birth. Perhaps this unexpected telephone call, for whatever reason it had been made, was a sort of lifeline.

He clutched at it. He said, "Yes, everything's wrong," and told Brian. It did not take very long.

When he was finished, Brian only said, "I see."

"I was going to write tomorrow and tell you. Or telephone . . . I'm sorry I didn't get around to telling you before."

"That's all right, old boy. Look. I'm coming up to London next week for the fatstock show at Smithfield. Would you like to meet?"

No comments, no postmortems, no unnecessary sympathy. "More than anything," Alec told his brother. "Come to my club and I'll give you lunch."

They fixed on a day and time.

"And what shall I tell Gerald?" Brian asked.

"Tell him I'll be at his wedding. I wouldn't miss it for all the tea in China."

Brian rang off. Slowly Alec replaced his own receiver. The past is another country.

Images filled his mind, not only of Chagwell, but now, thinking of Gerald, of Tremenheere as well. The old stone house at the very end of Cornwall, where palm trees grew, and camellias and verbena, and scented white jasmine covered the sides of the glass houses in the walled garden.

Chagwell and Tremenheere. They were his roots and his identity. He was Alec Haverstock and he would cope. The world had not come to an end. Gabriel had gone; parting from her had been the worst, but now the worst was over. He had touched bottom and he could only start coming up again.

He stood up, and carrying his empty glass, went through to the kitchen to look for something to eat.

3

ISLINGTON

*I*T WAS FIVE O'CLOCK before Laura finally reached home. The breeze had dropped and Abigail Crescent drowsed sleepily in the golden sunshine of late afternoon. For once, the street was almost deserted. In all likelihood, her neighbors were sitting in their tiny gardens or had taken their children off to neighborhood parks for the solace of grass underfoot and shady trees overhead. Only an old lady, with a shopping trolley and an ancient mongrel on a leash, was making her way down the pavement. As Laura drew up in front of her house, even they disappeared, like rabbits down a burrow, descending steps into some basement flat.

She gathered up the day's shopping, her handbag, and her dog and got out of the car, crossed the pavement, and went up the stairs to her front door. She always had to remind herself that it was her own front door every time she found her latchkey and turned the lock. Because the house, which she had lived in for nine months, was still not totally familiar. She was not yet in tune with its moods nor its reactions. It was Alec's home, and it had been Erica's home, and Laura always entered it tentatively, unable to suppress the sensation that she was trespassing upon another person's property.

Now, the warm silence pressed in, thick as a fog. From below, from Mrs. Abney's domain, came no sound. Perhaps she had taken herself out or was still asleep. Gradually the humming of the refrigerator in the kitchen made itself heard. Then a clock ticking. Yesterday Laura had bought roses, filled a jug with them. Today their scent, from the sitting room, lay heavy and sweet.

I have come home. This is my home.

It was not a large house. Mrs. Abney's basement and, above it, three stories—two rooms at each level and none of them particularly spacious. Here, the cramped hall and stairway; on one side the sitting room, on the other the kitchen, which also served as dining space. Above, the main bedroom and bath room and Alec's dressing room, doubling as a study. Above again—with dormer windows and sloping ceilings—the attics. A nominal guest room, usually stacked with suitcases and an overflow of furniture, and the nursery, which had once been Gabriel's. That was all.

She set Lucy down and then went into the kitchen to unload the groceries and the chops she had bought for supper. Here were pine fitments, blue-and-white china, a scrubbed table, wheel-back chairs. French windows opened onto a teak deck, and from this a flight of wooden steps led down into a small paved garden, where grew a flowering cherry and a few tubs of geraniums. Laura unbolted these windows and threw them open. Air stirred through the house. Outside on the deck were a couple of garden chairs and a small, wrought-iron table. Later, when Alec came home, and while the chops grilled, they would have their drinks out here, in the dusky twilight, watching the sun drop out of the sky, savoring the coolness of evening.

Perhaps that would be the right time to tell him about not going to Scotland. Her heart sank at the thought, not because she was afraid of him, but because she dreaded spoiling things for him. The kitchen clock stood at ten minutes past five. He would not be home for more than an hour. She went upstairs and took off her clothes, pulled on an airy wrapper, and lay down on her own side of the enormous double bed. Half an hour, she promised herself, and then she would have a shower and change. Half an hour. But almost instantly, like a person dropping down a well, she was asleep.

There was a hospital: long corridors, white-tiled, the hum of half-consciousness loud in her ears, white-masked faces. Nothing to worry about, she was being told. Nothing to worry about. A bell started to jangle. Perhaps there was a fire. Someone had tied her down. Nothing to worry about. The bell went on ringing.

She opened her eyes and lay staring at the ceiling. Her heart was still hammering with the fright of the dream. Automatically she lifted her wrist and looked at her watch. Half past five. The bell rang again.

For airiness, she had left the door open, and now she heard Mrs. Abney coming up from the basement, making heavy weather of the climb, a step at a time. Laura lay motionless, listening. She heard the click of the latch, the front door opening.

"Oh, Mrs. Boulderstone, it's you!"

Daphne. *Daphne?* What was Daphne doing here at half past five in the afternoon? What on earth could she be wanting? Perhaps, hopefully, Mrs. Abney would think Laura was out, and send her away.

"I've been ringing for *hours*." Daphne's high-pitched voice was clearly audible. "I was sure somebody had to be in, because Mrs. Haverstock's car's there."

"I know. I had a look for myself when I heard the doorbell ringing. Perhaps she's up in her room." Hope died. "Come along in, and I'll pop up and see."

"I hope you weren't asleep, Mrs. Abney."

"No. Just frying a fishcake for my tea."

Now, Mrs. Abney was climbing the stairs again. Laura sat up with a jerk, pushed aside the light cover, swung her legs over the side of the bed. Sitting there, dizzy and disorientated, she saw Mrs. Abney appear at the open door, stopping only to give it a token rap on the panel with her knuckled fist.

"You're not asleep, then." Mrs. Abney, with her frizzy gray hair and her bedroom slippers and her heavy support hose, which did nothing to conceal the ropelike knots of her troublesome varicose veins. "Didn't you hear the bell?"

"I *was* asleep. I'm sorry you had to answer the door."

"Ringing and ringing it was. Thought you must be out."

"I'm sorry," Laura said again.

"It's Mrs. Boulderstone."

From downstairs, Daphne was listening in to this exchange. "Laura, it's me! Don't get out of bed, I'll come up—'

"No . . ." She didn't want Daphne in her bedroom. "I won't be a moment."

But her protests did no good, because the next moment Daphne was there. "Goodness, I'm sorry. I never imagined you'd be in bed at this hour. Poor Mrs. Abney. Thank you so much for coming to my rescue. Now you can get back to your fishcakes. We were quite worried about you, Laura. Thought you'd disappeared for good."

"She never heard the bell," Mrs. Abney explained unnecessarily. "Well, if you're all right, then." And she left them, her bedroom slippers treading heavily away down the creaking stair.

Daphne pulled a comic face at her departing back view. "I did try to telephone, but there wasn't any reply. Were you out?"

"I went to have tea with Phyllis in Hampstead."

Daphne tossed her bag and her sunglasses down onto the end of Laura's bed and moved to the dressing table to check her appearance in Laura's mirror. "I've been having my hair done. It was boiling under the dryer."

"It looks very nice." You could tell, not just by her perfectly coifed cap of silvery hair, but by the rich lacquered smell of her, that Daphne had come straight from the beauty salon. She looked, Laura decided in a hopeless sort of way, quite amazingly chic, in thin cotton trousers and pale pink silk shirt. Her figure remained slender as a child's, and as always she was deeply tanned, impeccably made up, scented and elegant. "Who does it for you?"

"A boy called Antony. He's queer as a coot, but he cuts well." Apparently satisfied with the way she looked, Daphne turned from the mirror and sank into a small pink velvet armchair that stood by the window. "I'm exhausted," she announced.

"What have you been doing all day?"

"Well. I had some shopping to do. . . . I got a divine pair of knickerbockers in Harrods, I thought they'd do for Glenshandra. I've left them in the car, otherwise I'd show them to you. And then I had a gorgeous lunch in the Meridiana, and then I had to come all the way to Euston to pick up a package for Tom. It's a new salmon rod, made for him in Inverness, and they sent it down on the train. *So* . . . as I was coming this way, I thought I'd come and see you and we could finalize all our plans for going north. Doesn't that sound businesslike?"

She lay back in the chair, stretching out her legs. Her eyes, large and of an amazing blue, moved around the room. "You've changed things in here, haven't you? Isn't that a new bed?"

Her lack of perception, of tact, was something that Laura, painfully diffident herself, had never got used to.

"Yes. It is new. Alec bought it when we got married."

"And new curtains as well. That's a very pretty chintz."

It occurred to Laura that Daphne must have been in this room a thousand times before, gossiping with Erica, just as she now sat and chatted to Laura. She imagined them trying on new clothes, sharing confidences, discussing some party, making plans. Her thin wrapper felt crumpled and sweaty. More than anything, she wanted a shower. She wanted Daphne to go away and leave her alone.

As sometimes occurs on truly desperate occasions, she was visited by a brainwave.

"Would you like a drink?"

"Adore one," said Daphne promptly.

"You know where Alec keeps the drinks . . . in that cupboard in the kitchen. There's gin there, and tonic. And a lemon in the fridge . . . and some ice. Why don't you go down and help yourself and I'll be with you in a moment. I have to get some clothes on. I can't stay here for the rest of the day, and Alec will be home soon."

At this Daphne perked up visibly and needed no further persuasion to fall in with Laura's impromptu plan. She pulled herself out of the chair, collected handbag and sunglasses, and went downstairs. Laura waited until she heard cupboard doors opening and the clink of glass. Only then, when she was certain that Daphne would not suddenly appear again, like a Jack-in-the-box, did she get to her feet.

Fifteen minutes later, showered and dressed, she went down and found Daphne relaxed on the sofa, with a cigarette lighted and her drink on the table at her elbow. The sitting room was full of evening sunlight and the scent of roses, and Daphne had found a new *Harpers and Queen,* and was flipping through its glossy pages, but when Laura appeared, she tossed the magazine down and said, "You haven't changed this room at all, have you? I mean, apart from a few bits and pieces?"

"There wasn't much point. It's pretty enough as it is."

"Do you like living here? I always think Islington's a bit back of beyondish. It takes such hours to get anywhere."

"It's handy for the City."

"That's what Alec always said—stubborn old devil. Which was the reason that Erica made him buy Deepbrook."

Laura, taken aback, could think of no rejoinder to this. Never before had Daphne come up with such a direct, almost provocative, reference to the past. Why now? Perhaps because there was no Tom here to put a brake on her outspokenness. She and Laura were alone, and she obviously felt that there could be no need for delicate references, tactful evasion. Laura's heart sank and she felt trapped.

Daphne smiled. "We never talk about Erica, do we? We all tiptoe around the subject as though it were forbidden. But after all, it happened; it's past history now. Water under the bridge."

"Yes, I suppose it is."

Daphne's eyes narrowed. She lit another cigarette and then said, "It must be strange being a second wife. I've often thought it must be strange for you. A whole new experience, and yet it's all happened before, to another woman. It's a classic situation of course."

"How do you mean?"

"Well, think of Jane Eyre, or the second Mrs. de Winter in *Rebecca.*"

"Except that Alec is neither a bigamist nor a murderer."

Daphne looked blank. Perhaps she was not as well-read as she made out. Laura thought about explaining, and then decided against it. She saw that Daphne's glass was empty.

"Have another gin and tonic."

"Adore it." This seemed to be her stock reply when offered a drink. She held out the glass. "Or would you like me to get it for myself?"

"No. I'll do it."

In the kitchen, she poured the drink, filled the glass with ice. Daphne had been out for lunch—doubtless with one of her mysterious admirers. Doubtless, too, she had been plied with martinis and wine. Laura wondered if, possibly, she was slightly drunk. What else could explain her extraordinary burst of frankness? She looked at the clock and longed for Alec to come home and rescue her from this situation. She carried the glass back into the sitting room.

"Oh, gorgeous." Daphne took it from her. "Aren't you having anything?"

"No. I'm . . . not really thirsty."

"Well, cheers!" She drank, and then set the glass down again. "I was just thinking . . . you know, it's nearly six years since Erica went to America. It doesn't seem possible that it was so long ago. I suppose, as we all get older, time flies by more quickly . . . or something. But it doesn't seem so long." She settled herself more comfortably in her corner of the sofa, tucking her feet up beneath her, the very picture of a woman getting down to an intimate chat. "She was my best friend. Did you know that?"

"Yes, I think I did."

"We were at school together. We were always friends. It was I who introduced her to Alec. At least, I didn't introduce them, because she was in Hong Kong, but I brought them together. When they got married, I was terribly thrilled, but I was also just the teensiest weensiest bit jealous. You see, Alec was one of my first boyfriends. I knew him before I met Tom. Silly to feel that way about a man, but let's face it, there's no love like a first love."

"Unless it's the last love."

Daphne's expression was at once surprised and hurt, as though she had just been bitten by a worm. "I wasn't being bitchy, I promise you. Just making a tiny confession. After all, he is a very attractive man."

"I expect," said Laura, in some desperation, "you missed Erica very much."

"Oh, dreadfully. At first I couldn't believe that she wasn't coming back, and then the divorce came through and Alec sold Deepbrook, and after that I knew we'd never go back. It was like the end of an era. Weekends without Deepbrook to escape to seemed very strange. We worried about Alec, too, being on his own so much, but he took up with his brother again and used to disappear off to Devon on Friday evenings. I expect he's taken you there?"

"To Chagwell, you mean? Yes, we've been, we went for Easter. But mostly we just stay here." (Those weekends were the best of all. Just the two of them and Lucy, the door closed and the windows open and the little house to themselves.)

"Do you like them? Brian Haverstock and his wife, I mean. Erica couldn't stand going there. She said the furniture was covered in dog's hairs and the children never stopped screaming."

"With such a big family, it's bound to be fairly disorganized and rowdy . . . but it's fun, too."

"Erica couldn't stand undisciplined children. Gabriel was charming." She stubbed out her cigarette. "Does Alec ever hear from Gabriel?"

This was getting worse and worse. Uncontrollable. Laura lied. "Oh, yes," and was astonished at her own coolness.

"She's probably a real little American by now. Young people out there have such a marvelous time. I suppose that was why she never came back to this country to see Alec. He always imagined that she would. Each year he'd start making noises about her joining us at Glenshandra, and he'd book a room for her in the hotel and get himself all organized. But she never came. Talking of which," she went on, with no change of expression in her voice, "that's really why I came to see you, not to talk about my past life. Glenshandra. Are you all prepared to face the frozen north? I hope you've got heaps of warm clothes, because it can be bitterly cold on the river, even in July. One year it rained nonstop and we nearly froze. And you'll need something formal for the evenings, just in case we get asked out for dinner. That's the sort of things husbands never remember to tell you, and there isn't a shop for a hundred miles, so you can't go out and buy anything."

She stopped and waited for Laura to make some response to this. Laura could think of nothing to say. Daphne rattled on.

"Alec told us that you'd never actually fished, but you are going to try it, aren't you? It'll be boring otherwise, left at the hotel all on your own. You don't look very excited at the prospect. Aren't you looking forward to it?"

"Well . . . yes . . . but . . ."

"There's nothing wrong, is there?"

She would have to know sooner or later. Everybody would have to know. "I—I don't think I'm going to be able to come."

"Not *come?*"

"I've got to go into hospital. It's just a small thing . . . a small operation, but the doctor says I've got to rest up afterwards. She says I can't go to Scotland."

"But *when?* When do you have to go into hospital?"

"In a day or two."

"But does that mean *Alec* can't come?" Daphne sounded appalled at this prospect, as though without Alec the entire holiday was doomed to disaster.

"Yes, of course he can. There's no reason for him to stay."

"But . . . won't you *mind?*"

"I want him to go. I want him to come with you all."

"But *you.* Poor you. What a wretched thing to happen. And who's going to look after you? Mrs. Abney?"

"I'll maybe go and stay with Phyllis."

"You mean, your aunt, who lives in Hampstead?"

A car was drawing up in the street outside. The engine stopped; a door slammed. Laura prayed for it to be Alec. "That's why I went to see her this afternoon." Footsteps; his key in the lock. "That's Alec now."

They met as he opened the front door, and she had never been so glad to see him.

"Laura . . ."

Before he had time to kiss her, she said in clear tones, "Hello, isn't it lovely, Daphne's here."

He froze, one arm around his wife, the other hand still holding his briefcase. "Daphne?" He looked amazed.

"Yes, it's me!" Daphne called from the sitting room. Alec put down his briefcase and shut the door behind him. "Isn't that a nice surprise for you?"

He went through the open door, with Laura behind him, and stood there, with his hands in his pockets, smiling down at Daphne.

"What are you doing here?"

She smiled back at him, tilting her head, so that her earrings bobbed to one side.

"Just having a little girlish gossip. I had to pick up a parcel at Euston and it seemed a good opportunity. It's not often I'm in this neck of the woods."

He stooped to kiss her upturned face. "Lovely to see you."

"I really came to talk to Laura about Glenshandra. . . ."

Behind Alec's back Laura made an agonized face, but Daphne either did not notice this frantic telegram or else was too engrossed in Alec to pay attention, ". . . but she's just told me that she isn't going to be able to come."

In that instant, Laura could have strangled Daphne. Or strangled herself for having been such a fool as to confide in her.

Alec turned and looked at her, frowning and completely at a loss. "Not able to come . . . ?"

"Oh, Daphne, Alec doesn't *know* about it yet. At least he didn't until you told him."

"And you wanted to tell him yourself! How ghastly, and now I've let the cat out of the bag. Tom's always telling me I talk too much. I had no idea. . . ."

"I *told* you. I only saw the doctor this afternoon!"

"I didn't know you were going to see the doctor," said Alec.

"I didn't want to tell you. Until I'd been. Until I knew. I didn't want you to be worrying. . . ." To her horror she heard the break in her own voice. But Alec heard it too and came to her rescue, stemming her distress and confusion.

"We don't need to talk about it now, you can tell me later. When Daphne's gone."

"Oh, darling, is that a hint? Does that mean I've got to take myself off?"

"No, of course not. I'm going to have a drink. Let me give you another."

"Well'—she cradled her glass in her hand—"perhaps a tiny one. Not too strong, though, because I've got to drive myself home, and Tom will kill me if I bash up the car."

She went at last. They watched the weaving back view of her car disappear around the curve of the crescent.

"Hope she doesn't kill herself," said Alec. They went indoors and he shut the door. Laura instantly burst into tears.

Almost as instantly he had his arms around her.

"Now come along. Calm down. What's all this about?"

"I didn't want *her* to be the one to tell you. I wanted to tell you myself, when we were having a drink. . . . I didn't mean to tell her, but she went on and on about Glenshandra and in the end I couldn't do anything else . . ."

"That doesn't matter. All that matters is you. . . . Come along." With his arm around her he led her into the sitting room, pushed her gently down where Daphne had sat, and lifted her feet up on to the sofa. The cushion under Laura's head smelled of Daphne. She couldn't stop crying.

"I . . . kept putting off going to see Doctor Hickley because I didn't want to be told I'd have to have another operation, and because I thought perhaps everything would sort itself out. But it hasn't. It's just got worse."

Tears were streaming down her face. He sat on the edge of the sofa and gave her the clean linen handkerchief out of his top pocket. She blew her nose, but it didn't seem to do much good.

"When have you got to go into hospital?"

"In a day or two. Doctor Hickley's going to ring me. . . ."

"I'm sorry. But after all, it's not the end of the world."

"It will be if it doesn't work this time, because if it happens again . . . she says I'll have to have a hysterectomy, and I don't want that to happen. I'm frightened of that happening . . . I don't think I could bear it . . . I want to have a baby . . . I want to have your baby. . . ."

She looked up at him, but she could not see his face because it was drowned in her own tears. And then she couldn't see it, because he had gathered her up into his arms, and her own face was buried against the warm comfort of his shoulder.

He said, "It won't happen again."

"That's what Phyllis said, but we don't know." She wept into his navy-blue, chalk-striped suit. "I want to *know.*"

"We can't know everything."

"I want a child. . . ." *I want to give you a child to make up for Gabriel.*

Why couldn't she say it? What was wrong with their marriage that she couldn't bring herself to say Gabriel's name? What was wrong with their marriage that Alec never mentioned his daughter, wrote letters to her from the privacy of his office, and, if she ever replied to these letters, kept these a secret from Laura? There shouldn't be secrets. They should be able to talk about anything, tell each other everything.

It wasn't even as though she had gone without trace. Upstairs in the attics was her room, filled with her furniture, her toys, her pictures, her desk. On the chest of drawers in Alec's dressing room stood Gabriel's photograph, the drawing that she had done for him, proud in its silver frame. Why couldn't he realize that this refusal to admit even her existence was creating a void between them that Laura was incapable of crossing?

She sighed deeply and pulled away from him, and lay back on the pillow, hating herself for crying so much, for looking hideous, for being so unhappy. His handkerchief was already sodden with her grief. She tugged viciously at its hemstitched corner. She said, "If I can't give you a child, I can't give you *anything.*"

Being Alec, he came out with no comforting cliché. But after a little he said, in a marvelously normal way, "Have you had a drink?"

Laura shook her head.

"I'll get you a brandy." He stood up and went out of the room. She heard him moving around the kitchen. Lucy, disturbed by his presence, got out of her basket. Laura heard the scratch of her claws on the linoleum. Then she came into the room and ran to jump up into Laura's lap. She licked Laura's face and, tasting salt tears, licked it again. She curled up and went back to sleep. Laura blew her nose again and pushed a straggling lock of dark hair away from her face. Alec returned with whiskey for himself and a little glass of brandy for Laura. He gave it to her and pulled up a low stool and sat facing her. He smiled and she smiled back, feebly.

"Better?"

She nodded.

"The brandy's medicinal," he told her. She took a mouthful and felt it slip, burning, down her throat and into her stomach. Its strength was comforting.

"Now," he said, "we'll talk about Glenshandra. Doctor Hickley says you're not to come?"

"She says I can't."

"And there's no question of the operation being postponed?"

Laura shook her head.

"In that case we'll have to call Glenshandra off."

She took a deep breath. "That's what I *really* don't want. I really don't want you not to go."

"But I can't leave you here alone."

"I—I thought we could get a nurse in or something. I know Mrs. Abney couldn't manage by herself, but we could perhaps get somebody to help her."

"Laura, I couldn't leave you here."

"I *knew* you'd say that. I just *knew* you'd say that."

"Well, what did you expect me to say? Laura, Glenshandra doesn't matter."

"It does matter. You know it matters." She began to cry again, and there was no way she could stop the flood of tears. "You look forward to it all year, it's your holiday, you have to go. And the others . . ."

"They'll understand."

She thought of Daphne's face of horror, Daphne saying, *Does that mean Alec can't come?*

"They won't understand. They'll just think I'm being as useless and boring about this as they do about everything else."

"That's unfair."

"I want you to go. I want you to. Don't you realize that's why I'm so miserably upset, because I know I'm ruining everything for you?"

"You can't go into hospital and have an operation if you're in this state."

"Then think of something. Phyllis said you'd be able to think of something."

"Phyllis?"

"I went to see her this afternoon. After Doctor Hickley. I thought I'd ask her if I could go and stay with her when I come out of hospital, because I thought if you knew I was with her, then you'd go to Glenshandra, but she can't have me because she's going to Florence. She says she'll put it off, but I can't let her do that . . ."

"No, of course we can't let her do that."

"I told her it's the first time in my life I wished I had a family of my own. A real family, with masses of close relations. I've never wished that before. I wish I still had a cozy mother, and I could go and stay with her and she'd put hot-water bottles in my bed."

She looked at him to see if he was smiling at this useless fancy, but he was not smiling. He said gently, "You haven't got a family, but I have."

Laura thought about this, and then said, with a notable lack of enthusiasm, "You mean Chagwell?"

He laughed. "No. Not Chagwell. I love my brother and his wife and their brood of children very much, but Chagwell is a house where you can stay only if you are in the rudest of health."

Laura felt relieved. "I'm glad you said that, and not me."

He said, "You could go to Tremenheere."

"Where's Tremenheere?"

"Cornwall. The very end of Cornwall. Heaven on earth. An old Elizabethan manor and a view of the bay."

"You sound like a travel agent. Who lives there?"

"Gerald and Eve Haverstock. He's my uncle, and she's a darling."

Laura remembered. "They sent us crystal wineglasses for a wedding present."

"That's right."

"And a sweet letter."

"Right again."

"And he's a retired admiral?"

"Who didn't get married until he was sixty."

"What a complicated family you have."

"But all charming. Like me."

"When were you at this place . . . Tremenheere?" The word was difficult to say, especially after a neat brandy.

"When I was a boy. Brian and I spent a summer holiday there."

"But I've never met them. Gerald and Eve, I mean."

"That doesn't matter."

"We don't even know if they can have me to stay."

"I'll ring them later on and fix it."

"What if they say no?"

"They won't say no, but if they do, we'll think of something else."

"I'll be a nuisance."

"I don't think so."

"How would I get there?"

"I'll drive you down once you're out of hospital."

"You'll be at Glenshandra."

"I shan't go to Glenshandra until you're safely delivered. Like a parcel."

"You'll miss some of your holiday. Some of the fishing."

"That won't kill me."

She had finally run out of objections. Tremenheere was a compromise, but it was at least a plan. It would mean meeting new people, living in a stranger's house, but as well it meant that Phyllis would go to Florence and Alec would go to Scotland.

She turned her head on the cushion and looked at him, sitting there, with his drink cradled between his knees. She saw his thick hair, black, streaked with white, like silver fox fur. His face, not conventionally handsome, but arresting and distinguished, the sort of face that seen once could never be forgotten. She saw his tallness, easily disposed upon the low stool, his long legs spread, his hands clasped loosely around his glass. She looked into his eyes, which were dark as her own, and he smiled, and her heart turned over.

He is, after all, a very attractive man.

Phyllis had said, *Can you see a man of Alec's integrity having an affair with his best friend's wife?* But how Daphne would love having him at Glenshandra on his own.

The thought filled Laura with a pain that was ludicrous, because she had spent the last half hour persuading him to go. Ashamed of herself, filled with love for Alec, she put out her hand, and he took it in his own.

"If Gerald and Eve say they can have me, and if I say that I'll go, you promise you'll go to Scotland."

"If that's what you want."

"That is what I want, Alec."

He bent his head and kissed the palm of her hand and closed her fingers around the kiss as though it were some precious gift.

She said, "I probably wouldn't be much good at fishing anyway . . . and you won't have to spend all your time trying to teach me."

"There'll be another year."

Another year. Perhaps in another year, everything would be better.

"Tell me about Tremenheere."

4

TREMENHEERE

T HE DAY HAD BEEN PERFECT. Long, hot, sun-soaked. The tide was out, and the beach, viewed from the sea, where Eve, after an energetic swim, drifted blissfully on the rise and fall of gathering waves, revealed itself as a curve of cliff, a sickle of rocks, and then the wide, clean sweep of the sand.

It was, for this particular beach, crowded. Now, at the end of July, the holiday season was at its peak and the scene was littered with bright spots of color: bathing towels and striped windbreaks; children in scarlet and canary-yellow bathing suits; sun umbrellas and huge, inflatable rubber balls. Overhead, gulls swooped and screamed, perched on the clifftops, dived to devour the flotsam of a hundred picnics, dropped in the sand. Their screams were matched by human cries, which, across the distance, pierced the air. Boys playing football, mothers shrieking at wayward toddlers, the happy screams of a girl being mobbed by a couple of youths who appeared to be trying to drown her.

The sea at first had seemed icy, but the swim had got her circulation going and now she was aware only of a marvelous, invigorating, salty coolness. She lay on her back and watched the cloudless sky, her mind empty of anything save the physical perfection of now.

I am fifty-eight, she reminded herself, but had long since decided that one of the good things about being fifty-eight was the fact that one took time to appreciate the really marvelous moments that still came one's way. They weren't happiness, exactly. Years ago, happiness had ceased to pounce, unawares, with the reasonless ecstacy of youth. They were something better. Eve had never much liked being pounced on, by happiness or anything else. It had always frightened and disconcerted her to be taken unawares.

Lulled, as though in a cradle, by the movement of the sea, she let herself be gently washed ashore by the incoming tide. Now, the waves gathered their puny momentum, curved into shallow breakers. Her hands touched sand. Another wave, and she lay, beached, letting the incoming tide flow over her body, and after the depths in which she had been swimming, the water now felt actually warm.

That was it. It was over. There was no time for more. She got to her feet and walked up onto the blistering sand toward the outcrop of rock where she had left her thick white towel robe. She picked up the robe and pulled it on, felt it warm against the cold wetness of her shoulders and arms. She tied the sash, pushed her feet into thong sandals, started the long walk up toward the narrow footpath that led to the clifftop and the car park.

It was nearly six o'clock. The first of the holiday people were starting to pack up, the children, reluctant, protesting, howling with exhaustion and too much sun. Some people were already well tanned, but others, who had perhaps arrived only yesterday or the day before, were boiled pink as lobsters and were in for a couple of days of agony and peeling shoulders before they could safely venture out again. They never learned. It happened every hot summer, and the doctors' surgeries were filled with them, sitting in rows with flaming faces and blistered backs.

The cliff path was steep. At the top, Eve paused for breath, turning back to look at the sea, framed between two bastions of rock. Inshore, over the sand it was as green as jade, but farther out lay a ribbon of the most intense indigo blue. The horizon was hazed in lavender, the sky azure.

A young family caught up with her, the father carrying the toddler, the mother dragging the older child by the hand. He was in tears. "I don't want to go 'ome termorrer. I want to stay 'ere for another week. I want to stay 'ere forever."

Eve caught the young mother's eye. She was close to exasperation. Eve could identify with her. She remembered being that age, with Ivan, a stocky little blond boy, clinging to her hand. She could feel his hand, small and dry and rough, in her own. Don't be angry with him, she wanted to say. Don't spoil it. Before you know where you are, he'll be grown up and you'll have lost him forever. Savour every fleeting moment of your child's life, even if he does, from time to time, drive you out of your mind.

"I don't want to go 'ome." The drone continued. The mother made a resigned face in Eve's direction and Eve smiled back wryly, but her tender heart bled for the lot of them, who tomorrow would have to leave Cornwall and make the long, tedious journey back to London; to crowds, and streets and offices and jobs and buses and the smell of petrol fumes. It seemed grossly unfair that they should have to go and she should stay. She could stay here forever, because this was where she lived.

Walking toward her car, she prayed for the heat wave to continue. Alec and Laura were arriving this evening in time for dinner, which was the reason Eve could not linger on the beach. They were driving down from London, and tomorrow morning, at some ungodly hour, Alec was leaving again, to make the unimaginably long drive to Scotland and his salmon fishing. Laura would stay at Tremenheere for the next ten days or so, and then Alec would return to take her back to London.

Alec, Eve knew. Pale and stony-faced, still pole-axed by his newly broken marriage, he had come to their wedding, and she had always loved him for this. Since then, slightly less shattered, he had come, once or twice, to stay with Gerald and Eve. But Laura was a stranger. Laura had been ill, in hospital. Laura was coming to Tremenheere to recover.

Which made it even more necessary for the weather to go on being conveniently perfect. Laura would have breakfast in bed and lie, peacefully, in the garden with no person to bother her. She would rest and recover. When she was stronger, perhaps, she, Eve, would bring her here, and they would bask on the beach and swim together.

It made everything so much easier if the weather was good. Living here, in the farthest corner of Cornwall, Eve and Gerald were inundated each summer with visitors: relations, friends from London, young families unable to afford the hideous cost of hotels. They always had a good time because Eve made sure that they did, but sometimes even she became disheartened by constant rain and unseasonable winds, and although she knew perfectly well that it wasn't, she could never quite get rid of the idea that it was all her fault.

These reflections got her into her car, which was boiling hot, despite the fact that she had parked it in the meager shade of a hawthorn bush. Still bundled in her towel robe, and with the air from the open window cold on her damp hair, she started for home. Up the hill from the cove and onto the main road. Through a village and along by the edge of the sea. The road crossed the railway by means of a bridge and then ran, parallel to the railway lines, toward the town.

In the old days, Gerald had once told her, before the war, here had been only agricultural land, small farms and hidden villages with tiny square-towered churches. The churches still stood, but the fields where the broccoli and the early potatoes had grown were now lost to development and progress. Holiday homes and blocks of flats, petrol stations and supermarkets, lined the road.

There was the heliport that served the Scilly Islands and then the big gates of a mansion house that was now a hotel. Once there had been trees beyond the gates, but these had been cut down and space made for a glittering blue swimming pool.

Between this hotel and the start of the town, a road turned up to the right, signposted to Penvarloe. Into this road Eve turned, away from the stream of traffic. The road narrowed to a lane, high hedged, winding up onto the hill. At once she was back in rural, unspoiled countryside. Small fields, stone-walled, where herds of Guernseys grazed. Deep valleys, dark with thickets of wood. After a mile or so, the road curved steeply and the village of Penvarloe lay ahead, low cottages clinging to the edge of the street. She passed the pub—where tables stood out on the cobbled forecourt—and the tenth-century church, embedded, like some prehistoric rock, surrounded by yews and ancient, leaning gravestones.

The village post office was also the general store and sold vegetables, fizzy drinks, and deep-frozen goodies for the holiday trade. Its open door (for it did not close until seven o'clock in the evening) was flanked with crates of fruit, and as Eve approached, a slender woman, with a mop of curling gray hair, emerged through this door. She wore sunglasses and a pale blue, sleeveless dress and carried a wicker basket of shopping. Eve tooted her horn, and the woman saw her and waved, and Eve slowed the car and drew up at the side of the road.

"Silvia."

Silvia Marten crossed the pavement and came over to talk, stooping, supported by a hand on the roof of the car. From a distance, despite the gray hair, her appearance was incredibly youthful, so that close up, the lined weather-beaten skin, the sharp angle of her jawbone, the sagging flesh beneath her chin, were somehow shocking. She set down her basket and pushed her sunglasses to the top of her head, and Eve stared up into those amazing eyes, neither yellow nor green, very wide, very open, and fringed with thickly mascaraed lashes. Her eyeshadow was a pale translucent green and her eyebrows immaculately shaped and plucked.

"Hello, Eve." Her voice was deep and husky. "Have you been swimming?"

"Yes, I went to Gwenvoe. I've been busy all day and I simply had to have a cool-off."

"How energetic you are. Didn't Gerald want to come with you?"

"He's been cutting the grass, I think."

"Are you going to be in this evening? I've got some chrysanthemum cuttings I promised him, and I've run out of space in my greenhouse. Thought I might bring them up, take a drink off you."

"Oh, how sweet of you. Of course." Then she hesitated. "The only thing is, Alec and Laura are arriving sometime. . . ."

"Alec? Alec Haverstock . . . ?" she smiled suddenly, and her smile was disarming as a small boy's grin, transforming her expression, dissolving the tautness of her features. "Is he coming to stay?"

"Not to stay. Just for a night. Laura's staying on for a bit, though. She's been in hospital; come for a rest cure. Of course'—she slapped the flat of her hand against the driving wheel—"I always forget you've known Alec for so long."

"We used to play on the beach centuries ago. Well . . . I . . . won't come this evening. Another time."

"No." Eve could not bear to disappoint Silvia, to imagine her returning to her empty house, to spend the rest of this lovely day on her own. "Come. Come anyway. Gerald would love to see you. If you ask him he'll make us some Pimms."

"Well, if you're *sure.*"

Eve nodded.

"Heaven, then; love to come." She picked up her basket again. "I'll just take this home and collect the cuttings. Be about half an hour."

They parted, Silvia walking up the street in the direction of her little house, Eve to pass her and drive on, through the length of the village and a hundred yards or so beyond the last cottage. Now, she was running alongside the garden of Tremenheere. There was a stone wall, and thick clumps of rhododendrons beyond. The gates stood open, and the drive curved around a stand of azaleas and stopped in a sweep of gravel below the front door. This was framed in honeysuckle, and as Eve got out of the car, she could smell its heavy fragrance, drowsy and sweet in the warmth of the breezeless evening.

She went, not indoors, but in search of Gerald, through the escallonia archway that led into the garden. She saw the sweep of the lawn, newly cut, neatly striped into two shades of green. She saw her husband on the flagged terrace, supine in a long chair, with his old sailing hat on his head, a gin and tonic conveniently to hand, and the *Times* on his lap.

The sight of him was, as always, eminently satisfying. One of the best things about Gerald was that he never pottered. Some husbands Eve knew pottered the day away, always apparently on the go, but never actually achieving anything. Gerald was always either intensely busy or intensely idle. He had spent the day cutting the grass; now he was going to be lazy for an hour or two.

Her white coat caught his eye. He looked up and saw her, laid down the newspaper, took off his spectacles.

"Hello, my darling." She reached his side, put her hands on the arms of his chair, leaned down to kiss him. "Did you have a lovely swim?"

"Quite delicious."

"Sit down and tell me about it."

"I can't. I've got to go and pick raspberries."

"Stay for a second."

She sat at his feet, cross-legged. Scented thyme grew between the cracks of the flagstones, and she pulled up a tiny sprig and crushed it between her fingers, releasing the herby, aromatic smell.

She said, "I've just seen Silvia. She's coming round for a drink. She's got some chrysanthemum cuttings for you. I said you'd maybe make us some Pimms."

"Can't she come another evening? Alec and Laura will probably arrive while she's here."

"I think she'd like to see Alec. They said they wouldn't be here until dinnertime. Perhaps—' She had been going to suggest that they should invite Silvia to stay for dinner, but Gerald interrupted her.

"You're not to ask her to stay for dinner."

"Why not?"

"Because Laura won't feel like meeting new people, not just yet. Not after two days in hospital and a long drive on a hot day."

"But it's so embarrassing when people come for a drink and then one has to bundle them off home because it's time to start eating the soup. It seems so inhospitable."

"You wouldn't know how to be inhospitable. And with a bit of luck, Silvia will have gone before they arrive."

"You're heartless, Gerald. Silvia's lonely. She's all alone. After all, it's not very long since Tom died."

"He's been dead for a year." Gerald never minced words nor talked in platitudes. "And I'm not heartless. I'm very fond of Silvia and I find her extremely decorative and amusing. But we all have our own lives to live. And I won't have you exhausting yourself, looking after all your lame ducks at the same time. They must wait in a tidy queue and take their turn. And this evening it's Laura's turn."

"Gerald, I do hope she's nice."

"I'm sure she's charming."

"How can you be so sure? You couldn't stand Erica. You said that she drove a wedge between Alec and his family."

"Never said that. Never met the woman. It was Brian who couldn't stand her."

"But men who remarry nearly always follow a pattern. I mean, the second time around they often marry somebody the spitting image of the first wife."

"I don't think that's happened with Alec. Brian approves of this one."

"She's terribly young. Only a bit older than Ivan."

"In that case, you will be able to look on her as a daughter."

"Yes." Eve thought about this, holding the sprig of thyme to her nose and looking at the garden.

From the terrace and the house the newly cut lawn sloped away, flanked by glossy-leaved camellias, which in May were a riot of pink and white flowers. The prospect, carefully landscaped by some long-dead gardener, enclosed the distant view much as a frame surrounds a painting. She saw the bay, the wedge of blue sea, dotted with the white sails of small boats.

Still worrying about Silvia she said, "If we asked Ivan as well he could make up an even number for dinner, and we would tell Silvia—'

"No," said Gerald. He fixed Eve with a stern blue eye. "Absolutely no."

Eve capitulated. "All right." They smiled, understanding, in total accord.

She was his first wife, and he was her second husband, but she loved him—although in a totally different sort of way—as much as she had loved Philip Ashby, Ivan's father. Gerald now was sixty-six—balding, bespectacled, white-haired, but still as distinguished and attractive as he had been when Eve first met him, as her husband's commanding officer, and quite the most eligible bachelor in the service. Active and energetic, he had retained his long-legged (all the Haverstocks had long legs), flat-stomached physique, and at parties was constantly surrounded by quite young ladies or cornered in sofas by elderly ones who remembered Gerald as a young man and had never ceased to be charmed by him. Eve didn't mind all this in the slightest. On the contrary, it made her feel quite smug and proud, because at the end of the day, she was the female he searched for and claimed, and took home to Tremenheere.

Gerald had put on his glasses and was once more immersed in the cricket scores. Eve got to her feet and left him there, going indoors.

The British Empire was built by naval officers with private fortunes. Although Gerald Haverstock was born a hundred years or so too late to take part in this enterprise, the principle of the old saying still applied. His success in the service was due, in the larger part, to his own courage, ability, and resource, but as well, he had the courage to take risks and to gamble on his career. He could do this because he could afford to. He loved the navy and was keenly ambitious, but promotion, although desirable, was never financially essential. As a commanding officer, faced with nerve-racking dilemmas involving the future safety of men, expensive equipment, and even international relations, he had never taken the easy, the timid, nor the obvious way out. This dashing behavior paid off and earned for Gerald a reputation for coolheaded nerve, which had stood him in good stead and finally earned his right to a flag officer's ensign on the front of his large, black, official car.

He had, of course, been lucky as well, and Tremenheere was part of his luck. It was bequeathed to him by an elderly godmother when he was only twenty-six. With the estate went a sizeable fortune, originally amassed by astute dealings with the Great Western Railway, and Gerald's financial future was assured for the rest of his charmed life. It was thought then that he might leave the navy, settle in Cornwall, and take up the existence of a country squire, but he loved his job too much for this, and Tremenheere was left, until the day he retired, to run, more or less, on its own momentum.

A local land agent took over the administration, a tenant was found for the home farm. At times, for long periods, the house was let. Between lets, a caretaker kept an eye on the place, and a full-time gardener tended the lawns and the flowerbeds and kept the two walled gardens neatly dug and filled with rows of vegetables.

Sometimes, home from abroad and with a long leave under his belt, Gerald stayed there himself, filling Tremenheere with family, nephews and nieces, and his own naval friends. Then the old house came to life again, ringing with voices and laughter. Cars stood parked by the front door, children played French cricket on the lawn, doors and windows stood open, enormous meals were partaken around the scrubbed kitchen table or, more formally, in the paneled, candlelit dining room.

The house took all this unorthodox treatment in its stride. It remained, like an elderly sweet-tempered relation, undisturbed, unchanged: still filled with the old godmother's furniture, the curtains she had chosen, the faded prints on the chairs, the Victorian furniture, the silver-framed photographs, the pictures, the china.

Eve, brought here as Gerald's bride six years ago, had made only a few changes. "It's dreadfully shabby," Gerald had told her, "but you can do what you want with it. Do the whole place over if you want to." But she hadn't wanted to, because Tremenheere, to her, seemed perfect. There was a peace about it, a tranquility. She loved the ornate Victoriana, the low-lapped chairs, the brass bedsteads, the faded floral carpets. She was reluctant to replace even the curtains, and when one by one they finally shredded to pieces and fell apart, she spent days searching through pattern books from Liberty trying to find designs that would match, as closely as possible, the original chintzes.

Now, she entered the house through the French windows that led from the terrace into the drawing room. After the brightness of the day outside, the interior seemed very cool and dim, and smelled of the sweet peas that, this morning, Eve had arranged in a great bowl and placed on the round marquetry table that stood in the middle of the room. Beyond the drawing room, a wide, oak floored passage led to the hall, and from this spacious entrance, a square wooden staircase with carved newels rose past a soaring window to the upper floor. Here were old portraits, a carved armoire that had once contained linen. The door to their bedroom stood open, and inside the room felt airy, the rose-trellised curtains stirring in the first breeze of the evening. Eve pulled off her towel robe and her bathing suit and went into the bathroom and took a shower, washing the salt out of her dried hair. Then she found clean clothes, a pair of pale pink jeans, a cream silk shirt. She combed her hair, which had once been blonde and was now nearly white, put on some lipstick, and sprayed herself with cologne.

She was now ready to pick raspberries. She left her room and went down the passage to the door that stood at the top of the back stairs leading to the kitchens. But, holding the door handle, she hesitated, changed her mind, and instead went on down the passage to where once had been the nursery wing, and where now May lived.

She tapped on the door. "May?"

No reply.

"May?" She opened the door and went inside. The room, which was at the back of the house, smelled stuffy and airless. The window had a charming view of the courtyard and the fields beyond, but was firmly shut. In old age May felt the cold and saw no point in suffering what she called howling drafts. As well as being stuffy, the room was crowded, not only with the original Tremenheere nursery furniture, but as well with May's bits and pieces, which she had brought with her from Hampshire: her own chair, her varnished tea-trolley, a fireside rug, hectic with cabbage roses, which May's sister had once hooked for her. The mantelpiece was crowded with china mementoes from forgotten seaside resorts, jostling for place with a plethora of framed snapshots, all of which depicted either Eve or her son Ivan as small children, because once, in the long distant past, May had been Eve's nursery maid and had remained, willy-nilly, to become—in the not so distant past—Ivan's nanny.

A table stood in the middle of the room, where May sat to do the mending or eat her supper. Eve saw the scrapbook, scissors, the pot of paste. The scrapbook was a new ploy for May. She had bought it in Woolworth's on one of her weekly outings to Truro, where she would lunch with an old friend and potter around the shops. It was a child's scrapbook, with Mickey Mouse on the cover, and already beginning to bulge with cuttings. Eve hesitated, and then turned the pages. Pictures of the Princess of Wales, a sailing boat, a view of Brighton, an unknown baby in a pram—all clipped from newspapers or magazines, neatly arranged, but without any apparent reason or cohesions.

Oh, May.

She closed the book. "May?" Still no reply. A sort of panic filled Eve's heart. Nowadays, she was always anxious for her, fearing the worst. A heart attack, maybe, or a stroke. She crossed to the bedroom door and looked inside, steeling herself to discover May prostrate on the carpet or dead on the bed. But this room too was empty, neat, and stuffy. A small ticking clock stood on the bedside table, and the bed lay smooth beneath May's own crocheted counterpane.

She went downstairs and found May where she had feared to find her, in the kitchen, pottering about, putting things away in the wrong cupboards, boiling up a kettle. . . .

May wasn't meant to work in the kitchen, but she was always sneaking down there when Eve wasn't looking, in the hope of finding some dishes to wash or potatoes to peel. This was because she wanted to be useful, and Eve understood this and tried to make a point of giving May small harmless chores like shelling peas or ironing napkins, while Eve cooked the dinner.

But May stumbling around the kitchen on her own was a perpetual anxiety. Her legs had become unsteady, and she was always losing her balance and having to grab onto something to stop herself from falling. As well, her sight was bad and her coordination beginning to fail, so that the most mundane of tasks, like chopping vegetables, making tea, or going up and down stairs, became occupations fraught with danger. This was Eve's nightmare. That May would cut herself, or scald herself, or break a hip, and the doctor would have to be called, and an ambulance would arrive to wheel May off to hospital. Because in hospital, without doubt, May would be a terror. They would examine her and probably be insulted by her. She would do something mad and irrational, like stealing another patient's grapes or throwing her dinner out of the window. The authorities would become suspicious and officious and start asking questions. They would put May into a home.

This was the nub of the nightmare, because Eve knew that May was becoming senile. The Mickey Mouse scrapbook was only one of her disconcerting purchases. About a month ago she had returned from Truro with a child's woollen hat, which she now wore like a tea cozy, pulled down over her ears, whenever she went out of doors. A letter that Eve had given May to post, she found three days later in the door of the refrigerator. A freshly made casserole May dumped into the pig bucket.

Eve unloaded her anxieties on to Gerald, and he told her firmly that she was not to start worrying until there was something to worry about. He didn't care, he assured her, if May was nutty as a fruitcake, she was doing no person any harm, and provided she didn't set fire to the curtains or scream blue murder in the middle of the night, like poor Mrs. Rochester, she could stay at Tremenheere until she turned up her toes and died.

"But what if she has an accident?"

"We'll cross that bridge when we get to it."

So far there had been no accident. But, "Oh, May darling, what are you up to?"

"Didn't like the smell of that milk jug. Just going to give it a scald."

"It's absolutely clean; it doesn't need scalding."

"You don't scald jugs in this weather, and we'll all be coming down with diarrhea."

She had once been quite round and plump, but now, at nearly eighty years old, had become painfully thin, the joints of her fingers gnarled and twisted as old tree roots, her stockings wrinkled on her legs, her eyes pale and myopic.

She had been a perfect nanny, loving, patient, and very sensible. But even as a young woman, she had held strong views, attended church each Sunday, and was a passionate believer in strict temperance. Old age had rendered her intolerant to the point of bigotry. When she first came with Eve to live at Tremenheere, she refused to go to the village church, but joined some obscure chapel in the town, a grim edifice in a back street, where the minister preached sermons on the horrors of drink and May, with the rest of the congregation, renewed her pledges and raised her cracked voice in joyless praise.

The kettle boiled. Eve said, "I'll pour the water into the jug," and did so. May's expression was sour. To placate her, Eve had to think of something for May to do. "Oh, May, I wonder if you'd be an angel and fill up the salt cellars for me, and put them on the dining room table. I've laid it and done the flowers, but I forgot about the salt." She was searching in cupboards. "Where's the big bowl with the blue stripe? I want it for picking raspberries."

May, with a certain grim satisfaction, produced it from the shelf where the saucepans lived.

"What time are Mr. and Mrs. Alec coming?" she asked, although Eve had already told her twenty times.

"They said they'd be here in time for dinner. But Mrs. Marten's bringing some cuttings for us . . . she should be here any moment, and she's going to stay for a drink. If you hear her, tell her the Admiral's on the terrace. He'll look after her till I get back."

May's mouth pursed over her dentures, her eyes narrowing. This was her disapproving face, which Eve had expected, because May approved neither of drink nor of Silvia Marten. Although it was never mentioned, everybody—including May—knew that Tom Marten had died of an excess of alcohol. This was part of Silvia's tragedy and had left her not only widowed but with very little money. It was one of the reasons Eve was so painfully sorry for her and tried so hard to help her and be kind.

As well, May thought Silvia a flighty piece. "Always kissing the Admiral," she would mumble complainingly, and it wasn't any good pointing out that she had known the Admiral for most of her life. May could never be convinced that Silvia did not have ulterior motives.

"It's nice for her to come here. She must be dreadfully lonely."

"Hm." May remained unconvinced. "Lonely. I could tell you some things you wouldn't like to hear."

Eve lost her patience. "Well, I don't want to hear them," she said, and put an end to the conversation by turning her back on May and going out through the door. This led directly into the spacious courtyard, sheltered from the winds, and now somnolent with evening sunshine. The four sides of this quadrangle were formed by garages, the old coach house, and a cottage where undergardeners had once lived. Beyond a high wall lay one of the vegetable gardens, and in the center of the courtyard was a pigeon cote, where a flock of white doves roosted, cooing gently and fluttering about in brief bursts of flight. Strung between the pigeon cote and the garage wall were lines of washing, shining white pillowcases and tea towels, and not-so-shining white nappies, all crisp and dry. All about stood a variety of tubs, planted with geraniums or herbs. There was the spicy scent of rosemary.

When Gerald retired and returned to Tremenheere to live for good, the coach house and the cottage had long stood empty. Derelict, unused, they had become repositories for broken garden machinery, rotting harnesses, and rusting tools, all of which offended his navy-engrained sense of order. Accordingly he had gone to some trouble and expense to reconstruct and convert them. Furnished and equipped, they were rented out, in short lets, as holiday homes.

Now, both the houses were occupied, but not by holiday people. Ivan, Eve's son, had been living in the coach house for nearly a year, paying Gerald a generous rent for this privilege. The undergardener's cottage was inhabited by the mysterious Drusilla and her fat brown baby Joshua. They were Joshua's nappies that hung upon the washing line. So far, Drusilla had paid no rent at all.

Ivan was not at home. His car was gone and his front door, flanked by wooden tubs of pink pelargoniums, closed. This was because early this morning, he and his partner Mathie Thomas had loaded Mathie's truck with samples of furniture from their little factory at Carnellow and had driven to Bristol, in the hopes of getting regular orders from some of the big stores there. Eve had no idea when they would be back.

Drusilla's door, however, stood open. There was no sign of Drusilla or her baby, but as Eve stood there, from inside the little house a sweet piping started up, and the warm, scented evening was filled with the floating strains of music. Eve, listening, charmed, recognized Villa-Lobos.

Drusilla was practising her flute. Heaven knew what Joshua was doing.

She sighed.

I won't have you exhausting yourself, looking after all your lame ducks.

So many lame ducks. Silvia and Laura and May and Drusilla and Joshua and . . .

Eve pulled her thoughts to a stop. No. Not Ivan. Ivan was not a lame duck. Ivan was a man of thirty-three, a qualified architect, and totally independent. Exasperating, perhaps, and far too attractive for his own good, but still perfectly capable of taking care of himself.

She would go and pick raspberries. She would not start worrying about Ivan.

By the time she had finished this, Silvia had arrived. Eve came through the French windows on to the terrace to find her and Gerald sitting there, looking relaxed and civilized and chatting lazily. While Eve picked raspberries, Gerald had stirred himself and arranged a tray of drinks, glasses and bottles, sliced lime, and a bucket of ice, and this stood between them on a low table.

Silvia looked up, saw Eve, and raised her glass. "Here I am, being perfectly looked after!"

Eve drew up another chair and sat beside her husband.

"What do you want my darling?"

"A Pimms would be delicious."

"With lime, too, what a treat. . . ." Sylvia said. "Where do you get limes? I haven't seen one for years."

"I found them in the supermarket in the town."

"I shall have to go and buy some before they all go."

"I'm sorry I wasn't here when you came. Did you find Gerald all right?"

"Well, not exactly'—Silvia smiled her small boy's grin—"I went into the house and was calling, rather pathetically, because there didn't seem to be anybody about, and May finally came to my aid and told me Gerald was here. I must say'—Silvia crinkled her nose—"she didn't look exactly delighted to see me. But then, come to think of it, she never does."

"You mustn't take any notice of May."

"She is a funny old thing, isn't she? Do you know I met her in the village the other day, and it was sweltering hot and she was wearing the most extraordinary woollen hat. I couldn't believe it. She must have been boiling."

Eve leaned back in her chair and shook her head, smiling, torn between anxiety and amusement.

"Oh, dear, I know. Isn't it awful? She bought it in Truro a couple of weeks ago and she's been wearing it ever since." Automatically, she lowered her voice, although it was unlikely that May—wherever she was —would overhear. "She bought herself a scrapbook, too, with Mickey Mouse on the cover, and she's started cutting things out of the paper and sticking them in."

"There's nothing very heinous about that," Gerald pointed out.

"No. It's just . . . unpredictable. Odd. I've got to the point when I never quite know what she's going to do next. I—' She stopped, realizing that she had already said too much.

"You don't think she's going off her head?" Silvia sounded horrified, and Eve said stoutly, "No, of course I don't." She had her own private fears, but no one else was allowed to. "She's just getting old."

"Well, I don't know, but I think you and Gerald are a pair of saints, looking after the old girl."

"I'm not a saint. May and I have been together for most of my life. For years she looked after me, and then Ivan. She was always there when things went wrong, like a rock in times of crisis. When Philip was so ill . . . well, I couldn't have lasted the course without May. No, I'm not a saint. If anybody's a saint, Gerald is, taking her on when he married me, and giving her a home."

"I didn't have much option," Gerald pointed out. "I asked Eve to marry me, and she said that if she did, I'd have to marry May as well." Having poured his wife's drink, he now handed it to her. "A fairly shaking thing to be told."

"Didn't May mind leaving Hampshire and coming to live down here?"

"Oh, no, she took it all in her stride."

"She was at our wedding," Gerald enlarged on this, "wearing the most fantastic hat, like a cake tin covered in roses. She looked like a very old, very cross bridesmaid."

Silvia laughed, "Did she come on your honeymoon as well?"

"No, I put my foot down there. But by the time we got back to Tremenheere she was already installed, with a nice little list compiled of things to complain about."

"Oh, Gerald, that isn't fair. . . ."

"I know. I'm only teasing. Besides, with May here, I get my shirts ironed and my socks darned, despite the fact that they take about an hour to find, because she's always put them away in the wrong drawer."

"She does all Ivan's laundry as well," said Eve, "and I'm sure she's longing to get her hands on Joshua's pale gray nappies and give them a good boil. Actually, I suspect she's longing to get her hands on Joshua as well, but so far she's made no move. I expect she's torn between her nanny instincts and the fact that she hasn't quite made up her mind yet about Drusilla."

"Drusilla." Silvia repeated the improbable name. "When you come to think of it, she couldn't be called anything but Drusilla, could she? Totally outlandish. How long is she staying here?"

"No idea," said Gerald peaceably.

"Isn't she a bit of a nuisance?"

"No nuisance at all," Eve assured her. "We see very little of her. She's really Ivan's friend. In the evenings they sometimes sit outside her house on kitchen chairs and have a glass of wine. What with the washing line and the doves cooing, and the geraniums, and both of them looking faintly bohemian, Tremenheere suddenly feels like Naples, or one of those little courtyards you unexpectedly come upon in Spain. It's nice.

And then at other times, you can hear her practising her flute. She was playing this evening. It's rather romantic."

"Is that what she and Ivan are doing now? Drinking wine beneath the shade of the washing line?"

"No, Ivan and Mathie have been in Bristol all day, trying to drum up some business."

"How's the factory going?"

Gerald answered, "All right as far as we know. They don't seem to be going bankrupt. Silvia, your glass is empty . . . have another."

"Well'—she made a show of glancing at her watch—"won't Alec and his wife be here in a moment . . . ?"

"They aren't here yet."

"I'd love one, then . . . but after that I must take myself off."

"I feel awful," said Eve, "not asking you to stay for dinner, but I think Laura will be feeling exhausted, and we'll probably have an early meal, so that she can get to bed."

"I can't wait to meet her."

"You must come for dinner another evening, when I know how much social life she can cope with."

". . . and I'd love to see Alec."

"You can see him when he comes back to fetch her, and take her back to London."

"The last time he was here Tom was still alive. . . . Oh, thank you, Gerald. Do you remember? We all went out for dinner at the Lobster Pot."

Yes, thought Eve, *and Tom got paralytically drunk.* She wondered if Silvia remembered this too, and then decided that she didn't, otherwise she would never have mentioned that occasion in the first place. Perhaps the passing months since Tom's death were being kind to Silvia, clouding memory over, so that the bad moments were fading and only the happy ones remained. This happened to other people, she knew, but it had never happened to Eve. When Philip died, there had been no bad memories, only the recollection of twenty-five years of good companionship and laughter and love. She had been blessed with so much good fortune; Silvia, it seemed, had had so little. Life, when it came to handing out the goodies, was really dreadfully unfair.

The sun was now low in the sky. It was cooler, but the midges were beginning to bite. Silvia slapped one away and leaned back in her chair, gazing out over the newly cut lawn.

She said, "Tremenheere always looks so fantastically neat. Not a weed in sight. Not even on the paths. How do you keep them down, Gerald?"

"I'm afraid I spray them with weed killer," Gerald admitted.

"Tom used to do that, too, but I just use the hoe. Somehow I think it makes a better job, and at least they don't all come up again. Talking of which, I got buttonholed by the vicar, and he told me you were running the garden stall for the fête next month. Do you need any plants?"

"I certainly do."

"I'm sure I can find something in my greenhouse for you." Silvia had finished her second drink. Now, she laid down the empty glass and reached for her bag, preparing to depart. "I took some cuttings of those little geraniums with the delicious lemon-scented leaves. . . ."

Eve stopped listening to them. Out of the silence of the evening, she had heard the soft purr of a car coming up the road from the village. It changed down, came through the gate; there was the scrunch of tires on gravel. She sprang to her feet. "They're here."

The others got up and they all made their way across the lawn and through the escallonia arch to greet the new arrivals. In front of the house, alongside Silvia's shabby little car, stood parked a beautiful dark red BMW coupé. Alec had already got out of the car and was holding the door open for his wife, a hand under her elbow to help her out.

Eve's first impression was of a girl much younger than she had expected. A slender girl, with dark eyes and thick dark hair, loose upon her shoulders. She wore, like a teenager, faded Levis and a loose blue cotton shirt. Her feet were bare in open sandals, and she carried in her arms a small long-haired dachshund (which looked, thought Eve, like a cross between a fox and a squirrel), and the first thing she ever said to Eve was, "I am so sorry. I hope you don't mind having Lucy to stay as well as me."

Silvia trundled home in her little car. There was a new and unexplained rattle from the engine and the choke didn't seem to be working properly. Her gate, with the name *Roskenwyn* painted upon it, stood open. A pretentious name, she always thought, for such a small and ordinary house, but that was what it had been called when she and Tom bought it, and they had never got around to thinking up anything better.

She parked outside her door, collected her handbag off the seat, and went indoors. The cramped hallway seemed deathly quiet. She looked for letters, forgetting that the postman had already passed, leaving none for her. She dropped her handbag at the foot of the stairs. The silence pressed upon her, a physical thing. Silence, stirred only by the slow ticking of the clock on the upstairs landing.

She went across the hall and into her sitting room, an apartment so small that there was room only for a sofa and a couple of armchairs and desk, with bookshelves over it. In the grate lay the dusty ashes of a fire, although she had not lit one for days.

She found a cigarette and lit it and stooped to switch on the television; she punched the buttons to change channels, was bored by everything, and switched it off. After the moment's burst of meaningless voices, silence pressed in upon her again. It was only eight o'clock. She could not, reasonably, go to bed for at least two hours. She thought of pouring herself a drink, but already had had two with Eve and Gerald, and it was best to be careful with alcohol. Supper, then? But she felt no healthy pang of hunger, no inclination to eat.

A glass door stood open, leading out into her garden. She threw the half-smoked cigarette into the empty fireplace and went out of doors, stooping to pick up a pair of scissors from a wooden basket. Now, with the sun nearly gone, the lawn lay dark with long shadows. She crossed the grass toward her rosebed, began aimlessly to snip off a few dead heads.

A wayward briar became entangled in the hem of her dress, snagging the material. Impatient, angry, she jerked it free, but in her clumsiness caught her thumb on a jagged thorn.

She gave a little cry of pain, holding up her hand to inspect the damage. From the tiny agonizing wound blood swelled. A dot of blood, a bead, a trickle. She watched its progress, a miniature scarlet river, flowing down into the palm of her hand.

As though in sympathy, tears welled in her eyes, brimmed, overflowed. She stood there in the gloomy twilight, numbed by the misery of loneliness, bleeding, and weeping for herself.

The room that they had been given seemed, after Abigail Crescent, enormous. It had a pinkish, flower-patterned carpet, a fireplace, and two long windows, curtained in faded chintz, with tasselled ropes to hold them back. The brass bedstead was of a size to match, and the linen sheets and the pillowcases on the great, downy pillows were elaborately hemstitched and embroidered. There was a mahogany dressing table for Laura and a tall chest of drawers for Alec, and beyond an open door was their own bathroom. The bathroom had once been a dressing room, but conversion from one to another seemed to have been achieved simply by replacing the bed by a bath, so that it too was carpeted and had a fireplace and even one or two rather comfortable-looking chairs.

Laura lay in bed and waited for Alec. She had retired straight after dinner, suddenly overcome with physical exhaustion, but Alec had remained downstairs, in the dining room, drinking a glass of port with Gerald and putting the world to rights, with their chairs pushed back from the table and the air redolent with the scent of cigar smoke.

Laura found the house comfortingly reassuring. Wobbly after the operation, easily prone to tears and apprehensions, she had felt naturally nervous about coming on this long visit, being left by herself, abandoned to strangers. She had kept these fears to herself, in case Alec at the last moment changed his mind and decided to give up all thoughts of Glenshandra and the salmon that were waiting to be hooked out of the river, but as the long car journey progressed and they drew closer by the minute to their destination she had fallen silent.

She had been afraid that Tremenheere would be overwhelmingly grand; that the glittering Gerald would be frighteningly sophisticated; that she would find nothing to say to Eve; and that both Eve and Gerald would think her a dreary ninny and would curse the day they had let Alec talk them into this undertaking.

But it was going to be all right. Their genuinely delighted faces, their obvious fondness for Alec, the warmth of their welcome had dispelled Laura's doubts and melted her shyness. Even the appearance of Lucy they had taken in their stride. And the house, far from being grand, was in fact rather shabby in the very nicest and most comfortable sort of way. Laura had been allowed, at once, to have a bath, which was what she needed more than anything in the world, and after that they had a glass of sherry in the drawing room and then moved into the dining room, which was paneled and candlelit, and hung with Victorian seascapes of great detail and charm, and dinner was grilled trout and a salad, and raspberries smothered in Cornish cream.

"They're our own raspberries," Eve had told her. "Tomorrow we'll pick some more. Even if we don't eat them all, we can put them in the freezer."

Tomorrow. Tomorrow Alec would be gone.

She closed her eyes and moved her feet, which were beginning to get cramped because Lucy, under the quilt, was lying upon them. Her body, beneath the cool, smooth linen sheet, felt flat and insubstantial . . . denuded in some extraordinary way. The operation had left her in no sort of pain, but drained of energy and heavy with lassitude, and it was bliss to be, at last, in bed.

She was still awake when Alec came. He closed the door and came over to the bed to kiss her forehead. Then he turned back the quilt and lifted Lucy from her hiding place and put her in her basket by the fireplace. Lucy's expression at this treatment was one of cold reproach, but she settled in her basket and stayed there. She knew when she was beaten.

He stood with his back to Laura and emptied his pockets, placing his keys, watch, small change, and wallet in a neat row on the top of the chest of drawers. He loosened his tie and pulled it off.

Watching him, Laura decided that security was lying in bed and watching your husband get ready to join you. She remembered, years ago, some minor childhood illness, being allowed to sleep with her mother. Lying in her mother's bed as she lay now and seeing, through eyes heavy with drowsiness, her mother brush her hair, cream her face, slip on her filmy nightgown.

Alec turned off the lights and got into bed beside her. Laura raised her head from the pillow, so that he could slip an arm beneath it. Now they were really together. He turned toward her, laying his other hand against her rib cage. His fingers moved slowly, caressing, comforting. Through the open windows the warm night air flowed in upon them, laden with mysterious scents and small unexplained country sounds.

He said, "You're going to be all right."

It was a statement of fact and not a question.

She said, "Yes."

"They love you. They think you're charming." She could hear the smile in his voice.

"It's a lovely place. They're lovely people."

"I'm beginning to wish I weren't going to Scotland."

"Alec!"

"Tremenheere always has this effect on me."

To this remark, thought Laura, other women, other wives more sure of themselves, would say teasingly, *Tremenheere! I hoped it was me that you didn't want to leave.* But she had neither the heart nor the courage to risk such coyness.

She said, "The moment you go through that gate, you'll start looking forward to Glenshandra." The others would be there already, waiting for him. His old friends. He would be absorbed into his old, pre-Laura life, about which she knew too little and yet too much. Her eyes filled with tears. But this is what I *want* him to do. She said, doing her best to sound down-to-earth, "In magazines, they're always telling you that being apart every now and then adds spice to a marriage."

"Sounds like a cookery recipe."

The tears fell. "And ten days isn't *really* very long."

She wiped the tears away. Alec kissed her. "When I come back for you," he told her, "I shall expect to find you fat and sunburned and well again. Now, go to sleep."

He had set an alarm, which rang at five thirty the following morning, shrilling them both awake. He got out of bed, and Laura lay, sleepily, while he bathed and shaved, and then she watched him dress and put his few things into an overnight bag. When he was ready, she too got out of bed and pulled on her dressing gown. She lifted Lucy out of her basket, and they went out of the room and down the stairs. The old house and its occupants slept on. Alec unlocked the front door and they went out into the chill, misty dawn. Laura set Lucy down and stood, shivering, watching while he stowed his bag in the car, found a duster, and wiped the morning dew from his windshield. He tossed the duster back into the car and turned to her.

"Laura."

She went to his side, was enfolded in his arms. Through his sweater, his shirt, she could hear the beating of his heart. She thought of him throughout the coming day, bombing his way north on the great motorways that led to Scotland.

She said, "Don't have a crash."

"I'll try not to."

"Stop for the night if you get too tired."

"I will."

"You're too precious to lose."

He smiled and kissed her, then let her go. He got into the car, fixed his seat belt, and slammed the door. He started the powerful engine. The next moment, he had gone, around the azaleas, through the gate, down the road through the village. She stood there, listening until there was nothing more to hear. Then she called to Lucy and went back indoors and up to their room. She was very cold, but when she got back into bed, it was lovely and warm because before they went downstairs Alec had switched on the electric blanket.

She slept until midday and awoke to find the room filled with bright noon sunshine. Out of bed, she went to the window and leaned out, her bare arms on the warm sill. The garden simmered in the heat of yet another good day. A man in overalls was working in one of the flower-beds; the distant sea was a cup of blue.

She dressed and went downstairs, and made her way to the kitchen, whence came sounds and voices. There she found Eve, in an apron, stirring something on the Aga stove and a very old lady sitting at the kitchen table, podding peas. They both looked up as she appeared.

"I'm sorry I'm so late."

"It doesn't matter a bit, you were meant to sleep. Did Alec get off all right?"

"Yes, at about quarter to six."

"Oh, Laura, this is May . . . you didn't meet her last night. May lives here with us."

Laura and May shook hands. May's hand felt cold from the peas and was knotted with arthritis.

"How do you do?"

"Pleased to meet you," said May and went on with her podding.

"Can I do something to help?"

"You don't have to. You're meant to be having a rest."

"I shall feel quite purposeless if I'm not allowed to do something."

"In that case"—Eve left her saucepan and stooped to a cupboard to find a bowl—"we'll need more raspberries for this evening."

"Where do I pick them?"

"I'll show you."

She led the way out into the courtyard and pointed out the door that gave on to the vegetable garden. "The canes are up at the far end, under a cage, because otherwise the birds eat all the fruit. And if you see somebody picking peas, it'll be Drusilla. I said she could take some for herself."

"Who's Drusilla?"

"She lives there, in that cottage. She plays the flute. She's got a baby called Joshua. I expect he's up there with her. She looks a bit odd, but she's quite harmless."

The vegetable garden was very old, the various beds neatly squared off from one another by hedges of box. Inside the sheltering walls it was very hot; no breath of breeze stirred. The air smelled of box and mint and thyme and newly turned earth. Laura walked up the path. At the end of this stood an enormous old-fashioned pram, containing a large baby. He wore no sun hat and no clothes at all and was as brown as a berry. Nearby, veiled in the green of pea vines, his mother was hard at work.

Laura stopped to admire the baby. Drusilla, disturbed, looked up, and their eyes met over the top of the peas.

"Hello," said Laura.

"Hello." Drusilla laid down her basket and came to chat, folding her arms and propping a shoulder against a post.

"What a nice baby."

"He's called Joshua."

"I know. Eve told me. I'm Laura Haverstock."

"I'm Drusilla."

Her accent was sensible North Country, which was somehow surprising, because her appearance was quite outlandish. She was a very small and thin girl—it was hard to believe that the lusty Joshua had sprung from such meager roots—with pale eyes and a great deal of bushy tow-colored hair, which did not look as though it had ever seen a pair of scissors. In an attempt to keep it under some sort of control, Drusilla had bound her head with a length of braid. Above this, her hair bulged like a bathing cap; below it stuck out sideways, thick and dry and frizzy.

Her clothes were no more conventional than her hairstyle. She wore a low-necked black vest, beneath which her breasts were flat as a child's. Over this, despite the heat, a velvet jacket, touched here and there with scraps of moth-eaten fur. Her skirt of heavy cotton was long and full, reaching nearly to her ankles. Her feet were bare and dirty.

To complete the bizarre assemblage of garments, Drusilla had added further adornment: a single dangling earring, set with blue stones; a string of beads around her neck and a silver chain or two. Bangles rattled on her thin wrists and there were many rings on her small and surprisingly elegant hands. You could see them playing a flute.

"Eve told me I'd find you here. I've got to pick some raspberries for her."

"They're over there. You came last night, didn't you?"

"That's right."

"How long are you staying?"

"About ten days, I think."

"Eve said you'd not been well."

"I was in hospital for a couple of days. Nothing very serious."

"You'll get better here. It's peaceful. It's got good vibes. Don't you think? Don't you think it's got good vibes?"

Laura said, yes, she did. She thought it had lovely vibes.

"She's a really nice person, Eve. She's good. She lent me that pram, because I didn't have one for Josh. Used to lug him around in an old grocery carton, and he weighs a bloody ton. Makes life a bit easier having a pram."

"Yes, it must."

"Well"—Drusilla heaved her shoulder from the support of the post—"I must get on with my picking. We're having peas for lunch today, aren't we, my duck? Peas and macaroni. That's what Josh loves. See you around."

"I hope so."

Drusilla disappeared once more into the thicket of leaves, and Laura, carrying her bowl, went in search of raspberries.

That afternoon, they lay on deckchairs in the garden, which Eve arranged beneath the dappled shade of a mulberry tree, because it was too hot to sit out in the full sunshine. Gerald had gone to Falmouth for some meeting to do with a sailing club, and May, after the dishes were done, had taken herself off upstairs to her own rooms.

"We could go to the beach," Eve had said, but after some discussion they had both agreed that it was too hot to get into the car and drive there, even with the lure of a swim at the end of the drive, and had settled for the garden. It was very pleasant, the air scented with roses and filled with birdsong.

Eve had brought her tapestry with her and was stitching industriously, but Laura was happy to be totally idle, simply watching Lucy, who, a small russet shape with pluming tail, was happily nosing through the borders and shrubberies after rabbit smells. Finally this delightful occupation palled, she came across the lawn and leaped lightly into Laura's lap. Her fur, beneath Laura's hands, felt velvety and warm.

"She is a charming little animal," said Eve. "So well behaved. Have you had her long?"

"About three years. She lived with me in my flat in Fulham and she used to come to the office with me and sleep under my desk. She's used to being well behaved."

"I don't even know what you did before you married Alec."

"I worked for a publisher. I was with them for fifteen years. It sounds rather unenterprising, staying in one place for so long, but I was happy there, and I ended up as an editor."

"Why unenterprising?"

"Oh, I don't know. Other girls seemed to do such adventurous things . . . like being cooks on yachts or hitchhiking to Australia. But I wasn't ever a very adventurous person."

They fell silent. It was very warm, even under the shade of the tree. Laura closed her eyes. Eve said, "I've started working seats for all the dining room chairs. I've only done two, and there are still eight to go. At the rate I'm going, I'll be dead before I finish them."

"It's such a lovely house. You've made it so pretty."

"I didn't make it pretty. I just found it pretty."

"It must be big to run, though. Don't you have any help?"

"Oh, yes. We have a gardener who lives in the village, and his wife comes in most mornings and gives me a hand. And then there's always May, although she's getting a bit past it now. . . . She's nearly eighty, you know. It's extraordinary to think of a person actually remembering life before the First World War, at the turn of the century. But May has total recall about her childhood, remembers every detail. What she *can't* remember is where she's hidden Gerald's socks or who it was who telephoned and left a message for me to ring them back. She lives with us because she was my nanny, and then she looked after Ivan."

Ivan. Alec had told Laura a little about Ivan. Eve's son, whom he had met at Eve and Gerald's wedding, to which—by some slipup in his social planning—he had brought, not one girl, but two, neither of whom could stand the sight of the other. Ivan, who had trained as an architect, joined a firm in Cheltenham and seemed set for a good solid career, only to blot his copybook by getting engaged to some girl and then deciding to disengage himself. This would not have been so bad, Alec pointed out, if he had not waited until the wedding invitations had been sent out, all the wedding presents had come in, and an enormous marquee was about to be erected for the reception. Before the repercussions of this outrageous behavior had even settled, Ivan had thrown up his job and come to live in Cornwall. Which did not make him sound a very reliable proposition.

"Ivan's your son, isn't he?"

"Yes. My son, not Gerald's. Of course, I keep forgetting, you haven't met him yet. He lives in the coach house at the back of the courtyard. He's been in Bristol, on business. I thought he'd be back by now. Perhaps that's a good sign. Perhaps he's sold lots of furniture."

"I thought he was an architect."

"No, he's started up a little factory in a disused chapel up at Carnellow . . . that's about six miles from here, up on the moor. He's got a partner, Mathie Thomas. He met him in a pub. Such a nice man."

"It must be lovely for you, having him so close."

"We don't see that much of him."

"Do he and Gerald get on?"

"Oh, yes. They're very fond of each other. But then, you see, Gerald was very fond of Ivan's father. He's known Ivan since he was quite a little boy."

"I think Gerald's a darling," said Laura and was astonished that she had, without thinking, come out with this totally spontaneous remark. But Eve was not disconcerted, simply delighted.

"Oh, isn't he? I am glad you think so."

"He's so good-looking."

"You should have seen him when he was a young man."

"Did you know him then?"

"Oh, yes, but not very well—for one thing, I was married to Philip, and for another, Gerald was Philip's commanding officer, and I felt very junior and respectful. Then, when they both retired, Gerald to Cornwall and Philip and I to Hampshire, we didn't see each other for a bit. But then Philip . . . became ill. And Gerald used to come and see him, on his way to London, or if he happened to be staying nearby. When Philip died, Gerald came to his funeral. And then he stayed with me for a day or two, to help untangle all the legal and financial problems and show me how to cope with things like insurance and income tax. I remember he mended a toaster that hadn't worked properly for months and gave me the most frightful row because I hadn't had the car serviced."

"Was your husband ill for long?"

"About six months. Long enough to forget about servicing the car."

"And then you married Gerald."

"Yes. I married him. Sometimes I look back at my life and I simply can't believe my good fortune."

"I feel that way too," said Laura.

"I'm glad you do. If Gerald is a darling, then Alec is too. You must be very happy with him."

"Yes," said Laura.

There was a small pause. She still lay with her eyes closed, but she imagined Eve beside her, with needle poised, looking up over the rims of her pale blue spectacles. Eve said, "He had a rough deal. We never met Erica or Gabriel. Gerald always says that Erica came between Alec and his family . . . the Haverstocks, I mean. But after the divorce, when he came to stay with us, he never talked about her, so we never really knew what happened."

"She ran away to America with another man."

"I think we knew as much . . . but little more. Not that we wanted to. Does he ever hear from her?"

"No."

"Does he ever hear from Gabriel?"

"I don't think so."

"So sad. How unhappy people can make each other. I always feel guilty, all the time, about Silvia Marten."

"She was here last night when we arrived?"

"I wanted to ask her to stay and have dinner with us all, but Gerald wouldn't let me."

"Who is she?"

"Oh, she's lived here always. She used to be Silvia Trescarne. When Alec and his brother were young, they came to Tremenheere for a summer holiday, and they used to play cricket with Silvia on the beach. She married a man called Tom Marten, and for a bit they were very happy, and very social, darting hither and thither from one party to another. But then Tom started drinking, and it seemed that he simply couldn't stop. It was terrible to witness . . . a sort of physical disintegration. He had once been quite attractive, but by the end he was repulsive, with a plum-colored face, hands he couldn't keep still, and eyes that could never quite meet yours. He died last year."

"How dreadful."

"Yes. Dreadful. And particularly dreadful for Silvia because she's the sort of woman who really needs a man in her life. There were always men around Silvia, like bees round a honeypot. They were usually Tom's friends, but he didn't seem to mind. Some women need that little extra bit of attention and admiration. I don't suppose it does any harm."

Laura was reminded, instantly, of Daphne Boulderstone. She said, "I know somebody just like that. She's the wife of Alec's friend. She's forever having intimate lunches with mysterious gentlemen. I don't know how she finds the time or the energy."

Eve smiled. "I know. One's imagination reels."

"She's so attractive. Silvia, I mean. She'll probably get married again."

"I wish she would. But the sad truth is that after Tom died, Silvia's admirers rather fell by the wayside. I suppose it became a different kettle of fish, once she was on her own and free to remarry. Nobody wanted a serious involvement."

"Does she?"

"Of *course!*"

"It doesn't follow. I've got an Aunt Phyllis. She's the prettiest thing you've ever seen and she's been widowed for years. She simply doesn't want to get married again."

"Was she, as they say, richly left?"

"Yes. She was," Laura admitted.

"I'm afraid that makes a terrible difference. Drinking yourself to death is an expensive way of committing suicide, and Tom left Silvia with very little money. That's one of the reasons I worry so much about her. I felt so mean letting her go home alone yesterday evening, when all of us had one another and were so happy together."

"Couldn't she come another evening?"

"Yes, of course," Eve cheered up. "We'll ask her for supper in a day or two, and when Alec comes back to collect you, we'll all go out for dinner together. Somewhere terribly smart. That's what Silvia really enjoys. An expensive dinner in a smart restaurant. It would be such a treat for her. And now, would you believe it, it's nearly half past four? What would you say to having tea out here in the garden?"

5

LANDROCK

Everything baked. Up in the vegetable garden, beyond the pea vines, the gardener toiled, stripped to the waist, planting young lettuces. On a browning patch of lawn, Gerald set up the sprinkler. The sun, shining through the spinning sprays of water, made rainbows. In the house, Eve drew down the drawing room blinds, and outside her cottage Drusilla sat on her doorstep while Joshua squatted beside her, digging up the corner of Eve's herb bed with an old tin spoon.

Wednesday. May's day off. She had to be driven to the station to catch the train to Truro and Laura volunteered for this job. She went to fetch Eve's car from the garage, backed it cautiously out, and waited for May by the back door. When May emerged, she leaned across to open the door for her and the old lady got in beside her. May was dressed up for her outing in a seemly brown dress patterned with squiggles and her child's woollen hat with the bobble on top. She carried her ponderous handbag and a plastic carrier patterned with a Union Jack, which made her look as though she were about to go and cheer royalty.

As instructed, Laura helped May buy her return ticket and saw her on to the train. "Have a good day, May."

"Thanks very much, dear."

She drove back to Tremenheere, parked the car once more in the shade of the garage. Drusilla and her child had disappeared, retreating to the cool of the cottage, and going into the kitchen, Laura saw that Gerald, too, had been defeated by the heat and was sitting at the kitchen table, drinking cold beer and reading the *Times*. Around him, Eve was trying to lay the table for lunch.

"Oh, Laura, you angel." She looked up as Laura came through the open door. "Did you get her off all right?"

"Yes." Laura pulled out a chair and sat facing Gerald's open newspaper. "But won't she expire in that hat?"

"Imagine. Trailing around Truro in this heat, wearing a tea cozy on your head. It's market day, too. Don't let's think about it. I've given up."

Gerald shut the *Times* and set it aside. "Let me get you both a drink." He pulled himself to his feet and went over to the fridge. "There's lager here, or orange juice. . . ."

They both opted for orange juice. Eve pulled off her apron, ran a hand through her short, silvery hair, and collapsed into a chair at the top of the long, scrubbed table.

"What time does she get back? May, I mean."

"About seven. Somebody has to go and fetch her from the train. We'll think about that later. What are we going to do with ourselves today? It's almost too hot to decide. . . . Oh, thank you, darling, how delicious."

Ice bobbed against the tall glasses. "Don't worry about me," said Laura. "I'm perfectly happy doing nothing in the garden."

"I suppose we could go to the beach." She touched Gerald's hand as he sat beside her. "What are you going to do, my darling?"

"I shall take a siesta. Get my head down for a couple of hours. Then when it's cooler, I shall maybe contemplate a little gentle hoeing. The border's like a jungle."

"You wouldn't like to come to the beach with us?"

"You know I never go to the beach in July or August. I object to being showered with sand, deafened by transistors, and anaesthetized by the smell of suntan oil."

"Well, perhaps—'

But he interrupted her. "Eve, it's too hot to be organized. Let's have something to eat and then decide what we're going to do."

Lunch was cold ham and crusty bread and butter and a dish of tomatoes. As they ate this delicious food, the simmering quiet of the day beyond the open door was broken by the sound of a car coming up from the gate and through the archway into the courtyard. There it stopped. A door slammed with a heavy thud. Eve laid down her fork and listened, turning her head toward the door. Footsteps came across the gravel and down the flagged walkway. A shadow fell across the patch of sunlight on the kitchen floor.

"Hello, there."

Eve smiled. "Darling, you're back." She turned up her face to be kissed. "Have you been in Bristol all this time?"

"Got back this morning. Hello, Gerald."

"Hello, old boy."

"And this'—he was looking down at Laura—"this has to be Alec's Laura."

His saying that—*Alec's Laura*— melted any shyness or restraint. He held out his hand, and Laura put her own into it and smiled up into his face.

She saw a young man of good height, but not as tall as Gerald or Alec. Broad-shouldered and very tanned, with blunt, boyish features, his mother's bright speedwell blue eyes, and thick fair hair. He wore a pair of washed-out cotton trousers patched over the knees and a blue-and-white checked shirt. A thick serviceable watch encircled one wrist, and around his neck, revealed by the low-buttoned shirt, hung a gold medallion on a thin silver chain.

"How do you do," they both said, formally and at the same time. This sounded ridiculous, and Ivan laughed. His smile was wide and ingenuous, disarming as his mother's, and Laura recognized the famous charm that had landed him in so much trouble over the years.

"Had any lunch?" Gerald asked him, and he let go of Laura's hand and turned to his stepfather.

"No, I haven't, actually. Is there any to spare?"

"Heaps," said his mother. She got to her feet and went to collect another plate, a glass, knives and forks.

"Where's May? Oh, of course, it's Wednesday, isn't it? Truro day. I should think she might die in this heat."

"How did you get on in Bristol?" Gerald asked.

"Very successful." He went to the fridge for a can of lager and came back to the table, drawing up a chair alongside Laura and letting Eve lay a place in front of him. He opened the can and reached for a glass and poured the lager neatly, with no head to it. "We got two orders from one store and a tentative order from another. The head buyer was away on holiday and the other chap didn't want to commit himself. That's why we were so long."

"Oh, darling, that is good. . . . Mathie must be thrilled."

"Yes, it's encouraging." Ivan leaned forward to cut himself a thick slice of bread. His hands, doing this, were neat and strong and competent, their backs, and his bare forearms, downed in sun-bleached hair.

"Where did you stay in Bristol?" Eve asked.

"Oh, some pub Mathie knew."

"Lots of traffic on the motorway?"

"Not too bad . . . middle-of-the-week stuff." He took a tomato and began to slice it. He said to Laura, "You've brought the good weather with you. I heard the forecast on the radio. It seems to be set fair for a few more days. How's Alec?"

"He's very well, thank you."

"I was sorry to miss him. But he's coming back for you, isn't he? That's fine, I'll see him then."

"You can come out to dinner with us," said Eve. "Laura and I have decided that one night, we're all going to go somewhere terribly expensive and grand for dinner, and we're going to ask Silvia to come with us."

"She'll love that," said Ivan. "Head waiters to hand and a quick fox-trot between courses."

"Who's going to pay the bill?" asked Gerald.

"You are, of course, my darling."

He was not in the least put out by this, as Eve knew he would not be. "Very well. But remember to ring and book a table in good time. And don't let it be that place where they gave us rotten scampi. Took me days to get over it."

Ivan made the coffee. "What are you all doing this afternoon?"

"Good question," said Gerald.

"Gerald's going to have a little nap. He says he won't come to the beach with us."

"Are you going to the beach?"

"We haven't decided." Eve took a sip of her coffee. "What are *you* going to do? Go up to the factory, I suppose?"

"No, I have to drive to Landrock. Old Mr. Coleshill's got some old pine pieces in . . . there's been a sale at some big house. He's given us first refusal, and if I don't go today, the dealers are going to find out about them."

Eve took another sip of coffee. "Why don't you take Laura with you?" she suggested. "It's a pretty drive, and she'd probably enjoy nosing round Mr. Coleshill's antiques."

"Of course," said Ivan at once. He turned to Laura. "Would you like to come with me?"

This unexpected suggestion took Laura unawares. "Well . . . yes. But, please, don't worry about me."

Eve and Ivan laughed. "We're not worrying," Eve told her, "and you don't have to go if you'd rather rest. But you might enjoy it. And the shop's filled with pretty china as well as a mass of dusty junk. It's fun nosing around."

Laura loved antique shops almost as much as she loved bookshops. "I think I'd like to come. . . . Would you mind if I brought my dog as well?"

"Not at all, provided it's not a Great Dane prone to car sickness."

Eve said, "She's a dear little dachshund, but I think she'd be happier left with me. She can play in the garden."

"That's settled, then." Ivan pushed back his chair. "We're off to Landrock. And on the way back, we'll maybe stop at Gwenvoe and have a bathe."

"I was there two days ago," his mother told him. "The tide's out just now and the swimming's perfect."

"Would you like that, Laura?"

"I'd love it."

"We'll leave in about fifteen minutes. I've got a couple of phone calls to make . . . and don't forget your swimming things."

His car was just what she had expected, an open coupé, which meant that the wind blew her hair from the back, all over her face. She tried to hold it back, but it was an impossible task, so Ivan produced an old silk scarf and she tied her head up in that, wondering how many of his girlfriends had already done just this thing.

They followed the main road for a mile or so, moving at great speed, and then turned off into a maze of winding high-hedged lanes. These, with their narrowness and blind corners, Ivan treated with respect and took at a leisurely pace. They trundled peacefully along, every now and then passing small villages or isolated farms, where the air was heavy with the smell of manure and farmhouse gardens bright with flowers. Fuchsias grew in the hedges, purple and deep pink, and ditches were filled with buttercups and tall, creamy stalks of cow parsley.

"It's so peaceful," said Laura.

"We could have taken the main road, but I always come to Landrock this way."

"If you build new furniture, why do you have to go and buy old furniture?"

"We do both. When I first met Mathie, he was in the pine-stripping business. Had quite a good little concern going and no shortage of material. But then stripped pine became suddenly very fashionable and all the London dealers were down, buying anything they could get their hands on. The supply started petering out."

"What did he do?"

"He couldn't do anything much. He couldn't afford to top their prices, and after a bit he couldn't supply his own customers. That's when I came in, a year ago. I met him in a pub, and he poured out his troubles to me over a glass of beer. He's such a good chap, I went the next day to look at his workshop, and I saw some chairs he'd made himself, and a table. I asked him why he didn't start up manufacturing the stuff himself, and he said he couldn't, because he hadn't the capital to buy machinery and generally shoulder all the overheads involved. So we went into partnership. I put up the money, and Mathie put up the expertise. We've had a few thin months, but I'm more hopeful now. I think it's beginning to pay off."

"I thought you were an architect."

"Yes, I am. I was a practising architect for a number of years, in Cheltenham of all places. But when I came down here to live I realized that there simply wasn't enough work. There was no call for a man with my qualifications. Anyway, designing furniture isn't that different from designing houses, and I've always liked working with my hands."

"Are you going to stay here always?"

"If I can. Provided I don't blot my copybook with Gerald and get flung out of Tremenheere. It's your first visit, isn't it? How do you like it?"

"It's heaven."

"Mind you, you're seeing it under ideal conditions. Just wait till the winds blow and the rain starts pouring down. You'd think it would never stop."

"I was a bit apprehensive about coming," she admitted, and somehow it was possible to do this, because he was an easy person to talk to. "You know, to stay, by myself, with people I'd never met. Even though they are Alec's relations. But the doctor said I wasn't to go to Scotland, and I didn't actually have anywhere else to go."

"What . . . ?" he sounded astonished. "No relations of your own?"

"No. Not one."

"I don't know whether to envy you or be sorry for you. Well, don't worry about it anyway. My mother's most favorite thing is looking after people. Every now and then Gerald has to put his foot down, but she persists. He grumbles that she's turned his house into a bloody commune, but he only becomes annoyed with all us hangers-on when he thinks that Eve's looking tired. Have you met Drusilla?"

"Yes."

"And the dreaded Joshua? I'm afraid Drusilla's coming to Tremenheere was my responsibility."

"Who is she?"

"I've really no idea. She turned up at Lanyon about a year ago, with the infant Joshua and a man called Kev. I suppose he was Joshua's father. He called himself an artist, but his pictures were so appalling that no person in his wildest moment would dream of paying good money for them. They lived in a little house on the moor, and then one evening when they'd been there about nine months, Drusilla turned up at the pub with her backpack and her flute case and her baby in a grocery carton and the news that Kev had decamped on her and gone back to London and another woman."

"What a brute."

"Oh, she was quite philosophical about it all. Not particularly resentful. Just homeless and broke. Mathie was in the pub that evening, and at closing time he took pity on her and took her home to his wife, and they looked after her for a couple of days, but it was obvious that she couldn't stay there, so I had a word with Gerald and she moved into the cottage at Tremenheere. She seems to have settled down very nicely."

"But where does she come from?"

"Huddersfield, I think. I don't know her background. I don't know anything about her. Except that she is a trained musician. I think she once played in an orchestra. You'll hear her practising her flute. She's very good."

"How old is she?"

"No idea. I suppose about twenty-five."

"But what does she live on?"

"Social Security, I imagine."

"But what will *happen* to her?" Laura persisted. She found this all fascinating, a glimpse into a life that she had never had to imagine.

"Again, no idea. Down here, we don't ask those sort of questions. But have no fears for Drusilla. She and Joshua are born survivors."

As they talked, the road had climbed, the terrain altered. Bosky lanes had given way to open countryside, reclaimed moorland, with distant views of rounded hills topped here and there with the engine houses of disused tin mines, piercing the skyline like jagged teeth.

They came to a sign, Landrock, and a moment later entered the village, not as picturesque as the others they had come through, but a collection of bleak stone terraces, built around a crossroads. On the four corners of this stood a pub, a newsagent, a post office, and a long rambling building that had once, perhaps, been a barn. It had small, dusty windows crammed with seductive junk, and over the door hung a sign.

WM. COLESHILL

SECONDHAND FURNITURE

BRIC-À-BRAC

ANTIQUES

Ivan slowed down and drew up at the pavement's edge. They got out of the car. Up here, on the hill, it was cooler, the air fresh. There did not seem to be anybody about. They went through the open door of the shop, down a step. Inside the temperature dropped by ten degrees or more, and there was the smell of damp and decay and musty old furniture and wax polish. It took some time to grow accustomed to the dark after the bright sunshine out of doors, and as they stood there, a stirring came from the back of the shop. A chair was pushed back. Out of the gloom, edging his way between cliffs of stacked furniture, emerged an old man in a sagging cardigan. He took off his glasses, the better to see.

"Ah . . . Ivan!"

"Hello, Mr. Coleshill."

Laura was introduced. Remarks were made about the weather. Mr. Coleshill asked after Eve; then he and Ivan disappeared into some dim recess to look at the pine furniture the old man had acquired. Left alone, and very happy, Laura pottered around, squeezing herself into inaccessible corners, tripping over coal scuttles, milking stools, broken umbrella stands, piles of china.

But she was not simply pottering, because she was looking for a

present for Eve. There had not been time before she left London to buy
a gift for her hostess, and she had felt badly arriving as she did, empty-
handed. When at last she came upon the pair of china figures, the shepherd and the shepherdess, she knew at once that they were exactly what
she had been searching for. She inspected them for cracks or chips or
mends, but they appeared to be in perfect condition, if a little dusty. She
blew at the dust and wiped the shepherd on the skirt of her dress. His
face was white and pink, his hat blue, encircled by tiny flowers. She
wanted them for herself, which is perhaps the best criterion of all when
giving presents. Holding her find, she made her way back to the main
part of the shop, where Ivan and Mr. Coleshill, having apparently trans-
acted their business successfully, were waiting for her.

"I'm sorry. I didn't realize how long I'd been. I found these. . . .
How much are they?"

Mr. Coleshill told her and she reeled. "They're genuine Dresden," he
assured her and turned them up in his dirty long-nailed hands to show
her the mark on the bottom. "Dresden and in perfect condition."

"I'll have them."

While she wrote the check, Mr. Coleshill went away and returned
with her purchase, bulkily wrapped in dirty newspaper. She gave him the
check and took the precious parcel from him. He went to the door to
open it for them and let them out. They said goodbye and got into the
car. After the chill of the shop, it was good to be warm again.

Ivan said, "I think you probably paid too much for them."

"I don't care."

"They're charming."

"They're for your mother. Do you think she'll like them?"

"For Eve? What a darling girl you are!"

"I'll have to wash them before I give them to her. They can't have
had a bath in years. And perhaps, on the way home, I could stop off
somewhere to get some pretty tissue paper. I can't give them to her
wrapped in dirty newspaper."

She looked at him. He was smiling. "You're obviously a person who
loves to give presents."

"Yes, I do. I always have. But . . . ," she added, in a burst of confidence, "before I married Alec I could never afford to give people the
sort of presents I really wanted to buy. But now I can." She hoped that
she did not sound mercenary. "It's a lovely feeling," she said apologeti-
cally.

"There's a gift shop in the town. We'll get some paper there when
we've had our swim."

Laura stowed the parcel at her feet, where it could not fall and break.
She said, "And you? Are you pleased with what you've bought?"

"Yes. Quite satisfied. Although like you I've probably been rooked.
But so what? He has to make a living. Now"—he started up the engine

—"let's forget about shopping and go to Gwenvoe and jump into the sea."

Silvia lay in the deck chair, where yesterday Laura had lain. After his stint of hoeing, Gerald had taken himself off to the town to deal with a few small masculine errands, and Eve had grasped the opportunity to calm her troubled conscience, and telephoned Silvia to ask her for tea. Silvia had accepted the modest invitation with alarming alacrity and come at once, walking the short distance up the road from her little house.

It was now five thirty, and they had had their tea. The remains of this stood on a low table between them, the empty teapot, the thin Rockingham cups and saucers, a few biscuits that had not been eaten. Lucy, who had decided that if she couldn't be with Laura, she might as well be with Eve, was curled up in the shade beneath Eve's chair. Eve was stitching at her tapestry.

She glanced at her watch. "I'd have thought they'd be home by now. I hope Ivan hasn't made Laura do too much. . . . At Gwenvoe he usually walks up the cliff path for a bit and swims from the rocks, but that really would be too much of a climb for her. I should have said something."

"I should think Laura's perfectly capable of looking after herself," said Silvia.

"Yes, I suppose so. . . ." Eve raised her head, needle poised. A car roared up through the village. "Talk of the devil, there they are now. I wonder if I should go and make a fresh pot of tea."

"Wait and see if they want one," said Silvia sensibly.

They listened. Car doors slammed. Voices could be heard. Laughter. Next moment Ivan and Laura appeared through the escallonia arch and began to walk across the sunlit grass toward the two watching, waiting women. Ivan and . . . yes, it was Laura. But so subtly changed from the pale girl who had arrived at Tremenheere two days ago that Eve, for an astonished second, scarcely recognized her. But of course it was Laura. Laura with her dark hair wet and sleek from swimming, wearing a loose sleeveless sundress that exposed long bare arms and legs already tanned to a warm honey brown. As they watched, one of her sandals came loose. She stood on one leg to deal with this, and Ivan put his hand on her arm to support her. He said something and she laughed.

Lucy heard her laughter. She sat up, pricked her ears, saw Laura, and ran to greet her, tail and ears flying. Laura, with her sandal fixed, stooped and gathered Lucy up into her arms and got her face licked for her pains. They came on, across the grass, the fair young man, the dark pretty girl, the little dog.

"Hello!" called Eve when they were within earshot. "We wondered what had happened to you. Did you have a lovely time?"

"Yes. Gorgeous. We're cool at last. Hello, Silvia, I didn't know you were here." Ivan stooped and kissed Silvia's cheek beneath the enormous black sunglasses, and then took the lid off the teapot.

"Anything left? I've got a hell of a thirst."

Eve laid down her tapestry. "I'll make some more," but Ivan stopped her, with a hand on her shoulder.

"Don't stir yourself, we'll get some for ourselves." He collapsed on the grass, leaning back on his elbows. Laura kneeled at Silvia's feet and set Lucy down beside her. She smiled at Silvia. "Hello!"

"Where did you take her?" Silvia asked Ivan.

"To Gwenvoe. It was packed with screaming people, but you were right. The swimming was perfect."

"I hope you're not too tired," Eve said to Laura.

"No. I feel marvelous. All refreshed." She kneeled there on the grass, glowing from her bathe, looking, thought Eve, about fifteen.

"Have you never been down to Cornwall before?" Silvia asked her.

"No. This is my first visit. When I was a child I lived in Dorset and we used to go to Lyme Regis in the summertime."

"Alec and I used to play on the beach here together when we were both very young. . . . I'm sorry I didn't have the chance to chat with him when he was here, but Eve's promised that we shall have a good gossip when he comes back to fetch you. He's gone to Scotland?"

"Yes. Salmon fishing."

"And you still live in London?"

"Yes. The house Alec's always had, in Islington."

"I used to go to London quite often, in the old days, when my husband was alive. It was always rather a treat. But I haven't been for ages. Hotels are so dreadfully expensive now, and everything costs so much . . . even taking a taxi practically bankrupts me."

"We've got a spare bedroom. It's not very smart, but you'd be more than welcome if ever you wanted to make use of it."

"How very kind."

"You just have to ask. Alec would love to have you, I'm certain. It's Abigail Crescent. Number thirty-three. Or you could telephone. Eve's got the number."

"Oh, I do think that's thoughtful. I'll maybe take you up on it one day."

"I really mean it. I wish you would."

Eve was talking to Ivan. "How did you get on with Mr. Coleshill?"

Silvia heard the name and joined in with their conversation. "Did you find any pretty things, Ivan?"

"Yes, it was a worthwhile trip. I got a beautiful dresser and some very nice wheel-back chairs. So good-looking, I think they might be worth copying. Mathie will be thrilled."

"Oh, darling, what a lovely, successful few days you've had," said Eve.

"I know. Laura and I have decided that we should celebrate. So there's going to be a cocktail hour in the coach house this evening. Or it might even be a champagne cocktail hour if I can find the right sort of bottles. Silvia, you're invited too. About seven o'clock."

Silvia turned her blind, black gaze in his direction. "Oh . . . I don't think—" she began, but Eve interrupted her.

"Now, don't start making excuses, Silvia. Of course you must come. It wouldn't be a proper party without you. And if you can't find any champagne, Ivan, I'm sure Gerald's—"

But no, said Ivan. "I'll go out and buy some and put it on ice. This is my party."

An hour later Laura was in her bath when Eve came to call her. "Laura, you're wanted on the telephone. Long-distance from Scotland. It must be Alec."

"Oh, heavens." She got out of the warm, scented water, wrapped herself in a large white towel, and went downstairs—her bare feet leaving damp marks on the polished treads—to where the telephone stood on a chest by the front door. She picked up the receiver.

"Hello."

"Laura."

He sounded very far away, as indeed he was.

"Oh, Alec."

"How are you?"

"I'm all right. Did you have a good drive?"

"Yes. Did it in one go. Got here about nine o'clock in the evening."

"You must be exhausted."

"Not really."

Laura hated the telephone. She always found it hard to speak naturally over the horrid instrument, or even to think of anything to say.

"What's the weather like?" she asked now.

"Pouring with rain and pretty cold, but the river's full and there are plenty of fish. Daphne caught her first salmon today."

Pouring with rain and pretty cold. Laura looked up and saw through the long windows the cloudless sky and sunbaked garden of Tremenheere. She might have been abroad, oceans away from her husband. She tried to imagine Glenshandra drenched and chill, but it was unimaginable, and this was not just because she had never been there. She thought of Daphne, booted and mackintoshed, wielding her hefty salmon rod . . . the talk in the evening over large whiskeys, sitting in some little lounge by a necessarily blazing fire. She was grateful not to be there, and this shameful gratitude immediately filled her with guilt.

"Oh, how lovely." She made herself sound pleased and enthusiastic, smiling into the telephone receiver as though Alec could see her. "Send her my love." And then, "Send them all my love."

"What have you been doing?" he asked. "Resting, I hope."

"Well, I rested yesterday, but today I met Ivan and we went to a lovely beach and swam."

"Ivan's back, then?"

"Yes. Yes, he got back this morning."

"How did Bristol go?"

"I think successfully. He's celebrating tonight. Has asked us all for drinks in his house." She added, "Champagne cocktails if we're lucky."

"Well, it sounds as though you're enjoying yourself."

"Oh, Alec, I am. I really am."

"Don't do too much."

"I won't."

"I'll ring you again."

"Yes, do."

"Goodbye, then."

"Goodbye . . ." She hesitated. "Goodbye, darling."

But she had hesitated too long, and he had already put down the receiver.

Eve, showered and changed into a thin dress, came out of her bedroom and made her way, by the back stairs, down to the kitchen. Here, after Ivan's party, they were all going to partake of an informal supper. She had already laid the table and it looked rustic and pretty, with checked napkins and white candles and a pottery jug filled with marguerite daisies.

Gerald, already changed, had gone to fetch May from the station. May always had her evening meal upstairs in her room, but Eve had set places for both Ivan and Silvia and now stood wondering whether she should set one for Drusilla as well. She didn't know if Ivan had invited Drusilla to what he insisted on calling his cocktail hour, but that didn't mean that she wouldn't come. With Drusilla, one never quite knew. In the end, she decided against it. If necessary an extra place could be added at the last moment.

Having made up her mind, she left the kitchen and went out into the warmth and herb-scented air of the courtyard. From their rooftop the doves cooed and murmured, indulged in sudden bursts of flight, their wings spread white against the deep blue sky. Ivan had no garden to his house; but she saw that he had arranged chairs and small tables in a companionable group outside his open front door. Silvia had already arrived and was sitting with a cigarette lighted and a wineglass in her hand. Ivan, talking to her, leaned against a table, but as his mother approached, he straightened.

"Come along. You're just in time for the first brew-up."

Silvia held up her glass. "Champagne, Eve. Such a treat."

She wore a dress of palest yellow, a dress that Eve had seen her wear often before, but which she thought particularly becoming. Her thick gray hair curled about her lively face like the petals of a chrysanthemum, and she had taken much time and trouble over her makeup. Gold studs shone in her earlobes, and around one wrist she had fastened her gold chain bracelet, jangling with old seals and charms.

Eve sat beside her. "Silvia, you *are* looking glamorous."

"Well, I felt I had to dress up for such an occasion. Where's Gerald?"

"He's gone to fetch May. He'll be here in a moment."

"And Laura?" said Ivan.

"She's on her way. Alec phoned from Scotland, so that probably delayed her a little." She lowered her voice. The door of Drusilla's cottage stood open. "Did you ask Drusilla?"

"No," said Ivan. He poured a glass of champagne for his mother and handed it to her. "But she'll probably appear," he finished comfortably.

At that moment they were joined by Laura, coming, as Eve had come, through the kitchen door and walking across the gravel toward them. She looked, thought Eve, deliciously pretty, in an airy dress of peacock blue lawn, delicately stitched and smocked. Her aquamarine earrings, set in diamonds, echoed this rich color, and she had darkened, with mascara, her long, bristly lashes, which had the effect of making her eyes appear luminous and very large.

"I hope I'm not late."

"Yes, you are," Ivan told her. "Dreadfully late. At least two minutes. I refuse to be kept waiting like this."

She made a comic face and turned to Eve. "This is for you," she said.

She had been carrying what Eve thought to be a small handbag, but which now she saw was a parcel, wrapped in pink tissue paper and tied with pale blue ribbon.

"For me?" She set her glass on the table and took the package from Laura's hand. "Oh, but how exciting. You shouldn't have bought me a present."

"It's really a hostess present," Laura explained, sitting down, "but I didn't have a chance to get one in London, so I bought it today."

With all of them watching, Eve undid the ribbons and the paper. First pink tissue and then white. The two little china figures were revealed. She had never seen anything so pretty and was wordless with delight.

"Oh . . . oh, *thank you.*" She leaned forward and kissed Laura. "Oh, how can I thank you? They're enchanting."

"Let me see," said Silvia and took one from her. She turned it up, as Mr. Coleshill had done, to inspect the mark. "Dresden." She looked at

Laura, and Laura met her topaz-colored gaze and silently begged her
not to refer to their astronomical price. After a second, Silvia got the
message and smiled. She turned the shepherd the right way up and set
him down on the table. "They are very lovely. How clever of you to find
them, Laura."

"I shall keep them in my bedroom," Eve announced. "All my most
precious things I keep in my bedroom, because I can enjoy them first
thing in the morning and last thing at night. Did you get them at Mr.
Coleshill's?"

"Yes."

"He's a dreadful old rogue," said Silvia, "but he does have some
good stuff mixed up with all that dusty tat. Even if you do have to pay
through the nose for it."

"Well," said Ivan, "like I said, he has to make a living. And Dresden's
rare these days."

"I shall wrap them up again, before they get broken." Eve began to
do this. "You really are a darling, Laura. Now tell me about Alec. How is
he?"

Laura began to tell her, but before she had time to say more than the
fact that Alec had arrived at Glenshandra safely, Gerald's car came
through the gate, drove past them all through the courtyard, and disappeared into the garage. In a moment he reappeared, with May at his
side.

May was still wearing her woollen hat, but definitely gone in the legs.
Eve, with a sinking heart, saw this immediately. She must have had a
tiring day and walked too far, and seemed glad of Gerald's support, his
hand beneath her elbow. In her other hand she carried her bag and the
Union Jack carrier, bulging mysteriously. Eve's heart sank even further
at the thought of what it might contain.

They halted.

"Did you have a good day, May?" Eve asked.

"Oh, it was all right." said May. But she did not smile. Her old eyes
looked at them all, moving from one face to another. They took in the
champagne bottles and the glasses. Her mouth folded over her dentures.

"You must be tired. Would you like me to come and get you a little
supper?"

"No, no, I'll manage." Firmly, she detached her arm from Gerald's.
"Thanks for coming to get me," she said to him, and then she turned
her back on them all. They watched her make her slow way toward the
house. She went through the door into the kitchen.

"Cross old thing," said Silvia.

The door closed, with some firmness, behind May.

"Silvia, you mustn't say things like that. She'd be terribly hurt if she
heard."

"Oh, Eve, come off it, she *is* a cross old thing. I've never been given such a look in my life. We might have been having an orgy."

Eve sighed. It was no good trying to explain to anybody. As Gerald came to join them, she looked up and caught Ivan's eye. Ivan knew what she was thinking, and he smiled reassuringly, before turning away and drawing up a chair for his stepfather.

His smile made Eve feel better, but not much. The occasion was so pleasant, the company so delightful, the champagne so delicious, the evening so beautiful, however, that it would have been morally wrong to waste it all in fretting over May. The present was now, and every precious moment of it to be appreciated.

The sun was sinking, the shadows lengthening. At this hour Tremenheere became a magic place. The blue hour. *L'heure bleu.* Eve recalled other, long-ago evenings spent with good friends and a bottle of wine on cool terraces after days of Mediterranean sunshine. Terraces wreathed in pink and purple bougainvillaea, the air resinous with pine. A full moon rising over a dark and silent sea. The sound of cicadas. Malta, where she had been married to Philip. The south of France on her honeymoon with Gerald.

She looked up and saw that Gerald was watching her. She smiled, and across the little space that divided them, he threw her a secret kiss.

Drusilla did not appear, but inside her cottage, as dusk gathered, she began to play her flute. By now, Ivan's cocktail hour was in full swing. They all seemed to have drunk a great deal of his champagne, and Silvia had started to tell Gerald an old anecdote that she knew always made him laugh, but as the first sweet notes floated out into the evening air, the laughter and the voices died away, and even Silvia fell silent.

Mozart. The Eine Kleine Nachtmusik. Magical. Extraordinary to think that the outlandish Drusilla should have, locked within her, this amazing talent. Listening, lost in pleasure, Eve remembered Glyndebourne and the first time Gerald had taken her. She decided that this occasion was not all that different, and the heady enchantment of Drusilla's music just as sweet.

When the little concert was over, they sat spellbound for an instant, and then spontaneously began to applaud. Gerald got to his feet. "Drusilla!" A standing ovation. "Drusilla! Bravo! Come and join us. You've earned a reward for giving us so much pleasure."

After a moment, she appeared in her open doorway and stood there, arms crossed and one shoulder propped against the lintel, a marvelously strange and picturesque figure, with her untamed mass of pale hair and her archaic clothes.

She said, "Did you enjoy it?"

" 'Enjoy' isn't a strong enough word. You play like an angel. Come and drink champagne with us."

Drusilla turned her head and, as May had done, looked them all over.

Her face was never, at the best of times, expressive, but now it was impossible to guess what she was thinking.

After a bit, "No, I won't," she said. "Thanks all the same."

And she went into her cottage and shut the door. She did not play her flute again.

6

PENJIZAL

*T*HE WEATHER WAS CHANGING, the barometer dropping. A wind had arisen, flowing in from the southwest, warm and blustery. On the horizon, clouds banked, in dark billows, but the sky remained blue, crossed by chasing banks of white cumulus. The sea, observed from the gardens of Tremenheere, no longer lay blue and flat as silk, but was whipped into flecks of surf. Doors slammed and windows rattled, and sheets and pillowcases and Joshua's nappies flapped and bellied on the washing line, making a noise like badly set sails.

It was Saturday, and Eve for once had her kitchen blissfully to herself. May had taken a pile of mending up to her room and, hopefully, would not appear again until lunchtime. Drusilla had gone down to the village to do her shopping, pushing Joshua in the old pram. In deference to the wind, she had wound a woollen shawl about her shoulders and as well, Eve was glad to notice, had put clothes on to Joshua: a nappy and a felted sweater that his mother had bought at a jumble sale.

Because it was a Saturday and the factory was closed, Ivan had placed his free day at the disposal of Laura and taken her off in his car to show her the north coast in general and Penjizal Cove in particular. Eve had packed a picnic for them and warned Ivan about letting Laura do too much or walk too far.

"She's been ill; you mustn't forget that. That's why she's here."

"You are a fussy old hen," he told her. "What do you think I'm going to do? Take her on a ten-mile hike?"

"I know what you're like, and I have a responsibility to Alec."

"What am I like?"

"Energetic," she told him, thinking that she could have said a great many other things.

"We'll have a picnic and we'll maybe have a swim."

"Won't it be terribly cold?"

"If the wind stays in this quarter, it'll be sheltered at Penjizal. And don't worry. I'll take care of her."

So, she was alone and it was eleven o'clock and she was making coffee for herself and Gerald. She put two cups on a tray with the milk and sugar and a ginger biscuit for Gerald and went out of the kitchen and down the passage to where he had his study. She found him sitting behind his desk, dealing with the paper work that nowadays seemed inevitable if one were to run any sort of an establishment. As she appeared, he laid down his pen, leaned back in his chair, and took off his spectacles.

He said, "The house seems quite extraordinarily quiet."

"Of course it does. There's nobody in it except you and me and May, and she's upstairs darning your socks." She put the tray in front of him.

"Two cups," he observed.

"One is for me. I shall sit and drink it with you and we shall have a companionable five minutes together with no interruptions."

"That'll make a nice change."

She picked up her cup and carried it over to the big chair by the window, where Gerald sometimes took an afternoon snooze or read the papers in the evening. It was a very comfortable and masculine chair, in which her small form was lost, but then this was a comfortable and masculine room, with paneled walls and photographs of ships and various other mementoes of Gerald's naval career.

"What's Laura doing?" he asked.

"Ivan's taken her off for the day in his car. I've given them a picnic. I think they're going to Penjizal to look for seals."

"I hope he behaves himself."

"I've told him not to let her get tired."

"I didn't mean that," said Gerald. He was fond of Ivan but had no illusions about him.

"Oh, Gerald, you must give him some credit. He's just being kind. Besides, Laura's Alec's wife, and she's older than Ivan."

"That's what I call an alternative defense. She's very pretty."

"Yes, she is, isn't she? I didn't think she'd be pretty. I thought she'd be rather a mouse. I think she *was* probably rather a mouse when Alec found her, but it's marvelous what a bit of loving care and some expensive clothes will do to even the plainest of women."

"Why do you think she was a mouse?"

"Oh, just things she's told me over the course of the last few days. An only child, parents killed in a car crash, brought up by an aunt."

"What, a spinster aunt?"

"No, rather a jolly-sounding aunt. A widow. They lived in Hamp-stead. But then when she grew up, she got herself a job and a little place of her own, and as far as I can gather, that was her life for the next fifteen years. She worked for a publisher's. She ended up as an editor."

"Which proves that she's not unintelligent, but doesn't prove that she was a mouse."

"No, but it does sound a little unadventurous. And Laura is the first to admit it."

Gerald stirred his coffee. "You like her, don't you?"

"Immensely."

"Do you think she's happy with Alec?"

"Yes. I think so."

"You sound doubtful."

"She's reserved. She doesn't speak all that much about him."

"Perhaps she's just being private."

"She wants to have a child."

"What's stopping her?"

"Oh, mysterious female complications. You wouldn't understand."

Gerald, that man of the world, accepted this sweeping statement with good grace. He said, "Would it matter very much if they didn't have a child?"

"I think it would matter to her."

"And Alec? Alec must be fifty now. Would Alec want a squalling brat about the place?"

"I wouldn't know." She smiled sweetly. "I haven't asked him."

"Perhaps if . . ."

The telephone on his desk suddenly rang. He said, "Oh, damn."

"Don't let's answer it. Let's pretend we're out. . . ."

But Gerald had already picked it up.

"Tremenheere."

"Gerald."

"Yes."

"It's Silvia . . . I . . . oh, Gerald . . ."

Eve could hear her voice quite clearly and was appalled to realize, instantly, that Silvia was in floods of tears.

Gerald frowned. "What's wrong?"

"Something horrible . . . ghastly . . . vile . . ."

"Silvia, what is it?"

"I can't . . . I can't tell you over the telephone. Oh, will you come? You and Eve? Nobody else. Just you and Eve . . ."

"What, come *now?*"

"Yes . . . right away. Please. I'm sorry, but there's nobody . . ."

Gerald looked at Eve. Frantically, she nodded.

"We'll come," he said. His voice was even, reassuring. "You just wait for us and try to calm down. We'll be there in five minutes or so."

Firmly, he replaced the receiver. Across the desk, before she could say more, he met his wife's agonized, questioning gaze.

"Silvia," he said unnecessarily. "So much for our companionable time together."

"Whatever was all that about?"

"God knows. Damned woman. She's hysterical about something." He stood up, pushing back his chair. Eve, too, got to her feet, still carrying the coffee cup. Her hand was shaking and the cup rattled in the saucer with a tiny tinkling sound. Gerald came and took it from her and set it down on the tray.

"Come along." He put his arm around her, supporting her, urging her gently forward. "We'd better take the car."

The road to the village was strewn with green leaves, blown from the trees. They turned into the gates of Silvia's house, and Eve saw that the front door stood open. Feeling physically sick with apprehension, she was out of the car before Gerald had even switched off the engine.

"Silvia."

As she ran into the house, Silvia emerged from the sitting room, her face distorted with distress, and the two women came together in the cramped hallway.

"Oh . . . Eve, I'm so glad to see you."

She fell into Eve's arms, weeping and incoherent. Eve held her close, patted her shoulder, murmured words of comfort that didn't really mean anything at all.

"There . . . there, it's all right. We're here."

Gerald, on the heels of his wife, firmly shut the door behind them all. He waited for a decent moment or two, and then said, "Now, come along Silvia. Calm down."

"I'm sorry . . . you are angels . . ." With an effort Silvia pulled herself together, drew away from Eve, felt up the sleeve of her sweater for a handkerchief, mopped pathetically at her streaming face. Eve was deeply shocked by her appearance. She had scarcely ever seen Silvia without makeup, and now she looked exposed, defenseless, much older. Her hair was awry, her hands, sunburned and rough from gardening, shook uncontrollably.

"Let us all go," said Gerald, "and sit down quietly. Then you can tell us all about it."

"Yes . . . yes, of course. . . ."

She turned and they followed her into her little sitting room. Eve, whose legs were beginning to feel like rubber, sat in a corner of the sofa. Gerald took hold of the chair by the desk, turned it, and settled himself there, upright and unflappable. He had obviously determined to bring some sense of order to the occasion.

"Now. What's this all about?"

Silvia told them, her voice unsteady, every now and then gasping with intermittent sobs. She had been into the town to do some shopping. When she returned, the morning post lay upon her doormat. A couple of bills and . . . this . . .

It lay on her open desk. She picked it up and gave it to Gerald. A small, plain brown business envelope.

"Do you want me to open it?" he asked her.

"Yes."

He put on his spectacles and took out the letter. A sheet of pale pink writing paper. He unfolded it and read its contents. It did not take a moment. After a bit, he said, "I see."

"What is it?" Eve asked.

He stood up and silently handed it across to her. Gingerly, as though it were contaminated, Eve took it from him. He sat down again and began, minutely, to examine the envelope.

She saw the child's lined writing paper, and sickly pictures of a fairy at the top. The message was composed by letters cut from newspaper headlines and neatly stuck to form words.

> *YoU WEnT WItH OTheR MEn*
> *anD DrOVE YoUR hUSbanD*
> *to dRiNK*
> *YOu ShoULd bE asHaMed OF*
> *YoURseLF*

She felt that for the first time in her life she was truly seeing evil, but on the heels of this repulsion came the most terrible fear.

"Oh, Silvia."

"Wh—what am I to do?"

Eve swallowed. It was very important to be objective. "How does the address on the envelope look?"

Gerald handed it over, and she saw that this had been printed, not very evenly, in separate letters, and by means of a rubber stamp. A child's printing set perhaps. A second-class stamp. Their local postmark and yesterday's date. That was all.

She gave the letter and the envelope back to Gerald.

"Silvia, have you the slightest idea who could have sent you such a horrible thing?"

Silvia, who had been standing by the window staring out at her garden, turned her head and looked at Eve. The amazing eyes, her best feature, were swollen with weeping. For a long moment Eve met her gaze. Silvia said nothing. Eve turned to Gerald, longing for reassurance, but he only watched her over the rim of his spectacles, and his expression was both grave and unhappy. All of them knew what the other was thinking. None of them could bring themselves to actually say the name.

Eve took a deep breath and let it out again in a long, trembling sigh. "You think it's May, don't you?"

Neither Gerald nor Silvia spoke.

"You think it's May. I know you think it's May. . . ." Her voice, rising, began to shake. She clenched her jaw against incipient tears.

"Do *you* think it's May?" Gerald asked quietly.

She shook her head. "I don't know what to think."

He looked at Silvia. "Why should May write you a letter like this? What possible motive could she have?"

"I don't know." The worst of her weeping seemed to be over, and she was calmer now, more like her usual self. With her hands deep in the pockets of her trousers, she came away from the window and began to pace the floor of the tiny sitting room. "Except that she doesn't like me."

"Oh Silvia . . ."

"It's true, Eve. It's never mattered particularly. It's just that for some reason May could never stand the sight of me."

Eve, knowing that it *was* true, sat in miserable silence.

Gerald said, "Even so, it's not sufficient motive."

"All right. So Tom drank himself to death."

Eve was shocked at her coolness and at the same time filled with admiration. To speak thus of her own personal tragedy seemed to Eve both sensible and very brave.

Gerald said, "I know May's strong views on drink and temperance sometimes become a little tedious, but why should she take them out on you?"

" 'Went with other men,' then. Is that what you're driving at, Gerald?"

"I'm not driving at anything. I'm trying to be objective. And I can't see that your friends, or your private life, are any concern of May's."

"They might be, if the friend was Ivan."

"Ivan." Eve's voice, even to herself, sounded shrill with incredulous disbelief. "You can't be serious."

"Why not? Oh, Eve, darling, don't look like . . . what I meant was, that sometimes, when you and Gerald are away from home, Ivan asks me up to the coach house for a drink . . . He's just being kind. Another time, he gave me a lift to a party over at Falmouth that we'd both been asked to. Nothing. *Nothing.* But I've seen old May spying away out of her upstairs window. Nothing goes on beyond that window that she doesn't know about. Perhaps she thought I was undermining his morals or something. Old nannies are always possessive, and after all, he was her baby."

Eve's hands clenched tightly together in her lap. She heard May's voice. *Hmmm. Lonely. I could tell you some things you wouldn't like to hear.*

She saw the scrapbook. The unexplained scrapbook, the newspapers, the scissors, and the paste.

She thought of May's Union Jack carrier bag, bulging mysteriously with things that she had bought on her day out. Had they included the fairy writing paper, the child's printing set?

Oh, May, my darling May, what have you done?

She said, "You mustn't tell anybody."

Silvia frowned. "What do you mean?"

"We mustn't tell anybody about this terrible thing."

"But it's criminal."

"May's a very old lady. . . ."

"She would have to be mad to send a thing like that."

"Perhaps . . . perhaps she is . . . a little . . ." She could not say the word *mad*. She finished, feebly, "confused."

Gerald was studying the envelope again. "It was posted yesterday. Did May go to the village yesterday?"

"Oh, Gerald, I don't know. She's always pottering up and down to the post office. It's her little bit of exercise. She gets her pension there and buys peppermints and darning wool."

"Would the girl in the post office remember seeing her?"

"She wouldn't have had to go into the post office. She always keeps a book of stamps in her bag. I'm constantly borrowing stamps from May. She could simply have posted the letter and come home again."

Gerald nodded, accepting this. They fell silent, Eve haunted by visions of May in her woollen hat making her slow way out of the gates at Tremenheere, down the road to the village, dropping the venomous envelope into the mouth of the scarlet letter box.

Silvia went to the fireplace, took a cigarette from a packet on the mantelpiece, and lit it. She stood looking down into the empty, un-cleared grate. She said again, "She could never stand me. I've always known that. I don't think I've ever had a civil word from the old cow."

"You *mustn't* call her that! You mustn't call May a cow. She isn't. She may have done this appalling thing, but that's because she's muddled and old. And if anyone gets to hear of it . . . if we tell the police or anyone we ought to tell, then there'll be questions, and . . . nobody will understand . . . and May really will go out of her mind . . . and they'll take her . . . and . . ."

She had tried so hard not to cry, but now she couldn't stop. In a single movement, Gerald had left his chair and come to her side on the sofa. His arms were around her, her face pressed to the familiar warmth of his chest. Shoulders heaving, she wept into the lapel of his naval blazer.

"There," said Gerald, comforting her in much the same way that Eve had comforted Silvia, with pats and gentle words. "That's all right. That's all right."

She finally pulled herself together and apologized to Silvia. "I'm sorry. It's we who came to help you, and now I go all to pieces."

Silvia actually laughed. Without much humor, perhaps, but she did at least laugh. "Poor Gerald, what a pair of females we are. I really feel badly about landing you with this, but I knew that you had to know. I mean, after the ghastly shock of opening the letter and reading those horrible words, I couldn't think of anybody but May." She had stopped her pacing and halted behind the sofa. Now she leaned down and kissed Eve's cheek. "Don't be upset. I'm not going to be upset about it anymore. And I know how fond you are of her. . . ."

Eve blew her nose. Gerald glanced at his wristwatch. "I think," he said, "that we should have a drink. I suppose, Silvia, you wouldn't have any brandy in the house?"

She had. They each had a snifter and talked things over. In the end they decided to do nothing, to tell nobody. If it was May who had sent the letter, Gerald pointed out, hopefully, she would have shot her bolt. Probably, by now, she would have forgotten all about it, so unreliable was her memory. But if anything remotely similar should happen again, then Silvia must let Gerald know at once.

She agreed to this. As for the letter, she intended burning it.

"I'm afraid you mustn't do that," Gerald told her gravely. "We never know. If things turn out badly, it might be needed as some sort of evidence. If you like, I'll keep it for you."

"I couldn't let you. I couldn't bear the thought of it contaminating Tremenheere. No, I'll shut it away in a drawer in my desk and forget all about it."

"You promise not to burn it."

"I promise, Gerald." She smiled. The familiar endearing grin. "What a fool I was to be so upset."

"Not a fool at all. A poison-pen letter is a frightening thing."

"I am so sorry," said Eve. "I'm so dreadfully sorry. In a way I feel personally responsible. But if you try to forgive poor May and understand the position I'm in . . ."

"Of course I understand." In silence, they drove the short distance home to Tremenheere. Gerald parked the car in the courtyard, and they went into the house through the back door. Eve crossed the kitchen and started up the back stairs.

"Where are you going?" Gerald asked.

She stopped, a hand on the banister, and turned to look down at him. She said, "I'm going up to see May."

"Why?"

"I shan't say anything. I just want to make sure that she's all right."

*   *   *

By the time lunch was finished, Eve had been overcome by a blinding, throbbing headache. Gerald observed that under the circumstances, this was hardly surprising. She swallowed two aspirin and took to her bed, a thing she very seldom did. The aspirin did their work, and she slept through the afternoon. She was awakened by the telephone ringing. Looking at her watch, she saw that it was past six o'clock. She reached out a hand and picked up the receiver.

"Tremenheere."

"Eve."

It was Alec, calling from Scotland, wanting to speak to Laura.

"She's not here, Alec. She went to Penjizal with Ivan, and I don't think they're back yet. Shall I tell her to ring you back?"

"No, I'll ring her later. About nine."

They exchanged a few more remarks and then rang off.

Eve lay for a little while and watched the clouds race across the sky beyond her open window. Her headache had, mercifully, gone, but for some reason she still felt very tired. Dinner must be prepared, however. After a bit, she got out of bed and went to the bathroom to take a shower.

The lane that led to the clifftop was rutted and winding and so narrow that the gorse bushes on either side scratched and scraped against the wings of Ivan's car. They were covered with yellow flowers and smelled of almonds, and beyond them lay fields where dairy cows grazed. These fields were small and irregular in shape, stitched into a patchwork by meandering stone walls. It was rocky terrain, and here and there out-crops of granite broke the surface of the rich green pasture.

The lane ended finally in a farmyard. A man on a tractor was loading dung on a forklift. Ivan got out of the car and went to speak to him, raising his voice to be heard over the sound of the tractor engine.

"Hullo, Harry."

" 'Ullo there, Ivan."

"All right if we leave the car here? We're going down to the cove."

"That's all right. It's in nobody's way there."

Ivan returned to the car, and the farmer continued his work.

"Come on," Ivan said to Laura and Lucy, "out you get!" He shoul-dered the haversack and, carrying the picnic basket, led the way toward the sea. The path narrowed to a stony track, plunging down into a tiny valley, where fuchsia grew in profusion and a small stream, concealed by hazel thickets, kept them company. As they neared the cliffs, this valley opened out into a deep cleft, thick with bracken and brambles, and the sea lay ahead.

Now the little stream revealed itself, bubbling down the hill through carpets of kingcups. They crossed a rough wooden bridge and paused at the rim of the cliff before descending farther.

Underfoot, sea pinks and heather grew in the tussock-grass, and the wind pounced upon them, salty and fresh, and blew Laura's hair all over her face. The tide was out. Here, there was no beach, only rocks, stretching to the rim of the sea. Wet with emerald seaweed, cruel and jagged, these rocks glittered and dazzled in the sunshine. From the ocean—the Atlantic now, she told herself—enormous waves, stirred up by the freshening wind, gathered themselves up—quite far out—to pour in upon the shore, breaking on the coastline in a fury of pounding white surf. The sound of this was ceaseless.

Beyond the breakers the sea stretched to the horizon and seemed to Laura's enchanted eyes to contain within its depths every shade of blue: turquoise, aquamarine, indigo, violet, purple. She had never seen such color.

She said, unbelieving, "Does it always look like this?"

"Heavens, no. It can look green. Or navy blue. Or, on a dark, cold winter evening, a particularly sinister shade of gray." He pointed— "That's where we're headed for."

She followed the line of his arm and finger, and saw, caught within a bastion of rocks, a large natural pool, shining in the sunlight like an enormous jewel.

"How do we get there?"

"Down this little path and over the rocks. I'll lead the way. Watch your feet, because it's treacherous. And perhaps you'd better carry Lucy. We don't want her going over the edge."

It was a long, tough scramble before they finally reached their destination, and took the best part of half an hour. But they were there at last. Laura edged her way around the final overhanging hazard and joined Ivan on a great flat rock, which sloped to the edge of the pool.

He wedged the picnic basket into a crevice, dropped the haversack, which contained their swimming things. He smiled at her. "Well done. We've made it."

Laura set Lucy down on her feet. Lucy went at once to explore, but there were no rabbit smells here. Only seaweed and limpets. After a bit she got bored and hot, found herself a shady corner, and curled up to sleep.

They changed at once and then swam, diving into cold, salty water, twenty feet deep or more, clear and blue as Bristol glass. The bottom of this was strewn with round, pale stones, and Ivan, diving deeply, brought one of these to the surface and placed it at Laura's feet.

"It isn't a pearl, but it will have to do."

After a little, they stopped swimming and came out and lay in the sunshine, sheltered from the wind by the surrounding rocks.

Laura unpacked the picnic, and they ate cold chicken, Tremenheere to-matoes, crusty bread, and peaches with the bloom still upon them, un-bruised and dripping with juice. They drank wine, which Ivan had cooled by the simple expedient of placing the bottle in a handy rock pool. There were shrimps in the pool, who scurried away when this strange object invaded their private world.

"They probably think it's a Martian," said Ivan. "A creature from outer space."

The sun beat down, the rocks were warm.

"There were clouds at Tremenheere," Laura observed, lying on her back and gazing at the sky.

"All blown away along the other coast."

"Why is it so different here?"

"A different coast, a different ocean. At Tremenheere we grow palm trees and camellias. Here, they can scarcely grow a tree, and escallonia's about the only shrub that can stand the wind."

She said, "It's like another country. Like going abroad."

"How many times have you been abroad?"

"Not very often. I went once to Switzerland in a party to ski. And Alec took me to Paris for our honeymoon."

"That sounds very romantic."

"It was, but it was only for a weekend, because he was in the middle of some enormous deal, and he had to get back to London."

"When were you married?"

"In November, last year."

"Where?"

"In London. In a registry office . . . It rained all day."

"Who came to your wedding?"

Laura opened her eyes. He lay beside her, propped on one elbow, looking down into her face.

She smiled. "Why do you want to know?"

"I want to be able to picture it."

"Well . . . nobody came, really. At least, Phyllis came, and Alec's driver, because we had to have two witnesses." She had already told him about Phyllis. "And then Alec took Phyllis and me out for Lunch at the Ritz, and then we caught the plane to Paris."

"What did you wear?"

She began to laugh. "I can't even remember. Oh, yes, I can. A dress I'd had for ages. And Alec bought me some flowers to hold. They were carnations and freesias. The carnations smelled of bread sauce, but the freesias smelled divine."

"How long had you known Alec?"

"A month, maybe."

"Were you living together?"

"No."

"When did you first meet?"

"Oh"—she sat up, resting her elbows on her knees—"at a dinner party. Very banal." She watched the surf pouring over the rocks. "Ivan, the tide's coming in."

"I know. It does. It's the natural course of events. Something to do with the moon. But we don't have to move just yet."

"Does it cover the pool?"

"Yes, which is why the water is so clean and clear. It gets laundered twice a day. And the sea covers where we're sitting and a great deal more besides. But not for another hour or so. If we're lucky and keep our eyes open, we'll see the seals. They always appear on a rising tide."

She raised her face to the breeze, letting it blow her wet hair back over her shoulders.

He said, "Go on about Alec."

"There's nothing more to go on about. We got married. We had a honeymoon. We went back to London."

"Are you happy with him?"

"Of course."

"He's so much older than you."

"Only fifteen years."

"Only." He laughed. "If I married a girl fifteen years younger than I am she'd be . . . *eighteen.*"

"That's old enough."

"I suppose so. But the very idea seems ludicrous."

"Do you think me being married to Alec is ludicrous?"

"No. I think it's fantastic. I think he's a very lucky man."

She said, "I'm lucky."

"Do you love him?"

"Of course."

"Did you fall in love with him? It's different from just loving, isn't it?"

"Yes. Yes, it's different." She bent her head and picked with her fingers at a crack in the rock, dislodging a tiny pebble. She lifted her arm and threw this, and it bounced on the rock and landed in the pool with a miniature splash. It sank, disappearing forever.

"So. You met Alec at a dinner party. 'This is Alec Haverstock,' your hostess said, and your eyes met over the cocktail tray, and . . ."

"No," said Laura.

"No?"

"No. It wasn't like that."

"How was it?"

She said, "It was the first time we'd met, but it wasn't the first time I saw Alec."

"Tell me."

"You won't laugh?"

"I never laugh at important things."

"Well . . . I actually first saw Alec six years before I met him. It was lunchtime, and I'd gone to see a girlfriend who worked in an art gallery in Bond Street. We were meant to be having lunch together, but she couldn't get away. That's why I went to see her. And it was quiet, and there weren't many people about, so we just sat and talked. And Alec walked in and spoke to my friend and bought a catalog, and then went to look at the paintings. And I watched him go and I thought, 'That's the man I'm going to marry.' And I asked my friend who he was. And she said Alec Haverstock. She said he often came in at lunchtimes, just to look around and sometimes buy pictures. And I said, 'What does he do?' And she told me . . . Sandberg Harpers, Northern Investment Trust . . . very successful, married to a beautiful wife, father of a beautiful daughter. And I thought, 'Funny. Because he's going to marry me.' "

She fell silent. Found another scrap of rock, threw it into the pool with some force.

"Is that all?" asked Ivan.

"Yes."

"I think that's amazing."

She turned to look at him. "It's true."

"But what did you do with your life during those six years? Sit and twiddle your thumbs?"

"No. Worked. Lived. Existed."

"When you met him at the dinner party, did you know then that his marriage had broken and he was divorced?"

"Yes."

"Did you leap at him, crying 'At last,' and fling your arms around his neck?"

"No."

"But you still knew?"

"Yes, I knew."

"And he, presumably, knew too?"

"Presumably."

"How fortunate you are, Laura."

"What, to be married to Alec?"

"Yes. But mostly, to have been so sure."

"Have you never been sure?"

He shook his head. "Not really. That's why I'm still a single, available, desirable, eligible bachelor. Or so I like to think."

"I think you're desirable," Laura told him. "I can't imagine why you're not married."

"That's a long story."

"You were engaged. I know that because Alec told me."

"If I start on that we'll be here till nightfall."

"Do you hate talking about it?"

"No, not particularly. It was just a mistake. But the gruesome thing was that I didn't realize it was a mistake until it was almost too late to do anything about it."

"What was she called?"

"Is that important?"

"I answered all your questions. Now it's your turn to answer mine."

"Oh, all right. She was called June. And she lived in the heart of the Cotswolds, in a beautiful stone house with mullioned windows. And in the stables were beautiful horses on which she used to ride to hounds. And in the garden was a blue, kidney-shaped swimming pool, and a hard tennis court, and a lot of statues and unnatural-looking shrubs. And we got engaged, and there were tremendous celebrations, and her mother spent the next seven months planning the largest, most expensive wedding the neighbors had witnessed in years."

"Oh, dear," said Laura.

"It's all water under the bridge. I turned tail at the last moment and fled, like the coward I am. I just knew that the magic wasn't there, that I wasn't sure, and I liked the poor girl too much to condemn her to a loveless alliance."

"I think you were very brave."

"Nobody else did. Even Eve was angry, not so much because I'd broken off the engagement, but because she'd bought a new hat, and she never wears hats."

"But why did you throw up your job? Surely you didn't have to throw up your job as well as your engagement."

"I had to, really. You see, the senior partner of my firm happened to be June's father. Tricky?"

Laura found this unanswerable.

It was seven o'clock before they got back to Tremenheere. Driving over the moor and down into the long, wooded valley that led to the village, they saw that the clouds to the south had thickened and moved inshore. After the brilliance of the north coast, this mist came as something of a surprise. The town was cloaked in it, invisible. It swallowed the low evening sun and was blown, in drifts, up from the sea toward them.

"I'm glad we didn't spend the day here," said Ivan. "we'd have been sitting in a fog with sweaters on, instead of sunbathing on the rocks."

"Is that the end of the good weather, or will the sun come back?"

"Oh, the sun'll come back. It always comes back. We could have another scorcher tomorrow. It's just a sea fog."

The sun always comes back. The confident way Ivan said this filled Laura with comfort. Optimism is a lovely thing, and one of Ivan's most endearing qualities was that he seemed to radiate optimism. She could not imagine him being downhearted, and if he ever was, then it would not last for long. Even the saga of his disastrous engagement and the loss of his job, which could in a less resilient man have been the source of much retrospective gloom, he had recounted with good humor, turning the whole episode into a joke against himself.

This optimism was catching. Sitting beside him in the open car, tired, sunburned, and salty, Laura felt carefree as a child and more hopeful about the future than she had for a long time. She was, after all, only thirty-seven. That was young. With a bit of luck, fingers crossed, she would be able to start a baby. Perhaps then Alec would sell the house in Islington and buy another, bigger, with a garden. And the house would be Laura's, not Erica's. And the nursery upstairs would be their baby's nursery, not Gabriel's. And when Daphne Boulderstone came to call, she would not be able to sit in Laura's bedroom and make remarks about the furniture and the curtains, because there would be no memories of Erica to justify them.

Now they were turning into the gates of Tremenheere, driving under the arch, stopping by Ivan's front door.

"Ivan, thank you very much. It's been the most perfect day."

"Thank you for coming." Lucy, curled up in Laura's lap, sat up and yawned and looked about her. Ivan caressed her head, pulled her long, silky ears. Then he picked up Laura's hand and kissed the back of it in the most natural and unconsidered way. "I hope I haven't exhausted the pair of you."

"I don't know about Lucy, but I haven't felt so well in years." She added, "Or so happy."

They parted. Ivan had a phone call to make; he would take a shower and change. Perhaps, later, they would all meet for a drink. It depended on what arrangements Eve and Gerald had made. He emptied the haversack and took the damp swimming things and slung them over the washing line, where they hung, sandy and unpegged, in the gathering mist. Laura carried the picnic basket into the kitchen. There was nobody about. She gave Lucy a drink of water and then unpacked the basket, throwing away the rubbish and washing up the plastic plates and glasses. She went out of the door and down the passage in search of Eve.

She found her, for once sitting down, in the drawing room. Because of the mist and the gloom of the prospect from the window, she had kindled a little fire, and this burned cheerfully in the grate.

She had already changed for the evening and was doing her tapestry, but as Laura came through the door, she set this down and took off her spectacles.

"Did you have a lovely day?"

"Oh, heavenly . . ." Laura flopped down into a chair and told Eve about it. "We went to Penjizal and it was gorgeous weather there, not a cloud in the sky. And then we swam and had lunch—thank you for the lunch—and sat and watched the tide come in. And we saw heaps of seals, all bobbing about with darling doggy faces. And then the tide *did* come in, so we went back onto the cliffs and spent the rest of the afternoon there, and then Ivan took me to Lanyon, and we had a beer in the pub, and then we came home. I'm sorry we're so late. I haven't done anything to help you with dinner or anything . . ."

"Oh, don't worry, that's all been seen to."

"You've lit a fire."

"Yes, I felt rather shivery."

Laura looked at her more closely. She said, "You're pale. Are you feeling all right?"

"Yes, of course. I—I had a bit of a headache at lunchtime, but I've had a sleep and I'm fine now. Laura, Alec called. Just after six. But he's ringing back at nine."

"Alec . . . What was he ringing about?"

"I've no idea. Probably just wanted a chat with you. Anyway, like I said, he's ringing back." She smiled. "You're looking wonderfully well, Laura. Quite a different person. Alec's not going to recognize you when he sees you again."

"I feel well," Laura told her. She pulled herself out of the chair and went to the door, headed for her bedroom and a bath. "I feel quite a different person." She went, closing the door behind her. Eve sat looking at the closed door, frowning a little. The she sighed, put on her spectacles again, and went back to her tapestry.

Gerald stood at his dressing table, chin raised, squinting into the mirror, pulling up the knot of his tie. A dark blue silk tie, patterned with red naval crowns. It settled neatly between the two crisp points of his collar. That done, he took up his ivory-backed brushes and attended to what remained of his hair, which was not very much.

Meticulously, he replaced the brushes, neatly lined up with his clothes brush, his stud box, his nail scissors, and the silver-framed photograph of Eve, taken on their wedding day.

His dressing room—as his sea cabin had been—was always a model of order. Clothes were folded, shoes placed in pairs, nothing ever left lying about. It even looked like a sea cabin. The single bed, where he sometimes slept if he had a cold, or Eve a headache, was narrow and functional, and neatly squared off under a navy-blue blanket. The dressing table was an old sea chest, with recessed brass handles at either side. The walls were lined with group photographs: his term at Dartmouth, and the ship's company of H.M.S. *Excellent,* the year that Gerald had been gunnery commander.

Order was engrained in him . . . order and a set of ethics by which he had lived his life, and he had decided long ago that the old, rigid maxims of the Royal Navy could be profitably applied to ordinary, day-today existence.

A ship is known by her boats.

That meant that if the front entrance of a house looked clean and scrubbed, with brass polished and floor shining, then visitors assumed that the rest of the house was just as spotless. It didn't necessarily have to be, and in the case of Tremenheere, frequently wasn't. It was just the first impression that mattered so much.

A dirty submarine is a lost submarine.

In Gerald's opinion this was particularly appropriate to the endless headaches of modern industry. Any establishment, mismanaged and inefficiently run, was doomed as well. He was, in the main part, a calm and easygoing man, but sometimes, reading accounts in the *Times* of strife, strikes, and picket lines, misunderstanding and noncommunication, he came near to grinding his teeth in rage, longing to be, not retired, but in action again, convinced that with a bit of sensible, seamanlike cooperation, all could be resolved.

And then the last, the final conceit. *The difficult we can do at once, the impossible may take a little longer.*

The difficult we can do at once. He put on his blazer, took a clean handkerchief from his drawer, and tucked it into his top pocket. He let himself out of the room, crossed the landing, to where a window looked out over the courtyard. Ivan's car was parked outside his door. Eve, Gerald knew, was having a sit-down in the drawing room. Quietly he went down the back stairs and through the deserted kitchen.

Outside, the mist had thickened and it was damp and cold. From far out to sea he could hear the faint, regular moaning of the coast-guard foghorn. He crossed the courtyard and opened the door of Ivan's house.

The impossible may take a little longer.

"Ivan."

From above he heard the sound of running water, as bath water gurgled down a drain. As well, Ivan had his radio on, a blast of cheerful dance music.

The door led straight into the spacious kitchen living room, which comprized the entire ground floor of the house. A table stood in the middle of this, and comfortable chairs were drawn up before a log-burning stove. Most of the furniture in the room belonged to Gerald, but Ivan had added things of his own: the blue-and-white china on the dresser, some pictures, a pink-and-red Japanese paper bird, suspended from the ceiling. An open flight of wooden steps, like a ship's ladder, gave access to the upper floor, where the old hay loft now contained two small bedrooms and a bathroom. He went to the foot of these and called again, "Ivan."

Abruptly, the radio was silenced. The water gurgled away. The next moment Ivan appeared at the head of the stairs, dressed in a small towel and with his wet fair hair standing on end.

"Gerald. Sorry I didn't hear you."

"I'm not surprised. I want a word."

"Of course, make yourself at home. I won't be a moment. It felt so damp and miserable, I lit the fire. I hope it hasn't gone out. Anyway, pour yourself a drink. You know where it is."

He disappeared, could be heard thumping about overhead. Gerald checked on the stove, which had not gone out. A faint warmth already emanated from its black iron walls. He found a bottle of Haig in the cupboard over the sink, poured a tot into a tumbler, and filled it with water from the tap. Holding this, he began to walk up and down the length of the room. Pacing the quarterdeck, Eve always called it. But at least it was better than sitting down, doing nothing.

Eve. *We won't tell anyone,* they had all agreed. *Oh, Gerald,* she had said, *we mustn't ever tell anyone.*

And now he was going to break his word, because he knew that he had to tell Ivan.

His stepson came down the steep stairs full tilt, like an experienced sailor, damp hair slicked down, and wearing blue jeans and a dark blue polo sweater.

"Sorry about that. You've got a drink? Is the fire all right?"

"Yes, it's going."

"Extraordinary how quickly it gets cold." He went to get himself a drink. "Up on the other coast it was really warm, not a cloud in the sky."

"You had a good day, then?"

"Perfect. How about you? What have you and Eve been up to?"

"We," said Gerald, "have not had a good day. That is why I'm here."

Ivan turned at once, the tumbler in his hand, half-filled with neat whiskey.

"I suggest you put some water in that, and then we'll sit down and I'll tell you."

Their eyes met. Gerald did not smile. Ivan turned on the tap and filled up the glass. He brought it over to the fireside and they sat facing each other across the white sheepskin hearthrug.

"Fire away."

Quietly, Gerald recounted to him the happenings of the morning. The hysterical telephone call from Silvia. Their instant response to her appeal. The letter.

"What sort of a letter?"

"A poison-pen letter."

"A . . ." Ivan's jaw dropped. "A poison-pen letter? You have to be joking."

"It is, unfortunately, true."

"Bu—but who's it from? Who the hell would write Silvia a poison-pen letter?"

"We don't know."

"Where is it?"

"She has it still. I told her to keep it."

"What did it say?"

"It said . . ." As soon as he had got home, and before he forgot the exact words, Gerald had written them down, in his neat script, at the back of his diary. Now he took his diary out of his breast pocket, put on his spectacles, opened the diary, and read aloud. " 'You went out with other men and drove your husband to drink. You killed him. You should be ashamed of yourself.' "

He sounded like a barrister, reading aloud in court the intimate details of some sleazy divorce. His cultured voice reduced to cool impersonality the ill-framed, evil-intentioned words. But the venom, still, was there.

"How revolting."

"Yes."

"Was it handwritten?"

"No, the classic method was used: letters cut from newspaper headlines and stuck on to writing paper. Child's writing paper. The envelope printed with a rubber stamp . . . you know the sort of thing. Local postmark, yesterday's date."

"Has she any idea who could have sent it?"

"Have you?"

Ivan actually laughed. "Gerald, I hope you don't think it was me!"

But Gerald did not laugh. "No. We think it was May."

"*May?*"

"Yes, May. May, according to Silvia, has never been able to stand the sight of her. May has this fetish about drink. You know that as well as we do. . . ."

"But not May." Ivan got to his feet, started pacing the floor, much as Gerald had paced it a few moments earlier.

"May is an old lady, Ivan. Over the last few months, her behavior has become odder by the day. Eve suspects she's going senile and I'm inclined to agree with her."

"But it's so out of character. I know May. She may not like Silvia, but deep down she's bound to be sorry for her. May can be maddening, I know, but she was never one to bear a grudge or be resentful. She was never wicked. You'd have to be totally wicked to think up a thing like that."

"Yes, but on the other hand, she's always held very strong views. Not just about drink, but moral behavior in general."

"What's that meant to mean?"

" 'You went with other men.' Perhaps she thinks Silvia's promiscuous."

"Well, she probably is. Was. Never did May any harm."

"Perhaps May thought she was being promiscuous with you."

Ivan swung around, as though Gerald had landed a blow at him. He stared, incredulous, at his stepfather, his blue eyes unblinking and blazing with indignation.

"With me? Who thought that one up?"

"Nobody thought it up. But Silvia's an attractive woman. She comes and goes at Tremenheere all the time. She told us that you'd driven her to some party . . ."

"So I did. Why waste petrol taking two cars? Is that being promiscuous?"

". . . and that sometimes, when we're away, you have her up here for a drink or a meal."

"Gerald, she's Eve's friend. Eve keeps an eye on Silvia. If Eve's away, I ask her here . . ."

"Silvia thinks that May has watched from her window and disapproved."

"Oh, for God's sake, what's Silvia trying to get me into?"

Gerald spread his hands. "Nothing."

"Well, it sounds like something to me. Next thing, I'll be accused of seducing the bloody woman."

"Did you?"

"Did I? She's old enough to be my bloody *mother!*"

"Did you sleep with her?"

"No, I bloody never did!"

The shouted words left a sort of vacuum behind them. In the silence that followed, Ivan tipped back his head and poured the last of his drink down his throat. He went to pour himself another. The bottle clinked against the side of the glass.

Gerald said, "I believe you."

Ivan filled the glass with water. With his back still turned to Gerald, he said, "I'm sorry. I had no right to shout."

"I'm sorry too. And you mustn't hold this against Silvia. She made not the smallest insinuation against you. It was just that I had to be sure."

Ivan turned, leaning with grace against the edge of the draining board. His quick anger had died, and he grinned ruefully. "Yes, I can see that. After all, my track record hasn't always been perfect."

"There's nothing wrong with your track record." Gerald put the diary back in his pocket, took off his spectacles.

"What are you going to do about the letter?"

"Nothing."

"What if there's another one?"

"We'll cross that bridge when we get to it."

"Is Silvia prepared to take no action?"

"Yes, only she and I and Eve know about it. And now you. And you will of course say nothing. Not even to Eve, because she doesn't know that I've told you."

"Is she very upset?"

"Very. I think more deeply upset than poor Silvia. She's frightened of what May might do next. She has nightmares about having to watch while poor May is wheeled off to some geriatric mental home. She protects May. Just as I protect Eve."

Ivan said, "Well, May protected us. She looked after me, and she stood by my mother all the time my father was ill and dying. She was like a rock then. Never faltering. And now this. Dear old May, I can't bear to think about it. We owe her so much." He thought about this. "I suppose we all owe debts to each other."

"Yes," said Gerald. "It's a sad business."

They smiled at each other. "Let me give you the other half," said Ivan.

Eve and Laura sat in the firelit drawing room, listening to a concert on BBC 2. The Brahms Piano Concerto. It was past nine o'clock, and Gerald, not wishing to spoil their pleasure, had taken himself off to his study to watch the news in there.

Laura lay curled up in one of the big armchairs, Lucy in her lap. Ivan had not reappeared. While she changed, Laura had heard his car go through the gate and take off up the hill in the direction of Lanyon. She guessed that he was off to the pub, perhaps to have a beer with Mathie Thomas.

Across the room, Eve stitched at her tapestry. She looked, thought Laura, tired this evening and very fragile, her fine skin taut over her cheekbones and dark bruises of fatigue beneath her eyes. She had spoken little, and it had been Gerald who made conversation over the grilled chops and fruit salad, while Eve picked at the delicious food and drank water instead of wine. Laura, watching her through sleepy, half-closed eyes, felt concern. Eve did so much, was always on the go, cooking and organizing and generally looking after them all. When the concert was finished, Laura would suggest bed. Perhaps Eve would let her make a hot drink for her, fill a hot-water bottle . . .

The telephone began to ring. Eve looked up from her work. "That'll be Alec, Laura."

Laura pulled herself out of the chair and went out of the room, with Lucy at her heels, down the passage to the hall. She sat on the carved chest and picked up the receiver.

"Tremenheere."

"Laura." The line was better this time, his voice as clear as if he spoke from the next room.

"Alec. I'm sorry I wasn't here when you called before. We didn't get back till seven."

"Did you have a good day?"

"Yes, it was lovely. . . . How is everything with you?"

"Fine, but that's not why I'm calling. Look, something's come up. I'm not going to be able to come back to Tremenheere to fetch you. As soon as we get back to London, Tom and I have got to go to New York. We only heard this morning. I got a phone call from the chairman."

"But how long have you got to be away?"

"Only a week. The thing is, we can take our wives with us. There's a fair amount of socializing to be done. Daphne's coming with Tom, and I wondered if you'd like to come too. It'll be pretty hectic, but you've never been to New York and I want to show it to you. But it would mean getting back to London under your own steam and meeting me there. How do you feel about it?"

How Laura felt was appalled.

This instinctive reaction to a suggestion made by Alec, whom she loved, and intended for Laura's pleasure, filled her heart with a sort of horrified guilt. What was wrong? What was happening to her? Alec was asking her to go to New York with him, and she didn't want to go. She didn't want to make the journey. She didn't want to be in New York in August, especially with Daphne Boulderstone. She did not want to sit in some air-conditioned hotel with Daphne while the men attended to their business, nor pound the sizzling pavements of Fifth Avenue, window-shopping.

But worse was the realization that she did not want to get the train back to London. Nor be torn by the roots from this lovely, carefree existence. Nor leave Tremenheere.

All this took only a second to flash, with hideous clarity, through her mind.

"When are you going?" she asked, stalling for time.

"Wednesday evening. We're flying Concorde."

"Have you booked a seat for me?"

"Provisionally."

"How—how long would we be in New York?"

"Laura, I told you. A week." And then he said, "You don't sound very enthusiastic. Don't you want to come?"

"Oh, Alec I do. . . . It's sweet of you to ask me . . . but . . ."

"But?"

"It's just that it's all a bit sudden. I haven't had time to take it in."

"You don't need much time. It's not a very complicated plan." She bit her lip. "Perhaps you don't feel up to it yet."

She grasped at this excuse, the proverbial drowning man with his wretched bit of straw. "Well, actually, I don't know if I do. I mean, I'm fine . . . but I don't know if flying's an awfully good idea. And New York will be so dreadfully hot. . . . It would be so awful if anything happened, and I spoiled it all for you . . . by being ill . . ." She sounded, even to herself, hopelessly irresolute.

"Well, don't worry. We can cancel the fourth seat."

"Oh, I am sorry. I feel so feeble. . . . Perhaps, another time."

"Yes, another time." He dismissed the idea. "It doesn't matter."

"When will you be back again?"

"The following Tuesday, I suppose."

"And what shall I do? Stay here?"

"If Eve doesn't mind. You'll have to ask her."

"And will you be able to come and fetch me then?" This sounded even more selfish than saying she would not go to New York with him. "You don't have to. I—I can easily catch the train."

"No. I think I'll be able to drive down. I'll see how things go. I'll need to contact you later about that."

He might have been planning some office meeting. The hated telephone separated them, rather than brought them together. She longed to be with him, to see his face, watch his reactions. To touch him, make him understand that she loved him more than anyone in the world, but she didn't want to go to New York with Daphne Boulderstone.

Not for the first time, she was aware of the gap that yawned between them. Trying to bridge this she said, "I miss you so much."

"I miss you too."

It hadn't worked. "How's the fishing?" she asked him.

"We're having a great time. Everyone sends their love."

"Ring me before you leave for New York."

"I'll do that."

"And I'm sorry, Alec."

"Think no more about it. Just a suggestion. Good night. Sleep well."

"Good night, Alec."

7

SAINT THOMAS

*A*T FIVE THIRTY IN THE MORNING, Gabriel Haverstock, who had lain awake since three, pushed aside the rumpled sheet and climbed silently out of her bunk. Across the cabin, a man still slept, his hair and stubbled chin dark against the pale pillow. His arm lay across his chest, his head was turned away from her. She pulled on an old tee shirt that had once belonged to him and made her way, barefoot, aft to the day cabin. She found a match and lit a ring on the small, gimballed gas cooker, filled a kettle and put it on to boil, and then went up the steps and out into the cockpit. There had been a dew, and the deck was damp, beaded with moisture.

In the dawn light, the waters of the harbor lay like a sheet of glass. All about, at their moorings, other boats slumbered, moving so slightly that it was as though they breathed in their sleep. Ashore, the dockside was beginning to stir. A car started up, and from the jetty a black man climbed down into a wooden dinghy, cast off, and began to row. Across the water, each dip of his oars was clearly audible. The boat moved out into the harbor, its wake causing only an arrow-shaped ripple.

Saint Thomas, United States Virgin Islands. During the night, two cruise liners had moved in under cover of darkness and tied up. It was like being unexpectedly invaded by skyscrapers. Gabriel looked up and saw, high on the superstructure, sailors working, winching cables, sluicing decks. Below them, the tall cliff of the ship's side was studded with rows and layers of portholes, behind which, in their cabins, the tourists slept. Later in the morning, they would emerge, wearing their Bermuda shorts and their hectically patterned fun shirts, to lean over the rail and gaze down at the yachts, just as Gabriel was gazing up at them now. Later, they would go ashore, slung with cameras and mad to spend their dollars on straw baskets and sandals and carved wooden statuettes of black ladies with fruit on their heads.

Behind her, in the cabin, the kettle began to boil.

She went below and made a pot of tea. They had run out of milk, so she cut a slice of lemon, put it in a mug, and poured tea over it. Carrying the mug, she went to wake him.

"Umm?" He turned when she shook his naked shoulder, buried his face in the pillow, scratched his head, yawned. He opened his eyes and looked up, saw her standing over him.

He said, "What time is it?"

"About a quarter to six."

"Oh, God." He yawned again, heaved himself up into sitting position, pulling the pillow from beneath him and stuffing it behind his head.

She said, "I made you some tea." He took the mug and tried a scalding sip. "It's got lemon in, because there's no milk."

"So I see."

She left him, poured another mug for herself, took it out into the cockpit, and drank it there. It was getting lighter by the minute, the sky turning blue. As the sun came up, it would burn all moisture away, in a drift of vapour. And then another day, another hot, cloudless, West Indian day.

After a bit, he joined her. He had dressed, was wearing his old dirty white shorts and a gray sweat shirt. His feet were bare. He stepped up onto the deck and went aft, busying himself with the painter of the dinghy, which had got fouled up with the stern anchor chair.

Gabriel finished her tea and went below again. She cleaned her teeth and washed in the tiny basin, put on jeans and a pair of canvas sneakers and a blue-and-white-striped tee shirt. Her red nylon kit bag, which she had packed last night, stood at the foot of her bunk. She had left it open and now stowed in it the last of her stuff—her sponge bag, her hairbrush, a thick sweater for the journey. There wasn't anything else. Six months of living on a boat had done nothing for her wardrobe. She pulled the ties at the top of the kit bag and tied them with a seaman-like knot.

Carrying this, and her shoulder bag, she went back on deck. He was already in the dinghy, waiting for her. She handed him the kit bag and then climbed down the ladder, stepped into the fragile craft, and sat on the forward thwart, holding the kitbag between her knees.

He started the outboard. It hiccupped and then fired, making a noise like a motor bicycle. As they moved out over the water and the distance widened, she looked back at the yacht—the beautiful, fifty-foot, single-masted sloop white-painted and graceful with her name, *Enterprise of Tortola,* emblazoned in gold upon her transom. Over his shoulder, she watched it go for the last time.

At the jetty, he tied up, tossed her luggage onto the dock, and heaved himself up after it. He gave her a hand and helped her up beside him.

Once, there had been a set of wooden steps for this purpose, but they had been blown away in some hurricane and never replaced. They walked down the dock and up the steps into the complex of the hotel. They went through the gardens past the deserted swimming pool. Beyond the reception building, beneath the palm trees, was a forecourt, where a couple of taxis stood, the sleepy drivers dozing. He woke one, who stretched and yawned, disposed of the kit bag, started the engine, and generally prepared himself for a trip to the airport.

He turned to Gabriel. "I suppose, then, this is goodbye."

"Yes. It's goodbye."

"Will I ever see you again?"

"I don't suppose so."

"It's been good."

"Yes. It's been good. Thank you for it."

"Thank you."

He put an arm around her shoulder and kissed her. He had not shaved and the stubble on his chin scratched her cheek. She looked into his face for the last time, and then turned and got into the taxi and slammed the door. The old car trundled forward, but she never looked back, so that she never knew if he waited until they were out of his sight.

From Saint Thomas she flew to Saint Croix. From Saint Croix to San Juan. San Juan to Miami. Miami to New York. At Kennedy, they lost her kit bag and she had to wait for an hour by the empty, turning carousel until it finally appeared.

She went out of the building into the warm, humid, New York dusk, the air foggy and smelling of fuel oil, and waited by the sign until an airport bus came her way. It was full, and she had to stand, strap-hanging, with her kit bag between her knees. At the British Airways terminal, she bought a ticket for London, and then went upstairs to sit for three hours, waiting for the flight to be called.

The plane was full, and she realized that she had been lucky to get a seat on it. She sat next to an elderly blue-haired lady who was making her first trip to Britain. She had been saving up, she told Gabriel, for two years. She was on a tour—most of the passengers were on the same tour—and they were going to see the Tower of London and Westminster Abbey and Buckingham Palace, and make trips farther afield as well. Edinburgh, for a day or two of the festival, Stratford-on-Avon.

"I just can't wait to see Stratford, and Anne Hathaway's cottage."

The excursion, to Gabriel, sounded mind-boggling, but she smiled and said, "How lovely."

"And you, dear, where are you going?"

"I'm going home," said Gabriel.

She did not sleep on the plane. There was not enough night to go to sleep. No sooner had they finished dinner than, it seemed, they were being handed hot towels to wash their faces and given glasses of orange juice. At Heathrow, it was raining. Soft, sweet English rain, like mist on her face. Everything looked very gentle and green, and even the airport smelled different.

Before she left Saint Thomas, he had given her some English money —a few ill-assorted notes from the back of his wallet—but there was not enough to pay for a taxi, so she caught the tube from Heathrow to King's Cross. At King's Cross she changed to another train that took her to the Angel.

From the Angel, she walked, her kit bag under her arm. It was not very far. She saw that changes were taking place in the once-familiar streets. A block of old houses had been bulldozed away and a new and enormous structure was going up in their place. A wall of wooden hoardings protected this building operation from the pavement, and these were spray-painted with graffiti. Skids Rule, she read, and Jobs not Bombs.

She went down the old Islington High Street and through the Campden Passage, between the shuttered jewelers and antique dealers, past the toy shop where once she had bought, in a dusty box labeled three shillings and sixpence, a doll's china tea set. She turned down a narrow, paved lane, and emerged into Abigail Crescent.

Abigail Crescent had not changed. A few more houses had had their faces cleaned, a neighbor had added a dormer window to his roof. That was all. The house where she had spent her childhood looked exactly as it always had, which was comforting, but her father's private parking space stood empty, which was not so comforting. Perhaps, although it was only half past eight in the morning, he had already gone to work.

She went up the steps and rang the bell. Inside the house, she heard it ringing, but no one came to the door. After a little she put her hand to her neck and drew from beneath her sweater a long silver chain, from which hung a latchkey. Long ago, when she was still at day school in London, her father had given her the key . . . in case of emergencies, he had said, but she had never had to use it, because there was always somebody there when she got home.

She used it now, turning the lock. The door opened, and as it did, Gabriel saw a figure making its slow way up the basement stairs toward her.

"Who's that?" The voice was shrill and sharp, even a little agitated.

"It's all right, Mrs. Abney," said Gabriel. "It's only me."

Mrs. Abney did all the things people are meant to do if they have turns or heart attacks. She stopped dead, gasped as if for air, placed her hand on her chest, clutched the banister.

"Gabriel!"

"I'm sorry, did I frighten you?"

"You certainly did!"

"I didn't think anyone was in. . . ."

"I was in all right and heard the bell, but I can't get up the stairs like a dose of salts, can I?"

Gabriel lugged the kit bag into the hall and closed the door behind her.

"Where have you sprung from?" asked Mrs. Abney.

"From the West Indies. I've been flying since . . ." It was too long ago to remember and, with time changes and jet lag, too complicated to try to explain. ". . . . oh, forever. Where's my father?"

"He's away. He didn't say anything about you coming."

"He didn't know I was coming. I suppose he's in Scotland."

"Oh, no. He's *been* to Scotland. Got back Wednesday . . . yesterday, that is. And flew off again yesterday evening."

"Flew off?" Gabriel's heart sank. "Where to?"

"New York. A business trip. With Mr. and Mrs. Boulderstone."

"Oh . . ." Gabriel's legs felt suddenly weak. She sat at the bottom of the stairs and bowed her head, pushing her fingers through her hair. He'd gone to New York. She'd missed him by only a few hours. Their planes must have crossed in the night, both of them traveling in the wrong direction.

Mrs. Abney, seeing her wilt with tiredness and disappointment, became motherly.

"There's nothing in the kitchen, because the house is empty. But why don't you come downstairs with me and I'll make you a cup of tea. . . . It'll seem like old times, having you there. Remember how I used to give you your tea after school when your mum was out? Just like old times."

Mrs. Abney's basement was another of the things that hadn't changed, dim and cozy as a badger's holt, with lace curtains shutting off what light seeped in from the area, and her little range, even in August, hot as a ship's boiler.

While Mrs. Abney put on a kettle and collected cups and saucers, Gabriel pulled out a chair and sat at the table. She looked around her, seeing familiar photographs, the framed calender of bluebells in a wood, the china dogs at either end of the mantelshelf.

She said. "Where's Dicky?"

"Oh, my little Dicky, he died. About a year ago. My nephew wanted to give me a budgie, but I hadn't the heart." She made the tea. "Do you want anything to eat?"

"No, just tea would be fine."

"You sure? When did you last have a meal?"

Gabriel couldn't remember. "Oh, sometime."

"I could do a bit of bread and butter."

"No, really."

Mrs. Abney sat facing her and poured the tea. She said, "I shall want to hear all your news. And about your mother. Mother's all right, is she? That's good. My goodness, it seems a long time since you went . . .

must be nearly six years now. How old are you now? Nineteen? Yes, I thought you must be just about nineteen. You haven't changed that much. Recognized you at once. Except your hair's short. And you've dyed it blond."

"No, I didn't dye it. It just bleached itself with West Indian sunshine and chlorinated swimming pools."

"You look like a boy. That's what I thought when I saw you standing there. That's why I got such a scare. Some nasty boys around the place these days . . . I have to take good care of the house when your father's away."

Gabriel took a mouthful of the tea, which was dark and sweet and strong, the way Mrs. Abney had always liked it.

"And his new wife . . . has she gone to New York too?"

"No. I told you, just the Boulderstones. No, the new Mrs. Haverstock's gone to Cornwall. She's been there for a bit." Mrs. Abney dropped her voice to a confidential whisper. "Had to have this little operation. You know, dear. Insides."

"Oh, dear."

"Anyway," Mrs. Abney continued in her normal tones, "the doctor wouldn't let her go to Scotland, so she went to Cornwall instead." She took another sip of tea and laid the cup down in the saucer. "To get better."

"Do you know where she is?"

"No, I don't know where. Mr. Haverstock didn't give me her address. Just to some relation of his, in Cornwall."

"There are dozens of Haverstocks in Devon and Cornwall. She could be anywhere."

"Well, I'm sorry, but I don't know where she is . . . except . . . a letter came yesterday evening. I think it came from Cornwall. Just wait and I'll get it." She got to her feet and went over to her sideboard and opened a drawer. "Your father's secretary drops by each morning and picks up all the mail, and deals with it in the office. But she hasn't come yet, and this is all I've got to give her."

She handed the envelope to Gabriel. A plain brown envelope with her father's name and the address apparently printed on, as though it had been done with a rubber stamp. The postmark was Truro, Cornwall, and in the opposite corner someone had written, in felt pen, Urgent, and underlined it.

"What an extraordinary-looking letter."

"It *might* be from Mrs. Haverstock. The new Mrs. Haverstock, that is," she added tactfully.

"I can't *open* it." She looked at Mrs. Abney. "Can I?"

"Well, I don't know, dear. It's up to you. If you want to get hold of Mrs. Haverstock and the address is in the letter, then I don't see why you shouldn't have a peep. Though I must say, it's a funny way to write the address. Must have taken hours."

Gabriel laid down the envelope and then picked it up again.

She said, "I really *have* to know where she is, Mrs. Abney. If I can't see my father, I have to see her."

"Then open it," said Mrs. Abney. "After all, 'Urgent' doesn't mean private."

Gabriel put her thumb beneath the flap and slit the envelope. She drew out a sheet of pale pink writing paper and unfolded it. Lined paper, headed by a stamp-size picture of a fairy. The lines of black, uneven print shouted at her like a bad-news headline.

> *YOur WiFe aT TreMEnhEeRe iS
> HaViNG AN AFfaIR wITh IvAN
> AShbY. ThOUgHt yOu shOUld KnoW
> A WEll-wisHEr.*

Her heart was hammering. She felt the blood drain from her face.

"Any use?" asked Mrs. Abney, craning her neck to peer.

Gabriel quickly folded the letter and stuffed it back into the envelope before Mrs. Abney should see.

"No. Yes. It's . . . not from her. Just a note from somebody else. But she's at a place called Tremenheere."

"There you are! Now you know." Her eyes narrowed. "Are you all right? You've gone deathly pale."

"Yes, I am all right, but I'm tired." She pushed the horrible envelope into the pocket of her jeans. "I haven't slept for hours. I think, if you don't mind, I'll go and lie down."

"You do that. Your bed's not made up, but it's been aired. You can get in under the blankets. Have a bit of shut-eye."

"Yes. You are kind, Mrs. Abney. I'm sorry I suddenly burst in on you, surprised you."

"It's nice to have you here again. Nice to have a bit of company with everyone away. Your dad'll be pleased when he knows you're back."

Gabriel went upstairs and into the sitting room. Picked up the telephone and dialed a number. A man answered. "Directory enquiries."

"I want a number in Cornwall, please. The name is Haverstock. I'm afraid I don't know the initial. And the address is Tremenheere."

"Hold on a mo."

She held on. He was a cheerful man, singing at his work. "Oh, when e'er the darkest cloud is in the sky, You mustn't sigh. And you mustn't cry. . . ."

The sitting room was much as she remembered it. The same curtains, the same covers on the chairs. The cushions that her mother had chosen. Some new ornaments, another picture or two . . .

"Tremenheere. Here we are. Penvarloe two three eight."

Gabriel, ready with a pencil, wrote it down.

"And it's Mist . . . ?"

"No, not Mister. Admiral, Admiral G. J. Haverstock."

She said, "Penvarloe," and then, sounding helpless, "Oh dear."

"What's wrong now?"

"I've got to get there by train. I wonder which would be the nearest railway station."

"I can tell you that." And he did so.

"How do you know?"

"The wife and I were down there for our summer holidays last year."

"How amazing."

"Amazing all right," said the cheerful voice. "Rained the whole bloody time."

She went out of the room, picked up her things, and trailed upstairs. On the first landing, she dropped the kit bag and went into her father's dressing room. It smelled, as it had always smelled, of Bay Rum. She opened the wardrobe and touched his clothes, lifting the sleeve of a tweed jacket and holding it against her cheek. She saw his salmon rod, in its canvas case, neatly stowed in a corner; his open desk, stuffed with his ordered confusion of papers and check stubs and some accounts, waiting to be paid. On the chest of drawers stood a photograph of herself, taken years ago, and a terrible drawing she had once done for him. As well there was a photograph of . . . Laura? Not a studio portrait but an enlarged snap, informal and laughing. She had a lot of dark hair and dark eyes and a lovely smile. She looked so happy.

Your wife at Tremenheere is having an affair with Ivan Ashby.

Gabriel went out through the door and closed it behind her. Dragging the kit bag again, she started up the last flight. *Your room will always be there,* he had promised her. *Waiting for you.* She opened the door and went in. Her bed, her books, her bears, her dollhouse. The Beatrix Potter frieze around the walls, the blue-and-white curtains.

The kit bag fell upon the floor with a soft thud. She kicked off her shoes and pulled back the covers and got into the bed. The blankets felt soft and warm, more comforting than any sheet. She stared at the ceiling, too tired to sleep.

Your wife at Tremenheere . . .

Too tired even to cry. She closed her eyes.

Later, she got up and had a hot bath and put on some other clothes. Another pair of jeans, another tee shirt, hauled, unironed, from the kit bag, but at least clean. She picked up her shoulder bag and let herself out of the house and walked around the corner to the local bank that her parents had always used. She asked to see the manager, identified herself, and was allowed to cash a check. With money to spend, she realized that she was ravenously hungry. She found a delicatessen and bought fresh bread, butter, a carton of milk, some pâté, and half a pound of tomatoes. When she got back to Abigail Crescent, she unloaded all this onto the kitchen table, and there assembled and consumed the impromptu meal. It was now nearly three thirty. She went through to the sitting room and rang Paddington Station and booked herself a sleeper on the night train. After that there wasn't anything to do except wait.

The station was at the end of the line. For the last mile or so of the journey, the railway ran alongside the sea, and when Gabriel opened the door of the train and stepped down onto the platform, it was to be met by the strong, salty smell of seaweed and fish, while overhead a lot of gulls, screaming into the fresh morning breeze, were flying about.

The platform clock stood at half past seven. She walked down the platform and out into the station yard. Beyond this was a harbor, filled with fishing boats and small pleasure craft. There was a taxi rank, with two or three cars lined up, so she went to the first and asked the man to take her to Tremenheere. "Got any luggage, 'have you?"

"Only this."

He opened the door, and she got in and he slung the red kit bag in after her.

"Is it very far?" she asked him, as he started up the road behind the station and then turned back in the direction from which the train had come.

"No, only a mile or two. Going to stay with the Admiral?"

"Do you know him?"

"No, I don't know 'im. Know *of* 'im. Lovely 'ouse 'e's got."

"I hope it's not too early for them. I'm not expected."

"Bound to be someone around."

Already, they had left the town behind them, turned up a winding lane, climbing a hill. There were little fields and farms and a lot of wild rhododendrons. Then a village. "This 'ere's Penvarloe," and then gates, and a short driveway, and a big and very beautiful stone Elizabethan house was revealed.

They stopped by the front door, which stood, irrefutably shut, locked against them. At the side of it was a wrought-iron bellpull, but the thought of actually pulling it and waking a houseful of sleeping people was more than Gabriel could face.

"Just drop me here, and I'll wait."

"Let's go round the back and see if there's anyone there."

The taxi moved on cautiously, under an archway and into a courtyard at the back of the house. Still, there was no sign of life. Gabriel got out and heaved her kit bag after her.

"Don't worry," she told the driver. "I'll be all right now. How much do I owe you?"

He told her, and she paid him and thanked him. He backed cautiously out of the courtyard, through the archway, and she heard him drive away. As she stood there trying to decide what to do next, the quiet was shattered by the sound of a window opening, and a man's voice said, "Are you looking for somebody?"

Not the big house, but the small house opposite, on the far side of the square. It had pink pelargoniums in tubs on either side of its door, and from the upper window a man leaned, his forearms resting on the stone ledge. He might have been totally naked, but Gabriel could only see his top half, so she couldn't be sure.

She said, "Yes."

"Who?"

"Mrs. Haverstock."

"You have a choice. We have two Mrs. Haverstocks here. Which would you like?"

"Mrs. Alec Haverstock."

"Hold on a moment," said the naked man, "and I'll come down and let you in."

Gabriel carried the kit bag across the courtyard and waited. She did not have to wait for long. A moment later, the door of the little house opened—he obviously never locked it—and he reappeared, barelegged and barefooted, but with the rest of him decently wrapped in a blue towel robe, the sash of which he was in the process of knotting around his waist. He was unshaven and his fair hair stood on end.

He said, "Hello."

"I'm afraid I woke you up."

"Yes, you did, or at least the taxi did. You're looking for Laura. She won't be up yet; none of them ever appear until about nine o'clock."

Gabriel looked at her watch. "Oh, dear . . ."

He picked up her kit bag and stood aside, holding the door open. "Come on in."

"But, aren't you . . . ?"

"Come on, it's all right. I can't go back to bed, even if I wanted to. I've got to get to work. . . ."

Gabriel went through the door, and he closed it behind them. She saw the big room, which appeared to serve all functions; the pleasant clutter of scrubbed pine and blue-and-white china; saucepans neatly ranged over a small electric cooker; a black stove with armchairs drawn up to its comfort. There was a table in the middle of the room, on which stood a brown jug filled with roses. From the ceiling, suspended by a thread, hung a pink-and-red paper bird.

She said, "What a nice room."

"I like it." She turned to face him. "Does Laura know you're coming?"

"No."

"Who are you?"

"Gabriel Haverstock." He stared. "Alec's my father."

"But you're in America."

"No, I'm not. I'm here. It's my father who's in America now. He flew to New York on Wednesday evening. Our planes must have crossed in the middle of the night."

"He didn't know you were coming, either?"

"No."

"How did you get here?"

"On the night train from Paddington."

"Well . . ." He seemed to be lost for words. "This is a turn-up for the books. Are you going to stay?"

"I don't know. That depends on whether anybody asks me."

"You don't sound very sure."

"I'm not."

"Do you know Gerald?"

"My father used to talk about him, but I've never met him."

"So you won't have met Eve?"

"No, I haven't met either of them. And I haven't met Laura."

He laughed, scratching the back of his head, the very picture of a man in perplexity. "What a jolly time everybody's going to have, meeting each other. Well, we'll just have to wait until they all stir their stumps. Would you like some breakfast?"

"Are you going to have some?"

"Of course I am. You don't imagine I go to work on an empty stomach."

He went over to the little cooker, switched it on, opened the fridge, took out a packet of bacon. Gabriel pulled a chair away from the table and sat and watched him. He looked, she thought, marvelously disheveled, like an advertisement for Eau Savage.

She said, "Where do you work?"

"I have part shares in a small furniture factory, up on the moor at a place called Carnellow."

"Have you lived here long?"

"Only a year." He plugged in the electric kettle, put bread in the toaster. "I rent this place from Gerald. It used to be a coach house, but he converted it." He found a tin and started spooning coffee into an enamel jug. "You've been in Virginia, haven't you?"

"Yes. But not for a bit. For the last six months I've been in the Virgin Islands, living on a yacht."

He turned to grin at her over his shoulder. "Have you? How fantastic. The lotus eater's dream. Is that where you've come from?"

"Yes. Saint Thomas to Saint Croix, Saint Croix to San Juan, San Juan to Miami, Miami to Kennedy, Kennedy to London . . ."

"London to Tremenheere."

"Right."

The crisp smell of bacon filled the room mingled with the aroma of coffee. From a cupboard he took plates, cups, saucers; from a drawer, knives and forks. He dumped all these on the table. "Be a good girl and lay the table, would you?" He went back to the cooker. "One egg or two?"

"Two," said Gabriel, who, once again, was feeling famished. She set out the china and the cutlery.

"What else do we need?" he asked.

She tried to remember traditional British breakfasts. "Marmalade? Honey? Porridge? Kidneys? Kedgeree?"

"Don't get overexcited."

"Butter, then."

He found some in the fridge, a pale yellow chunk on an earthenware dish, dumped it on the table, returned to his cooking.

He said, "What were the Virgin Islands like?"

"Full of mosquitoes."

"You have to be joking!"

"But perfect if you were at sea."

"Where were you based?"

"Saint Thomas."

"Where did you sail?"

"Everywhere. Saint John. Virgin Gorda . . ." His back view was the most attractive back view she had ever seen, even, dressed as he was, in a bathrobe and with his hair on end. He had the most beautiful, capable hands. . . . "Norman Island."

"Norman Island. Sounds like a hairdresser."

"The original Treasure Island. You know. Robert Louis Stevenson."

"Did he go there?"

"Must have."

He piled the bacon and eggs onto two plates, carried them over to the table. "Is that enough for you?"

"More than enough."

"I can add tomatoes. If you want mushrooms and kidneys, you'll have to wait while I make a quick dash down to the post office in the village."

"I don't want them."

"Coffee, then?"

"Lovely."

He sat down opposite her. "Go on about Norman Island."

"Nothing to go on about."

"Banyan trees and white strands."

"You've got it in one."

"Why did you leave?"

Gabriel picked up her fork in her right hand, saw that he was watching her, transferred the fork to her left hand, and picked up a knife in her right hand.

He said, "Transatlantic customs."

"I forget easily. I'm in Britain now."

"We are divided by a common language."

"But you make great ham and eggs."

"Why did you leave?"

She looked down at her plate, shrugged. "Oh, time to come home, I guess."

It was a delicious breakfast, but he did not linger. With his second cup of coffee in his hand, he told Gabriel that he had to go and shave. But before he did this, he went to open the door, to check on the morning situation in the big house.

"Not a movement. Nor a stir. It's only half past eight. There won't be a face at the window for another half hour." He came back into the room, leaving the door open. Sunshine was beginning to seep into the courtyard. A long golden diamond of it lay on the scrubbed wooden floor. "Can you look after yourself while I go up to dress?"

"Of course."

"You don't have to do the washing up"—he headed for the open staircase—"but it would be nice if you did."

She said, "I don't know who you are."

Halfway up, he turned, looking down at her from eyes as brightly blue as hummingbird feathers, or the water at Caneel Bay, or speedwells.

"I'm sorry, didn't I tell you? Eve's my mother."

"But I still don't know your name."

"It's Ivan Ashby."

He disappeared upstairs. His footsteps moved overhead. Presently she heard the radio turned on, cheerful, early-morning music. A tap ran water into a basin.

Ivan Ashby.

Gabriel pushed back her chair, gathered up the breakfast dishes, and took them to the sink. She washed everything up, stacking it neatly in a rack to dry. With this done, she went out into the courtyard. Overhead a flock of white doves fluttered, settling on the bleached tiles of a pigeon cote. No movement showed in the big house. An upstairs window still had the curtains drawn.

But there was another cottage in the courtyard, and this had already wakened. Smoke blew from the single chimney and the door stood open. As Gabriel watched, a figure appeared in this doorway, a girl, wearing a long dark skirt and a white garment, like a choirboys' surplice, touched here and there with bedraggled lace. She paused, savoring the warm freshness of the summer morning, and then, with a sort of timeless grace, settled herself on the doorstep in the sun.

Intriguing. A young woman emerging from her house at eight o'clock in the morning and simply sitting down, doing nothing, was a charming novelty.

> *What is this life so full of care.*
> *We have no time to stop and stare.*

Gabriel stared. The girl, becoming aware that she was being watched, looked up and saw her.

She said, "Hello."

"Hello," said Gabriel.

"Lovely morning."

"Yes." She began to walk over toward the cottage. "You've got the right idea."

The girl was quite young, with a small head made enormous by a frizzy mop of pale hair. Her feet were bare, her hands covered with rings. She said, "Where have you sprung from?"

She looked like an insubstantial gipsy, but her voice was bright and strong, with the long vowels of the North Country.

"I've just arrived. Got off the train this morning."

Gabriel had reached her side. The girl shunted herself along the doorstep, making space, and Gabriel sat beside her.

"I'm Drusilla," said the girl.

"I'm Gabriel."

"Have you come to stay?"

"I hope so."

"Join the club, then!"

"Do you live here?"

"Yes. I've got a baby inside. He hasn't woken up yet, that's why I'm sitting here. Nice to have a bit of peace."

"How long have you lived here?"

"Oh, a month or two. Before that I was out at Lanyon. But I've been down in this part of the world for about a year."

"Do you work here?"

"No, I'm not working. Just looking after Josh. I'm a flautist," she added.

"Sorry?"

"A flautist. I play the flute."

"Do you?" More and more intriguing. "Professionally?"

"That's right. Professionally. Used to play in an orchestra in Huddersfield—that's my hometown—but then the orchestra ran out of funds, and I haven't really worked since. I went to London to try to get a job there, but I didn't have any luck."

"So what did you do?"

"Well, I met this man. Kev. He was a painter. He had a little place in Earls Court, so I moved in with him for a bit. He didn't have much luck in London, either, so we decided to come down here. Some chums of his were here already, and they helped us find somewhere to live. We got this little house out on the moor at Lanyon, but it wasn't much of a place. Nothing like this. Didn't even have a lavatory."

"How old is your baby?"

"Ten months."

"And . . . are you and Kev still together?"

"God, no. He lit out on me. Went back to London. I had to get out of the cottage—the man who owned it wouldn't let me stay there on my own. Anyroad, I couldn't pay the rent."

"What did you do?"

"Couldn't do much, could I? Got out. Mathie Thomas—do you know Mathie Thomas?"

"I don't know anybody."

"He took me in for a night or two, and then Ivan found me this place. Ivan's Mathie's partner."

"He's just given me breakfast."

"Has he?" Drusilla smiled. "Isn't he smashing? I think he's a lovely person. Really fancy him. Wouldn't mind taking up with Ivan any day of the week."

". . . his mother . . . ?"

"Eve? She's a lovely person too. And the Admiral. Have you met the Admiral?"

"I told you, I don't know anybody."

"We're a regular commune, I can tell you." Gabriel had caught Drusilla in one of her expansive moods. "There's an old nanny as well, older than God she is, and twice as disagreeable." She thought this over. "No"—she wrinkled her nose—"that's not fair. She's not a bad old thing. She goes to Truro every Wednesday, it's her day off, and I asked her to buy a bottle of Ribena for Josh, because I can't get it in the post office, and she brought him back a little rabbit. Not a real one, a toy one, with a ribbon round its neck. He'd never had a toy like that before. I thought it was really kind of her. But her face when she handed it over! Sour as an old prune. Some people are funny, no doubt. There's none so queer as old folks."

"Who else is there?"

"There's Laura. Some relation of the Admiral's. Here to convalesce. She'd had an operation. She doesn't live here, though. Just staying. And then there are various hangers-on. You know, popping in and out. There's the gardener, and his wife—she helps in the house sometimes. And a woman called Mrs. Marten who lives in the village, but I can't stand her."

"Does she help in the house, too?"

"God, no. She's a friend of Eve's. I think she's a toffee-nosed bitch. Never handed me a good word, never so much as looks at Josh. And never a day passes but she isn't here for some reason or another. Taking advantage. You know."

Gabriel, who did not know but was loath to stem this flood of fascinating information, nodded.

"To tell the truth, I think she resents me being here, wants to be the only pebble on the beach. She was up for a drink the other evening. . . . They were all sitting outside Ivan's house in the sun and drinking champagne, and the Admiral asked me to join them. But when I saw her there as well, I said I wouldn't and came into the house and shut the door. And it was champagne they were drinking, too. I wouldn't have minded. . . ."

She stopped. From behind them, in the house, came the indignant wail of a small child, just woken, and thinking itself abandoned.

"That's Josh," said Drusilla and got up and went indoors. A moment later she appeared again, bearing the baby in her arms. She sat down and set him on his fat bare feet between her knees. He wore a shrunken nightgown and was immensely fat and brown, with sparse hair and black, boot-button eyes.

"Who's my duck, then?" Drusilla asked him tenderly and pressed a kiss into his fat neck.

He took no notice of her, being absorbed in Gabriel. After a bit he smiled, revealing a small tooth or two. Gabriel put out her hand and he clutched at her finger and tried to put it into his mouth. When she would not let him he roared in rage, and Drusilla bent to kiss him again, hold him close, rock him lazily to and fro.

"Did you . . . ?" Gabriel asked. "When you were having a baby, did you ever think about having an abortion?"

Drusilla looked up, wrinkling her nose in disgust.

"God no. What a gruesome idea. Not have Josh?"

Gabriel said, "I'm having a baby."

"Are you?" Drusilla's voice was not only delighted, but interested. "When?"

"Ages yet. I mean, I've only just realized that I am having a baby. You're the first person I've told."

"Get away."

"You won't say anything, will you?"

"I won't say a word. Do you know who the father is?"

"Yes, of course."

"Does he know?"

"No. And he isn't going to."

Drusilla smiled approvingly. This sort of independent stand was right up her street.

"Good for you," she said.

* * *

May, lying in bed, with her teeth in a tumbler beside her, awoke to the soft murmur of voices beneath her window. Last night, she had worked for a bit at her scrapbook, stuck in some lovely pictures, and then watched television till there was nothing left to watch. But in old age, sleep did not come easily, and the new day was dawning before she finally dropped off. Now . . .

She put a hand out and found her spectacles, fumbling, got them on. She picked up her watch. A quarter to nine. Changed days. In the old days, she'd been out of bed at six thirty, and sometimes sooner if there was a baby to be fed. The voices murmured on, making, she decided, a pleasant sound. She wondered who was there.

After a bit, she got out of bed, put in her teeth, and pulled on her dressing gown. She went to the window and drew back the curtains. Below, the courtyard lay washed in the first sunshine of another fine day. Outside Drusilla's cottage Drusilla sat with Joshua and a girl beside her. One of her funny friends, no doubt.

She did not lean out of the window, because that was not May's way. She watched them. The new girl wore trousers, had dyed-looking hair. May pursed her lips, settling her dentures. She saw Ivan come out of his house and walk across the courtyard toward the two girls.

"Anybody stirred yet?" he asked them. May opened her window. "I'm stirring," she told him. He stopped and looked up. "Morning, May."

"What are you all doing down there, chattering?" May wanted to know.

"May, be an angel and go and see if my mother's awake. Now. I've got to go to work and I want to see her before I leave."

"I'll have to get me clothes on."

"No time. Go now. You look smashing in your dressing gown."

May bridled. "Get away." But she shut the window and turned back into her room. She found her bedroom slippers and put them on, went out of the door and down the passage. Outside Gerald and Eve's bedroom, she paused, listening. They were talking. She knocked.

Eve sat up in her side of the big, padded bed, with a shawl around her shoulders, drinking her morning cup of tea. Gerald, up and dressed, was sitting at the end of her chaise longue tying his shoelaces. Encouraged by the continuing good weather, she was trying to talk him into the idea of a lunch picnic the following day. ". . . we could go to Gwenvoe and walk along the cliffs for a bit. I haven't been there for ages, and there wouldn't be any people there to kick sand in your face. Do say you'll come. I think we all need to get away from the house. . . ."

A knock on the door. Eve instantly felt apprehensive. After the letter, she felt apprehensive all the time, and even more so when May's face appeared around the edge of the door.

"May, what is it?"

"Ivan wants you. He's out in the courtyard."

"Ivan? What's happened? What's the matter?"

"I don't think anything's the matter. Just says he wants a word before he goes to the factory. Drusilla's out there too, and another girl . . . think she must be friend of Drusilla's. Got dyed hair."

"Heavens," said Eve.

"Ivan says to come."

"Thank you, May. I'll be there in a moment."

The door closed. "Gerald, why have I got to go and see Ivan and a girl with dyed hair?"

"Don't look so worried. It sounds interesting. I shall come with you."

"All the time, I think something terrible's going to happen. . . ."

"You mustn't." She turned back the covers and got out of bed, dropping her shawl. Gerald got to his feet and helped her on with her pale blue quilted robe. He said, "Do you think the girl with dyed hair belongs to Drusilla or to Ivan?"

Despite herself, Eve had to smile. "Oh, don't say things like that!"

"You know, Tremenheere was very dull until I married you. I hope she's not another lame duck."

"A lame duck with dyed hair?"

"The imagination boggles," said Gerald.

They went together down the back stairs and through the kitchen. The table was laid with three places for breakfast. Laura's tray waited on the dresser. Gerald unbolted the back door and opened it.

"We thought you were never going to appear," Ivan told them.

"What's so urgent?" Gerald asked. Eve looked over his shoulder. Drusilla's friend. She had been sitting on the doorstep of the cottage, but now she stood up and came toward them. She was tall and slender, long-legged. Her face brown, her hair the color of straw. She had, Eve had time to notice, remarkably beautiful gray eyes.

From her doorway, Drusilla and the baby watched.

"Do you know who this is?" Ivan asked. It was unlike Ivan to ask idiotic questions. How could she and Gerald know who she was? Eve shook her head.

"Gabriel," said Ivan.

Lucy was not well. In the middle of the night, she had woken Laura, standing on her back legs by the bed, scratching at the sheet and whining miserably. In the still darkness, Laura had carried her downstairs, unbolted the front door, and taken Lucy out into the garden, where she had promptly been sick. Upstairs again, she had drunk copiously from her water bowl and then gone back to her basket, digging her way in under her blanket, for warmth.

When Laura woke, she was still there, only her face visible, her eyes dark and reproachful, her silky ears drooping.

"How do you feel?" Laura asked her, but Lucy did not stir at the sound of her voice. She sighed and rested her chin on the edge of the basket and looked more miserable than ever.

She must have eaten something. For all her pretty looks, she was a terrible scavenger. Perhaps she had found the compost heap, or dug up a rotten bone. Perhaps she would have to be taken to the vet.

She looked at her watch. It was nearly nine o'clock and another beautiful morning. It seemed sinful still to be lying in bed, but she was not allowed by Eve to appear downstairs until she had eaten her breakfast, which Eve insisted on bringing up to her on a tray. Laura was now so totally recovered that she would have been happy to join the others in the kitchen and save Eve a trek up the stairs, but Eve so enjoyed this little bit of spoiling that it would have been churlish not to accept with good grace.

After a bit, she got up and cleaned her teeth and brushed her hair, and thought about Alec in New York. She immediately felt guilty again. She had written to him, an air letter, apologizing and trying to explain, but the letter somehow did not express what she wanted to say, and posting it had not made her feel any better. When he came back to Tremenheere to fetch her, it would be better. She would stop being so reserved. She would stop being polite about Daphne Boulderstone. Perhaps she would discover that Alec felt exactly the same about Daphne as Laura did, but had never actually put his feelings into words, and then they would laugh together, and everything would be all right.

She crouched by Lucy's basket, touched the little dog's head, put the back of her hand to Lucy's nose, which was warm and feverish. She was there when Eve's footsteps came down the passage from the top of the back stairs, and Eve's light tap sounded on the door.

"Eve, I'm up."

Eve appeared, carrying the wicker breakfast tray. She was still in her quilted robe and looking more cheerful than she had looked for days.

She put the tray down on the bed and said, "Are you feeling strong?"

Laura stood up. "Why?"

"Really strong? Ready for a surprise? A lovely surprise."

A lovely surprise. She could only think of Alec. But it wasn't Alec who followed Eve through the door and there stopped, not smiling exactly, but looking secret and a little bit wary. She was very young, with short, bleached hair and huge gray eyes that met Laura's, unblinking.

Nobody said anything, and it was Eve who had to break the silence.

"Laura, it's Gabriel. It's Alec's Gabriel."

*   *   *

"But where have you come from?"

"Saint Thomas. The Virgin Islands."

Eve had left them, and they sat on the big bed together, Gabriel with her legs curled beneath her and her back supported by the great brass bedstead.

"Did you see your father?"

"No. He'd already left for New York." She went on, explaining exactly what had happened. Her journey home sounded to Laura like a nightmare, but Gabriel seemed to take it all in stride. She had gone back to Islington and seen Mrs. Abney, spent a day in London, and then come to Tremenheere.

She had come to Tremenheere, not to see Alec, but Laura. It was Gabriel, and she was home. She was a person, a girl, a daughter, sitting on the end of Laura's bed. No longer a name that nobody mentioned. No longer a photograph, a drawing, a deserted attic room filled with a child's possessions. She was here. Within touch. Gabriel.

"We must let Alec know you've come."

"No, don't," said Gabriel. "He'll only worry, and there's nothing to worry about. Eve said he'd be coming back to fetch you, so let's surprise him then. It's only for a few days. Let's keep it a secret from him."

"But don't you have to go back to America?"

"No, I don't have to go back."

"But . . . what will you do?"

"I thought I might stay in England."

"But that would be *marvelous*. I can't think of anything nicer. And Alec . . . oh, Gabriel, he's missed you so much. I know he missed you so much."

Gabriel said, "Yes." She got off the bed and stood with her back to Laura, looking out of the window. "What a heavenly place this is. And palm trees too. It's like the West Indies all over again." She squatted beside Lucy.

"Yes. But she's not well. She was sick in the night. Luckily, she told me, and I got her out into the garden in time. I think she's eaten something. She's called Lucy."

Watching Gabriel, she realized what had been subconsciously puzzling her. "Gabriel, how did you find me? How did you know I was here, at Tremenheere?"

"Oh," Gabriel leaned forward to stroke Lucy. "Mrs. Abney knew. She told me."

"Alec must have told her before he left for New York."

"Yes," said Gabriel. "I guess so." She straightened up. She said, "I'm going downstairs. Eve said she'd give me a cup of coffee. I'll leave you to have your breakfast in peace. Your boiled egg will be hard as a stone if you don't eat it soon."

"When I come down," said Laura, "let's talk. There's so much I want to ask you."

"Sure. We'll sit in the garden and gas."

Gabriel closed the door behind her and went to the head of the great staircase. She stopped there, hesitating, then put her hand into the pocket of her jeans and took out the creased brown envelope. *Your wife at Tremenheere is having an affair with Ivan Ashby.*

Tough and young, with the resilience and open-mindedness of her generation, Gabriel had been shocked by the evil intent of the letter, but not shocked by the actual accusation. Now, within a couple of hours of arriving at Tremenheere, she had met both Ivan and Laura. An almost frighteningly attractive man, of whom one could believe almost anything. But a woman who looked and behaved like a total innocent, naïve in her transparent pleasure at Gabriel's appearance. Faced with an unknown step-daughter, she could, under any circumstances, have been wary, suspicious, or even jealous, but no trace of these emotions had shown in her candid delight, and her patent sincerity was clear as glass.

For the first time, Gabriel knew stirrings of suspicion. For the first time it occurred to her that it was possible that the letter was totally untrue. In which case, who hated Laura and Ivan so much that they had fabricated such a dangerous slander?

She went downstairs. As she crossed the polished hall, she saw the kitchen door open, and Gerald emerged, carrying his newspaper. He did not see Gabriel, but walked away from her, headed down the passage.

"Gerald."

He turned. She went toward him. "Do you think I could talk to you for a moment?"

He took her into his study, a pleasant room, smelling of cigars and books and wood ash.

"Is this where you come to read the paper?"

"Yes." He was a very good-looking man. "Gets me out of the way. Sit down, Gabriel."

She sat, not in the armchair he indicated, but in an upright one, so that they faced each other across his desk.

She said, "You've been so kind . . . I'm sorry I didn't let you know I was coming, but there really wasn't time."

"Delighted. Delighted to see you. Delighted to meet you, for that matter."

She said, "I've just told Laura that Mrs. Abney—she's the housekeeper at the house in Islington—that she told me where I could find Laura. But that wasn't true."

"How did you know she was here, then?"

Gabriel said, "I opened this," and she laid the envelope on his blotter.

Gerald, leaning back in his chair, did not move. He sat looking at the brown envelope and then raised his eyes and met Gabriel's. His expression was grave. He said, "I see."

"What do you see?"

"There has already been a similar letter. Sent to a friend of ours in the village . . . a poison-pen letter."

"Well, this is another. I opened it because I saw the Truro postmark and I knew Laura was somewhere in Cornwall. Mrs. Abney and I thought it would be all right."

"Did you show it to Mrs. Abney?"

"No. I haven't shown it to anybody."

He sighed deeply and picked it up. "It was posted in Truro, on Wednesday."

"Yes, I know."

He took the letter out and read it. Then he put his elbow on the desk and covered the bottom half of his face with his hand. He said, "Oh, God."

"It's horrible, isn't it?"

"You had breakfast with Ivan. Did you say anything to him?"

"No, of course not. Nor to Laura. I told you. You're the first person I've shown it to."

"What a good girl you are."

"Who wrote it?"

"We don't know."

"But what about the other one. Didn't you follow the first letter up?"

"No. For . . . reasons . . . we let it slide. We hoped there wouldn't be a second letter. Now, I'm beginning to think we made a mistake."

"But it's criminal to write things like that. It's a crime."

"Gabriel, there's no word of truth in it. You know that, don't you?"

"I wondered. But how do we *know* it isn't true?"

"Because I know Ivan and I know Laura. Believe me, I've lived long enough, and I've seen enough of my fellow men to know very well if something—clandestine, as this infers—was going on under my roof. Ivan's my stepson, not always the most discreet or sensible of men, but he would never be such a fool, or such a knave, as to seduce Alec's wife. As for Laura'—he spread his hands—"you've met her yourself. Can you see her doing a thing like that?"

"No, I can't," Gabriel admitted. "I'd worked that out for myself. But there must be *some* justification. . . ."

"Oh, a couple of outings together. To an antique shop . . . for a picnic. Ivan's a kind fellow. He enjoys the company of any attractive woman, but basically his intentions are triggered off by a sheer goodness of heart. And it's landed him in trouble, I can tell you, over the years."

Gabriel smiled. It was like having a weight lifted from her heart to hear Ivan described in such glowing terms, even if he was Gerald's step-son, and Gerald was bound to be slightly biased.

"In that case, what are we going to do?"

"Perhaps we should get in touch with your father."

"No, we mustn't do that."

"Not even to let him know you're here?"

"Let's keep it a surprise. After all, he hasn't seen me for six years, and he thinks I'm still in Virginia. . . . It's not as though he'll be worry-ing."

"I'd be happier telling him."

"Oh, don't. Please don't. If you don't mind me staying on here until he comes, that's what I'd rather do."

Gerald gave in. "All right."

"But I still don't know what you're going to do about the letter."

"Will you leave that to me?"

"I think we should tell the police."

"I will if we have to, but for Eve's sake I'd rather not."

"What's Eve got to do with it?"

"Everything," he told her. "I'll explain another time. The first letter made her ill with worry, but she's looking better now than she has for days, and I'm hoping that your unexpected appearance has put it out of her mind. Meanwhile, I think you should try to do that too. It's not your responsibility any longer. So why don't you just enjoy yourself? Go and sit in the sun in the garden. Go and find Laura and make friends."

When she left, he read the letter again, then put it back into its enve-lope and stowed it away in the breast pocket of his old tweed jacket. He got to his feet and went out of the study and back to the kitchen, where he found Eve in her cooking apron, chopping vegetables for soup.

"Darling."

He kissed her. "I have to go out for half an hour."

"Are you going into the town? I need some groceries."

"Not just at the moment. I'll go later, though, if you want."

"You are a love. I'll make a shopping list."

He opened the back door. She said, "Gerald." He turned. She smiled her old smile. She said, "She's sweet, isn't she? Gabriel, I mean."

"Charming," said Gerald and went out.

In his car he turned left at the gate and headed up the hill on the road that led over the moor. After a mile or two he came to a fork and a signpost, one arm of which pointed to Lanyon, the other to Carnellow. He took the road to Carnellow.

It had once been an isolated tin-mining village. A couple of rows of blank-faced cottages, a ruined engine house and stack, a bleak chapel. Up here, high on the moor, even on the stillest day, there was always a wind. When he got out of the car, this wind whined in his ears, and all about him, the moor rolled, patched here and there with emerald green of bog, tall grasses leaning in the breeze.

From the old chapel came the clangor of activity. The whine of a circular saw, the banging of wooden mallets. The original doorway had been opened up into an aperture the size of a double garage, and heavy doors, on runners, were pushed aside to reveal the interior of the workshop. Over this entrance was a new sign, recently erected: Ashby and Thomas.

Outside the factory, timber was stacked, seasoning beneath a makeshift shelter. There were a couple of vans and Ivan's car. Shavings, like ringlets, blew about. He could smell the sweet, new-sawn wood.

A boy appeared, carrying a chair, which he was loading into one of the vans.

"Good morning," said Gerald.

"Ullo."

"Is Ivan in there?"

"Yes, 'e's about somewhere."

"Get him, would you? Say it's Admiral Haverstock."

The boy, perhaps impressed by Gerald's authoritative manner as much as his title, set down the chair and disappeared, only to return a moment later with Ivan beside him. Ivan in shirt sleeves and a pair of old-fashioned bib-and-brace overalls.

"Gerald."

"Sorry to disturb you. Won't take a moment. Let's go and sit in the car."

He told Ivan the sorry tale and showed him the second letter. As Ivan read it, Gerald saw his fist clench on his knee so tightly that the knuckles turned white. As Gerald had said, Ivan said, "Oh, God."

"Nasty business," said Gerald. "But this time, of course, I know it's not true."

Ivan said drily, "Well, that's a good start anyway. What a filthy thing. And you say Gabriel read it in London and brought it with her! She must have thought I was a real four-letter man."

"She knows there's no word of truth in it. I told her so and I got the impression that she was happy to believe me."

"You don't still think it's May."

"Well, who is it, old boy?"

"You don't think . . . ? I wondered about this after the first letter, but I didn't say anything. You don't think it could be Drusilla?"

"Drusilla?"

"Yes, Drusilla."

"Why should it be her? What would she get out of writing scurrilous poison-pen letters?"

"I don't know. Except that"—Ivan began to look faintly embarrassed—"well, after I helped her, you know, fixed for her to come and live in the cottage . . . she did come over one evening and made it quite plain that she was grateful and if she could repay me in any way, she'd be more than pleased. But it wasn't anything to do with . . . loving. Just a business proposition."

"Did you take her up on it?"

"No, of course I didn't. I thanked her and said she didn't owe me anything and sent her home again. She bore no grudge." He thought about this, and added, "Apparently."

"Would Drusilla be capable of writing a thing like that?"

"She's a funny girl. I don't know. I don't know her. None of us does. We don't know her background, we don't know what makes her tick. She's a mystery."

"I agree with that. But why should she want to hurt Silvia?"

"No idea. I don't think she's particularly fond of Silvia, but that hardly merits sending the poor woman a poison-pen letter. And Drusilla certainly doesn't have strong views about drink. She enjoys her jar."

Gerald thought this over. "Ivan, that letter was posted in Truro on Wednesday. Drusilla never goes farther than the village. She can't, with the baby in the pram. There's no way she could get to Truro."

"She could have asked May to post the letter for her. In an odd fashion, they seem to have made friends. May sometimes gets things for her when she's in Truro, stuff for Joshua that Drusilla can't buy in the village. So why shouldn't she have posted a letter for Drusilla?"

It all seemed perfectly reasonable. And so impossibly awful that Gerald wished that, like Eve, he could somehow put the whole sorry business out of his mind.

Ivan said, "What are we going to do now?"

"I suggested to Gabriel that we should get in touch with Alec, but she wouldn't let me. She doesn't want him worried. Anyway, he'll be here by Tuesday."

"Gerald, we have to do something before he comes."

"What?"

"Don't you think we should get the police in?"

"And what if it *is* May?"

After a bit, Ivan said, "Yes, I see your point."

"Let's leave it for another day."

Ivan smiled at his stepfather. "You're not acting in character, Gerald. Procrastinating. I thought naval time was five minutes beforehand."

"It is."

" 'The difficult we can do at once, the impossible may take a little longer.' "

"Don't you quote myself at me. And perhaps this is an impossible one. Perhaps it will take a little longer. When will you be back, Ivan?"

"I'll maybe take a make and mend, be home for lunch. You look like a man who needs a little moral support." He got out of the car, slammed the door behind him. "See you later."

Gerald, his heart filled with affection and gratitude, watched him go. When Ivan had disappeared back into his workshop, Gerald started up the engine of his car and drove back to Tremenheere.

"It wasn't so bad at first. It wasn't as bad as I thought it was going to be. Virginia's beautiful, and Strick had this lovely place, on a bluff above the James River. It was an enormous house, with acres of land all around, green pastures for the horses, and white split-rail fences. And there were dogwoods and wild oaks, and in front of the house a garden with a vast swimming pool and tennis courts. It was so mild and so sunny, even in winter. And I had a huge room all to myself and a bathroom as well, and there were servants. A cook and a housemaid, and a colored butler called David, who came to work each day in a pink Studebaker. Even the school my mother sent me to was all right. It was a boarding school and I imagine, wildly expensive, because all the girls' parents seemed to be just as rich as Strickland was, and after a bit, when they'd got used to the idea of me being English and having a British accent, I became a sort of novelty, and it wasn't so difficult to make friends."

They were in the garden together, under the mulberry tree. They had carried out a rug and some cushions, and lay, side by side, on their stomachs, like a couple of schoolgirls exchanging confidences. Being like that somehow made it easier to talk.

"Were you never lonely?"

"Oh, heavens, yes. All the time, really, but it was a funny sort of loneliness. A little part of me that I carried around all the time, but it was hidden. Very deep. Like a stone at the bottom of a pond. I mean, I never ever felt that I belonged, but it wasn't too difficult to behave as though I did."

"What about when you weren't at school."

"Even that wasn't too bad. They knew I didn't want to ride, so they left me alone. I've never, actually, minded being alone, and besides, there were usually people around the place. Friends staying, with children of my age, or people coming for tennis, or to swim." She smiled. "I can swim really well, and I can even play tennis too, though I'm not what you call a champion."

"Gabriel, why did you never come back and see your father?"

Gabriel looked away, pulled at a tuft of grass within reach, shredded it between her fingers.

"I don't know. It just never worked out. At first I thought I'd come back and be with him when he went to Glenshandra. That was where we really were together, just him and me. He used to take me out on the river with him, and we spent hours . . . just the two of us. I wanted to go to Glenshandra, but when I tried to tell my mother, she said she'd fixed for me to go to summer camp, and why not leave it for this year. There'd be other years. When you're only fourteen, it's not easy to argue and get your own way. And my mother is an almost impossible person to argue with. She has answers for absolutely everything, and in the end you're always defeated. So I went to summer camp, and I thought my father would write and be furiously angry with us all. But he didn't. He just said the same thing. Perhaps next year. And that hurt me, because I guessed perhaps he hadn't cared as much as I thought he would."

"Did he write to you?"

"Yes, he wrote. And I got presents at Christmas and for my birthday."

"Did you write back?"

"Oh, yes. Thank-you letters."

"But he must have missed you so much. Those five years when he was all on his own. He must have longed to have you with him. Just sometimes."

Gabriel said, "He should never have let me go. I wanted to stay with him. I told my mother that, and she said that it was impossible. Apart from the practical problems, he was too busy, too involved with his work. His job always came before anything else."

"Did you tell your father?"

"I tried to. He came to see me at the school in England, and we walked around the games field, but somehow by then it was too late to get through to him. All he said to me was, 'I have too many commitments. You need your mother.' "

"And you've never forgiven him for that?"

"It's not a question of forgiving, Laura. It's a question of adapting. If I hadn't adapted, I'd have become a screwed-up mess, the sort of nutty kid who has to be wheeled off to the local headshrinker. And once I'd adapted, it was too late to go back, even for a little while. Do you see that?"

"Yes," said Laura slowly. "I think I do see. I think you did very well. At least you accepted an impossible situation and made some sort of a life for yourself."

"Oh, I made a life all right."

"What happened when you left school?"

"Mother wanted me to go to college, but I jibbed at that. We really had a row, but for once, I stuck my toes in and won, and did what I wanted to do, which was to study fine arts at a place in Washington."

"How fascinating."

"Yes, it was great. I had a little apartment and a car of my own, and if I wanted to, at weekends, I could go back to Virginia and take my friends. Mother didn't approve of any of the friends, who all voted

Democrat and had long hair, but apart from that it was O.K. At least, it was for a bit . . ."

"Why only for a bit . . . ?"

Gabriel sighed and pulled up another piece of Gerald's lawn. She said, "I don't know if you know anything about Strickland Whiteside."

"No. Nothing. Alec's never spoken of him. I'm afraid he hardly spoke about your mother."

"After I left school . . . I don't know, nothing happened, but I used to catch Strickland watching me, and I felt sleazy, and I knew things weren't the same any longer. I started taking some trouble to keep out of his way. That's one of the reasons I went to Washington, to get away from Virginia. But of course, finally, when I'd got my little degree, I had to go back, and the first night I was home, my mother went to bed early, and Strickland made the most violent pass at me. He'd had a few drinks and I think he was feeling a bit randy, but it was horrible."

"Oh, Gabriel."

"I knew I couldn't stay. The next morning I told my mother I was going to New York, to stay with a girl who'd been a friend of mine at school. She bucked slightly, but she didn't raise any objections. Perhaps she had an idea of what was going on in Strickland's pin-brain, but if she did, she gave no indication. She's always been a very controlled person. I never saw her lose control of any situation. So I called the girlfriend, packed, and got myself to New York. I thought I'd get a job or something, but New York was never my scene, and the first morning I was there, I caught sight of my reflection in one of the Fifth Avenue store windows and I thought, 'What the hell are you doing here?' Anyway, after two days I still hadn't found anything to do, but as it turned out that didn't matter. Because that evening we went to a party down in Greenwich Village, and I met this man. He was British and funny and nice; we talked the same language, were on the same wavelength. And oh, the joy of being with someone who laughed at the same idiotic things as I did. Anyway, he took me out for dinner and said that he had this yacht down in the Virgin Islands, and he'd asked some friends down for a cruise, and would I like to go too. So I went. It was great. The most beautiful yacht, and heavenly sailing, and gorgeous romantic little coves with white sand and palm trees. And then the two weeks were over, and all the others went back to New York, but he stayed on. And so did I. I stayed with him for six months. We lived together for six months. I said goodbye to him two days ago. Two days. It feels like two years."

"But who was he, Gabriel?"

"I suppose you'd call him an upper-class drifter. I told you, he was English. He'd been in the army. I think he had a wife somewhere. A lot of money, because he didn't have a job, and it costs something to keep a fifty-foot sloop in the Virgin Islands."

"Were you happy with him?"

"Oh, sure. We had a great time."

"What was his name?"

"I'm not going to tell you. It's of no account."

"But if you were happy, then why did you come back to England?"
Gabriel said, "I've started a baby."

There was a silence, which was not a silence at all, because the garden
was filled with birdsong. Then Laura, inadequately, said, "Oh, Gabriel."

"I only realized that I had—about a week ago."

"Have you seen a doctor?"

"No, nothing like that, but I'm perfectly sure. And at the same time,
I knew that if I wasn't going to have a child, if I was going to have an
abortion, I had to move pretty quickly. But that wasn't the only reason I
came straight home. The real reason was that I wanted my father. I just
wanted him. I needed him. I needed to tell him, and to talk to him, and
to hear his advice and . . . oh, just to be with him, Laura. And then
when I got to London and he wasn't there, I thought that the only
thing I could do was to find you and talk to you."

"But you didn't even know me."

"I had to tell somebody."

Laura's eyes filled with tears, and swiftly, ashamedly, she brushed
them away. She said, "I've never had very strong views about abortion. I
mean, I've never campaigned either way, for or against. But hearing you
even say the word fills me with such horror and revulsion. . . . Oh,
Gabriel, you mustn't have an abortion!"

Gabriel grinned. "Don't worry. I've already decided I couldn't go
through with it. I decided this morning, when I was talking to Drusilla,
before you were all awake. When I saw that great fat baby of hers, I was
suddenly, absolutely, sure that I wanted this one."

"Does the father know about it?"

"No, I didn't say anything."

"Oh, darling . . ." The tears started again. "So silly to cry, but I
can't help it. Perhaps I shouldn't be, but I'm happy for you."

"You don't think Alec's going to flip when we tell him?"

"You know him better than that."

"What I'd really like to do," said Gabriel, "is to come back to London with you both . . . maybe stay till the baby's born."

"Stay as long as you want."

"We'll be a bit of a tight fit in that little house."

"We'll get Alec to buy us a bigger one, with a garden."

They laughed together, two women conspiring gently against the
man they both loved. "It's what I've always wanted. Not a bigger house,
but a baby. But I'm thirty-seven now, and every now and then my
insides go mad, and so far I haven't been very lucky. That's why I had
to have this operation. That's why I'm here and why I didn't go to

Glenshandra or New York with him. But if I can't have a child, then you
having one . . ."

"Will be the next best thing?"

"No. Never that. Never next best."

A movement from the house disturbed them. Looking up, they saw
Gerald emerge onto the terrace through the French windows from the
drawing room. They watched while he collected the folded garden furniture, set it up in the sunshine around the white iron table. When this was
done, he picked up some small piece of rubbish—a matchstick perhaps—
and stooped to pull a stray weed or two from between the stone flags.
Then, apparently satisfied that all was shipshape, he disappeared indoors.

"What a marvelous guy," Gabriel observed.

"Yes, marvelous. He was always Alec's hero. Poor man. A bachelor
for sixty years, and here he is with a houseful of women. So many of us.
Women on their own. Women without men. Old May, up in her room,
darning socks and with her life behind her. Drusilla, with nobody but
her baby. Silvia Marten, Eve's friend, coming and going, hungry for
company. She's probably the loneliest of all. And you. And me."

"You, lonely? But Laura, you have Alec."

"Yes, I have Alec. And it's been very nearly perfect."

"What's missing?"

"Nothing's missing. Just another lifetime that I had no part of."

"You mean my mother. And Deepbrook. And me."

"You most of all. Alec would never talk to me about you. It was like a
barrier between us and I never had the confidence nor the resolution to
break it down."

"Were you jealous of me?"

"No, I don't mean that." She lay, trying to work it out, to find the
right, tremendously important words. "I think I was lonely for the same
reason as Alec. You weren't a barrier, Gabriel, but a void. You should
have been there, with us, but you weren't."

Gabriel smiled. "Well, I'm sure here now."

"How about Erica? Will she be worrying about you?"

"No. She thinks I'm still cruising round the Virgin Islands with a jolly
party of socially acceptable New Yorkers. When my father gets back and
the future's a little clearer, I'll write to her, tell her what's happening."

"She'll miss you."

"I don't think so."

"Is she ever lonely? Is she one of the lonely ones?"

"Never. You see, she has her horses."

They stayed there for a little longer, and then Laura looked at her
watch, stirred herself, and sat up.

"Where are you going?" Gabriel asked.

"I've been neglecting Eve. I must go and help her. We're such a
houseful and she does all the cooking herself."

"Shall I come too? I'm a dab hand at peeling potatoes."

"No, you stay. You're allowed to be lazy on your first morning. I'll give you a shout when it's time for lunch."

She went across the grass, the breeze blowing her pink cotton skirt, her long hair. She climbed the steps onto the terrace and disappeared into the house. Gabriel watched her go, and then rolled over onto her back, the cushion beneath her head.

The baby was there. Would be born. She laid a hand on her abdomen, cherishing the future. A tiny seed, already growing. An entity. Last night on the train, she had scarcely slept, and because of this or, perhaps, delayed jet lag, she was all at once overcome with drowsiness. With her face to the sun, she closed her eyes.

Later, she stirred. Consciousness came gently, tranquilly. There was another sensation, one at first unrecognized, and then remembered from long ago, from childhood. Security, like a warm blanket. A presence.

She opened her eyes. Ivan, cross-legged, sat beside her on the rug, watching her, and his being there seemed so natural that she felt none of the normal embarrassment of a person found asleep, vulnerable and defenseless.

After a bit, he said, "Hello."

Gabriel said the first thing that came into her head, which was, "You weren't having an affair with Laura."

He shook his head. "No."

She frowned, trying to think what had made her say this, when they had not before even spoken of the letter. As though he knew what was going on in her head, he said, "Gerald showed me the letter. He came up to Carnellow to show it to me. I'm sorry about everything. Sorry it was written, but mostly sorry that it was you who had to read it."

"I only opened it because I wanted to find Laura. And I think it's a mercy that I did. It could have been so dangerous, Ivan. If Alec had read it before he went to New York, it could really have been very dangerous."

"It can't have made meeting Laura for the first time very easy."

"No. But in the last few days I seem to have done a lot of things that weren't easy."

"I just hate that you had that uncertainty about us. Even if it was only for a single day."

"It wasn't your fault."

"There's already been one like it. Gerald told you."

"Yes, he told me. But, like he said, it was a pack of lies. It's no longer my responsibility." She stretched, yawned, and sat up. The garden was dazzled in sunshine, scented with wallflowers. The sun had moved, and beneath the mulberry tree the grass lay dappled in light and shadow. "How long have I been asleep?"

"I don't know. It's half past twelve. I was sent out to tell you it will soon be lunchtime."

He was wearing a pale blue shirt, open-necked, the sleeves rolled up and away from his wrists. Beneath this, against the brown skin of his chest, she saw the glint of a silver chain. His hands, which she had already decided were beautiful, hung loosely between his knees. She saw his wristwatch, the heavy gold signet ring.

"Do you feel like something to eat?" he asked.

She dragged her eyes away from his hands and looked up into his face. "Do you always come home for lunch?"

"No. But today I'm taking a make and mend."

"Sorry?"

"Six months in a yacht and you don't speak the language! Naval slang for a half-day."

"I see. And what are you going to do with it?"

"Nothing, I think. How about you?"

"Sounds a good idea."

He smiled and got to his feet, and put out a hand to help Gabriel up. "In that case," he said, "let's do nothing together."

They were all sitting around the kitchen table, having a drink before lunch, and waiting for May. When she appeared cautiously descending the back stairs, it was immediately obvious, from the sour displeasure on her wrinkled features, that something was very amiss.

"May, what is it?" Eve asked.

May folded her hands over her stomach, set her mouth, and told them. The door of Laura's bedroom had been left open. Lucy had got out of her basket, found her way along the passage to May's room, and had there been extremely sick in the middle of May's good rug.

At five o'clock that evening, Laura, carrying a punnet of tomatoes, walked down to the village by herself. She and Eve had picked the tomatoes together. They came from the Tremenheere greenhouse, and with the warm weather, dozens of them had ripened at the same moment. They had spent the afternoon concocting soups and purées, and yet there were pounds left over. Drusilla gladly accepted a bowlful, and a basket was set aside for the vicar's wife, but still there were more.

"Why do the beastly things all have to come at once?" Eve wanted to know, flushed in the face from all this culinary effort. "I can't bear to waste them." Then she was visited by a brainwave. "I know, we'll give them to Silvia."

"Doesn't she have her own?"

"No, she grows just about everything else, but not tomatoes. I'll give her a ring and see if she'd like some." She went off to the telephone and returned triumphant. "She's simply delighted. She says she's been buying them in the post office, and they're overcharging. We'll take them down later."

"I'll take them down if you like."

"Oh, would you? You've never seen her garden, anyway, and it's a dream, and she's always glad of someone to chat to. And perhaps she'd like to come to Gwenvoe with us tomorrow." Over lunch, she had finally persuaded her reluctant husband into agreeing, not only that a Saturday picnic would be a good idea, but that he would take part and accompany them all. "If she would, tell her we'll bring the food, and one of us will pick her up. We'll have to take two cars anyway."

As she came around the corner of the house, Laura had glanced into the garden. At the far end of the lawn Ivan and Gabriel sat cross-legged, talking. They had been there all afternoon, apparently engrossed, like a pair of old acquaintances catching up on the news of a lifetime. Laura was glad that he had not taken her off for the day on one of his energetic and exhausting expeditions. She felt protective as a mother about Gabriel.

She had not been to Silvia's house, but it was not difficult to find. The gate stood open, with the name on it, Roskenwyn. Laura went up the short gravelled drive and in through the open front door.

"Silvia."

There was no reply, but the sitting room door stood open, and on the other side of this, a glass door led out into the garden. Here, she found Silvia, on her knees, working at her border with a small weeding fork.

"Silvia."

"Hello." She sat back on her heels, the fork held loosely in her hand. She was in old jeans and a checked shirt, her face as usual almost concealed by her huge dark glasses.

"I've brought you the tomatoes."

"Oh, you are an angel." She dropped the fork and stripped off her earth-stained gloves.

"Don't stop if you don't want to."

"But I do want to. I've been at it all afternoon." She got to her feet. "Let's have a drink."

"It's only five."

"It doesn't need to be alcohol. I'll make a cup of tea if you like. Or we could have some lemonade."

"Lemonade would be delicious."

"Right." She took the basket from Laura's hand. "I'll bring it out. You can move around my garden and say ooh and aah, and when I come back you can tell me how good it's looking."

"I don't know much about gardens."

"Even better. I like uncritical admiration."

She disappeared into the house and Laura, obediently, walked around the beautifully staked and tended borders, which were a mass of flowers in every shade of pink and blue and mauve. No red, or orange, no yellow. Delphiniums stood high as a tall man, and smoky lupins smelled of every summer Laura could remember. Silvia's roses were almost indecently flamboyant, thickly planted, and with heads as large as saucers.

Sitting on Silvia's little patio, with the tray of lemonade between them, "How on earth do you grow roses like that?" she asked.

"I feed them. Horse manure. I get it from the farmer up the road."

"But don't you have to spray them and all that sort of thing?"

"Oh, yes. Like mad. Otherwise they get bitten to death by greenflies."

"I don't know much about gardening. In London we've only got a sort of yard with a few tubs."

"Don't tell me Gerald hasn't got you weeding yet? He's a great one for organizing what he calls work parties."

"No. Nobody's got me doing anything. Except pick a bit of fruit. I've been treated like the most expensive sort of guest."

"Well, it's certainly worked." Silvia turned her blank, black stare onto Laura's face. "You look marvelous. Better each day. Today, you look particularly well. You've lost that rather . . . anxious expression."

"Perhaps I'm not anxious anymore."

Silvia had finished her lemonade. Now she reached for the jug and refilled her glass. "Any particular reason?"

"Yes, a very particular one. Gabriel's with us. Alec's daughter. She arrived this morning, off the night train."

Silvia put the jug back on the tray. "Gabriel. But she's in Virginia, isn't she?"

"She was, but she's come home. Nobody was expecting her. It was just the most wonderful surprise."

"I thought she never visited her father."

"She didn't. And this isn't a visit. She's staying. She's going to live with us. She's not going back."

It occurred to Laura then that happiness was a strange thing, at times as uncontrollable as grief. All day, she had felt as though she were walking on air, and now was suddenly visited by the compulsion to share this happiness, to confide. And why not Silvia, who had known Alec since they were children, and had seen him at Tremenheere in his loneliness. "We'll be a family. And I've only just discovered that that was what I always wanted. That's what has been missing."

"Missing in your marriage?"

"Yes," Laura admitted. "Marrying a man who was married before, for quite a long time, to another woman . . . it's not always very easy. There are great chunks of his life that are shut away from you, like a locked room where you're not allowed inside. But now Gabriel's back, it's going to be different. It's as though she were the key that unlocks the door." She smiled at her own inadequacy. "I'm afraid I'm not very good at explaining. It's just that, now, I know everything's going to be marvelous."

"Well, I hope you're right," said Silvia. "But I wouldn't allow yourself to be too euphoric. You've only known the girl for a day. After a month of living with her, you'll probably be glad to see the back of her. She'll go off and find herself a flat of her own. They all do, these young things."

"No. I don't think she will. Anyway, not for a bit."

"What makes you so sure?"

Laura took a deep breath and then let it all out again without saying anything. Silvia said, "You're looking guilty, like a woman with a secret."

"I am. I haven't even told Eve yet because it isn't my secret to tell."

"Laura, I'm the soul of discretion."

"All right. But don't say anything." She smiled, because just being able to say it, aloud, filled her with joy. "She's going to have a baby."

"*Gabriel* is?"

"You mustn't be shocked. You mustn't sound shocked."

"Is she going to get married?"

"No. That's why she's coming back to London with us."

"What on earth is Alec going to say?"

"I think he's going to be so thrilled that she came back to him, that the fact that she's pregnant simply won't matter."

"I don't understand you. You look as though you were telling me you'd started a baby yourself. All radiant."

"Perhaps," said Laura, "that's a bit how I feel. I'm happy for Gabriel and Alec, but mostly I'm happy for myself. That's selfish, isn't it? But you see, Silvia, from now on, we're all going to be *together*."

With all this excitement, it wasn't until she was leaving that Laura remembered the other message she had to give Silvia.

"I nearly forgot. We're all going for a lunch picnic to Gwenvoe tomorrow, and Eve wondered if you'd like to come with us."

"Tomorrow, Saturday?" Silvia, as Gerald was constantly doing, stooped and pulled a weed from between the gravel chips of her driveway. "Oh, what a bore. I can't. I've got an old girlfriend staying at the Castle Hotel in Porthkerris, and I promised I'd go over and see her. I'd much rather come to Gwenvoe, but I can't let her down."

"What a shame. But I'll explain to Eve."

"I thought something was missing," said Silvia suddenly. "Where's your little dog? She's always with you."

"She's not well. May's not talking to anybody because Lucy got into her room and was sick on May's rug."

"What's wrong with her? The dog, I mean."

"I think she's eaten something. She's a dreadful scavenger."

"The beaches begin to be filthy at this time of the year."

"I never thought of that. Perhaps I won't take her to Gwenvoe tomorrow. Anyway, she gets so hot in the sand, and she won't go into the sea, because she doesn't like getting her fur wet."

"Like a cat."

Laura smiled. "Yes, just like a cat. Silvia, I must go."

"Thanks for bringing the tomatoes."

"Thank you for the lemonade."

Laura walked away from her. At the gate, she turned to wave and then disappeared behind the wall. Silvia stood outside her house. She looked down and saw another weed, groundsel this time. She stooped and jerked it out, and its fragile roots were covered in damp brown earth, dirtying her hands.

Gerald sat on a rock, in the shade of another one, and watched his family swimming. His assorted family, he corrected himself. His wife, his great-niece, her stepmother, and his own stepson. It was five thirty in the evening, and he was ready to go home. They had been here since noon, and although they had the spot to themselves, he was looking forward to a shower, a gin and tonic, the cool drawing room, and the evening paper, but just as he had started to make noises about departing, Eve and the others all decided to swim again.

They were at Gwenvoe, but not on the beach. Instead, on leaving the car park, they had walked half a mile or so along the cliff path, and then dropped down onto the rocks. At first the sea had been far out, but as the afternoon slipped by, the tide came in, filling a deep gully, which split the face of the cliff like a fiord, and forming a natural pool. The water here was the deepest turquoise, clear and sparkling in the evening sunshine. Which was why nobody had been able to resist it.

Except Gerald, who had had enough and chose to observe. Eve, his darling Eve, who was perfectly seaworthy, but the only person he had ever seen who could swim in a totally upright position, and Gerald had never got around to solving the sheer mathematics of this extraordinary feat. Laura was more conventional, with her unambitious breast stroke, but Gabriel swam like a boy, head down, brown arms moving smoothly, slipping through the water in a beautifully professional crawl. At intervals, she and Ivan would clamber up onto a convenient ledge and dive. She was waiting now to do this thing, perched on the rock like a sleek wet mermaid, wearing the smallest bikini Gerald had ever seen, her brown body sparkling with droplets.

Eve and Laura came out at last, sat beside him, rubbing at their hair with towels, dripping all over the sizzling rock.

Gerald asked wistfully, "Do you think we could go home now?"

"Oh, my darling." Eve reached up her face and gave him a cool, salty kiss. "Of course. You've been very good and not complained once. And I think I've had enough for the day, although it's always sad to end a day when it's been so perfect."

"You should always leave a party when you're still enjoying yourself."

"Anyway, I must get back and start thinking about dinner. By the time we've got everything packed up and we've walked back to the car . . ."

She slid down the straps of her bathing suit, preparing to get dressed. "How about you, Laura?"

"I'll come with you."

"And the others?"

They looked toward Ivan and Gabriel. Gabriel was in the water in the pool, treading water, looking up to where Ivan stood, high above her, poised to dive.

"Ivan," Gerald called.

He relaxed, turned his face in their direction. "What is it?"

"We're going now. What do you want to do?"

"We'll stay for a bit, I think. . . ."

"All right, we'll see you later."

"Leave some of the baskets for me to carry."

"We'll do that."

At Tremenheere, he drove the car under the archway and parked in the courtyard. Drusilla and Joshua were there, playing with a rubber ball, Joshua chasing it on his hands and knees, as he had not yet mastered the art of walking. He wore a grubby cotton vest and nothing else, and as they got out of the car, he sat on his fat brown bottom to observe them.

"Have a good day?" Drusilla asked.

"Perfect," said Eve. "How about you?"

"We went up to the walled garden and I turned the hose on Joshua. I hope you don't mind."

"What a good idea. Did he like it?"

"Thought it was a great joke. Couldn't stop laughing."

They carried the picnic baskets into the kitchen. After the warmth out of doors, it felt marvelously cool.

"I think," said Laura, "I'll just run up and see how Lucy is, give her a little walk in the garden."

"What a good thing we didn't take her," said Eve. "She'd have hated it being so hot."

Laura ran up the back stairs, and Eve began unpacking the remains of the picnic—always, she thought, a distasteful job, and the sooner accomplished the better. While she was doing this, Gerald joined her, carrying the hamper that had contained the wine bottles and the coffee thermos.

Eve smiled at him. "Darling, it was lovely that you came with us. It wouldn't have been the same without you there. Just leave that, and go up and have a shower. I know you're longing for one."

"How did you guess?"

"You've got a sort of hot and sweaty look. I'll clear up, it won't take me a moment. I'll stack it all in the dishwasher, and—'

"Eve."

Laura, calling from upstairs.

"Eve!"

They heard the panic in her voice, shrill as a scream for help, and looked at each other, their eyes meeting in apprehension. Then, with accord, they dropped what they were doing and made for the stairs. Eve was first, down the passage, and in through the open door of Laura's bedroom. They found her standing there, with Lucy in her arms. The little bowl that Laura had left filled with milk was empty, and it seemed that she had struggled from her basket and tried to reach the door, for there were small pools of vomit all across the carpet. The smell was sour and sickening.

"Laura."

The dog's supple body was strangely rigid, her usually silky fur staring, her back paws dangling pathetically. Her eyes were open, but sightless and glazed, and her lips curled back from her pointed teeth in an agonized snarl.

She was, quite obviously, dead.

"Laura. Oh, Laura." Eve's instinct was to embrace, to touch, to comfort, but somehow she could do none of these things. She put out her hand and laid it on Lucy's head. "She must have been much sicker than any of us realized. Poor little thing . . ." She dissolved into tears, hating herself for succumbing, but it was all too tragic, and she was incapable of controlling her distress. "Oh, Gerald."

Laura did not cry. Slowly she looked from Eve's face to Gerald's. He saw her dark eyes blank with the misery of loss. After a little, "I want Alec, then" she told him.

He went to her side, gently loosened the frantic grip of her fingers, and took Lucy's body away from her, holding it against his chest. He left the women and went out of the room, and carried Lucy downstairs to the kitchen. He found a cardboard grocery carton and there, decently, laid the little body, covered it with the lid. He carried the box out into the woodshed, set it down on the floor, and came out, closing the door behind him. Later, he would dig a grave and bury Lucy in the garden. But now, there were more urgent things to be done.

It being a Saturday made everything infinitely more complicated. In the end, with the assistance of directory enquiries, he obtained the home telephone number of Alec's chairman at Sandberg Harpers and put a call through to him. By the greatest of good fortune he caught that eminent gentleman at home, explained the bare facts of his dilemma, and was given, in return, a New York number at which Alec might be reached.

It was now six thirty. One thirty in New York. He put the call through, but was told there would be a little delay. If he would care to stay by the telephone, he would be rung back. He set down the receiver and sat back to wait.

It was while he was doing this that Eve came to find him. He looked up as she came into his study.

"Is Laura all right?" he asked.

"No. She's desperately shocked. She didn't cry, she just started shivering. I put her to bed with the electric blanket on. I gave her a sleeping pill. I couldn't think of anything else to do."

She came to his side, and he put his arms around her and for a little they said nothing, just indulged in wordless, mutual comfort. After a bit, she drew away from him and went to sit in his big armchair. She looked, he thought, desperately tired.

She said, "What are you doing?"

"Waiting to speak to Alec. I've put a call through to New York."

She looked at her watch. "What time is it there?"

"One thirty."

"Will he be there?"

"I hope so."

"What are you going to say to him?"

"I'm going to tell him to get the first plane home."

Eve frowned. "You're going to tell him to come home? But Alec . . ."

"He has to come. It's all too serious."

"I don't understand."

"I didn't want to tell you. But there was another of those dreadful letters. And Lucy didn't die from natural causes, Eve. She was poisoned."

8

ROSKENWYN

𝒟AWN. SUNDAY MORNING. The great jet dropped out of the sky above London, circled once, lined up on the runway at Heathrow, and floated down to a perfect landing.

Home.

Alec Haverstock, with no luggage save a small grip, which he carried, went straight through Immigration and Customs, across the terminal, and out into the cool, gray damp air of an English summer morning.

He looked for the car and found it. His own dark red BMW, with Rogerson, the office driver, standing alongside. Rogerson was a formal fellow, and although it was Sunday, and officially his day off, he had come to the airport in full rig: peaked cap, leather gloves, and all.

"Morning, Mr. Haverstock. Have a good flight?"

"Yes, fine, thank you." Although he had not slept at all. "Thank you for bringing the car."

"That's all right, sir." He took Alec's bag and stowed it in the boot. "She's all filled up—you shouldn't have to stop for a bit."

"How are you getting back to town?"

"I'll take the tube, sir."

"I'm sorry to have to put you to so much trouble on a Sunday. I appreciate it."

"Anytime, sir." His gloved hand received Alec's grateful fiver discreetly. "Thank you very much, sir."

He drove, and the morning lightened all about him. On either side of the motorway small villages slowly came to life. By the time he was in Devon, church bells had started to ring. By the time he crossed the bridge over the Tamar, the sun was high in the sky and the roads were filling with aimless Sunday traffic.

The miles flashed by. Now it was sixty, now fifty, now forty to Tremenheere. He crested a rise, and the road ran downhill to the northern estuaries, and sand dunes, and the sea. He could see the small hills, crested with monoliths and cairns of granite that had stood there since before the very beginning of time. The road swung south, into the sun. He saw the other sea, shimmering with sun pennies. There were yachts out—some small regatta, perhaps—and the narrow beaches were lined with screaming, happy holiday-makers.

Penvarloe. He turned up the hill and into the familiar, quiet lanes and was through the village and out the other side in the same moment, turning in through the remembered gates.

It was half past twelve.

He saw her at once. She was sitting on the front doorstep of Tremenheere, with her knees drawn up to her chin, waiting for him. He wondered how long she had been there. As he drew up and stopped the engine, she rose slowly to her feet.

He unlatched his safety belt and got out of the car, and stood by the open door looking at her. Across the small distance that separated them he saw the beautiful gray eyes, the best thing that she could have inherited from her mother. She had grown tall and long-legged, but she hadn't changed. Once, her hair had been long and dark, and now it was short and bleached the color of straw. But she hadn't changed.

She said, "You took your time," but the tough words were belied by the shake in her voice. He slammed the car door shut and held out his arms, and his daughter said, "Oh, Daddy!" and burst into tears, and catapulted herself into his embrace, all at one and the same time.

Later, he went upstairs in search of his wife. He found her in their bedroom, sitting at the dressing table, brushing her hair. The room was neat and airy, the bed made. Lucy's basket was gone. In the mirror, their eyes met.

"Darling."

She dropped the brush and turned into his arms. He pulled her to her feet, and for a long moment they embraced, her slenderness held so close that he could feel the beating of her heart. He kissed the top of her clean, sweet-smelling head, touched her hair with his hand.

"Darling Laura."

She said, into his shoulder, the words sounding muffled, "I didn't come down because I wanted you to see Gabriel first. I wanted her to be the first one to see you."

"She was waiting." He said, "I'm sorry about Lucy."

He felt her shake her head, wordless, not wanting to talk about the tragedy, not trusting herself to speak.

He did not say, "I'll buy you another," because that would be like telling a bereaved mother that you would buy her another child. For Laura, there could never be another. A new puppy, perhaps, in time, but never another Lucy.

After a little, he held her gently away from him and stared down into her face. She looked brown and marvelously better, but dreadfully sad. He put his hands on either side of her head, with his thumbs touching the dark smudges beneath her eyes as though they were marks that he could rub away.

She said, "Did you speak to Gabriel?"

"Yes."

"Did she tell you?"

"Yes."

"About the baby?" He nodded. She said, "She came home to you, Alec. That's why she came home. To be with you."

"I know."

"She can stay with us."

"Of course."

"She's had a bad time."

"She's survived it."

"She's a lovely person."

He smiled. "That's what she said about you."

"You would never speak about her, Alec. Why would you never speak about Gabriel to me?"

"Did that worry you so much?"

"Yes. It made me feel so dreadfully inadequate, as though you thought I didn't love you enough. As though I hadn't enough love for you to let Gabriel be part of our life together."

He thought that over. He said, "It sounds complicated. I think we'd better sit down. . . ." Taking Laura's hand, he led her to the old sofa that stood in front of the window. He sank into the corner of this, drawing her down beside him, still holding her hands within his own.

He said, "You have to listen. I didn't talk about Gabriel, partly because I didn't think it was fair to you. My life with Erica was over years ago, and Gabriel physically left me then. In truth, by the time I married you, I'd given up all hopes of ever seeing her again. As well, I *couldn't* talk about her. It was as simple as that. Losing her, seeing her go, was the worst thing that ever happened to me. Over the years, I shut the memory away, like something shut in a box, with the lid tightly closed. That was the only way I could live with it."

"But now you can open the box."

"Gabriel's opened it herself. Escaped. Free. She's come home."

"Oh, Alec."

He kissed her. He said, "You know, I've missed you so much. Without you with me, Glenshandra lost its magic. I kept wanting the holiday to be over, so that I could get home to you. And in New York, I kept thinking that I saw you, in restaurants and on sidewalks, and I'd look and the girl would turn round, and I'd see that she didn't look in the least like you, and my imagination had been playing me tricks."

"Did it matter very much, leaving New York in the middle of your business and coming back? When . . . Lucy died, I told Gerald that I wanted you, but I never thought he'd go to all that trouble to get you here."

"Tom's still there. He's quite capable of handling things on his own."

"Did you get my letter?"

He shook his head. "Did you write?"

"Yes, but it wouldn't have got to you. It was only to say how sorry I was about not coming with you."

"I understood."

"I hate telephones."

"So do I. I use them all the time, but they're impossible instruments if you're trying to get close to someone."

"Alec, it wasn't just that I didn't want to fly, or that I was still feeling ill. It was just that . . . I couldn't . . ." She hesitated, and then it all came out in a rush ". . . I couldn't face a week in New York with Daphne Boulderstone."

For a second Alec was silenced into blank astonishment. And then he started to laugh. "I thought you were going to tell me something horrendous."

"Isn't that horrendous?"

"What, being driven around the twist by Daphne Boulderstone? My darling, we all are, constantly. Even her husband. She's the most maddening woman in the world. . . ."

"Oh, Alec, it isn't just that. It's that . . . she always . . . well, she makes me feel an idiot. As though I don't know anything. That day she came to see me, she went on about Erica, and Erica's curtains and things, and how she'd been Erica's best friend, and nothing was the same after Deepbrook was sold, and how she'd been your friend before she even met Tom, and how important first loves were, and . . ."

Alec laid his hand over her mouth. She looked up and saw his eyes sympathetic, but still, dancing with amusement.

He said, "That's the most garbled sentence I've ever heard in my life." He took his hand away. "But I do understand." He kissed her mouth. "And I'm sorry. It was stupid of me to even imagine you'd have wanted to spend a week with Daphne. It was just that I wanted you so much to be with me."

"They're like a club, the Boulderstones and the Ansteys. One that I can never belong to . . ."

"Yes, I know. I've been very unperceptive. Sometimes I forget how much older we all are than you. I've been involved with them so long that sometimes I lose track of the real essentials."

"Like what?"

"Oh, I don't know. Like having a beautiful wife. And a beautiful daughter."

"And a beautiful grandchild."

He smiled. "That too."

"We'll be a bit of a squash in Abigail Crescent."

"I think I've lived in Abigail Crescent long enough. When we get back to London, we'll look for a bigger house. One with a garden. And there, no doubt, we shall all live happily ever after."

"When do we have to leave?"

"Tomorrow morning."

She said, "I want to go home. Eve and Gerald have been unbelievably kind, but I want to go home."

"That reminds me." He looked at his watch. "I had a word with them before I came to find you. Lunch is at half past one. Are you feeling hungry?"

"I think I'm too happy to be hungry."

"Impossible," said Alec. He stood up and pulled her to her feet. "Look at me. And I can't wait to get my teeth into Eve's cold roast beef and new potatoes."

". . . so that's the situation. After Silvia received that first letter, we were all, reluctantly, pretty sure that poor old May was responsible. Had composed it in a moment of total lunacy. In her old age, she behaves very oddly every now and again, and it seemed at the time a reasonable explanation. But when Gabriel produced that second letter, the one that was addressed to you, Ivan suggested that it could possibly be Drusilla who was writing them, the girl who lives in the cottage. She's apparently quite a nice creature, but as Ivan pointed out, a complete mystery to all of us. She came here to live because she had nowhere else to go. And I think, probably, she rather fancied Ivan." He shrugged. "I don't know, Alec. I really don't know."

"And then Lucy!"

"Yes. And this horror leaves me without explanations at all. Even if she was stark staring bonkers, May could never, would never, do such a thing. And Drusilla's a sort of earth-mother type. I simply can't see her taking life."

"You're sure the dog was poisoned?"

"Absolutely no doubt. That's why you had to come back from New York. As soon as I saw the dog I was filled with fears for Laura."

It was now three o'clock in the afternoon, and they had been closeted together in Gerald's study since lunchtime. Finally, they seemed to have come to the end of the road. The letter and its envelope lay on the desk between them, and Alec now took it up and read it yet again. The black, uneven words were burned into his memory, as though his brain had taken a sharp, clear-edged photograph, but still he felt compelled to read them, just once more.

"We haven't got the first letter?"

"No, Silvia has it. She wouldn't let me take it. I told her not to destroy it."

"Perhaps, before we make any further decisions, I'd better see it. Anyway, if we do have to take . . . further steps . . . we'll need it for evidence. Perhaps I'd better go down and see Silvia. Do you think she'll be there?"

"Give her a ring," said Gerald. He picked up his telephone, dialed the number, and handed the receiver across to Alec. He heard the ringing tone. After a moment, "Hello" came Silvia's cheerful, husky voice.

"Silvia, it's Alec."

"Alec." She sounded delighted. "Hello! You're back?"

"I wondered, are you going to be around for the next hour?"

"Heavens, yes. I'm always around."

"Thought I might walk down. Come and see you."

"Lovely. I'll be in the garden, but I'll leave the front door open. Just walk through. See you."

Out of doors, the warmth of the slumberous Sunday afternoon was tempered by a cool breeze, blowing off the sea. It was very quiet, and for once Tremenheere was deserted. Ivan had taken Gabriel off in his car, with a vacuum flask of tea and their swimming things packed into a haversack. Eve and Laura, both looking exhausted, had been persuaded by their husbands to take to their beds and rest.

Even Drusilla and Joshua were gone. During the morning, observed by Ivan, a very small, old, open car had rattled into the courtyard, driven by one of Drusilla's mysterious friends, a large man with a biblical beard. On the back seat of the car was parked, like an upright passenger, an enormous black 'cello case. There had been a discussion with Drusilla, and presently they had all driven off together, Drusilla with Joshua on her knee. As well, she had taken her flute, so presumably some unimaginable musical occasion was planned. Ivan had watched them drive away and reported all this to the others over lunch.

Eve became quite excited. "Perhaps this is a new romance for Drusilla."

"I wouldn't count on it," said Ivan. "They looked quite bizarre, but very sedate, setting off. I'm sure they're just going to make beautiful music together, but not the kind you envisage."

"But . . ."

"I shouldn't push it, if I were you. I should think the last thing Gerald needs right now is a bearded cellist moving in to Tremenheere."

So much for Drusilla. So much for everybody. Alec walked through the gate and down the road toward the village. There was no traffic in the shady lane, but somewhere from across the valley came the barking of a dog. Above him, the topmost branches of the trees shivered in the wind.

He found Silvia, as she had said that he would, in her garden. She was working in her rosebed, and as he walked across the garden toward her, it occurred to him that, with her slender figure, her brown arms, and her curly mop of gray hair, she looked like an advertisement for some life insurance company. Invest with us and your retirement will be carefree. All that was missing was the handsome, white-haired husband, snipping away at the dead heads and smiling because he had no financial worries.

All that was missing. He remembered Tom, but Tom had not been handsome and white-haired. Tom, the last time Alec had seen him, had become shambling and shifty-eyed, with a beetroot-colored face and hands that shook unless they were firmly clasped around a glass.

"Silvia."

She turned her face toward him. She was wearing sunglasses, so that he could not see her eyes, but at once she smiled, appearing delighted to see him.

"Alec!" She edged herself out from among her roses and came to meet him. He kissed her.

"This is a lovely surprise. I didn't know you were back from New York. And I hardly had a glimpse of you when you were here before, leaving Laura."

"I was just thinking about Tom. I don't think I ever wrote to you when he died. And there wasn't time that other evening to say anything. But I was sorry."

"Oh, never mind. Poor old Tom. It was strange without him at first, but I suppose I'm getting used to it now."

"Your garden's looking fantastic, as it always does." There were tools lying on the grass. A rake and a hoe, a pair of scissors, a small fork. A wheelbarrow was filled with weeds and dead rose heads and prunings. "You must work like a beaver."

"It keeps me busy. Gives me something to do. But I'm going to stop now and talk to you. I'll just go and wash my hands first. Would you like a cup of tea? Or a drink?"

"No, I'm fine. What about all this stuff? Would you like me to put them away?"

"Oh, you are an angel. They live in the potting shed." She started toward the house. "I shan't be a moment."

He gathered up the things and carried them to the small garden shed that stood in a corner of the garden, discreetly disguised by a trellis, smothered in clematis. Behind the shed was a compost heap and the remains of a bonfire, where Silvia had been burning garden rubbish. Alec went back for the wheelbarrow and dealt with that as well, tipping its contents onto the top of the compost heap and then setting the barrow neatly against the back wall of the shed.

There was earth on his hands. He took out his handkerchief and wiped them. As he did this, he glanced down and saw that on her bonfire, Silvia had disposed of not only rubbish from her garden, but also old newspapers, cardboard packets, letters. Half-burned scraps of paper, inevitably, had survived, littered around the blackened ash. Scraps of paper. His hands were still. After a bit, he put his handkerchief away and stooped to pick up one of these. A corner—a triangle, charred along its longest edge.

He went back into the garden shed. It was neatly kept and very orderly. Long-handled tools leaned against one wall, small tools hung from a pegboard. There were stacks of earthenware flowerpots, a box of white plastic labels. At eye level was a shelf, ranged with packets and bottles. Grass seed, rose food, a bottle of methylated spirits. A can of engine oil, some fly repellent. A packet of Garotta for the compost heap. His eye moved down the shelf. A large green bottle with a white cap. Gordon's gin. Thinking of poor old Tom, he lifted it down and read the label. The bottle was still half full. Thoughtfully, he set it back in its place, stepped out of the shed, and walked slowly back toward the house.

As he went into the living room, Silvia appeared through the other door, rubbing cream into her hands. She had not taken off her dark glasses, but had combed her hair and doused herself in perfume. The room was heavy with its musky fragrance.

She said, "It's *so* lovely to see you again."

"It's not actually a social visit, Silvia. It's about that letter you got."

"That letter?"

"The poison-pen letter. You see, I got one too."

"You . . ." She looked horrified, as the meaning of this sunk in. *"Alec!"*

"Gerald tells me that you still have the one that was sent to you. I wondered if I might have a look at it."

"Of course, Gerald said I had to keep it, otherwise I'd have burned the horrible thing." She went to her desk. "It's here somewhere." She opened a drawer, took it out, handed it to him.

He drew, from the brown envelope, the sheet of paper. Brought from his pocket the second one, which had been addressed to him. He held them, fanned like a pair of playing cards.

"But they're exactly the same! A child's writing paper."

"So is this," said Alec.

It was the charred scrap that he had found. Pink, and lined, with the sickly little fairy only half burned away.

"What's that?" Her voice was sharp, almost indignant.

"I found it at the edge of your bonfire. I saw it when I emptied your wheelbarrow."

"I didn't ask you to empty the wheelbarrow."

"Where did it come from?"

"I've no idea."

"It's the same paper, Silvia."

"So what?" All this time, she had been wringing her hands, rubbing in the cream. Now she suddenly stopped doing this and went to the mantelpiece to find a cigarette. She lit it and flung the matchstick into the empty grate. Her hands were shaking. She took a long drag on the cigarette, blew out a plume of smoke. Then she turned to face him, her arms folded across her chest, as though she were trying to hold herself together.

"So what," she said again. "I don't know where it came from."

He said, "I think you sent that first letter to yourself. So that you could send the second letter to me, and nobody would even think of suspecting you."

"That's not true."

"You must have bought a packet of the child's writing paper. You'd only have needed two sheets. So you burned the rest."

"I don't know what you're talking about."

"You wanted everybody to think it was May. You posted the first letter locally. But the second time, you drove to Truro and posted that one there. On a Wednesday. That's the day that May always goes to Truro. It arrived in London the following day, but by then I'd already left for New York. So I never saw it. It was Gabriel who found it. Gabriel opened it, because she wanted to find out where Laura was staying, and she thought some clue might be in the letter. As it happens, you told her everything she wanted to know, but it wasn't a very nice way for her to find out."

"You can't prove anything."

"I don't think I have to. I just have to try to find out *why*. I thought we were friends. Why send me this sort of malevolent rubbish?"

"Rubbish? How do you know it's rubbish? You haven't been here, watching them, seeing them. Carrying on together."

She sounded like May at her most disagreeable.

"But why should you want to come between me and my wife? She's done nothing to harm you."

Silvia had finished her cigarette. She stubbed it out viciously, flung it into the hearth, fumbled for another.

She said, "She has everything."

"Laura?"

She lit the cigarette.

"Yes. Laura." She began to pace up and down the small room, still holding herself as though she were icy cold, up and down, like a tigress in a cage.

"You were part of my life, Alec, part of growing up. Do you remember, when we were all children, you and I and Brian, playing cricket on the beach, and climbing the cliffs and swimming together? Do you remember, once, you kissed me? It was the first time a man ever kissed me."

"I wasn't a man. I was a boy."

"And then I didn't see you for years and years. But then you came back to Tremenheere, and your first marriage was finished and I saw you all over again. Do you remember, we all went out for dinner. You and Eve and Gerald and Tom and I . . . And Tom got drunker than usual, and you came back with me and helped me get him to bed. . . ."

He did remember, and it was not an occasion that he enjoyed remembering. But he had come because it was obvious that Silvia could not cope on her own with a totally inebriated husband, six feet tall, sodden with alcohol and likely at any moment to pass out or be violently sick. Between them, he and Silvia had somehow got him into the house, upstairs, onto his bed. Afterwards, they had sat in this room, and she had given him a drink, and he—feeling pitifully sorry for her—had sat and talked for a little.

". . . you were so sweet to me that night. And that was the first time I thought about Tom dying. That was the first time I faced the fact that he would never get better, never dry out. He didn't want to. Death was all that was left for him. And I thought then, 'If Tom dies—when Tom dies—then Alec will be there, and Alec will take care of me.'" Just a fantasy, but when you left me that night, you kissed me with such tenderness that all at once it seemed perfectly reasonable and possible."

He did not remember kissing her, but he supposed that he had.

"But Tom didn't die. Not for a year. By the end it was like living with a shadow, a nonentity. A sort of wraith, whose only aim in life was to get his hand around the neck of a whiskey bottle. And by the time he did die, you'd married again. And when I saw Laura I knew why. She had everything," she repeated, and this time the word came out through teeth clenched with envious rage. "She's younger and she's beautiful. She has an expensive car, and expensive clothes and jewelry that any woman would give her eyes for. She can afford to buy expensive presents. Presents for Eve, and Eve is *my* friend. I can never give Eve presents like that, Tom left me so broke, I can scarcely make ends meet, let alone buy presents. And everybody went on and on about her, as though she were some sort of saint. Even Ivan. Especially Ivan. Before, Ivan used to come and see me sometimes, ask me up for a drink if I was feeling blue, but once Laura arrived, that was it; he had time for no one but her. They used to go off together, did you know that, Alec? God knows what they were up to, but they'd get back to Tremenheere all secret and laughing, and your wife looking sleek and smug as a cat. It was true, what I told you. It was true . . . they had to be lovers. Fulfilled . . . that's how she looked, I know. I can tell. Fulfilled."

Alec said nothing. Filled with sadness and pity he listened, watching the tireless figure pacing to and fro, hearing the voice, which was deep and husky no longer, but shrill with desperation.

". . . do you know what it's like to be alone. Alec? Really alone? You were without Erica for five years, but you can't know what it's like to be truly alone. It's as though your unhappiness is contagious, and people keep away from you. When Tom was alive there were always people coming around, friends of his, even at the end when he was so impossible. They came to see *me*. But after he died, they didn't come anymore. They left me alone. They were afraid of involvements, afraid of a woman on her own. The last few years of his life Tom was no use to me, but I . . . managed. And I wasn't ashamed of it either, because I had to have some sort of love, some sort of physical stimulus to keep me going. But after he died . . . Everyone was so sorry for me. They talked about the empty house, the empty chair by the fire, but they were all too delicate to mention the empty bed. That was the worst nightmare of all."

He began to wonder if, possibly, she were a little mad. He said, "Why did you kill Laura's dog?"

"She has everything. . . . She has you and now she has Gabriel. When she told me about Gabriel, I knew that I'd lost you forever. You might have chucked *her* over, but you'd never leave your daughter. . . ."

"But why the little dog?"

"The dog was ill. It died."

"She was poisoned."

"That's a lie."

"I found a Gordon's gin bottle in your toolshed."

She almost laughed. "That would be one of Tom's. He used to keep them hidden everywhere. After a year I'm still finding bottles stashed away."

"This one didn't have gin in it. It was labeled. It's Paraquat."

"What's Paraquat?"

"A weed killer. Just about the most deadly poison there is. You can't buy it in a shop. You have to sign for it."

"Tom must have got it. I never use weed killer. I don't know anything about it."

"I think you do."

"I don't know anything." She flung her cigarette out through the open garden door. "I tell you I don't know anything." She seemed about to turn on him. He caught her by the elbows, but she jerked herself away, and in doing this, her hand caught her sunglasses and knocked them off. Revealed, unprotected, her strange-colored eyes stared into his. The dark pupils were hugely distended, but there was no life, no expression there. Not even anger. It was disturbing. Like looking into a mirror and finding no reflection.

"You killed the dog. Yesterday, when they were all at Gwenvoe. You walked up the road and into the open house. May was in her bedroom, Drusilla and her baby out at the back. There was nobody there to see you. You simply walked up the stairs and into our bedroom. You put probably just the smallest drop of Paraquat into Lucy's milk. That's all it would have needed. She didn't die at once, but she was dead by the time Laura found her. Did you really think, Silvia, did you honestly imagine that May would be blamed?"

"She hated the dog. It had been sick in her room."

"Have you any conception of the agony of mind you've put Eve through? No woman could have a better, kinder friend than Eve, but if this had gone the way you meant it to go, there wouldn't have been a thing Eve could do to help May. You were prepared to crucify the pair of them, just to satisfy a fantasy that could never have been more than a shred of your imagination. . . ."

"That's not true. . . . You and I . . ."

"Never!"

"But I love you . . . I did it for you, Alec . . . you . . ."

Now she was screaming the words at him, trying to get her thin arms around his neck, turning up her blank-eyed face in a travesty of passion, her mouth open and hungry for some physical assuagement of her pathetic and unbearable need. "Can't you see, you fool, I did it for you . . . ?"

The force of her assault on him was manic, but he was a good deal stronger than she, and the distasteful struggle was over almost as soon as it began. In his arms, he felt her go limp. As he held her, she sagged against him and began, horribly, to cry. He picked her up in his arms and carried her to the sofa, and laid her down, arranging a cushion beneath her head. She went on weeping, a dreadful sound, choking and gasping, her head turned away from him. He drew forward a chair, and sat and watched her, waiting until hysteria was spent. At last, she lay still, exhausted, her breathing heavy and deep, her eyes closed. She looked like a person who had suffered a devastating fit, as though she were slowly coming out of a coma.

He reached out and took her hand. "Silvia."

Her hand in his was lifeless. She gave no indication that she had heard him speak.

"Silvia. You must see a doctor. Who is your doctor?"

Presently she sighed deeply and turned her tear-ravaged face toward him, but she did not open her eyes.

"I'll call him. What's his name?"

"Doctor Williams." It was no more than a whisper.

He laid down her hand and left her there, and went out to the hall where the telephone stood. He looked up the number in her own private book, found it written in her neat hand. He dialed, praying that the doctor would be in.

He was, and answered the call himself. Alec, as clearly and simply as he could, explained what had happened. The doctor listened.

When Alec had finished, "What's she doing now?" he asked.

"She's quiet. She's lying down. But I think she's a very sick woman."

"Yes," said the doctor. And then, "I've been afraid something like this might happen. I've been seeing her, on and off, since her husband died. She's been under great stress. It wouldn't have taken much to trigger this off."

"Will you come?"

"Yes. I'll come. I'll come now. Will you stay there with her until I arrive? I'll be as quick as I can."

"Of course."

He went back to Silvia. She seemed to be sleeping. Grateful for this, he took a rug from the back of a chair and covered her, tucking the soft wool around her shoulders and over her feet. Looking down into her lined, unconscious face, racked with tension and spent despair, she seemed to him as old as May. Older, for May had never lost her innocence.

When at last he heard the doctor's car, he left Silvia and went out to meet him. He saw that the doctor had brought a nurse with him, a bustling woman in a white apron.

"I'm sorry about this," said Alec.

"I'm sorry too. Good of you to call. Good of you to stay with her. If I want to get hold of you, where will you be?"

"I'm staying at Tremenheere. But I have to go back to London tomorrow morning."

"If I need to, I can always get in touch with the Admiral. I don't think you can do any more. We'll take over now."

"Will she be all right?"

"There's an ambulance on the way. Like I said, it's out of your hands now."

Walking slowly back up the road to Tremenheere, Alec found himself recalling, not the shattering confrontation that had just taken place, but that long-ago time when he and Brian had been boys, staying with their dashing young uncle Gerald, and tasting the first heady sip of adulthood. Perhaps this was what happened to very old people. This was why May could remember in minute detail the Sunday School picnics and snowy Christmases of her childhood, and yet had no recollection of what she had done the day before. Hardening of the arteries, the medical profession called it, but perhaps the causes lay deeper than the physical disintegration of the extremely elderly. Perhaps it was simply a withdrawal, a rejection of the reality of failing sight, failing hearing, unsteady legs, and hands that fumbled, crippled with arthritis.

So now, Silvia was, in his memory, fourteen again. A child, but, for the first time, patently aware of the potential heady excitement of the opposite sex. Her legs and arms were long and skinny and brown, but her tiny breasts belied this childishness, and her red-gold mop of hair framed a face filled with a promise of great beauty. The three of them had played cricket and climbed cliffs, with the innocence of all youngsters of their age, but swimming together, as though the cold salt sea washed away the timid inhibitions of puberty, was a different matter altogether. Tumbling in the surf, their bodies touched. Diving, they came together underwater, hand met hand, cheek brushed against cheek. When, finally, Alec plucked up the courage to kiss her, a boy's first fumbling kiss, she had moved her face so that her open mouth touched his lips, and after that, the kiss wasn't such a fumbling affair after all. So much she had taught him. She had so much to give.

In all his life he could not remember feeling so tired. Never a man to yearn for the comfort of alcohol, he found himself, now, deeply in need of an enormous drink. But that would have to wait. Reaching Tremenheere, he went indoors through the open front door and stood for a moment in the empty hall, listening. There were no voices, no sound. He climbed the great, polished oak staircase, went along the passage to their bedroom, gently opened the door. The curtains were still drawn against the sunlight, and in the great double bed, Laura slept. For a moment he watched her, her dark hair spread on the white pillow, and was overwhelmed by tenderness and love. His marriage to her was the most important thing in his life, and the thought of losing her, for any reason, filled him with anguish. Perhaps they had both made mistakes, been too reserved, too respectful of the other's privacy, but he promised himself that from now on they would share everything fate flung their way, good or bad.

Her face, in sleep, was untroubled and innocent, so that she looked much younger than her years. And it occurred to him then, with a sort of amazed gratitude, that she *was* innocent.

She, of all of them, knew nothing of the malevolent letters. She did not know that Lucy had died because she had been poisoned. It was important that she should never know. She stirred, but did not wake. Quietly, he went from the room, closing the door behind him.

Eve and Gerald were nowhere in the house. Searching for them, Alec made his way through the deserted kitchen and out into the courtyard. Here, he saw that Drusilla and her friend had returned from their outing. His car, resembling nothing so much as a very old sewing machine on wheels, stood parked, apparently held together with knots of string and bits of wire. He and Drusilla and Joshua were outside her cottage. A rocking chair had been carried out, and in this the friend sat, looking like some ancient prophet, with Joshua squatting at his feet. Drusilla sat on the doorstep and was playing her flute.

Alec, diverted from his intent by the charming scene they presented, stopped to look and listen. Drusilla's music pierced the air with all the clarity and precision of water dropping into a fountain. He recognized "The Lark in the Clear Air," an old North Country song, which she probably carried with her from her childhood. It was the perfect accompaniment for a summer evening. Her friend, rocking gently in his chair, sat and watched her. Joshua, bored with playing on the ground, all at once struggled to his feet, hauling himself upright against the man's knees. He leaned forward and lifted the child into his lap, bare bottom and all, and held him, cradled in the curve of his massive arm.

So maybe Ivan had been wrong. Maybe Drusilla and her friend were going to make more than beautiful music together. He looked a nice sort of fellow, and Alec, silently, wished them well.

The last note died away. Drusilla lowered her flute and looked up and saw him standing there.

He said, "Well done. That was beautiful."

"Are you looking for Eve?"

"Yes."

"They're up in the garden picking raspberries."

He found himself comforted by this little encounter. Tremenheere had not lost its magic, its gift of soothing the spirit. But even so, as he went through the door in the wall and up the path between the box hedges, his heart was heavy as that of a man about to break the news of a tragic family bereavement. As he approached, they stopped their picking, their faces turned toward him. It seemed an eternity since Alec had last seen them, and yet it took only moments to relate the somber details of the afternoon. They stood there, in the sunshine, in the scented, tranquil walled garden, and it was all told in a few bare, painful sentences. It was finished. Over. They were still together. Relationships had survived, undamaged. It seemed to Alec nothing short of a miracle.

But Eve, being Eve, had thoughts only for Silvia.

". . . an ambulance? A nurse? Oh, dear heaven, Alec, what are they going to do to her?"

"I think they'll take her to hospital. She needs caring for, Eve."

"But I must go and see her . . . I must."

"My darling," Gerald laid a hand on her arm. "Let it be. For the moment, let it be. There's nothing you can do."

"But we can't abandon her. Whatever she's done, she has nobody but us to turn to. We can't abandon her."

She turned to Alec, appealing to him. He said, "She's sick, Eve." Still she did not understand. "She's had a nervous breakdown."

"But . . ."

Gerald abandoned euphemisms. "My darling, she has gone off her head."

"But that's ghastly . . . tragic . . ."

"You must accept it. It's better for you to accept it. If you don't, then you have only one alternative, and that is infinitely worse. We suspected both Drusilla and May; two totally innocent women might have been blamed for something they knew nothing about. And that is what Silvia wanted. To destroy not only Alec and Laura's marriage but May as well . . ."

"Oh, Gerald—' Her hand went over her mouth, shutting off the rest of the sentence. Her blue eyes filled with tears. "May . . . my darling May . . ."

She dropped her basket of fruit and turned away from them, running down the path in the direction of the house. Her going was so sudden that Alec, instinctively, started after her, but Gerald put out a hand to stop him.

"Leave her. She'll be all right."

May was sitting at her table, pasting pictures into her scrapbook. Lovely, it had been, hearing Drusilla play that nice tune. Funny girl she was. Got a new admirer by the looks of things, though May had never been much of a one for beards. She'd found some nice photos in the Sunday papers. One of the Queen Mother in a blue chiffon hat. She'd always had a pretty smile. And a comic one of a kitten in a jug with a bow round its neck. Pity about Mrs. Alec's little dog. Nice little creature, even if it had been sick on her rug.

Because she was so deaf, she did not hear Eve coming down the passage, and the first thing she knew was her door bursting open and Eve there in the room. Such a start it gave her that she was quite annoyed and looked up crossly over her spectacles, but before she had time to say a word, Eve was across the room and on her knees at May's side.

"Oh, May . . ."

She was in floods of tears. Her arms were around May's waist, her face buried in May's meager bosom.

"Oh, darling May . . ."

"Well, whatever's all this about?" asked May in the rallying tones she had used when Eve was a very small child and had cut her knee or broken her doll. "My word, what's upset you? All those tears. And all about nothing, I shouldn't wonder. There now." Her gnarled arthritic hand stroked the back of Eve's head. Such a pretty blond she'd been, and now she was quite white. "There now." Oh well, thought May, we're none of us getting any younger. "There. Nothing to cry about. May's here."

She had no idea what all the fuss was about. She was never to know. She never asked, and she was never told.

9

HOMES

LAURA WAS ALONE IN HER BEDROOM, doing the last of the packing: emptying drawers, checking on the contents of the wardrobe, trying to remember where she had put a red leather belt or whether it was already in her suitcase. She had left Alec and Gabriel at the breakfast table, eating the last of the toast and drinking a second cup of coffee. As soon as they had finished, and Alec had assembled their various bits of luggage, they would be leaving. The car waited at the front door. Tremenheere was almost over.

She was in the bathroom collecting her sponge and toothbrush and Alec's shaving things, when there came a knock on the bedroom door.

"Hello?"

She heard the door open. "Laura." It was Gabriel. Carrying all the various bits and pieces, Laura emerged from the bathroom.

"Oh, darling, I won't be a moment. Is Alec making impatient noises? I've just got to get these things sorted, and then I'll be ready. Is your suitcase in the car? And I've got a bottle of Elizabeth Arden somewhere . . . or have I put it in?"

"Laura."

Laura looked at her.

Gabriel smiled. "Listen to me."

"Darling, I'm listening." She put the things down on the bed. "What is it?"

"It's just that . . . would you mind most frightfully if I didn't come back with you? If I stayed here . . . ?"

Laura was taken aback, but did her best not to show it. "But of course. I mean, there's no rush. If you want to stay on for a bit, why shouldn't you? It's a good idea. I should have thought of it myself. You can join us later."

"It's not like that, Laura. What I'm trying to say is that . . . I don't think I'll be coming to London at all. After all," she added unnecessarily.

"You won't . . . ?" Thoughts flew, undisciplined, in all directions. ". . . but what about the baby?"

"I'll probably have the baby here."

"You mean, you're going to stay here with Eve?"

"No." Gabriel laughed ruefully. "Laura, you're being dreadfully thick. You're not making it the least bit easy for me. I'm going to stay with Ivan."

"With I—" Laura felt, quite suddenly, all weak at the knees and found it necessary to sit down on the edge of the bed. She saw to her surprise that Gabriel, rather endearingly, was blushing.

"Gabriel!"

"Does that horrify you?"

"No, of course it doesn't horrify me. But it is a little surprising. . . . You've only just met him. You scarcely know him."

"That's why I'm going to stay with him. So that we really can get to know each other."

"Are you sure this is what you want to do?"

"Yes. I'm sure. And he's sure too." When Laura did not reply, Gabriel came to curl up on the bed beside her. "We've fallen in love, Laura. At least, I think that's what happened to us. I don't know for certain, because it's never happened to me before. I never really believed in it. And as for falling in love at first sight, I always told myself that was just a lot of sentimental twaddle."

"It isn't," Laura told her. "I know, because I fell in love with your father at first sight. Before I even knew who he was."

"Then you understand. You don't think I'm behaving like an idiot. You don't think it's all a wild figment of my imagination, or something to do with hormones or being pregnant."

"No. I don't think that."

"I'm so happy, Laura."

"Do you think you'll marry him?"

"I expect so. One day. We'll probably walk down to the church in the village, just the two of us, and come back man and wife. You wouldn't mind if we did that, would you? You wouldn't mind losing out on all the hassles of a family wedding?"

"I don't think you should ask me that. I think you should ask Alec."

"Ivan's downstairs now, telling him what I'm telling you. We thought it would be easier that way. For everybody."

"Does he know about the baby?"

"Of course."

"And he doesn't mind?"

"No. He says, in a funny way, it just makes him more certain that this is what he wants."

"Oh, Gabriel." She put her arms around her stepdaughter, and for the first time they embraced, hugging enormously, kissing with a true and tender affection. "He's such a special person. Almost as special as you are. You both deserve all the happiness in the world."

Gabriel drew away. "When the baby comes, will you come back to Tremenheere? I'd like you to be around when it's born."

"Wild horses wouldn't keep me away."

"And you're not upset about me not coming back to London with you after all?"

"It's your life. You must live it your way. Just know that your father's always there if you need him. You didn't realize it before, but that's the way it's always been."

Gabriel grinned. "I guess so," she said.

She was still there, still endeavoring, in a bemused fashion, to finish the packing, when Alec came to find her. As he opened the door, she straightened from her suitcase, a hairbrush in one hand and the elusive bottle of Elizabeth Arden in the other. For a long moment they looked at each other across the room, in silence, not because they had nothing to say, but because words were unnecessary. He shut the door, with some force, behind him. His expression was serious, his features set grimly, the corners of his mouth turned down, but his eyes, bright with amusement, gave him away. And Laura knew that he was laughing, not at Ivan and Gabriel, but at themselves.

It was he who broke the silence. "We look," he told Laura, "the very picture of two long-suffering parents, trying to come to terms with the dotty inconsistencies of the younger generation."

She dissolved into laughter. "Darling, however hard you try, you'll never sound like a Victorian father."

"I wanted you to believe I was enraged."

"You haven't succeeded. You don't mind?"

"Mind? That's the understatement of the year. I'm punch-drunk with body blows, most of them beneath the belt. Ivan and Gabriel." He cocked an eyebrow. "What do you think about it?"

"I think," said Laura, stowing the bottle and the hairbrush, and shutting the suitcase. "I think they need each other." She fastened the locks. "I think they're in love, but I think they like each other too."

"They don't know each other."

"Oh, yes, they do. They made friends right away, and they've been together constantly over the last two days. He's a very kind man, and

Gabriel, for all that veneer of toughness, needs kindness. Especially now, with the baby on the way."

"That's the other extraordinary thing. He doesn't give a damn about a baby being on the way. Just makes him more sure than ever that he wants to spend the rest of his life with her."

"Alec, he loves her."

At that, he had to smile, shaking his head. "Laura, my darling, you're a romantic."

"I think Gabriel's probably a romantic too, although she doesn't want to admit it."

He thought this over. "There's one good thing about all this. If she stays here, I won't need to go hunting for a bigger house."

"Don't count on it."

"What does that mean?"

"I'm coming back to Tremenheere when Gabriel has the baby. That's eight months' time. I may be pregnant myself by then. You never know."

Alec smiled again, his eyes filled with love. "That's right," he said, "you never know." He kissed her. "Now, are you ready? Because they're all hanging around downstairs in the hall, waiting to see us off. My father always used to say, if you're going, go. Let's not keep them waiting."

She shut the last of the cases, and he picked them up and made for the door, but Laura lingered for a last look around. Lucy's basket was gone, for Gerald had burned it. And Lucy was buried here, at Tremenheere, in the garden. Gerald had offered to have a little headstone carved, but somehow that did not seem quite right, so instead Eve had promised to plant a rose over the spot where Lucy lay. An old-fashioned rose. *Perpétué et Félicité,* perhaps. Darling little pale pink flowers. Just right for Lucy.

Perpétué et Félicité. She thought of Lucy, running across the grass toward her, eyes shining, ears streaming, tail whisking with delight. It was a good way to remember her, and *Félicité* meant happiness. Her eyes had misted with tears—it was still impossible to think of Lucy without tears—but she brushed them swiftly away and turned and followed her husband through the door.

Behind them, the deserted room lay empty and still, but for a curtain stirring, caught by the summer morning breeze.

THE CAROUSEL

1

My MOTHER STOOD in the middle of her pretty sitting room, filled with September sunshine, and said, "Prue, you must be going out of your mind."

She looked as though she were about to burst into tears of disappointment, but I knew that she would not, because tears would destroy her faultless maquillage, would make her face swell, turn down her mouth, and accentuate unbecoming lines. However exasperated, she would never cry. Her appearance mattered to her almost more than anything else, and now she stood across the hearth rug from me, immaculately turned out in a raspberry pink woollen suit and a white silk shirt, with her gold earrings and her charm bracelet, and pretty silvery hair crisp and curly.

She struggled, however, to contain a conflict of destructive emotions: anger, motherly concern, but mostly disappointment. I felt very sorry for her.

I said, "Oh, come on, Ma, it's not the end of the world." Even as I said it, it sounded pretty feeble, which it probably was.

"For the first time in your life, you seem to have got involved with a really suitable man . . ."

"Darling, 'suitable's' a terribly old-fashioned word . . ."

"He's charming, he's steady, he's got a good job, and he comes from the right sort of family. You're twenty-three and it's time you settled down, got married and had children and a home of your own."

"Ma, he hasn't even *asked* me to marry him."

"Of course he hasn't. He wants to do it properly—take you home, introduce you to his mother. There's nothing wrong with that. And it's obvious the way his mind is running. You only have to see the two of you together to know that he's wildly in love with you."

"Nigel is incapable of being wildly anything."

"Honestly, Prue, I don't know what you're looking for."

"I'm not looking for anything."

We had had this conversation so often that I knew my part word for word, as though I had sat down and learned it by heart. "I've got everything I want. A job I like, a little flat of my own—"

"You can hardly call that one-room basement a flat—"

"And I don't feel like settling down."

"You're twenty-three. I was nineteen when I was married."

I nearly said, *and divorced six years later,* but I didn't. However maddened by her, you couldn't say things like that to my mother. I knew that she had a will of iron and an inner core of steel, which nearly always ensured that she got her own way, but there was something vulnerable about her—her delicate build, her enormous blue eyes, her rampant femininity—that precluded harsh words.

So I opened my mouth and then shut it again, and looked at her hopelessly. She gazed back at me, reproachful but not reproaching, and I understood for perhaps the thousandth time why my father, from the moment they set eyes on each other, had been lost. They had married because she was totally irresistible, and he was exactly what she had been searching for ever since she first realised that there was such a thing as an opposite sex.

My father is called Hugh Shackleton. In those days he worked in London, in a merchant bank in the City, with a life-style that was solid and a future that was bright. But he was basically a fish out of water. The Shackletons were a Northumberland family, and my father had been brought up there on a farm called Windyedge, where the pasture fields ran down to the cold North Sea and the winter gales blew straight in from the Ural Mountains. My father never lost his love of the country, or ceased to yearn for it. When he married my mother, the farm was being managed by his older brother, but about the time that I was five years old, this brother tragically was killed in a hunting accident. My father travelled to Northumberland for the funeral. He stayed away for five days, and by the time he returned to us, his mind was made up. He told my mother that he intended resigning from his job, selling the house in London, and returning to Windyedge.

He was going to be a farmer.

The rows and arguments, the tears and recriminations that followed this announcement are amongst the earliest of my truly unhappy memories. My mother tried everything to make him change his mind, but my father remained adamant. In the end she fired her final gun. If he returned to Northumberland, he would return alone. Rather to her surprise, he did this. Perhaps he thought that she would follow, but she could be just as stubborn. Within the year they were duly divorced. The house in Paulton Square was sold and my mother moved to another, smaller one, near Parson's Green. I, naturally, stayed with her, but I always went to Northumberland for a couple of weeks every year, just to keep in touch with my father. After a bit he married again; a shy, horsy girl whose tweed skirts were always slightly seated and whose clear and freckled face had never known so much as the touch of a powder puff. They were very happy. They are still very happy. And I am glad.

But for my mother it was not so easy. She had married my father because he seemed to conform to a pattern of masculinity that she could understand and admire. She never delved beneath the veneer of the pin-stripe suit and the briefcase. She had no wish to uncover any hidden depths. But the Shackletons were full of surprises, and to my mother's horror, I inherited most of them. My dead uncle had not only been a farmer but an amateur musician of some achievement. My father in his spare time stitched the most beautiful tapestries. But it was their sister Phoebe who was the true rebel. An artist and an accomplished painter, she was a character of such originality, with such careless regard of day-to-day conventions, that my mother had a hard time coming to terms with her sister-in-law.

As a young woman Phoebe had based herself in London, but in her middle years she wiped the dust of the city from her shoes and went to live in Cornwall, where she cohabited happily with a charming man, a sculptor, called Chips Armitage. They never married—I think because his wife would not divorce him—and when he died he left his little Victorian Gothic house in Penmarron to Phoebe, and she had lived there ever since.

Despite this small social hiccup my mother could not completely write Phoebe off, because Phoebe was my godmother. Every now and then my mother and I would be invited to stay with her. The letters always made it perfectly clear that Phoebe would be happy to have me on my own. But my mother feared her bohemian influence, and on the princi-ple that if she couldn't lick the Shackletons, she would join them, she always—at least when I was a child—accompanied me on these visits.

The first time we travelled to Cornwall, I was filled with anxiety. I was only a child, but I knew well that my mother and Phoebe had nothing in common, and I dreaded two weeks of disagreements and prickly si-lences. But I underestimated Phoebe's perception. She took care of the situation by introducing my mother to Mrs. Tolliver. Mrs. Tolliver lived in the White Lodge at Penmarron and had a perfectly conventional little circle of friends, who were charmed to include my pretty mother in their bridge afternoons and small dinner parties.

With them, she would contentedly play cards on the bright days while Phoebe and I walked on the beach, or set up our easels by the old seawall, or drove inland in the battered old Volkswagen that Phoebe used as a mobile studio, to climb the moor and lose ourselves in landscapes that lay drowned in a white and shimmering light that seemed reflected from the very sea itself.

Despite my mother's antagonism, Phoebe exerted enormous influences on my life. Unconscious influences, in the shape of my inherited talent for drawing. And other, more practical influences—pressures, maybe—which bolstered my determination to study in Florence, to go to art school, and which finally culminated in getting me my present job with the Marcus Bernstein Gallery in Cork Street.

And now it was because of Phoebe that we quarrelled. Nigel Gordon had come into my life some months ago. He was the first totally conventional person I had ever even mildly liked, and when I brought him home to meet my mother, she could not hide her delight. He was charming with her, flirting a little and bringing her flowers, and when she learned that he had invited me to Scotland to stay with his family and meet his mother, her excitement knew no bounds. She had already bought me a pair of tweed knickerbockers to wear "on the moor," and beyond this I knew that her imagination was in full flight to the final climax of engagement notices in the *Times,* engraved invitations, and a London wedding with me in a white creation designed to look well from the back.

But at the last moment, Phoebe had put an end to all these pretty fancies. She had, of all things, broken her arm, and the day she returned from hospital to Holly Cottage, her little house, with the arm rigid in a plaster cast, she telephoned to beg me to come and keep her company. It wasn't that she couldn't perfectly well look after herself, but she was not able to drive the car, and to remain immobilized until the cast came off was more than she could bear.

As I listened to her voice over the phone, I was filled with an extraordinary sense of relief, and it was only then that I admitted to myself that I didn't want to go north to stay with the Gordons. I was not ready to become so deeply involved with Nigel. Subconsciously I had been longing for some sound excuse to wriggle out of the arrangement. And here it was, presented to me on a plate. Without even hesitating, I told Phoebe that I would go. Then I told Nigel that I couldn't go to Scotland. And now I was telling my mother.

She was, predictably, devastated.

"Cornwall. With Phoebe." She made it sound like the worst sort of dead end.

"I must go, Ma." I tried to make her smile. "You know she's hopeless at driving that old car of hers, even with two arms."

But she was beyond amusement. "It's so rude, crying off at the last moment. You'll never be invited again. And what will Nigel's mother think?"

"I'll write to her. I'm sure she'll understand."

"And with Phoebe . . . you'll meet nobody with Phoebe except a lot of unwashed students and extraordinary women in hand-woven ponchos."

"Perhaps Mrs. Tolliver will come up with some suitable man for me."

"It's nothing to joke about."

I said, gently, "It is *my* life."

"You've always said that. You said it when you took yourself off to live in that gruesome basement in Islington. Islington, of all places."

"It's very trendy."

"And when you enrolled at that horrible art school . . ."

"At least I've got a perfectly respectable job. You must admit that."

"You ought to be married. And then you wouldn't have to have a job."

"Even if I were married, I wouldn't want to give it up."

"But, Prue, it's not a future. I want you to have a proper life."

"I think it is a proper life."

We eyed each other for a long moment. Then my mother sighed deeply, resigned and apparently mortally wounded. And I knew that for the time being, the argument was over.

She said, sounding pathetic, "I'll never understand you."

I went to give her a hug. "Don't try," I told her. "Just cheer up and go on liking me. I'll send you a postcard from Cornwall."

I had decided not to drive a car to Penmarron but to travel by train. The next morning I took a taxi to Paddington, found the right platform and the right coach. I had reserved a seat, but the train was not full; by the middle of September the flood of holidaymakers had ceased. I had just stowed my luggage and settled myself in a seat when there was a tap on the window, and I looked up and saw a man standing outside, carrying a briefcase in one hand and a bunch of flowers in the other.

It was, astonishingly, Nigel.

I got up and went back to the door and stepped down onto the platform. He was walking towards me, smiling sheepishly.

"Prue. I thought I wouldn't find you."

"What on earth are you doing here?"

"I came to see you off. Wish you bon voyage." He held out the bunch of flowers, which were small and shaggy yellow chrysanthemums. "And to bring you these."

I was, despite myself, very touched. I recognised that his coming here to the station was a generous gesture of forgiveness, and to make it clear that he had understood why I was letting him down. This had the effect of making me feel more of a heel than ever. I took the flowers in their collar of crisp white paper and buried my nose in them. They smelt delicious. I looked up at him and smiled.

"It's ten o'clock. Oughtn't you to be at your desk by now?"

He shook his head. "No hurry."

"I didn't realise you were so high up in the banking world."

Nigel grinned. "I'm not, but I don't exactly have to clock in. Anyway, made a phone call. Said I'd been held up." He had a solid, mature sort of face, with fair hair beginning to thin on top, but when he grinned like that, he looked quite boyish. I began to wonder if I was mad, abandoning this personable man in order to go and nurse my unpredictable aunt Phoebe. Perhaps my mother had been right, after all.

I said, "I'm sorry about letting you down. I wrote to your mother last night."

"Perhaps, another time . . ." said Nigel generously. "Anyway, keep in touch. Let me know when you get back to London."

I knew that he would be waiting for me, if I asked him. Ready to meet my train, to drive me back to Islington, to pick up the threads of our relationship as though I had never been away.

"I'll do that."

"I hope your aunt recovers quickly."

"It's only a broken arm. She's not ill."

There came a short, uncomfortable pause. Then Nigel said, "Well . . ." He moved forward to kiss my cheek. It was more of a peck than a kiss. "Good-bye, and have a good journey."

"Thank you for coming. Thank you for the flowers."

He stepped back, made an indeterminate gesture of farewell, turned and walked away. I watched him go, making his way through the shifting confusion of porters, barrows, families with suitcases. At the barrier he turned back for a final time. We waved. Then he was gone. I got back into the train, stowed the flowers in the luggage rack and sat down once more. I wished that he had not come.

I was very much a Shackleton, but every now and then stray emotions would float to the surface of my mind, which I recognised as stemming straight from my mother. This was just such a time. I must be mad not to want to be with Nigel, to become involved with him, even to spend the rest of my life with him. Normally, I bucked like a horse at the very idea of settling down, but at this moment, sitting in the train, gazing out the window at Paddington Station, it suddenly seemed enormously attractive. Security; that's what this dependable man would give me. I imagined living in his solid London house, going to Scotland for my holidays; only working if I wanted to, and not because I needed the money. I thought about having children . . .

A voice said, "I'm sorry, is this seat taken?"

"What . . . ?" I looked up and saw the man standing there in the aisle between the seats. He carried a small suitcase, and there was a child beside him, a small thin girl about ten years old, dark haired and wearing round, owllike spectacles.

"No, it's not taken."

He said, "Good," and lifted the suitcase up into the rack. He did not look in the mood for any sort of pleasantry, and a certain impatience of manner made me not ask him to watch out for my bunch of chrysanthemums. He was dressed, as Nigel had been, for some City office, in a navy chalk-striped suit. But the suit sat ill upon him, as though he had lately put on a good deal of weight (I imagined enormous expense-account luncheons), and as he reached up with the suitcase, I had a direct view of his expensive, bulging shirt and straining buttons. He was dark, and once, perhaps, had been good-looking, but now his jowls were heavy, his complexion florid, and his greying hair worn long on the back of his collar, possibly to atone for the lack of it on top.

"There you are," he said to the little girl. "Go on, sit down."

She did so, cautiously, perched on the very edge of the seat. She carried a single comic paper and wore a red leather purse slung by a strap across one shoulder. She was a pale child, with hair cut very short, exposing a long and slender neck. This, and her spectacles, and her expression of stoic misery gave her the appearance of a small boy, and I was reminded of other small boys I had observed on station platforms, dwarfed by stiff new uniforms, fighting tears, and being told by beefy fathers how much they were going to enjoy being at boarding school.

"Got your ticket all right?"

She nodded.

"Granny'll meet you at the junction."

She nodded again.

"Well . . ." He ran a hand back over his head. He was obviously longing to be off. "That's it, then. You'll be all right."

Once more she nodded. They looked, unsmiling, at each other. He began to move away and then remembered something else.

"Here . . ." He felt in his breast pocket, produced a crocodile wallet, a ten-pound note. "You'll need something to eat. When it's time, take yourself along to the restaurant car and get some lunch."

She took the ten-pound note and sat looking at it.

"Good-bye, then."

"Good-bye."

He went. At the window he paused to wave and give a cursory smile. Then he disappeared, hurrying in the direction of some sleek, showy car that would restore him to the safe, masculine world of his business.

As I had already told myself that Nigel was nice, I now told myself that this man was horrible and wondered why such an unengaging person had been given the job of seeing the little girl off. She sat beside me, still as a mouse. After a little she reached for her handbag, undid the zipper, put the ten-pound note inside, and shut the zipper again. I thought about saying something friendly to her, but there was a shine of tears in her eyes behind the spectacles, so I decided, for the moment, to leave well alone. A moment later the train started to move, and we were off.

I opened my *Times*, read the headlines and all the gloomy news, and then turned with a pleasant sensation of relief to the Arts page. I found what I was looking for, which was the review of an exhibition that had opened a couple of days before in the Peter Chastal Gallery, which was only a couple of doors away from where I worked for Marcus Bernstein.

The artist was a young man called Daniel Cassens, and I had always been interested in his career because, when he was about twenty, he had spent a year in Cornwall living with Phoebe and studying sculpture with Chips. I had never met him, but Phoebe and Chips had become very fond of him, and when he left them to continue his career in America, Phoebe had followed his progress avidly and enthusiastically as if he had been her own son.

He had travelled and spent some years in America and then had taken himself on to Japan, where he had engrossed himself in the intricate simplicities of Oriental art.

This latest exhibition was a direct outcome of his years in Japan, and the critic was enthusiastic, revelling in the tranquillity and formality of Daniel Cassens's work, praising the controlled brushwork of the watercolours, the subtlety of detail.

". . . This is a unique collection," he finished his piece. "The paintings are complementary, each one a single facet of a total and rare experience. Take an hour or so off from your daily round and visit the Chastal Gallery. You will certainly not be disappointed."

Phoebe would be delighted, and I was glad for her. I closed the paper and looked out the window and saw that we had left the suburbs behind and were now out into the country. It was a damp day, with large grey clouds rolling across the sky, revealing every now and then a patch of limpid blue. Trees were beginning to turn, the first leaves to fall. There were tractors ploughing out in the fields, and cottage gardens, as we rocketed past, were purple with Michaelmas daisies.

I remembered my small companion and turned to see how she was getting on. She had not yet opened her comic or unbuttoned her coat, but the tears had receded and she seemed a little more composed.

"Where are you going to?" I asked her.

She said, "Cornwall."

"I'm going to Cornwall, too. Whereabouts are you going?"

"I'm going to stay with my grandmother."

"That'll be nice." I thought about this. "But isn't it term time? Shouldn't you be at school?"

"Yes, I should. I'm at a boarding school. We all went back, and then the boiler blew up, so they closed the school for a week till it's mended and sent us all home again."

"How terrible. I hope nobody was hurt."

"No. But Miss Brownrigg, our headmistress, had to go to bed for a day. Matron said it was shock."

"I'm not surprised."

"So I went home, but there's nobody there but my father. My mother's on holiday in Majorca. She went at the end of the holidays. So I've got to go to Granny."

She didn't make it sound a very attractive prospect. I was trying to think of something comforting to say to jolly her along when she picked up her comic and settled down, rather pointedly, to read it. I was amused but took the hint, found my book, and began to read. The journey progressed in silence until the waiter from the restaurant car made his way down the train to tell us that luncheon was being served.

I laid down my book. "Are you going to go and have some lunch?" I asked her, knowing about the ten-pound note in her bag.

She looked agonised. "I . . . I don't know which way to go."

"I'm going. Would you like to come with me? We could have lunch together."

Her expression changed to one of grateful relief. "Oh, could I? I've got the money, but I've never been on a train by myself before, and I don't know what I'm meant to do."

"I know, it's muddling, isn't it? Come along, let's go before all the tables get booked up."

Together we made our way down the lurching corridors, found the restaurant car, and were shown to a table for two. There was a fresh white cloth, and flowers in a glass carafe.

She said, "I'm a bit hot. Do you think I could take off my coat?"

"I think that would be a good idea."

She did this, and the waiter came to help her, and fold the coat, and lay it over the back of her seat. We opened the menus.

"Are you feeling hungry?" I asked her.

"Yes I am. We had breakfast *ages* ago."

"Where do you live?"

"In Sunningdale. I came up to London with my father in his car. He drives up every morning."

"Your . . . ? Was that your father who saw you off?"

"Yes." He hadn't even kissed her good-bye. "He works in an office in the City." Our eyes met, and then she looked hastily away. "He doesn't like being late."

I said, soothingly, "Few men do. Is it his mother you're going to stay with?"

"No. Granny's my mother's mother."

I said, sounding chatty, "I'm going to stay with an aunt. She's broken her arm, and she can't drive her car, so I'm going to look after her. She lives at the very end of Cornwall in a village called Penmarron."

"Penmarron? But I'm going to Penmarron too."

This was a coincidence. "How extraordinary."

"I'm Charlotte Collis. I'm Mrs. Tolliver's granddaughter. She's my granny. Do you know Mrs. Tolliver?"

"Yes, I do. Not very well, but I do know her. My mother used to play bridge with her. And my aunt is called Phoebe Shackleton."

And now her face lit up. For the first time since I had set eyes on her, she looked a natural and excited child. Her eyes were wide behind the spectacles, and her mouth opened in a delighted gasp of surprise, revealing teeth too big for her narrow face.

"*Phoebe!* Phoebe's my best friend. I go and have tea with her and things, every time I go and stay with Granny. I didn't know she'd broken her arm." She gazed into my face. "You . . . you're not Prue, are you?"

I smiled. "Yes, I am. How did you know?"

"I *thought* I knew your face. I've seen your photograph in Phoebe's sitting room. I always thought you looked *lovely.*"

"Thank you."

"And Phoebe used to tell me about you when I went to see her. It's lovely going to tea with her, because it's not like being with a grown-up person and I'm allowed to go on my own. And we always play with the carousel that used to be a gramophone."

"That was mine. Chips made it for me."

"I never knew Chips. He was dead before I can remember."

"And I," I told her, "never knew your mother."

"But we go and stay with Granny most summers."

"And I am usually there at Easter, or sometimes for Christmas, so our paths have never crossed. I don't think I even know her name."

"It's Annabelle. She was Annabelle Tolliver. But she's called Mrs. Collis now."

"And do you have brothers and sisters?"

"One brother. Michael. He's fifteen. He's at Wellington."

"And the boiler at Wellington hasn't blown up?"

It was an attempt to add a little levity to the conversation, but Charlotte did not smile. She said, "No."

I studied the menu and thought about Mrs. Tolliver. My memories of her were of a tall, elegant, and rather chilling lady, always immaculately turned out, her grey hair neatly groomed, her skirts pleated and pressed, her long, narrow shoes polished like chestnuts. I thought of White Lodge, where Charlotte was going to stay, and wondered what a child would find to do in those neatly manicured gardens, that quiet and orderly house.

I looked across the table at the child and saw that she, too, with furrowed brow, was trying to decide what she would have for lunch. She seemed a sad little person. It couldn't have been much fun, being sent home from school simply because the boiler there had blown up. Unexpected and probably unwanted, with your mother abroad and no person to take care of you. It couldn't have been much fun, being put by yourself on a train and shunted off to the end of the country to visit your grandmother. I wished, all at once, for Mrs. Tolliver to be dumpy and cozy, with a round, warm bosom and a passion for knitting dolls' clothes and playing Clock Patience.

Charlotte looked up and saw me watching her. She sighed hopelessly. "I don't know what I want."

I said, "A moment ago you told me you were feeling very hungry. Why don't you have everything?"

"All right." She decided on vegetable soup, roast beef, and ice cream. "And do you think," she added wistfully, "there might be enough money over for a Coca-Cola?"

What is there so magical about travelling by train to Cornwall? I know I am not the first person to have known the enchantment as the line crosses the Tamar by the old Brunel railway bridge, as though one were entering the gates of some marvellous foreign country. Each time I go I tell myself that it cannot be the same, but it always is. And it is impossible to pinpoint the exact reasons for this euphoria. The shapes of the houses, perhaps, pinkwashed in the evening sun. The smallness of the fields; the lofty viaducts soaring over deep, wooded valleys; the first distant glimpses of the sea? Or perhaps the saintly names of small stations that we rocket through and leave behind, or the voices of the porters on the platform at Truro?

We reached St. Abbatt's Junction at a quarter to five. As the train drew alongside the platform, Charlotte and I were ready by the door, with our suitcases and my bunch of chrysanthemums, by now distinctly worse for wear. When we stepped down from the train, we were assailed by a blustering west wind, and I could smell the sea, salty and strong. There were palm trees on the platform, rattling their leaves like old, broken umbrellas, and a porter opened the door of the guards' van and manhandled out of it a crate of indignant hens.

I knew that Mr. Thomas was going to come and meet me. Mr. Thomas owned the only taxi in Penmarron, and Phoebe had told me over the telephone that she had engaged his services. As we walked up towards the bridge, I saw Mr. Thomas waiting, bundled up in an overcoat as though it were winter and wearing on his head the hat that he had bought at a jumble sale and that had once belonged to some noble chauffeur. When he was not driving a taxi, he was a pig farmer, and for this occupation he had another hat, felt, and of great antiquity. Phoebe, who had a Rabelaisian wit, once wondered what sort of hat he wore when he was getting into bed with Mrs. Thomas, but my mother had pursed her lips and lowered her eyes and refused to be amused, so Phoebe had not wondered it again.

There was no sign of Mrs. Tolliver. I could feel Charlotte's anxiety.

"Perhaps your grandmother's waiting on the other side of the bridge."

The train, which never stopped long anywhere, drew out. We scanned the opposite platform, but the only person who waited was a fat lady with a shopping bag. Not Mrs. Tolliver.

"Maybe she's sitting in the car in the station yard. It's a cold evening to be standing about."

"I hope she hasn't forgotten," said Charlotte.

But Mr. Thomas was to reassure us. "Hello, my dear," he said to me, coming to meet us and to relieve me of my case. "How are you? Nice to see you again. Have a good journey, did you?" He looked down at Charlotte. "You're Mrs. Tolliver's little girl, aren't you. That's right. My orders are to pick up the pair of you. Take the little girl to White Lodge, and then you on to Miss Shackleton's. Travel together, did you?"

"Yes, we did; we met on the train."

"Your aunt would have come, but she can't drive her car with that dratted arm of hers. Come on now," he turned to Charlotte, "give me your case, too, easier to carry two than one . . ."

And thus burdened, he trudged up the wooden steps and over the bridge, and Charlotte and I followed him. Settled in his taxi, which had molting leather seats and always smelt faintly of pig, I said, "I hope Mrs. Tolliver hasn't broken her arm, too."

"Oh, no, she's lovely." In Cornwall, lovely means well. "Nothing wrong with her. But didn't seem much point two cars coming . . ." And with that he started up his engine, and the taxi, after backfiring twice, ground into gear and shot forward up the hill that led to the main road.

I sat back and felt annoyed. Perhaps it was the most sensible thing to do, arranging for Charlotte and me to share the taxi, but it would have been more welcoming if Mrs. Tolliver had come to the station to meet Charlotte herself. It was, after all, a drive of only two miles. Charlotte was looking away from me, out the window, and I suspected that once more she was fighting tears. I didn't blame her.

"That was a good idea, wasn't it, for us to share the taxi?" I tried to sound enthusiastic, as though I approved.

She did not turn round. She said, "I suppose so."

However, we had arrived. We were here. Along the main road on that windy afternoon, and down the hill beneath the oak trees. Past the gates of what used to be the Squire's house, and then into the village. Nothing ever seemed to change. Up the hill again, past the cottages and the shops, an old man walking his dog, the petrol station, the pub. We turned down the road that led to the church and the sea, the copse of ancient oaks, the farm with its slated steadings, and so to the open white gates of White Lodge.

Mr. Thomas changed down with a hideous clash of gears and turned into these gates. We came up the short drive, between overhanging trees, and I saw the swept verges and the fading banks of hydrangea. We rounded a clump of these and drew up on the gravel sweep in front of the house. It was a stone house, whitewashed and solid. A wisteria clambered up the wall to the upstairs windows, and a flight of stone steps rose to the closed front door. We all got out of the taxi, and Mr. Thomas went up the steps to ring the bell. The wind suddenly blew up a gust and swept a scatter of dead leaves into a whirlpool at our feet. After a short wait, the door was opened and Mrs. Tolliver appeared. She looked just the same as I had remembered her and came down the steps towards us with her smoothly coiffed grey hair and her slender, elegant figure. Her face was neatly arranged in a smile of welcome.

"Charlotte. Well, here you are." She stooped to kiss the child briskly. She straightened up. I am tall, but she was taller. "Prue. How very nice to see you. I hope you didn't mind sharing the taxi."

"We didn't mind in the least. We met on the train in London, so we've travelled all the way together."

"How very nice. Now, Charlotte, is this your suitcase? In you come. There's just time to wash your hands, and then we'll have tea. Mrs. Curnow's made a sponge cake. I expect you like sponge cake."

Charlotte said, "Yes." It did not sound convincing. She probably hated sponge cake. She would much have preferred fish fingers and chips.

". . . And Prue, I hope you find Phoebe well. Perhaps you'll come for lunch one day. How is your mother?"

"She's well."

"I'll get all the news some other time. Come along now, Charlotte."

"Good-bye," Charlotte said to me.

"Good-bye, Charlotte. Come and see us."

"Yes, I will."

I waited by the taxi until they had gone up the steps and through the door. Mrs. Tolliver carried the suitcase, and Charlotte, still clutching her comic, trod cautiously at her heels. She did not turn to wave. The door closed behind them.

2

*I*T SEEMED ALL WRONG that Charlotte should have been given a reception of such little warmth, while I, twenty-three years old and perfectly able to stand on my own two feet, had Holly Cottage waiting for me, and Phoebe. At Holly Cottage there was no driveway; just a patch of gravel between the gate and the house. At Holly Cottage the garden was a mass of dahlias and chrysanthemums, the front door stood open to the evening breeze, and from an upstairs window a pink cotton curtain blew in the wind, like a person waving a cheerful greeting. No sooner was the taxi turning in at her gate than Phoebe herself appeared. Her left arm was strapped up in a bulky white plaster cast, but her right arm signalled its own exuberant welcome, and she came running forward so unexpectedly that Mr. Thomas very nearly ran her over.

Before the car had stopped, I was out of it and into Phoebe's one-armed embrace. The one I gave back to her did double duty for both of us.

"Oh, my darling," she crowed, "what an angel. Never thought you'd be able to come. Couldn't believe it. I'm going nearly insane trying to get myself about. Can't even ride a bicycle . . ."

Laughing, I let her go, and we stood back and looked at each other with the greatest of satisfaction. Looking at Phoebe is always a pleasure. Unpredictable, but always a pleasure. She was at that time well into her sixties, but it has always been impossible to equate Phoebe to the passing years.

I saw the thick stockings, the stout boots, the worn and faded blue-jean skirt. Over these she wore a man's shirt and cardigan (probably inherited from Chips); there were gold chains about her neck, and a tartan scarf, and on her head, inevitably, a hat.

She always wore hats, broad-brimmed, deep-crowned, rather dashing. She had taken to wearing them to protect her eyes, while painting out of doors, from the cold, white glare of the Cornish light, and they had become so much part of her that she very often forgot to take them off. This one was a rich brown, decorated with grey gull feathers stuck into the ribbon band. Beneath its kindly shade, Phoebe's face, the skin netted with lines, twinkled and smiled at me. The smile revealed teeth that were even and white as a child's, and her eyes were the deepest speedwell blue, their brightness challenged only by the turquoise-and-silver earrings that dangled on either side of her face.

I said, "You're a fraud. You may have broken your arm, but you're as beautiful as ever."

"What rubbish! Do you hear that, Mr. Thomas, she says I'm beautiful. She must be either mad or blind. Now, what's this? Your suitcase. And what are the dead flowers for? I don't want any dead flowers . . ." Holding the poor things, she began to laugh again. "Now, Mr. Thomas, you'll have to send me a bill. I can't pay you just now—I've mislaid my handbag."

"I'll pay, Phoebe."

"Of course you won't. Mr. Thomas doesn't mind, do you, Mr. Thomas?"

Mr. Thomas assured her that he didn't. He got back into his taxi, but Phoebe pursued him in order to put her head through the window and ask after Mrs. Thomas's bad leg. Mr. Thomas began to tell her, at some length. Halfway through his dissertation, Phoebe decided she'd had enough. "So glad she's better," she said firmly, and withdrew her head from the window. Mr. Thomas, halted in full spate, was not in the least disconcerted. It was just Miss Shackleton, and heaven only knew, she had some funny ways. The old taxi was set into motion once more and the next moment had sped away, scattering gravel through the gate and up the road.

"Now." Phoebe took my arm. "Let's get indoors. I want to hear all the news."

Together we went through the open door and into the house. I stood in the hall, looked about, and loved everything for being the same. I saw the polished floors scattered with rugs; the uncarpeted wooden staircase that led to the upper floor; the whitewashed walls hung, haphazard, with Phoebe's tiny, jewel-bright oil paintings.

The house smelt of turpentine and wood smoke and linseed oil and garlic and roses, but its greatest charm was the effect of airy lightness engendered by pale colours, lacy curtains, straw rugs, and polished wood. Even in the middle of winter, it always felt summery.

I took a deep breath, savouring it all. "Heaven," I said. "Heaven to be back."

"You're in the same old room," said Phoebe and then left me, heading for the kitchen. I knew she would spend some time trying to resuscitate Nigel's poor flowers, even though she had more than enough of her own. I picked up my case and went upstairs to the room that had been mine since I was a very small girl. I opened the door and was assailed by a gust of cold air pouring in from the wide open window. I shut the door, and everything stopped billowing. Putting down my case, I went to the window and leaned out to gaze at the familiar view.

The tide was out, and the evening smelt of seaweed. You were never far from the sea smells at Holly Cottage, because the house had been built on a grassy bluff overlooking a tidal estuary, which penetrated inland like a huge lake and was filled and emptied each day by the tides.

Below the house was a wide seawall, where once a single-line railway siding had led to a busy shipyard. The shipyard was closed now and the railway sleepers removed, but the wall still stood, solid as a cliff. At high tide the water reached nearly to the rim of this wall, and in summer it made a good place to swim, but at low tide there was nothing but acres of empty sand, with a few weedy rocks and shallow pools scattered here and there and a dozen or so derelict fishing boats that had been pulled up on the shingle winters ago and for some reason never floated again.

On this, the south side of the house, the garden was unexpectedly large. An irregularly shaped lawn, edged here and there with random flower beds, sloped down to a boundary hedge of escallonia. In the middle of this was a gate, and over the gate the clipped escallonia had been trimmed into an arch, which gave the garden a charmingly formal and old-fashioned aspect. To the right, beyond a high brick wall, where Chips Armitage used to grow peach trees, was a sizeable vegetable garden, and at the bottom of this, scarcely visible from the house, he had built his studio. All I could see was the pitch of the slate roof and, sitting on it, a single herring gull. As I watched, it spread its wings, screaming defiance at nothing in particular, and then took flight, soaring and gliding away, out over the wet, empty sands.

I smiled, closed the window against the cold, and went down to Phoebe.

We sat facing each other across the hearth rug, with a blazing log fire to warm us, and the light outside gradually dying into evening. There was a big brown teapot on the trolley, hand-painted earthenware cups and saucers, a plate of fresh scones, yellow farm butter, and homemade cherry jam.

"You didn't make these scones, Phoebe. You couldn't, with only one hand."

"No, Lily Tonkins made them this morning. Darling woman, she comes in every day, and she's simply taken over the kitchen. I never realised what a marvellous cook she is."

"But how did you break your arm?"

"Oh, my dear, too stupid. I was down in the studio looking for some old folios of Chips's . . . I knew they were on the top shelf of his bookcase, and I stood on a chair, and of course some worm, unknown to me, had burrowed into the wood, and the leg gave way, and down I came!" She roared with laughter as though it were the best joke in the world. She was still wearing her feathered hat. "Very lucky not to break my leg. I came back to the house, and by great good fortune there was the postman, delivering the afternoon mail. So I hopped in beside him and he drove me to the cottage hospital and they tied me up in this tiresome cast."

"You poor thing."

"Oh, never mind, it doesn't hurt much; it's just a nuisance, and maddening not being able to drive. I've got to go back to the hospital tomorrow to let the doctor see it . . . I suppose he thinks I'm going to get gangrene or something . . ."

"I'll drive you . . ."

"You won't have to, because they're sending an ambulance. I've never been in an ambulance before. I'm rather looking forward to it. Now, how's Delia?"

Delia was my mother. I said she was well.

"And what sort of a train journey did you have?" Before I could tell her, she remembered the arrangement she had made with Mrs. Tolliver. "Heavens, I forgot to ask about Charlotte Collis. Did Mr. Thomas remember to collect her at the station as well?"

"Yes."

"How fortunate. I hope you didn't mind sharing the ride with her. Personally, I thought Mrs. Tolliver might have gone to fetch the poor child herself, but she seemed to think it was pointless if Mr. Thomas was going anyway."

"I thought she might have come to meet her, too."

"How is she, poor little mite?"

"She seemed a bit anxious. Not at all excited at the thought of staying with her grandmother. The only person she showed any enthusiasm for was you. She adores you."

"It's funny, isn't it. You'd think she'd rather be with children of her own age. Except that there aren't many children in this village, and even if there were, she's always been something of a loner. The first time we met, I found her wandering on the beach by herself. She said she was out for a walk, so I asked her back for tea and rang Mrs. Tolliver to say she was with me. After that she came quite often. She's fascinated by my pictures and paints and sketchbooks. I gave her a sketch pad and some felt pens for herself, and she has a remarkable talent and a marvellous imagination. Then she loves being told stories; hearing about Chips and all the stupid things he and I used to do together. Extraordinary, really, in such a young child."

I said, "You know, I don't think I ever knew that Mrs. Tolliver had a grandchild. I don't think I ever realised that she had a daughter. Or a husband, for that matter. What happened to Mr. Tolliver?"

"He died, some years ago. When Chips and I first came here, he was still alive, and they lived in great style. You know the sort of thing—a Bentley in the garage and two gardeners and a cook and a housemaid.

Annabelle was impossibly spoiled and indulged—a real only child. But then Mr. Tolliver had a heart attack—keeled over on the seventh green of the golf course—and never recovered. After that nothing was quite the same again. Of course, Mrs. Tolliver never said anything—she's the most reserved woman I know—but the big car was sold and a general cutting back rather obviously took place. Annabelle had been sent to some ridiculously expensive school in Switzerland, and she had to leave and come home and attend the local Comprehensive. She simply hated it. I think she felt that life had deliberately humiliated her. Silly girl."

"What was she like?"

"Very beautiful, but without the vestige of a brain. After she was married and had her little boy, she used to come down for the summers and stay with her mother, and every time there were three or four love-lorn fellows dancing attendance. At a party you couldn't see her for men. Just like bees round a honey pot."

"She's in Majorca just now. Charlotte told me that much."

"I know. I've heard all about that. I think Mrs. Tolliver rather felt that she should come back and look after Charlotte herself. She was annoyed about the school boiler blowing up. She felt it was inefficient. I was horrified. It might have killed all the children. But Mrs. Tolliver was far more concerned at the prospect of having Charlotte to stay."

"But doesn't she like Charlotte?"

"Oh, I think she quite likes her," Phoebe told me in her airy way. "But she's never been interested in children, and I think she finds Charlotte very dull. And, as well, she's never had the child on her own before. I think she's wondering what on earth she's going to do with her."

Outside, the wind was getting up, rattling the window sashes and whistling around the corners of the house. It was nearly dark, but the room in which we sat was warm with dancing firelight. I reached for the kettle that simmered on a brass hob near the flames and refilled the teapot.

"What about Annabelle's husband?"

"Leslie Collis? I could never stand him, gruesome man."

"I thought he was gruesome, too. He didn't even kiss Charlotte good-bye. How did Annabelle meet him?"

"He was staying at the Castle Hotel in Porthkerris with three other stockbrokers, or whatever it is he does in the City. I don't know how they met, but the moment he set eyes on her, that was it."

"He couldn't have been attractive."

"In a funny way, he was. He had a certain sort of dark, flashy charm. Spent money like water, drove around in a Ferrari."

"Do you think Annabelle was in love with him?"

"Not for a moment. Annabelle was in love only with herself. But he could give her everything that she'd ever wanted, and she didn't like being poor. And of course Mrs. Tolliver encouraged it madly. I don't think she ever forgave her poor husband for leaving her in straitened circumstances, and she was determined that Annabelle should marry well."

I thought about this. Then I poured myself another cup of tea and lay back against the cushions of the deep and friendly old chair. I said, "I suppose all mothers are the same."

"Don't tell me Delia's been at you again."

"Oh, no, she's not been at me. But there's this man . . . he brought me those chrysanthemums . . ." And I told her about Nigel Gordon and the invitation to Scotland.

Phoebe listened sympathetically, and when I had finished, she said, "I think he sounds very nice."

"He is. That's the trouble. He's terribly nice. But my mother's already got wedding bells banging to and fro and keeps reminding me that I'm twenty-three and ought to be settling down. Perhaps if she didn't go on about it so, I might marry him."

"You mustn't marry him unless you can't imagine life without him."

"That's just it. I can. Quite easily."

"We all need different things from life. Your mother needs security. That's why she married your father, and a fat lot of good it did her, because she never took the time to get to know him before she made that spectacular entrance up the aisle. But you're a special person. You need more than a man to bring you flowers and pay the bills. You're intelligent and you're talented. And when you do settle down with a man, it is absolutely vital that he makes you laugh. Chips and I laughed all the time, even when we were poor and unsuccessful and didn't know how we were going to pay the grocer's bill. We were always laughing."

I smiled, remembering them together. I said, "Talking of Chips, did you know that Daniel Cassens has an exhibition on at the Chastal Gallery? I read a rave review in the *Times* this morning."

"I read it too. So exciting. Dear, clever boy. I intended going up to London for the opening day, but then I went and broke this stupid arm and the doctor said I wasn't to travel."

"Is he in London? Daniel, I mean."

"Heaven knows where he is. Probably still in Japan. Or Mexico, or somewhere mad. But I'd love to see that exhibition. Perhaps, if I'm able, I'll come back to London with you and we'll go together. What fun that would be! Something to look forward to."

That night I had a dream. I was on some island—a tropical island, palm-fringed and white-sanded. It was very hot. I was on a beach, walking down towards the silent, glass-clear sea. I meant to swim, but the water, when I reached it, was only inches deep, scarcely covering my ankles. I walked for a long time, and then, all at once, the sand fell steeply away, and I was out of my depth, swimming, and the water was dark as ink and the current like a rushing river. I felt myself borne along on its flow, towards the horizon. I knew that I should turn back, swim for the beach, but the current was too strong, and there was no resisting it. So I stopped fighting and let myself be carried along, knowing that I could never return, but so marvellous was the sensation of going with the tide that I did not care.

I woke with the dream still sharp and clear in my mind. I could remember every detail of it. I lay in bed, thinking about the clear water and the sensation of peace as I was borne along in the wash of that warm and tranquil sea. All dreams have meaning, and I wondered how some professional would analyse this one. It occurred to me, in an unworried sort of way, that it might be about dying.

3

THE EARLY MORNING turned into a beautiful day. Breezy and bright, the blue sky was patched with large, sailing white clouds blown in from the Atlantic. The sun blinked in and out of these clouds, and during the morning the flood tide slowly filled the estuary, creeping up the sands, filling the tide pools, and finally, by about eleven o'clock, reaching the seawall below the house.

Phoebe had gone to keep her appointment at the Cottage Hospital, borne there in some style by the local ambulance. For the trip she had donned yet another hat, black velours, bound by a tussore scarf, and she had waved enthusiastically through the open window as though she were setting off on a jaunt. She would be back for lunch. I had offered to prepare this, but Lily Tonkins, already busy with the vacuum cleaner, said that she already had a bit of lamb in the oven, so I found a sketch pad and a stick of charcoal, stole an apple from the fruit bowl, and took myself out of doors.

And now, at eleven o'clock, I sat on the grassy slope above the seawall, with the sun a dazzle on the wind-ruffled waters of the estuary and the morning freshness filled with the scream of gulls. I had done a rough sketch of the derelict fishing boats with their ramshackle chains and anchors, their empty masts piercing the sky. As I filled in some detail of a weather-scarred hatchway, I heard the morning train from Porthkerris come through the cutting behind Holly Cottage and draw up at the little halt by the edge of the shore. It was a very small and infrequent train, and a moment or two later it gave a hoot and moved on again, around the curve of the line and out of sight.

So engrossed was I in maddening perspectives that I was scarcely aware of this happening, but when I next looked up to study the keel of an upended dinghy, a movement caught the corner of my eye. I looked and saw a solitary figure walking towards me. He approached from the direction of the station, and I presumed that he had alighted from the train, crossed the line, and so followed the track of the disused siding. There was nothing unusual about this. People often took the train from Porthkerris to Penmarron and then walked back to Porthkerris, following the footpath that led for three miles or more along the edge of the cliff.

I lost interest in my drawing. I laid down the sketch pad, picked up my apple, and began to eat it. I watched the stranger's progress. He was a tall man, long-legged, with an easy, loping stride. His clothes at first were simply a blur of blue and white, but as he came closer I saw that he wore denim jeans and a faded shirt, and over this a white knitted jacket, the sort that people bring home from holidays in Ireland. The jacket was unbuttoned, flying open in the wind, and a red and white handkerchief, like a gipsy's, was knotted around his throat. His head was bare, his hair very dark, and though he did not appear to be in any sort of hurry, he was covering the ground at considerable pace.

He looked, I decided, a man who knew where he was going.

Now he had come to the far end of the seawall. Here he paused and looked out over the dazzling water, shielding his eyes from the glare. A moment later he moved on once more, and it was then that he spied me, sitting there in the long grass, eating my apple, watching him.

I thought that he would probably walk past me, perhaps with a casual "good morning," but as he drew level with me, he stopped and stood there, with his back to the water, his hands in the pockets of that voluminous jacket, his head tilted back. A gust of wind ruffled his dark hair. He said, "Hello."

His voice was boyish, his demeanour youthful, but his thin, brown face was not a boy's face, and there were strong lines etched around his mouth and his deeply set eyes.

"Hello."

"What a lovely morning."

"Isn't it?" I finished my apple and tossed the core away. A gull instantly pounced on it and bore it off to consume in private.

"I just got off the train."

"I thought you must have. Are you going to walk back to Porthkerris?"

"No, as a matter of fact, I'm not." And with that he began to climb the grassy slope, picking his way between the bramble patches and the clumps of bracken. When he reached my side, he collapsed, a sprawl of long boney limbs. I saw his old canvas shoes had holes in the toes, and the warmth of the sun made his jacket smell sheepy, as though it had been knitted straight off some oily fleece.

I said, "You can walk by the cliffs if you want to."

"Ah, but then you see, I don't want to." He spied my sketch pad and before I could stop him had picked it up. "That's very nice."

I hate people looking at my work, especially when it's not even finished. "It's just a scribble."

"Not at all." He surveyed it for a moment longer and then laid it down without further comment. He said, "There is a deadly fascination about watching a flood tide. Is that what you've been doing?"

"For the past hour."

He felt in his capacious pocket and brought out a thin packet of cigars, a book of matches, and a dog-eared paperback, obviously much read and consulted. Interest stirred when I saw that it was *Vanishing Cornwall* by Daphne du Maurier. The book of matches had "The Castle Hotel Porthkerris" printed upon it. I felt like a detective and as though, already, I knew quite a lot about him.

He selected a cigar and lit it. His hands were beautiful; long and narrow, with spade-tipped fingers. On one wrist he wore a cheap and unremarkable watch, on the other a chain of gold links, very old-looking and heavy.

As he put the matches and the cigars back into his pocket, I said, "Are you staying at the Castle?"

He looked up in surprise and then smiled. "How did you guess that?"

"Deduction. Matches. Sharp eyes."

"Of course. How stupid of me. Well, I spent last night there, if you can call that staying. I came down from London yesterday."

"So did I. I came by train."

"I wish I had. I got a lift. I hate driving. Hate cars. I'd much rather sit and look out of the window or read a book. Infinitely more civilized." He settled himself into a more comfortable position, leaning on an elbow. "Are you on holiday, or staying here, or is this where you live?"

"Just staying."

"In the village?"

"Yes. Right here, actually."

"What do you mean by right here?"

"In the house up there."

"Holly Cottage." He began to laugh. "Are you staying with Phoebe?"

"Do you know Phoebe?"

"Of course I know Phoebe. That's why I'm here. To see her."

"Well you won't find her just now, because she's gone to the Cottage Hospital in an ambulance." He looked horrified. "It's all right, she hasn't had a stroke or anything, just broken her arm. It's been put in a cast, and the doctor wants to have a look at it."

"Well, that's a relief. Is she all right?"

"Of course. She'll be back for lunch."

"And who are you? A nurse, or one of her perpetual students?"

"No, I'm a perpetual niece."

"You wouldn't by any chance be Prue?"

"Yes, I would." I frowned. "But who are you?"

"Daniel Cassens."

I said, ridiculously, "But you're in Mexico."

"Mexico? Never been to Mexico in my life."

"Phoebe said you were probably in Mexico or somewhere mad."

"That was charitable of her. In fact, I've been in the Virgin Islands, on a boat with some American friends, but then somebody said there was going to be a hurricane, so I decided the time was ripe to get out. But back in New York, I was instantly bombarded with cables from Peter Chastal to say I had to be in London for the opening day of this exhibition he's mounted for me."

"I know about that. You see, I work for Marcus Bernstein. We're practically next door to Peter Chastal. And I read the reviews of your exhibition. I think you've got a success on your hands. Phoebe read it, too. She was enormously thrilled."

"She would be."

"Were you at the opening?"

"Yes, I was. I finally made it. At the last moment I gave in and caught a flight over."

"Why were you so reluctant? Most people wouldn't miss it for anything. All the champagne and the adulation."

"I hate my own exhibitions. It's the most ghastly form of exposure, like putting one's children on display. All those eyes, staring. Makes me feel quite ill."

I understood. "But you did go?"

"Yes, for a little. But I wore a disguise—dark glasses and a concealing hat. I looked like an insane sort of spy. I only stayed for half an hour, and then when Peter wasn't looking, I slunk away and went and sat in a pub and tried to decide what to do next. And then I got talking to this man, and I bought him a beer, and he said that he was driving to Cornwall, so I hitched a lift with him and arrived last night."

"Why didn't you come and stay with Phoebe?"

Without thinking I asked the question and immediately wished that I hadn't. He looked away from me, pulled at a tuft of grass with his hand, and let the wind blow it from his fingers.

"I don't know," he said at last. "So many reasons. Some high-minded, some not so."

"You know she would have welcomed you."

"Yes, I know. But it's been a long time. It's eleven years since I was here. And Chips was alive then."

"You worked with him, didn't you."

"Yes, for a year. I was in America when he died. Up in the Sonoma Valley in northern California. I was staying with some people I knew who had a vineyard. Phoebe's letter took a long time to find me, and I remember thinking then that if nobody ever told you that people you love have died, then they would live forever. And I thought then that I could never come back to Cornwall. But dying is part of life. I've learned that since. But I hadn't learned it then."

I thought of the carousel that Chips had made for me out of an old gramophone; he and Phoebe laughing together; the smell of his pipe.

"I loved him, too."

"Everybody did. He was such a benevolent man. I studied sculpture with him, but I learned from Chips a lot about living that, when you're twenty, is infinitely more important. I never knew my own father, and it always made me feel different towards other people. Chips filled that gap. He gave me a great sense of identity." I knew what he meant, because that was just the way I felt about Phoebe. "Coming down from London yesterday, I kept having second thoughts; wondering if I was doing the right thing. It isn't always wise to return to the place where you've been young and dreamed dreams. And had ambitions."

"Not if your dreams and ambitions came true. And surely that's happened for you. The Chastal exhibition must have proved that. There can't be a painting left unsold . . ."

"Perhaps I need to be unsure of myself."

"You can't have it all."

We fell silent. It was noon now, and the sun was very warm. I heard the soft buffet of the breeze, the lap of water against the seawall. Across the flooded estuary, from the distant causeway, came the hum of passing cars. A flock of gulls fought over a piece of rotting fish.

He said, "You know, once, centuries before Christ, in the Bronze Age, this estuary was a river. Traders sailed all the way from the eastern Mediterranean, around the Lizard and Lands End, laden to the gunwales with all the treasures of the Levant."

I smiled. I said, "I've read *Vanishing Cornwall*, too."

"It's magic." He opened the book and it fell open at a much-studied page, and he read aloud:

For the watcher to-day, crouching amidst the sand dunes and the tufted grass, looking seaward to where the shallows run, imagination can take a riotous course, picturing line upon line of high-prowed, flat-bottomed craft, brightly coloured, their sails abeam, entering the river with the flood tide.

He closed the book. "I wish I had that sort of perception, but I haven't. I can only see the here and the now, and try to paint it the way it happens to me."

"Do you take that book everywhere with you?"

"No. But I found it in a shop in New York, and when I first read it I knew that someday, sometime, I had to come back to Cornwall. It never leaves you. It's like a magnet. You have to return."

"But why to the Castle Hotel, of all places?"

Daniel looked up at me, amused. "Why? Don't you think I fit in there?"

I thought of the rich Americans, the golfers, the twin-setted ladies playing bridge, the genteel teatime orchestra.

"Not exactly."

He laughed. "I know. It was a fairly incongruous choice, but it was the only hotel I could remember and I was tired. Jet-lag tired, London tired, everything tired. I wanted to get into an enormous bed and sleep for a week. And then when I woke up this morning, I wasn't tired any longer. And I thought about Chips and knew that all I wanted to do was come and see Phoebe again. So I walked down to the station and caught the train. And then got off the train and met you."

"And now," I told him, "you're coming back to the house with me, and you're going to stay for lunch. There's a bottle of wine in the fridge and Lily Tonkins has got a bit of lamb in the oven."

"Lily Tonkins? Is she still going?"

"She runs the house. She's doing all the cooking as well just now."

"I'd forgotten Lily." He picked up my sketch pad once more, and this time I didn't mind. He said, "You know, you're not only exceptionally pretty, but you are talented as well."

I decided to ignore the bit about being pretty. "I'm not talented. That's why I work for Marcus Bernstein. I found out the hard way that there was no hope of me earning a living by being an artist."

"How wise of you to realise," said Daniel Cassens. "So few people do."

Together, with the sun on our backs, we climbed the slope of the hill. I opened the wooden gate in the escallonia hedge, and he went ahead of me, cautiously, as a dog will go, nosing his way into once-familiar territory. I shut the gate. He stood looking up at the face of the house, and I looked, too, and tried to see it with his eyes, after eleven years away. To me, it looked as I had always known it. I saw the pointed Gothic windows, the garden door open to the brick terrace and the morning's warmth. There were still geraniums blooming in their earthenware tubs, and Phoebe's ramshackle garden chairs had not yet been put away for the winter.

We walked up the gentle slope of the lawn, and I led the way indoors.

"Phoebe?" I opened the kitchen door, from whence came delicious smells of cooking lamb. Lily Tonkins was at the kitchen table, chopping mint, but she stopped when I appeared.

"She got home about five minutes ago. Went upstairs to change her shoes."

"I've brought a visitor for lunch. Is that all right?"

"Always plenty to eat. Friend of yours, is it?"

Daniel, behind me, moved into view. "It's me, Lily, Daniel Cassens."

Lily's mouth fell open. "Aw, my dear life." She laid down the chopping knife and put a hand to her meager chest, conveying heart-stopping shock. "The sight of you! Like a body out of the past. Daniel Cassens. It must be nearly twelve years. What are you doing here?"

"Come to see you," he told her. He walked around the table and stooped to kiss her cheek. Lily gave a crow of laughter and went pink. "You villain. Turning up like a bad penny. Just you wait till Miss Shackleton sets eyes on you. Us thought you'd forgotten all about we."

The Cornish frequently mix their pronouns, but Lily did this only under great stress, her voice shrill with excitement. "Did you know she'd broken her arm, poor soul? Been at the hospital all morning she has, but the doctor says she's doing nicely. Wait now, till I give her a shout." And she disappeared into the hall, and we heard her calling upstairs to Miss Shackleton to come down immediate, because there was some lovely surprise waiting for her.

Daniel followed her, but I stayed in the kitchen because for some reason I felt that if I witnessed their reunion I should probably burst into tears. As it was, it was Phoebe who cried. I'd never seen her cry before, but they were tears of joy and over in a moment. But still, she cried. And then we all found ourselves back in the kitchen, and I took the wine out of the refrigerator and Lily forgot about chopping mint and went to find some glasses, and the occasion then and there suddenly turned into a tremendous celebration.

He stayed for the rest of the afternoon. The day, which had started so brightly, became overcast, with low clouds blowing in from the sea on a rising wind. There were showers, and it became chilly, but none of this mattered, for we were indoors by the fire, and the hours flew by in talk and reminiscence and a general catching up on everything that had been happening to both of them.

I had little to add to the conversation, but that did not matter. Listening was a joy, because not only did I feel that I was involved with both of them as people but because my interests and my work were relevant to everything that they discussed. I knew about this painter; I had heard of that exhibition; I had actually seen that particular portrait. Phoebe spoke of one Lewis Falcon, who was now living in a house out at Lanyon, and I remembered him because we had held an exhibition of his work at Marcus Bernstein's not two years before.

And we talked about Chips, and it was not like talking about a person who had died six years ago but as though at any moment he would walk into the firelit room to join us, sink into his own sagging armchair, join in the discussion.

Finally, they got onto the subject of Phoebe's own work. What was she doing now? Daniel wanted to know, and Phoebe laughed in her usual self-deprecating way and said that she had nothing to show him, but under pressure she admitted that there were a few canvases that she had completed last year, whilst on holiday in the Dordogne, but she had never got around to sorting them out and they were down in Chips's studio, still stacked haphazardly beneath dust sheets. Daniel at once sprang to his feet and insisted on seeing them, so Phoebe found the studio key and pulled on a raincoat and they set off together, down the brick path, to go and search them out.

I did not accompany them on this expedition. It was half past four and Lily Tonkins had gone home, so when I had collected our coffee mugs and washed them up, I laid a tea tray, found a fruitcake in a tin, and took the empty kettle off the Aga to fill it at the sink.

The sink in Phoebe's kitchen was beneath the window, which was pleasant, because it meant that while you were washing up, you could enjoy the view. But the view now was lost, drowned in a mistlike rain. The clouds were low, the wet, emptying sands of the estuary reflecting their leaden darkness. Flood tide, ebb tide. They made a pattern of time, like the minute hands of a clock, ticking life away.

I felt philosophic, peaceful. And then, suddenly, very happy. This happiness caught me unawares, as I used to be caught unawares by the random ecstasies of childhood. I looked around me, as though the source of this reasonless euphoria could be seen, pinned down, remembered. I saw everything in that familiar kitchen with a rare and heightened perception, so that each humble and ordinary object appeared both pleasing and beautiful. The grain of the scrubbed table, the bright colours of the crockery on the dresser, a basket of vegetables, the symmetry of cups and saucepans.

I thought about Daniel and Phoebe, rooting around together in Chips's dusty old studio. I was glad that I had not gone with them. I liked him. I liked his beautiful hands and his light, quick voice and dark eyes. But there was also something disturbing about him. I was not sure if I wanted to be disturbed.

He had said, "You are not only exceptionally pretty, but you are talented as well."

I was not used to being told I was pretty. My long straight hair was too pale, my mouth too big, my nose snub. Even Nigel Gordon, who—

according to my mother—was in love with me, had never actually got around to saying that I was pretty. Smashing, maybe, or sensational, but never pretty. I wondered if Daniel was married and then laughed at myself, because my thought processes were so painfully obvious, and because it was exactly the question that my mother would have asked. My own self-ridicule broke the spell of that extraordinary moment of perception, and Phoebe's kitchen dissolved into its usual mundane self, left neat by Lily Tonkins before she had donned her head scarf and bicycled home to get her husband's tea.

When tea was over, Daniel pushed back his cuff, looked at his watch, and said that he must go.

"I wish you were staying here," said Phoebe. "Why can't you come back here? Fetch your things and then come back to us."

But he said that he wouldn't. "Lily Tonkins has got quite enough on her plate looking after the pair of you."

"But we'll see you again? You're down for a little?"

He stood up. "A day or two, anyway." It sounded vague. "I'll be back to see you."

"How are you going to get back to Porthkerris?"

"There's probably a bus . . ."

I said, "I'll drive you in Phoebe's car. It's a mile to the bus stop and it's still raining and you'll get soaked."

"Don't you mind?"

"Of course I don't mind."

So he said good-bye to Phoebe and we went out and got into her battered old car, and I backed it cautiously out of the garage and we drove off, leaving Phoebe silhouetted in the lighted doorway of Holly Cottage, waving her good arm and wishing us a safe journey, as though we were setting off on some marathon rally.

We bowled up the hill through the rain, past the golf club, onto the main road. "You're so clever to drive," he said admiringly.

"But you can surely drive a car. Everybody can drive a car."

"Yes, I can drive, but I simply hate it. I'm a total fool about anything mechanical."

"Have you never had a car?"

"I had to have one in America. Everybody has a car in America. But I never really felt at home with it. I bought it secondhand, and it was enormous, long as a bus, with a radiator like a mouth organ and huge, phallic headlights and exhaust pipes. It had automatic gears, too, and electrically operated windows, and some sort of super-charged carburetor. I was terrified of it. When I'd had it three years, I finally sold it, but by that time I'd only just worked out how to operate the heater."

I began to laugh. I suddenly thought of Phoebe saying, when you settle down with a man, it is absolutely vital that he makes you laugh. Nigel, it was true, had never made me laugh much. On the other hand, he was a wizard with cars, and spent a good deal of his spare time either with his head under the hood of his M.G., or else prone beneath it, with only his feet sticking out, and conversation reduced to requests for a larger monkey wrench.

I said, comfortingly, "You can't be good at everything. If you're a successful artist, it would be too much to ask to be a mechanic as well."

"That's what's so fantastic about Phoebe. She paints like a dream. She could have made a really great name for herself if she hadn't happily subjugated her talent in creating a home for Chips . . . and for all the stray students like myself who lived with them and worked with them and learned so much from them. Holly Cottage was a sort of refuge for so many young and struggling artists. There were always immense, delicious meals, and order and cleanliness and warmth. You never forget that sort of security and comfort. It instills in you a standard of good living—and I mean 'good' in the true sense of the word—for the rest of your life."

It was marvellously satisfying to hear another person state aloud what I had always felt myself about Phoebe, and yet, somehow, had never been able to express.

I said, "We're the same, you and I. When I was a child, it was just about the only time I ever cried, when I had to say good-bye to Phoebe, and get on the train and go back to London. And yet once I was home again, back with my mother, and with my own room, and all my own things around me, it was all right. And by the next day, I was always quite happy again, and involved, and glued to the telephone, ringing up all my friends."

"The tears would have been the direct result of the insecurity of two different worlds touching. Nothing makes one more miserable."

I thought about this. It made sense. I said, "I suppose so."

"Actually, I can't imagine you being anything but a happy little girl."

"Yes, I was happy. My parents were divorced, but they were both wise and intelligent people. And it all happened when I was very little, so that it didn't leave what you might call a lasting scar."

"You were lucky."

"Yes, I was. I was always loved and I was always wanted. You can't ask more than that out of any childhood."

Now the road sloped and curved towards Porthkerris. Through the murk, the lights of the harbour sparkled far below us. We came to the gates of the Castle Hotel, and turned in, and made our way up the winding drive, the avenue of oak trees. There was an open space, with tennis courts and putting greens, and then a wide gravel sweep in front of the hotel. Lights shone from windows and the glassed revolving door.

I drew up between a Porsche and a Jaguar, pulled on the brake and turned off the engine.

"I can't help feeling very slightly out of place. Do you know, I've never been here before. Nobody's ever been rich enough to bring me."

"Come in and I'll buy you a drink."

"I'm not suitably dressed."

"Neither am I." He opened the door. "Come on."

We left the car, looking dusty and forlorn between its aristocratic neighbors, and Daniel led the way through the revolving doors, and inside it was tremendously warm and thickly carpeted and expensive-smelling. It was that slack period between tea and cocktail time, and there were not many people about; only a man in golf clothes, reading the *Financial Times,* and an elderly couple watching television.

The hall porter gave us a cold glance, then recognised Daniel and hastily rearranged his expression.

"Good evening, sir."

"Good evening," said Daniel and headed straight in the direction of the bar. But it was my first visit to the Castle, and I wanted to linger and inspect. Here was a writing room, and here, visible through open double doors, an overheated, overupholstered apartment arranged as a card room. In this, by a blazing fire, sat four ladies around a bridge table. I paused for a moment, my attention caught; the scene was so reminiscent of some play from the thirties. I felt that somewhere I had seen it all before: the long brocade curtains, the chintz-covered chairs, the set piece of the elaborate flower arrangement.

Even the ladies wore the correct clothes: the cashmere cardigans, the strings of good pearls. One smoked a cigarette with a long ivory holder.

"Two no trumps."

"Prue." Daniel, impatient, had retraced his steps to urge me on. "Come *on.*"

I was about to follow him when the lady who faced me across the card table looked up. Our eyes met. I had not instantly recognised her, but now I was face to face with Mrs. Tolliver.

"Prue." She looked politely pleased to see me, though I found it hard to believe that this was so. "What a surprise."

"Hello, Mrs. Tolliver."

"What are you doing here?"

I did not want to go and talk to them, but confronted by the situation, I couldn't think of anything else to do. "I . . . I was just looking around. I've never been here before." I moved forward into the room, and the other ladies looked up at me from their hands of cards with smiling mouths and eyes that did not miss a detail of my windblown hair, my old pullover, my faded jeans.

Mrs. Tolliver laid down her cards and introduced me to her friends.

". . . Prue Shackleton. You must know Phoebe Shackleton, who lives at Penmarron. Well, Prue is her niece . . ."

"Oh, yes. How nice," said the ladies in their various ways, obviously longing to get on with their game.

"Prue was so kind to Charlotte yesterday. She travelled down with her from London on the train."

The ladies smiled again, approving of this. I realised with some dismay that I had not thought of Charlotte all day. For some reason this made me feel guilty, and the guilt was not assuaged by the sight of Mrs. Tolliver sitting here in her element and playing bridge.

I said, "Where is Charlotte?"

"At home. With Mrs. Curnow."

"Is she all right?"

Mrs. Tolliver fixed me with a cold eye. "Is there any reason she shouldn't be?"

I was taken aback. "No reason . . ." I met her eye. "It's just that, on the train, she seemed very quiet."

"She's always quiet. She never has much to say. And how did you find Phoebe? Not bothered by her broken arm? I'm so glad. Is she with you now?"

"No. I just drove someone back . . . he's staying here . . ."

I remembered Daniel then, standing behind me, and in some confusion turned to include him in this little encounter and introduce him to Mrs. Tolliver.

"Daniel, this is Mrs . . ."

But he wasn't behind me. I saw only the open doors and the empty foyer beyond.

"Your friend took one look at us and left," one of the other ladies remarked, and I turned back and saw them laughing as though it were a joke. I smiled too.

"How silly of me. I thought he was still there."

Mrs. Tolliver picked up her cards once more and arranged them in a neat fan. "So nice to have seen you," she said. I found myself, for no reason, blushing. I made my excuses, said good-bye to them, and left.

Back in the foyer, I searched for Daniel. There was no trace of him, but I saw the lighted sign of the Cocktail Bar and headed for it, and found him, a solitary figure, sitting on a high stool with his back to me.

I was indignant. "What did you go off like that for?"

"Bridge-playing ladies aren't really my scene."

"They aren't my scene either, but sometimes you have to talk to people. I felt such a fool. I was going to introduce you and you'd evaporated into thin air. It was Mrs. Tolliver, from Penmarron."

"I know. Have a drink."

"If you knew it was Mrs. Tolliver, that was even ruder."

"You sound like an etiquette writer. Why should I be bothered with

Mrs. Tolliver? No, don't tell me, because I don't want to know. Now I'm having a Scotch. What do you want to drink?"

"I don't know if I want a drink." I was still feeling put out.

"I thought that having a drink was what we'd come to do."

"Oh, all right." I climbed up onto the stool beside him. "I'll have a lager."

He ordered it for me. We then proceeded to sit in silence. At the back of the bar the shelves of bottles were backed by mirrored glass, and our two reflections gazed back at us from behind them. Daniel took out a cigar and lit it, and the barman brought me my lager and made a few remarks about the weather. He gave us a dish of peanuts. When he had gone back to the other end of the long bar, Daniel said, "All right, I'm sorry."

"What for?"

"For insulting Mrs. Tolliver, and for being bloody to you. I am in fact quite often bloody. It's as well to know before we embark on some deathless friendship." He looked at me and smiled.

"You didn't insult her." I added ruefully, "To be perfectly truthful, I don't much like her either."

"How do you come to be on such intimate terms with her?"

"Talking to someone at a bridge table isn't exactly being intimate."

"But you do know her quite well?"

"No, I don't. But my mother used to play bridge with her when we came down to stay with Phoebe. And then yesterday I travelled down on the train from London with her little granddaughter, Charlotte Collis. Her mother is Annabelle Tolliver. She was sitting next to me and she looked rather miserable, so we went and had lunch together. There was . . ." I decided not to go into the details of Charlotte's predicament, ". . . some complication, and she can't be at her boarding school, so she's spending a week with Mrs. Tolliver. Phoebe says she's a lonely child; she's always at Holly Cottage, just to have someone to talk to."

Daniel, quietly smoking his cigar, said nothing. I wondered if I was boring him stiff and looked to see if he was politely stifling yawns. But he wasn't. He was simply sitting, his elbow propped on the bar, his profile showing no expression, his eyes downcast. The smoke of his cigar made a fragrant, curling plume.

I took a mouthful of delicious icy lager. "Mrs. Tolliver didn't really want her to stay, according to Phoebe. She didn't even come to the junction to meet Charlotte off the train, and Charlotte and I had to share Mr. Thomas's taxi. And now, today, Mrs. Tolliver's playing bridge, and she's left the child with her housekeeper. It can't be much fun for Charlotte. She's only about ten. She should be with other children."

After a little, Daniel said, "Yes." He put out his half-smoked cigar, grinding the stub into the ashtray as though he had a grudge against it.

He finished his drink and set down the empty glass, then turned and smiled at me and said, surprisingly, "Tomorrow. Will you come and have lunch with me?"

Taken unawares, I did not immediately reply. He went on, swiftly, "That is, if Phoebe can spare you. And lend you her car again."

"I think she could. I don't think she'd mind."

"Ask her, then, when you get back."

"All right. Shall I come here? To the hotel?"

"No. I'll meet you in the Ship Inn on the harbour in Porthkerris. We'll get a ploughman's lunch and a glass of beer, and if it's fine we'll go and sit on the harbour wall and pretend we're tourists."

I smiled. "What time?"

He shrugged. "About half past twelve."

"All right." I was very pleased that he had asked me. "Half past twelve."

He said, "Good. Now finish your lager and I'll take you back to the car."

We emerged from the revolving doors, ejected into wet darkness. We found Phoebe's car, and Daniel opened the door for me, but before I could get into it, he had put his hand around the back of my neck and drawn my face towards his and kissed my mouth. His face was damp with the rain, and for an instant we stood there, and I felt the cool pressure of his cheek against my own.

We said good night. I drove giddily back to Penmarron, feeling drunk, as though I had consumed a great deal more than a single half-pint of lager.

I was bursting to tell Phoebe about everything and to indulge in more long and illuminating discussions about Daniel and Mrs. Tolliver and Charlotte, but when I got back to Holly Cottage, I disturbed her dozing by the fire, and when she woke up, she admitted that she was very tired. Her arm ached, the cast was heavy, the day had been long and exciting. She looked tired, too, her face, beneath the obliterating brim of her hat, thin and shadowed. So I told her only that Daniel had asked me to have lunch with him the next day and asked if this would be all right and if I could borrow her car. She was, as I had known she would be, perfectly agreeable, so I went off to the kitchen and poured her a glass of restoring wine, and then I made scrambled eggs and we ate them in front of the fire.

After that, although it was only half past eight, she decided that she would go to bed, so I helped her upstairs and switched on the electric blanket and drew the curtains against the chilly darkness. When I left her, cozy in her huge bed, she was reading a book by the light of the bedside lamp, but as I shut the door and took myself downstairs, I knew that very soon she would be asleep.

4

NEXT MORNING I was out of bed before she could be, and downstairs. It was too early for Lily Tonkins, so I laid a tray for Phoebe's breakfast, made coffee and toast, and carried the lot upstairs. She was already awake, watching through her open window the sun climb the sky. When I appeared through the door, she turned her head on the pillow and saw the tray and said, with all her usual energy, "You are an idiot, Prue; you know I never have breakfast in bed."

"You are this morning." She pulled herself up on her pillows, and I laid the tray across her knees and went to close the window.

"Red sky at morning, shepherd's warning. I suppose it's going to rain today."

"Don't be so gloomy. You haven't brought a coffee cup for yourself."

"I thought you'd like to be left in peace."

"I hate being left in peace. I like chatting over breakfast. Go and get a mug." She took the lid off the coffee pot and peered inside. "You've made enough for ten people; you'll have to help me drink it."

In bed, which was about the only place she did not wear one of her dashing hats, she looked different: feminine; older, perhaps; vulnerable. Her thick, wiry hair hung in a plait over one shoulder, and she was wrapped in a fleecy shawl. She looked so comfortable that I said, "Why don't you stay there for the morning? Lily Tonkins can cope with everything, and there's not much that you can do to help with only one arm."

"I might," said Phoebe, not committing herself. "I just might do that. Now go and get a mug before the coffee gets cold."

I fetched not only a cup but a bowl of cereal as well, and ate it sitting on the edge of the great, carved pine bed that Phoebe and Chips had shared for all those happy, sinful years. She had once told me that everything she really enjoyed in life was either illegal, immoral, or fattening, and then had roared with laughter.

But somehow they had got away with it, she and Chips. Even in this small, parochial village, they had ridden out the inevitable storm of prejudice by sheer strength of character coupled with their disarming charm. I remembered Chips playing the organ in church when the regular organist had flu, and Phoebe busily baking enormous, lopsided cakes for the Women's Institute tea.

She cared for everybody, and yet for no person's opinion. I looked at her eating toast and marmalade and loved her. She caught my eye. She said, "How nice that you're having lunch with Daniel. What time are you meeting him?"

"Half past twelve at the Ship Inn in Porthkerris. But I won't go unless you promise me that you'll be all right."

"For heaven's sake, I'm not in a wheelchair. Off you go. But I shall want to hear all about it when you get back. Blow-by-blow descriptions." Her eyes twinkled, her cheeks bunched up in wicked laughter, and she was so obviously back to her normal good spirits that I started to tell her about the previous evening and our encounter with Mrs. Tolliver.

". . . And it was very embarrassing, because I thought Daniel was just behind me, and I said something stupid like, 'I want you to meet my friend,' and when I turned round, he wasn't there. Disappeared. Bolted to the bar."

"Did Mrs. Tolliver see him?"

"I've no idea." I thought about this. "Does it make any difference?"

"No-o-o . . ." said Phoebe.

I frowned at her. "Phoebe, you're holding something back."

She laid down her coffee cup and gazed abstractedly out the window. After a bit she shrugged and said, "Oh, well, I don't suppose it matters talking about it now. It all happened so long ago, anyway. Water under the bridge. And it wasn't anything very desperate even then."

"What wasn't desperate?"

"Well . . . when Daniel was living with us, when he was a very young man, Annabelle Tolliver came down from London to spend the summer with her mother, and . . . well . . . I suppose you could say that they had a little fling. A flingette," she added hopefully, trying to make it sound trivial.

Daniel and Annabelle Tolliver. I stared at Phoebe. "You mean, he fancied Annabelle."

" 'Fancied.' " She chuckled. "Such a lovely old-fashioned word. Like 'frock.' Nobody wears frocks anymore." She gave a sigh and got back to the point. "No. Not exactly. If truth be told, I think it was Annabelle who fancied Daniel."

"But she must have been much older than he was."

"Oh, certainly. At least eight years."

"And married."

"Yes, married, too. But I told you, that never made much difference to Annabelle. She had a child by that time. Michael. He must have been about four years old. Poor child, even then I remember, he looked exactly like his father!"

"But . . ." Phoebe's endless digressions did nothing to clarify the situation. "What *happened?*"

"Oh, heavens, nothing happened. They used to go to parties together, picnics on the beach, swimming. She had a very flashy car that summer. It had a hood you could put down, and they used to drive all over the place together; very dashing they looked, too. Very eye-catching. Oh, you can imagine it, Prue."

I could. Only too clearly. "But I wouldn't have thought that Daniel . . ." I stopped, because I wasn't sure what I did think.

"You wouldn't have thought that Daniel was the social type. Perhaps he wasn't, but he was a very attractive young man. Still is, for that matter. And it must have flattered his ego to have her so eager to spend her time with him. I told you, she was beautiful. There were always queues of men swooning around her like lovesick cows. Or do I mean lovesick bulls? But Daniel was always a very quiet person. I think it was his quietness that intrigued Annabelle."

"How long did this go on?"

"The whole summer, on and off. It was just a little flirtation. Perfectly harmless."

"What did Mrs. Tolliver have to say about it?"

"Mrs. Tolliver never says anything about anything. She's the sort of woman who truly believes that if you don't look, it will go away. Besides, she must have realised that if it wasn't Daniel, it would have been some other man. Perhaps she reckoned that he was the lesser of a lot of other evils."

"But the little boy . . . Michael?"

"There was a starchy nanny taking care of him. He never got in the way at all."

"And her husband . . ." I could hardly bear to say his horrid name. "Leslie Collis?"

"He was left in London, running his office. I suppose living in some service flat or other. I've no idea. It's not important, anyway."

I thought carefully through this extraordinary revelation. I finally said, "Then last night . . . you think that's why Daniel didn't want to talk to Mrs. Tolliver."

"Maybe. Maybe he just didn't want to get involved with four bridge-playing ladies."

"I wonder why he didn't tell me himself."

"There was no reason he should. It has nothing to do with you, and it was a total nonevent, anyway." She poured herself more coffee and said, quite briskly, "You're not to make anything of it."

"I'm not. I just wish it had been anybody but Annabelle Tolliver."

Red sky at morning, shepherd's warning. But it was the sort of day when you couldn't be sure what would happen to the weather. A warm, west-wind sort of day, with gusts that tore leaves from trees and sent them flying and flecked the indigo sea with white horses. The sky was a brazen blue swept by high clouds, and the very air seemed to glitter. From the top of the hill above Porthkerris, I could see for miles, long beyond the lighthouse to the distant spur of Trevose Head. From the harbour far below me, a solitary fishing boat butted out into the choppy sea, making for the deep water beneath the cliffs of Lanyon.

The way led steeply downhill, through the narrow streets of the little town. Most of the summer visitors had now departed. Only a handful, looking chilly in shorts, stood about outside the news agent's or made their way down the hill to where a bakery was redolent with the smell of fresh, hot pastries.

At Porthkerris the Ship Inn stands, where it has stood for three hundred years or more, on the harbour road by the old quay where the fishermen used to land their pilchards. I drove by it, but there was no sign of Daniel, so I found a place to park the Volkswagen and then walked back along the cobbles and went in, dipping my head beneath the low, smoke-blackened lintel. Inside, after the brightness of the day, it was very dark. A small coal fire burned in the grate, and an old man sat by this, looking as though he had sat there all his life or had, perhaps, grown up out of the floorboards.

"Prue."

I turned. Daniel was sitting in the deep window seat with an empty pint tankard on a wobbly table that had been made out of a barrel. He stood up, easing himself from behind this table, and said, "It's too good a day to have lunch indoors. What do you think?"

"So what shall we do?"

"Buy something. Eat it on the beach."

So we went out again and down the road until we reached one of those convenient shops that seem to sell everything. We bought fresh pastries, so hot that the man had to wrap them in newspaper. We bought a bag of apples, and some chocolate biscuits, and a packet of paper cups, and a bottle of dubious red wine. When the kindly man realised we were going to drink it right away, he threw in a corkscrew as well.

We went back out into the sunshine and crossed the cobbled street, and climbed down the stone steps that were dry at the top and coated with green weed at the bottom. The tide was on its way out and had left behind it a sickle of clean yellow sand. There was a cluster of rocks pounded smooth by the seas of centuries, and we settled ourselves on these, sheltered from the wind and with the sun on our faces. Screaming gulls wheeled in the windy air, and from where some men worked peacefully on a boat came the pleasant sounds of hammer blows and muted voices.

Daniel opened the bottle of wine, and we unwrapped the pastries. I was suddenly very hungry. I bit greedily into mine, and it was so hot that I nearly scalded my mouth and bits of steaming potato fell out of the pastry onto the sand, to be spied and scooped up in an instant by a great, greedy gull.

I said, "This was a brilliant idea."

"I have them, every now and again."

And I thought that if it had been Nigel, we would in all probability have been lunching at the Castle Hotel, with white tablecloths and waiters hovering, hampering conversation. Daniel had taken the cork out of the bottle; now he took a mouthful of wine, considered its taste, and swallowed it.

"An amusing and unpretentious little wine," he said, "if you don't mind it being stone cold. I don't suppose it improves its bouquet, drinking it out of a paper cup, but beggars can't be choosers. The only alternative seems to be the neck of the bottle." He took a bite out of his pastry. "How's Phoebe this morning?"

"She was tired last night. She went to bed early, and this morning I took her up her breakfast in bed, and she promised she'd stay there till lunchtime."

"What would she have done if you hadn't been able to come to Penmarron and take care of her?"

"She'd have managed. Lily would have looked after her, but Lily can't drive, and Phoebe hates being without her car."

"Were you able to get away from work just like that? What does Marcus Bernstein do without you?"

"I was on holiday anyway for two weeks, so that was no problem. He'd already engaged a temp to take over while I was away."

"You mean you had two weeks' holiday and you weren't going to do anything with it? What were you going to do, stay in London?"

"No. As a matter of fact, I was meant to be going to Scotland."

"Scotland? For heaven's sake, what were you going to do there?"

"Stay with people."

"Have you ever been to Scotland?"

"No. Have you?"

"Once. Everybody kept telling me how beautiful it was, but it rained so hard that I never found out if they were telling the truth or not." He took another mouthful of pastry. "Who were you going to stay with?"

"Friends."

"You're being cagey, aren't you? You might as well tell me all, because I'll just go on asking questions until you give me some answers. It's a boyfriend, isn't it?"

I would not look at him. "Why should it be?"

"Because you're far too attractive not to have some man languishing with love for you. And you've got the most extraordinary expression on your face. Confused nonchalance."

"I'm sure that's a contradiction of terms."

"What's he called?"

"Who?"

"Oh, stop being coy. The boyfriend, of course."

"Nigel Gordon."

"Nigel. Nigel's one of my most unfavorite names."

"It's no worse than Daniel."

"It's a wet name. Timothy's a wet name, too. So is Jeremy. And Christopher. And Nicholas."

"Nigel is not wet."

"What is he, then?"

"Nice."

"What does he do?"

"He's an insurance broker."

"And he comes from Scotland?"

"Yes. His family lives there. In Inverness-shire."

"What a frightfully good thing you didn't go. You'd have hated it. A great unheated house, with bedrooms cold as refrigerators and baths encased in mahogany, like coffins."

I said, "Daniel, you make more ridiculous sweeping statements than any man I've ever met."

"You won't marry him, will you, this Highland insurance broker? Please don't. I can't bear the thought of you in kilts and living in Inverness-shire."

I very nearly laughed but managed to keep a prim face. "I wouldn't be living in Inverness-shire. I'd be living in Nigel's desirable residence in South Kensington." I threw what remained of my pastry to the gulls and helped myself to an apple, rubbing it to a shine on the sleeve of my sweater. "And I wouldn't have to work, either. I wouldn't have to go trudging off to Marcus Bernstein's every morning. I could be a lady of leisure, with time to do all I want to do, which is paint. And it wouldn't matter if nobody bought my pictures, because my husband would be there, ready and willing to pay all the bills."

He said, "I thought you thought like Phoebe. I'm disillusioned."

"Perhaps sometimes I think like my mother. She likes life to be neat and squared off and conventional and safe. She adores Nigel. She's longing for me to marry him. She can't wait to start planning a wedding. St. Paul's, Knightsbridge, and a reception in Pavilion Road . . ."

"And a honeymoon at Budleigh Salterton, with the golf clubs in the boot of the car. Prue, you can't be serious."

I took a great bite of the shiny apple. "I might be."

"Not about a man called Nigel."

I was beginning to feel irritated. "You know nothing about him. And anyway, what's so bad about getting married? You think the world of Phoebe, you thought the world of Chips. But, you know, they would have been married, years ago, if only Chips could have gotten a divorce. But he couldn't. So they compromised, and made the very best of their life together."

"I don't think there's anything wrong in getting married. I just think it's insane to get married to the wrong person."

"I suppose you've never made that mistake."

"No, as a matter of fact, I haven't. I've done just about everything else. Made every other sort of mistake, but getting married wasn't one of them." He appeared to be considering this state of affairs. "Never even thought about it, as a matter of fact."

He smiled at me, and I smiled back, because for no particular reason I was filled with gladness, simply because he had never married. And yet I was not surprised. There was something nomadic, free, about Daniel, and I found I was envious of this.

I said, "I wish there was time in life to do everything."

"You've got time."

"I know, but already I seem to be in a sort of rut. I like the rut. I like my job and I'm doing exactly what I want to do, and I love Marcus Bernstein, and I wouldn't change my job for anything in the world. But sometimes, on a certain sort of morning, I drive to work, and I think, I'm twenty-three and what am I doing with my life? And I think of all the places I long to see. Kashmir and the Bahamas and Greece, and Palmyra. And San Francisco, and Peking and Japan. I would like to have been to some of the places you've been to."

"Then go. Go now."

"You make it sound so simple."

"It can be. Life is as simple as you make it."

"Perhaps I haven't got that sort of courage. But still, I would like to have done some of the things you've done."

He laughed. "Don't wish that. Some of it was hell."

"It can't still be hell. Everything's going so well for you now."

"Uncertainty is always hell."

"What are you uncertain about?"

"About what I'm going to do next."

"That shouldn't be too frightening."

"I'm thirty-one. Within the next twelve months I've got to make some sort of a decision; I'm frightened of drifting. I don't want to drift for the rest of my life."

"What do you want to do?"

"I want . . ."

He leaned back against the knobby granite of the harbour wall and turned his face to the sun and closed his eyes. He looked like a man who longed for the oblivion of sleep. "When this exhibition at Peter Chastal's is over and finished with, I want to go to Greece. There's an island called Spetsai, and on Spetsai there is a house, square and white as a sugar cube. And there's a terrace with terra cotta tiles on the floor, and geraniums in pots along the tops of the wall. And below the terrace there's a mooring and a boat with a white sail like the wing of a gull. Not a big boat. Just large enough for two." I waited. He opened his eyes. He said, "I think I shall go there."

"Do that thing."

"Would you come?" He held out his hand to me. "Would you like to come and visit me? You just told me you wanted to go to Greece. Would you come and let me show you some of its glories?"

I was very touched. I laid my hand in his and felt his fingers close about my wrist. How different this was, how frighteningly different, from the invitation Nigel had painfully offered me, to visit his mother in Inverness-shire. Two different worlds. *The insecurity of two different worlds touching.* I wondered if I was about to burst into tears.

"One day," I told him, in the voice of a mother placating an insistent child. "One day, maybe, I'll be able to come."

The sky clouded and it grew cold. It was time to stir ourselves. We gathered up the picnic rubbish and found a little bin by a lamp post, and threw all the trash into that. We walked back to where I had left Phoebe's car, and there was the smell of rain in the air and the sea had turned angry and leaden.

Red sky at morning, shepherd's warning. We got into the car and slowly drove back to Penmarron. Phoebe's heater did not work, and I felt cold. I knew that there would be a fire ablaze at Holly Cottage, and possibly crumpets for tea, but I wasn't thinking about these things. My mind was filled with images of Greece, of the house above the water and the boat with a sail like the wing of a gull. I thought of swimming in that dark Aegean sea, the water warm and clear as glass . . .

Memory stirred.

"Daniel."

"What is it?"

"That night I got off the train from London, I had a dream. It was about swimming. I was on a desert island, and I had to walk a long long way through shallow water. And then all at once it was deep, but so clear I could see right to the bottom. And once I had started to swim, there was a current. Very fast and strong. It was like being swept down a river."

I remembered again the sensation of peace, of blissful acceptance.

"What happened then?"

"Nothing. But it was nice."

"Sounds a good dream. What brought it to mind?"

"I was thinking about Greece. Swimming in Homer's wine-dark seas."

"All dreams have meaning."

"I know."

"What do you think that one signified?"

I told him, "I thought perhaps it was about dying."

But that was before Daniel had come into my life. Now I was wiser, and I knew that the dream was not about dying at all but loving.

When we got back to Holly Cottage, there was no sign of Phoebe. The firelit sitting room was empty, and when I called up the stair, thinking that perhaps she had spent the whole day in her bed, there was no reply.

But sounds of clashing crockery and opening drawers came from the kitchen. I went down the hall with Daniel behind me to open the door and investigate, only to discover Lily Tonkins engaged in whisking up a bowl of batter.

"You're back then," she said. She did not look too pleased to see us, and I wondered if she was in one of her cross moods. Lily could get very cross. Not with us in particular but just with the world in general, which included her morose husband, the cheeky girl who worked in the grocer's, and the man in the town hall who dealt with Lily's pension.

"Where's Phoebe?" I asked.

Lily did not look up from her task. "Gone down to the water."

"I hoped she'd stay in bed today."

"Stay in bed?" Lily set down the bowl with a thump and faced me with her arms akimbo. "Some chance she's had of staying in bed. We've had that little Charlotte Collis here all day, ever since ten o'clock this morning. I'd just taken Miss Shackleton a nice cup of tea and was polishing up the brasses when I heard a ring at the bell. Dratted nuisance, I said to myself, and went to the door, and there she was. And been here ever since."

"Where's Mrs. Tolliver?"

"Gone over to Falmouth for some meeting—Save the Children or Save the Church or something. Seems funny to me. I mean, I can understand some people don't like looking after children. There are some that do and some that don't. But she's that little girl's granny. No business to be up and about all the time, playing cards and saving things. Somebody's got to look after the little girl."

"Where's Mrs. Curnow?"

"Betty Curnow, she's there all right, up at White Lodge, but she's got her own work to do. Mrs. Tolliver can't be bothered to look after the child, then she should pay some other person to do the job."

"So what happened?"

"Well, I let her in, poor little soul, and I said Miss Shackleton was still in bed and you were out, gone for lunch. So she went up the stairs to see Miss Shackleton, and I heard them talking together. Talk, talk, you'd think that child had never had a soul to talk to the way she carries on when she's here. Then she came down, the little girl, and said Miss Shackleton was getting up and getting dressed. And that vexed me because I knew she needed a good rest. So I went up and gave her a hand with her clothes, and then down she came and phoned Betty Curnow and said that we were keeping Charlotte here and giving her lunch. Luckily there was a bit of cold lamb, and I peeled a few potatoes and made a custard, but it's not right Miss Shackleton being landed with the child to take care of, and her with that bad arm and everything."

I had never seen Lily so loquacious or upset. She was concerned, and naturally so, for Phoebe. But, as well, she had a kind heart. The Cornish love children, and Lily was no exception. She had decided that Charlotte was being neglected, and all her hackles were well and truly up.

I said, "I'm sorry. I should have been here to help you."

Daniel had listened to all this in silence. Now he said, "Where are they?"

"Went down to the shore to do their drawing. That's what they like to do when they're together, like a pair of old women." She turned from the table and went to the sink to peer out the window. Daniel and I followed her. We saw the empty estuary, the deserted sands. But at the far end of the seawall we could discern the two distant figures: Phoebe, unmistakable in her hat, and the child beside her, wearing a scarlet anorak. They had taken camp stools with them and sat side by side, very close. There was something touching about the pair of them. Oblivious to the rest of the world, they looked as though they had been washed up by some unimaginable storm and forgotten.

As we stood there, there came the first sharp rattle of raindrops against the glass of the window, and Lily said, "There now!" as if she had forecast this very thing happening. "That's the dratted rain come on. And Miss Shackleton won't even notice. Once she starts her sketching, that's the end of it. Might as well shout your heart out, and she'd never take notice. And her with that cast on her arm, poor soul . . ."

The time had obviously come to intervene. "I'll go and get them," I said.

"No." Daniel laid a restraining hand on my arm. "It's pouring. I'll go."

"You'll need a mackintosh, Daniel," Lily warned him, but he found an umbrella in the hall and set off armed with that. I watched his progress, the umbrella held high over his head, as he walked down across the lawn and disappeared through the gate in the escallonia hedge. Moments later he came into view once more, making his way along the edge of the seawall towards the two unsuspecting artists.

Lily and I turned away from the window. "What can I do to help you?" I asked.

"You could lay the table for tea."

"Let's all have it in here. It's so nice and warm."

"I'm making a batch of pancakes." She picked up her bowl and started whisking again. She looked more cheerful, having aired her grievances, and I was grateful for this.

I said, "Tomorrow I'll do something with Charlotte. Take her somewhere in the car, perhaps. She's been on my conscience ever since I arrived, only there doesn't seem to have been much time to arrange anything."

"Mind, she's a nice enough little girl."

"I know. But somehow that only makes it worse."

The table was laid, the drop scones made, and the kettle boiling, and still they had not returned.

"That Daniel," observed Lily. "He's as bad as the rest of them. Probably forgot what he went for, and he's sat down with them to paint a picture for himself . . ."

"I'd better go." I found an old raincoat of Phoebe's and a man-eating sou'wester that had once belonged to Chips and let myself out the garden door. It was now raining hard and very wet, but as I crossed the grass Daniel and Phoebe appeared at the gate, Daniel holding the camp stools under one arm and the umbrella high over Phoebe's head with the other. Phoebe, except for her hat, was dressed as though for a sunny outing, and her cardigan, buttoned bulkily over her plaster cast, was sodden, her shoes and stout stockings mud-splashed. She carried in her good hand her painting bag, a sturdy and familiar piece of equipment made of canvas, and as Daniel opened the gate for her, she looked up and saw me.

"Hello! Here we are, a lot of drowned rats!"

"Lily and I wondered what had happened to you all."

"Charlotte hadn't quite finished, and she wanted to."

"Where is she?"

"Oh, coming. Somewhere," said Phoebe, airily.

I looked past her, down the hill, and saw Charlotte at the foot of it. She stood with her back to me, peering into the depths of a dripping bramble bush.

I said, resigned, "I'd better get her," and set off down the wet and slippery slope. "Charlotte! Come along."

She turned and looked up and saw me. Her hair clung to her head, and her glasses were misted with rain.

"What *are* you doing?"

"I'm looking for blackberries. I thought there might be some."

"You're not meant to be looking for blackberries, you're meant to be coming up to the house for tea. Lily's made pancakes."

She moved reluctantly. "All right." Even the lure of hot pancakes did not kindle much enthusiasm. I thought that it would be easy to be maddened by her, and yet I understood her reluctance to end an afternoon spent in Phoebe's delightful company. I remembered myself at Charlotte's age, trailing home after a day with Phoebe, spent perhaps on the beach or picking primroses or riding in the little train to Porthkerris. It had always been an effort to drag oneself back to routine, and meals, and everyday, mundane life.

I held out my hand to her. "Do you want a pull up the hill?"

She took her hand out of her anorak pocket and gave it to me. It felt thin and small and wet and cold. I said, "What you need is a good rubdown with a towel and a hot drink." We set off up the slope. "Did you have a good afternoon with Phoebe?"

"Yes. We've been drawing."

"I don't suppose you even noticed the rain."

"No, not really. My paper was beginning to get a bit wet, but then that man came and held the umbrella over it and I could finish."

"His name is Daniel."

"I know. Phoebe's told me about him. He used to live with her and Chips."

"He's a famous artist now."

"I know that, too. He said my drawing was very good."

"What did you draw?"

"I tried to draw some gulls, but they kept flying away, so I did a made-up picture."

"That was enterprising."

"He said it was very good."

"I hope you haven't left it behind?"

"No. Phoebe put it in her bag."

Breathless by now, we toiled on in silence. We reached the gate. I opened it, and as Charlotte went through, I said, "I've been wondering how you've been getting along. I would have rung you up or asked you to tea, only I've been so . . ." I hesitated, searching for the right word. "Busy" seemed scarcely truthful.

"It's not much fun," said Charlotte with a child's uncompromising honesty.

I made a cheerful face. "Well, perhaps tomorrow we could do something together." I shut the gate behind us. "Go somewhere in the car if Phoebe doesn't need it."

Charlotte considered this. Then, "Do you think," she said, "that Daniel would like to come too?"

As soon as we were inside the kitchen, Lily, half-irritated and half-laughing, pounced on Charlotte, unzipping her drenched jacket, kneeling to struggle with the buckles of her sandals.

"I don't know, some people can be that silly. Miss Shackleton, well, I've never seen a soul so wet. I told her to go upstairs and change down to the skin, and all she would do was laugh and say it didn't matter. It'll matter all right when she gets pneumonia. Didn't you notice the rain?"

"Not really," said Charlotte.

Lily produced a dry towel, removed Charlotte's spectacles, carefully dried the lenses, and then gently put them on again, setting them straight across the bridge of Charlotte's small nose. Using the same towel, she began to dry the child's hair, rubbing as though she were drying a wet puppy, scolding on. I left them to it and went to take off the mackintosh and the sou'wester and drape them over the radiator in the hall to dry.

The door to Phoebe's sitting room stood open. On the far side the fire blazed, the flames reflected in the brass fender and on all the little polished knickknacks that stood about—a copper jug, a silver photograph frame, a luster bowl. In front of the fire, with an elbow on the mantelpiece and a foot on the fender, stood Daniel. The profile of his downcast face was reflected in the mirror that hung above the mantelpiece, and in his hand he held a sheet of paper, which he appeared to be studying.

I came through the door, and he looked up.

"I've got Charlotte. She's with Lily, getting dried. She was looking for blackberries." I went to stand beside him, spreading my cold hands to the warmth of the fire. "What are you looking at?"

"This little picture she's done. She's very good."

He handed it to me and moved away from the fireplace to sink, recumbent, in the roomy depths of Chips's old armchair. He looked tired, his chin sunk on his chest, his long legs stretched out in front of him. I looked at Charlotte's drawing and saw at once what he meant. It was a child's effort, but imaginative and cleanly drawn. She had used felt pens, and the bright primary colours reminded me of Phoebe's own brilliant little oils. I saw the red boat bowling across a cobalt sea, the sail curved and set full in the wind. There was a small figure at the helm wearing a cap with a seagoing peak, and on the foredeck a large, whiskery cat.

I smiled. "I like the cat."

"I like the whole thing."

"It's a very cheerful picture. And that's odd, because I don't think she's a particularly cheerful child."

"I know," said Daniel. "It's reassuring."

I put the drawing on the mantelpiece, propped against Phoebe's clock. "Tomorrow I said I'd take her somewhere. She isn't having much of a time with her grandmother. I thought we could go somewhere in the car."

"That would be kind."

"She seemed to think it would be more fun if you came, too."

"Did she," said Daniel. He did not seem overexcited at the prospect. I wondered if he was already tiring of feminine company, or perhaps the idea of a day spent with Charlotte and myself had no allure for him. I wished now that I had said nothing about it. "You've probably got better things to do."

He said, "Yes," and then, "We'll see."

We'll see. He sounded like the adults who used to infuriate me as a child by using those very words when they were unable, or possibly unwilling, to commit themselves.

Chips had made the carousel for me. It was mine. He had said when he gave it to me that if I wanted, I could take it back to London, but I chose not to. The carousel was part of Holly Cottage, and I was such a traditionalist that I chose to leave it here.

It lived where it always had, in the bottom half of the huge French bombe cabinet that stood at one end of Phoebe's sitting room. That evening, after tea had been cleared away and washed up, Charlotte went to take it out. She carried it carefully and set it on the table in front of the fire.

Chips had made it from an old-fashioned gramophone. He had removed the lid and the needle arm and cut a circle of plywood the same size as a regular record, with a hole in the middle to fit over the gramophone's central spindle. This disc was painted a bright scarlet, and the animals were fixed around its perimeter. These, too, had been cut from plywood with Chips's little jigsaw. There was a tiger, an elephant, a zebra, a pony, a lion, and a dog, each coloured with its own stripes or spots and each sporting a brightly painted saddle with tiny bridles and reins made of golden cord.

Various games could be played with it. Sometimes, along with building blocks, farmyard people, and a few wooden animals left over from a defunct Noah's Ark, it became part of a fairground or a circus. But mostly I played with it just as it was, winding the handle to power the mechanism and switching the lever that made the turntable revolve. There was, as well, another lever to regulate the speed. You could start it up very slowly (to give people time to get on, Chips used to say) and then speed it up until the animals whirled so fast you could scarcely see them.

Charlotte did this now. It was like watching a spinning top. Finally the mechanism ran down, and the carousel came slowly to a halt.

She crouched down on her heels and moved the turntable with her hand, gazing at the face of each animal in turn.

"I simply don't know *which* is my favorite."

"The tiger was always mine," I told her. "He has such a fierce face."

"I know. He's a bit like the tigers in *Little Black Sambo,* isn't he. And you know, when the animals go round really fast they look a bit like the *Little Black Sambo* tigers going round the tree and turning into butter."

"Perhaps," said Phoebe, "Lily made our pancakes out of tiger butter, just the way Little Black Sambo's mother did."

"Why did you have to make old-fashioned gramophones go fast and slow? I mean, there's everything on my father's stereo at home, in Sunningdale, but I don't think there's a switch to make it go fast or slow."

"It was great fun," Phoebe told her. "You could put an ordinary record on very slowly and it sounded like an enormous Russian singing basso profundo. And then you'd make it go quickly and it was all squeaky and high. Like a mouse singing."

"But *why?* Why did that happen?"

Phoebe said, "I haven't the faintest idea," which was always her very sensible reply to a question to which she had no answer.

Charlotte turned to me. "Do you know?"

"No, I don't."

"Do you?" She turned to Daniel.

He had been silent all this time. He had, for that matter, been silent through most of tea. Now he was back in Chips's armchair, apparently watching the carousel with the rest of us and yet in some way remote and withdrawn. Now we all looked at him expectantly, but he had not even realised that Charlotte had spoken to him, and she had to say it again. "Do you, Daniel?"

"Do I what?"

"Do you know why the music goes squeaky when it's fast and basso profundo when it's slow?"

He considered this question with some care and then suggested that perhaps it had something to do with centrifugal force.

Charlotte screwed up her nose. "What's *that?*"

"It's what makes your spin dryer work."

"I haven't got a spin dryer."

"Well, when you're a big girl, perhaps you'll have one, and you'll look at it working, and then you'll know what centrifugal force is."

Charlotte began to wind the gramophone handle again. Above us, on the mantelpiece, Phoebe's clock struck five.

Phoebe said gently, "Charlotte, perhaps it's time you went home."

"Oh, do I *have* to?"

"No, you don't have to, but I said you'd be back about five."

Charlotte looked up, her expression all set to whine. "I don't want to go. And I can't walk back, because it's raining."

"Prue will take you in my car."

"Aw . . ."

Terrified of tears, I said quickly, "And don't forget, we've got a date for tomorrow. We're going out together in the car. Do you want me to come and fetch you?"

"No. I hate being fetched because I hate waiting. I'm always afraid people won't come. I'll come here. I'll walk down like I did this morning. What time shall I be here?"

"Oh, about half past ten?"

"All right."

Daniel had heaved himself to his feet. "Where are you off to?" Phoebe asked him.

"I must go, too," he told her.

"But I thought you were going to stay for dinner with Prue and me. Lily's made a chicken casserole . . ."

"No, really . . . I should get back. I've got a phone call to make. I promised Peter Chastal I'd get in touch with Lewis Falcon, and I've done nothing about it . . ."

"Oh, all right," said Phoebe, who always instantly accepted other people's decisions and never tried to argue. "Then you'd better go with Prue, and she'll drive you back to Porthkerris after she's dropped Charlotte."

He looked at me. "Do you mind?"

"Of course not."

But I did mind, because I wanted him to want to have dinner with Phoebe and me.

"Good-bye, Phoebe." He went to give her a kiss, and she gave him an affectionate little pat on the arm; letting him go, asking no questions.

That's the way I've got to be, I told myself, as I went to fetch my coat. *If I don't want to lose his friendship that's the way I've got to be.*

In the car, he sat in front, while Charlotte perched on the backseat, leaning forward so that the pale blur of her face hung between us.

"Where shall we go tomorrow?" she wanted to know.

"I don't know. I hadn't thought. Where's a good place?"

"We could go up to Skadden Hill. We'd maybe find blackberries. And there's lots of rocks on the top of the hill and one of them has got a giant's footprint on it. Really. A real, huge footprint."

Daniel said, "You could go to Penjizal."

"What happens at Penjizal?" I asked.

"There's a cliff walk, and at low tide a great deep rock pool, and the seals come into it and swim there."

Charlotte instantly forgot about Skadden Hill. Giant's footsteps were tame compared to seals.

"Oh, let's go there. I've never seen seals, at least not close to."

I said, "I don't even know where Penjizal is."

"Will you show us, Daniel?" Charlotte banged on his shoulder with her fist to get his whole attention. "Will you come with us? Oh, do come with us."

Daniel did not at once respond to this impassioned appeal. I knew that he was waiting for me to intervene, perhaps make some excuse for him, but I stayed selfishly silent. Through the windscreen wipers' fan of clear glass I saw the road ahead, awash with muddy water; the oak trees, black against the sky, lashed with rain.

"Please," Charlotte persisted.

He said, "I might."

But she stuck to her guns. "Does that mean yes or no?"

"Well, all right . . ." He turned his head to grin at her. "Yes."

"Oh, *good.*" She actually clapped her hands. "What shall I bring, Prue? Shall I bring my gum boots?"

"Perhaps you'd better. And a proper raincoat in case it's wet."

"But we'll have a picnic, won't we, even if it's raining?"

"Yes, we'll have a picnic. We'll find somewhere to eat it. What do you like? Ham sandwiches?"

"Yes. And Coke."

"I don't think we've got any Coke."

"I think Granny's got some. And if she hasn't I'll go and buy some. They sell it in the village shop."

We had reached the gates of White Lodge. I drove through them and up the short drive, and the house, as before, waited for us, curtained in the rain, its face closed and blank, giving nothing away. We drew up at the foot of the steps, and Daniel got out in order to let Charlotte emerge from the backseat. He stood looking down at her. She was holding the picture she had drawn. Phoebe had taken it down from the mantelpiece and given it to Charlotte as we were on the point of leaving.

"Don't forget this," she had said, and added hopefully, "Perhaps you'd like to give it to your grandmother."

But now Charlotte held it out to Daniel. "Would you like to keep it?" she asked him shyly.

"I'd like to very much. But isn't it for your grandmother?"

"Not really. She won't want it."

"In that case, I'll take it." He did so. "Thank you. I shall treasure it."

"I'll see you tomorrow then. Good-bye. Good-bye, Prue, and thank you for bringing me home."

We watched her climb the steps to the front door. As Daniel got back into the car beside me, the door opened. A wedge of yellow light shone out into the murk, and we saw Mrs. Tolliver standing there. She waved —perhaps to say thank you, perhaps to say good-bye—and then drew Charlotte indoors.

5

WE SET OFF FOR PORTHKERRIS. It was only a short journey, but it was made that evening, by Daniel and me, in total silence. Sometimes silences between two people are comfortable things; sometimes they speak more loudly than words. On other occasions they become strained and tense, and this was one of them. I wanted to break the constraint, to start some trivial conversation, but in the face of such noncooperation I could think of no words for the tall, quiet stranger who sat beside me. His hand, still holding Charlotte's present, lay against his knee. His head was turned away from me. He stared out at the drenched, grey-green fields, the stony walls, the rain. There seemed to be nothing to say.

We reached the gates of the hotel at last, turned up the driveway, parked with all the expensive cars. On that gloomy evening even the opulent Castle Hotel had an abandoned appearance, like a sinking liner, with its few lighted windows reflected in a sea of puddles.

I turned off the engine and waited for Daniel to get out of the car. Now there was only the sound of the rain drumming on the roof and the sough of wind blown up from the sea far below us. Listening, I heard the distant breakers crashing on the shore. Daniel turned his head and looked at me. "Will you come in?"

I couldn't think why he had even bothered to ask me. "No. You have to get in touch with Lewis Falcon. And I should get back . . ."

He said urgently, "Please. I want to talk to you."

"What about?"

"We can have a drink."

"Daniel . . ."

"Please, Prue."

I switched off the headlights and we got out of the car. Once more the revolving doors injected us into that warm, scented, carpeted, over-heated interior. Today, perhaps because of the inclement weather, there were more people about. They sat grouped around tea tables, read their newspapers, chatted over knitting. The air was thick with late-afternoon boredom. Daniel headed for the bar, but it was too early and it had not opened yet.

He stopped before the shuttered door and said, "Bloody hell," so loudly that one or two pairs of eyes were raised to observe us. I felt embarrassed. I knew how we looked, untidy and incongruous; Daniel in his worn jeans and the sweater of dark rough wool; myself in an old navy blue duffle coat that had seen better days, and with my hair windblown and uncombed.

I wanted to go away. "I don't want a drink, anyway."

"I do. Come on, we'll go up to my room."

And without waiting for my response to this suggestion, he set off up the wide staircase, his long legs taking the steps three at a time. Because there didn't seem to be anything else to do, I followed him, aware of the interest that our behaviour was arousing. I knew that we would be suspected of the very worst, but so concerned was I by Daniel's behaviour, so apprehensive for myself, that I didn't care anyway.

His room was on the first floor, at the end of a long, wide passage. He took the key from his pocket and went in, turning on the lights, and I followed him and saw that he had been given one of the best rooms in the hotel, facing out over the small nine-hole golf course. The greens and fairways of this golf course sloped to a little wood, and so high on the hill were we that the sea's horizon lay above the topmost branches of these trees. This evening the horizon was not visible, but the window of Daniel's room stood open, and the wind poured in upon us and sent the long curtains flapping like badly set sails.

He shut the door and went to close the window. The curtains ceased their frantic dance. I looked at the large, comfortably furnished room, with its unexpected features that made it feel more like a bedroom in some well-loved country house than an impersonal hotel. There was a fireplace, and over this a pretty mirror, framed in rose-colour glass. Chintz-covered armchairs were drawn up before the fireplace, and the same chintz skirted the dressing table. A television set stood on a low table, and beside this was a small refrigerator. There were even flowers on the mantelpiece and a round basket of fresh fruit by the wide double bed.

When he had shut the window, Daniel went to switch on the electric fire. Sham logs instantly flickered. He was still holding Charlotte's picture. Now he placed it carefully in the middle of the mantelpiece. In the mirror I could see his quiet reflected face.

I watched him and waited.

He said, "She's my child."

Beyond his reflection, I could see my own, my face a pale blur, my hands deep in the pockets of my coat; the whole image distorted by some flaw in the glass so that I appeared ghostly, like a person drowned.

It was suddenly very hard to speak. I said, "Charlotte," and the word came out as a whisper.

"Yes, Charlotte." He turned from the fireplace, and across the room our eyes met. "She's my child."

"But why are you saying this?"

He said again, "She's my child."

"Oh, Daniel."

"You see, all those years ago, I had a love affair with her mother. I wasn't in love with Annabelle, she was married to another man, she already had a child. Everything was against us. But still, contrary to any sort of reason, it happened. And Charlotte is the outcome of a long, hot summer of what must have been total madness."

I said, "I know about it. I mean, I know about you and Annabelle Tolliver."

"Phoebe told you."

"Yes."

"I thought she might tell you. In fact, I was pretty sure that she would."

We stared at each other. My mind, like a panicky rabbit, scuttled to and fro, getting nowhere. I tried to remember the words that Phoebe had used. *I think it was Annabelle who fancied Daniel. Daniel was a very quiet person. It was a total non-event anyway.*

I said. "But I thought . . . I mean . . . I didn't realise . . ."

He rescued me from my delicate floundering. "You thought we'd just had a little walk out. I always hoped that that was what Phoebe and Chips thought too. But you see, it wasn't nearly as innocent as that."

"You're . . . you're sure she's your child?"

"I knew the moment I saw her this afternoon, sitting there on her camp stool, at the end of the sea wall. In the cold and the rain, trying to finish her picture. Prue, you've gone as white as a sheet. I think we'd better both have a drink."

I watched him go to open the refrigerator. He took out glasses and ice and soda water and a bottle of whisky and set these on the top of the cabinet.

"Daniel, I don't drink whisky."

"I haven't anything else." He unscrewed the top of the bottle.

I said, "She doesn't even look like you."

"She doesn't look like Annabelle, either. But I have a photograph of my mother when she was just about that age. Nine or ten. Charlotte is my mother all over again."

"Did you know that Annabelle was having your baby?"

"She said she was."

"Wasn't that enough?"

"As things turned out, no."

"I don't understand."

He shut the refrigerator door and stood leaning against it, a tumbler in either hand. "Prue, take off your coat. It makes you look impermanent. Besides, it's probably damp. You mustn't catch a cold."

I thought this the most irrelevant observation, but I did as he said, unbuttoning the coat and taking it off and laying it over the back of a chair. He held out my drink and I went to take it from him. The glass was icily cold.

I said again, "I don't understand, Daniel."

"You can't understand unless you understand about Annabelle." He frowned. "Did you never meet her? When you were staying with Phoebe?"

"No, our paths never crossed. I suppose because she used to come down in the summer, and I was usually in Northumberland then, with my father."

"That would explain it."

"Were you in love with her?" I sounded cool, as if it were of no importance.

"No, I wasn't in love with her. Come to think of it, I didn't even like her very much. But there was something . . . amazing about Annabelle that rendered every other emotion meaningless. I was twenty and she was twenty-eight. Married and a mother. None of that mattered, either."

"But didn't people . . . talk? Surely Phoebe and Chips . . ."

"They knew, of course, but they imagined it was just a jolly flirtation. And Annabelle was clever. She played the field. There were always plenty of other men."

"She must have been very beautiful." It was hard to keep the wistful note from my voice, but I had never been described as "amazing" and knew that I never would be.

"No, she wasn't beautiful. But she was very tall and slender and she had a face like a Siamese cat, with a neat little nose and a long upper lip and a smile that was full of secrets. 'Enigmatic,' perhaps, the word is. Her eyes were astonishing. Enormous, slanted, a very dark grey."

"How did you meet her?"

"Phoebe and Chips carted me off to this party. I didn't want to go, but they said I had to, I'd been invited, and I'd get boring if I did nothing but work. And Annabelle was there. I saw her the moment I walked into the room. She was over on the far side, surrounded by other women's husbands. I saw that face and my fingers itched to draw her. I suppose I was staring, because she suddenly looked up, straight at me, as though she'd known all along that I was there. And I forgot about drawing her." He gave a rueful grin and shook his head. "It was like playing a game of rugger and then getting a great kick in the guts."

"That's never happened to me."

I hoped my timid attempt at levity would make him smile, but he didn't seem to hear it, for now he was pacing up and down the room with his glass in his hand as though it were physically impossible for him to talk and stand still at the same time.

"The next time we met, it was on the beach. I'd got a surfboard, a Malibu, from Australia. A friend had brought it for me from Sydney. There was a north wind that day, and the rollers were pouring in from miles out. I surfed until the tide changed, and when I came in, blue with cold because I couldn't afford a wet suit, I saw Annabelle sitting up on the dunes, watching me. I had no idea how long she'd been there. She wore a red skirt and her hair was loose and black and blowing in the wind. There wasn't anyone else on the beach that grey day, and I knew that she was waiting for me. So I climbed up to where she sat, and we talked and smoked her cigarettes, and the rushes all around us were flattened by the gale. I remember thinking that they looked like stroked fur. And later we walked home, and the golf links smelled of wild thyme. And a couple of men, golfers, passed us, and I saw them looking at Annabelle and then at me, and there was envy in their faces. It made me feel good. And that's the way it always was; going into a pub with her, or sitting beside her in the car, with the roof down and the sun on our faces. We'd stop at traffic lights, and people on the pavements would turn their heads, and stare, and smile."

"They were probably thinking what a good-looking couple you made."

"More likely asking themselves what a sensational creature like Annabelle was doing with a callow, gangling boy."

"How long did this go on for?"

"Two months. Three months. It was a very hot summer. She said it was too hot to take her little boy back to London. So she stayed at Penmarron. She was always there."

"Did she talk about her husband?"

"Leslie Collis? Not much. Rumour had it that she'd married him for his money, and she certainly didn't talk of him with much obvious affection. That didn't bother me. I didn't want to know about him. I didn't want to think about him. I didn't want to feel guilty. If you're really determined, it's quite possible to stuff an uneasy conscience out of sight. I'd never realised that I had that ability. It made things much easier."

"Perhaps, at twenty, that's the way you're meant to live life."

He smiled. "You sound old and wise. Like Phoebe."

"I wish I were."

He was still pacing, a caged tiger, up and down the charming, pretty room. He said, "It was about this time of the year, the middle of September. Only it wasn't raining like it is now. They went on and on, the sunshine and the warmth. So that I was taken unawares when Annabelle suddenly announced that she was going back to London. We were on the beach again. We'd been swimming. It was a flood tide, one late afternoon. The tide had come in over the warm sand, and the sea was the colour of jade and very warm. We were sitting having a cigarette, and she told me about going back to London, and I waited for utter desolation, and then realised that I wasn't desolate. In a funny way, I was relieved. I wanted it to stop now, while we were still having fun. I didn't want it to get stale. Besides, I knew that I had to get back to work. Painting has always been the most important thing in my life, and it had started tugging at me. I wanted to turn my back on everything else and concentrate on my painting, drown myself in it. My year with Chips was just about over. I wanted to travel, to learn. I planned to go to America.

"I started to say something trivial, but Annabelle interrupted me. It was then that she told me she was having a baby. She said, 'It's your child, Daniel.'

"You know, when I was young, growing up, I used to scare the pants off myself by imagining just such a situation. A girl, pregnant by me. A girl I didn't want to marry. Paternity suits, furious fathers, shotgun weddings. Nightmarish. And now it had happened, only it wasn't happening that way. She went on talking, and it gradually sank into my paralysed brain that she wanted nothing of me. She didn't want me to act as correspondent for a divorce; didn't want me to elope; didn't want me to marry her. She didn't want money.

"I felt there had to be a catch in it somewhere. Finally, when she stopped talking, I said, 'What about your husband?' and Annabelle laughed and said that he wouldn't ask any questions. I told her I couldn't believe this; no man would accept another man's child. But Annabelle said that Leslie Collis would, to save his own face and his pride; he hated more than anything else in the world to be made to look foolish. He minded what his colleagues thought of him, what people said about him. He'd built up for himself this hard-headed image, and he would let nothing destroy it. And then she looked at the expression on my face and she laughed again, and she said, 'Don't worry, Daniel, he won't come gunning for you.'

"I said, 'But it's my baby,' and she threw her cigarette away and pushed her hair out of her face and said, 'Oh, don't bother about the baby. It'll have a good home,' and she made it sound as though she were talking about a dog."

He was still now, the restless pacing stopped. He stood in the middle of the room, looking down into his glass. There was still some whisky left in the bottom, and with a quick movement of hand and head, he tipped the last of it down his throat. I hoped that he would not pour himself another. He seemed to me, in this frame of mind, a man happy to drink himself into oblivion. But he went and put the empty glass back on top of the refrigerator and then, noticing that it was now dark, moved to the window and drew the heavy curtains, shutting away the dismal night outside.

He turned to face me. "You're not saying anything."

"I can't think of anything intelligent to say."

"You're shocked."

"That's a ludicrous word to use. I'm in no position to be shocked. I'm in no position to take up any sort of attitude. But for your sake, I'm sorry it happened."

"I haven't told you everything yet. Do you want to hear the rest?"

"If you want me to hear."

"I think I do. I . . . . I haven't talked like this for years. I'm not sure if I could stop now, even if I wanted to."

"Have you never told anyone before?"

"Yes. I told Chips. At first I thought I wouldn't. I couldn't. For one thing, I was too ashamed. Leslie Collis wasn't the only man who hated to look foolish. But I was never much good at hiding my feelings, and after a couple of days of idiocy, shambling around Chips's studio and dropping things, he lost patience with me and came out with it, and said what the hell was the matter with me, anyway. So I told him then. I told him everything, and he never interrupted; never said a word. Just sat there in his saggy old chair, smoking his pipe and listening. And when I'd finished, got it off my chest, the relief was so great that I couldn't think why I hadn't told him straight away."

"What did he say?"

"He didn't say anything for a bit. Just went on smoking and gazing into space. Mulling things over. I didn't know what he was thinking. I half-expected to be told to go and pack my bags and never darken the doors of Holly Cottage again.

"But finally he knocked the ash out of his pipe and put it in his pocket and said, 'Young man, you are being taken for a ride.' And then he told me about Annabelle. He said that she had always been amoral, openly promiscuous. That summer was no exception. As for the baby, there was another man, a farmer from over Falmouth way, married and with a family of his own. In Chips's opinion, there was every likelihood that he was the father of Annabelle's baby. And Annabelle must know this.

"When he came out with this, I was in more of a quandary than ever. Half of me was relieved. But, as well, I felt cheated. My pride was badly bruised. I knew I was deceiving Leslie Collis, but it gave my newly found manhood a kick in the teeth to be told that Annabelle had been two-timing me. That sounds despicable, doesn't it?"

"No. It's understandable. But if it was true, why did she say the baby was *yours?*"

"I asked Chips that very question. And he told me that that had always been Annabelle's way. It was no fun creating havoc if she couldn't leave behind her a trail of guilt and remorse. Unbelievable, isn't it?"

"It sounds unbelievable to me. But if Chips said that, then it has to be true."

"I knew that, too. He went and saw Annabelle that very evening.

Had it out with her. He walked up to White Lodge and got Annabelle on his own. At first she tried to bluff it out, insisting that it could be nobody's child but mine. But then he faced her with what he had told me. About the other man. And when he came out with his name, Annabelle broke down and admitted that he was right. It wasn't necessarily my child. She just liked to think that it might be. I never saw her again. She went back to London a couple of days later, taking the little boy and his nanny with her. And Chips and I agreed that it was time that I went, too. I'd been marking time for far too long."

"Does Phoebe know about all this?"

"No. I didn't want her to know, and Chips agreed that it would be better if she didn't. Hopefully, there would be no repercussions, and there was no point in upsetting her or creating any sort of trouble with Mrs. Tolliver. Penmarron is a small village. They had to go on living there, both of them part of a fairly tight community."

"What a wise man Chips was."

"Wise. Understanding. I can't begin to describe to you his kindness to me at that time. Like the very best sort of father. He fixed everything for me, even lent me some money to see me through till I found my feet. He gave me letters of introduction to friends of his in New York, but most important, he sent me off with a letter of introduction to Peter Chastal in London. In those days the gallery had been going only for a couple of years, but he'd already earned something of a name for himself in the art world. I took a great folio of my work for him to look at, and by the time I left for America, he'd agreed to exhibit for me and act as my agent. And that's what he's done ever since."

I thought of the ecstatic review I had read on the train. "He's done well for you."

"Yes. I've been fortunate."

"Chips used to say it was no good having a talent if you didn't work at it."

"Chips used to say a lot of sound things."

"Was it working that kept you away for eleven years?"

"I like to think so. I don't like to think I was trying to escape from what had happened. But perhaps I was. Running. Further and further away. New York first, and then Arizona, and then San Francisco. It was while I was there that I first became interested in Japanese art. There's a big Japanese community in San Francisco, and I found myself involved with a group of young painters. The longer I worked with them, the more I realised how little I knew. The traditions and disciplines of Japanese painting go back for centuries. It fascinated me. So I went to Japan, and there I became a student again, sitting at the feet of a very old and famous man. Time ceased to have any meaning. I was there for four years. Sometimes it seemed like a few days. At others, eternity.

"This exhibition at Peter Chastal's is a direct result of those years. I told you I didn't want to come back for it. Opening days do genuinely terrify me. But as well, I was afraid of coming back to England. On the other side of the world it was possible not to think about Annabelle and the child that might be mine. But coming back . . . I had nightmares about being in London and seeing Annabelle and my child walking up the pavement towards me."

"Wasn't coming to Cornwall something of a risk?"

"It all seemed predestined. Meeting a stranger in a pub, being offered a lift. I very nearly didn't come, but I wanted so much to see Phoebe again."

I thought back to yesterday. I remembered how quietly he had sat at the bar downstairs while I chattered on about Mrs. Tolliver and Charlotte. "Daniel, when I told you Charlotte was here, at Penmarron, staying with her grandmother, you must have realised that she was the baby."

"Yes, I realised. And I knew, too, for sure, inevitably, that I was going to meet her. It was all part of some extraordinary pattern, out of my control. When we got to Phoebe's this afternoon and got out of the car and went into the house, I knew that Charlotte was around, somewhere. I knew even before Lily told us. And as I walked out of the house and down the hill and along the seawall to fetch them back for tea, I kept telling myself that after all these years of uncertainty, I was finally going to know.

"They didn't notice me coming. They were both far too engrossed in their work. And then Phoebe caught sight of me and said my name. And Charlotte looked up, too. And there was that little face. And I knew then that, without knowing it, Annabelle had told me the truth."

So that was it. I seemed to have been standing forever, listening to Daniel's voice. My back ached, and I felt drained and exhausted. I had no idea what hour it was. From downstairs, from the busy heart of the hotel, came sounds and smells. Voices, the distant clash of dishes, the thin strains of an orchestra playing something undemanding out of *The Sound Of Music*. Sometime I had to return to Holly Cottage, to Phoebe and the chicken casserole. But not yet.

I said, "If I don't sit down I shall die." And I went over to the fireplace and collapsed in one of the chintz-covered armchairs. All the time we had talked the little fake flames had licked cheerfully around the pretend logs. Now I sat back, with my chin buried in the collar of my sweater, and watched them flickering busily, getting nowhere.

I heard Daniel pour himself another drink. He brought it over and sat facing me in the other chair. I looked up, and our eyes met. We were both very solemn.

I smiled. "So now you've told me. And I don't know why you told me."

"I had to tell someone. And for some reason, you seem to be part of it all."

"No. I'm not part of it." It was about the only thing of which I was certain. Otherwise the situation in which Daniel now found himself seemed to have no solution. I thought about it for a bit and then went on. ". . . and I don't think that you're part of it, either. It's over, Daniel. Finished. Forgotten. Water under the bridge. You thought that Charlotte might be your child; now you know that she is. That's all that's changed. Charlotte is still Charlotte Collis, Leslie Collis's daughter, Mrs. Tolliver's granddaughter, and Phoebe's friend. Accept that and forget about everything else. Because there really is no alternative. The fact that you've discovered the truth is irrelevant. It alters nothing. Charlotte was never your responsibility and she isn't now. You have to think of her as a little girl you met on the seawall who happens to share your talent for drawing and whose face reminds you of your mother's."

He did not answer me at once. And then he said, "If that were all I had to come to terms with, it wouldn't be so bad."

"What do you mean, exactly?"

"I mean exactly what you observed in the train, and what Lily Tonkins, who is nobody's fool, instantly put her finger on. Charlotte not only has to wear spectacles, but she bites her fingernails, she is lonely, she is unhappy and apparently neglected."

I looked away from him, turning to the fire for diversion. If it had been a proper one, I could have filled in the difficult moment by some small business with a poker or a fresh log. As it was, I found myself at a loss. I knew, and Phoebe knew and Lily Tonkins knew, that everything Daniel had just said was in all probability true. But to agree with him now could do no good for Charlotte and would only make the situation even more difficult for Daniel to accept.

I sighed, searching for words. "You mustn't take everything that Lily says quite literally. She's always been inclined to overdramatize things. And you know, little girls of Charlotte's age aren't always very easy to understand. They become secretive and withdrawn. As well, I think she's rather a shy child . . ."

I looked up and met his gaze again. I smiled, making my face cheerful and matter-of-fact. ". . . And let's face it, Mrs. Tolliver would never win a competition for the world's coziest granny. That's why Charlotte's so fond of Phoebe. And anyway, I don't suppose she's having a bad time staying at White Lodge. I know there are no other children to play with, but that's because all the other children in the village are back at school. And despite what Lily said, I'm sure Betty Curnow spends a bit of time with her and is kind. You mustn't let things exaggerate themselves in your mind. Besides, tomorrow we're taking her out for a picnic. You haven't forgotten that, have you? You said you'd take us to Penjizal and show us the seals . . . you can't back out now."

"No. I won't back out."

"I understand why you were reluctant to come with us. It won't be very easy for you."

He shook his head. "I don't see that a single day is going to make much difference, one way or another, taken in the context of two separate lifetimes."

I tried to work this out. "I don't know what that means, but I'm sure you're right."

He laughed. Downstairs the orchestra had switched from *The Sound Of Music* to *The Pirates of Penzance*. I could smell delicious food.

I said, "Come back with me. To Holly Cottage. Phoebe would love it so much. We'll eat Lily's casserole, the way we planned. She's cooked enough to feed an army."

But he said that he would not come.

I looked at the empty whisky glass on the floor between his feet.

"You promise me you won't sit here all evening and drink yourself into a coma?"

He shook his head. "How little you know me. How little we know each other. I don't drink that way. I never have."

"But you'll get something to eat? You'll have dinner?"

"Yes. Later. I'll go downstairs."

"Well, if you won't come, then I must go on my own. Phoebe will think I've forgotten about her or crashed the car or something ghastly."

I got out of my chair and so did Daniel. We stood, like people at a formal party when it is time to leave.

"Good night, Daniel."

He put his hands on my shoulders and stooped to kiss my cheek. When he had done this, I stood for a long moment, looking up into his face. I put my arms around his neck and drew his head down to mine and kissed his mouth. I felt his arms come around me, felt myself held so close that I could feel the beating of his heart through the thick, rough wool of his sweater.

"Oh, Prue."

I laid my cheek against his shoulder. Felt his lips caress the top of my head. It was the most gentle of embraces, without passion, without apparent significance. So why did I suddenly feel this way, aching with a need I had never known before, my legs weak, my eyes burning with ridiculous, unshed tears? Could loving a person happen so suddenly? Like a rocket, fired into a dark sky, exploding into infinity and carrying with it a trail of shimmering, many coloured stars.

We stood silent, holding each other, like children clinging for comfort. It didn't seem to matter about not talking. Then Daniel said, "That house in Greece. I don't want you to think I didn't mean it when I asked you to come and visit me."

"Are you asking me to come with you now?"

"No."

I drew away from him and looked up into his face. He told me, "I can't go on running away from the inside of my own head. Maybe someday, sometime." He kissed me again, briskly this time, becoming practical, glancing at his wristwatch. "You must go. The casserole will be burned to nothing and Phoebe will think I've ravished you." He fetched my coat from the chair and held it out for me, and I put my arms into the sleeves, and he turned me around and did up all the buttons down the front.

"I'll come downstairs with you." He went to open the door, and we walked together, side by side, down the long corridor towards the head of the stairs. We passed rows of closed bedroom doors behind which people we had never known had loved and honeymooned and holidayed and laughed, and quarrelled and made up the quarrels with laughter.

The foyer, when we reached the foot of the stairs, now presented its most festive face. Guests emerged from the bar or made their way towards the restaurant or sat around those same little tables with cocktails before them and dishes of nuts. The hum of conversation, raised in order to be audible above the sound of the orchestra, was considerable. The men wore black ties and velvet dinner jackets, and the ladies were in evening skirts or sequinned caftans.

We walked through it all, causing a slight stir with our unexpected appearance, like ghosts at a feast. Conversations faltered as we walked by; eyebrows once more were raised. We reached the main door and were turned out into the darkness and the night. It had stopped raining at last, but there was still a wind keening through the high branches of trees.

Daniel looked up at the sky. "How will it be tomorrow?"

"Fine, perhaps. The wind may blow all the bad weather away."

We came to the car. He opened the door for me. "When shall I meet you?"

"About eleven. I'll come for you, if you want."

"No. I'll get a lift over to Penmarron or catch a bus or something. But I'll be there, so don't go without me."

"We have to have you there, to show us the way."

I got into the car, behind the wheel.

He said, "I'm sorry about this evening."

"I'm glad you told me."

"I'm glad, too. Thank you for listening."

"Good night, Daniel."

"Good night."

He slammed the door shut, and I started the engine and set off down the curving drive, following the beam of the headlights; away from him. I do not know how long he stood there after I had gone.

6

WE TALKED THAT EVENING, Phoebe and I, far into the night. We indulged in memories, recalling the days when Chips was alive. We went even further back, to Northumberland, to Windyedge, where Phoebe had spent her childhood, running wild and riding her shaggy pony along the margins of those cold and northern beaches. We spoke of my father, and the contentment he had found with his new wife, and she remembered expeditions when they were all children together, to Dunstanbrugh and Bambrugh, and midwinter meets, with the pink coats of the huntsmen bright as berries in the frosty air and the foxhounds streaming across the snow-streaked fields.

We talked about Paris, where she had been a student, and the little house in the Dordogne she and Chips had bought one affluent year and to which she still returned for annual painting trips.

We talked about Marcus Bernstein, my job, my little flat in Islington.

"Next time I come to London, I shall come and stay with you," she promised.

"I haven't got a spare room."

"Then I shall sleep on the floor."

She told me about the new Society of Arts that had just been formed in Porthkerris and of which she was a founding member. She described for me the house of an old and famous potter, who had returned to Porthkerris to spend his final years in the warren of narrow streets where he had been born eighty years before, the son of a fisherman.

We talked about Lewis Falcon.

But we did not speak of Daniel. As though we had made some secret agreement, neither Phoebe nor I mentioned his name.

Past midnight she went at last to bed. I followed her up the stairs to draw her curtains and turn down the quilt and help her off with her more awkward clothes. I took a hot-water bottle downstairs and filled it from the boiling kettle and finally left her, warm in her huge and downy bed, reading her book.

We said good night, but I did not go to bed. My mind was seething, as alert and restless as if I had pumped myself with some enormously stimulating drug. I could not face lying in the darkness, waiting for sleep that I knew would not come. So I returned to the kitchen and made a mug of coffee and took it back to the fireside. The flames had died to a bed of grey ash, so I threw on more logs and watched them kindle and flare, and then curled myself up into Chips's old armchair. Its battered depths were comforting, and I thought about him and longed for his presence. I did not want him dead; I wanted him alive, here, in this room with me. We had always been very close, and now I needed him. I needed his counsel.

Like the very best sort of father. I thought of Chips, his pipe in his mouth, listening as the young Daniel told him about Annabelle Tolliver and the baby. Annabelle, with her dark hair and her cat face and her grey eyes and her secret smile.

It's your child, Daniel.

There were other voices. Lily Tonkins. *Mrs. Tolliver can't be bothered to look after the child, then she should pay some other person to do the job.* Lily shrill with indignation, beating out her resentment on a bowl of batter.

And my mother, exasperated because I would not conform to the pattern that she had endeavoured all her life to cut for me.

Honestly, Prue, I don't know what you're looking for.

I had told her that I wasn't looking for anything. But there was a word—"serendipity." It was such an odd, strange-sounding word that I had once looked it up in a dictionary.

serendipity *n:* faculty of making happy discoveries by accident

I had discovered. Daniel. Watched him walking from the little railway station, along the old seawall, towards me, into my life. This evening, "How little we know each other," he had said, and up to a point, that was true. A day. Two days. Too short, one would have said, to achieve anything but the most superficial relationship.

But this was different. For me time and events had become miraculously encapsulated, so that I felt as though I had lived an entire lifetime with him in the course of the past twenty-four hours. It was hard to realise that I had not known him forever, that our two separate existences were not already spun together, like strands in a single skein of wool.

I wanted it to go on being this way. I was prepared to let him go his way, as Phoebe had let him go. I was wise enough for that. But I did not want to lose him. And I knew that the odds were against me. Partly because Daniel was the man that he was—an artist, restless, seeking, he would always need to be free. But infinitely more formidable was the memory of Annabelle, the existence of Charlotte.

Charlotte. Who knew what traumas Charlotte had suffered, foisted upon a man who was not her father and who must surely know that he was not her father. I had taken an instant dislike to him during those brief moments I had seen him on the train, watched his impatience with the little girl and recognised a total lack of affection as he thrust the ten-pound note into her hand, as though he were paying off some tiresome debt.

And Annabelle. So much unhappiness to answer for. *It was no fun creating havoc if she couldn't leave behind her a trail of guilt and remorse.* She had done that, all right, with her wayward passions, destructive as a hurricane. Now the hurricane seemed to have blown up again, and I was afraid because I could see it tearing Daniel and me apart forever.

I can't go on running away from the inside of my own head.

I thought of the house in Greece, the sugar-cube house above the sea, with the whitewashed terrace and the bright geraniums. A scrap of poetry, half-learned, half-forgotten, flew like a ghost through the back of my mind.

Oh, love, we two shall go no more to lands of summer beyond the seas.

From the mantelpiece, Phoebe's clock chimed a single, silvery note. One o'clock. I laid down the empty coffee mug and with an effort pulled myself from the deep comfort of Chips's armchair. Still not sleepy, I went over to Phoebe's radio and fiddled with knobs, searching for some early-hour music. I found a recorded programme of classic pop, recognised a tune that dated back to the years of my growing up.

God bless you,
You made me feel brand new
For God blessed me with you.

The toy carousel still stood on the table where Charlotte had played with it. It had never been put back in its cupboard, and now I went to do this, for fear that dust should seep into its ancient mechanism and cause it to grind to a final halt. I couldn't bear to think of it broken, forgotten, never played with again.

I simply don't know which is my favourite . . .

I wound the handle and gently released the lever. Slowly, sedately, the brightly painted animals revolved, their tinselly bridles sparkling in the light from the fire, like decorations on a Christmas tree.

Without you,
Life has no meaning or rhyme
Like notes to a song out of time.

There was always tomorrow. I could not be sure whether I dreaded the day we had planned or looked forward to it. There seemed to be too much at stake. I only knew that we would go, the three of us, to Penjizal and look for the seals. Beyond tomorrow I could not imagine, simply hope that some good would come of our being together. For Daniel's sake. For Charlotte. And, selfishly, for myself.

The mechanism ran down; the turntable slowly came to a halt. I stooped and lifted the carousel off the table and put it away in its cupboard; closed the doors, turned the key. I put the guard in front of the fire, switched off the radio, turned off the light. In the darkness, I went upstairs.

I awoke early, at seven, to the sound of a big old herring gull screaming at the new day from the roof of Chips's studio. My drawn curtains framed a sky of the palest blue veiled in a haze reminiscent of the hottest days of summer. There was no wind, no sound but the cry of the gull and the whisper of an incoming tide, trickling to fill the gullies and sand pools of the estuary. When I got up and went to the window, it was very cold, almost as though there had been a frost. I smelt the seaweed, tarry rope, and the clean saltiness of fresh seawater surging in from the ocean. It was a day made to order for a picnic.

I dressed and went downstairs and made coffee for myself and breakfast for Phoebe. When I took this up to her, I found her already awake and sitting up against the pillows, not reading but simply gazing with pleasure as the warmth of the sun on that perfect autumn morning burned away the last of the mist.

I put the breakfast tray on her knees.

"These are the sort of mornings," she said without preamble, "that I'm certain one remembers when one is very, very old. Good morning, my darling." We kissed. "What a day for a picnic."

"Come with us, Phoebe."

She was tempted. "It depends where you're going."

"Daniel's going to show us the way to Penjizal. He said something about a tidal rock pool where the seals come and swim."

"Oh, it's so beautiful! You'll be enchanted. But no, I think I'd better not come. The path down the cliffs is a little too precipitous for a person with only one arm. It would be too tiresome for you if I lost my balance and went flying over the cliff into the sea." She went into gales of her usual laughter at the very idea. "But the walk down from the farmhouse at the top is magical. There are wild fuchsias everywhere, and in summertime the valley is humming with dragonflies. What are you going to take with you to eat? Ham sandwiches? Have we got any ham? What a pity you can't make cold casserole sandwiches, there's so much left over from last night. I wonder if Daniel got in touch with Lewis Falcon. I've heard that he's got the most beautiful wild garden out there at Lanyon . . ."

She chattered on, her conversation, as always with Phoebe, darting from one intriguing subject to the next. It was tempting to forget about the day ahead; to lose all sense of time and simply to settle down to spending the rest of the morning sitting there on the end of Phoebe's downy bed. But, with the coffee pot empty and the sun's rays shining obliquely through the open window, I heard from downstairs the slamming of the kitchen door and knew that Lily Tonkins had arrived on her bicycle.

I looked at Phoebe's clock. "Heavens, it's past nine o'clock. I must get moving." I climbed reluctantly off the bed and started to gather up cups and plates, stacking them on Phoebe's tray.

"So must I."

"Oh, don't get up. Stay there for another hour or so. Lily likes it when you do that. She can get on with her polishing without having to shunt you around all the time."

"I'll see," said Phoebe, but as I went out the door, I saw her reach for her book. She was reading C. P. Snow, and I envied her her warm bed and that wonderful sonorous prose and guessed that it would be midday at least before she put in an appearance downstairs.

In the kitchen I found Lily tying on her apron.

"Hello, Prue, how are you this morning? Lovely, isn't it? Ernest said last night, this was what was going to happen. He said that wind was going to blow the dirty weather away. And coming down the road from the church, you'd think it was warm as June. Had a good mind not to come in to work today; just go down to the beach and put my feet in the tide."

From the hall, the telephone began to ring.

"Now," said Lily, as she invariably did when this happened, "who can that be?"

"I'll go," I said.

I went back to the hall and sat on the old carved chest where the telephone lived and picked up the receiver.

"Hello."

"Phoebe?" A woman's voice.

"No. This is Prue."

"Oh, Prue. This is Mrs. Tolliver. Is Phoebe there?"

"I'm afraid she's still in bed."

I expected her to apologise for the early call and to say that she would ring back later. But instead she persisted. "I must speak to her. Can she come to the telephone?" And there was an urgency to her voice, an unsteadiness, that filled me with nameless apprehension.

"Is anything wrong?"

"No. Yes. Prue—I have to talk to her."

"I'll get her." I laid down the receiver and went upstairs. As I put my head around Phoebe's door, she looked up placidly from her book.

"That's Mrs. Tolliver on the telephone. She wants to speak to you." I added, "She sounds very odd. Upset."

Phoebe frowned. "What's it about?" She laid down her book.

"I don't know." But my imagination had already scurried ahead. "Perhaps it's something to do with Charlotte."

Not hesitating any longer, Phoebe pushed back her covers and got out of bed. I helped her into her dressing gown, putting her good arm into the sleeve and wrapping the rest of its voluminous folds around her like a cape. I found her slippers. Her thick hair still lay in a plait over one shoulder, and her reading spectacles had slipped down her nose. She led the way down to the hall, sat where I had sat, picked up the receiver.

"Yes?"

The call was obviously important, and, possibly, private. Perhaps, realising this, I should have taken myself off out of earshot to the kitchen. But Phoebe sent me a glance that beseeched me to stay at hand, as though she expected to need my moral support, so halfway down the stairs, I sat, too, watching her through the bannister rails.

"Phoebe?" Mrs. Tolliver's voice was clearly audible from where I perched. "I'm sorry I had to get you out of bed, but I have to speak to you."

"Yes."

"I have to see you."

Phoebe looked a little nonplussed. "What, right away?"

"Yes. Now. Please. I . . . I think I need your advice."

"I hope Charlotte's all right?"

"Yes. Yes, she's all right. But please come. I . . . I really want to speak to you very urgently."

"I shall have to get dressed."

"Just come as soon as you can. I shall expect you." And before Phoebe could raise any objections, she had rung off.

Phoebe was left sitting there, holding the humming receiver. We looked at each other blankly, and I could tell by her face that she felt just as apprehensive as I did.

"Did you hear all that?"

"Yes."

Phoebe thoughtfully replaced the receiver, and the humming sound ceased.

"What on earth can be wrong? She sounds quite demented."

From the kitchen we could hear Lily wielding the floor polisher and singing hymns. This was a sure sign that she was feeling on top of the world.

"Guard us, oh, thou Gre-hate Je-he-hovah . . ."

Phoebe stood up. "I'll have to go."

"I'll drive you in the car."

"You'd better help me get dressed first."

Back in her bedroom, she took from cupboards and drawers a selection of garments even more haphazard than usual. When she was ready, she sat at her dressing table, and I did her hair, replaiting it and winding it up into a knob at the back of her head, and holding it while she skewered it into place with her old-fashioned tortoiseshell pins.

I knelt to lace up her shoes. This done, "You go and get the car out," she told me. "I'll be down in a moment."

I found my coat and pulled it on and let myself out of the house. The pearly, brilliant morning shimmered all about me. I opened the garage and persuaded the old car to start. I had backed it out of the garage and was waiting by the front door when Phoebe appeared. She had put on one of her largest and most dashing hats, and, for warmth, had draped across her shoulders a brilliant poncho of wool, doubtless woven by some Middle Eastern peasant. Her spectacles were sliding down her nose; her hair, fresh from my inexpert hands, already looked as though it was about to collapse. None of this mattered. What did matter was that for once in her life she did not have a smile on her face, and this alone was enough to make me angry with Mrs. Tolliver.

She bundled herself into the seat beside me and we set off.

"What I can't understand," said Phoebe, giving her hat a tug to settle it even further down on her head, "is why me? I'm no particular friend of Mrs. Tolliver's. She's far more intimate with those nice ladies she plays bridge with. Perhaps it is something to do with Charlotte. She knows how fond I am of the child. That's it. It must be—" She stopped, abruptly. "Prue, why are we going so slowly? You're still in second gear." I changed up to third, and we continued our journey at a slightly increased speed. "We're meant to be in a hurry."

"I know," I said. "But I want to tell you something and I don't want to get to Mrs. Tolliver's before I've finished."

"What are you going to tell me?"

"It may have nothing to do with what she's going to talk about. But, on the other hand, I have an uncomfortable feeling that it has. I don't know whether I ought to say anything. But whether I ought to or not, I'm going to."

Phoebe sighed deeply. "It's about Charlotte, isn't it?"

"Yes. Daniel's her father."

Phoebe's worn hands stayed where they were, quietly clasped in her lap. "Did he tell you so?"

"Yes. He told me yesterday."

"You could have said something last night."

"He didn't ask me to."

We were moving so slowly that I had to change down again as the car ground on up the slight slope towards the church.

"So they did have an affair, he and Annabelle."

"Yes. You see, it wasn't just a little flingette after all. At the end of that summer, Annabelle told Daniel she was having his baby. And Daniel confided in Chips. And Chips pointed out that it wasn't necessarily Daniel's baby; it could easily be some other man's. And Chips confronted Annabelle with this, and she finally admitted to him that she couldn't be sure whose child it was."

"I always wondered why Daniel went off so precipitately to America. I mean, he'd been talking about it all summer, and I knew he planned to go. But all at once he was going. And then he'd gone."

"And didn't come back for eleven years."

"When did he realise she was his child?"

"As soon as he set eyes on her, sitting there on the seawall trying to finish her picture in the rain."

"*How* did he know?"

"Apparently she looks just the way his mother looked as a little girl."

"So there's no doubt."

"No. Not in Daniel's mind. No doubt."

Phoebe fell silent. Presently she sighed again, a long, troubled sigh. She said inadequately, "Oh, dear."

"I'm sorry, Phoebe. It's not a very nice thing to have to tell anyone."

"Perhaps in a strange way I already knew. I always had such a close relationship with Charlotte, just as I used to have with you. Just as I used to have with Daniel. And there were little things about her . . . mannerisms . . . that were strangely familiar. The way she holds a pencil, with her fingers all bunched up around it. Daniel holds a pencil that way."

"Chips never said anything to you?"

"Not a word."

"Perhaps I shouldn't have, either. But if you're going to be faced by some appalling revelation from Mrs. Tolliver, it's as well to have a few facts at your fingertips."

"I've got those all right. What a proper turn-up for the books." She added, without much hope, "Perhaps it's just going to be about the Women's Institute tea. And then your bombshell will have been all for nothing."

"It's not my bombshell. And if I hadn't told you, Daniel would have. And you know as well as I do that this isn't going to be about the Women's Institute tea."

There was no time for more. Even driving at my deliberate snail's pace, we had already covered the short distance between Holly Cottage and White Lodge. Here were the gates, the neatly kept drive, the gravel sweep in front of the formal house. But today the front door stood open, and as we drew up at the foot of the steps, Mrs. Tolliver came through the door and down the steps towards us. I wondered if she had been waiting for us just inside the hall, sitting on one of those ugly, uncomfortable chairs that are not meant to be used for sitting on but other purposes, like dumping overcoats and leaving parcels.

There was nothing outwardly dishevelled about her. I saw the usual well-cut skirt, the simple shirt, a cardigan of deep coral, the good pearls around her throat and set in the lobes of her ears, the well-coiffed grey hair.

But the inner turmoil was all too evident. She appeared distraught, her face blotched as though recently she had actually been crying.

Phoebe opened the door of the car.

"Phoebe, how good of you . . . how very good of you to come." She stooped to help Phoebe out and caught sight of me sitting behind the driving wheel. I smiled weakly.

"Prue had to come," said Phoebe briskly. "To drive me. You don't mind if she comes in, too, do you?"

"Oh . . ." Mrs. Tolliver obviously did mind, but it was a good indication of her immediate distress that this single word was as far as her objection went. "No. No, of course not."

I didn't want to go in in the very least. In the course of the last two days I'd had enough of the Tollivers, but Phoebe obviously wanted me with her, so trying to appear both disinterested and colourless, I too got out of the car and followed the two women up the stone steps and into the house.

The hall was flagged in stone, scattered with Persian rugs of great antiquity. A graceful staircase with a wrought-iron bannister curved to the upper floors. I closed the front door behind me, and Mrs. Tolliver led us across the hall and into her drawing room. She waited as we passed through the door and then closed it firmly, as though wary of possible eavesdroppers.

It was a large and formally furnished room, with long sash windows facing out onto the garden. The morning sun had not yet penetrated these windows, and the atmosphere was chilly. Mrs. Tolliver gave a shiver.

"It's cold. I hope you're not cold . . . so early . . ." Her instincts as a hostess rose to the surface. "Perhaps . . . light a fire . . . ?"

"I'm not in the least cold," said Phoebe. She chose a chair and sat firmly down in it, still bundled in her garish poncho and with her solid legs crossed at the ankle, like royalty. "Now, my dear. What is this about?"

Mrs. Tolliver crossed to the empty fireplace and stood there, supporting herself with a hand laid along the edge of the mantelpiece.

"I . . . I really don't know where to begin . . ."

"Try the beginning."

"Well." She took a deep breath. "You know the reason Charlotte is with me?"

"Yes. The boiler at her school blew up."

"That, of course. But the real reason is that her mother—Annabelle—is in Majorca. That was why there was nobody to take care of her at home. Well . . . I had a telephone call last night, at about half past nine . . ."

She took her hand from the mantelpiece and felt up her cuff and produced a tiny, lace-edged handkerchief. As she went on talking, she played with this, looking to me as though she were trying to tear it to pieces.

"It was my son-in-law, Leslie Collis. Annabelle has left him. She's not coming back. She's with this man. He's a riding instructor. South African. She's going back to South Africa with him."

The enormity of her statement silenced the lot of us. I was thankful that I was expected to say nothing, but I looked at Phoebe. She sat unmoving, and I could not see the expression on her face, because it was obliterated by the brim of her hat.

At last, "I am so sorry," she said, and there was a whole world of sympathy in her voice.

"But you see, that isn't the end of it. I . . . I really don't know how I'm going to tell you."

"I imagine," said Phoebe, "that it's got something to do with Charlotte."

"He says that Charlotte is not his child. Apparently he always knew this, but he accepted her for Michael's sake, because he wanted to keep his home together. But he's never liked the child. I always knew that he never had any time for her, though of course I had no idea exactly why. It used to distress me when I stayed with them. He was so impatient with her, sometimes it seemed as though she could do nothing right."

"Did you say anything?"

"I didn't want to make trouble."

"She's always seemed to me to be rather a lonely little girl."

"Yes. Lonely. She never fit in. And she was never pretty and engaging, the way Annabelle used to be. I don't want you to think that Leslie was *unkind* to her. It was just that all his time and affection seemed to be centred on Michael . . . and there wasn't enough left over for Charlotte."

"What about her mother?"

Mrs. Tolliver gave an indulgent little laugh. "I'm afraid that Annabelle was never very maternal. Like me. I was never very maternal, either. But when Annabelle was a child, things were easier. My husband was alive then, and we were able to afford a nanny for Annabelle. I had help in the house as well. Things were easier."

"Did your son-in-law know that Annabelle was having an affair with this man . . . the riding instructor?"

Mrs. Tolliver looked embarrassed, as though Phoebe had deliberately offended her. She looked away, toying with a china shepherdess that stood upon the mantelpiece. "I . . . I didn't ask him that. But . . . you know Annabelle, Phoebe. She was always . . ."

She hesitated, and I waited with interest. How does a mother describe her only daughter who is, by all accounts, a nymphomaniac?

". . . attractive. Full of life. Leslie was in London all the time. They didn't see a great deal of each other."

"So he didn't know," said Phoebe bluntly. "Or perhaps he just suspected."

"Yes. Perhaps he just suspected."

"Well," said Phoebe, coming to the point. "So what is now going to happen to Charlotte?"

Mrs. Tolliver set the china figure down neatly, exactly, in its customary position. She looked back at Phoebe and her mouth was trembling, but whether with incipient tears or indignation, I could not tell.

"He doesn't want Charlotte back. He said that she's not his child and she's never been his child, and now that Annabelle has left him, he intends washing his hands of Charlotte."

"But he can't do that," said Phoebe, her hackles rising at the very suggestion of such behaviour.

"I don't know whether he can or not. I don't know what to do."

"Then she must be with her mother. Annabelle must take her to South Africa."

"I . . . I don't think that Annabelle will want her."

The enormity of this silenced both Phoebe and myself. We stared, unbelieving, at Mrs. Tolliver, and a flush crept up her neck.

At last Phoebe said bluntly, "You mean that Charlotte would get in Annabelle's way."

"I don't know. Annabelle . . ." I waited for her to tell us next that Annabelle had no more fondness for Charlotte than Leslie Collis had. But Mrs. Tolliver could not bring herself to come out with this. "I don't know what I'm trying to say. I feel torn in all directions. I'm sorry for the child —but, Phoebe, I cannot have her here. I'm too old. This isn't a house for a child. I haven't got a nursery, I haven't even got any toys. Annabelle's dollhouse went years ago, and I gave all her children's books to the hospital."

I thought, *No wonder Charlotte loved the carousel.*

"And I have a life of my own. My own commitments, my friends. It isn't as though she seems particularly happy here. She mopes around most of the time, without saying or doing anything. I admit, I find her difficult. And Betty Curnow only comes in in the mornings. It isn't as though I have good help. I . . . I don't know which way to turn. I'm at my wit's end."

Tears had never been far away. Now, at the end of her tether, she lost control. The tears of older women are ugly. Perhaps ashamed of them or wishing to spare us embarrassment, she turned from the fireplace and took herself over to the long window, where she stood, her back to us, as though admiring her own garden. There came the sound of painful sobs.

I knew that I was very much in the way and longed for escape. I looked beseechingly in Phoebe's direction and caught her eye.

Phoebe said instantly, "You know, I think a nice hot cup of coffee would do us all good."

Mrs. Tolliver did not turn, but presently in a choked voice she said pathetically, "There's no one to get it. I sent Betty Curnow and Charlotte up to the village. Charlotte wanted to buy some Coca-Cola. We've . . . we've run out. And it seemed a good excuse to get her out of the house. I didn't want her here while I spoke to you . . ."

I said, "I can get coffee."

Mrs. Tolliver blew her nose. This seemed to help a bit. Slightly recovered, she looked at me over her shoulder. Her face was blurred and swollen. "You won't know where to find anything."

"I can look. If you don't mind me going into your kitchen."

"No. Not at all. How kind . . ."

I left them. Let myself quietly out of the drawing room and shut the door and leaned against it, like people do in films. I couldn't like Mrs. Tolliver, but it was impossible not to feel dreadfully sorry for her. Her well-organised existence seemed to be collapsing about her head. Annabelle was, after all, her only child. Now Annabelle's marriage had come to pieces and she was off with her new love to the other end of the world, abandoning both her children and all her responsibilities.

And yet I knew that the bitterest blow of all to the pride of a woman like Mrs. Tolliver was the shaming revelation that Charlotte was not Leslie Collis's child but the unfortunate result of one of Annabelle's many love affairs.

I wondered if she had any idea which love affair it was. For all our sakes, I hoped not.

And Charlotte. *That little face.* I couldn't think about Charlotte. I pulled myself away from the door and went in search of Mrs. Tolliver's kitchen.

By a process of trial and error, opening cupboard doors and pulling out random drawers, I finally assimilated a tray, cups and saucers, a sugar bowl, some spoons. I filled the electric kettle and found a jar of instant coffee. I decided that we could do without biscuits. When the kettle had boiled, I filled the three cups and carried the tray back to the drawing room.

They were still at it, but Mrs. Tolliver, in my absence, seemed to have stopped crying and pulled herself together. Now she sat in a wide-lapped Victorian chair, facing Phoebe.

". . . Perhaps," Phoebe was saying, "your son-in-law will have second thoughts about Charlotte. After all, she has a brother, and it's always been considered very wrong to split up families."

"But Michael is so much older than Charlotte. So much more mature. I don't believe they've ever had very much in common . . ."

She looked up as I appeared through the door, and at once a polite smile turned up the corners of her mouth. She was a lady to whom social graces came automatically, even in times of stress.

"How kind, Prue. So clever." I set down the tray on a low stool. "Oh," a small frown creased her brow. "You've used the best teacups."

"I'm sorry. They were the first I found."

"Oh. Well, never mind. It won't matter for once."

I handed Phoebe her coffee. She took it and stirred it thoughtfully. I sat down, too, and for a moment there was silence, broken only by the tinkling of stirring teaspoons, as though we were gathered together for an enjoyable occasion.

Phoebe broke this silence. "In my opinion," she said, "I think there can be no question of Charlotte returning home. At least until things have simmered down and your son-in-law has had time to sort himself out."

"But her school."

"Don't send her back to that school. I don't like the sound of it, with the boiler blowing that way. It must be very inefficiently administrated. She's far too young for boarding school, anyway, and there can be no point in her returning there if her home life is in pieces. Enough to give any child a nervous breakdown." She sat with her cup and saucer in her lap and looked long and hard at Mrs. Tolliver. "You have to be very careful. You don't want the responsibility of Charlotte, and I can understand that, but for the moment, as far as I can see, you've got it. A life in your hands. A young, sensitive life. She is going to be hurt enough when she knows about her mother. Let us all see that she is not hurt any more than she has to be."

Mrs. Tolliver started to say something, but Phoebe, with unusual bluntness, overrode her.

"I said, I understand your situation. Things are going to be very difficult. For that reason I think it would be much better if you were here on your own, without Charlotte around the place, listening to talk and possibly overhearing telephone calls which she should not. She's an intelligent child, and she'll know instinctively that something is wrong. So I suggest that you simply tell her she's coming to live with me for a little while."

Oh, darling Phoebe. Oh, blessed Phoebe.

"I know I'm a bit of a crock just now, but Prue's with me for another ten days and Lily Tonkins is always a tower of strength in times of emergency."

"But, Phoebe, that's too much."

"I'm very fond of Charlotte. We shall get along very well."

"I know that. And I know that she is devoted to you. But . . . oh, don't think I'm not grateful . . . it will seem so strange to everybody. Leaving me, her grandmother, and coming to stay with you. What will people think? What will they say? This is a small village, and you know both Lily Tonkins and Betty Curnow will talk."

"Yes, they will talk. People always talk. But all the talk in the world is better than having that child hurt any more. Besides," Phoebe said as she set down her empty coffee cup, "we've both got broad shoulders, and," she gave a little chuckle, "let's face it, surely we're getting a bit long in the tooth for a scrap of gossip to bother us. So what do you say?"

Mrs. Tolliver, with obvious relief, finally succumbed.

"I don't mind admitting it would make things very, very much easier for me."

"Will you be in touch with your son-in-law again?"

"Yes. I said I would ring him up tonight. Yesterday evening we were both of us getting a little too emotional. I think he'd probably had far too much to drink. Not that I blame him for that, but neither of us was making much sense."

"In that case you can tell him that Charlotte's coming to stay at Holly Cottage for a little. And you can tell him as well that she's not going back to that boarding school. Perhaps we could get her into the local school here. You could talk it over with him."

"Yes. Yes, I'll do that."

"That's settled, then." Phoebe stood up. "Now Charlotte has already arranged to come to Holly Cottage this morning. Prue is taking her on a picnic. Pack a bag and let her bring that with her. But don't say anything to the child about her mother."

"But she'll have to be told."

"You are family, far too close, too involved. I shall tell her."

For a moment I thought that Mrs. Tolliver was going to object to this. She took a breath to say something but then met Phoebe's eye and didn't say it after all.

"Very well, Phoebe."

"It will be easier if I tell her. For all of us."

At the same snail's pace we trundled homewards. Down the drive of White Lodge, through the gates, past the oak copse. We turned the corner by the church, and the road to home sloped down and away from us, and we could see the whole long blue lake that was the estuary, the floodwaters dazzling with sun pennies.

"Prue, stop the car for a moment."

I did as she said, drawing the car in to the side of the road and switching off the engine. For a little we sat like two aimless tourists, gazing at the familiar view as though we had never seen it before. On the far shore, the gentle hills, patchworked in small fields, drowsed in the morning's warmth. A red tractor, minimised by distance to toy size, was out ploughing, drawing in its wake a flock of screaming white gulls.

At the end of the road, in the lee of the shore, Holly Cottage waited for us, hidden beyond the crest of the hill, slumbering in the sheltered sunshine. But here on the brow of the slope, the sea breezes were never still. Now the thin wind flattened the pale grasses in the roadside ditches and blew the first of the leaves from the topmost branches of the trees that bordered the ancient churchyard.

"So peaceful," said Phoebe, sounding as though she were thinking aloud. "You'd think that here, the end of the world, you'd be safe. I thought so, when I first came to live here with Chips. I thought I'd escaped. But there is no way you can escape reality. Cruelty, indifference, selfishness."

"All those things are part of people, and people are everywhere."

"Destroying." Phoebe thought this over for a bit, and then said in a changed voice, "Poor woman."

"Mrs. Tolliver. Yes, I'm sorry for her, too. But still, I wonder why she chose to confide in *you.*"

"Oh, my dear, it's obvious. She knows I'm an old sinner. She'll never forget that Chips and I lived in happy sin for years. She could talk to me, where she could never have confided in her other friends. Colonel Danby's wife, or the bank manager's widow from Porthkerris—they'd have been appalled. And, of course, what's hurting most of all is her pride."

"I thought that, too. But you were marvellous. You always are marvellous, but this morning you were more marvellous than usual."

"I don't know about that."

"I just hope you haven't bitten off more than you can chew. Supposing Leslie Collis really does refuse to have anything more to do with Charlotte; you'll be landed with her indefinitely."

"I wouldn't mind."

"But Phoebe . . ." I stopped, because you can't say to a person you love, You're too old, even if you think that she is.

"You think I'm too old?"

"Other things, too. You've as much a life of your own as Mrs. Tolliver. Why should you be the one who gives it all up? And let's face it, we're all getting older. Even I'm getting older . . ."

"I'm sixty-three. If I manage to stay alive and kicking for another ten years, I shall still be only seventy-three. That's a young woman when you think of Picasso or Arthur Rubenstein."

"What have they got to do with it?"

"And by then Charlotte will be twenty and well able to take care of herself. I really don't see that that's much of a problem."

The windscreen of the Volkswagen was dirty. I found in some pocket a grubby rag and began to try in a desultory sort of way to clean the glass.

I said, "When I was in the kitchen getting the coffee, did she make any reference to Daniel?"

"None."

"You didn't say anything?"

"Heaven forbid."

I was making the smears on the windscreen, if anything, worse. I stuffed the rag back into its hiding place.

"He's coming here, you know, this morning, for the picnic. I offered to fetch him in the car, but he said he'd make his own way."

"That's just as well."

I looked at her. "You're going to tell Daniel about all this?"

"Of course I shall tell him. I shall tell him everything. Three heads are better than two, and I'm sick and tired of all of us keeping secrets from each other. Perhaps if we hadn't kept secrets, none of this would have happened."

"Oh, Phoebe, I hardly think so."

"Maybe you're right. But let's start being completely frank and truthful; then we'll all know where we stand. Besides, Daniel has a right to know."

"What do you think he'll do?"

"*Do?*" Phoebe gazed at me blankly. "Why should he do anything?"

"He's Charlotte's father."

"Leslie Collis is Charlotte's father."

It was just what I had said to Daniel, sitting with him by the pretend fire; trying to be down-to-earth and sensible, jollying him along. But surely, now, things were taking a different course.

"He may not *be* responsible," I pointed out, "but that's not going to stop him feeling that way."

"And what do you imagine he's going to do about it?"

"I don't know."

"In that case, I can tell you. Nothing. Because there is nothing that he can do. And because even if there were, he wouldn't do it."

"How do you know?"

"Because I know Daniel."

"I know him, too."

"I only wish you did."

"What's that supposed to mean?"

Phoebe sighed. "Oh, nothing. It's just that I'm afraid you've fallen in love with him."

Her voice, as always, was inconsequential, as though she were talking of something of no importance. As a result, I was taken unawares. I said, trying to sound as casual as she did, "I don't think I know what falling in love actually means. It's always been a sort of nonword with me. Like 'forgive.' I never understand the word 'forgive.' If you don't forgive, then you're mean and resentful and grudge-bearing; and if you do, then you're smug and sanctimonious."

But Phoebe would not be waylaid into this interesting discussion. She stuck to her point.

"Well, 'love,' then. Perhaps that's an easier word to define."

"If you want definitions, then I feel as though I've known him always. I feel as though already we've shared a past. And I don't want to lose him, because I think we need each other."

"Did you feel this way before he unfolded to you the great saga of Annabelle?"

"I think so. Yes. So you see I'm not just feeling sorry for him."

"Why should you be sorry for him? He has everything—youth, a terrifying talent, and now fame and money and all the material things that go with them."

"But how can you discount what happened between Daniel and Annabelle? He's felt guilty for eleven years because he didn't even know if the child was his or not. Wouldn't you feel sorry for any man who had that load of guilt on his back for eleven years?"

"The guilt was of his own making. And he didn't need to run away."

"Perhaps he didn't run away. Perhaps he did what Chips told him to do, which was the only possible, reasonable thing."

"Did he speak about this to you?"

"Yes. And he asked me to go to Greece with him. To Spetsai. That was before he told me about Annabelle and Charlotte. But afterwards we talked about it again, and he said that it wouldn't be any good, because he couldn't go on running away from the inside of his own head."

"Would you have gone? To Greece?"

"Yes."

"And afterwards?"

"I don't know."

"That's not good enough for you, Prue."

"You sound like my mother."

"At the risk of sounding like your mother—who, incidentally, is nobody's fool—I have to say it. You don't know Daniel. He is a true artist: impermanent, restless, impractical."

"I know he's impractical." I smiled. "He told me once that he had a car, and at the end of three years he'd only just learned how to work the heater."

But Phoebe ignored my small attempt at humour and went on doggedly.

"He's unreliable, too, because he's always lost in his own form of creation. It makes him, in a way, negative. Maddening."

"Oh, come off it, Phoebe, you know you adore him."

"I do, Prue, I do. But face him with day-to-day decisions and responsibilities, and I could never truly predict how he would react."

"Are you talking about Daniel as a prospective husband?"

"I wouldn't intrude that far."

"You knew him when he was twenty. You can't judge him by the person he was eleven years ago. He's a man now."

"Yes, I know that. And people mature, of course. But do their personalities change so much? You're such a special person, Prue, I wouldn't want you ever to be hurt. And Daniel could hurt you. Not deliberately, but by the sins of omission. His work fills his life, and I don't know how much room there is left over for personal things like loving people and being with them, and taking care of them."

"Perhaps I could take care of him."

"Yes, perhaps you could, for a little while. But I think not indefinitely. I don't see how it could be possible to stay forever with a man who I knew was afraid of permanency, emotional involvements, becoming trapped."

It was no good arguing with her. I sat saying nothing, gazing ahead of me through the dusty windscreen and seeing nothing. The funny thing was that we both seemed to be on the same side. She put out her hand and laid it over mine. Her fingers were warm, but I could feel the cold, hard pressure of her bulky, old-fashioned rings.

"Don't create fantasies about Daniel. They will probably never come true. And if you expect nothing of him, you will at least never be disappointed."

I was thinking of Charlotte. "I don't believe he will run away from this."

"And I believe that he has no alternative. Perhaps you should run away, too. Go back to London. Get your life in perspective. Ring up that nice young man who brought you the dead chrysanthemums."

"Oh, *Phoebe.*" It took a small effort even to remember his name. "They weren't dead when he gave them to me."

"When you see him again, you may feel quite differently about him."

"No. I shan't do that. Anyway, he doesn't make me laugh." Nigel Gordon. I knew that now I should probably never get to go to Scotland.

"Well, you must make up your own mind." She gave my hand a pat and then sat back in her seat with her hands in her lap. "I've said it. Interfered. Cleared my muddy conscience. Now perhaps we'd better go home and break the news about Charlotte coming to stay to Lily Tonkins. If anything's going to stop her singing "Guard Us Oh Thou Great Jehovah," then that is. On the other hand, she always enjoys a drama, so maybe she'll take it quite well. As well, Charlotte will be turning up at Holly Cottage at any moment, and we've got the picnic to organise, as if life wasn't already sufficiently complicated."

I had forgotten the picnic. Now, starting the engine and letting off the brake, I wished that Phoebe had not found it necessary to remind me.

"Well, I don't know," said Lily when we told her about Charlotte coming to stay. "Leaving her granny and coming here. Seems funny." She looked from Phoebe's innocent face to mine. I hastily smiled, brightly and blankly. "I suppose, come to think of it, it's not all that surprising. The child's here most of the time whenever she's meant to be staying with Mrs. Tolliver. Just as easy to make up a bed and be done with it."

Phoebe looked relieved. "You are good, Lily. And I hope it won't be too much extra work. I know you've got enough to do as it is just now, but once my arm's out of this dratted cast . . ."

"Don't you worry, Miss Shackleton, we'll manage lovely. Any road, she's no trouble. Quiet little soul. Doesn't even eat much." She moved her eyes once more from Phoebe's face to mine. She frowned. "There's nothing *wrong*, is there?"

There was a small pause. Then Phoebe said, "No. Not really. But Mrs. Tolliver finds it . . . awkward having Charlotte living at White Lodge. I don't think they find it too easy to get on together, and we all decided it might be better if she came here for a bit."

"Well, certainly more fun for her," Lily pointed out. "Betty Curnow's a nice enough person, but she was never much of a one for fun. Miss La-di-dah we used to call her when we were all at school together, and marrying up with a sanitary inspector didn't make her any more free and easy."

"Yes. Well, maybe Joshua Curnow isn't the jolliest of men, but I'm sure he's made Betty a marvellous husband," said Phoebe soothingly before bringing Lily back to the matter at hand. "Where do you think Charlotte should sleep?"

"We'll put her in Mr. Armitage's old dressing room. The bed's made up; just needs a bit of an airing."

"And the picnic, don't forget. They're all going on a picnic."

"That's right. Ham sandwiches I've made, and a little salad in a plastic box. And there's chocolate cake with orange icing . . ."

"How delicious. I wish I were going . . . my favourite . . . what a lovely picnic . . ." And Phoebe took herself off upstairs to divest herself

of her poncho and change her shoes. We heard her footsteps cross the
floorboards above us.

I said, "You are a tower of strength, Lily. That's what Phoebe always
says about you."

"Get away," said Lily, pleased.

"I can help you. Give me something to do to help you."

"You can string beans for dinner tonight. One thing I can't abide is
stringing beans. Give me a carrot to peel or a turnip and I'm happy as a
sandboy. But fiddley old beans I can't abide . . ."

So I was in the garden, in the sunshine, in one of Phoebe's rickety old
garden chairs, stringing beans, when Charlotte finally arrived. I heard
the sound of a car and laid down the knife and the basket and went
through to the front of the house, only to find both Phoebe and Lily
there before me. Betty Curnow had brought Charlotte, driving Mrs.
Tolliver's car. Charlotte was already out of it, and Lily had opened the
boot and was lifting out her suitcase. Charlotte wore her grey flannel
coat, with her red handbag slung across one shoulder. Her travelling
clothes. I wondered how she had felt, putting them on; dressing herself
for another journey, another house; shunted from pillar to post because
nobody wanted her, nobody could be bothered to take care of her.

"Hello, Charlotte."

She turned and saw me. "Hello." She was very pale, unsmiling. Her
spectacles were crooked. Her hair looked greasy, as though in need of a
good wash, and somebody—perhaps Charlotte herself—had parted it
carelessly and pinned back the front lock with a blue plastic slide.

"This is fun. Do you want to come upstairs and look at your bedroom?"

"All right."

Lily and Phoebe were engaged in conversation with Betty Curnow, so
I took the suitcase, and we started together towards the front door. But
then Charlotte remembered her manners and stopped.

"Thank you very much, Mrs. Curnow, for bringing me."

"That's all right, love," said Betty Curnow. "See and be a good girl,
now."

We went upstairs. The little room that had been Chips's dressing
room was next to mine. Lily had been through it like a dose of salts, and
it smelt strongly of polish and clean, starched linen. Phoebe had found
time to pick flowers for the dressing table, and the open window framed
the same view that I enjoyed, of the garden and the escallonia hedge and
the flood tide of the estuary beyond.

The room was so small and delightful, so exactly the right size and
shape for a little girl, that I expected a spark of enthusiasm. But Charlotte seemed unseeing; her expression showed nothing.

I set down her suitcase. "Do you want to unpack now, or later?"

"If I could just get Teddy out."

Teddy, flattened, was on the top of the suitcase. She lifted him out and set him on her pillow.

"What about everything else?"

"It doesn't matter. I'll do it later."

"Well . . . if you'd like to take off your coat, you can come down to the garden and help me. I'm stringing beans for Lily Tonkins and I could do with a bit of help."

She took off her red shoulder bag and laid it on her dressing table, then unbuttoned her grey flannel coat. I found a hanger and put it away in the wardrobe. Under the coat she wore a blue T-shirt and a faded cotton skirt.

"Do you need a sweater?"

"No. I'm all right."

We made our way downstairs again. In the chest in the hall I found an old car rug, in the kitchen took a second knife from the drawer. We went back out into the garden. I spread the rug and we sat on it together, with the basket of beans and Lily's largest saucepan between us.

"The knives are very sharp. You'll be careful not to cut yourself?"

"I've strung beans heaps of times."

Pause.

"Isn't it a lovely day? You haven't forgotten about our picnic, have you?"

"No."

"Daniel's definitely coming. He'll be here any moment now. He said he'd try and get a lift over from Porthkerris."

Pause.

"I wanted Phoebe to come with us to Penjizal, but she said that she was frightened that the wind would blow her over the edge of the cliff. Did you remember to bring the Coca-Cola?"

"Yes. Mrs. Curnow said she'd give it to Lily."

"Lily's made us ham sandwiches, just the kind you wanted. And a chocolate cake . . ."

Charlotte looked at me. "You don't have to cheer me up, you know."

I felt, and with some reason, extremely foolish.

I said, "I'm sorry."

She went back clumsily to slicing her bean.

"Charlotte . . . didn't you want to come and stay with Phoebe?"

"I've never stayed before."

"I . . . I don't know what you're trying to say."

"Something's happened. And nobody wants to tell me."

I was apprehensive. "What makes you say that?"

She did not reply, but a movement behind me caught her eye and she looked up, over my shoulder. I turned and saw Phoebe emerging through the garden door. She still wore her hat but had abandoned the gaudy poncho, and now her knotted scarf fluttered in the breeze like a little flag, and the sunlight winked back at us from the gold chains slung about her neck. She lugged, in her good arm, a deck chair, and I got up and went to take it from her and set it up by the rug where we sat. She sank into it, her knees jutting beneath the folk weave of her skirt.

There seemed no point in prevaricating. I caught and held her eye. "Charlotte and I were just talking." Phoebe's gaze was calm and untroubled. I knew that she understood. I settled down on the rug once more and picked up my knife. "She's wondering why she's here."

"Mostly," Phoebe told her, "because we want you."

"Mummy's not coming back from Majorca, is she?"

"Why do you say that?"

"She isn't coming, is she?"

"No," said Phoebe.

I selected a bean and began, very neatly, to string and slice it.

"I knew," said Charlotte.

"Would you like to tell us how you knew?"

"Because she had this friend. He was called Desmond. He used to come and see her. He had a riding school quite near our house in Sunningdale. They used to go riding together, and then he'd come back and have a drink or something. He was called Desmond. She went to Majorca with him."

"How do you know that?"

"Because there was one night at the end of the holidays. Before I went back to school and the boiler blew up. Daddy was in Brussels on business. And I had to get up in the middle of the night to go to the bathroom, and then I was thirsty, and I thought I'd go downstairs and get some Coke out of the fridge. I'm not meant to, but I do sometimes. And then when I was halfway down the stairs I heard voices. I heard a man talking and I thought perhaps it was a burglar. I thought perhaps it was a burglar and he was going to shoot Mummy. But then he said something and I knew it was Desmond. So I sat on the stairs and listened. And they were talking about Majorca. She told Daddy she was going on holiday with an old school friend. I heard her telling him at breakfast one morning, but I knew she was going with Desmond."

"Did you say anything?"

"No. Daddy never listens to me anyway, and I was frightened."

"Frightened of your father?"

"No. Just frightened. Frightened of her going and never coming back."

"Did you know that your father rang your grandmother last night?"

"I wasn't asleep. I heard the phone ringing. Granny's drawing room is under my bedroom. You can hear people talking, but you can't hear what they say. But I did hear her say his name. He's called Leslie. And I knew it was him. And I thought perhaps he'd just rung up to see how I was. But this morning everything felt so horrible, I knew it hadn't just been that. And Granny was all funny and cross, and then she sent me and Betty Curnow up to the village to buy Coke. So I knew something was wrong, because I'm always allowed to go to the village by myself."

"I think your grandmother didn't want you to overhear. To be distressed."

"And then when we got back again, Mrs. Curnow and me, Granny said I was coming to stay with you."

"I hope you were pleased."

All the time that she had been speaking, Charlotte had sat with downcast eyes, fiddling with a runner bean that she had slowly and deliberately torn to shreds. Now she looked up at Phoebe, her eyes anxious behind the lenses of her unbecoming spectacles. She was being very brave. "She isn't ever coming back, is she?"

"No. She's going to go and live in South Africa."

"What will happen to us? To Michael and me? Daddy can't look after us. At least, he wouldn't mind looking after Michael. They're always doing things together, like going shooting and watching rugger matches and things like that. But he wouldn't want to look after me."

"Maybe not," said Phoebe. "But I would. That's why I asked your grandmother if I could have you to stay with me."

"But not *forever?*"

"Nothing is ever forever."

"Won't I ever see Daddy and Michael again?"

"Yes, of course you will. After all, Michael is your brother."

Charlotte screwed up her nose. "He's not always very kind. I don't like him that much."

"Even so, he is your brother. Perhaps, next holidays, he'd like to come and stay with me as well. But I expect your grandmother might like to have him."

"She didn't want me," Charlotte pointed out.

"You mustn't think that. She just doesn't find it very easy to have a person of your age around the place. It's called not being good with children. Lots of the nicest people are like that."

"You're good with children," Charlotte told her.

"That's because I like them." Phoebe smiled. "Particularly you. That's why, for the time being at any rate, I want you to stay here."

"What about my school?" Charlotte was still being very wary. "I have to go back to school at the end of the week."

"I had a word with your grandmother about that. Do you like your boarding school?"

"No, I hate it. I hate having to be away all the time. And I'm much the youngest; there's nobody younger than me, not boarding. There are day girls, but they're all friends and they do things together at the weekend, and they don't want me. I wanted to be a day girl, too, but Mummy said it was much better to be a boarder. I don't know why it should be better. I thought it was horribler."

"Then you wouldn't mind too much if you didn't go back?"

Cautiously, Charlotte considered this. For the first time a gleam of something hopeful crossed her face. "Why? Don't I have to?"

"No, I don't think you do. If you're going to live with me, then it would be much easier for all of us if you went to our local school. Nobody's a boarder there, and I think you'd enjoy it."

"I'm not very good at lessons."

"People can't be good at everything. You're good at drawing and making things. And if you like music, they have a very good music master, and they have a proper orchestra and give concerts. I know one boy, he's only your age, and he plays the clarinet."

"Could I go there?"

"If you wanted, I think it could be arranged."

"I do want it."

"Then you'll stay with me?"

"You mean . . . never go back to Daddy?"

"Yes," said Phoebe gently. "Perhaps that is what I mean."

"But . . . you just said . . . you said nothing is ever forever." Her eyes were filling with tears, and it was almost too painful to watch. "I can't stay with you . . ."

"Yes you can. For as long as you like. So you see, although the worst has happened, the world hasn't come to an end. You can talk about things, to Prue and to me. You haven't got to keep everything to yourself any longer. Don't go on trying to be brave. It doesn't matter about crying . . ."

It was a dam burst of tears, uncontrollable. Charlotte's mouth went square in the manner of all weeping children, but the sobs that racked her small frame sounded more like the suffering grief of an adult.

"Oh, Charlotte . . ."

Phoebe leaned forward in her chair, her arms—the good arm, and the stiff one in its plaster cast—outflung, an open invitation to comfort and love. At any other time the effect of this typically expansive gesture might have been comic, but it wasn't funny now. ". . . come away, my darling."

And Charlotte scrambled to her feet and flung herself into the lop-sided embrace, winding her arms tightly around Phoebe's neck, burying her face in Phoebe's shoulder, knocking Phoebe's hat askew.

I picked up the beans and the saucepan and went indoors. Because it was their own private moment. Because she was Daniel's child. And because I thought I might be going to cry as well.

*   *   *

The kitchen was empty. Through the open back door I could see Lily out on the drying green, pegging out a line of snowy tea towels. Now she was onto another hymn.

Do no sinful action
Speak no angry wer-erd.

I put the beans and the saucepan down on the end of the scrubbed pine table and went upstairs to my bedroom. I had made my bed this morning, but since then Lily had been what she called through the room, which meant a strong smell of floor polish and everything on my dressing table arranged in a straight line. I sat on the edge of the bed and after a little realized that I wasn't going to cry after all. But I felt drained, disoriented, as though I had spent the last three hours in a dark cinema, absorbed in some deeply emotional film, and was now back in the street again, dazzled by the light, blundering my way along an unfamiliar pavement; incapable.

Mummy's not coming back from Majorca, is she? Daddy never listens to me anyway. He wouldn't want to look after me. I wanted to be a day girl, but Mummy said it was much better to be a boarder. My grandmother doesn't want me.

Oh, dear Lord, the things we do to our children.

The window was open, the curtains stirring in the warm breeze. I got off the bed and went to the window and leaned out of it, my elbows on the sill. Below me on the grass, Phoebe and Charlotte still sat. The tears seemed to be over, and now all that could be heard was the companionable murmur of their conversation. Charlotte was back on the rug again, cross-legged, absorbed in making a daisy chain. I looked down at her bowed head, the vulnerable back of her neck. I remembered being her age. My parents were divorced and I lived with my mother, but never was I unloved, unwanted, shunted off to boarding schools. I remembered travelling to Northumberland to stay with my father, willing the train to travel faster and faster as we rocketed north. I remembered being met by him at Newcastle Station and racing up the platform to be swept into his sturdy, tweed-smelling embrace.

I remembered my mother's little house in London, the bedroom she decorated for me exactly the way I wanted it. The clothes she bought me, which were the clothes that I was allowed to choose for myself. The fun of dancing classes in the winter, and Christmas parties; being taken to the pantomime at the Palladium and the *Sleeping Beauty* at Covent Garden.

I remembered shopping in Harrod's, the tedium of buying school clothes rewarded by the treat of a chocolate milk shake at the soda fountain. And summer outings down the Thames, by boat, with a party of small friends and all the shivery anticipation of a visit to the Tower of London.

And always Cornwall, and Penmarron. And Phoebe.

Oh, my darling, how lovely to see you again.

Phoebe. I was suddenly filled with nameless apprehensions for her. What had she taken on, so impulsively, so lovingly? She was sixty-three and had already fallen from a worm-ridden chair and broken her arm. Supposing she had not simply broken her arm, but her hip, or her neck? Supposing she had struck her head and lain there, on the studio floor, concussed, with nobody knowing or coming to look for her? My imagination turned and fled but immediately came up with alternative and even more horrendous fabrications.

I thought of Phoebe driving her old car. She had never done this with much concentration, since she was always being diverted by the goings-on in the roads and streets down which she trundled, quite often on the wrong side of the white line, believing that provided she continued to blow the horn, nothing too dreadful could happen.

Supposing she had a heart attack and died? It happened to other people; why should it not happen to Phoebe? Supposing one summer day she went swimming from the old seawall, as she liked to do. Supposing she dived, wearing her old-fashioned bathing suit and her plastic bath hat, and never came up again? There seemed no end to the possible fatalities, and if anything happened to Phoebe, then who would take care of Charlotte? Once more my mind scurried ahead, searching for a solution to this hypothetical problem.

Who would have her? Myself? In a basement flat in Islington? My mother? Or perhaps my father? He was the sort of man who would take in any lame dog. I tried to picture Charlotte at Windyedge, but somehow nothing quite fit. My young stepmother would welcome any child who would ride her horses, muck out stables, clean tack, and go hunting, but she would have little in common with a small girl who only wanted to play the clarinet and draw.

These gloomy thoughts might have gone on forever, but at that moment I was brought back to reality by the sound of the morning train from Porthkerris, rattling through the cutting behind the house. It appeared busily around the curve of the single line to draw up at the halt, looking like a toy train, the kind that is wound up with a key. For a moment it stood there, and then somebody blew a whistle and waved a green flag, and it moved on, pulling away from the station and leaving behind it on the empty platform a single, lonely figure.

Daniel. Come for the picnic.

As soon as it was clear, he jumped down onto the line, crossed it, climbed a fence, and started down the track, past the small anchorage where the sailing boats bobbed at high tide and so onto the old seawall. He wore blue jeans, a navy blue sweater, a white canvas smock.

I watched his approach, ambling long-legged, his hands in his pockets, and longed for him to be the sort of person to whom I could run with all my problems, just as I used to run into the arms of my father on Newcastle Station. I wanted to be embraced, reassured, loved. I wanted to gabble out to him everything that had occurred on that endless morning, and to be told that nothing mattered, I was never to worry again, he would deal with everything . . .

But Phoebe, who loved Daniel, was wiser than I.

Face him with day-to-day decisions and responsibilities and I could never truly predict how he would react.

I didn't want him to be that sort of person. I wanted him to take charge. To have taken charge. I watched him coming and knew that if what was happening to us all were a story I was making up, then this moment would be the beginning of the end. He would have everything solved, decisions taken and plans formed. I devised a film, slow motion, soft focus: Daniel coming through the gate in the escallonia hedge to run in floating strides up the slope of the lawn. To embrace Phoebe, scoop his child up into his arms, call me down from my open window in order to plan our future together. Violins would soar. "The End" would appear upon the screen. Credits would roll and we would all live happily ever after.

Don't create fantasies about Daniel. They will probably never come true. Instead, reality. Phoebe would take him aside, relate to him bluntly what had happened. No more secrets, Daniel. Annabelle has taken off and nobody else wants Charlotte. Nobody else wants your daughter.

And he? What would he do? I did not want to think about it. I did not want to know what was going to happen next.

He had moved out of sight, hidden from my view by the slope of the bank and the height of the hedge. I closed my window and turned back to my room. In the mirror over my dressing table I caught sight of my reflection, and my appearance was so appalling that I spent the next five minutes doing things to improve it. Washed my face with a scalding-hot flannel, scrubbed my nails with Phoebe's lavender-scented soap, brushed and combed my hair. I took a fresh cotton shirt from a drawer, changed my shoes, applied mascara, sprayed scent.

"Prue!" Charlotte's voice.

"I'm here. In my bedroom."

"Can I come in?" The door opened, and her face appeared around the edge of it. "Daniel's here."

"I saw him get off the train."

"But Phoebe's taken him down to the studio. She says she wants to show him something that belonged to Chips. She says they'll be about ten minutes. What a lovely smell!"

"It's Dior. I always use it. Want a squirt?"

"Don't you mind?"

"Don't take it all."

She sprayed on some scent, breathing in the perfume with an ecstatic expression on her face. I picked up my comb and tidied her hair for her, straightening the parting and refastening the plastic slide.

When this was done, I said, "Perhaps we should go down to the kitchen and start packing our picnic basket. And it might be a good idea if you found your Wellingtons and an anorak."

"But it won't rain today."

"This is Cornwall . . . you never know what it's going to do."

So we were in the kitchen when Phoebe eventually came to find us. I saw her through the window, walking slowly up the brick path that led from the walled garden and the studio. She came towards us like an old person. She was alone. She came through the garden door and saw us standing, waiting for her. She told us that Daniel had gone. He would not, after all, be able to come with us on the picnic. He was sorry.

"But he promised . . ." Charlotte kept saying, near to tears. "He *said* he'd come . . ."

Phoebe would not meet my eyes.

So we never got to go to Penjizal. Somehow, by then, none of us had the heart to go anywhere. We ate the picnic right there, in the garden of Holly Cottage. We never saw the seals.

It was evening before I got Phoebe to myself. Charlotte was engrossed in television, and I cornered my aunt by the sink.

"Why did he go?"

"I warned you," said Phoebe.

"Where did he go?"

"I've no idea. Back to Porthkerris, I suppose."

I said, "I'm going to take the car. I'm going to go and see him."

"Don't do that."

"Why not? You can't stop me."

"Ring him first, if you must. Talk to him. Make sure that he wants to see you."

I went straight to the telephone. Of course he would want to see me. I dialled the number of the Castle Hotel, and when the girl on the switchboard answered, I asked for Daniel Cassens. But she put me through to the Reception desk, and a girl's voice told me that Mr. Cassens had gone, checked out, and left no forwarding address.

7

I WASHED CHARLOTTE'S HAIR and trimmed the ragged ends with Phoebe's sewing scissors. Clean, it was the colour of chestnuts shot through with unexpected copper lights.

Phoebe telephoned the headmaster of the local school and took Charlotte for an interview. She returned home full of excitement. She would have a new uniform, navy-blue and white. They had a pottery wheel in the art room. She was going to learn how to play the clarinet.

We watched, on television, a pretty girl showing us how to make a dolls' house out of cardboard boxes. We took the car into Porthkerris, and went to visit the wine merchant and were given four sturdy crates that had once held bottles of Scotch whisky. We bought a Stanley knife, and little pots of paint and some brushes. We bought tubes of glue. We came home and began to measure and mark out the door, the windows. The kitchen was littered with sheets of newspaper, scraps of card, all the tools of our trade.

Now there was a new moon in the night sky. It hung in the east, a silvery eyelash, and its pale reflection hung in the black waters of the estuary, drowned in trembling slivers of light.

"Prue."

"What is it?"

"Where has Daniel gone?"

"I don't know."

"Why did he go?"

"I don't know that, either."

"Is he ever coming back?"

"I expect he will. One day."

"People always go away. People I like. When Michael first went to school, the house was funny without him. All quiet and empty. And I had a nanny once, when I was very little, about six. I really liked her. But she had to leave and go and look after her mother. And now Daniel's gone."

"You scarcely know Daniel."

"But I've always known about him. Phoebe used to tell me about him. She used to show me bits in the newspaper about him, when he was having exhibitions and things in America. And she used to tell me about him."

"But, still, you scarcely knew him. You only met him for a day or so."

"I didn't want him to go away. It wasn't just the picnic. It wasn't just not seeing the seals. We can do that any time."

"Then what was it?"

"I wanted to tell him things, show him things. I wanted to show him the dolls' house. I wanted to *ask* him things. Daddy never has time to answer properly if you ask him things. And Daniel doesn't talk to you as though you're little, he talks as though you are a grown up person. He'd never tell you that you were being a nuisance or that you were stupid."

"Well . . . perhaps you have a lot in common. You're interested in the same sort of things. Perhaps that's why you feel so close to him."

"I wish he would come back."

"He's a busy man. An important man. And now he's a famous man. He has so many things that he has to do. And an artist is . . . different from other men. He needs to be free. It's hard for someone like Daniel to put down roots, to stay in the same place all the time, and be with the same people."

"Phoebe's an artist, and she stays in the same place."

"Phoebe is different. Phoebe is special."

"I know. That's why I love her. But I love Daniel too."

"You mustn't love him too much, Charlotte."

"Why not?"

"Because it's no good loving a person too much, if you may never see them again . . . oh, don't start to cry. Please don't cry. It's just that it's true, and it's no good either of us pretending that it isn't."

We painted the door red, the frames of the windows black. Lily found an old dress box, and we cut the roof from the lid of this and scored a central line and bent it into a gable. We painted tiles.

One day it rained, and there was a great wind, and Charlotte and I walked over the golf links and down to the beach. There was sand blowing everywhere, and the breakers poured into the shore from half a mile out or more. The rushes on the dunes were flattened by this wind, and the sea gulls abandoned the coast and flew inland to float and scream over fields of newly turned plough.

* * *

No letter came for Charlotte, no postcard from South Africa. We learned, through Betty Curnow and Lily Tonkins, that Mrs. Tolliver had gone to spend a few days with a friend at Helford. Which made three people who had run away.

We constructed furniture for the doll's house out of empty matchboxes; we painted wallpaper. We raided Phoebe's rag bag and made carpets from scraps of tweed with fringed ends. Just like real, said Charlotte when we laid them, and she closed the door of the dolls' house and put her face to the window, loving the smallness of everything, the little, safe, miniature world.

One night, "I can't bear to see you looking so unhappy," Phoebe told me, but I pretended that I had not heard her, because I did not want to talk about Daniel.

He was gone. Back to his nomadic, searching, restless life. Back to his painting, his exhibition, Peter Chastal. Perhaps, by now, back to America. Much later, when he felt able, maybe he would send me a postcard. I saw it, dropping through the letter box of my front door in Islington. A brightly coloured picture of the Statue of Liberty, perhaps, or the Golden Gate bridge, or Fujiyama.

Having a wonderful time, wish you were here. Daniel.

There was a future. My future. My job, my flat, my own friends. I would go back to London and pick up the threads again. But on my own, as I had never been alone before.

I had the dream again, the swimming dream. It was the same as before. The water first shallow, and then deep and warm. The racing current. The sensation of being swept along by this flood, not struggling but acquiescent. Not dying, I reminded myself at the end of the dream. Not dying, but loving. So why did I wake with tears wet on my cheeks?

The passing days had lost their names, just as I had lost all sense of their passing. Then suddenly it was a Tuesday and time to be practical. Phoebe had decided the previous evening that I should drive her and Charlotte into Penzance, where we would buy the new navy-and-white school uniform. Perhaps, as a treat, we would have lunch in a restaurant or go down to the harbour and see if the Scilly Islands steamer was in.

But these plans did not come off, because early that morning Lily Tonkins rang to say that Ernest, her husband, had been taken poorly. Phoebe answered the telephone call, and Charlotte and I stood around and listened to the quaking voice over the line.

"Up all night," Lily told Phoebe.

Phoebe said, "Oh, dear."

Lily enlarged on the details. Phoebe's face took on an expression of horror. "Oh, *dear.*" After this she hastily agreed that on no account was Lily to abandon her ailing husband until the doctor had seen him. She rang off. Lily was not coming to work today.

We hastily changed our arrangements. I would stay at Holly Cottage to do a bit of sketchy housework and cook the lunch, and Mr. Thomas, in his trusty taxi, would be asked to make the trip into Penzance with Phoebe and Charlotte.

Charlotte was slightly indignant about this.

"I thought we were going to have lunch in a restaurant."

"It wouldn't be any fun without Prue," Phoebe told her briskly. "We'll do it another day, when I have to go and see the bank manager or have my hair done."

A telephone call was duly made, and Mr. Thomas turned up in ten minutes with his chauffeur's hat on his head and the wheels of his car encrusted in pig manure. Phoebe and Charlotte clambered in, and I waved them away and then returned indoors to deal with the morning chores.

They were not very arduous. Lily cleaned the house so thoroughly every day that once I had made the beds, scoured the bath, and cleared the ashes out of the sitting room grate, everything looked more or less as usual. I went into the kitchen, made a cup of coffee and started to peel potatoes. It was a grey, still day, with rain in the air. When I had finished the potatoes, I pulled on a pair of rubber boots and went down to the vegetable garden to cut a cauliflower. As I returned to the house, I heard the sound of a car coming down the road towards the house. I looked at my watch and saw that it was only an hour since Phoebe and Charlotte had set off. There was no way that the shopping expedition could be over so soon.

The car came over the railway bridge, and I knew then that it was heading for Holly Cottage, for we were the last house on the road, and at the end of it lay only the dead end, the padlocked iron gates of the old shipyard.

I hurried back inside. In the kitchen I laid my knife and the cauliflower on the draining board, and then, still wearing Lily's apron and my boots, went through the hall and out the front door.

There, on the gravel, was parked an unfamiliar car. An Alfa-Romeo, long and sleek, dark green and travel-stained. The driver's door was already open, and behind the wheel, his eyes on my face, sat Daniel.

On that still, misty morning, there was little sound. Then, from far away, I heard the scream of some gulls flying low over the empty sands of the estuary. Slowly, he climbed out of the car and straightened himself cautiously, arching his back, and putting up a hand to massage the back of his neck. He was wearing his usual strange assembly of clothes, and there lay the dark shadow of stubble on his chin. He shut the car door behind him, and it closed with a solid expensive-sounding thud. He said my name.

That proved it was true. He wasn't in London. He wasn't in New York. He wasn't in San Francisco. He was here. Back. Home.

I said, "What are you doing?"

"What do you think I'm doing?"

"Who's car is that?"

"Mine." He began to walk stiffly towards me.

"But you hate cars."

"I know, but it's still mine. I bought it yesterday." He reached my side and put his hands on my shoulders and stooped and kissed my cheek, and his chin felt rough and scratchy against my skin. I looked up at him. His face was colourless, grey with tiredness, but his eyes were bright with secret laughter.

"You're wearing Lily's apron."

"Lily's not here. Ernest's ill. You haven't shaved."

"Didn't have time. I left London at three o'clock this morning. Where's Phoebe?"

"She and Charlotte have gone to do some shopping."

"Aren't you going to ask me in?"

"Yes . . . yes, of course. I'm sorry. It's just that you were the last person I expected to see. Come along. I'll make you some coffee, or bacon and eggs if you want something to eat."

"Coffee would be fine."

We went back indoors. The house felt warm after the chilly dampness outside. I led the way through the hall and heard him close the front door behind us. In the kitchen I saw the cauliflower and the knife by the sink where I had left them, and for a moment, so disoriented was I, found myself wondering what I had intended doing with them.

I filled the electric kettle and plugged it in and switched it on. When I turned around, I saw that Daniel had pulled out a chair and was sitting at the head of the long scrubbed pine table. He had an elbow on the table and was rubbing his eyes with his hand, as though it were possible to erase exhaustion.

He said, "I haven't driven so far or so fast in my life, I don't think." He took his hand away and looked up at me, and I had forgotten the darkness of his eyes, the pupils round and dark as black olives. He still looked exhausted, but there was something else about him, an exhilaration, perhaps, that I could not fathom, because I had not seen it in him before.

I said, "What made you buy a car?"

"I wanted to get back to you all, and it seemed the quickest way."

"Have you found out how the heater works?"

It wasn't much of a joke, but it helped break the tension.

He smiled. "Not yet. Like I told you, I've only had it for a day." He crossed his arms on the tabletop. He said, "Phoebe told me, you know. About Annabelle and Leslie Collis and Mrs. Tolliver."

"Yes. I know."

"And Charlotte."

"Yes."

"Was Charlotte disappointed about the picnic?"

"Yes."

"I couldn't stay, Prue. I had to get away. By myself. Do you understand?"

"Where did you go?"

"I went back to Porthkerris. I walked back, over the dunes and along the cliffs. When I got back to the Castle Hotel, I packed my suitcase without any clear idea of what I was going to do next. But then, when it was packed, I picked up the telephone and rang Lewis Falcon. I'd been meaning to get in touch with him ever since I got down here, but somehow with one thing and another I'd never got around to it. He was great. I told him who I was and said that we'd never met. And he said that he knew who I was, because he'd heard about me through Peter Chastal, and why didn't I come out to Lanyon to see him? So I said I'd do that, but what I needed was a bed for a couple of nights, and he said that would be okay too. So I checked out and got a taxi to drive me to Lanyon.

"He's a marvellous man. Immensely likeable, totally uncurious. With him, I found I could switch off; as though I were pulling down a great fireproof safety curtain between myself and everything that Phoebe had told me. The psychoanalyst's seventh veil, perhaps. He showed me his studio, and we looked at his work, and we talked shop as though nothing else existed for either of us.

"That was all right for a couple of days, and then I knew that I had to get back to London. So he drove me to the station and I caught the morning train.

"When I got to London I went to the gallery to see Peter. I was still in this extraordinary state of mind . . . it was like being insulated from reality. The curtain was still down, and I knew that Annabelle and Charlotte were behind it, but for the time being they had simply ceased to exist, and all I could do was carry on with my ordinary life as though nothing had happened. I didn't say anything about them to Peter. The exhibition is still on, the gallery still full of visitors. We sat in his office and ate sandwiches and had a glass of beer, and watched them through the glass of the door as though they were goldfish in a tank. Those were my pictures they were looking at, but I couldn't relate myself either to the pictures or to them. Nothing seemed to have anything to do with me.

"Then I left Peter and I went out and started walking. It was a beautiful afternoon. I walked for miles along the embankment, and eventually I realized that I'd reached Millbank and I was standing outside the Tate Gallery. Do you know the Tate?"

"Yes."

"Do you go there?"

"Often."

"Do you know the Chantrey collection?"

"No."

"I went up the steps and into the gallery. I made for the room where the Chantrey collection is hung. There's a picture in it by John Singer Sargent. It's an oil. Quite big. Two little girls in a garden at night, lighting Japanese lanterns. They're wearing white dresses with frilled collars. There are lilies growing and pink roses. It's called *Carnation Lily, Lily Rose*. One of the little girls has short, dark hair and a very thin, delicate white neck, like the stem of a flower. She could be Charlotte.

"I don't know how long I stood there. But after a bit, very slowly, I realized that that safety curtain was going up, and little by little I was being flooded with—extraordinary instincts I'd never known I possessed. Tenderness. Protectiveness. Pride. And then anger. I began to be angry. Angry with all of them. Annabelle, and her husband and her mother. But most of all angry with myself. What the bloody hell was I doing, I asked myself, when she was my child, and I was her father, goddamn it. What the bloody hell was I doing, unloading all my responsibilities onto Phoebe? The answer was painfully simple. I was standing there doing nothing, which was what I had been doing for the past three days. Running on the spot, we used to call it at school. Getting nowhere. Achieving absolutely bugger all.

"I left the picture, and I went downstairs and found a telephone. I rang Directory enquiries and got Mrs. Tolliver's telephone number. And then I rang White Lodge. Mrs. Tolliver wasn't there . . ."

"She's visiting a friend in Helford," I told Daniel. I might just as well not have spoken.

". . . but her housekeeper answered the telephone and I told her that I was a friend of Leslie Collis and I wanted to get in touch with him, and she was able to give me the name of the firm where he works in the City."

The kettle was boiling, but we both seemed to have forgotten about coffee. I switched it off and then went to pull out a chair and to sit at the other end of the table, so that Daniel and I faced each other down its long scrubbed length.

"So, another phone call. I rang Leslie Collis. I said I wanted to see him. He began by saying that it wasn't convenient, but I insisted it was urgent, so he finally said that he could give me fifteen minutes or so if I could come right away.

"I went out of the Tate and got a taxi and went to his office. The City was looking very beautiful. I'd forgotten how beautiful it is, with all those ponderous buildings and narrow streets, and everywhere sudden unexpected glimpses of St. Paul's. One day I must go back and do some drawings . . ."

The words died. He had lost the thread of what he was telling me.

"Leslie Collis," I reminded him gently.

"Yes, of course." He put up his hand and ran his fingers through his hair. He began to laugh. "It was the most ludicrous interview. In the first place, I was looking even more reprehensible than I usually do. Again, I don't think I'd shaved, and I was wearing the shirt I'd worn on the train, and a pair of sneakers with holes in the toes. He, on the other hand, was all resplendent in his City gear, starched collar, pinstripe suit. We made the most incongruous pair of antagonists. Anyway, I sat down and started to talk, and as soon as I mentioned Mrs. Tolliver and Charlotte, he immediately decided I'd come to blackmail him, and he was on his feet, shouting me down, threatening to call the police. And then I started shouting, too, just to try and make myself heard, and for a moment or two there was total pandemonium with both of us accusing each other, claiming responsibility, disclaiming responsibility, blaming each other, blaming Annabelle.

"But finally, just as I'd decided he was going to keel over with a heart attack and leave me with a corpse on my hands as well as everything else, it got through to him that I wasn't a villain come to bleed him white. After that things got a bit better. We both sat down again, and he lit a cigarette, and we started all over."

"You didn't *like* him, did you?"

"Why? Didn't you?"

"When I saw him that morning on the train, I thought he was the most horrible man."

"He's not that bad."

"But saying he never wants Charlotte again . . ."

"I know. That's rotten. But, in a way, I see his point of view. He's an ambitious man. He's worked his butt off all his life to make a lot of money and achieve his ambitions. I think he probably genuinely adored Annabelle. But he must have known all along, from the very first, that she could never be faithful to him. Even so, he stuck to her, gave her everything she wanted, bought the house in Sunningdale so that the boy could be brought up in the country. She had a car of her own, a maid, a gardener, holidays in Spain, total freedom. He kept saying, 'I gave her everything. I gave that woman bloody everything.' "

"Did he know from the first that Charlotte wasn't his baby?"

"Yes, of course he knew. He hadn't seen Annabelle for three months, and then she came back from Cornwall and told him that she was pregnant. And that's a pretty good kick in the balls for any self-respecting man."

"Why didn't he end it then?"

"He wanted to keep the family together. He's devoted to his son. He didn't want to lose face with his friends."

"He never liked Charlotte, though."

"It's hard to blame him for that."

"Did he say he didn't like her?"

"More or less. He said she was sly. He said she told lies."

"If she did, it was his fault."

"That's what I told him."

"That must have gone down well."

"Oh, it was all right. By then we'd reached the stage when all the cards were on the table, and we could insult each other as much as we liked, with no offence given or taken. It was almost as though we'd made friends."

It was hard to imagine. "But what did you *talk* about?"

"We talked about everything. I told him that Charlotte was going to stay with Phoebe, and in the end he finally admitted that he was grateful. And he was also quite pleased to hear that she wasn't going back to that school. Annabelle had chosen it for the child, but in his opinion it had never been worth the massive fees he'd had to fork out each term. I asked about the boy Michael, but Collis seemed to think that he was no problem. He's fifteen and apparently mature, well able to look after himself, do his own thing. I think the general feeling was that he'd outgrown his mother and, considering the way she was carrying on, would be better away from her influence. Leslie Collis is going to sell the house in the country and get a place in London. He and the boy will live there together."

"I'm sorry for Michael."

"I'm sorry for him, too. I'm sorry for everybody in this unholy mess. But I believe he'll probably be all right. The father thinks the world of him, and they appear to be the best of friends."

"And what about Annabelle?"

"He's spoken to his lawyer, and divorce proceedings are already underway. Leslie Collis is not a man to let the grass grow under his feet."

I waited for him to go on, but he didn't, so I said, "Which leaves us back at square one. What's going to happen to Charlotte? Or didn't you talk about her?"

"Of course we talked about her. That was the whole object of the exercise."

"Leslie Collis knows you're her father?"

"Sure, that was the first thing I told him. And he doesn't want her back."

"What about Annabelle? How does she feel about Charlotte?"

"She doesn't want her either, and even if she did, I don't think Leslie

Collis would let her have the child. Call it sour grapes if you will, but it's the best thing that could happen to Charlotte."

"Why?"

"Because, my darling Prue, if Leslie Collis doesn't want Charlotte and neither does Annabelle, then the way is clear for me to adopt her as my own."

I sat still as stone, staring at him in incredulous disbelief.

"But they won't let you."

"Why not?"

"You're not married."

"The law has changed. Now a single person is allowed to adopt. It takes longer to get through the courts; there's obviously a bit more red tape to be cut, but it is eventually perfectly possible. Provided, of course, that Annabelle agrees to it, and I honestly don't see why she shouldn't."

"But you haven't got a house. You haven't got anywhere to live."

"Yes I have. Lewis Falcon is off to the south of France to work there for a couple of years, and he said he'd rent me his house at Lanyon and the studio if I wanted them. So I'll be around. I don't suppose I'd be able to have Charlotte to live with me until the adoption is through the courts, but I'm hoping that Phoebe might be able to continue as her official foster mother until then."

"It sounds . . . Oh, Daniel, it sounds too good to be true."

"I know. And as I said, the extraordinary thing was that by the end of all this, it was almost as though Leslie Collis and I had made friends. We seemed to understand each other. Finally we went out to lunch together, to a scruffy place where none of his colleagues would spy him with a down-and-out like me. And at the end of the meal, there was another ludicrous pantomime while we both tried to pick up the bill. Neither of us wanted to owe the other anything. So in the end we split it down the middle and each paid half. And then we went out of the restaurant, and we said good-bye, and I promised to be in touch. And he walked back to his office, and I got into a taxi and went back to the gallery to see Peter Chastal.

"I knew I had to get a good lawyer, and I've never even had a bad one, because Peter's always done everything for me. I've never even had an accountant, either, or a banker, or an agent. Peter's handled everything ever since that first day when I went to him, raw and inexperienced, sent by Chips. He was marvellous. He put me in touch with his own lawyer, and he went and found out how much money I had put away, which is about ten times more than I thought I had, and then he said it was about time I matched up to this new family-man image and got over my dread of anything mechanical and bought myself a car. So I went out and did. And then Peter and I had dinner together, and after that I knew I couldn't wait another moment to see you all, so I got into the car and drove back to Cornwall."

"And now Phoebe and Charlotte aren't even *here*." I couldn't bear it for him.

But he only said, "I'm glad they're not. Because the most important thing I've got to tell you concerns you. Actually, it's not so much telling you as asking you. I'm going to Greece. For a holiday. In about ten days' time. I've told you about the house on Spetsai, and I've already asked you to come with me, but now I'm asking you again. I've got two seats booked on a flight to Athens. If Lily and Phoebe can cope with Charlotte, will you come with me?" The sugar-cube house that I had told myself I would never see. The whitewashed terrace with the geraniums, and the boat with a sail like the wing of a gull. "Come with me, Prue."

My mind raced ahead. I would have to do things, arrange things, tell people. My mother. Marcus Bernstein. And, somehow I should have to write a letter to poor Nigel Gordon.

I said, "Yes."

Down the length of the table our eyes met and held. He suddenly smiled. He said, "How little we know each other. Was it you who said that, or I?"

"It was you."

"After two weeks in Greece we'll know each other so much better."

"Yes. I expect we will."

"And after that—after we get home—perhaps we could think about coming back to Lanyon together. We'd have to get married first, but we don't need to think about that just now. It's better that way. After all, we don't either of us want to commit ourselves, do we?"

I knew that there was nothing I wanted more. And from the way Daniel was looking at me, I had a pretty good idea that he felt the same way.

I smiled, too. "No," I told him. "We don't want to commit ourselves."

When Mr. Thomas's taxi returned bearing Phoebe and Charlotte and all their shopping, we were still in the kitchen, though no longer sitting at either end of the table. We heard the ancient vehicle come grinding down the road and turn in at the gate, and we went out together to greet them.

Mr. Thomas was flummoxed by Daniel's car, which, unexpectedly parked in front of the house, had left him no room to turn. Phoebe was already out of the taxi, dramatic in her best brown tweed cape, and trying to give him directions.

"Left hand down, Mr. Thomas. No, I don't mean left, I mean right . . ."

"Phoebe," said Daniel.

She turned and saw him.

"Daniel!"

Mr. Thomas and his problems were forgotten. Disgusted, he switched off his engine and sat there, brooding, trapped, the radiator of his car nose-to-nose with Daniel's, the back wheels hard against the red brick kerbstone that protected Phoebe's border.

Daniel moved to meet her halfway. They embraced enormously, and her hat was knocked sideways.

"You wicked villain." She thumped his shoulder lovingly with her good fist. "Where have you been?"

But she did not give him time to tell her, because just then, over his shoulder, she caught sight of me standing there in Lily's apron and with a smile on my face that I could do nothing about. She let go of Daniel and came to me, and although she had no idea of what had happened, what was happening, what was going to happen, I saw my own happiness reflected in her face, and we held each other very tightly and laughed together, because Daniel had come back, and everything was suddenly so completely all right.

And Charlotte. At the same instant we remembered Charlotte. We looked and saw her cautiously alighting from the back of the old car, her arms filled with a perilous pile of wrapped boxes and packages. I knew that she had watched us all, was holding back, probably telling herself that she, Charlotte, had no place in all these loving reunions. Carefully, with her foot, she closed the door of the taxi. When she turned, her chin clamped over the topmost parcel, she found herself confronted by Daniel. Slowly her face tilted up to stare into his, her eyes unblinking behind the owlish spectacles. For a moment there was silence as they looked at each other. And then Daniel smiled and said, "Hello, my love. I'm back again."

He held wide his arms. It was all she needed.

"Oh, Daniel . . ."

The parcels began to slip. She let them go and flung herself at him, and he caught her and swung her up in his arms, round and round, and the packages lay unheeded where they had tumbled, higgledy-piggledy onto the gravel.

ABOUT THE AUTHOR

In addition to writing *The Shell Seekers*, which dominated national best-seller lists for two years, and the three novels that appear in this collection, *September, Voices in Summer,* and *The Carousel*, ROSAMUNDE PILCHER has produced two collections of short fiction, *The Blue Bedroom and Other Stories* and *Flowers in the Rain,* as well as twenty novels over the past four decades. More than twelve million copies of her books are in print. Mrs. Pilcher lives on her family farm in Scotland with her husband, Graham. When not writing, she is a passionate gardener and keeps an eye on a variety of guests, children, and animals.